Malice & Surrender

BROOKLYN CROSS

BROOKLYN CROSS

Copyright © May 2023

MALICE & SURRENDER
Snake - Box Set
Lost Souls MC

Written by: Brooklyn Cross

FIRST EDITION.

ASIN: 978-1-998015-12-2

ISBN: 978-1-998015-13-9

ALL RIGHTS RESERVED.

Edited by: R. Mudawar

Cover Art: Dazed Designs

Cover Models: Jord Liddell & Rhiannon Carr

Photographer: Craig Devlin Photography

Book Cover Disclaimer: Individuals depicted in the images on the cover and anywhere are models and solely used for illustrative purposes.

This book may not be reproduced or used in whole or in part by any means existing without the author's written permission. Author Brooklyn Cross.

This book is a work of fiction, and any resemblance to persons, living or dead, or places, events, or locales is purely coincidental. The characters, incidents, and dialogues in this book are productions of the author's imagination and are not to be construed as real.

The ideas represented in this book are not factual representations of anyone's thoughts affiliated with Author Brooklyn Cross, or of any of the trademarked acknowledgments mentioned in this story. This story is simply a work of fiction.

Trademark Acknowledgements

The author Brooklyn Cross acknowledges the trademarked status and trademark owners of familiar wordmarks, products, actors' names, television shows, books, characters, video games, and films mentioned in this fiction work.

✸ Created with Vellum

ALSO BY BROOKLYN CROSS

Lost Souls MC

(Motorcycle Club - Dark 3.5-4.5 Spice 3.5-4.5)

Malice

Surrender

Showbiz

Handcuffed

Other Books in the Lost Souls World by T.L. Hodel

Adversaries

Frenemies

Warfare (Coming 2023)

The Righteous Series

(Vigilante/Ex Military Romance - Dark 3-4 Spice 3-4)

Dark Side of the Cloth

Ravaged by the Dark

Sleeping with the Dark

Hiding in the Dark

Redemption in the Dark

Crucified by the Dark

Dark Reunion (Coming 2023)

The Consumed Trilogy

(Suspense/Thriller/Anti-Hero Romance - Dark 4-5 Spice 3-4)

Burn for Me

Burn with Me

Burn me Down (Coming 2023)

The Buchanan Brother's Duet

(Serial Killer/Captive Horror Romance - Dark 4-5 Spice 3-5)

Unhinged Cain by Brooklyn

Twisted Abel by T.L Hodel

The Battered Souls World

(Standalone Books Shared World Romance/Dramatic/Women's Fiction/All The Feels- Dark 2-3 Spice 2-3)

The Girl That Would Be Lost

The Boy That Learned To Swim (Coming Soon)

The Girl That Would Not Break (Coming Soon)

The Brothers of Shadow and Death Series

(Dystopian/Cult/Occult/Poly MMF Romance - Dark 3-4 Spice 3-4)

Anywhere Book 1 of 3

Backfire Book 1 of 3 by T.L. Hodel

Seven Sin Series

(Multi Author/PNR/Angel and Demons/Redemption - Dark 2-5 Spice 3-5)

Greed by Brooklyn Cross

Lust by Drethi Anis

Envy by Dylan Page

Gluttony by Marissa Honeycutt

Wrath by Billie Blue

Sloth by Talli Wyndham

Pride by T.L. Hodel

MALICE

That was what
Raine was to me,
the story that was waiting
to be finished and I needed
to decide how I wanted
it to end.
Kaivan

WARNING

THIS IS A DARK MMFM (WHY CHOOSE) MOTORCYCLE CLUB ROMANCE NOVEL AND IS INTENDED FOR MATURE AUDIENCES ONLY.

THIS BOOK IS FOR SALE TO ADULTS ONLY, AS DEFINED BY THE COUNTRY'S LAWS IN WHICH YOU MADE YOUR PURCHASE.

THIS BOOK MAY CONTAIN DARK HUMOR, EXPLICIT SEXUAL CONTENT, GRAPHIC VIOLENCE, COARSE LANGUAGE, DUB/NON CONSENSUAL SCENES, STALKING, MULTIPLE KINKS, TRAUMA, MEMORIES OF ABUSE, PTSD FAMILY LOSS, DRUG/TOBBACO/ALCOHOL USE AND SCENES THAT DEAL WITH SENSITIVE AND MATURE SUBJECT MATTER.

FOR A COMPLETE BREAKDOWN OF THE CONTENT WARNINGS, PLEASE SEE BROOKLYN CROSS'S WEBSITE WWW.BROOKLYNCROSSBOOKS.COM

AKNOWLEDGEMENT

It is with love and appreciation that I say thank you to all those that have stood by my side through my author journey. Who picked me up during my lowest moments and continue to make me smile. I could not do this without each of you.

PLAYLIST

PAGE 1

VENOM - EMINEM
A LITTLE BIT STRONGER - SARA EVANS
A LITTLE BIT DANGEROUS - CRMNL
BAD HABITS - ED SHEERAN
FORGET ME - LEWIS CAPALDI
BUTTERFLY - CRAZY TOWN
SURVIVOR - NATHANIEL RATELIFF
BUTTONS - SNOOP DOGG & PUSSYCAT DOLLS
I WANNA BE YOU - MANESKIN
BREATHE - SKITZ KRAVEN
LIMIT TO YOUR LOVE - JAMES BLAKE
SHE KEEPS ME UP - NICKELBACK
NEVER GONNA LET YOU GO - ESTHERO
YOU WORRY ME - NATHANIEL RATELIFF
PEACHES - JUSTIN BIEBER
GUNS+AMMUNITION - JULY TALK
BAD BUY - BILLIE EILISH
THE KIND OF LOVE WE MAKE - LUKE COMBS
MEMORY - KANE BROWN X BLACKBEAR
HOLD ON, WE'RE GOING HOME - DRAKE
THE NEXT EPISODE - DR DRE
ANTI-HERO - TAYLOR SWIFT
SOMETHING TO LOSE - LANDON TEWERS
SHIVERS - ED SHEERAN
I THINK I LIKE WHEN IT RAINS - WILLIS
RUN AWAY TO MARS - TALK

PLAYLIST

PAGE 2

NEVER LEAVE - BAILEY ZIMMERMAN
BURY A FRIEND - BILLIE EILISH
I WALK THE LINE - HALSEY
LAST RESORT - PAPA ROACH
TAKE WHAT YOU WANT - POST MALONE
HERO - CHAD KROEGER
APOLOGIZE - TIMBALAND
WRECKING BALL - MILEY CYRUS
FUNHOUSE - PINK
STERO HEARTS - GYM CLASS HEROES
TOXIC - BRITNEY SPEARS
CENTURIES - FALL OUT BOY
SUGAR, WE'RE GOIN DOWN - FALL OUT BOY
ATTENTION - CHARLIE PUTH
SATELLITE - GUSTER
OUT TA GET ME - GUNS N' ROSES
TREEHOUSE - HE IS WE
ME, MYSELF & I - G-EAZY X BEBE REXHA
COMING UNDONE - KORN
SEX AND CANDY - ALEXANDER JEAN
CONFETTI - CHARLOTTE CARDIN
PIECE OF MY HEART - JANIS JOPLIN
COMING FOR YOU - OFFSPRING
RESCUE ME - ONEREPUBLIC
SLOW HANDS - NIALL HORAN
SANGRIA - BLAKE SHELTON

ECLIPSE

SPECIALTY SHOTS

APPLE PIE - 1OZ SOUR GREEN APPLE, 1OZ CINNAMON WHISKY

BLUEBERRY BLITZ - 1OZ BLUE BERRY VODKA, 1 OZ BLUE CURACAO

PEACH LIPS - 1/2 OZ SPICED RUM, 1/2 OZ BANANA LIQUEUR, 1OZ PEACH SCHNAPPS

NIGHTCAP - 1/2OZ CREME DE MENTHE, 1/2OZ KAHLUA, 1/2OZ COFFEE LIQUEUR, TOP WITH CHOCOLATE MILK

BEND OVER SALLY - 1OZ TEQUILA, 1OZ SOUR RASPBERRY LIQUEUR

FROST BITE - 1OZ COFFEE LIQUEUR, 1OZ MAPLE WHISKEY

SPANK ME - 1OZ LIMONCELLO, 1OZ COCONUT CREAM LIQUEUR

PIG ROASTED - 1OZ SALTED CARAMEL LEQUEUR, 1 OZ SMOKY WHISKEY

BIG DADDY - 1/2OZ CHERRY LIQUEUR, 1/2OZ BANANA LEQUEUR, 1/2OZ BLUE VODKA

1

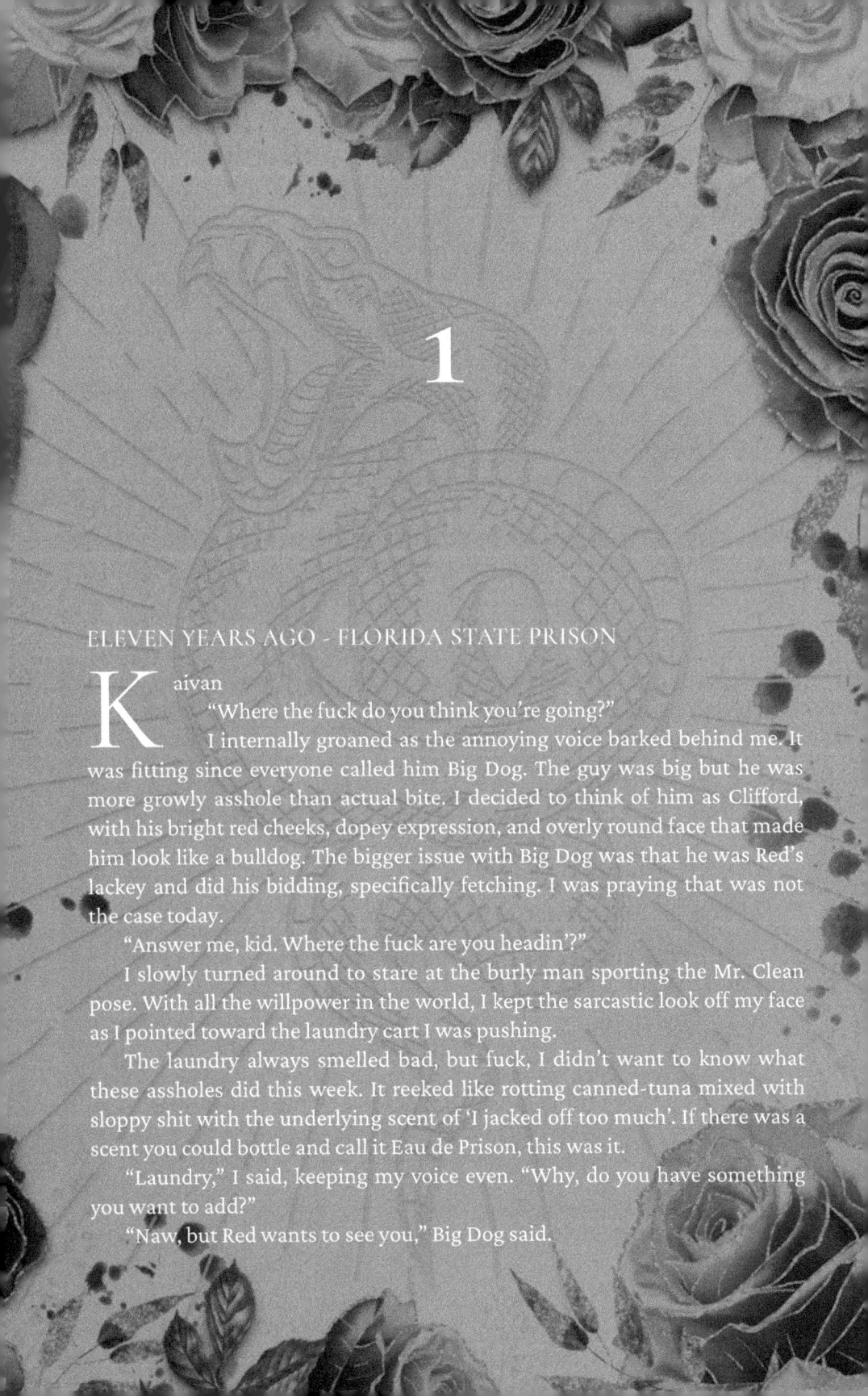

ELEVEN YEARS AGO - FLORIDA STATE PRISON

K aivan

"Where the fuck do you think you're going?"

I internally groaned as the annoying voice barked behind me. It was fitting since everyone called him Big Dog. The guy was big but he was more growly asshole than actual bite. I decided to think of him as Clifford, with his bright red cheeks, dopey expression, and overly round face that made him look like a bulldog. The bigger issue with Big Dog was that he was Red's lackey and did his bidding, specifically fetching. I was praying that was not the case today.

"Answer me, kid. Where the fuck are you headin'?"

I slowly turned around to stare at the burly man sporting the Mr. Clean pose. With all the willpower in the world, I kept the sarcastic look off my face as I pointed toward the laundry cart I was pushing.

The laundry always smelled bad, but fuck, I didn't want to know what these assholes did this week. It reeked like rotting canned-tuna mixed with sloppy shit with the underlying scent of 'I jacked off too much'. If there was a scent you could bottle and call it Eau de Prison, this was it.

"Laundry," I said, keeping my voice even. "Why, do you have something you want to add?"

"Naw, but Red wants to see you," Big Dog said.

Nightmare initiated. This wasn't good. You wanted to avoid Red, not end up in his crosshairs. I learned that the first day I watched him and his pack of goons attack a guy who looked to be doing nothing but minding his own business. They messed him up so badly that the guards had to ship him to the hospital. That dude never came back, and Red's crew never got in trouble.

For the last six weeks, six days, and almost six hours, I'd kept my head low and under his radar, or at least I thought I had. It was a bad omen to be summoned at this time of day. He would want to see me for only three reasons, and I wanted nothing to do with any of them.

Option one, Red wanted to recruit me as part of his group. He would demand that I fuck someone up—and preferably kill them—to prove my loyalty. I had no interest in being part of his goon squad and didn't want to kill some random guy just because he told me to.

Option two, he wanted to use me as bait for someone else to get their stripes, then I would have to defend myself. I was pretty big for eighteen, and I could hold my own in a fight, but adding time to my sentence was on my Fuck-No list.

The only other option...he wanted to make me his bitch. There was no way I was letting that happen. I would rather die than let that man—a walking cesspool of disease—stick his cock up my ass. Not that I ever wanted any cock tearing my ass apart, but definitely not his. I didn't care if a dude wanted to fuck another dude, but it had never been my jam.

"No, I gotta get this to the laundry room," I said, and turned away from his shocked expression. The wheels squeaked as I pushed the cart, but I was immediately whipped around by a meaty hand gripping my shoulder.

Yanking out of Big Dog's hold, I snarled at him, standing nose to nose as I clenched my fists. "Don't fucking touch me."

Big Dog had eighty pounds on me easily, but I wasn't letting him intimidate me. This place was eat or be eaten, and I refused to be someone's meal.

"You have big kahunas, kid, but Red will knock you down a peg or two." Big Dog leaned in, but I refused to back down. "You need to learn your place."

"I think you mean cojones, and you need to learn to brush your teeth. Your breath fucking reeks, man. Get out of my face." His eyes narrowed into slits. "My place is to be left alone, and that's what I want you to do." I glared back and heard his neck crack as he tilted it from side to side.

"Oh, I'm gonna have so much fun with you." Big Dog stepped off to the side and pointed in the direction he wanted me to go. "Walk. Now. Or I tell Red that you disobeyed a direct summons, and you won't last another day."

I was fucked either way now. If I ignored him and stayed in the laundry room, I could avoid whatever Red had planned for tonight, but I would be labeled a pussy, and it wouldn't save me tomorrow. If I went...well...it wasn't like I was going anywhere for another five hundred and thirteen point four weeks, so I might as well get it over with.

Looking longingly at a pile of dirty clothes was not something I ever thought I would do, but I did now. Sad when handling men's cum splattered clothes was a better option than where I was headed. Then again, there were many things I didn't think would ever happen in my life. Being tossed in prison to rot for a crime I didn't commit was currently sitting in first place. Hopefully, whatever Red had planned wouldn't knock that into number two.

I glanced up as we walked and shook my head when I spotted that the camera's light wasn't blinking, which meant that it was turned off. It seemed to be a conspiracy all on its own that random hallways at all hours of the day would no longer be recording. It was even more mysterious that the heads of the different groups that ran this place all seemed to know when they would be down.

I felt like I was walking the plank as we weaved through the maze that took us to the far side of the prison and the set of showers that were barely ever used, at least not for washing. I'd already spent an entire week cleaning and mopping in this section, and the constant grunting and moans coming from this disgusting tiled hole in the wall would've made you think it was filled with farm animals.

I swallowed hard as I stepped inside, and the three goons I'd seen beating the random dude were standing around with their arms crossed. All eyes turned my way as I stepped inside. My muscles flexed and twitched, ready for the fight that was coming.

It was easy to spot the red-headed man whose beard matched the vibrant shade on his head. The scraggly strands looked like shit, but it made him stand out among the crowd.

Red was sitting on the counter by the sinks. I knew without him even opening his mouth what he wanted with me. Red's eyes openly roamed over my body, and I fought the urge to fidget under his stare.

"What are you in for?" Red asked as he leaned back on the counter and spread his legs wide. Any other guy, in any other place at any other time, I would've said he was simply relaxing, but that was not what was happening here.

The goons in the room began to do their slow shuffle as if I wouldn't notice them blocking my only escape route.

I didn't want to say why I was here. The fact that it wasn't true wouldn't matter. The moment I opened my mouth and the words rape tumbled out, it was game over. There was a code in prison. If you hurt women, you were an automatic target to be someone's bitch until the day you got out. But it was worse for those who hurt kids. Most didn't last a full day, and the ones who did wish they hadn't.

Red would have me bent over the counter so fast it would make my head spin. That may happen anyway, but I wasn't giving anyone here an open-season ticket.

"Armed robbery," I muttered, unable to think of anything better.

"Oh yeah? Robbery of what?"

Lifting my shoulders, I let them drop. "Whatever I could get my hands on. Why do you want to know? Are you looking to acquire something when I get out?"

"Oh, I plan on acquiring something all right."

He smirked, and I could feel my blood pressure rising. I was used to this feeling, this anticipation of bad shit about to happen. I had it so many times in foster care that I lost count. Until I got to the Collins family. Their place hadn't been a walk in the park either, but at least I didn't worry every time I laid my head down that someone would try to beat me, or worse. I was also a fuck load tougher. So if he wanted me, he was forcing it, and I would fight with my last breath before I submitted.

"I have it on good authority that you're a sick fuck and liked to diddle your sister," Red said, and then laughed. The sound echoed off the walls of the large space.

I didn't need any reminders of what had landed me in this fucking place. Raine was my foster sister, we were best friends until she didn't come home one night, and the police dragged me from my bed. They told me I was being arrested for rape and drove me to the precinct, where I spent so many hours in the interrogation room that I didn't even know what day of the week it was.

They never got me to break and implicate myself in something I didn't do, but it didn't matter. Stupid fucking public defender was a useless dick, and I ended up with a shit plea deal. So here I was with a ten-year sentence hanging over my head. I'd promised myself I wouldn't end up like my old man, but I guess some shit was simply unavoidable.

"Not sure where you heard that from, but it was a fucking lie. I wouldn't do that shit," I snarled. My muscles tensed, and my hands curled into fists as the goons stepped closer. I glared at them, sizing them up. This wasn't the first time I'd been outnumbered.

Red slid off the counter and took a step in my direction. "What a shame. I was hoping you were a freak. It would make what I plan to do to you so much more entertaining." Red got up in my personal space. "Wouldn't that have been ironic? You in here for diddling your sister, and then you get your ass tapped. It would've been a sweet circle of events."

"Apparently, our ideas of entertaining differ," I drawled.

Red smiled, but it did nothing to ease the hard lines on his face. "You have a smart mouth. I wonder how smart it will be when I have my cock shoved so far down your throat that you choke to death on it."

I inched closer and squared off with Red. There was no way I was backing down. "If you put your cock anywhere near my mouth, I'll fucking bite it off." I snapped my teeth together, the sound loud in the otherwise quiet bathroom.

Red looked behind me, and I knew the goons had moved closer. "You believe this kid?" The guys chuckled. "I kinda like you, but you're not getting out of this. Hold him down," Red ordered. "I'm going to be the first to teach your ass a lesson."

Not giving them a chance to grab me, I spun. My elbow sailed backward into Red's face with a hard crack.

"Ah fuck! You broke my nose." The sound was music to my ears.

I barely felt the impact and used the same arm to land a hard right hook along the jaw of the goon closest to me. Like a comic strip, blood and a tooth flew from his mouth.

Fighting was second nature to me. I'd been fighting for everything from the day I was born. I fought to breathe through the umbilical cord wrapped around my neck. Fought to keep my mother alive when gang members—pissed off at my father—decided to teach him a lesson by killing her. I fought for my next meal when my father forgot I existed. Fought to not be a punching bag for fucktards in the foster homes I bounced around in. Fighting to stay alive in this rat hole called life was all I knew.

The guy I hit stumbled back from the blow and left a shot open for me to get my foot up and into the second guy's gut. He stepped back and doubled over, grabbing his stomach. That blow should've laid him out flat. Damn, I wish I had my shitkickers on instead of these stupid white running shoes.

The third goon pushed his buddy out of the way and growled like a wild animal as he swung at me. This guy was the largest of the three and had more muscle in one arm than I had on my entire body. But that also made him slow. Ducking under his large fist, we danced around until I landed a solid strike to his kidneys. The goon winced and closed his eyes for just a moment; but that was all I needed. I stepped back and brought my foot up, landing a sidekick to his jugular. He clutched at his throat, eyes bulging as he tried to get air. I watched him for one satisfactory moment as he dropped to his knees.

I'd maneuvered enough to dash out the door, and I might've had a shot if fucking Big Dog hadn't stuck around. I hadn't seen him still hanging out in the entryway. I saw the man a second before I was slammed into like a battering ram. We crashed to the floor and skidded backward in a heap. All the air was driven out of my lungs, but I didn't care. Gasping for breath, I fought for my life.

Big Dog held the front of my jumper in one hand, and I raised my arms up just in time for his fist to crack down hard. The side of my face, shoulder, and arms all fell victim to his blows, despite the guard I held firmly in place. I tried to drive my knee or fist into any part of Big Dog's body that would force him to let go, but the guy was like the Pillsbury Doughboy, with just a bit more muscle. It felt like my fist was sinking in and being pushed back out.

Another massive fist cracked me across the face, and little stars exploded behind my eyes as the metallic taste of blood filled my mouth.

"Get him up," Red ordered, and I was hauled to my feet. "Put him on the counter, face down. I'm going to enjoy this." Red grabbed my jaw before the guys could drag me across the floor, and his meaty fingers dug in painfully. "I was going to break you in slowly because I was feeling generous, but..." I grunted as his fist slammed into my stomach and once more drove the air from my lungs.

"Now I'm going to teach you what it means to be in my waters. Your tight little asshole will be ripped apart by the time we all get our fill. It'll be a winking mess for longer. And if I have to teach you another lesson in manners, I'll cut your balls off." A shank pressed against my jugular, and I was tempted to jab myself into the sharp blade so this didn't happen. With my shit ass luck, they would sodomize my corpse, and I would have to hover over my body and watch. "I own your ass now, pup."

I tensed as he stepped back and cocked his fist. This time I was at least expecting it and flexed my muscles against the blows. Coughing and unable to breathe, I fought the two men as they dragged me across the floor, my sneakers squeaking like they were revolting as well.

"Fuck," I yelled as they forced me face-first onto the counter. It was cold and damp from what I could only hope was water. I kicked my legs out at anything I could and didn't care how ridiculous I looked doing it.

"Hold him still, for fuck's sake," Red barked.

Two more sets of hands joined in, each pair taking a leg and pulling them apart. My heart was beating so hard that I could hear the thumping echoing back at me through the surface of the counter. A hand gripped the back of my jumper and the panic that had been building reached new heights at the sound of tearing material.

"Look at that ass. Mmm hmm," Red said, his large hand cracking off my right ass cheek.

I snarled, and turned my head as best I could. "Get the fuck away from me. Or so help me, I'll rip your tongue from your head and shove it up your ass, so you'll know how you taste."

Red glared at me and raised his hand to strike again when a deep voice I didn't recognize boomed inside the room.

"Let him go, Red," a man I couldn't see said.

"Fuck you, Mannix. This guy is mine. He broke my fucking nose. I deserve payback," Red argued.

"The thing is, I don't see it that way." This voice was a lot more threatening than the whiny sound of Red's higher pitch. "You see, the kid here has already agreed to be part of my crew. So, technically, you're encroaching on my territory. Don't hand me some line that he wandered over here all on his own, either. We both know better."

I could make out a shadow along the wall, and I strained my neck to see who the hell this guy was. My eyes landed on the biggest man I'd ever seen. I didn't know where he came from, but I hadn't seen him before, and he was definitely someone you remembered.

The standard issue jumper looked too small and was open at the top. Even with my limited view, I could tell the guy was jacked. Tattoos covered every inch of his deep brown skin, but my attention was drawn to the reaper on his neck. His glare was focused on Red, and those eyes screamed do not mess with this guy. He also looked like the type who was used to people following his orders.

Great, now I'd been claimed by another leader. Why not have multiple people wanting my ass today? The fucking stars were not aligned in my favor.

"What do you mean, he's your territory? Where's his tattoo?" Red held his arm out in my direction.

Mannix stepped in close to Red, and I held back a smirk as Red craned his neck up to look at him.

"He was supposed to get it today after his duties in the laundry room, but he never showed up."

How the hell did this guy know my schedule? I'd never even seen his face before. "But then I heard you were down here, and I had a feeling that you were once more trying to steal something that wasn't yours," Mannix snarled.

"Do I need to remind you what I said would happen if you did that again?" His voice dropped even lower. "What I would take from you?"

The tone of his voice made me shiver, and it wasn't even directed at me. The room was so quiet it was like everything, including the air, had been sucked out. I swallowed as I waited to see what way this would go.

Red stepped back, and I could no longer see him from my position. "Fuck, fine, you can have him. He's more trouble than he's worth," Red said. "Let's go," he grumbled, and the men holding my arms and legs let go like I was a hot potato.

Pushing myself up from the counter, I washed my hands and scrubbed at my face, horrified to think how many hairy asses and cum shots had landed on this counter.

Mannix casually stood as I washed. My eyes flicked to his light, amber-colored ones. Time to face the music. I couldn't delay any longer. Turning, I looked up at the man who still had a solid five inches on my six-four frame.

"Why did you do that?" I asked, wary of the answer.

"I was keeping an eye on you, and some things just can't be explained." He lifted a big shoulder and let it drop. "You're officially under my protection, but one day, you'll owe me a favor. That's how this place works." His lip curled up with a smirk. "Come on. I'll get you back to your cell in one piece. With your ass hanging out like that, hard to say what would happen." He smiled wide and held out his hand. "Everyone calls me Mannix."

"Kaivan, but everyone calls me Snake."

2

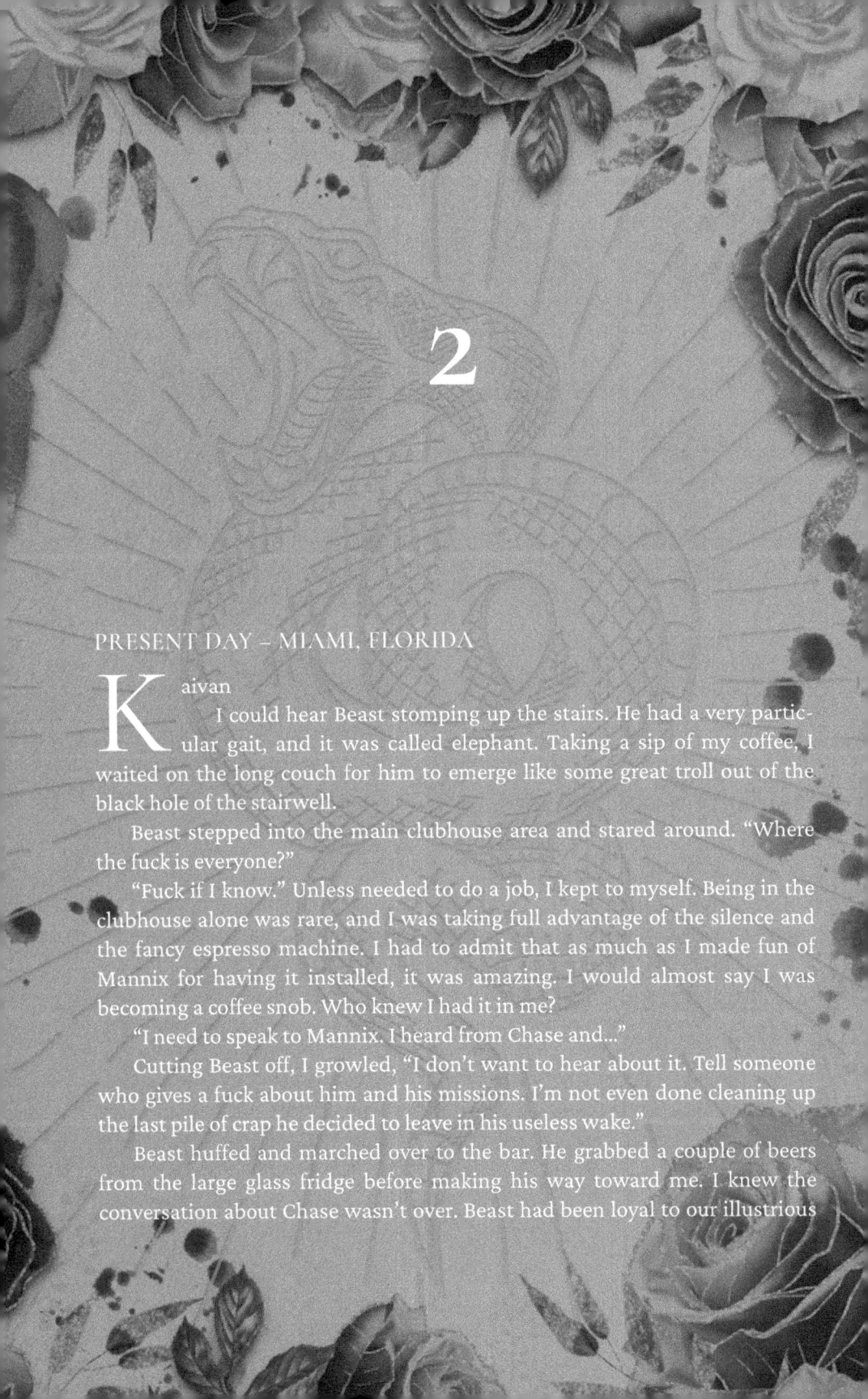

PRESENT DAY – MIAMI, FLORIDA

Kaivan

I could hear Beast stomping up the stairs. He had a very particular gait, and it was called elephant. Taking a sip of my coffee, I waited on the long couch for him to emerge like some great troll out of the black hole of the stairwell.

Beast stepped into the main clubhouse area and stared around. "Where the fuck is everyone?"

"Fuck if I know." Unless needed to do a job, I kept to myself. Being in the clubhouse alone was rare, and I was taking full advantage of the silence and the fancy espresso machine. I had to admit that as much as I made fun of Mannix for having it installed, it was amazing. I would almost say I was becoming a coffee snob. Who knew I had it in me?

"I need to speak to Mannix. I heard from Chase and…"

Cutting Beast off, I growled, "I don't want to hear about it. Tell someone who gives a fuck about him and his missions. I'm not even done cleaning up the last pile of crap he decided to leave in his useless wake."

Beast huffed and marched over to the bar. He grabbed a couple of beers from the large glass fridge before making his way toward me. I knew the conversation about Chase wasn't over. Beast had been loyal to our illustrious president for far longer than I'd been in prison, so he gave the guy a break at every turn. I, on the other hand, had no reason to do so. Mannix inducted me into the Lost Souls, and two weeks and four days after my release, I had to go to some place called Ashen Springs to save a girl I'd never met. Like a fucking magic trick, Chase Mathers came back from the dead and popped out of whatever hole he'd crawled into to claim he was the rightful leader of the MC.

From that moment on, it had been one clusterfuck after another or Chase's complete absence. I did get a damn good blowjob out of his old lady while he was out whoring around. He disappointed me again when he didn't try to kill me. That would've been fun. Mannix filled me in on Chase's history like that would make me feel sorry for him and maybe shed a tear or two. Not likely. What I saw was a piece of shit who couldn't handle the crap in his life head-on and decided to hide like a motherfucking coward. I had no time for cowards, and they certainly didn't get my respect.

It shocked me every day that his old lady, Naomi, stayed with him. What she saw in him, I could never say. He certainly wasn't worth the effort she put into getting him clean after the shit he pulled. Then again, I guess that was the crazy you chose when you got yourself knocked up. Personal opinion, she would be better off raising that baby alone. Hell, even crazy-ass Ava would've been a better choice than Chase Mathers. That girl was no coward. Strange and off her rocker for sure, but no coward.

"You do know that at some point you're going to have to accept that Mathers is our Prez and show some respect, or you'll be out on your ass," Beast drawled in that lazy fatherly voice he put on whenever he thought one of us was saying something stupid. The bottle hissed as he popped the top off and settled back in the chair across from me like he was my motherfucking therapist.

I didn't need a therapist. Okay, that was a lie. I probably needed a therapist, but I didn't want to fix what was wrong with me. My wrong had me smiling wide as I slit someone's throat open. It was what had kept me alive for twenty-nine years and three glorious months.

"Actually, I don't have to do shit. Mathers doesn't deserve my respect, and he certainly shouldn't have yours," I argued and took a swig of my coffee. "I respect you, and I respect Mannix. Until that man proves he deserves to be at the helm, he can go to hell for all I care."

Beast shook his head and muttered something with the word fuck thrown in multiple times, which pulled at the corner of my lip.

"What are you drinking?" Beast asked as he sniffed the air and looked at my porcelain cup.

I looked from the large biker down to the black coffee and saw my reflection in the liquid. Time changed everyone, and it certainly changed me. Mannix would tell me something all philosophical like, 'time is but the journey we choose to take between one life and the next...and with each new journey you take...blah, blah, blah.' Mannix was always hitting me with crap like that. I didn't even know where he got that shit—probably scribbled on some bus stop.

"Coffee, black," I said, and chugged the rest before it got cold. Nothing worse than cold coffee. Well, there were a couple of things, but it was up there on my list.

"Why you drinkin' that?" Beast looked up at the clock on the wall. "You planning on going dancing with those Weasel members tonight?"

My lip curled up, and to anyone other than Beast and a small handful of others, it would look malicious, and it was, but he also knew it wasn't directed at him. Becoming an enforcer for a motorcycle club had never been one of my life plans. Looking back, this was where I was always going to end up. That happened when your father was an enforcer for an MC and got sent away for three life sentences when you were nine years, two months, and ten days old.

"Yup. I have two dance partners who are in need of a lesson tonight," I said and stood to stretch out the tight muscles in my back. I'd spent four hours in the gym today, and my shoulders were officially telling me off.

That was something else that time had changed. I was no longer the eighteen-year-old punk who landed in prison with a smart mouth and very few skills or muscles to back it up. No, I trained hard, worked out harder, and now I was feared more than any other enforcer in all the southern states. Life goals pushed me to make sure that title spread to all corners of the great U.S. of A.

If you were on my list, you were a dead man, and I always left you looking like the spectacle you were meant to be. Why have a nice corpse for opposing members to clean up? That didn't leave a lasting impression.

"I said soon. I didn't mean you needed to go tonight," Beast said.

"No time like the present," I said, and lit up my smoke.

"But I just got here," Beast complained as I wandered over to the bar and put the coffee mug on the counter. Smiling, I shot Beast a teasing glance on my way to the door.

"Which is exactly why I'm leaving." I smirked as Beast swore.

Jogging down the stairs, I pushed my way out into the cool fall night and took a deep breath. I fucking loved Halloween, and I was going to make the most of it. Unable to help myself, I glanced at the dilapidated amusement park next door and snorted as I watched Wilder scurry around, covered in a camouflage of garbage and old stuffed toys. He looked like some creepy ass creature out of a horror flick. I actually found him highly entertaining, and the fact that he scared just about everyone made him A-OK in my mind.

Wilder moved out of sight in the darkness, but I knew he would still be keeping an eye on me. Crazy? Maybe. I think the term crazy was tossed around a little too much and a little too easily these days.

My two bikes stood out from the rest like a sore thumb, or in this case, a sexy middle finger to everyone else. Everyone here rode a sled of some sort, but I was never much of a joiner, so I went and got myself an Indian instead of a Harley. I thought Roach was going to faint the day I rode in on it. That was the second best day of my life. The top spot was held by getting my get-out-of-jail-free card stamped.

My second ride was a chopper. The midnight black paint glistened under the lights of the parking area. The custom paint job of snakeskin—which could only be seen at certain times of day—made you do a double take. When I rode, it looked like the skin was moving under the paint, making my heart pound and my cock hard.

I knew that even though Roach would never say it, he was jealous as hell over my ride. I'd seen him eyeing it up more than once, but I told him girls didn't dig insects on a paint job. A few choice words were thrown my way that day.

Roach had arrived at the pen when I reached the midway point of my sentence. I remembered the day well. I'd celebrated being on the back half by talking one of the guards into getting me a chocolate cupcake. It helped that I saved that particular guard from having his throat slit in a riot. Every year after that, on the same day, that guard brought me a small treat. Might have been a cupcake or a couple of cookies, but it was a gift, not a favor. I would find it left in my cell just before lights out. There was only one thing that I found tasted sweeter. It came with a cute smile and lips that could suck the chrome off a tailpipe.

Choosing the chopper for tonight, I straddled the girl and shivered as she fired up. I nodded to the guys running the gate as I got close and slipped out onto the dark road. This was a shit part of town, but it felt like home. Much like a rat would still call a sewer home, this was where I belonged.

As I got closer to Miami beach, the traffic thickened, and so did the number of people on the sidewalks. The wide assortment of costumes ranged from cute fuzzy bunnies to terrifying monsters and everything in between. I rolled up to a red light, and a group of girls dressed as different female superheroes squealed and began jumping up and down as they waved.

I smirked and winked at the girls. They were fucking hot, and if I weren't on the job tonight, one of them would've been fucked hard and fast, bent over my bike. I would make sure she couldn't stand before I brought her back to her friends, then maybe took another for a tour. My cock thickened in my jeans as I stared at the long legs of the stunning blonde dressed up like Supergirl. She could be my Supergirl any day.

The light went green, and Supergirl kissed her hand and blew the kiss in my direction. Being the gentleman I was, I grabbed it out of the air and pretended to eat that shit. Her face went scarlet.

The steady breeze coming off the water hit me in the face and blew my hair back. I decided a long time ago that nothing was ever going to smell as sweet as the ocean. Sitting on the beach in the middle of the night with a drink was my favorite pastime. Aside from killing and fucking, both of which I took very seriously.

My only experience with pussy before being locked up was Mrs. Collins, my foster mother. She was decent to look at and lonely with her husband away all the time. He was a long-distance trucker and was only home two nights out of the week. I had no loyalty to either of them, so when her hand landed on my thigh one night while watching a movie, I didn't move away.

It had taken me by surprise, and I sat tense through the rest of the movie, but I learned that it was her testing the waters. She had her plan in place, and I would end up the main event. Not that I cared at the time. I needed the experience, and she was willing to fuck me as much as I wanted.

At seventeen, I was hard most of the day, and my hand became pretty boring. Now that I was a free man, I didn't waste a second of being buried balls deep inside some willing participant. More women at once were always welcome. I had two hands, a mouth, and a cock, all happy to get involved.

Pulling into one of the parking areas along the beach, I had to maneuver around the throngs of people that crossed back and forth between wanting food and drink and partying on the sand. A large truck was parked in the last spot at the end, with one of the local DJ's logos splashed across the door.

Perfect. Turning around, I slowly pushed the chopper backward until it hopped the curb, completely hidden from view behind the truck. A barricade, a large bush, and another parking lot blocked the other side. There were a lot of cameras around, but this particular parking lot had its cameras smashed a week ago. I knew this cause I was the one who had taken them out. You needed to pre-plan this shit, and it was fucking unwise to wander around killing people without a plan. For example, paying to know where these two assholes were going to be was a well thought out plan. Not having a plan would get your ass thrown back in the pen as quick as a look.

I double-checked my clip and knives before grabbing the Scream mask from the pouch on my bike. Stuffing the gun into the back of my jeans, I pulled on the Scream mask and wandered along the path of writhing bodies.

A group of partiers had opted for the painted body look over actual clothes and were rubbing all up on each other. My step paused for half a second as I considered joining them. The hard nipples of the girl painted like a butterfly were calling to me as she bounced up and down, and my mouth was watering for a taste.

"Fuck, that was hot," I grumbled as I forced myself to look away.

I spotted the bar area I was after and began wobbling on my feet like I was already drunk. Grabbing an open bottle of tequila from a girl's hand, she gave me a dirty look until I pulled her against my body and danced in a circle, grinding against her bare pussy with my leg.

She bit her lip and waved as I let go and continued on my way. Damn, I needed a raise. Passing all this goodness up deserved a bonus. The music was booming at this end with the massive speakers set up. My eyes locked in on the two men at the stand-up bar, each with multiple women pressed against them.

They were already hammered and sloppy from whatever alcohol and drugs they'd consumed. I pushed through the bodies dancing and swaying to the thumping beat. Colorful lights flashed in time to the music as the DJ on stage waved his arm in the air.

I had two choices. I could make this quick and seamless, in and out before the guys knew what hit them, or I could wait them out and make this a real party when they decided to leave.

As I glanced around the party, my eyes found the naked asses of women inches away from my fingers. It was Halloween, after all, and body paint was more common than clothes tonight. The one time of year that everyone let loose and became someone else. Someone dark and dangerous they wished they always could be.

I was already dark and dangerous, but I'd lost ten years of my life to a prison that handed us a cookie decorated like a ghost or a pumpkin on Halloween and then told us lights out. That was when we prayed that the real goblins and ghouls surrounding us wouldn't kill us in our sleep.

This was living, and this was what had been stolen from me. A sliver of bitterness uncoiled from where it lurked in my stomach. No, I was going to wait them out, and I had pretty good odds of getting my cock sucked too. That was a two-for-one special if I ever heard it.

Raine

3

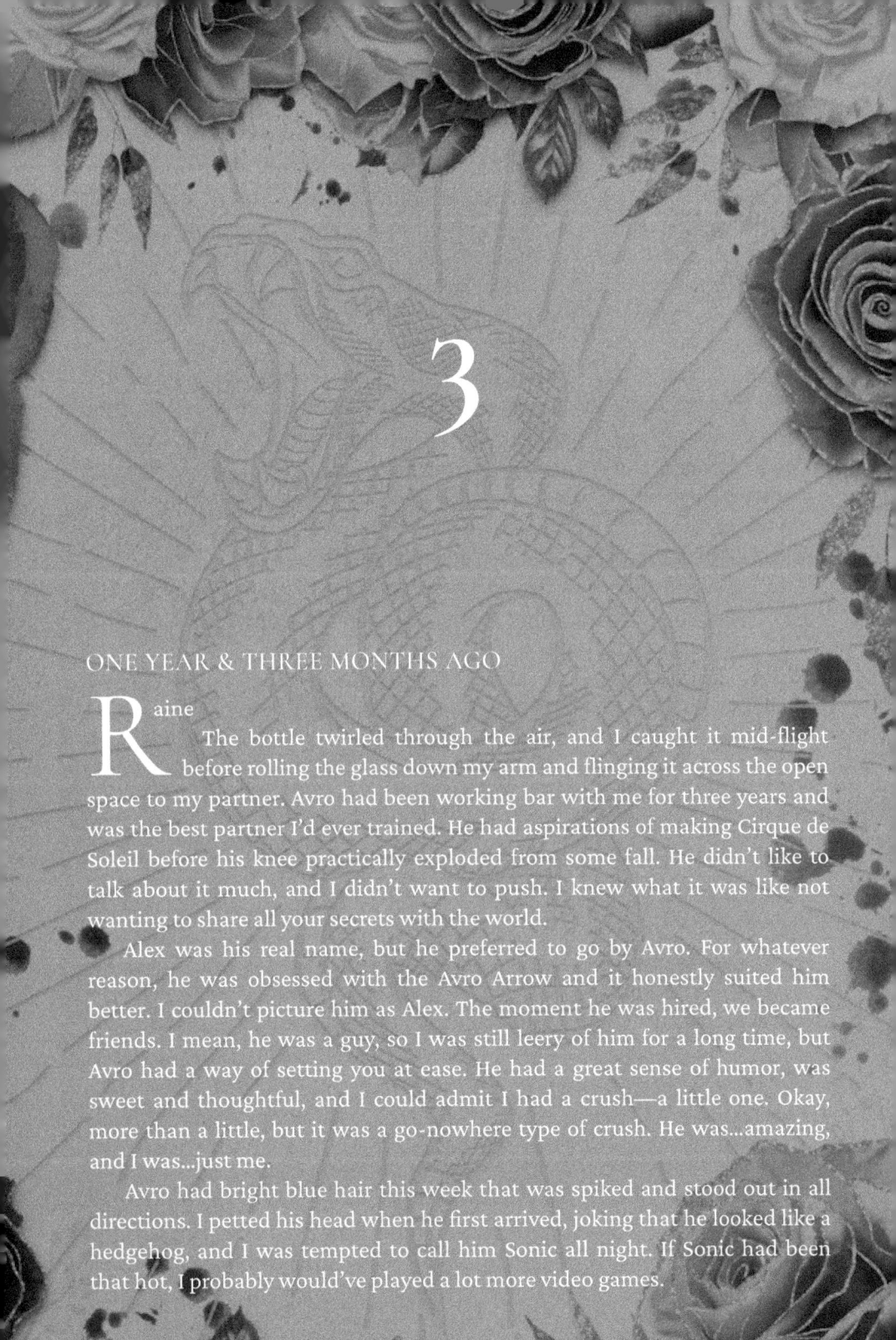

ONE YEAR & THREE MONTHS AGO

Raine

The bottle twirled through the air, and I caught it mid-flight before rolling the glass down my arm and flinging it across the open space to my partner. Avro had been working bar with me for three years and was the best partner I'd ever trained. He had aspirations of making Cirque de Soleil before his knee practically exploded from some fall. He didn't like to talk about it much, and I didn't want to push. I knew what it was like not wanting to share all your secrets with the world.

Alex was his real name, but he preferred to go by Avro. For whatever reason, he was obsessed with the Avro Arrow and it honestly suited him better. I couldn't picture him as Alex. The moment he was hired, we became friends. I mean, he was a guy, so I was still leery of him for a long time, but Avro had a way of setting you at ease. He had a great sense of humor, was sweet and thoughtful, and I could admit I had a crush—a little one. Okay, more than a little, but it was a go-nowhere type of crush. He was...amazing, and I was...just me.

Avro had bright blue hair this week that was spiked and stood out in all directions. I petted his head when he first arrived, joking that he looked like a hedgehog, and I was tempted to call him Sonic all night. If Sonic had been that hot, I probably would've played a lot more video games.

He jumped up, grabbed the glass, and—in a move that would've broken my back—flipped through the air to loud applause before sending the glass back. I tossed him three bottles next. He rolled them up his arms and over his back. We had two smaller bars set up with other bartenders, but people loved having their drinks served by one of us, so I filled glasses as quickly as I could in between performances. I'd been fascinated with the movie *Cocktail* as a teen. I couldn't even remember how many times I'd made Kaivan watch it with me.

My smile faltered at the thought of him. He was the one person I'd trusted in this world, and he turned on me just like everyone else in my life. You couldn't trust anyone, not really. Sometimes I didn't even know if I could trust myself. You never knew what was lurking below the surface. Even with Avro, I'd relaxed around him more than once. Fantasizing about what his lips would taste like and wondering if his shoulders and abs were as firm as they looked. I squashed those thoughts as quickly as they started.

I'd learned the hard way that everyone had their own agenda. The key was to figure out what they were after so you could stay ahead of the fallout.

The crowd was jumping tonight, and as the song switched to a mash up of a fun dance song and "edamame" by bbno$, the cheers got louder. Drinks waved in the air, and I couldn't keep from wiggling to the music.

I fucking loved this job. It was the only time I got out of my head and felt like a person, not a victim or loner, who stayed locked away in her small ratass house. The large bell on the wall rang, and all the regulars knew what was coming. With skill that only came from a shit ton of practice, Avro and I raced to get the tall stacks of shot glasses laid out along the bar.

I punched my arm in the air as the clock counted down to the start of the game. Avro stood at the far end of the bar and smiled as I stuck my tongue out at him. The sound of the buzzer was loud, but it still got drowned out by the roar of the rowdy crowd. Grabbing two bottles off the shelf, I started pouring shots. They were always something of our own creation and the only free round we offered the crowd, or at least those who could fight to get close enough.

It was amazing how excited people got over the prospect of two ounces of alcohol, but they did. They would push and shove and get into fights to be one of the few who would get the shot for free.

"Woohoo!" I screamed as I managed to pull ahead by one shot. We met in the middle, and whoever got there first forced the other person to do a specific trick or task or, in Avro's case, a dance on the bar.

This was not a new idea, but when you freshened it up, made it a competition, and offered free shit, people would keep coming in like the place was the bloody Field of Dreams. The little test glass in front of me was filled with a combination of green apple and cinnamon. I called this one my Apple Pie, and it was a bar favorite. By the bright blue color of Avro's drink, he was doing Blueberry Bomber, which was a combination of blueberry vodka and Blue Curcacao. The owner hadn't been overly excited to give away free alcohol, but he quickly changed his mind when he saw how many extra people it brought in, who then spent way more than the small freebee.

Now that ass got his picture taken for social media posts about the most popular spots in Miami, and Eclipse was quickly rising to the top of the scene. I guess I couldn't complain. I got to keep all my tips, and he gave me a two-thousand-dollar bonus for the idea, which I squirreled away for a rainy day.

"Yeah," I cheered and did a little twirl as I finished filling my last shot and held up the bottles.

Avro finished filling his and offered me one of his drinks as he conceded his loss. I drank it back and held the glass in the air.

"Go," I yelled above the music, and hands struck out like a bunch of vipers and snatched the glasses off the long bar. I wiggled backward and pointed to Avro and then the bar. "Dance, dance, dance," I chanted and got the crowd involved as my face was plastered on the massive screen, flashing the word 'dance' in neon colors.

Avro lived to dance, so this was never really a punishment. If he could, he would be on a stage somewhere full-time and not here slinging drinks with me. With a nifty maneuver, he leaped up on the top of the bar and swayed his ass back and forth, sending the women into a wild frenzy.

The guy was so smokin' hot that you'd burn your hand just touching him. Not a part of his body wasn't cut and ripped to perfection. He always wore contacts that stood out against the color of his hair, and he had the best smile. It was warm and friendly but also said, 'I would strip you naked and lick your body in all the right places.'

He was the kind of hot that made straight men in the crowd second-guess their sexuality. I'd seen more than one man who'd come in with a woman have to adjust themselves. Avro slowly peeled his T-shirt off and put it between his legs like he was riding it. A woman in the front screamed and collapsed as Avro winked at her.

I nodded to the bouncer and pointed to the woman on the floor. Not that anyone paid attention while Avro was on the bar. He ran and slid only to end up on his stomach, and even though I'd seen him practice this and knew what was coming, I couldn't peel my eyes away from the Magic Mike move. He looked like he was fucking the bar as he easily held himself up for all to see his hips working.

Yup, definitely the best job in the world.

It was three in the morning before the bouncers managed to get the last stragglers out of the bar and lock the doors.

"Is it just me, or are the crowds getting more insane?" Avro said as he thumbed through the wad of cash he made. "Fuck, five grand! Damn, at this rate, I might be able to afford that place I was telling you about."

"Only you make that kind of cash. That little move..." I thrust my hips like I was fucking the side of the bar and made him laugh. "Does them in every time."

"True, but you could make this too if you showed them a little more. You know, maybe put a cute bra-type top on under your tank so you could take it off."

Grabbing a towel and the cleaner, I squirted the sanitizer all over the bar and turned my back on Avro. He had no idea why I wouldn't want to do that, and I had no intention of letting him find out. Some scars were better left hidden.

"Just not my thing, but I'm happy for you, Avro. You're fucking good at this, even if it wasn't what you set out to do." I shot him a smile.

"Thanks. Oh, I had a few ideas for some new moves. They are a little trickier than what we normally do, but I know we can do it, and the crowd will love it."

I shrugged as I kept moving so we could get out of here. "Sure, you know I'm always open to learning new routines."

We chatted happily until our portion of the cleanup was completed. Then we changed out of the clothes soaked in alcohol, and only God knew what else. Pulling the hood up on my sweatshirt, I searched through my backpack and pulled out my cell. I had a dozen missed calls. Putting the pack on, I followed Avro out the door and unlocked my phone.

"You want a ride home?" Avro offered. "I promise no drive-thru, no detours, and I'll only take the route you say. You can even keep the window down," he teased.

I smiled, embarrassed that he knew me so well that he was already prepared for me to refuse the offer. I'd gotten many rides from him when we finished late at night, but I always had to talk myself into it. It was stupid, and I hated the fear that crept up simply because I was trapped in a small space with a man.

"That would be great. I hate walking home this late," I said.

The simple black sedan with blacked-out windows was nice but totally opposite to his personality. Avro was always over the top with everything. It made me wonder what his home looked like. Even though we'd worked together awhile now, I'd never once seen his place; and it wasn't for lack of trying on his part.

I didn't know if he was interested in me or used the friend hangout excuse to get me alone. Just the thought of going over to his place sent fear racing through my body and choked off my air supply. It was horrible that one incident ten years ago still had me terrified to be alone with a man, but it was the truth. Kaivan had been my best friend, and I thought I knew him. Not in a million years would I have ever thought he would hurt me, but he did.

Avro put on the radio and described what he wanted to do for the new routine. It was so normal and so us that I relaxed. In a blink, he pulled up to the front of my shoebox.

Hopping out, I leaned on the open window. "Thanks, and I love those ideas. Wanna arrive an hour early tomorrow, and we can practice?"

"Fuck yes." He held out his fist for me to bump, making me laugh. "I'm not leaving until you're inside safely," he said.

He was probably a great guy. It wasn't like I thought all men were evil or anything. I just didn't know which ones were, and I didn't trust my instincts to tell me when I was in danger.

Waving to Avro, I closed the door and locked it before making my way into the kitchen and sitting down to listen to the messages on my cell.

"Raine Eastman, I'm social worker Harvey Johnson. Can you give me a call when you get this message?" I jotted down the phone number, confused about why he had called me. I hadn't spoken to a social worker in many years.

I hit the button to go to the second message. "Hi there, Raine. This is Harvey calling again. This is not news I wanted to leave in a message, but I feel you should be aware that Kaivan McMillan was released today. If you need anything, please call me at..."

I didn't hear anything else left in the message as the phone fell from my shaking hands. Jumping up, I ran to the cupboard and grabbed the bottle of anxiety meds that I'd managed to stop taking.

"Oh, no," I cried out as the stubborn lid flew off the pills and the bottle dropped from my shaking hands.

Dropping to the floor, I curled up in the corner by the sink and pulled my knees to my chest. "No, this can't be happening. No."

Please, dear God, don't let him look for me. Please let him have forgotten all about me.

Raine

4

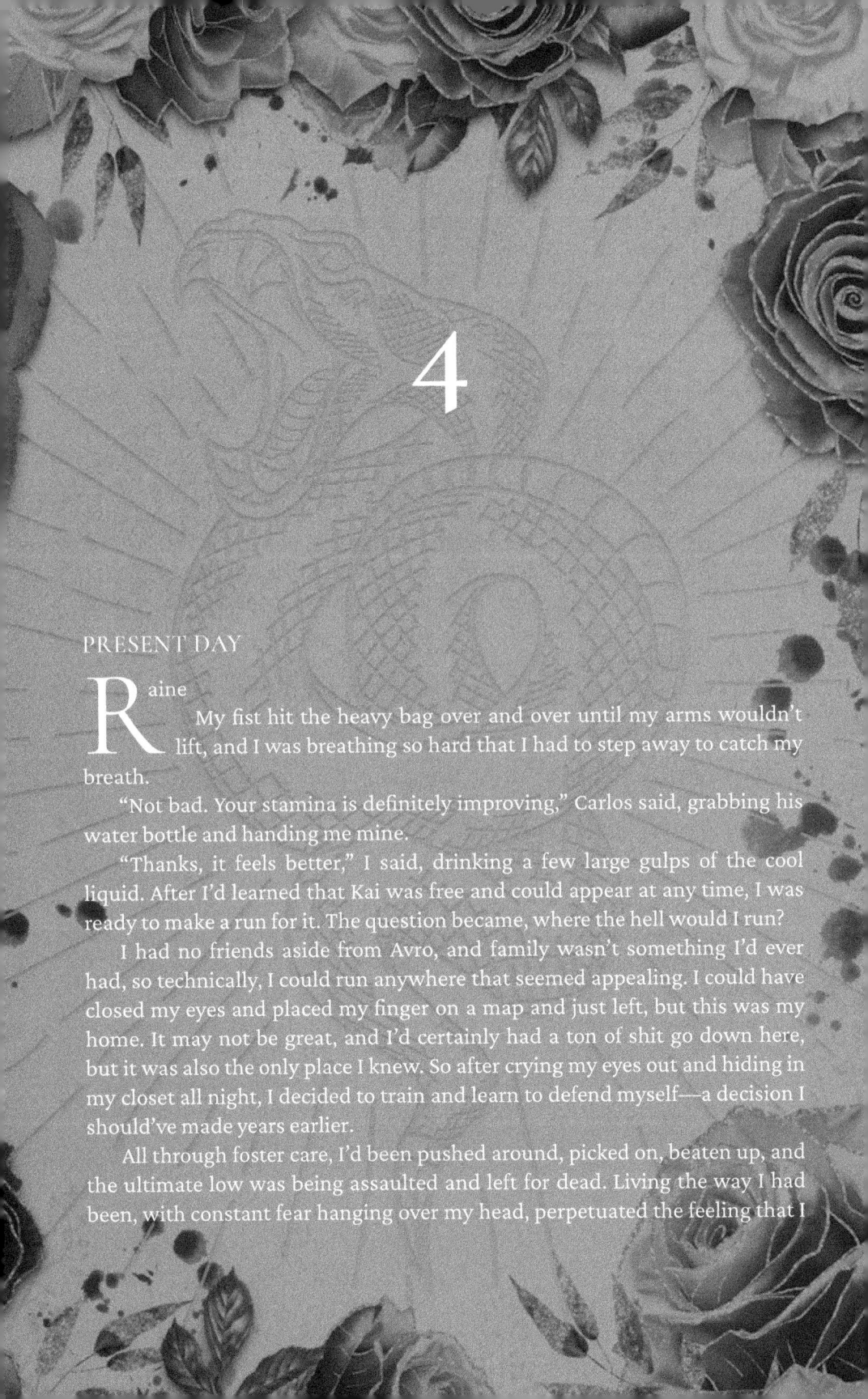

PRESENT DAY

R aine

My fist hit the heavy bag over and over until my arms wouldn't lift, and I was breathing so hard that I had to step away to catch my breath.

"Not bad. Your stamina is definitely improving," Carlos said, grabbing his water bottle and handing me mine.

"Thanks, it feels better," I said, drinking a few large gulps of the cool liquid. After I'd learned that Kai was free and could appear at any time, I was ready to make a run for it. The question became, where the hell would I run?

I had no friends aside from Avro, and family wasn't something I'd ever had, so technically, I could run anywhere that seemed appealing. I could have closed my eyes and placed my finger on a map and just left, but this was my home. It may not be great, and I'd certainly had a ton of shit go down here, but it was also the only place I knew. So after crying my eyes out and hiding in my closet all night, I decided to train and learn to defend myself—a decision I should've made years earlier.

All through foster care, I'd been pushed around, picked on, beaten up, and the ultimate low was being assaulted and left for dead. Living the way I had been, with constant fear hanging over my head, perpetuated the feeling that I was a victim and could be again. Was it still possible? Sure, but now I had skills I could use, and more than that, somewhere in the process of learning to fight, I found the backbone I never knew I had.

I couldn't decide on which discipline I liked until I tried MMA. It was the freedom to use so many techniques that I preferred. My first fight was last week, and even though it was entry division, I walked out of there with a win. It was a shot of courage in my arm.

"Do you have any more fights coming up that I could enter?" I asked and grabbed the towel that Carlos tossed my way.

"Maybe. I'll take a look around and see if there is anyone in flyweight over the next couple of months. I'm sure we can find something for you to enter," Carlos said. "You good to train on Sunday morning?"

"No, I better not. Saturday night is our biggest night at Eclipse, and we're expecting a VIP that will make the place extra busy. Probably won't get home until like eight or nine in the morning."

"Damn, okay. Wanna let me in on who the VIP is?" He smiled, but I'd been sworn to secrecy. The agent of Grimhead Crew had made it clear that he wanted the appearance of his client and the impromptu concert to be a complete secret until they arrived.

"All I can say is that you will want to stop by and make sure to do it early, or you won't get in at all," I smiled wide.

"Damn, that big, huh? I'm in. It's my girl's birthday, and I promised that I had something special planned. My bad that I didn't get something figured out sooner, and this will make me look like an awesome boyfriend." Carlos laughed.

"Your girlfriend won't hear it from me. Just remember to arrive early and get close to the large bar area, and I'll be sure to hook you up with a couple of free drinks," I said, pulling the hoodie over my head.

I needed to get home and get ready for work. Apparently, there was a lot to prepare for when a celebrity came. I'd been given a massive list of musts and only two more days to get it done.

It would be easier if I just showered here, but stripping down naked in strange places was still on my 'No' list. I'd managed to start showering after my shift when it was just Avro around. He never made me feel uncomfortable or did something like test the door. I don't know why he would, but of all people, he was the one I secretly wished had tried. Some fantasies were just too big.

The juice bar had my green sludge ready for me and waiting on the counter. Smiling, I took a sip and held up the drink that, in reality, made me want to vomit.

"Why do I drink this?" I mumbled as I wandered down the street.

I couldn't believe it was already Halloween. It wouldn't be long until Christmas was here and then New Years, and just like that, another year would be gone. Another year older, not sure about wiser, but it felt like I was racing against a clock I couldn't see. A group of kids excitedly screamed as they ran past in their costumes, their parents trailing behind. A real smile graced my lips as I watched the little angel and the pirate run, holding hands. This time of year always made me think of Kai. Halloween was his thing, and I'd fallen in love with the day just as much because of his enthusiasm.

I hated how everything still made me think of him, wonder about him, and worry about him finding me. It didn't matter that over a year had passed since his release, and he hadn't magically appeared on my doorstep. The nagging concern was always there. The worst part was that I missed him. I hated him, and I missed him. How did those two things work?

"Come on, put it on. I spent all my savings to get these costumes for us," Kai said, his smile wide like a child.

"You do realize that we are too old for trick-or-treating?" I asked, holding up the Cat Woman costume. I hated to admit that it looked cool. Cool and I were not exactly on speaking terms. I was more punk/grunge mixed with total geek and a dash of loser, which was not a sexy combination.

"I'm not saying we go and collect candy, but I know of a couple of parties we can crash. Or if you don't want to do that, the beach will be wild, and before you say it, I know we can't buy any drinks." He held up a pirate's hat and snarled at me. "Argh, matey."

Bursting out laughing at the ridiculous look, I nodded my head. "Okay, fine, you win, but only if you promise never to do that again."

"Aw, come on, I need to be able to do it for at least the rest of the night. I mean, I have to remain in character." I lifted a brow at him and crossed my arms over my chest as I held firm. If I didn't, that was all I would hear all night long, and he would do it twice as much just to annoy me. "All right, fine, I promise."

An hour later, I felt like everyone we passed on the street to get to the beach was staring at me. "Why did you have to get the boots so tall? I can barely walk in these," I complained as I tried to walk in the teetering heels that added four inches to my five-foot-four height.

"Stop complaining. You look amazing, and all the guys are staring." Kai smiled

like this was a good thing. I didn't like people staring. In fact, I did everything I could to avoid the very reaction that made Kai puff out his chest.

"I don't like all the guys staring," I whispered and inched closer to Kai as a couple of guys walking toward us openly gawked at my outfit.

"Ignore them. You're here with me."

I knew he didn't mean it like a date, but my heart sped faster in my chest, and I bit my lip as he wrapped his arm around my shoulders and gave it a quick reassuring squeeze before taking his arm back. I didn't want him to. I wanted him to continue to walk like I was his girl and not just his pal or the annoying foster sister.

Just like he said, the beach was crazy with people of all ages. You could easily tell the college groups from everyone else. They were far sexier and a whole lot wilder. A guy ran by and almost knocked me over as he chased a football.

"Hey, watch where you're going," Kai called out, his face dark as he glared at the guy. Kai stepped in close with his back to me, and I could smell the cologne he wore. Unable to help myself, I sucked in a deep breath and sighed. He was always so tough and abrasive, like he needed to take on the world, and yet under the hard shell was this sweet guy. I never told him that. He would probably have a heart attack if anyone thought he was sweet.

"Sorry about that," the guy said. I stepped out from behind Kai, and instantly the new guy's eyes roamed over the skin-tight leather. "Damn, do you want to party with us?"

I shook my head no as Kai suddenly grabbed my hand. "Not a fucking chance. She's with me."

The guy licked his lips and then lifted his muscled shoulders in a shrug. "Suit yourself. It's your loss." He jogged off and tossed the ball to the group of guys waiting.

It felt strange to have Kai touch me like this. That was twice very close together. We'd been staying with the same foster family for five years now, and other than a handshake when I first arrived or the fist bumps that were mandatory after a particularly good round of Call of Duty, we never touched. I looked down at our joined hands and could admit it felt nice. I had no idea how to make him see me as more, but every time he touched me like this, a jolt of excitement shot through my body.

Kai was a couple of years older, and next year, he would head off to college, and I'd be left behind. It didn't sit right. I detested the idea of him leaving for whatever college he chose. He'd already started to take off most weekends to go see the campuses. Kai was smart, much smarter than my C+ grades, but he never applied himself. He was too busy playing games and talking about how much ass he was going to get while away at school with his friends.

His new thing was street fights. I didn't like them. They were dangerous, and he always came home late with a split lip or a black eye. I'd even seen a large purple bruise that wrapped his side when he was pulling on a shirt, but he didn't want to talk about it. I was too young, or as he put it, he wanted to protect me, but I didn't need his protection. What I wanted, he had no interest in.

I'd gone out on a movie date, and as soon as Kai found out, he miraculously showed up at the theater with his friends and a couple of girls. I was furious. Not only was he there to keep an eye on me like an annoying brother, but all the jealousy I ignored when I saw him with girls reared its ugly head. The entire situation was a disaster, and I apologized to my date and said I wasn't feeling well, then took off for home, fuming the whole way.

We'd always promised to be each other's best friend, but it felt like it should be so much more. Yet, he was at home less, talked less, and it felt like he was already gone and pulling away. I was fifteen, and he was seventeen, and I knew that the closer he got to his eighteenth birthday, the more I looked like the dopey foster sister hanging onto his shirt and begging for his attention.

At least, that was how it felt. As soon as the guys moved far enough away, Kai let go of my hand, and the little pitter-patter in my chest crashed and burned.

"Fuck, guys like him are annoying. I should've laid his ass out," Kai said.

"Right. You and who exactly? That guy was huge," I said, and Kai turned his head to look at me.

"I'm ripped," he argued, his dark brows furrowed, making his blue eyes more intense.

"Uh-huh," I said and walked toward the quieter area of the beach.

I left him to either follow or not, but I needed to sit down before these tall boots were the death of me. There were still beach chairs left out from earlier in the day that had been missed during clean up. I dropped down on the chair that doubled as a lounger, groaning, and kicked my feet up.

"What does uh-huh mean?" Kai parked himself in the chair beside mine.

I rolled my head in his direction. "It means that you might be, but he's still a college guy with a bunch of friends, and you're...well, you're just you."

"I'm hot," Kai argued and then turned himself so he was sitting like I was.

"I'm just sayin', you're seventeen, and that dude was like twenty-five." I had no idea why he was angry, but I could feel the tension rolling off him. The breeze off the water felt nice as it hit my face.

"Yeah, and the guy is also a perv. He was going to take you to his friends and want to do all sorts of things that you're just not ready for," Kai argued.

That bristled my anger. "Oh, really? And who says I'm not ready? Maybe I want to be ready. Maybe I wanted to be ready with him, and if so, that is my business," I bit out. Who the hell did he think he was? Telling me I wasn't ready for sex. He didn't get a say in the matter. No one but me did.

"Fine, whatever. You want to be a college guy's slut. Who am I to tell you differently? Just remember that they can be charged with rape. You're still a minor." The way he said minor hurt. It was like he was purposely picking at the fact that we were growing further apart every day.

We were silent for a long time, the strange tension between us just sitting there. I didn't know what to say and didn't want to argue with Kai. He was my only friend.

"I wouldn't, you know," I finally said.

"What?" Kai turned his head to look at me, and I felt him staring at the side of my face. I couldn't look at him, the earlier nervousness was back, and my stomach felt all weird.

"I said I wouldn't. I mean, sleep with that guy. I wouldn't fuck that guy. There, I said it." I scowled at the ocean like it was the water's fault for making me feel this way.

"Good. I didn't want to have to kill him," he said.

I did look over at Kai then. I couldn't tell if he was serious or what his tone meant. His face held no emotion and gave none of his thoughts away.

Unsure what to say about the murderous announcement. I decided he was simply joking and asked the next best question. "You ever wonder if people who don't celebrate Halloween come here and wonder what the fuck is wrong with everyone? I mean, can you picture getting off a plane and everyone outside the airport is dressed up like this?" I pointed to my Cat Woman outfit and smiled.

It took a second, but the impish grin returned to his features, and the hard stare from a moment ago disappeared. "Can you imagine if they saw the pair of guys dressed up like a toaster and a condom back there?"

We both laughed, and just like that, the awkward tension burst, and once more, we were simply two best friends hanging out.

I finished the last of my disgusting healthy drink just as I reached my front door. A honk from the road made me jump and turn. My heart rate tripled for a second until my eyes found Avro, who'd pulled up in his car.

"Fuck girl, you're running late. Hurry up, and I'll give you a ride to work."

"Okay," I called out and pushed open the door. Nervous energy made me shiver, but it was time that I put Kai and all the shit he put me through in the past. I was done letting the memory of him control me any longer. Taking a deep breath, I turned around again.

"Did you want to wait in here?"

"That's okay. I know you won't be long, and I have a couple of calls I need to make," Avro yelled back and picked up his phone.

The lone butterfly that always flitted around when Avro was near floated to the pit of my stomach. Now that I wanted him to come in, I was hurt by his refusal. Was I ever going to stop being a confused mess?

I'd officially banished Kai McMillan from my life and my mind, and yet the lasting effects continued to touch all corners of my life.

Snake

5

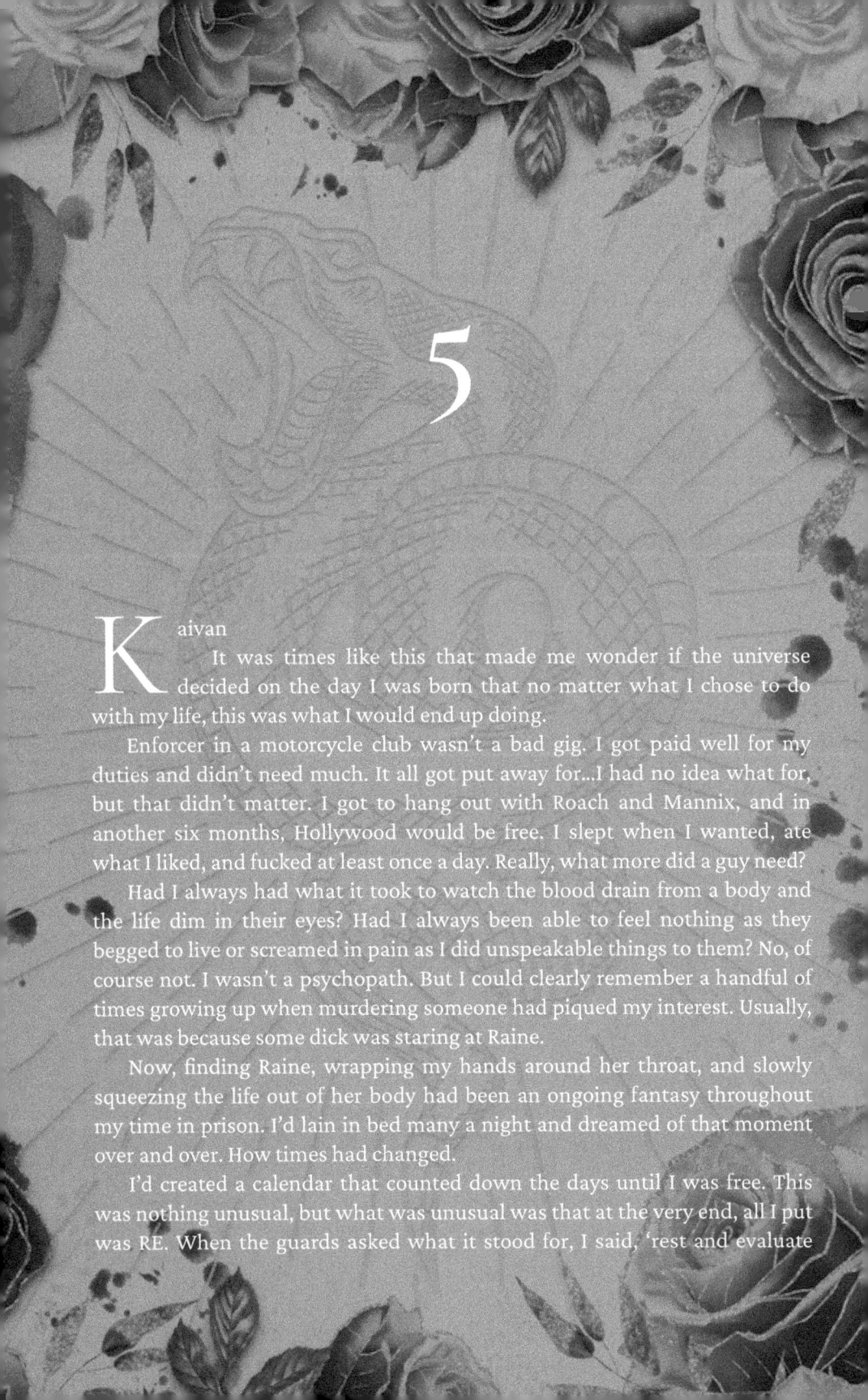

Kaivan

It was times like this that made me wonder if the universe decided on the day I was born that no matter what I chose to do with my life, this was what I would end up doing.

Enforcer in a motorcycle club wasn't a bad gig. I got paid well for my duties and didn't need much. It all got put away for…I had no idea what for, but that didn't matter. I got to hang out with Roach and Mannix, and in another six months, Hollywood would be free. I slept when I wanted, ate what I liked, and fucked at least once a day. Really, what more did a guy need?

Had I always had what it took to watch the blood drain from a body and the life dim in their eyes? Had I always been able to feel nothing as they begged to live or screamed in pain as I did unspeakable things to them? No, of course not. I wasn't a psychopath. But I could clearly remember a handful of times growing up when murdering someone had piqued my interest. Usually, that was because some dick was staring at Raine.

Now, finding Raine, wrapping my hands around her throat, and slowly squeezing the life out of her body had been an ongoing fantasy throughout my time in prison. I'd lain in bed many a night and dreamed of that moment over and over. How times had changed.

I'd created a calendar that counted down the days until I was free. This was nothing unusual, but what was unusual was that at the very end, all I put was RE. When the guards asked what it stood for, I said, 'rest and evaluate what to do with my life now I am free.' The parole board had been very impressed with that answer. Bunch of idiots.

It stood for Raine Eastman, the girl who ruined my life. Finding her and making her pay had been my singular goal for so long, but once I was free, I'd been too busy. I joined the Lost Souls officially, and only a few short months after my release, Mathers left a path of murder and destruction in his wake as he got high on the shit we were supposed to sell.

I'd spent almost every waking hour since that moment cleaning up one disaster after another for fucking Chase. This included killing innocent people who'd seen him do it because his sloppy ass made them a liability. I didn't mind killing. In fact, I enjoyed it most of the time now, but to have to shoot a grandmother of three because Mathers couldn't keep his head screwed on straight was not my idea of a good time. I mourned for her. I didn't want to fucking mourn anyone. I hated him all the more for turning me into a full-fledged monster. For turning me into my father.

I missed a lot while I was locked up but spending the little bit of time I had in a day to hunt down Raine and make her pay was not as enticing as it once was. Secretly, a part of me worried that I would have nothing left to keep me going once she was six feet under. Roach would've laughed his ass off at me if I had told him that.

I made the mistake of mentioning Raine to Chase one day, and he offered to take care of the bitch for me. I almost punched him out. I didn't know what to make of the strange emotions, but for now, I didn't want that chapter of my life to end. She changed me, made me into the man who could rip another's heart out without blinking. I hadn't even decided if what happened had been the best story ever written or the worst that could've happened. That was what Raine was to me, a story waiting to be finished, and I needed to decide how I wanted it to end.

I took a moment to look around at my work and smiled. Blood coated the floor and decorated the walls like I'd tried my hand at abstract art and just happened to be using red paint. It was truly amazing how much blood was in the human body. It was equally impressive how it flew when you were cutting someone up.

The Weasel Legionnaires used this warehouse to store their overflow. It was a fair distance outside of the city and not manned unless they needed to get something. These two asswipes were supposed to be on guard duty for Halloween while the rest of the club was out partying. I still couldn't get over the fucking name. Who the fuck wanted to be part of a motorcycle group with that rat shit name? Weasel Legionnaires? What idiot came up with that?

I glanced over at the man screaming like a little pansy in the corner. His eyes were filled with terror as he stared at the severed head in my hands. Surprisingly, his screams could barely be heard over the movie *Saw*, which played in the background. It was a little dramatic, even for me, but it seemed fitting. Besides, I liked it, and having it playing was sick, psychological warfare. I wished with all my heart that I could be a fly on the wall when this club of assholes found their two members and cleaned up this mess.

A really sick part of me hoped they didn't show up for a couple of days, so it would give the flesh time to rot in the heat.

I'm a sick fuck, but I loved it.

The first guy was already dead. Cutting him up had taken some work, even using the table saw in the corner. It would've helped if he hadn't been alive and trying to escape, but the living gave me much better screams.

Now those parts decorated the empty warehouse and hung from the rafters with rope, like bloody, crimson snowflake decorations. I was surprised that the guy had as much fight in him as he had, considering the massive quantities of alcohol I'd watched him consume. He'd done more little white lines off the bar than I could count, which made it impressive that he could stand, let alone scream and fight while I slowly chopped him up.

The second man—Mutt, was his name—screams reached all new levels as I ripped the two eyes out from the severed head and threaded the rope between the sockets like I was making a cranberry string.

"Oh fuck, oh fuck, oh fuck," Mutt said, then leaned over to heave for the eighth time.

I had no idea how he still had that much puke in his system. I'd asked Mutt earlier if the other guy's name was Jeff, but he didn't get the joke and said, 'No, it's Vic.' No one watched good comedy these days or had a fucking sense of humor.

"Snake man, I'm so sorry. I'll tell you whatever you want to know. Name it, and it's yours. Just please don't kill me," he said as I tossed the head like a ball over the steel beam and tied it off so that it swung slowly back and forth like a grotesque piñata. This had been a lot messier than planned, but when I got them here, and they had a saw...I mean, who can resist that? It was fucking kismet.

"Why?" I turned around to face Mutt.

"W-why w-what?" he stammered.

"Why shouldn't I kill you? I mean, I already know when your guns arrive if I wanted them. I already know it was your crew that tried to hijack our last drug shipment, and..." I held up a bloody finger. "I also know that you've been trying to take over areas that used to be the Reapers' and then claiming that it had always been yours. Those belong to the Lost Souls, and we are not fans of thieves or liars." I smiled wide and made sure to curl up the corners of my mouth like I was the goddam Joker. The wide-eyed look as the guy pissed himself was exactly what I wanted.

The movie was just getting to the good part, where the guy cut off his own foot, and I stared at the screen for a moment as those screams filled the room.

"I swear to you, I had nothing to do with any of that. I mean...I was part of the crew that tried to hit your shipment, but I only did that cause I was ordered to. You know what it's like when you have a boss you need to answer to," he pleaded. "Come on, man. I didn't want to. In fact, I told them it was a stupid idea."

Mutt wasn't wrong. He was mid-level at best, and not following orders would've been a death sentence. But he chose to be in an MC and do their bidding, which was the other side of the coin. If we planned on taking over the Weasels' network and area, I would've gone after the leader, not Mutt. We just needed them to know that we saw the crap they were pulling, and we wouldn't take any shit. Attacking and taking over areas caused other issues you never saw coming. It was better to keep the devil you knew as your neighbor than the one you didn't know at all.

"I believe you," I said, and he slumped against the wall and smiled. "But it doesn't mean I'll let you live either."

Mutt's face paled once more. "What if you keep me alive so I can give Rip a message for you?"

"A message? What is this high school? You wanna pass a love letter for me while you're at it? Maybe draw dicks and tits all over it."

Mutt looked confused. It was official. I was never going to make it as a stand-up comedian.

"I just thought I could relay the message not to mess with you guys or your shit, and I can be the voice of reason at meetings. Or I can join the Lost Souls. I mean, I never wanted to be a Weasel," he offered, nodding his head enthusiastically.

I marched across the floor, weaving my way around the puddles of blood, and with each step, Mutt shook harder. Shake, little Mutt, shake. I lived for that look now. Roach said that Chase had set loose the devil inside of me, and he was right. After fifty, I lost count of just how much blood I'd spilled in the name of the Lost Souls. So much that I craved it a little too much.

In all fairness, I'd been on the path already. A few people in the pen met their fate at the end of my blade. No matter the group or the member, they gave me a wide berth when I walked down the hall. I remembered all too well the day I killed Red and forced Big Dog to lick my shoes. Those were memories that warmed the furthest reaches of my blackened heart.

Squatting down, I stared at Mutt, his eyes wide and frozen in place like a fucking gecko. I waved my hand toward the far concrete wall.

"So what you're saying is, using your blood to write the message, don't fuck with L.S., isn't going to cut it?" I leaned my elbows on my knees and felt the blood dripping off my hands. "Hmm?"

Mutt swallowed, his Adam's apple bobbing as he did. I could almost see the mice in his brain running on little wheels as he tried to think of something to say.

"I'm waiting for an answer," I drawled. "Preferably, one in the next minute."

"Um...they aren't very good at reading." Mutt accentuated each word slowly.

My lip curled up before I laughed, and Mutt followed suit. His tone was more tense, with good reason.

"You know, that is the funniest shit anyone has ever said to me. Probably accurate too."

Technically, I didn't have to kill both. I didn't even have to kill Vic. My orders were to scare The Weasels into backing off—the how was left up to me. I glanced at the glowing red clock near the television, surprised to see it was already ten in the morning. After they left the beach, it took me exactly four hours and twenty-two minutes to capture the two men and kill Vic. Even with a hard night of drinking, the club would be coming around soon, and as much fun as a shootout with them would be, it wasn't the brightest idea.

The seconds ticked on as I thought. Mutt's eyes followed me like a wary, beaten animal. I pushed to my feet and marched over to the industrial sink with the harsh-smelling orange soap. Washing my hands and scrubbing under my nails before I wiped off my leather jacket. At least it was the morning after Halloween. Riding home looking like I was part of a horror movie would seem normal. Drying my hands off, I made my way to the exit.

"Where are you going?" Mutt called out.

My brow arched in his direction. "What? Do you want me to stay?"

"Um...no, but are you coming back?" His voice was hesitant.

"Do I have a reason too?"

"Nooo," Mutt said, drawing out the 'o' and making me smirk.

"Then I guess you answered your own fucking question. Make sure you hold up your end of the deal. Rip better step back and leave the Lost Souls' areas, or I will be back, and I won't just make a spectacle of one of you. I'll slit every single one of your throats while you're sleeping."

Mutt nodded. "Um, can I ask one thing?"

Wow, this guy didn't know when to quit. "What?"

"Can you cut me loose? They aren't going to be here for a few days," he said.

I groaned. Why did he have to say that? Why couldn't he just keep his mouth shut? Some people didn't know when not to look a gift horse in the mouth. Now I was tempted to kill him again.

No, be good. Go home. Get fucked. Get some sleep. My inner voice chanted as the part of me that loved to kill sat up and grinned wickedly in my mind.

"You know, Mutt, you owe me one." I turned to face him. "One day, I'm gonna collect a favor from you because that is how this life works. When I do, you'll do exactly what I ask when I ask you to do it, or you will end up worse than your buddy, Vic. Do you understand?"

Mutt nodded; his lips pressed tight together. I walked over to where I'd piled their crap, grumbling to myself the entire time. Snatching up the phones, I made my way around the blood to Mutt and laid them down. Mutt's hands were tied behind his back, but he could still reach the phone. It would take him a few tries to get it open, kind of like a game.

At least he was smart enough to keep his mouth shut this time as I marched for the door and pushed my way out into the sun. A few sweetbutts would be in early, getting the club ready for later. My cock had a date with one, and then I needed some sleep.

I was getting too old for these all-night parties.

Avro

6

Avro

"I can do this," I mumbled and got out of the car. "You're just asking her to go to the beach as a friend. Nothing wrong with that."

Other than the fact that you're completely in love with the girl, the annoying voice in my mind retorted.

No one asked you. I grumbled to myself.

Wiping my hands off on my track pants, I stared at Raine's front door. It was a pretty shade of blue, with little pots of flowers outside—nothing too much or overstated, like her. The lawn needed some tending unless she was going for the dirt look.

We'd been working together and friends for four years, and all that time, I managed to keep my feelings under wrap. Raine reminded me of a deer. If you moved too quickly, she would startle and take off. I knew that sensation all too well. If it weren't for Jace, I would still be like that.

"You've got this. Just act like your normal self," I whispered under my breath as I knocked hard on the door.

I heard the sound of feet on stairs, and Raine called out that she was coming. The thin curtain beside the window moved, and my heart skipped a beat when my eyes locked with Raine. I smiled and waved.

Okay, that felt stupid.

The door swung open, and there she was, looking like she belonged somewhere other than Florida. She wore a thick sweater and yoga pants like it was freezing outside when it was almost ninety, yet she pulled it off and was as stunning as ever. Her big blue eyes shone, and her short platinum-blonde hair looked adorable. I was staring at her lush lips as she nibbled on her bottom one and had to force myself to look up into her eyes.

"Avro, is everything okay? Nothing is wrong with the bar, right?" She peered out the door like she could see the place from here.

"No, no, everything is fine. I just stopped by to see what you're doing today. I mean, other than work later?" I swallowed the lump in my throat and prayed that it didn't sound as lame as it did in my head.

"Um...well." She crossed her arms. "Not much. I have to pick up a few groceries this weekend."

"Great. Do you want to go to the beach with me?" Her face blanched. "Just to hang out. I hate going alone. I mean, I will, and I've done it before, but I was hoping to have someone go with me for a change. They have a belly dancing festival going on. I thought it might be cool to check out," I said in one long rambling breath and promptly wanted to smack myself on the forehead. Could I sound any more lame?

Raine sucked the lip she'd been nibbling on into her mouth, and I stuffed my hands in my pockets to keep from wringing them.

Please say yes, please say yes.

"If you don't want to hang out with me, then..."

Her face morphed into a horrified expression. "No, it's not that. People and I don't exactly get along, and that sounds like a lot of people."

My brow lifted, and I couldn't help the laugh from escaping. "You do know what you do for work, right?"

A vivid shade of pink spread across her cheeks, making her look more adorable. Raine was this unique combination of sexy and adorable. She had no idea what the hell she did to me.

"Okay, I guess one day won't kill me. Come in, and I'll go grab my stuff." Raine took off upstairs. I stepped over the threshold like it was the holy grail. This was the first time I'd ever been inside her space. In all this time, we'd never been to one another's homes. Until a year ago, I couldn't even get her in my car, and she still turned me down more than she accepted.

"Mind if I look around?" I called up the stairs.

"Knock yourself out. There isn't much to look at," she yelled back.

There was a moderately sized television in the corner, a long grey couch with a matching recliner, and a single coffee table. There were a couple of pictures on the wall, but my brows knit together when I realized they were the ones that came with the frames. The only personal item was a picture of

Raine outside the club when the addition was completed and we held the ribbon cutting ceremony. I knew she wasn't close with her foster family, but that was all she said. It bothered me that she didn't want to open up, but then again, I hadn't told her about everything in my life, so who was I to cast stones?

The kitchen was just as small, but it wasn't the size that bothered me. The lack of anything that screamed this was Raine Eastman's place did. It could've been any Airbnb along this road.

"I'm ready," Raine called out, and I spun around to see her as she reached the bottom of the stairs.

My mouth fell open at the sight of her, and I had to snap my mouth shut. She wore a cute pair of shorts and a tank top with a bikini underneath. Sandals on her feet and a large beach bag slung over her shoulder completed her look.

"Why are you staring at me like that? Do I look bad?" Raine went to the hallway mirror to inspect herself, but I shook my head.

"No, you look amazing," I managed to say before making things awkward.

I could be so smooth at work because it meant nothing to me. It was acting, and I'd done that all my life, but when it was real, I always got tongue-tied. It was as if my brain didn't understand what words were anymore.

"Oh, okay, great. Thanks." Raine cleared her throat. "I brought clothes so we can head straight to work after. I was going to arrive a little early to make sure I didn't forget anything on the list from the Grimhead Crew's manager. I mean, who asks for freshly sliced oranges on a sugar-rimmed glass that is half full of ice cubes and gummies?"

I smirked at her annoyed expression and how her nose wrinkled up like she was smelling something gross. Did I tell her now that I knew the lead singer? In fact, I knew him better than anyone else in my life.

"And don't even get me started on the fresh, green matcha tea that needs to be made during intermission by a professional tea maker. What is a tea maker? I didn't even know such a thing existed until I had to hire one for this event. There are so many requests that I'm starting to wonder if this manager of theirs is only asking for this stuff to see if we will do it."

Raine wasn't far off the mark with that one. Jace had complained more than once about how Allen loved to screw with venues like that. The band would always take the stuff and hand it out to fans if it wasn't used, but Jace thought it was stupid and needless.

"Are we going to get going?" Raine asked, opening the door.

Okay, tell her later it was. It wasn't as simple as saying, 'oh, by the way, I know him.' Nope, that statement always came with a ton of questions, and I didn't want to answer them right now.

It wasn't even ten in the morning, and the sun was so hot that I felt beads of sweat already forming. Weather like this had a special place in the go fuck yourself part of my heart. Every shitty thing that happened to me over the years came when we had one of these intense heat waves that would undoubtedly get worse before ending in a torrential downpour.

It rained like God was trying to cool down the earth, but it was useless. Instead, everything became extra muggy, and the driving force of it tore up crops and flowers, caused leaks in your roof and snakes to show up in the most terrifying places. So yeah, this weather was fun for a day at the beach, but I would be looking over my shoulder for the inevitable shitstorm that followed.

"The nice thing about the festival is that it's only a couple miles from the club, so there's a good chance that we will be extra busy tonight," I said as we got into my car.

"That's true, and the tips will be flowing."

We sat in comfortable silence, but I had the biggest urge to grab her hand and kept glancing at her from the corner of my eye. She wore oversized sunglasses that were all the fashion and looked like a supermodel. All she needed was a fancy convertible to complete the look.

It didn't take much to find the festival. The beach was swarming with people in some form of skirt and bikini top. As usual, when something fun was going on, there was not a parking spot to be had. I ended up parking quite a ways down the road.

"Hope you're okay with walking?"

"Doesn't bother me at all. Although, if we want a quieter spot later, this is nice to come back to," Raine said, pushing open the car door.

My mind raced with all the possibilities of being alone with her on a quiet stretch of beach. I couldn't keep my feelings from her anymore, and Jace spontaneously coming to town and wanting to meet her forced my hand. The question remained, would she run or not?

Raine hid well under her humor and big personality while working. The moment you took her away from the bar, the unease shone through. I knew without asking that she'd been through something traumatic. All this time, brick by brick, I'd been putting pieces into place to make sure she knew she could trust me. I might have been able to push faster if I were Jace, but I wasn't, and it was only around a year ago that I started to see her open up and not be as guarded around me. I was terrified she would go back into her shell if I said the wrong thing or pushed too hard.

We walked along the beach toward the ever-growing crowd of people, and I made sure to walk close enough that our fingers would brush every few strides. If she noticed, she didn't say, but more importantly, she didn't move away. I kept the victory smile to myself.

A large group of guys ran past, all shouting about something exciting. They looked to be from the local campus, most likely frat boys. I suddenly felt very old thinking that. I wasn't that much older than they were, yet it seemed like we were worlds apart.

There were only three things that could make frat boys run that fast. The first was free alcohol and lots of it. The second was anything to do with sex. The kinkier, the better. The third was a fight, especially if it was brewing for a while.

"What do you think that's all about?" Raine said as we closed in on the large group of guys, all holding phones and cheering. "Maybe someone famous?"

"Not a hundred percent sure," I said. The question was answered a moment later when some girls arrived and whistled loudly, calling for more space to be made. The sea of bodies parted, and my mouth fell open.

There, parked on the beach, were three pickup trucks with their tailgates down. That on its own wasn't unusual. There were always tailgate parties along this section of the beach that went unchecked. What was mind-numbingly shocking were the six girls naked from the waist down, sitting two per truck bed with their knees spread open. As soon as a girl was free, a new guy would step up and stick his fingers in her pussy to take a selfie.

"Do they even know or care where those fingers have been?" I was unable to stop myself from asking the obvious question. Raine looked up at me. "What? It's unhygienic."

Raine laughed, a smile breaking out across her face that made the rest of the madness fade away.

"All I know is that I will not be hopping up there to join them. The last thing I want is my kitty plastered all over social media for the rest of my life. Thanks, but no thanks."

The crowd was getting rowdy with the alcohol flowing. With the overly testosterone-infested situation, there would be a fight yet. I could feel the charge in the air.

"Over this way." I nodded toward the shoreline, where fewer people gathered. We veered in that direction. "I can tell you one thing for certain. I wouldn't want to be the cop sent here to shut this down."

"No kidding," Raine said.

Movement caught my eye. Some guy was running in our direction but not looking. A football soared through the air, and there was no way he would get to it in time. I instinctively wrapped my arm around Raine's waist. She tensed but didn't jump away as I pulled her away from the torpedoing ball. I smacked it out of the air and glared at the guy that almost ran into us, my muscles ready for impact.

"Oh shit. Sorry, man," the guy said as he bent and picked up the ball. I cocked a brow at him as I told him to get the fuck away from me with my eyes.

I hadn't always been tough. In fact, one would say that I used to be the nerdy kid who got shoved in lockers and books knocked out of my hands or money stolen at lunch. The only thing that saved me from any of those things was Jace. We were polar opposites when we first met, yet we became fast friends. He only needed to look in an asshole's direction, and they would run the other way. I hadn't mastered that yet, but I was getting there.

"Thanks, I didn't even see that coming," Raine said when the guy jogged away.

"No problem." I kept my arm around her waist and counted down in my head till she pulled away. She was tense at first, but I couldn't contain my smile as she relaxed into me.

"What are you smiling about?" Raine asked.

"Just enjoying the beautiful day with one of the best people I know," I said, dancing around my words carefully.

"We're almost at the festival. Did you want to remove your sandals and walk in the water?" I suggested.

"Sure."

It felt like a race to get them off. As Raine picked up her shoes, and I gripped her hand, making her squeal as we ran for the water.

"Oh my god, nooo," she said. The protest was half-hearted as she laughed and squealed when the next wave crashed into our legs. We were soaked to our knees in a blink. She glared up at me, smiling with fake anger. "Jerk."

"I wanted to get you wet," I said, and her face turned every shade of pink before her eyes flicked away from mine. "Do you like to swim?" I quickly asked.

"Not really, at least not in the open water like all those people." Raine pointed to the large group of swimmers floating on inflatables, splashing, or playing water volleyball. "I do like pools, though. Less likelihood that I'm going to run into something creepy."

I smirked. "I guess that depends on the pool."

We looked at one another as that comment filled our minds with whatever terrifying images we conjured, then laughed hard.

"It's great to see you smile for real. You have a beautiful smile," I said.

My lips tingled with the urge to kiss her, but I held myself in check. Today was already a big win and a step forward. I had plans to push more tonight and hoped that she would be thinking about today when tonight finally came. Everything inside me was a jittery mess with the thought of Jace and Raine in the same room. I wanted this to go well.

No, I needed this to go well.

Raine

I wasn't sure what had gotten into Avro. I was shocked when he showed up at my door, but I couldn't say no to a day out with him. He was like a supermodel and could have posed for any magazine or book cover.

Yet, as we walked along the beach, he seemed completely oblivious to the stares he got. Could he be interested in me? No, that was a ridiculous thought. Or was it? Did I want him to be? I was nervous to admit that I did. It felt like I was setting myself up to be hurt if I let him in and created this whole idea of what we could be, only to have him laugh and say, 'I only meant as friends.'

The meter other people had to tell them that someone liked them was all skewed in my head. Mine spun in confusion all day long. We stopped and watched the long line of professional belly dancers. I wiggled to the music while Avro tried to match them, and of course, he was freaking amazing at it. Once again, I wondered why the hell this guy stuck around here, working in a club as a bartender when he was so talented. I tripped over my own feet while walking. He probably knew ballet. I'd been terrible at sports in school, while I knew he loved basketball and had been offered a full scholarship because he was that good.

Everyone clapped as he joined the line, earning heated stares from those watching. A tug of jealousy bloomed in my chest. It had flared before at work, but it was part of his job to flirt with the patrons and keep them buying drinks. Out here, he was sort of with me. At least, that was how it felt. This feeling was something I hadn't had for a very long time. Annoyed with myself, I swept it aside. There was no point in fantasizing about something that was never going to happen.

I couldn't stop smiling, and for the first time since I was a teen, I giggled as he danced toward me. My whole body felt like it was on fire with each step closer. He was wearing aqua-colored contacts today that matched the water at my back, but it was the intense look in his eyes that had me squirming.

"Wow, that is a lot harder than it looks." He looked over his shoulder and waved. "Thank you for the dance," he called out.

"Any time," came the reply, and I ground my teeth together as I glared at the girl.

"Did you want one of those slushies?" Avro pointed to a stand selling an assortment of cool treats along the boardwalk. "I could really use something cold."

"Yeah, sounds great." I didn't expect him to take my hand again, but when he did, I nibbled on my bottom lip and tried not to look as giddy as I felt. He was the first person in so long that made me feel a hundred percent safe and comfortable.

Nope, there was no place for Kai on this lovely day, and I dusted those thoughts to the side.

"Why don't you stay here? No need for both of us to stand in that long line in the sun," Avro offered as we stepped under the shade of tall palm trees.

"Are you sure?"

"Of course. What flavor do you want?"

I smiled wide. "Surprise me."

"Oh, I plan on it," he said and jogged away, but the glint in his eye and curl of his lips made me feel like we were no longer talking about the slushies.

More of the crowd from down the beach filtered up this way. Either they had gotten their fill, or the trucks had been shut down. I was staring down at my sandals, thinking I needed a new pair, when a hand grabbed my ass.

Yelping, I jumped forward and spun around to find a guy I'd never met.

"Damn girl, that is a damn fine ass. It would look amazing bouncing on my cock," he said, his blue eyes glazed with alcohol while his blonde hair waved in the breeze.

My relationship meter might be broken, but my creep-o-meter worked just fine.

"Don't touch me."

"Oh, you're feisty. I like it." He stepped in my direction, so I mirrored and stepped back. My hand balled into a fist while my other one gripped the handle of my bag tighter. The first thing Carlos taught me was anything could be used as a weapon.

"Don't be like that. I know you want this." Of course, the drunk asshole had to grab his cock. Why did guys do that? Did they actually think we liked it? "I mean, I'm Dennis Copland. No one can resist me."

He took another step, and I backed up once more. I would hit him if I needed to, but I preferred he just went away. An assault charge was not what I had planned for my Saturday.

"I don't care who you are. Back the fuck up," I said. I kept my tone even, but if looks could kill, he would've been dead.

"Oh, come on. You must know who I am. Everyone around here does." He cocked his hip and smiled. I was sure that had fooled some poor girl who thought pretty-boy looks and frat-boy swagger was impressive. That was not me.

"Nope, never heard of you, and I don't want to. Now, are you going to move along, or am I?"

Dennis continued to stand there and stare at me like that would somehow get me to change my mind.

"Fine, I'll move," he said, backing up a few steps. Dennis rolled his eyes and crossed his arms over his chest.

Figuring that was far enough away, I turned around to find Avro when a hand clamped onto my shoulder.

"No one turns me down, especially not some washed-up bitch like you," Dennis snarled.

Moving on instinct, I spun and knocked his arm away before stepping in close and driving my knee up into his crotch. The pain registered on his features instantly. Shoving him hard, he landed on his ass in the sand.

"I said, don't touch me," I growled at the jerk as Avro stepped up beside me.

I jumped a little when his arm brushed mine, and I immediately hated that I did.

"I was going to come over and kill this guy, but it looks like you have it all taken care of," Avro said casually. I looked up at him as he held out the slushie.

"Bitch, I think you broke my dick," Dennis groaned, still in the fetal position on the ground.

"Consider yourself lucky that's the only thing she broke, asshole. Don't touch my girlfriend again," Avro said, his voice as hard as steel.

Excited energy fluttered in my chest at the word girlfriend. Of course, just like another time in my life, it was said to get rid of a scumbag, but I couldn't help feeling that this time, it meant more. I took the red drink from his hand, and Avro immediately put his arm around my shoulder as he guided us away from Dennis and the crowd he was drawing.

"Why did you say that?" I asked.

He shrugged. "Unfortunately, guys like that only respect one thing, and that's a bigger, meaner guy. Sexist? Yes, but it doesn't make it any less true. Besides, you already embarrassed him in front of all those people." Avro leaned closer to my ear, and a shiver traveled down my spine. "And, if I stayed any longer, I was going to punch him. No one touches you..."

My mouth ran dry, and I quickly sipped on the cold slushie. It almost sounded like Avro was saying that I was his. My body heated all over, and it felt like a million degrees.

"And then everyone wonders why I don't people," I said and looked over my shoulder, but there was no sign of the jerk. Sighing, I played over the interaction and decided my mistake was turning my back on him. No matter how stupid I looked, I shouldn't have taken my eyes off him.

"Hey, are you okay?" Avro asked as the silence stretched on between us.

"Yeah, I'm just not feeling the fun beach vibe anymore. I'm sorry, that guy gave me the creeps, and I keep playing it over in my mind, trying to figure out what I could've done to avoid it altogether." I glanced up at him, and he was frowning.

"Raine, there is nothing you should have to do. That's the point. He shouldn't have touched you at all, and that's not on you." Avro pulled me closer, and I sighed, feeling completely relaxed with him around.

God, that felt good. To be touched and not be afraid. I didn't want the day to end, but I'd lost the mojo.

"Would you mind if we just headed to the club now? I really should make sure everything is set for tonight."

"Of course, but, Raine...try not to let that loser get to you. Jerks like that are a dime a dozen, and they win if you let them stop you from doing what you want. Don't give them that kind of power."

Avro smiled, but there was sadness in his eyes. Was he just sad about the day ending early, or was there more under the hooded stare? I suddenly wanted to know everything about him. Things I'd never asked to keep myself from falling more than I should. Wrapping my arm around his waist, I hugged him.

"Thanks, I needed to hear that, and thank you for an incredible day."

Snake

7

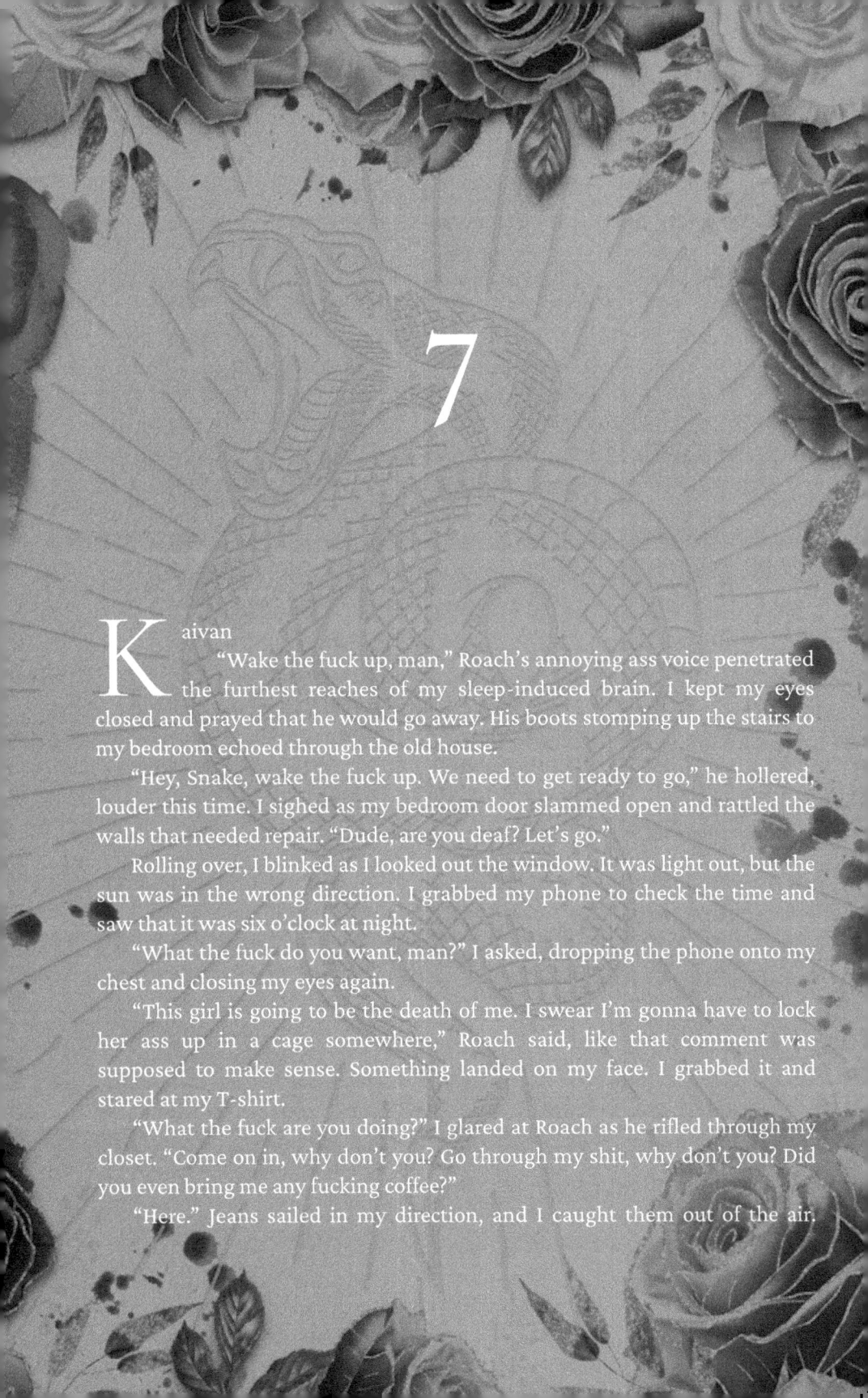

Kaivan

"Wake the fuck up, man," Roach's annoying ass voice penetrated the furthest reaches of my sleep-induced brain. I kept my eyes closed and prayed that he would go away. His boots stomping up the stairs to my bedroom echoed through the old house.

"Hey, Snake, wake the fuck up. We need to get ready to go," he hollered, louder this time. I sighed as my bedroom door slammed open and rattled the walls that needed repair. "Dude, are you deaf? Let's go."

Rolling over, I blinked as I looked out the window. It was light out, but the sun was in the wrong direction. I grabbed my phone to check the time and saw that it was six o'clock at night.

"What the fuck do you want, man?" I asked, dropping the phone onto my chest and closing my eyes again.

"This girl is going to be the death of me. I swear I'm gonna have to lock her ass up in a cage somewhere," Roach said, like that comment was supposed to make sense. Something landed on my face. I grabbed it and stared at my T-shirt.

"What the fuck are you doing?" I glared at Roach as he rifled through my closet. "Come on in, why don't you? Go through my shit, why don't you? Did you even bring me any fucking coffee?"

"Here." Jeans sailed in my direction, and I caught them out of the air.

"Coffee and pizza are downstairs. We need to go soon before they open the doors and don't let us in. You can eat on the way."

"Is someone dying?" I asked as Roach continued to stomp around my room like a cave dweller. I was expecting him to scratch his dick and grunt at me.

"Not yet, but I may be before the night is through," he mumbled, making me shake my head.

"Am I getting to kill someone?" I still didn't know what the fuck he was talking about, but I pulled the T-shirt on over my head, thankful I'd taken the time to shower when I got in.

"You really need to paint or something. This place looks like hell," Roach mumbled and tossed me a pair of socks from my drawer.

"I'm not going anywhere until you explain what the fuck is going on. You're not making any sense, and get out of my drawers. Shit, man, what are you, the warden?" I growled at my friend, and he slammed the drawer shut.

"I'll tell you when you get downstairs," he said, disappearing out the door.

"Hey?" I called out.

"What?"

"Is this a dress-up or get-bloody type of party?"

"I don't know. I guess dress-up. I don't expect anyone to get bloody, but with this girl, anything is possible," Roach grumbled as he stomped down my stairs.

Nothing like being woken up by the Tasmanian Devil. The guy was aptly nicknamed cause he was as annoying as any insect I'd ever come across. Holding up the jeans, I glared at them and wondered how Roach knew I liked these. It was creepy that he knew me that well. I couldn't have gone into his room and picked out an outfit that fast.

Yanking the jeans and socks on, I gave myself a once-over in the mirror. Then I strapped on my stylish leather cuffs, dropped my silver chain around my neck, and ran a hand through my hair. Guess that was about as dressed up as I got. The bathroom was next, and the fucker was just gonna have to wait.

Five minutes later, I wandered into my kitchen and watched Roach pace the floor.

"Shit, man, that took long enough." He spun around and looked at me. "Meh, you look okay, I guess. I can always bribe the bouncers."

"Break into my home, wake me up, and insult me. Keep it up. You're on a roll." I snatched the coffee off the kitchen table and popped the lid. It smelled like burnt tires. "Where the hell did you get this?"

"The gas station down the street," Roach said, pulling a piece of pizza from the box and stuffing his face with it. He was chewing so fast I would've guessed he was in a food-eating contest. Walking to the sink, I poured the coffee down the drain. "Hey, I got that for you."

"Yeah, you're trying to fucking poison me is what you're trying to do. I don't drink that shit. If you want me to go anywhere with you, then two things need to happen. The first is we hit a coffee shop of my choice on the way, cause I need the caffeine. Second, you tell me what the hell is going on."

He was jittery, like he'd taken something, but that wasn't Roach. He smoked and drank but steered clear of drugs, so I knew this was all him.

"Can we get going first?" he said and held out the box of pizza. One look at the black olives with four different meats and extra cheese had my stomach turning.

I held up my hand. "No thanks."

"What, you watching your figure?" he mumbled around the mouthful of food.

"Do you want me to come with you or not? Cause I'm very tempted to tell you to go fuck yourself and go back to bed."

He licked his fingers and dug around in his jacket, pulling out his truck keys. "Fine, coffee and tell you what's what. I got it. Now let's go. We're taking my truck."

I grabbed my clean leather jacket, locking the door on my way out, while he jogged to the shiny black vehicle. As always, I glanced over at the amusement park between my house and the club property. I didn't like the idea of living there with everyone. Maybe it was cause for ten years I had to live with too many fucking people I didn't want to. Living here, on this old farm with a couple hundred acres to myself, was nice.

Besides, I had a great view of Wilder's crazy-ass antics, and that made me smile. There was no sign of him tonight, but that didn't mean anything. He was one of those types who could be standing right in front of you, and you wouldn't see him unless he wanted you to.

"Are you coming, Grandpa?" Roach called out, and I cracked my knuckles.

"I'd kill him if he wasn't such a good friend." Stomping down to the truck, I hopped into the passenger side and stole one of his cigarettes from the pack on the dash. Lighting up, I took a pull and blew it out the open window as we drove down my long driveway to the road.

"All right, out with it. What are we doing and why?"

"I need to keep an eye on Lane," Roach said, and I cocked an eyebrow at him. "She's going to this bar tonight. She got word from the other sorority sisters that some famous band would be there singing, and she decided to go.

So we need to go. No group of horny band guys is getting their hands on Lane."

"Are we talking about Lane as in Hollywood's sister?" I was trying to keep up with his train of thought.

"Yes, who else would I be talking about? I only know one Lane," Roach said.

"You know, I really want to stab you right now," I grumbled, and took another pull on the cigarette before tossing the rest out the window. This cutting-back thing sucked ass.

"Why exactly are we stalking Hollywood's sister now? He asked you to look out for her, not turn into her personal bodyguard. Next thing you know, you'll be singing Whitney Houston songs about love," I said, and batted my eyes at Roach.

"Fuck you. It's not like that. I'm just taking my role seriously. Would you want to be in charge of a college girl while her brother trusts you to keep her safe? Especially after what Hollywood has already been through?"

"I guess not." I yawned and wished we were doing anything but going to some bar, club, or whatever this place was. "So, where are we going?"

"Do you listen to anything I say?" Roach looked over like I was a four-year-old who hadn't done my chores.

"I try really hard not to."

"So funny. Eclipse, it's down by the beach, you know, the one with the fancy lights on the patio area?"

"No, actually, I don't," I said.

"I don't get it. Why can't she be some geek that likes to be a hermit and stay in her room? And why does she always have to go out looking like she's ready to fuck everything? If someone so much as touches her, I'll cut off their hand."

Crossing my arms over my chest, I stared at the side of Roach's face and his twitching jaw muscle.

"You like her," I said, and his eyes snapped to mine.

"No, I don't."

"Yeah, you do."

"No, I fucking don't. The last time I wasn't making sure she stayed out of trouble, I found her at the clubhouse taking her shirt off." Roach gave me his full attention, his eyes wide. "Do you know what Hollywood would've done to me if he found out that she fucked one of the guys at the club? I'd be a dead man. D.E.A.D, man."

"Dramatic much? First, none of the guys were going to fuck the girls, at least I don't think, but I'm sure she fucked a ton of guys before her big bro put the chastity belt in place." Roach narrowed his eyes, and I couldn't resist poking at him. "Look at her. She's a smoke show and totally fuckable. We could've given her a good old roasted spit job that night if you hadn't chased her off," I said and waited for it.

"Don't you dare fucking touch her. You lay one finger on her fucking head, and I'll blow your dick off," Roach growled, his eyes murderous, which made me snort and then laugh.

"Yup, you don't like her at all," I said.

"You're a prick. I'm only fired up 'cause Hollywood is my bro, and if roles were reversed, he would look out for my sister. I can't let her get hurt or into trouble."

"I didn't know you had a sister," I said.

"I don't."

I shook my head and tried to right the insanity train. "Okay, fine, so you basically want me along for babysitting duty. Check. I now understand what we are doing and why. Next question, how far away is this place?"

"Dude, it's Eclipse. Fuck, do you pay attention to anything? We pass it almost every day. It's like twenty from here," Roach said as he wheeled into the coffee shop he knew I liked. I had no clue why he didn't just come here in the first place if he planned to try to bribe me.

I'd heard of this bar, but it wasn't my type of hangout. I preferred the quieter and a whole lot seedier spots or just stayed at the clubhouse. These popular bars were all the same. A million fucking people rubbing up against you, but with way too many clothes on. Jerks who thought they were tough when they had no idea what it was actually like to kill someone, and the booze was always way overpriced.

"Is this going to be a regular thing? The whole stalk her all over Florida?"

"If the girl would learn to stay put, then no. I really should invest in that cage. Do you think I could get away with putting her in a cage? Hollywood would be fine with it if it kept her safe, wouldn't he? I could give her pillows and food, and she would need a toilet," Roach mumbled as he tapped his chin. I didn't know if he was actually asking me this ridiculous question, so I stayed quiet. "Hollywood gets out in six months. I could make it work. College kids go MIA all the time to party, and I could force her to keep her studies up."

No, he didn't like this chick at all. Totally normal fucking reaction. I rolled my eyes at Roach. Maybe he didn't see it, but you would have to be blind not to see how he felt for this girl.

"I say no to the cage. Hollywood is not going to like his sister in a cell like he is," I said.

"Hmm, you may have a point."

I stared out the window as the sun set. There was only one girl I'd ever loved or wanted for more than getting my cock wet, and now I hated her.

Pushing the thought of Raine from my mind, I sighed and focused on the road, no longer paying attention as Roach talked. One of these days, I was going to miss something important, but that wasn't tonight.

Roach pulled into the beach parking lot and immediately swore as we watched a group of girls wearing so little it could pass as beach wear walk by the truck. Roach ducked low as Lane looked over and waved.

"Smooth, man. Totally suave. She didn't see you at all," I mocked and pushed open my door.

"Shut up, man," Roach snarled back and swore as Lane held up her finger to her friends and reversed course. She was heading straight for the truck, and I leaned against the hood, loving every fucking second of this.

Roach couldn't have looked any guiltier if he had tried as he slipped from the driver's seat and met the cute little blonde as she stepped up to the truck with her hands on her hips.

"Cole, are you following me?"

My brows lifted at the use of Roach's real name. He didn't tell many people what it was unless forced to, but I couldn't picture her having to force him to do much of anything. He looked more like he was ready to dissolve into a little puddle at her feet for a taste. Pathetic.

"No, of course not. I heard that there is a special headliner here tonight, Grim Man Garbage Bag, you know...." Roach stopped and looked over at me, but I wasn't helping him out of this mess.

Lane looked completely unimpressed as she lifted an eyebrow at Roach. "You mean Grimhead Crew?"

"Yeah, them. I was only joking. Ha, ha." He pretended to laugh.

I smirked at how ridiculous Roach was acting, earning a dirty glare from him. If this was his 'I'm acting totally cool and aloof routine,' it seriously needed work. Given even a sniff of opportunity, he would have this girl in the back of the truck fucking her hard. Oh, Hollywood was going to love that when he got out. I smiled wide. Okay, this night was making me feel a little better.

"Whatever. Look, Cole, I know that Nate has you watching me. My brother is such an ass. Of course, my brother would send his friend to spy on me. You don't need to. I'm not going to do anything stupid."

"Define stupid," Roach said.

Lane made an angry huff sound and stomped away.

"Wow, you are slick, just like butter on a hot summer day," I drawled, smiling at Roach. This night was far more entertaining than I initially thought it would. Watching Roach humiliate himself was a sport for me.

Raine

8

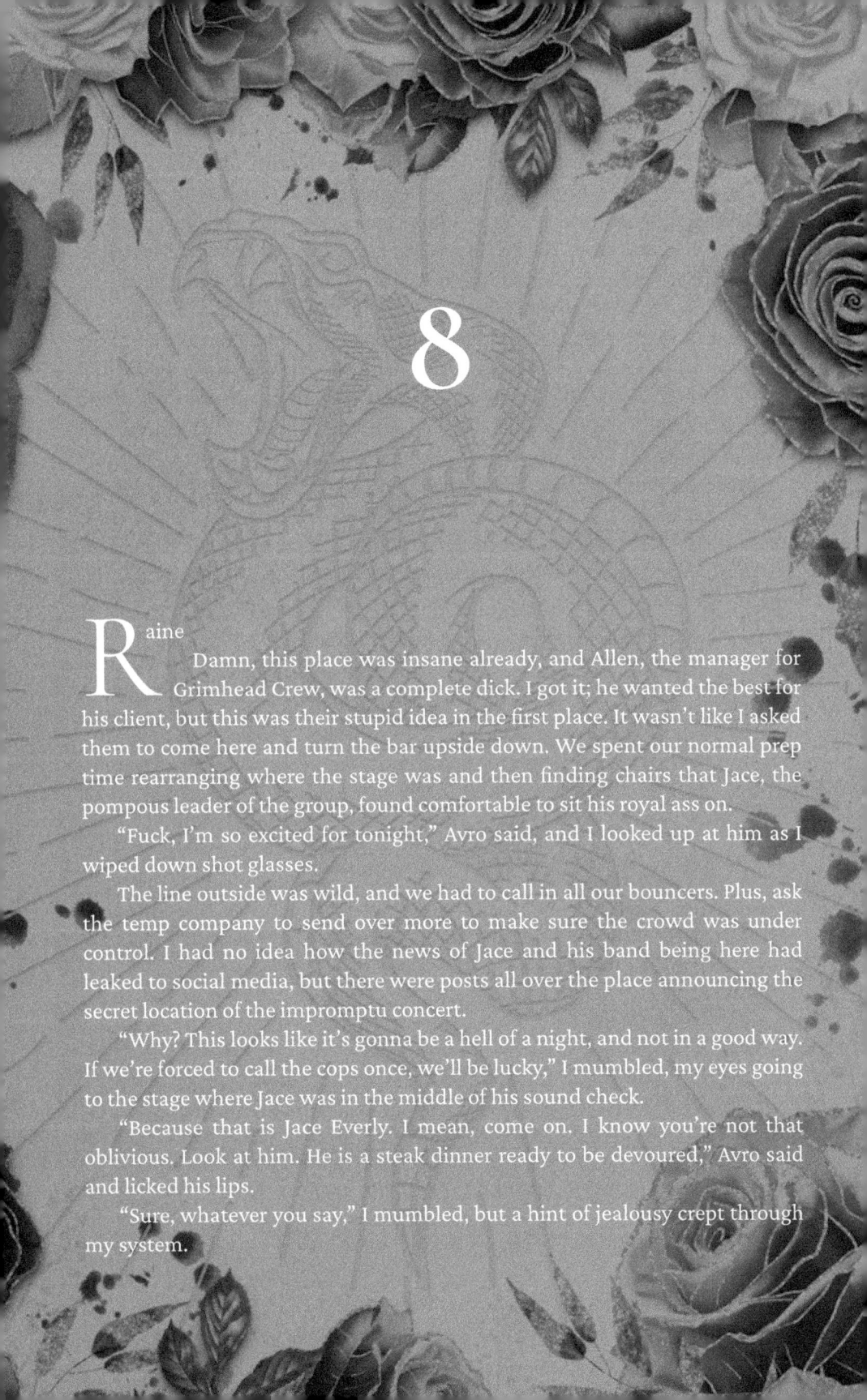

Raine

Damn, this place was insane already, and Allen, the manager for Grimhead Crew, was a complete dick. I got it; he wanted the best for his client, but this was their stupid idea in the first place. It wasn't like I asked them to come here and turn the bar upside down. We spent our normal prep time rearranging where the stage was and then finding chairs that Jace, the pompous leader of the group, found comfortable to sit his royal ass on.

"Fuck, I'm so excited for tonight," Avro said, and I looked up at him as I wiped down shot glasses.

The line outside was wild, and we had to call in all our bouncers. Plus, ask the temp company to send over more to make sure the crowd was under control. I had no idea how the news of Jace and his band being here had leaked to social media, but there were posts all over the place announcing the secret location of the impromptu concert.

"Why? This looks like it's gonna be a hell of a night, and not in a good way. If we're forced to call the cops once, we'll be lucky," I mumbled, my eyes going to the stage where Jace was in the middle of his sound check.

"Because that is Jace Everly. I mean, come on. I know you're not that oblivious. Look at him. He is a steak dinner ready to be devoured," Avro said and licked his lips.

"Sure, whatever you say," I mumbled, but a hint of jealousy crept through my system.

Avro was openly bi-sexual, and we'd never dated or been intimate on any level. Today at the beach was the most non-work interaction we'd ever had, and it was very PG. Yet, the fact that he was staring at Jace like he was food, and Jace was openly staring back, bothered me.

I continued to take in the rock star with his mop of shock-white hair, part of it hanging in his eyes. I hated to admit it, but he somehow pulled it off, and it looked great on him. His matching silver eyes practically glowed under the spotlights. It made me wonder if they were contacts or somehow a trick of the light that was all him. He had that air of arrogance that all those who found popularity had. I hated that attitude. Just because you became famous didn't give you the right to treat people like dirty pieces of toilet paper stuck to your shoe.

Jace looked over, and he smiled as our eyes locked. Forcing my stare away, I pointedly looked up at Avro, who seemed more flustered than any of the girls outside.

"Okay, fine, the guy is hot. You planning on leaving me here to run off with the circus?"

Avro's lips curled up as his eyes found mine. He was wearing all black tonight that matched his dyed black hair in a sexy gothic way. He even put in cat-eye contacts that made his intense stare seem more unnerving than usual. He leaned against the bar, staring directly into my eyes.

"What is that I smell?" I looked around and down at the glass before sniffing my black tank top. He laughed at my confused look. "I mean, is that jealously I detect in your voice?"

My face heated, and I kept my eyes trained on the next shot glass I picked up. "No, of course not. What would I have to be jealous over?"

"Absolutely nothing unless...you wanted there to be," he said. The sultry tone had shivers racing down my spine.

I cleared my throat. "I'm just concerned I need to find a new bartender," I said, giving him a pointed look.

"Are you sure about that?" he asked, leaning in a little closer.

We'd worked together for a long time, and it had taken me a while to accept that I was genuinely attracted to Avro. The thing was, I hated the idea of dating. Others loved the thrill of getting dressed up and going out for the night with someone, but I liked comfy clothes and a movie. More unnerving was that I hadn't had sex since my attack. That was eleven years ago. Forget a duster. I needed a whole cleaning company to remove the cobwebs in that cave.

Shit, I'd practically hidden in my house this entire time. I wasn't even sure how to flirt with Avro. Was that something people even did anymore? Should I shoot him a text—when and where to meet—and then we could sit and stare at our phones? That seemed to be the norm now. We worked together, and...he was my only friend. Dating and sex could ruin that, and then what? Emotions were far too confusing.

"I'm sure that I want to get this done before those doors open," I said, pointing to the tall stack of shot glasses still needing to be wiped down. I loved it when they first came out of the kitchen, all clean. They were warm to the touch, and something about that fresh smell comforted me, but I hated the little spots that would dry on them if we didn't wipe them.

"You can't fool me, Raine. I saw that tough exterior crack for a little while today, and very soon, you're finally going to let me in," Avro said.

I bit my lip as it felt like he was talking about things far more intimate than the words that came out of his mouth.

"I'll be right back. Get those cleaned and ready. We don't have much time left before that swarm outside is all over us."

"I know what I want all over me," Avro said as I walked behind him.

As I glanced over my shoulder, he looked at me and then at Jace before finding my eyes again. Oh, I knew what he was thinking, and now I knew he'd stepped out of reality to wander around in fantasy land with candy canes and gumdrops.

Shaking my head, I wandered into the back and down the short staircase to the downstairs storage area. There was no point in one of us leaving the bar to get the extra cases of our most popular in the middle of the shift. We had runners, but I'd yet to find one that didn't make me want to follow them around to make sure they didn't destroy the place. We had more glasses and alcohol wasted when runners touched them than at any other time. Flicking on the bright fluorescent bulbs, I searched the shelves until I found the bottles I wanted.

Grabbing the clipboard off the rack for the aisle, I marked down what was taken and picked up the case, moving it to the bottom of the stairs.

I wondered why all these places put the storage in the booze cache area. It did help keep the stuff cool, but it wasn't like you wanted to party down here. The supplies were heavy, and it was irritating to lug them up and down all the time. A short escalator leading directly to the bar would be amazing.

I walked back to the farthest aisle to grab the next case when I heard someone coming down the stairs.

"Avro, you can take that first box up. I'm going to grab a few more of the faves," I called out as I grabbed an empty box to fill with various extra bottles.

Bending over, I reached to the back of the bottom shelf and pulled out the last case of tequila we had. That wasn't good. It must have been missed on the previous order. Pulling open the top of the box, I counted twelve bottles and sighed. There would be enough for tonight, but I would have to change my specialty shot for the challenge. Straightening, I turned and yelped when I saw Jace leaning against the shelving.

"Jesus H, you just scared the shit out of me. Are you lost?" My voice dripped with sarcasm to cover my initial fear.

I tried to ignore the burning in my gut like I'd just taken a shot. Up close, I could see his eyes, and the fact that they weren't contacts and filled with heat that had me stepping back before I forced myself to stop. I was no longer that same teen who was assaulted, and I knew how to defend myself. I proved it earlier, didn't I?

"Only in your eyes," Jace said, and my mouth fell open a second before I laughed.

"Does that actually work on anyone?"

"Usually, it has people panting at my feet." His brows furrowed, and he crossed his arms, pulling the T-shirt he wore tight across his chest.

He was built a lot like Avro. They had that same tall, athletic body, with broad shoulders and a narrow waist. I could almost picture the hard abs under the shirt, but I kept my eyes firmly on his face.

"Ah, well, I'm not most girls," I said and went to walk around him, but he stepped into the way and grabbed the box I was carrying.

"I'll take this," he said, pulling it from my hands.

Instead of turning and walking toward the exit, he placed it on a high shelf that I would need to get the step stool to reach. I opened my mouth to give him shit when he stepped into my personal space, and I found myself backed up against the shelving unit. His hands gripped the shelf on either side of my waist as he leaned in close enough that I could feel the demanding heat from his body as it pressed into mine.

"What are you doing?"

I knew it was a stupid question. My heart was pounding hard, and the normal anxiety I had managed to control came racing back. I placed my hands on his chest to push him away, or maybe keep him from coming any closer. He was doing something weird to my head. The crippling fear was twisting into something else that I wasn't sure I liked any better. I felt the hard muscle under his T-shirt and suddenly wanted to run my fingers all over his body. This wasn't right for so many reasons. Avro was at the top of that list.

Jace looked down at my hands, which had yet to push him away, and smirked as his eyes found mine. He made a noise between a groan and a growl that did all sorts of wrong to my body.

Jace released the shelf on one side, and I immediately looked at my escape route, only to have him grip my chin in his fingers. He tilted my head up, forcing me to look into his eyes.

"I do like a challenge," he said, and I was tempted to pull a Dennis Copland on his ass. "Fuck, you're hot." He lowered his head to the side of my neck, and I was sure he could see my pulse pounding out of control under my skin. "I would eat you up if you let me."

I felt paralyzed, unsure of what to do next as my mind swam from all the new endorphins. My stomach twisted into a pile of knots. For a moment, I contemplated following through on my knee-to-the-crotch idea, but ending up on the front page of every paper and media outlet as the girl that made Jace Everly unable to have children was not the headline I ever wanted to make. I never wanted to be on any front page for anything, especially not for something like that. If I thought I was an outcast before, that certainly would take it to all new heights.

"Is that so? Well, I'll be more than just a challenge. I'm not interested. Can you please step back now?" I asked, trying hard to sound in control even when I felt like I was spinning out.

Jace inched closer to my lips, and I pushed myself back into the shelving unit until the sharp bite of the shelf pressed into my spine and forced me to stop moving.

"Raine...I like how that sounds, but you need a nickname. Something sweet and feisty, just like you. Don't you think?" His lips were a breath away from mine.

"How do you know my name?" We hadn't spoken since he arrived. Jace just smiled.

"Yo, Raine, you down here? They're about to open the doors," Avro called out, and I'd never been more relieved to hear his voice.

I could hear the soft sigh leave Jace's mouth as he pulled back and released me from the cage he'd made with his arms.

"Back here," I managed to call out. "I'm going to need that back." I pointed up to the box Jace had set up high, and his lips curled up like he found me amusing.

He grabbed the box, and I gave him the best *fuck you* look I could muster. "You can bring that, since you've put me behind schedule."

I left him standing in the aisle like he was no more than an employee and spotted Avro picking up the box at the bottom of the stairs. I grabbed a couple of whiskey bottles on the way past to give my hands something to do and didn't even care that I didn't write it down.

Avro looked up as he picked up the box, and his mouth dropped open, but nothing came out.

"Nothing was going on," I answered before he could ask the question. "Jace here had a question about his setup and was nice enough to offer to carry the box." I glared over my shoulder at the guy who I would be happy if I never saw again. "Isn't that right, Jace?"

"Oh, I definitely had a question about the setup, all right," he said, his voice dripping with sarcasm. It felt like he meant something else, and I narrowed my eyes, but he was no longer looking at me and was staring at Avro instead.

I couldn't deal with this or them right now. I needed to get back to work. Maybe I was excreting extra pheromones or something. First Avro all day, then Dennis, and now Jace. It made me worry. What the hell did the rest of the evening have in store for me?

I did not just put that out to the universe. I did not put that out to the universe.

I looked up at the ceiling as I stepped out of the cellar. "I take it back. I never thought that or said anything," I whispered under my breath, but already, it felt like I'd just sealed my fate with something a whole lot worse.

Snake

9

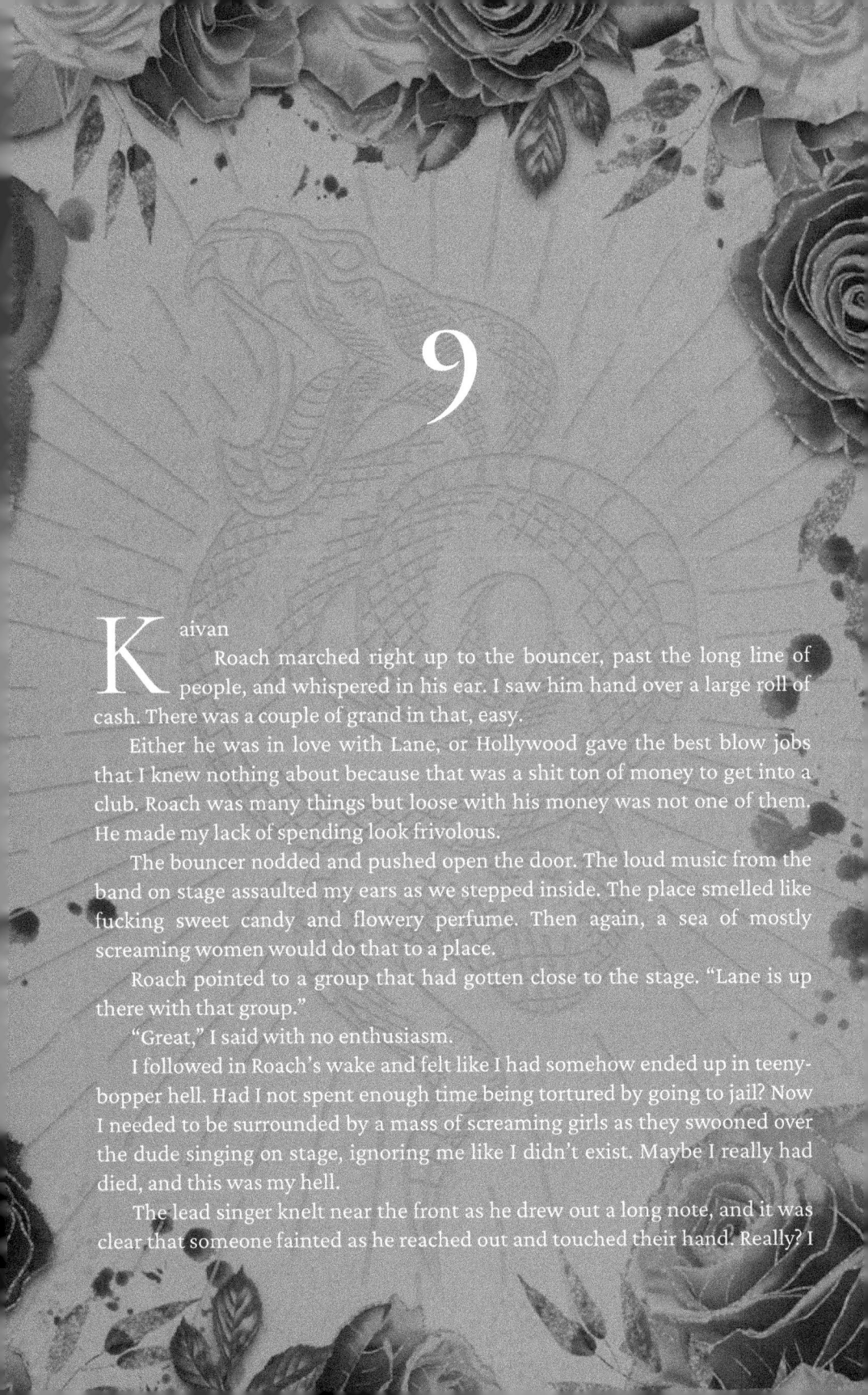

Kaivan

Roach marched right up to the bouncer, past the long line of people, and whispered in his ear. I saw him hand over a large roll of cash. There was a couple of grand in that, easy.

Either he was in love with Lane, or Hollywood gave the best blow jobs that I knew nothing about because that was a shit ton of money to get into a club. Roach was many things but loose with his money was not one of them. He made my lack of spending look frivolous.

The bouncer nodded and pushed open the door. The loud music from the band on stage assaulted my ears as we stepped inside. The place smelled like fucking sweet candy and flowery perfume. Then again, a sea of mostly screaming women would do that to a place.

Roach pointed to a group that had gotten close to the stage. "Lane is up there with that group."

"Great," I said with no enthusiasm.

I followed in Roach's wake and felt like I had somehow ended up in teeny-bopper hell. Had I not spent enough time being tortured by going to jail? Now I needed to be surrounded by a mass of screaming girls as they swooned over the dude singing on stage, ignoring me like I didn't exist. Maybe I really had died, and this was my hell.

The lead singer knelt near the front as he drew out a long note, and it was clear that someone fainted as he reached out and touched their hand. Really? I needed a drink, but the main bar was on the other side of the club, and that meant wading through the throngs of hysterical females to get there. That felt a little like I was taking my life in my hands. I nudged Roach's shoulder.

"I'll keep an eye on your girl, but you're going to get me a drink for being dragged into this," I yelled into his ear.

"She's not my girl." He glared at me.

"Don't give a fuck. I want a drink." He nodded, and I watched as he was swallowed up by the sea of people.

Leaning against the wall out of the way, I kept one eye on Lane and the other on the stage. I could admit that the music wasn't terrible. It wasn't what I usually listened to, but it didn't make my ears bleed. The guy looked around my age, maybe a little younger, but it was his attitude that grated me the wrong way. He reminded me too much of the guy I was before I went to prison. Full of cockiness, potential, and dreams. This guy was the walking epitome of what I could've been.

Lane and the other sorority girls she came with jumped up and down, clapping as the singer made his way to their end of the stage. I snorted as he grabbed Lane's hand and kissed her knuckles. If Roach saw that, this guy was going to lose his cock later.

The song wrapped up with a bang, and the lead singer bowed and blew kisses to the crowd. "Next up, we have the Eclipse challenge," he said, and the crowd went bananas.

I covered my ears as a swarm of screaming people turned toward the bar. What the hell was wrong with this place?

"Time is on the clock," the singer said and pointed to the massive clock, showing three minutes, on a countdown clock at the opposite end of the room. Beside it was a massive projector screen as big as any movie theatre. I was drawn in like the rest of the crowd, waiting to see what would happen.

"The contestants are ready!"

The camera panned to the bar and showed a guy looking like he'd just stepped out of a gothic vampire porno. My eyebrow raised at not only the outfit but the man himself. Some dudes had it all, and it seriously wasn't fair. He looked like he could either be on the cover of goth weekly as the next hot thing or strip it off and go full Magic Mike. You shouldn't be allowed to have both types of hot. What was left for the rest of us?

"In our first corner, we have Avro, who is tall, dark, and sexyyy." If this guy decided he didn't want to sing anymore, he could make it as an emcee, cause he had the flare down. "Avro is coming in at six foot three and has a fetish for making you melt with his moves on the bar," the singer said, and his voice dipped suggestively, which caused another round of cheers. Of course, this guy would confirm that the bartender Avro could dance on the bar. If not, why not? Come on, seven circles of hell.

"In our other corner, we have Raine, who comes in at five-four and is the spicy underdog. Raine takes no shit, and boys, don't let that hot little body fool you. She has moooves," he said and bit his lip.

My eyes snapped away from the stage to the screen, and my world narrowed on the face that was smiling and waving to the crowd. Those big blue eyes were the same, the thick full lips hadn't changed, and that smile could still stop a car in its tracks. Her cheeks were pink with the same look of embarrassment she always got when called out. It made her look ripe for eating.

My heart stopped as the world stood still. Leaning harder into the wall to keep myself from falling over from the shock, I watched every little move she made. From the flick of her pinky to the wink she gave the other bartender.

She was still stunning, still made me jittery, and now hard as a rock. The old bitterness and anger kicked open the door and marched to the surface until I was grinding my teeth, and my knuckles cracked as my fist clenched. Fate was a bitch, and she had a sick fucking sense of humor.

"And go!"

The clock on the wall began to count down, and as it did, Raine poured drinks like the devil himself was chasing her. She had two bottles per hand, and she would move on every few seconds, filling the massive lineup of shot glasses spread across the length of the massive bar. She smiled and looked over at the second bartender coming from the other direction, and a growl rippled from my throat as he gave her a flirty look.

The crowd cheered louder and louder as they neared the center of the large, curved bar, and by only a glass, the guy finished filling his first, raising his shot in the air before knocking it back. Everyone got quiet as the bartender held a finger over his mouth. Even the music stopped playing, and I could almost feel the heartbeat of the crowd as they waited to see what would happen next.

"As my prize tonight," he called out and then paused, as if making sure that he had everyone's attention. "I want a kiss from..." He held up his finger, and all the girls squealed and began jumping around, waving their hands in the air as they begged to be chosen. "Her," he said, and his finger pointed at Raine.

My nostrils flared, and my arms fell from where they'd been crossed over my chest. As the camera flicked back to Raine, she looked genuinely shocked as her mouth hung open, and her face went from soft pink to bright red. Then again, this girl was a liar. She could've been fucking this guy ten minutes before the place opened and probably still pulled off the act. She had certainly gotten away with a much harder performance.

"Kiss, kiss, kiss, kiss!" The chant went up around me as the bar began cheering the two on.

The bartender wrapped his arm around Raine's waist, and as he did, her face paled like she might faint. With a show of dipping her over, he said something against her lips that the mic couldn't make out before he kissed her. It was not a little peck on the lips. The guy made a show of it for the screaming audience as her jaw relaxed and her hand went to his cheek. The seconds ticked on, and rage rolled through my system like a desert storm.

I could feel her throat under my hand and the look on her face as she gasped for air and scratched at my arm. I was breathing hard as I seethed, glaring at the screen, at Raine all happy with her lips on another man. My cock ached as I pictured taking from her what she'd accused me of doing. Pushing her face down onto the bed and fucking her hard, making her scream my name.

"Yo, Snake! What the fuck is up?"

I glared at Roach, and he stepped back from me, holding up the drinks like a shield.

"Damn, man, what the hell happened? You look like you're ready to kill everyone in the room."

I glanced back up at the screen once more, showing the lead singer on stage as he fanned himself like the kiss had been hot. The music started back up, and within moments, all the girls shrieked again.

"I'm going to kill her," I mumbled, and Roach looked around.

"Who?"

"Raine, I'm going to fucking kill that bitch." My eyes found Roach again. "She's going to regret the day she ever crossed me."

Raine

"What the hell was that, Avro?" I paced the office and pointed toward the bar, which was still just as loud.

"What do you mean?" he asked, making me want to strangle him. He fucking knew what I meant.

I paused in my pacing to glare at him. "Don't give me that. You know exactly what I'm talking about. The kiss. You freaking made me kiss you. Out there. In front of all those people. And...what was with the sweet, *I've wanted to do this for so long*, statement?"

He leaned against the wall, his lip slightly curled up like he was amused with himself. "Made? That's a bit harsh. And what I said was true. I have wanted to kiss you for a long time. Was it terrible? Did you not want me to kiss you?"

"That's not the point," I said and rubbed my eyes.

My stomach was all fluttery, and it was like the kiss had ripped off the final bit of blinders which had allowed me to keep the friend line firmly in place. It didn't help that the kiss was exactly as I imagined it would be. Hot and yet somehow sweet, just like the man himself.

"It is the point," Avro said and walked across the room until he could sit on the edge of my desk.

I'd only been the manager for six months, but I had to say that having my own office made me feel pretty badass as I ranted. I went to walk past him, and he snaked an arm around my waist, forcing me to stop.

"Raine, look at me." Avro ran his hands down my arms until he could hold my hands, and even that little touch made me nervous and agitated, like I had too much adrenaline running through my veins. "Did you like the kiss? It's a simple question with a simple answer. Yes or no?"

I swallowed hard and wished I had superpowers to disappear as I stared into his eyes. "Of course I liked it. How could I not? But that's not the point."

"Why isn't it the point?" he asked.

My mouth fell open, and my brain went blank as I fumbled through all the reasons and excuses in my mind, but I couldn't find one that made sense right now. I'm sure there was at least one reason, but staring into his eyes made my brain mush.

"Because we're friends," I finally managed to get out. "And this is our place of work." I licked my lips. "And what if this ruins..."

Avro stood, and whatever argument I had died on my tongue. Avro didn't hesitate and dropped his lips to mine. Just like the first time, a warmth burned bright in my gut as our lips moved in sync. He made me feel like I was floating in warm water while eating a rich chocolate cake.

"Come over tonight. We won't do anything you don't want to," he said, breaking the kiss.

My head was light, and my lips tingled.

"I...I...I don't know," I said, moaning as he softly kissed the side of my neck, spiking my pulse.

"Spend more time with me. You know me, Raine, and at some point, you need to stop being terrified that everything will turn into whatever horror movie you have playing in your mind. I'd never hurt you, and I'd never let anyone else hurt you." I shivered and grabbed hold of the statement that hit too close to home. "But I'm done pretending that all I want is to be friends," he whispered, and I shivered. "I've wanted to be more than friends for a very long time."

"Who said I think everyone is a horror movie waiting to happen?" My eyes fluttered closed as he trailed his lips along the side of my neck.

"Because right now, it's written all over your face. And because, at one time, you would move away from me if you felt I was too close. You kept your eyes on me no matter what we were doing and refused to have me at your back. You always carried a box cutter, even when we had no boxes to open. Every move I made, you reacted as if I was going to beat you," Avro said softly.

I hated that he saw that part of me. I thought I did a good job hiding it from the world. In my mind, I was still that scared version of myself, screaming wildly and saying no. Every man was potentially one of my attackers, and any moment alone with a guy, no matter who it was or where it was, had a hidden agenda. It was the part of my brain I was trying to learn to control rather than have it control me.

"Okay, I'll come over."

I could feel his grin against my neck. "Oh, you naughty boss you, pulling me into your office to proposition me," he teased as he stood up straight.

The door opened just then, and the office filled with Jace's voice and cheering people as he sang another song.

"Sorry, am I interrupting?" Mr. Allen Lawrence, Jace's agent, asked. I rolled my eyes up at Avro before plastering a smile on my face. I stepped around Avro as we turned to face the man I wanted to choke.

"May I speak to you alone, Ms. Eastman? I have a few things I'd like to go over," Allen said.

"Of course, Mr. Lawrence, come on in," I said, happy that I could pull off the professional attitude. I held up my finger as he stepped forward. "But next time, wait until I say you can enter before opening my door. Just a professional courtesy, I'm sure you understand."

Avro lifted an eyebrow that only I could see, but I knew he was impressed. So was I.

"I'll go help with the bar again," Avro said, giving me a wink that was both sexy and calming.

Had I been blind to his affection all this time? He was always funny and flirtatious, but he'd dated so many people that I lost count after ten. Was he trying to make me another one of his numbers? I kicked myself mentally and shoved away the nagging doubt that no one would want me unless it were to hurt me. That was the kind of mentality that had made me scared to leave the house, and I was never going back to that person ever again.

"All right, Mr. Lawrence, what can I help you with?"

Snake

10

Kaivan

The ride back to the clubhouse was quiet. No matter what Roach asked, I didn't dare speak, or I might've leaped across the console and killed him simply for being there. We pulled into the Lost Souls parking lot, where I kept my bikes even when I was at home. I didn't even wait for the truck to come to a full stop before I hopped out and stomped to my bike. Roach didn't try to stop me. He knew me well enough to know that someone was going to die, and he didn't want to end up on my list.

I was going back to that bar and waiting as long as it took to see Raine and follow her home.

The image of my hands on Raine and her screaming as she fought me was so vivid that my step faltered mid-stride. Oh, the evil she conjured in my mind. The old darkness that filled me and kept me going night after night in the pen was once more taking over.

Mannix used to say I looked possessed when I got this angry, and he wasn't far off the mark. It felt like that, too. Like the world was narrowing in, and all I saw was red. He also told me that I needed to harness it, or I would end up back behind bars before I was even released. He hadn't been wrong about that, either. For the most part, I was able to, but there were just some times in life when you tossed all that control aside and simply did what felt right.

"Hey!" a voice called as I reached my bike. I was so consumed that I hadn't noticed that anyone else was out here with me. "Over here," the gravelly voice came again, and I looked over to see Wilder's version of the swamp monster hanging onto the chain-link fence. He blended with the chaotic background so well that I would never have noticed him.

He was always dressed up in the strangest outfits. This time he was coated in mud, a blanket of grass and water dripping from his body. Had he been lying in the water with the gators? If he was, the guy was crazier than I thought, or one hell of an animal whisperer.

I didn't have time for whatever he wanted, but considering Wilder rarely spoke—and he could probably sneak down my chimney or find a way inside my walls—it was better that I played along rather than ignore him. There was no telling what the hell this guy would do.

I walked over to the fence and stuffed my hands in my pockets. "Hey, man," I said. "What's up?"

"You need help killing whoever you're going after? I have skills that are itching to be used," Wilder said.

"I'm sure you do, but no, not this time." I stared at the long pieces of seaweed tied to the getup. "Can I ask why you're dressed like the swamp monster?"

"'Cause you can never be too careful," he said and nodded, so I nodded along with him.

"Okay. Did you want me for something?" My own hands were itching to get on Raine's fair skin.

"Oh, yeah. You fuck a lot of girls, right?"

Of all the questions that Wilder could've asked me, this was one I wasn't prepared for. I had no idea the guy knew what a girl was. He rarely spoke, and when he did, it was about guns, bombs, or how someone was after him. I didn't know if that last part was true, but regardless, women was not where I thought this conversation was headed.

"Um...yeah, I do alright, I guess. If you consider a couple of girls a week a lot, then yes." This conversation felt fucking weird, but now that I was into it, it was like quicksand, and I had no idea how to back the fuck out.

"Is it normal for a girl to cry after getting fucked?"

My brow furrowed as I thought about how to answer this landmine of a question from Wilder.

"Are we talking like that was the best fuck of my life crying, or are we leaning more toward crying for real?"

He looked confused.

"I mean, is she like, *oh my god, what just happened* type of crying? Or is she trying to get away from you?" I figured it was best to clarify the issue.

"Hmmm, difficult to say. She can't get away," he said, and my mouth fell open. Did he just admit to keeping someone hostage? "Tell me, what's the difference? Does the crying sound different? I mean, tears are tears, right?"

"Well, yes, but there is a difference," I said as I tiptoed around the image of Wilder attempting to have sex with someone in a cell or maybe chained to a wall. Not that I didn't think the guy could get his dick hard, but the idea of him having sex and not with a farm animal was a different story.

Wilder sighed like I was being difficult, so I tried to explain. "Let's try this. If the girl is crying after being fucked, but she's all like, *oh, Wilder, that was amazing. Yes, give me more. I want to take your cock down my throat. Do it again. I can't get enough.* Then that is good, and she liked it, so I would lean toward normal."

"Would her voice go that high pitched?" he asked, and I had to hold back from smacking myself on the forehead.

"Maybe, I don't know. Look, if she's screaming at you to get away from her and says she never wants you near her again while the tears are falling, then I'm going to say that falls under the not normal column." Lifting my shoulders, I let them fall. "Does that make sense?"

He rubbed his cheek, leaving behind a dirty streak. "Huh, okay. I think I need to go back to the drawing board," Wilder said, then bent low as he ran across the property.

I watched him until I couldn't see him any longer, then shook my head and stomped back to my bike. There was some shit you just couldn't explain, and that conversation was one of them. I feared for any girl who caught his eye.

Jumping on my bike, I revved her and flew out the open gates. I didn't bother to stop even though a car was coming, and the sound of the horn had me flipping the guy off. One year, three months, and two days ago, I was released, and I would go back to that hellhole just for the satisfaction of seeing Raine die by my hand.

There were still cars in the customer parking lot, so chances were that Raine was still inside. It didn't matter now that I knew where she worked. How fucking close she was this entire time. I was willing to sit outside this place every single night. Grabbing the smokes from my jacket, I parked the bike down a side street and sat there with the engine off, my eyes on the door as I waited. I held the cigarette between my lips and remembered the first time I tried one.

• • •

I'd stolen a couple of smokes from Mr. Collins's pack and snuck out back. It was late, and no one was awake. I sat down to lean against the tree. It had been a strange six weeks, and I wasn't sure what I thought about all that had happened. It was six weeks to the day that I'd taken the garbage out to the garage, and Mrs. Collins followed me. It took me all of ten seconds to know what she was after. It wasn't hard to guess after the whole movie situation that this was coming. When she grabbed my cock through my track pants, I almost came on the spot. No one other than myself had ever touched me like that.

In a garage, up against the chest freezer, was not how I thought I would lose my virginity, and the fact that she acted like it wouldn't be a one time thing kinda wigged me out. I mean, it was a shit ton better than my hand, but it felt...weird. She was my foster mother.

Did that make me a man now? At least I didn't have to go to college a virgin. So why was it that I felt guilty? I didn't care about Mr. Collins. The guy was never home, and when he was, he was a jerk or ignored us, but I did care about Raine.

Fuck, I shouldn't feel bad. She was practically still a kid, and I would be gone in a couple months, but there was a definite nagging sensation in my gut.

I pulled out the first smoke and the little book of matches and stared at them. My father liked to smoke. I remembered it clearly. The red and white pack he kept rolled up in the sleeve of his T-shirt. I'd always thought it was so cool how he sat on his motorcycle with one hanging out of his mouth and my mother sitting on his lap. The faint scent of smoke that clung to his clothes. At least I thought it was cool until I got a little older, and I realized that he was a fucking asshole, and my mother was miserable.

"Hey, can I sit?"

I jumped at the soft sound of Raine's voice as she stepped around the tree and sat down before I answered.

"By all means, join me," *I said sarcastically.*

The sweet, shy smile on Raine's face fell. She looked down at her hands, blonde hair hanging around her face, and I kicked myself for snipping at her. What had been happening between me and Mrs. Collins wasn't her fault, and neither was my feelings for her that I wasn't supposed to have. Every time I was near her was a conflict and battle of wills.

"I can go. I didn't mean to bug you," *she said, and I sighed.*

"No, I'm fine. Just in a mood, guy stuff, before you go asking. Here, you want one?" *I held out a cigarette for her to take, and she shook her head.*

"That's what gave me my asthma. At least that's what the doctor says."

I pulled the little match across the flint, and the flame rushed to life. I did what I'd seen a thousand times and sucked back hard on the smoke as I lit the end. Imme-

diately, I began to cough and gag at the terrible taste and burning sensation sticking to the back of my throat. I had asthma as a kid, but I'd grown out of it and wanted to see why everyone liked these things. So far, I was not impressed.

"You okay?" Raine asked and got up on her knees to rub my back.

I winced away from her touch as my dick stirred in my pants. See, this was exactly why I couldn't be around her anymore, and I definitely didn't need her trying to make me feel better. That was not how this situation was supposed to work. She crossed her arms in a huff.

"Fine, choke to death, see if I care," she grumbled. "I don't even know why I bother hanging out with you anymore. It's obvious you don't want me around. I don't know what I did to piss you off, but if you don't want to be my friend, just say so." Her eyes filled with tears, but I didn't know what to say.

She didn't piss me off. Of course, I wanted her around. I wanted her around too much. I wanted to hold her hand and kiss her and all the shit you would do if you were dating someone, but she was my foster sister and two years, two weeks, and two days younger.

Raine stood, and I grabbed her hand and tugged, though I wasn't sure why. "Don't go." She had the prettiest eyes I'd ever seen, and how she looked at me now with her very Raine attitude made me smile. "Please?"

I added in a little pout for good measure, and she laughed. "Fine."

"I still want to be your friend. I've just got a lot going on, and I've been off. Nothing to do with you," I lied. It had a lot to do with her, but none of it I could share.

She sat back down beside me, and it felt good to have her nearby. She laid her head on my shoulder, and for a few minutes, everything felt right.

Raine had already been here when I arrived, and she was the same now as that day. Sassy, a straight shooter who preferred her jeans and hoodies over anything else. She thought she was awkward, while I thought she was adorable. Of course, now that I was a few weeks from eighteen and she was only fifteen, I felt like I was a creep.

"You gonna keep doing those fights?" she asked, and I lifted her much smaller hand into mine, staring at it. Hers looked so sweet and innocent next to my much larger, newly tattooed one.

"Yeah, the money is good. I need to pay for college somehow." I shrugged. "They're not bad. The key is knowing who you should fight and who to stay away from."

"I guess so," she said, and I knew she wanted to complain more. She already had, and I told her more than once that she had to stop worrying so much.

"You know what you want for your birthday yet?" I asked, and she shrugged. "That's not an answer."

"What I want is impossible." She looked back at the house and then at me. "Ever just want to run away and go somewhere else?"

"Not really. Where would I go?" I linked our fingers together. This was dangerous territory. I should tell her I was too old to be her best friend while I walked away. Yet I couldn't make myself do it.

"I don't know. Just somewhere different. Somewhere that has snow at Christmas and mountains to hike, someplace that doesn't have so many mean people, and no one would bother us," she said, and I raised an eyebrow at that.

"Us?"

"Yeah, you're my best friend. Of course, I want you to come with me. I mean, only if you wanted to," she quickly added.

Hooking the long hair behind her ear, all I could think about was kissing her. "We better go in before they realize we're missing. Don't want anyone to get the wrong idea."

"Yeah, that would be terrible," she said and let go of my hand.

The way she said it bothered me. It was like she wanted more too, or maybe I was projecting. I'd learned in school that was a thing. Mind you, they weren't talking about what I had going on, but was pretty sure it didn't matter the emotions.

As she turned to walk away, I grabbed her arm and pulled her back. I wrapped her up in my arms and held onto her, not saying a word. I expected her to protest or at the very least ask what I was doing, but instead her arms slowly wrapped around my waist. I never wanted to let her go, she was the first and only good thing in my life.

Tossing the finished butt on the ground, I leaned back on the bike and watched for my prey. There was a lot of shit in this life that I could get over and move on from, but not this, never this. Her reprieve was over. Fate had stood up and pointed me in the direction I needed to go. Raine Eastman was going to pay for what she did. If it was the last thing I did, she would know the mistake she made the day she named me as the man who assaulted her.

Raine

11

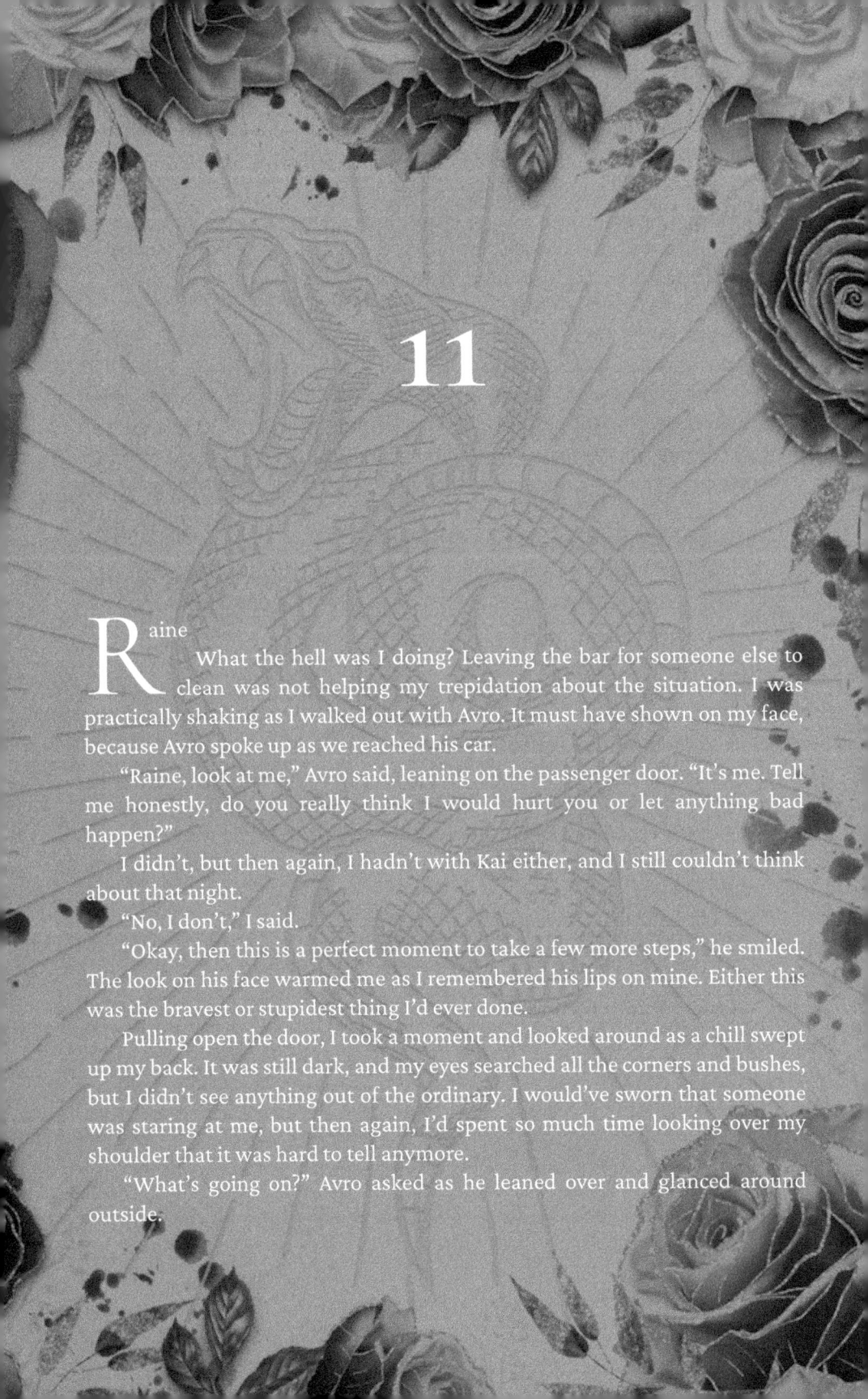

Raine

What the hell was I doing? Leaving the bar for someone else to clean was not helping my trepidation about the situation. I was practically shaking as I walked out with Avro. It must have shown on my face, because Avro spoke up as we reached his car.

"Raine, look at me," Avro said, leaning on the passenger door. "It's me. Tell me honestly, do you really think I would hurt you or let anything bad happen?"

I didn't, but then again, I hadn't with Kai either, and I still couldn't think about that night.

"No, I don't," I said.

"Okay, then this is a perfect moment to take a few more steps," he smiled. The look on his face warmed me as I remembered his lips on mine. Either this was the bravest or stupidest thing I'd ever done.

Pulling open the door, I took a moment and looked around as a chill swept up my back. It was still dark, and my eyes searched all the corners and bushes, but I didn't see anything out of the ordinary. I would've sworn that someone was staring at me, but then again, I'd spent so much time looking over my shoulder that it was hard to tell anymore.

"What's going on?" Avro asked as he leaned over and glanced around outside.

"Nothing, I just thought...it's nothing," I said, slipping into the car. "Where is your place?" I felt stupid that I didn't know. What kind of friend didn't bother to find out where he'd moved?

"Not far, I was leaving it as a surprise, but I managed to get a three-story near the beach. I finally took possession a few months ago. The tips have been great lately, and I put a huge deposit down to buy the place."

"Avro, that's amazing," I said.

He smiled wide, his real smile, not the one he gave to the crowd at the bar. It was sexier than the fake one he presented to the customers. I glanced out the window to the world passing by and watched the glistening water shimmering in the moonlight. Everything was so quiet and peaceful. Not so very long ago, I saw that beach at this time of night in the same light as I saw everything else...a place to be attacked. Avro turned the radio on, and "Old Town Road" played, making us laugh.

"That routine is still my favorite," he said.

"I have no idea how you talked me into getting up on the bar and pretending you were a horse." I shook my head and laughed at the memory.

"It was pretty epic. We still get requests for that routine," Avro said as we pulled into a pretty area.

His place was nestled in a great location where all the homes looked out toward the beach. The parking was at the back of the house, and I was shocked to see Avro had enough room to park six cars with space. That was rare. Getting out, I looked down the long alley. It seemed like a quiet spot.

"Are you kidding me? I'm never getting up on that bar again. It is one of my top three most embarrassing moments. I was so happy when we switched to a different routine. Although, tonight may have topped it," I said as Avro looked over his shoulder at me.

"Never say never," Avro teased.

"It's a really quiet area you found here." Only two other places had cars or lights.

"Most spots are rented to those coming in for spring break or Christmas. The rest of the time, it's like I have no neighbors at all."

I was startled when a loud motorcycle drove by. Why was I so jumpy? It had been months since I felt this way. I guess some shit was harder to shake. Avro opened the door, turning on lights as he went. Stepping up to the threshold, I stopped.

Avro happily talked as he walked through the house. Mentally berating myself, I stepped through the door and closed it behind me. Maybe it wasn't being alone with Avro or in his space that made me edgy. Perhaps it was because I knew he wanted to be more than friends, and I didn't know how to handle that. I wasn't sure how to navigate the feelings that felt like a mass of scrambled wires inside me.

"I mean, look at that view," Avro said as I entered the large room that was a cross between a living room and a games room. There was an almost ceiling-height speaker in the corner, an air hockey table, and a pair of dart boards. A massive television was mounted on the far wall, and three couches made a horseshoe shape for viewing. He even had a small bar with an assortment of bottles almost as extensive as at work lining the shelf.

This room said party, while my home said spinster. All I needed was a bunch of cats to complete the look.

"Well?" I looked at Avro and realized I didn't know what he'd been saying. I guess my blank, blinking stare told him I didn't have a clue. "What do you think so far?"

"I think this is pretty incredible." I walked over to stand near the tall bay windows and stared out at the water.

"Come on. I'll give you the rest of the tour."

From one room to the next, I followed him, amazed by his style and ability to maximize the space given. There wasn't a single thing out of place. I was a total slob and always had been. Tossing my jacket and bag wherever and living out of a laundry basket was normal.

We made our way upstairs, and the wooden steps and glass railing were as impressive as everything else. There were very few images on the walls, and the ones Avro did have were either nature shots or photos of himself at different performances before his accident. They'd been blown up to poster size and framed.

I paused at a small image at the top of the stairs. It was a newspaper clipping announcing his acceptance as a headliner in the newest Las Vegas Cirque performance. The date on it was six years ago before he damaged his knee doing a difficult trick. It was so bad that he ended up backing out of the show. He had multiple surgeries to stabilize his knee, and the doctors told him he couldn't go back to the extreme dancing and performances he'd been doing.

"You coming or what? This is the best room in the house," Avro said as he stuck his head out of a door. My heart ached for what he'd lost. To work that hard, to dream that big, then to have it all ripped away in a blink was heartbreaking.

"Coming," I said and tore myself away from the clipping. I was starting to realize just how cut off I'd been. Knowing it and understanding it were two different things.

I knew Avro had given up his dream, which was how he ended up at Eclipse. He would've found that transition difficult, but did I understand what he went through? The pain and rehabilitation of each surgery just so he could walk again, let alone do what he did four nights a week at the bar? Was he sore? Did the knee ever ache? Did he come home and stare at the wall of what could have been? I wanted to wrap him up in a hug and tell him I was sorry for never asking, and not being the kind of friend he deserved.

I walked up to the door Avro had disappeared into, and my mouth dropped open as I looked around the bedroom. It was massive, like he'd taken all the bedrooms on this side of the house and made himself one large space with a wall of glass facing the water. The bed was gigantic and took up almost half the room. He also fit a sitting area with a coffee machine right there for when you rolled out of bed. The balcony looked brand new, stretching the entire length of the bedroom, complete with tables and chairs.

"Avro, this is wow...just wow," I said, stepping into the room.

I hadn't been in a guy's bedroom since Kai. I'd sat on his floor or spun around on his desk chair, but as an adult, this was new. I wasn't a virgin—that had been stolen from me—but there'd been no one since.

Avro leaned against one of the supports for the windows, staring outside, and all my earlier fear returned. I felt like a child. At twenty-six, I'd only ever been kissed twice. Once when I was fifteen, and tonight. My pulse pounded in time with my hammering heart.

Avro was one of those people that made you do a double take on the street to make sure your eyes weren't playing tricks on you. I glanced at my reflection and wondered what the hell he saw in me. Of all the elegant and beautiful people out there, why me? I was suspicious. What could Avro really want? Did I doubt he was my friend? No, but today was different. Sure, I'd fantasized about being with him. Kissing him and running my hands over his body, but I'd never let my mind travel off the trail of fantasy. Today at the beach confirmed that I wanted someone in my life, but I wasn't even in the same league as Avro, let alone the same game. Fuck, I wasn't even in the same sport.

"This is my favorite spot. I love this room and the view. I'll be happier when it is officially all mine," he said, breaking me out of my thoughts. "I know the guy that owns the place next door wants to sell and I'm thinking of making an offer and rent it out until I can afford to attach the two places together."

"You should be proud of yourself," I said, and I meant it from the bottom of my heart.

I'd done nothing useful with my life and hated who I'd been for so long. Seeing what Avro made of a bad situation only gave me more determination to make better choices. What did I want to do with my life? Did I want to be a bar manager forever? Did I want to own my spot one day?

Avro turned to stare at me.

"I didn't get a chance to tell you, but Grimhead Crews's agent decided to have them do a second performance tomorrow night. Well, I guess that is later tonight now. Anyway, Allen said that social media is going crazy, which has given him a few more ideas for PR."

I rubbed my face, not sure how much more I wanted to be forced to hang around Jace Everly and his intense silver eyes that made my stomach toss and turn.

"Don't get me wrong, we made a killing off having him there, but he's just so full of himself, and...." I struggled to get out the right word.

"So, um...yeah, about Jace...." Avro started and then stopped when his doorbell rang. "Well, that was terrible or perfect timing," he grumbled. "I may have invited Jace over, too," he said, walking out of the room. My mouth fell to the floor.

"What? Why? What's going on?" I followed him down the stairs as the bell rang again.

Avro looked out the peephole and swore under his breath before putting his hand on the door. "I'm so sorry, it was only supposed to be Jace," he said, and opened the door.

Are you fucking kidding me?

There had to be at least twenty people outside. Members of the Grimhead Crew band walked in first, each with a pair of girls on their arms. DJ Club Chaos and his entire entourage were next, but the man at the back of the group had my earlier nerves bouncing around inside of me like a million hummingbirds. He seriously invited Jace Everly over? When? How? Why?

Jace stepped through the door like he owned the place, and it suddenly felt a whole lot smaller. Surprisingly, he didn't have a girl on each arm. Why that made me more nervous instead of less was a mystery. As the door closed, Jace pushed the hood of his sweatshirt off his head and there he was in all his sexy, arrogant glory.

"Party area is that way." Avro pointed toward the living room. "Feel free to wander and use any room except my bedroom. If I catch you in there, I'll toss you out," he said.

The group all seemed in agreement. At least they did now, but who knew what would happen once they had some drinks?

Jace stared at me as he walked by, and our eyes locked. My stomach flipped inside out at the memory of him in the storage room with me and the irrational feelings he caused. Unable to help myself, I rubbed my hands on my jeans like that would remove the feel of his chest from my memory.

There was something about Jace that sucked you in. My insides were a jittery mess, but I forced myself not to show any emotion. I lifted my brow in question as he continued to stare, silently asking what the fuck he wanted. Jace smirked and looked away. I was pretty sure I knew what he was doing, and it bothered the shit out of me.

As everyone fell into a comfortable groove talking or pouring drinks, I recognized the character flaw in myself. Socializing was something I rarely did, and I preferred it that way. Despite how much I loved my job, when the show was done and people were gone, I was happy to be alone. I couldn't remember if, as a child, I felt comfortable plunking myself down in the middle of a group and talking. It didn't matter what the topic was. I always felt uncomfortable in a group. The bar was easy. Something separated me from the crowd, and I knew what they wanted: alcohol. I didn't have to make conversation. I could just pretend to be someone else.

Avro pulled a release on the wall, and everyone cheered as the bookcase pulled out to show off a secret compartment. It reminded me of those fold-up beds, except this was full of DJ equipment. In seconds, the quiet house had turned into a loud party.

Staying just outside the living room, I quickly turned toward the kitchen. I needed a drink, and I wasn't walking in front of all those people to get to the alcohol.

I opened the fridge and stared at the perfectly arranged containers of food. They were labeled with the contents and the date it went into the container. Was Avro for real? This level of organization was intense. I mean, he kept his side of the bar looking immaculate, but I didn't realize his obsession stretched over everything until now. The entire house was the same way, and I was secretly envious. I could only imagine what he thought when he walked into my tiny bird house of a home. Would he faint when he saw my bedroom and my clothes hanging off every available space?

Other than two large bottles of champagne, there wasn't any alcohol in the fridge—just homemade fruit or vegetable juices. Closing the door, I stared at the stainless-steel appliance and wondered if I should stay or go. I wanted to spend time with Avro—the chemistry between us was there—but I was still waiting for him to jump up and yell, just joking. Like he would realize I was a walking mess and wouldn't want anything to do with me.

"Here, I made you this," Avro said, startling me as he stepped into the doorway. He looked sheepish as he rubbed the back of his neck. "Sorry, I should've given you a heads up about Jace, but I didn't want you to back out, and I didn't know about everyone else…shit, there's no excuse. I should've told you he was coming."

He'd removed the cat-eye contacts, yet I could still picture him purring as he begged forgiveness. I almost smirked as the CATS musical began to play in my mind.

"I may not have made the best decision, but you're here now, and I want to spend time with you. We don't have to go in there." He smiled wide, and I couldn't stay annoyed with him. "Forgive me?" he said and bit his lip. Was it hot in here?

"When did you and Jace become so close that you invited him over?" I took the drink, sniffing at what he'd made.

"Well, that's the other thing I need to tell you." He rubbed the back of his neck. "I actually know him really well."

"Come again?"

"We grew up together," he said, and other than the music in the other room, neither of us moved or made a sound.

"Did you know he was coming to the bar?" I was annoyed and hurt that he hadn't told me this sooner. I'd bitched about the man all day.

"Minutes before you did." He held up his hands. "I swear."

Did it really matter now? Maybe, no, yes, no. "I don't like secrets, Avro," I said.

"And yet we all keep the darkest and saddest parts of us hidden until we're ready, including you," he said, and I swallowed hard.

"Touché," I smirked. "It smells like peaches," I commented and took a sip. I closed my eyes as I tried to pick out what else was in the drink. This was a game we played when making new concoctions for the customers. "With a hint of banana and spiced rum."

"Not bad. Can you do that with every drink?" Jace's smooth-yet-annoying voice was loud, and I opened my eyes.

He was just behind Avro and seeing them standing so close to one another was picture worthy. I had the urge to whip out my cellphone and have a fangirl moment, but that was so not happening.

Avro seemed totally at ease with a rock star in his home, which seemed odd regardless of their knowing one another. Who was this calm with a celebrity? Again, just another reason why Avro and I were on different levels. I should've set the drink down and said goodnight before I ended up hoping for something that was never going to be possible. All I could think was, why the hell was I here?

My eyes roamed over the two walking gifts to eyeballs everywhere. They were pretty close in height and build, and the sensuality oozing off of them made me squirm. It was so hot all of a sudden that I had to grip the glass harder to stop myself from whipping off my hoodie to try and cool off.

"Most drinks. Avro has tripped me up a time or two, but I always get it right when I taste it," I said. Even though Jace hadn't said anything or given me the once-over that most guys did, it still felt like he was touching me.

"Would you prefer to sit in here?" Avro pointed to the table.

"Sure," I answered.

"You not into the party scene?"

I didn't want to answer Jace. In fact, I hoped he would turn around and walk away, but instead, he followed us to the table and sat down across from me.

Avro took the chair beside me and casually draped his arm on the back of mine. His presence was comforting, despite my attraction. He had a calm aura and a way of setting me at ease when I felt like I should be spinning out.

"I prefer the quiet after a long night of loud music," I said, sipping the drink that was a punch of flavor to my tastebuds I licked my lips and stared at the glass in wonder. "Wow," I said. "That is really good."

"I had the same thought," Jace said. I looked up to see him staring at my lips.

Avro's fingers touched my shoulder and squeezed like he was trying to comfort me, but I couldn't stop the jump from the light contact. "Don't push so hard, Jace. This was just supposed to be a get-to-know-us. She's not ready for all that," Avro said.

I was instantly transported back in time. I'd heard those words before when I was only fifteen. They pissed me off then and pissed me off now. No matter how long I'd known Avro, he didn't get to make those decisions for me. Wasn't ready for what? I was a grown-ass woman. If I wanted to jump out of a plane, I could. If I wanted to go partying at a sex club, I could. If I wanted to buy a gold car that cost more than I made in fifty years, I could. Not that I would do any of those things, but it wasn't the point.

"Don't give me that look," Avro said before I opened my mouth. "Getting you here without bolting down the street was tough enough, and don't deny it. I've been asking you to come over at least twice a week for months," he said, lifting a brow that made me squirm.

"So," I said, my back bristling.

"Fine, tell me honestly; do you really think you're up for whatever Jace has planned?"

He tilted his head and stared at me, waiting for an answer. I would never know what came over me at that moment, but the second I opened my mouth, I knew I was fucked. Not only had I painted myself into a corner, there was a very good chance that Avro had prepped and pampered the pillow under my ass in my honor. I could see him in my mind holding out my favorite drink and patting the seat beside him while a little smile played on his lips that screamed, got ya.

"I don't know. Maybe I am." Easily top three of the stupidest things I'd ever said to date.

Avro's lips curled up exactly like they had in my mind, and I swallowed hard. His eyes were more intense without the cat-eye contacts in. They were naturally amber, and I loved the unique shade. Why he chose to hide them behind fake spring green and vampire red was beyond me.

My eyes flicked between the two men, and I knew I'd bitten off more than I could chew. Maybe it was an overreaction, but now that I'd opened my mouth, I wasn't backing down.

"Don't just say that because you think you need to," Avro said softly against my ear so only I could hear.

I sucked in a sharp breath, my body lighting up with him so close, and I squirmed in my seat. He smelled so good. He always did, but I wasn't normally close enough to pick up on the scent of a cool sea breeze and fresh citrus that made me want to bury my face in his neck and breathe deeply.

"I think she's lying, Avro," Jace said.

My eyes lifted to his, and it wasn't what he said or even how he said it. It was the look in his eyes. It was the same look I'd gotten from Kai many times.

"I am not." I clenched my teeth together.

"Oh yeah? Then prove it," Jace whispered, and the hairs on the back of my neck stood up. His eyes locked with mine, and I felt like I was trapped in a snare.

Avro glared at Jace. "Raine, you don't need to do this," he said softly, his fingertips brushing against my neck and making me shiver.

Jace leaned back in the chair and crossed his arms as he stared me down.

"Yeah, I do," I said. "It's time I stop running."

I had no fucking clue what I was signing up for, and maybe I should've asked, but all I saw was another guy telling me I couldn't do something, and I wasn't having it.

Jace smiled, the look sexy and terrifying at the same time as my pulse jumped. He slowly stood and looked down at Avro and me.

"Are you two coming?"

Oh fuck.

Avro

12

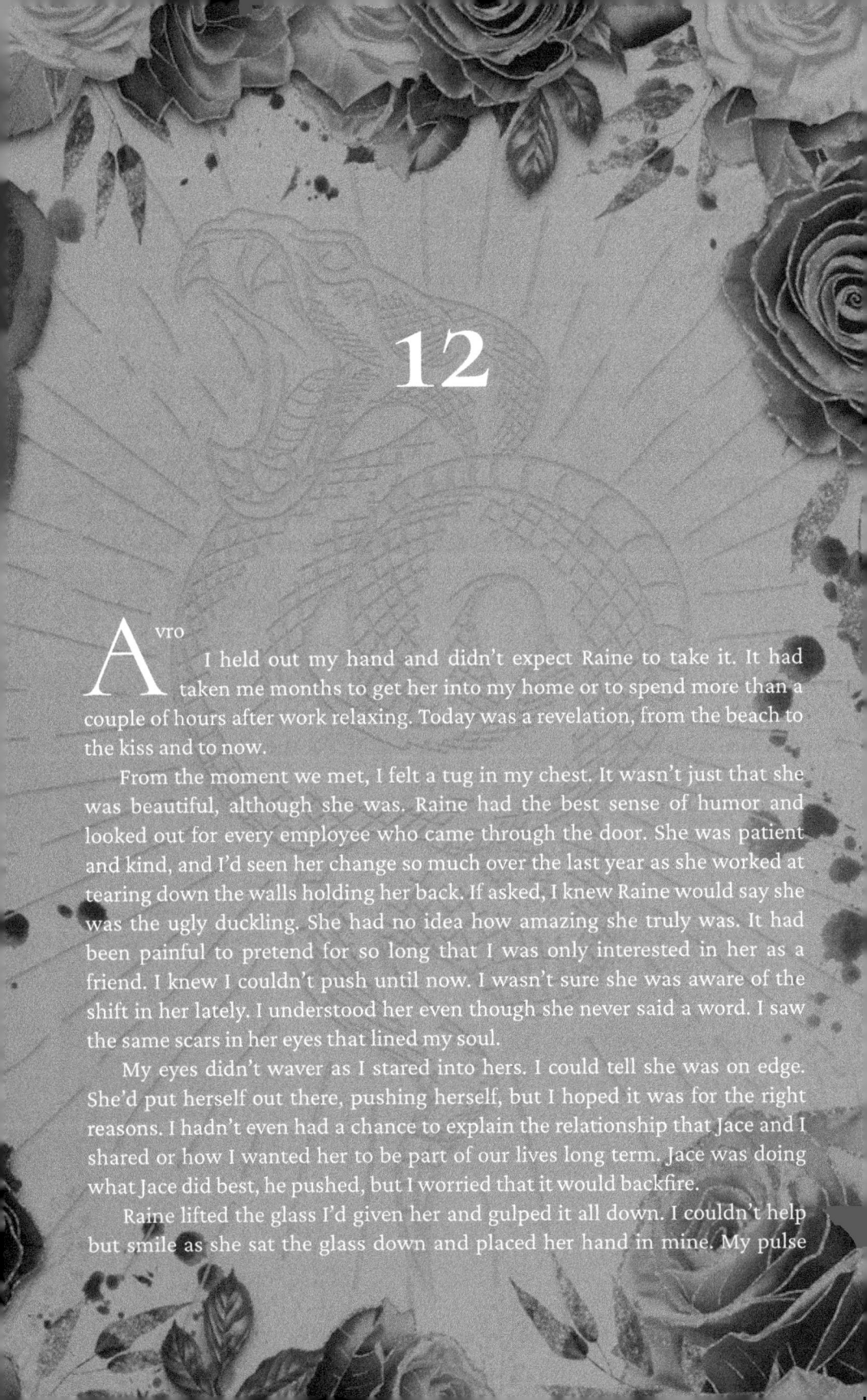

Avro

I held out my hand and didn't expect Raine to take it. It had taken me months to get her into my home or to spend more than a couple of hours after work relaxing. Today was a revelation, from the beach to the kiss and to now.

From the moment we met, I felt a tug in my chest. It wasn't just that she was beautiful, although she was. Raine had the best sense of humor and looked out for every employee who came through the door. She was patient and kind, and I'd seen her change so much over the last year as she worked at tearing down the walls holding her back. If asked, I knew Raine would say she was the ugly duckling. She had no idea how amazing she truly was. It had been painful to pretend for so long that I was only interested in her as a friend. I knew I couldn't push until now. I wasn't sure she was aware of the shift in her lately. I understood her even though she never said a word. I saw the same scars in her eyes that lined my soul.

My eyes didn't waver as I stared into hers. I could tell she was on edge. She'd put herself out there, pushing herself, but I hoped it was for the right reasons. I hadn't even had a chance to explain the relationship that Jace and I shared or how I wanted her to be part of our lives long term. Jace was doing what Jace did best, he pushed, but I worried that it would backfire.

Raine lifted the glass I'd given her and gulped it all down. I couldn't help but smile as she sat the glass down and placed her hand in mine. My pulse spiked with her touch. The hope I'd kept tempered bloomed in my chest as she stood.

"Coming?" I said, my eyes meeting Jace's.

"Better believe it," he said.

"Whoa, I'm...ah...you mean both of you, right now? But..." Raine started, but I wasn't letting her get this far and not at least shed one more layer to the protective walls she'd wrapped around herself.

Cupping Raine's face, I dropped my lips to hers and tenderly kissed her lips. I was met with tension and nervousness that I could taste on my tongue as she opened her mouth. Fuck, I wanted her so bad.

I wanted to sit her on the counter and fuck her until she was spent and passed out in my arms. As our lips moved together, I felt her take a shuddering breath, and her body relaxed against mine. I groaned as she opened her mouth, and I explored, tasting the sweet peach flavor that lingered. I was greedy and wanted it all. I wanted her to melt into my body, but that required trust, and I already knew that would take more time.

A hand grabbed my ass a second before Jace's lips found the side of my neck, and the feel of the two of them pressed up against me had my heart pounding like a trapped animal. This was my fantasy.

Before Jace was the big shot star, we were each other's person. We still were. Best friends didn't come close to what we shared. Most didn't know that Jace grew up an hour from here. We lived on the same street, met in preschool, and had been close since Jace punched a kid in the face for picking on me. Jace was also the first guy I was interested in other than girls. He was my first tentative kiss as I explored who I was and realized that my interest in him stretched beyond simple curiosity.

The real confusion came when I still found girls hot and dated them as easily as guys. Of course, my girlfriends I brought home; the guys were kept a secret except for Jace. My parents had no idea for years that we were anything more than best friends who played video games, rode bikes, and were on the basketball team together.

"Fuck, I've missed you," Jace whispered in my ear as he pressed his body harder into my back, pushing me harder into Raine. Our relationship had changed multiple times over the years, but one thing remained the same. We realized that no matter what, we couldn't live without each other.

Was it possible to be in love with two people at the same time? I hadn't known for sure until now, but my feelings for Jace had never diminished, no matter what part of the world he traveled to or how long he was gone.

Raine started as a fascination, this beautiful woman who dressed in the worst outfits, as if she were purposely trying to hide and never be noticed. But I noticed. I noticed everything about Raine. How her smile lit up the room, and her blue eyes sucked you into their pretty depths and made your heart beat fast. I also noticed that she had a big heart and found a way to help anyone who needed it. She was tough with a quick wit and was beyond talented, especially behind the bar. She was dedicated to anything she put her mind to, and she made me feel better, no matter the shit I had going on.

By my third month, I was more than fascinated, and by the end of the first year, she was the reason I never left Eclipse. Jobs came and went, but the people that made you feel whole, you hung onto them with both hands.

I needed Jace to want Raine, and Raine to want Jace. I wouldn't hide my relationship with Jace from her and try to sneak him in later. That wasn't right, and it wasn't who we were. It was both of us, or I had to choose, and fuck, I didn't want to have to make that choice.

Jace and I always had the same tastes, so with nervous anticipation, I hoped he found Raine as irresistible as I did. Then I had to pray that Raine wouldn't decide she'd rather punch Jace in the face, because he really loved to push those lines. It was his thing.

Jace coming back to town forced me to press things with Raine faster than I wanted. I hoped to lay out the entire situation and do dinner with them, but I should've known that would never happen. Jace had a style all his own, and he'd never been one to conform. I'd been talking about Raine for the last year, when Jace asked if I was in love with her. Of course, I told him yes, and he hadn't taken no for an answer about meeting her. Now apparently, he was going to see how far he could push her and there was nothing I could say or do to stop him other than throw him out of the house.

Raine didn't consider herself brave, but that was because she didn't see herself the way I did. Breaking the kiss with Raine, I admired her swollen lips and glassy eyes before turning my head to capture Jace's mouth. He was far more demanding, and his tongue immediately invaded my mouth as his hands roamed over my body. His kisses were always desperate. It felt like he was trying to devour every second we had together, a meal that would have to sustain him until the next time he passed through.

This wasn't the life I imagined for us. It certainly wasn't what I would've chosen, but it was the situation we were in currently. He was worried, or maybe jealous. I didn't know exactly, not that he ever had anything to worry about, but Jace talked his agent into letting the band do the show at the bar so that he could meet her. The show being a hit was just an added bonus.

His hand snaked around my waist, and Raine jumped as he slid it between our bodies. I broke the kiss and locked eyes with Raine once more. She was staring at the spot where Jace drew lines up my neck with his tongue as he teased me.

Raine's eyes held the desire I longed to see, but she was guarded.

"You still interested?" I lifted my brow. This was it, the moment of truth.

"I'm not sure. I thought the next logical step would be dinner or something. This is very lightning paced," she said. It might seem that way to her, but for me, it had been years of coaxing.

"We've eaten dinner at the bar after work almost every night for four years. We drank coffee and talked until all hours of the day and night as we discussed everything from a new routine to our dreams. Recently we streamed new movie releases on the screen in the bar when it was closed."

She smiled, the blush creeping across her cheeks. "You brought the popcorn," she said softly. Raine lifted her eyes from my chest. "You've been planning this a long time, haven't you?"

"Almost from the first day we met," I said, and her face deepened to a rose color. "I just didn't know how or when to tell you about my feelings or Jace, but I can promise that we won't make you do anything you don't want to do. If you want to stay in your clothes and just be upstairs with us, then that's fine. You want to touch us, but we don't touch you. That's also fine. You want to have a shower and pass out, then do it. All I'm asking is that you stay. Rip off a layer of the protective coating and take the leap."

I didn't want to give her the way out. I wanted to grab her hand, drag her upstairs, and make her scream as we fucked her senseless, and she begged to stay forever. We had a third in our relationship on a few occasions, but this felt different. I didn't want her to be a few nights of fun. I was desperate for Raine and Jace to get along. Adding her to our mix meant everything to me.

"Unless you're too scared," Jace said, lifting his mouth from where he was making a hickey I would have to cover later. I glared at him, but he completely ignored me. "You're sexy as fuck, Peaches, but you definitely don't seem like the type that can handle two men. Especially us. I think Avro was right. You're not ready for us. You may never be." He lifted his shoulder and let it drop. "No shame if you wanna go home."

Raine's eyes flared, and she narrowed her eyes at Jace. "Oh, really?"

I could feel her bristling, and the competitive edge she always had in spades at the bar was firing on all cylinders in her eyes.

Jace broke contact with my body, and I instantly missed his presence. There'd always been something about Jace that called to me, that had me on my knees begging.

He opened the fridge and smiled. "I do love your organization. I miss that on the road."

Reaching in, he pulled out the two bottles of champagne and the plate of chocolate-dipped fruit. Whenever Jace was in town, we made it a celebration. Those sexy-as-fuck eyes met mine first, then went to Raine. "Well, I don't see you moving to prove me wrong. Are you all talk?"

"Jace," I growled at him, but he just smirked.

Jace disappeared out of the room, and I knew that by the time we got upstairs, there was a good chance he would be fully naked.

I looked back at Raine. "I really want you to be part of this. Ignore Jace. Whatever you're good with is fine. He likes to run his mouth, but he'd never force you into something."

She bit her lip, and I could see the gears turning as those big blue eyes found mine.

"Alright, but no promises on how far I'll go, at least tonight. And, Avro...." She paused, and her eyes grew serious. "I need you to know it's only because it's you that I'm willing to try this."

Nothing could've wiped off the smile that spread across my face. Her trust in me was intoxicating. Dropping my head, I gave her a quick kiss.

"Thank you, and whatever you want is totally fair. I did kind of press fast forward on us."

Stepping away, I took her hand and led Raine through the house, past the crowd well on their way to turning my sitting area into an orgy. I didn't mind Jace's band mates. Allen held auditions and hired them after Jace was signed, so I never got the chance to know them well. They rarely came over when Jace was in town, and I didn't ask if that was their choice or by Jace's design. All I knew was that I was gonna need to sanitize the shit out of my room, but that was tomorrow's problem.

"Can I ask a question?" Raine said as we walked up the stairs. "What do you call this that you have with Jace? I mean, after the beach and the kiss, I thought you wanted to date me, but I can't quite figure this out. Am I an add-on to a fun night for you two?"

I stopped walking as I realized just how oblivious she was. Had I really done that good of a job hiding my feelings, or had Raine not picked up on any of my flirting, teasing, and suggestive ideas?

"Raine, I wasn't joking. I've wanted you since practically the first day we met. Jace has been in my life for as long as I can remember, but if you're willing, I want to bring you into our relationship. It would be our relationship, as in the three of us."

Her eyebrows shot up. "Like on a regular basis?"

"Like permanently. As in, it would be the three of us from now on," I said. "When Jace is away touring, you'll have to settle for just me." I smirked at her. "But when he's in town, it would be the three of us."

"So no one else is involved? You're not going to come home with someone from the bar, and Jace isn't in another relationship on the road?"

I swallowed hard, and my heart pounded in my chest. "No, just us three from now on," I said.

Jace was going to kill me for suggesting that. We'd agreed on an open relationship until he was done touring. He could have those one-night stands, and I could date whoever as long as there was no permanent attachment of any kind. My prepping for this moment hadn't just been to make sure Raine wouldn't run for the hills, but that Jace would be okay with closing off the open portion of our relationship.

The only thing was, I hadn't mentioned it to him yet. He had no idea I wanted to make us exclusive. He was gonna be pissed—I knew he would be pissed—but I opened my mouth, and the words tumbled out.

He was gone for months at a time, with women and men throwing themselves at him constantly. I didn't doubt that he loved me, but I understood the temptation when isolated and alone, which was why we'd agreed to this type of relationship.

"Permanent...oh, wow. That's...that's definitely a jump from friends."

"Is that really how you see me? Nothing more than a friend?" My gut ached at the idea that the feelings I'd had for so long weren't reciprocated, and I'd built this entire moment up in my head to be more than what it was.

"Well...." She went a bright scarlet, her fair skin showing the blush spreading to the tips of her ears. She looked away from my eyes, sighing, and I stood like a statue, waiting for her to respond. "I have thought about us as more than friends, but Avro, can we please be real for a moment? You are not someone who dates someone like me. Other than admitting to myself that a girl can dream, the train stopped there."

"Girl, I am tired of hearing you put yourself down. Rule number one if we are going to be together." I held up my finger to make sure I had her whole focus. "You will no longer be allowed to talk shit about yourself. You're amazing, understand? Come on," I said, not giving her the chance to respond.

I tugged at Raine's hand, and she didn't resist as we wandered into my bedroom, and I closed the door. Jace wasn't completely naked, which was shocking, but he was only in the black, silky boxers I'd given him, sprawled out on the bed like he didn't have a care in the world. The shiny material did nothing to hide how hard he already was.

My eyes trailed over his body. I never got sick of the sight of him. Hard abs that made my mouth water and long, muscled legs with tattoos running down his thighs. He had his arm behind his head, which only accentuated his chest. Never mind the face. He was currently holding a chocolate-dipped strawberry above his mouth, tracing the bottom with the tip of his tongue. My cock jumped and was instantly hard.

I smirked as I glanced down at Raine, her mouth hanging open at the sight of Jace. I always had the same reaction to him, and it was comforting to see that it wasn't just me he affected.

"Keep drooling, Raine. I like it when girls make a mess of my cock," Jace drawled, his eyes intense with the same challenge as downstairs.

Raine's mouth snapped shut, and I quickly intervened. "Fuck, Jace," I growled, my eyes pleading with him to rein it in. "Why don't you go shower," I suggested.

"Huh?" Raine looked up at me as I pulled my T-shirt off and tossed it aside. Her eyes roamed over my body, and she bit her lip. All the pent-up energy I tried to control went straight to my cock, begging to be touched behind the fly of my jeans.

Instead of repeating myself, I guided her to the bathroom and pulled a couple of massive fuzzy towels off the stand, handing them over. "Have a shower and try to relax. We're not going anywhere, and I won't barge in on you," I said.

"Are you sure about this? I mean...." I laid my finger on Raine's lips to stop the litany of reasons she came up with to stop this from happening. I was sure she already had a thousand and would come up with a thousand more if I let her. Some may even be legitimate concerns, but I didn't want to hear about them right now. Whatever they were, they could all be worked out later.

"You're safe. This is a safe space. Now go shower," I said and closed the door as I walked out.

Jace and I already shared a secret shower together at the club. There was a changing area that was never used upstairs, and while everyone else was cleaning, he'd talked me into taking the edge off. Honestly, he could talk me into doing it anywhere. That was one of his superpowers.

Magazines everywhere would've killed for a photo of Jace Everly lying like this, mostly naked, with a bottle of champagne in one hand and a strawberry in the other. Tattooed sleeves lined his arms and looked dark against the creamy-colored sheets. The barely contained bulge had my mouth watering, but he just couldn't resist and took it an extra step. I watched as he tipped the bottle of champagne to his chest. The liquid looked like gold as it dribbled out and left a trail down his abs before it was caught by the black silk material. I groaned at the sight.

No matter how many times we'd been together, my reaction was always the same. How did I end up being the chosen one? Was this even real? When was the dream bubble going to pop?

"Oops, I'm making a mess. You better lick it off," he teased, eyes shining with mirth. There were two things Jace never lacked: arrogance and a sarcastic sense of humor. He used both very well to hide the softness of the man underneath.

"Asshole," I muttered as I kicked off the flip-flops I'd worn home.

"Maybe," he said, as his hand slid down to the front of the boxers to grip his cock. He groaned, and the sound called to me like I was on the end of a rope and he was pulling me in.

My feet moved of their own accord, and I barely remembered moving as my eyes remained locked on him.

I knelt on the bed, and my mind registered that the shower had turned on, which was good. It meant Raine was fighting her fears, and that made me very happy for her.

"Well?" Jace asked as he dribbled more of the champagne on his skin. I licked at his body, not wanting to miss a single drop, and smirked when a new line of goodness traveled down and into my mouth.

"Don't think I forgot you cornering Raine in the storage area," I said, then drew a wet line up his chest with my tongue.

"I don't expect you to. I wanted to see how she'd respond. You know me."

That I did all too well. He loved pushing all the boundaries, every single one of them. Drawing gasps and moans from Jace, I moved up and down his body until I was satisfied I'd gotten all the champagne. Swirling my tongue, I finally reached his lips, and this time I was the aggressor and made sure he remembered why he missed me. Why he didn't want to board the plane and fly off. We were both breathless before I finally broke the kiss.

"I missed you too," I said. "Tell me, do you like her?" I held my breath for the answer. Jace's eyes went to the bathroom door and then back up to mine.

"I think she's smart and sexy as hell. I also think she is exactly what we've always wanted, but I have my reservations." He glanced at the door for a second time. "She's terrified, Avro. The bravado is covering something terrible. You must see it."

"Yeah, I know, she...she reminds me of me," I said quietly, and Jace searched my face.

"That may be difficult to unpack," he said, his fingers trailing down my arm. "You ready for that? I'm not here to help you."

"Were you ready to help me when I needed you?"

He licked his lips. "Fine, if this is what you want, I'm willing to give her a shot. Something about her gets under my skin," he said.

Dropping my lips to his nipple, I licked at the droplet of champagne I'd somehow missed.

"Fuck yes," Jace groaned, his hand gripping my hair.

Jace would give Raine a shot. Now all I needed was to get Raine to see that this was what she wanted too. Easier said than done with all the fear she had bubbling under the surface.

Raine

13

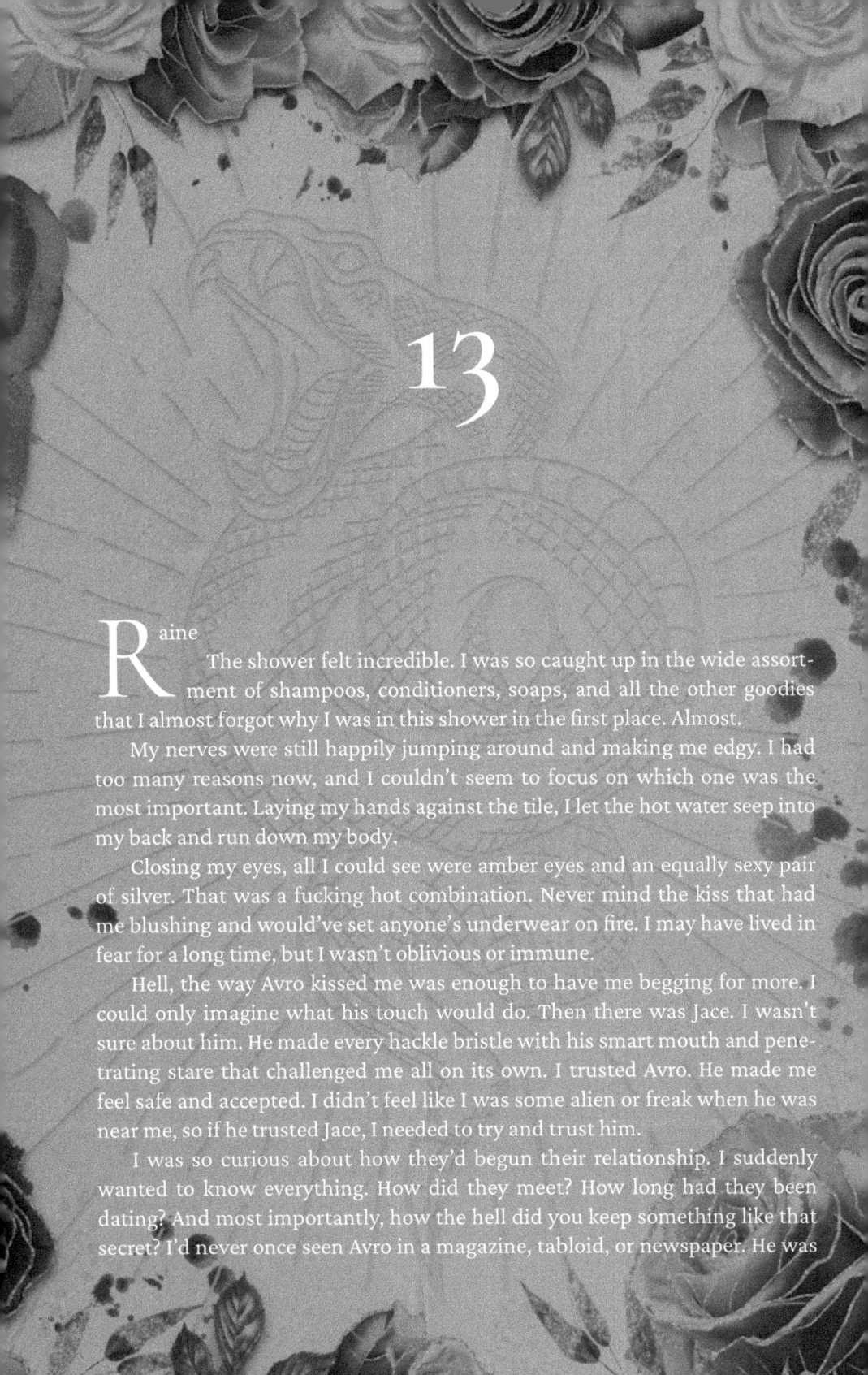

Raine

The shower felt incredible. I was so caught up in the wide assortment of shampoos, conditioners, soaps, and all the other goodies that I almost forgot why I was in this shower in the first place. Almost.

My nerves were still happily jumping around and making me edgy. I had too many reasons now, and I couldn't seem to focus on which one was the most important. Laying my hands against the tile, I let the hot water seep into my back and run down my body.

Closing my eyes, all I could see were amber eyes and an equally sexy pair of silver. That was a fucking hot combination. Never mind the kiss that had me blushing and would've set anyone's underwear on fire. I may have lived in fear for a long time, but I wasn't oblivious or immune.

Hell, the way Avro kissed me was enough to have me begging for more. I could only imagine what his touch would do. Then there was Jace. I wasn't sure about him. He made every hackle bristle with his smart mouth and penetrating stare that challenged me all on its own. I trusted Avro. He made me feel safe and accepted. I didn't feel like I was some alien or freak when he was near me, so if he trusted Jace, I needed to try and trust him.

I was so curious about how they'd begun their relationship. I suddenly wanted to know everything. How did they meet? How long had they been dating? And most importantly, how the hell did you keep something like that secret? I'd never once seen Avro in a magazine, tabloid, or newspaper. He was the full-time love interest of the guy who'd just hit the cover of Sexiest Man Alive, and no one freaking knew but me and maybe his bandmates? Was that possible?

Stepping out of the shower, I quickly dried off and realized I had no spare clothes. Fuck, I didn't even have my regular clothes. I glared at the door as I realized Avro had snuck in and taken them, but at least he left a large black robe in their place. It served me right for not locking the door. I looked at the handle and realized there was no lock, then paused.

I hadn't locked the door. I hadn't even tried. I'd stripped naked, got in the shower, and wasn't worried about locking the door. I covered my mouth as a well of emotion burst inside my chest. That was massive for me. It needed an award. I felt like I'd just climbed Everest and reached the peak.

I made my way over to the massive, intimidating mirror, stared at my shocked, smiling face, and took a moment to think.

This was a big step for anyone. This could be a whole new chapter in my life that I hadn't even dreamed of, or it could be a disaster. Avro was my best friend. Shit, he was my only friend, and if this went wrong, I'd be losing the one person in my life that I'd learned to trust and even lean on.

On the other hand, here I was in my twenties with all of one experience to my name, and I knew it was time for me to try to move past it. I needed to make strides to find out who I was and what I wanted for myself within a relationship dynamic. Was that both of them? I couldn't answer that. I didn't even fully understand it yet, but I knew I wanted to be with Avro, and that meant I wanted to try.

My heart fluttered, and my skin got hot as I pictured them out there on the bed together.

"Seriously, what the fuck is up with this?" I clutched the counter hard and leaned over as I tried to steady my breathing. The thoughts of them made me lightheaded.

The voice in the back of my mind was screaming that they only wanted to use and embarrass me. I was nothing more than a joke. The logical part of my brain told me that Avro was a great guy, and I felt in my gut that he was the same decent person I'd always known. Hell, he'd practically dated me without me even realizing it and had never made me feel uncomfortable. That took skill and patience.

The kiss at the bar and stealing my clothes aside, he'd never pushed or asked for anything that I hadn't been ready for, and somewhere along the line, I'd begun to see him as more than a friend. Hell, I tried to convince myself daily that we were only friends, but the pangs of jealousy would stand up and call me a liar every time. I couldn't even remember when I first fantasized about him, watched him work, and wondered, *what if?* I'd needed to drink extra water and had been tempted to stand in the walk-in freezer to cool off after watching him dance.

So why now? Why was he suddenly whisking me off to the beach and kissing me in front of a packed house? There had to be a reason for the rush and showing me all this now and all at once. I looked up, and the answer hit me. Jace. Fuck, this was wildly complicated.

It was like elementary school, and I was the item for show and tell. At least that was how it felt, even if Avro didn't mean it that way. The moment we knew Jace was coming to town, he'd been different. A little bolder and then he'd asked me out and kissed me in front of him. He was proving a point or showing me off, maybe. I wasn't sure, but I knew he was doing this because of Jace, whether Jace asked for it or not.

"Okay, enough thinking. You can do this," I said to myself, like I was giving someone a pep talk. "You're going to go out there and act like an adult, badass woman and fuck two men," I said, and I swear I watched my reflection take off out the door. "Who am I trying to kid? I'm not ready for that. I'll be lucky to get past kissing without having a coronary." I shook my shoulders and did a ridiculous little jog on the spot, like I was getting ready for the hundred-meter dash.

"Thank God they can't see this," I mumbled, then looked around the bathroom for a camera. "Okay, stop being crazy. Just walk out there. You've got this."

Grabbing the thick robe that was huge on me, I wrapped it tight around myself and tied it into place. Gripping the door handle, I took a final deep breath and opened the door. I froze as a very naked Avro kneeled on the bed, giving Jace the hottest blowjob I'd ever seen. Nothing could've prepared me for the stunning sight of these two men together.

My hands dropped to my sides, and my mouth fell open as Avro looked up, but his mouth never stopped working. I blew out a breath, trembling as a roaring heat spread throughout my body. My eyes followed his movements as his lips traveled up and down the long cock. I could feel my pulse in my throat, and my heart hammered inside my chest as the spark of passion flared into a raging inferno. I was shocked by my own wanton desire.

Jace was lying in the same position as when I'd left the room, but now he was fully naked, and Avro knelt beside him, facing me. Avro's eyes never strayed from mine, and I knew my face was bright red by now. I was so hot and turned on watching him.

"Fuck, that feels good," Jace groaned and leaned on his elbows so that I could see both of their faces clearly.

Jace's eyes met mine, and there was a smoldering heat so intense that it miraculously forced the temperature in my body higher. The house coat felt like too much clothing as I practically cooked inside the fuzzy material. Jace gripped the back of Avro's head and pushed down, forcing himself deeper into his mouth. Avro made a choking sound, and suddenly, the entire cock disappeared.

My hand instinctively went to my throat, and the earlier trembling became full-on body tremors. I couldn't decide if I was more excited by what I was watching or horrified that they wanted to do this with me.

"Fuck yes. Fuck, Avro," Jace's face darkened a moment before his head fell back, and he yelled Avro's name like there was no one for miles. His body jerked up, and I knew he was cumming. There was no denying it, as I rubbed my legs together, that watching the show made me wet.

Avro slowly lifted his head, his tongue drawing lines along Jace's shaft, and then licked the tip like Jace was a delicious treat. Those amber eyes turned to meet mine, and all the earlier courage I'd managed to muster took a swan dive out the window. Backing into the bathroom, I flicked the door closed and turned to lean against it. My hand clutched the fuzzy coat tight to my chest as I tried to calm the wild fluttering of my heart.

"Raine," Avro said a moment later, with a soft rap on the door.

I jumped like he'd pounded on it and gripped the material tighter as I stumbled away to sit down on the edge of the bathtub. I couldn't draw a breath and felt a panic attack coming on. I knew that if I kept it up, I was going to faint, and yet that didn't matter. My mind was screaming hysterically. It was like someone screaming, *Run! They're going to get you!* in my ear. What was it about panic attacks that left you spinning out of control? The harder you tried to stop them, the worse they became.

I didn't hear the door, but Avro was suddenly in front of me. His hands were on my knees, and his eyes locked with mine, but I couldn't understand a single word that came out of his mouth. It was all white noise, like someone had left a fan on, way too loud inside my brain.

Warm hands cupped my face, forcing me to stare into eyes that held so much warmth and compassion that they felt like a tender hug all on their own. He was exaggerating a breath in. I copied his action, and then he slowly blew out. I couldn't say how many times he made me do that before I could see without the spinning or hearing the loud hum.

"That's it. You're okay, Raine. I've got you. Just breathe," Avro said softly, and the sound of his voice brought tears to my eyes.

"I'm so sorry I'm ruining your night. I should go. I'm a mess, and I..."

"Shh, Raine. I said just breathe." He laid his finger on my lips, and I felt like such a fool. I couldn't believe that I'd had a panic attack over hot sex. I was completely insane. Anyone else would've run across the room and done a swan dive between them; yet here I was crying.

"I see your mind is still racing. Just focus on me and push all of that extra chatter aside." He cupped my chin, and even though I didn't want to, he forced me to keep staring into his eyes. "I said I've got you, and I meant it."

"But...."

"There is no but. I knew this would be hard for you and that you may not be able to follow through, but this is a huge step, Raine. You went from a few months ago not getting in a car with me to being in my home, showering, and sitting here in nothing but a bathrobe. From where I'm standing, those are massive strides."

I didn't say anything. All those things seemed so small and normal. They shouldn't be celebrated.

Avro smiled wide. "You kissed me in front of hundreds of people and went to the beach with me all alone. You came up here completely blind to what might happen. Raine, stop beating yourself up."

I shook my head. "Why do you even care? I've never told you what happened. I don't understand why you care this much."

"You don't understand because you refuse to see your worth. That needs to change. Second, I see in you the same emotional scars I carry around and battle every day. Even now, they creep up on me, but I've learned to control them, and you'll get there too," he said, and took one of my hands and placed it over his heart. "I was attacked and raped by someone that I thought I could trust. I see the same fear in you. You don't need to tell me now what happened, but I hope one day you will."

"Avro, I'm so sorry." I'd never have known if he hadn't said anything. He hid it so well. Something about the quiet admission made me feel more at ease. He truly understood and saw me. They weren't just words to placate me or calm me down.

"Don't be sorry," he smiled. "Here, I brought you this," Avro said. I looked to see what he picked up, and I laughed as I took in the fuzzy Minion pants and plain white T-shirt. "I knew you'd want your clothes clean for the morning, so I put them in the wash. Come on, stand up. I'll help you put this on."

He held my hand and helped me to my feet, and I couldn't explain it, but this felt like a monumental moment for me. Like I was finally finding my way off the roundabout I'd been stuck in. My heart swelled with Avro's nearness, and I was seeing him for the first time through eyes no longer tainted with crippling paranoia.

He helped slide the T-shirt over my head, and of course, it was way too large on me. As soon as it was in position, I let the towel fall.

Hanging onto his shoulders, I stepped into the sleep pants he held open for me and watched his hands as he tied the strings into a perfect bow.

"I bet you didn't think you would need to dress me tonight," I teased, my voice coming out as a whisper.

These last few hours had been the most intense I'd ever seen Avro, and when he laid his hands on my shoulders, I felt the weight of that gaze. "I would dress you a million times over again if it would keep you looking at me just like that."

My mouth curled up in a smile, and I couldn't stop blushing. Avro had that effect on me. I brushed it off at work, but here in this quiet moment, he wasn't performing for anyone. This was all him, the real him.

He ran his hands over my short hair. I'd kept it short since my attack. I could clearly remember the feel of the first guy's hand wrapping in the long length I'd been so proud of and pulling me back as I tried to run. I shuddered and pushed the image aside.

"I love your hair like this," he said, leaning down, his lips brushing against mine. "Will you lie with us to sleep?"

"Won't I just be ruining the little time you and Jace have together?"

"Do you mind if we play with one another?"

My mind drew a blank at that question. I'd never slept beside anyone other than Kai, and that was by accident while watching a movie or when I had a scary dream and would end up in his room on the floor. Kai would always be so angry when I did that and said that I was going to get him into trouble, but I just wanted to be close to him. He made me feel safe. Rather, he *had* made me feel safe.

To sleep in the same bed and then have them possibly have sex beside me sounded hot and all sorts of naughty at the same time. Surprisingly, I wasn't nervous about the idea.

"Is this normal?"

"You mean with three people?"

I nodded, and Avro cocked his head as he thought. "It's different for everyone." He rolled his shoulders. "Jace and I are very comfortable together and want you to feel the same. This shouldn't be a scary situation, Raine, or one where you are okay with me but scared of him." I nibbled on my lip as I thought about the teasers I'd already witnessed and knew I wanted to see more. "What does that mean exactly? That's open for discussion, but I can tell you that it means you can be with me or him or us together, and the same goes for us. There can't be any jealousy between us. That is the steadfast, hard, cut-and-dry rule. We have nothing if we don't have trust and are jealous of each other's individual time together."

My mind was reeling. This was a lot to toss at someone when they had a ton of experience, let alone me, who had none. What I did know was that I wanted to try. His confidence in me made me want to try.

"Okay," I said, and the smile that spread across Avro's face made it feel like everything in the world was rainbows and cotton candy. It was a lie, though; the world was far from that, but that was how he made me feel.

Avro linked our fingers together as we walked out of the bathroom. Jace was under the covers with his arm casually tossed over his head while the other lay on his abs, which always seemed to be flexed.

"Raine has agreed to sleep with us, but that's all for tonight," Avro announced, and even though I knew it wasn't his intention, it sounded like I was a kid coming over for a sleepover. I groaned as Jace's lip curled up like he was thinking the same thing.

Those inquisitive silver eyes found mine. "Alright, but if I want to fuck Avro, I'm going to," he said, and the image of Jace doing just that flashed before my eyes.

Damn, that image was hot. Maybe I was being corrupted, but I was already along for the ride. Unlike Avro, who asked if that would be okay, Jace just proclaimed he would do what he wanted. My eyes flicked between them, understanding their personality types and getting a glimpse of their dynamic. I nodded, not trusting my voice.

I thought for a moment that Avro would put me between them, but he lay down in the middle as we got on the bed. He held the covers up, pulling me into his body as I climbed in. He was so warm to the touch. I always bundled up when I went to bed with flannel pants and thick socks, sometimes a sweatshirt, but with the thin cotton material, the heat from his body soaked into mine. I sighed, and my muscles relaxed as I let myself be snuggled for the first time.

So this was what it felt like to be the little spoon. I flinched as an extra hand touched my stomach. I knew it was Jace, his hand was warmer, and his fingers were firmer. I couldn't see him or his hand, yet it felt like he'd just commanded us to stay put. Biting my lip, I was so tempted to lift the blanket and look at the two hands holding me.

"How do you feel?" Avro whispered, his breath fanning my ear.

It took a moment to assess myself because I didn't understand the subtle sensation that had taken over. I was never entirely calm; it always felt like I was looking around for a threat when there wasn't one, but right now, there was none of that.

"I feel...relaxed, actually. This is the safest and most peaceful I've felt in years." As I said the words, I let the truth and weight of them into my soul. It was as if one of the scars smoothed out and became whole once more.

"Good." Avro kissed my neck and found a way to cuddle closer. I was dwarfed by his tall frame, and I loved it.

For so long, the touch of another human had been terrifying, and a single tear trickled from my eye with the realization that there was hope for me yet.

Snake

14

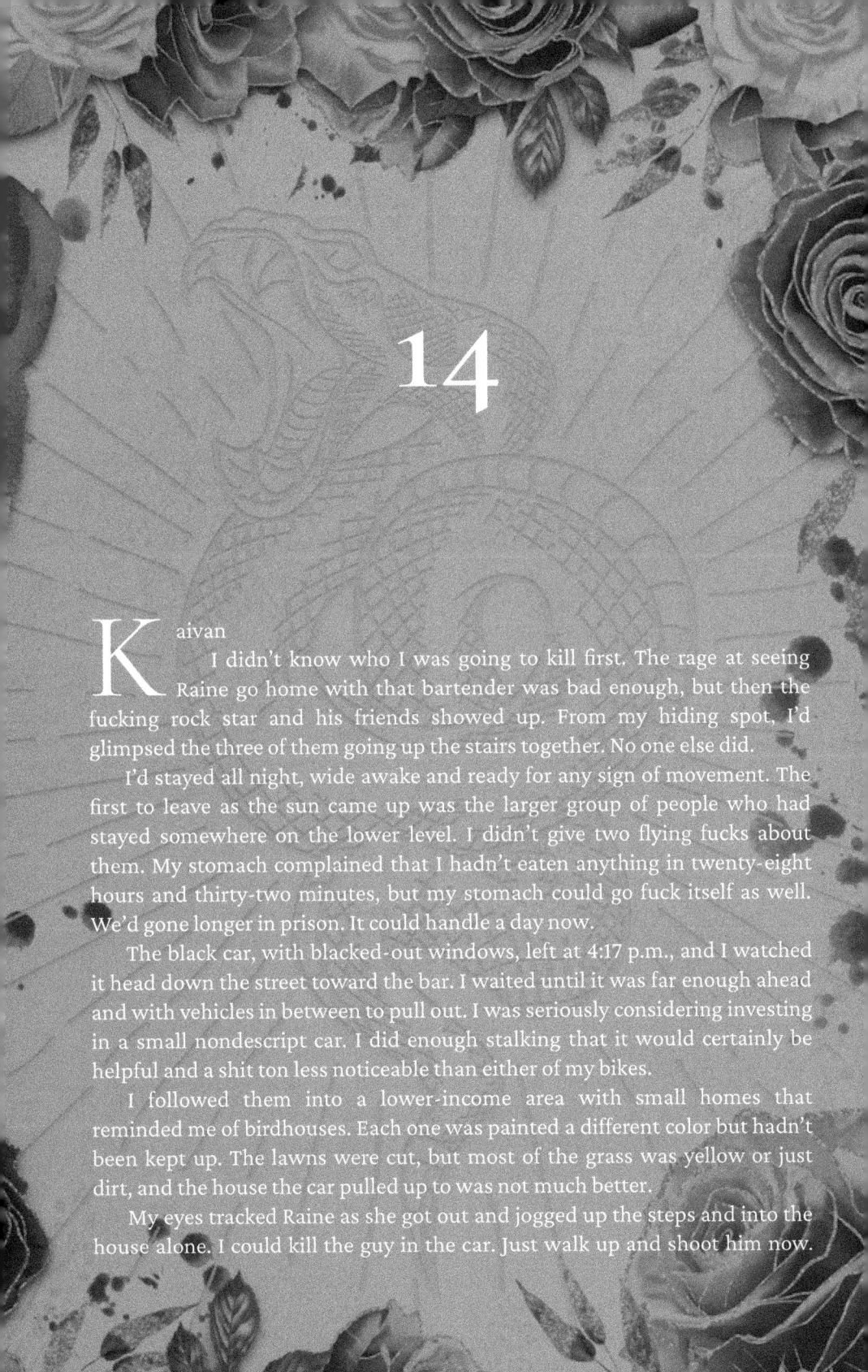

Kaivan

I didn't know who I was going to kill first. The rage at seeing Raine go home with that bartender was bad enough, but then the fucking rock star and his friends showed up. From my hiding spot, I'd glimpsed the three of them going up the stairs together. No one else did.

I'd stayed all night, wide awake and ready for any sign of movement. The first to leave as the sun came up was the larger group of people who had stayed somewhere on the lower level. I didn't give two flying fucks about them. My stomach complained that I hadn't eaten anything in twenty-eight hours and thirty-two minutes, but my stomach could go fuck itself as well. We'd gone longer in prison. It could handle a day now.

The black car, with blacked-out windows, left at 4:17 p.m., and I watched it head down the street toward the bar. I waited until it was far enough ahead and with vehicles in between to pull out. I was seriously considering investing in a small nondescript car. I did enough stalking that it would certainly be helpful and a shit ton less noticeable than either of my bikes.

I followed them into a lower-income area with small homes that reminded me of birdhouses. Each one was painted a different color but hadn't been kept up. The lawns were cut, but most of the grass was yellow or just dirt, and the house the car pulled up to was not much better.

My eyes tracked Raine as she got out and jogged up the steps and into the house alone. I could kill the guy in the car. Just walk up and shoot him now.

No, that was my irrational anger talking, and besides, the fucker did me a favor. I now knew where Raine lived, and as soon as the car left, I could sneak in and teach her a proper lesson.

That fucking car never left. Nope, it stayed there until she came back out. She had changed into a new outfit and carried a bag. A bag big enough to hold multiple nights' worth of clothing. My jaw cracked as I ground my teeth together.

She got back into the car, and I swore as it started back my way. I parked in a driveway with a truck and stayed on the bike with my jacket collar pulled up until the vehicle was long gone.

Not wanting to be seen later, I circled the area, learning all the potential hiding spots I could use to access the home, and then went past the bar. Sure enough, the sedan was in the parking lot, and my anger took on a life of its own.

Then Mannix called, and now here I was, as angry as a bear woken up during hibernation.

"Are you fucking joking?" I seethed.

My hand cracked down hard in the middle of the guy's face. Blood coated my fist and sprayed me with each new blow.

"Man, take it easy. The guy is dead already," Roach said. "We have a couple others you can spend this energy on instead."

My fist stopped mid-air, and I stared down at the mangled face. "Fine, lead the way," I growled, pushing myself to my feet. I wasn't even close to being tired. In fact, I was just getting warmed up.

"You know you're just making this a harder clean-up job, right?" Roach said as I reached where he was leaning against the wall, watching the show.

"Don't fucking care. You either get me fresh meat, or I go back to what I was doing," I said, eyeing Roach. He held his hands up like he was surrendering.

"Geez-us man, don't look at me like that. You freak me the fuck out." Roach pushed away from the wall of the beachfront property and led me down the hallway toward the bedrooms near the back. He pushed open the door, and two more guys were sitting on the floor, with their hands and feet tied up as they sat back-to-back with wide silver tape covering their mouths.

They started to beg for their lives, the sounds muffled through the tape, but I could understand them. They stopped when their eyes traveled from Roach's face to my bloodied shitkickers, and up to my face. In cartoon fashion, their eyes went wide at the same time. That's right, fuckers. Death has found you tonight.

"Gentlemen, let me introduce you to Snake. He's our enforcer, and he's just a little pissed off," Roach said and signed dramatically. "He really doesn't like it when people hurt those in our club." He lowered his voice to a whisper. "He scares me." Roach shivered, and the guys looked like they were going to faint.

"I found one more hiding in the carport. Stupid idiot tried to run out in the open, but he didn't get far," Mannix called out, but I was barely paying attention. "What the fuck? Did we use a sledgehammer on this guy's face?"

"Naw, just Snake's fist on a rampage," Roach answered and casually chewed on the end of a toothpick.

"Can I do whatever I want to them?"

I stepped farther into the room, and a moment later, Mannix pushed a third man through the door. As soon as he saw me, he tried to turn and run. My name and reputation held weight in more than just the MC circles. I'd done jobs for the Mafia, casino owners, and politicians who didn't want to get their hands dirty. I went after those who disrespected or hurt family members of the MC, but I was more than an enforcer. I'd graduated to gun-for-hire for the right price and the right favors.

"No, no, no, please," the guy said, who was trying to find a way out the door that was now filled with a wall of muscle as Mannix and Roach blocked the way. "Please, I didn't do it. I swear to God that I didn't touch Kitten," the guy begged.

I had no idea why we were here to begin with, and it honestly didn't matter. Mannix said he needed my help and to meet him here. Teach these guys what it meant to mess with Lost Souls' property. He wanted an example made out of them, which was like ringing a dinner bell in front of my face.

I yanked the one guy off the floor. He tried to scream through the tape and writhed around like that would make me let go.

"Yes, you can do whatever you want, Snake, but we need to be out of here in two hours and not a minute more. That guy Chase calls the Dragon is coming to make sure this property is..." Mannix looked around and shrugged. "Burnt to a crisp."

"That crazy psycho?"

Mannix and Roach lifted their brows at me. Probably not the best choice of words as I stood holding a knife to a man's throat and looking like I was auditioning for the lead in *Carrie*.

"Well, now, that doesn't leave me much time, but it will have to do." I ran the knife I was holding across the man's throat. He began to choke as he collapsed to the ground.

The man sitting on the floor dropped to his side and tried to roll away as I reached for him. That was the funniest shit I'd seen in a long time. He turned onto his stomach and used his face and body to inchworm toward the door.

Where the fuck did he think he was going?

"Please let me go, please. I'm telling you the truth, I never touched Kitten," the last man to join the party begged—sniveling sap.

"Which one is Kitten's father?" Mannix asked, and the guy pointed to the man trying to make his grand escape one inch at a time.

"Are you lying to me?" Mannix asked as he stared down at the guy begging for his life. Mannix always looked big, but today he looked like a giant beside the scrawny man.

I slammed my boot down in the middle of the inchworm's back as he reached the door. It was humorous for the first few seconds, but now I was just annoyed. I kept him pinned there while Mannix questioned the captive that didn't have tape on his mouth.

"No, no, I'm not lying. I never touched his daughter. He was the only sick fuck who did that," the man said, throwing the other one under the bus and letting us drive over him.

"But you are Steve, right?" Mannix asked, pulling a picture out of his pocket. He tapped the image and I couldn't see the photo well, but I knew the answer was yes just by the way he hesitated. He looked at the photo and then up into Mannix's eyes as if weighing what would be the wise answer.

"Um...well, yeah," he finally said.

"So you helped assault Kitten's underage friend, just not her? In a way, you still hurt one of the Lost Souls family," Mannix drawled, and I knew he was playing with the guy. He was never getting out of here, even if he said that he was the next coming of Christ.

"Um...I...I didn't know her friend was underage." Steve pointed to the man on the floor. "He said she was legal when I started fucking her," he blurted out, and Mannix's nose flared, his steely eyes turning hard as stone.

He leaned down closer to Steve, who wisely took a step back. "I didn't even know that part. She was too embarrassed to tell us exactly what happened, but thank you for the confirmation." Mannix was quick with his long knife. He stabbed Steve three times before the guy even registered that something was wrong.

In prison, you learned to work fast and kill faster. There was no hanging around or making it fun and drawn out like this. You killed your target, and you moved on.

Steve stumbled back and stared down at the red seeping into the front of his crisp white dress shirt. I would've killed these fuckers simply for what they did for a living. Fucking rich assholes always thought they could get away with anything. It was highly possible that if I'd been born into a wealthy family or had a rich lawyer, I wouldn't have ended up behind bars wasting the ten best years of my life.

I watched Steve fall to his knees, then sighed and looked at Mannix. "You just fucking killed my fun."

"You still have one. Besides, we don't have time for you to kill two," Mannix said, his voice calm. "You tend to dally." He wandered over to Steve, who was sadly still breathing, his mouth gaping open in shock.

"Dally? Like, as in dilly dally? What the fuck? Are you suddenly eighty?" Roach snorted as Mannix glared.

Mannix kicked out, and his massive shitkicker found the underside of Steve's chin. The sheer power sent him flying but also knocked him out cold. Now the asshole would die peacefully on top of it being quick.

"There, now you can focus on the one." He flicked his fingers at me like he was shooing a child. "Go on, get going. Take out whatever the fuck this is that's crawled up your ass on someone other than us, you ornery bastard."

"Fine, but for the record, you're no fun."

Putting my knife away, I bent down and lifted Kitten's father, who had tried to inch his way to freedom. With a heave, I tossed the pencil neck over my shoulder and marched out the back door. One nice thing about rich people, they liked space. I guess that was one thing we did have in common. I tossed the guy down on the beach. He made an oomph sound as he hit the sand. Taking a moment to arrange him so that he was facing the water, I yanked up hard on his arms tied behind his back, and the muffled scream was like a sweet lullaby as his shoulders dislocated with a loud pop.

Tears welled up in the man's eyes as I looped the rope holding his bound wrists over the fence post, and he hung there looking like a pathetic scarecrow. I worked quickly, cutting off the dress shirt, pants, and boxers. Taking a step back, I had to wonder what made someone hurt their own kid. He looked like a typical middle-aged dude.

There was nothing nefarious about him. There was no sign hanging around his neck that said, 'I like to rape little girls.' Had I looked like the type who would? Was that why they locked me up and tossed away the key? Was it because I'd been in and out of homes in the foster care system until I landed at the Collins' with Raine? Was it because I'd gotten into fights at school, was born into an MC family, had tattoos by the time I was seventeen, or had a father already in prison? Was it just expected I'd be the same? The joke was on them, because I wasn't until they locked me up.

Was that what they'd seen in me over this plain, nondescript guy? I couldn't help wondering what would've happened if it had been this douche with his crisp white shirt and polished shoes.

Didn't matter now. My justice would be so much worse than anything that ever would've happened on the inside. Yeah, he may have been laid over a table or two, but other than that, he would've survived. They liked to keep weak asswipes like this around so that they could have some easy fun or pawn off chores.

"Pwease, pwease don' 'ill me," he mumbled through the tape.

"And why exactly shouldn't I kill you?"

He mumbled apologies. From the little I'd been heard inside, this guy assaulted his own daughter, and they said I was an asshole. Kitten was Kickstand's house mouse. His family had taken her in a bit ago, but it was only recently that she'd confessed to them what had happened to her. We took hurting our members seriously, and that included everyone.

I gripped his chin in my hand. "Don't worry. The devil looks after his own. I'm sure you'll have a perfectly toasty seat to perch upon in hell." I smirked, the humor never reaching my eyes, as I stepped back and thought about what cut I wanted to make first.

The screaming began as the first cut was made. I glared into his eyes as I slowly sawed back and forth through the flaccid cock hanging between his legs, then held up my prize like I'd caught the biggest fish of the day.

"You weren't packing very much, were you? How did Kitten even feel this little thing?" I stretched it out like I was playing the accordion in front of the man to see.

I knew he vomited in his mouth, but it had nowhere to go, and I watched his face go green as he tried to swallow it back down.

"I hope you didn't eat too much," I said. "Would be a shame if you had a lot of seafood. Lobster and scallops coming back up would be nasty with its half-digested stench that fills your mouth and nose like it was already rotting." I already knew they'd been dining on a fancy lobster dinner by the remnants left in the kitchen.

Right on cue, he puked again, and I stepped back as bile was forced out his nose.

"This seems like a fascinating way to drown," I said, and laid the cock down on a rock so that I could continue my work.

By the time I was done, I was thoroughly impressed with what I'd accomplished in a short period of time. Mannix and Roach were walking along the path to where I displayed my pièce de résistance.

"What the fuck, man? I swear you get more sadistic with every passing day," Roach said as he screwed up his face at my work. "And I'm very fucking happy you like me."

"You just have no appreciation for a dramatic flare," I countered.

"That is certainly dramatic," Mannix drawled, his eyebrow cocking in my direction.

I looked back down at the man I'd decapitated, gutted, and set his head between his legs with a cock sticking out like his tongue.

"In all fairness, you said earlier that this man should be forced to suck his own cock, so really, it's your fault," I said and shrugged.

Mannix rolled his eyes at me. "Is whatever brewing in you settled down now, at least?"

"No," I growled out and clenched my knife harder.

"Wanna share?" Roach asked, crossing his arms.

"No."

"Are you safe to travel with?" Mannix asked, and it was my turn to stare at him like he was crazy.

"I'm pissed off. I don't have rabies."

"Are you sure about that? I've wondered for a long time if one of those rats in prison got to you," Mannix said and smirked.

I picked up the butt I'd smoked and smoothed the sand around the asshole's body. The guys took the hint and stepped onto the hard path as I made sure no print was left behind. I'd been very careful and was even nice enough to sanitize the cock before I shoved it in his mouth. Probably more than the girls, he decided to rape got.

Mannix handed me a towel and wet wipes to clean my face like we'd just eaten chicken wings and not killed four men. Putting everything in a bag, we marched around to the front of the house just as a nondescript white van pulled into the driveway. My hand instinctively reached behind my back for my gun when Mannix shook his head at me.

The guy that stepped out of the driver's side was a little taller than me and was almost as ripped as Mannix. His unusual lagoon-colored eyes found mine from under the shadow of the black hoodie, and I knew without asking this was Derek West. Chase started referring to him as the Dragon after Ava had called him that. I hadn't taken her seriously. I mean, it was hard to take anything that girl said seriously, but as it turned out, she wasn't far off the mark.

Fire followed this man like blood did me. We were one and the same in many ways, and true to our natures, neither of us spoke a word.

"We're done, and don't worry about the body in the back. He's kind of a message," Mannix said. "Feel free to cook all around him in case we missed anything, and here, can you destroy this as well?" Mannix held out the bag.

There was only a subtle nod from Derek as he took the bag and marched for the front door. I didn't see any tools and couldn't help wondering what he would use to start the fire. You would think it took longer to engulf an entire house in flames, but for this guy, it was only as long as it took for us to make our way the quarter mile down the beach to where our bikes were stashed.

Looking back over my shoulder, I saw the smoke rising steadily into the air in long black torrents while the glow of flames flickered through the trees like a fiery beast. The plain white van passed us before we got our bikes pulled from the shadowed corner of the lifeguard tower. We all paused to watch the Dragon drive away.

I didn't know where he came from or how Chase had met him, but he was one motherfucker I didn't plan on messing with. I'd seen what he did to the Reaper's hideouts. In one night, he killed more of their members than we had in a couple months. Even Chase's rampage couldn't compare to the fatalities. Derek West was more demon than human. That was high praise from me.

"Don't expect me back tonight. I have things I need to take care of." I left them staring after me as I rode back to where Raine worked.

She wasn't getting out from under my wrath that easily. I had a score to settle, and I was just getting warmed up.

Avro

15

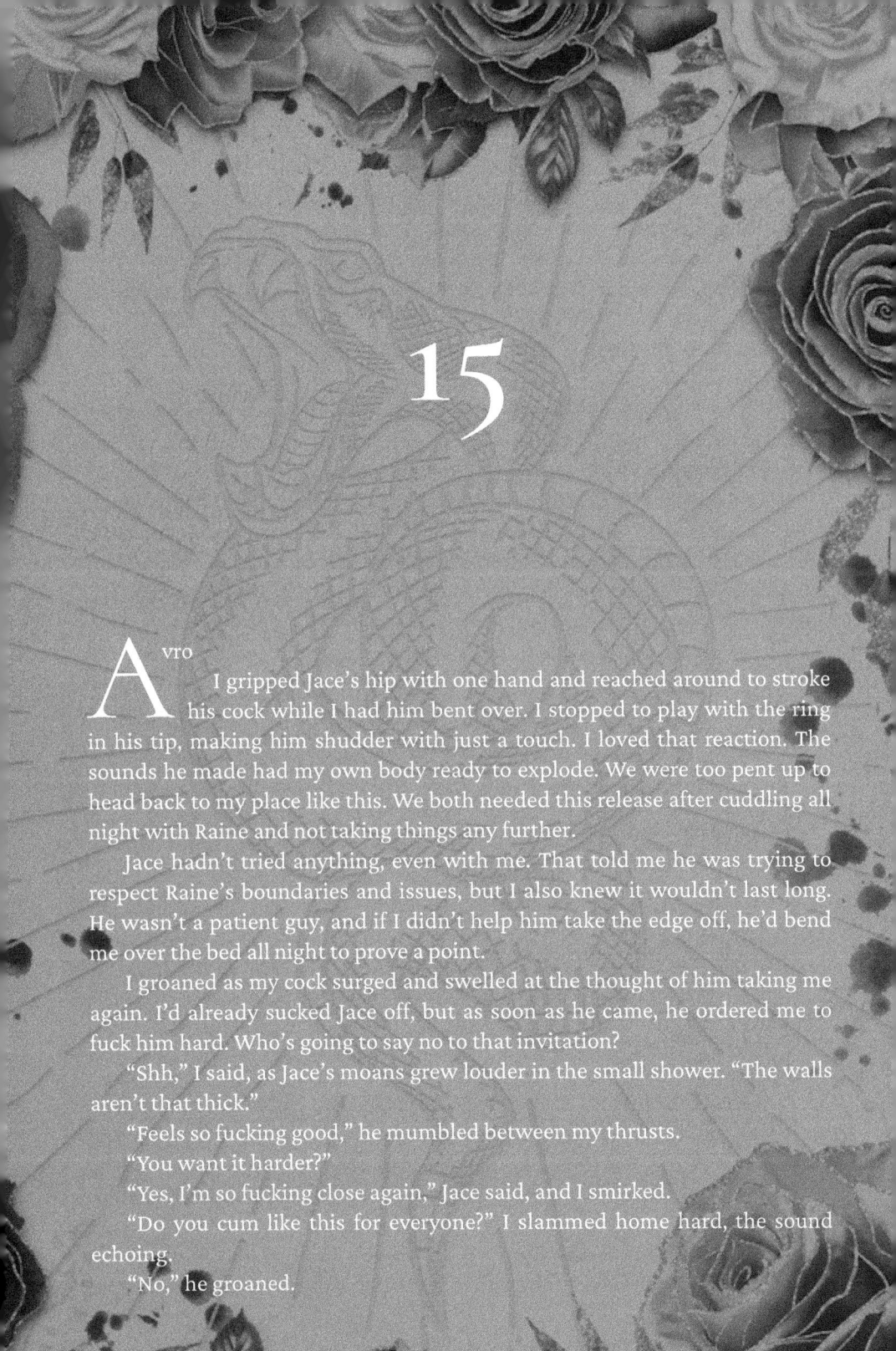

Avro

I gripped Jace's hip with one hand and reached around to stroke his cock while I had him bent over. I stopped to play with the ring in his tip, making him shudder with just a touch. I loved that reaction. The sounds he made had my own body ready to explode. We were too pent up to head back to my place like this. We both needed this release after cuddling all night with Raine and not taking things any further.

Jace hadn't tried anything, even with me. That told me he was trying to respect Raine's boundaries and issues, but I also knew it wouldn't last long. He wasn't a patient guy, and if I didn't help him take the edge off, he'd bend me over the bed all night to prove a point.

I groaned as my cock surged and swelled at the thought of him taking me again. I'd already sucked Jace off, but as soon as he came, he ordered me to fuck him hard. Who's going to say no to that invitation?

"Shh," I said, as Jace's moans grew louder in the small shower. "The walls aren't that thick."

"Feels so fucking good," he mumbled between my thrusts.

"You want it harder?"

"Yes, I'm so fucking close again," Jace said, and I smirked.

"Do you cum like this for everyone?" I slammed home hard, the sound echoing.

"No," he groaned.

"You sure about that? You didn't sound certain. If you can get it better elsewhere...." I smirked as Jace glared over his shoulder at me. I took that moment to pick up the pace, and his eyes rolled back, his mouth hanging open. "You didn't answer. Should I stop?"

"Don't you dare fucking stop. You know you're the only one I want."

I smiled wide and looked down to where my cock disappeared inside his ass. He felt incredible. That was the only word for how Jace made me feel with every touch. He always had. Closing my eyes, I let myself go, and there was no holding back.

"Holy fuck, yes," Jace yelled, and I was too lost in my own pleasure to care that everyone downstairs may have just heard me fucking Jace Everly. Trying to keep our relationship secret was a full-time job.

Where anyone else would wear it as a badge of honor and try to get themselves in a tabloid, I wanted nothing to do with that. The stardom, screaming fans, the red carpet, and fancy afterparties were his thing. What we had was ours alone. It was our private time to be who we really were and love one another without putting on a show.

Whenever he came to town, he always took different ways to get to our place. He never got caught up in any drama, so the paparazzi never chased him around waiting for their next big photo. Anything they did for publicity was always staged, and his manager would invite all the photographers. It didn't matter that it was fake. The pictures sold, which was all they cared about, so they left Jace alone the rest of the time.

Draping myself over his body, I clapped a hand over his mouth as he got louder. He groaned behind my hand, and his body shuddered a moment before he came. I couldn't hold back any longer and released his cock for him to finish off and gripped his hips with both hands.

My head fell back, staring up at the ceiling as my body pushed past that glorious peak. I opened my mouth, silently screaming, as my body went rigid with the powerful release that gripped me in its clutches. Legs weak and wobbly, I stumbled back and leaned against the tiled wall, trying to catch my breath.

Jace recovered first, turning to face me. I couldn't get over that this man was mine, and I was terrified that I would ruin it with the next thing I asked of him.

He molded himself to my body until no part remained untouched and bit my bottom lip.

"Fuck, I love you," he said.

There was a sadness in his eyes that I understood all too well. We only had a few more stolen hours, and then he was gone again. I hated it. Every damn second he was gone, I yearned for the next stolen day or night, but I would never ask him to give up doing what he loved. Music had been a lifeline for him during a very dark time, and he was amazing. His talent needed to be shared.

Cupping his face, I kissed him hard and tried to convey every last bit of emotion I felt into the kiss. "I love you too."

Our eyes locked, and neither of us moved, trying desperately to stop time, just for a little longer. Swallowing down the fear lodged in my throat, I held Jace tighter like that would help convince him to say yes.

"What is it? Something is wrong. I can tell by the way you're looking at me," Jace said, his muscles tensing. "Are you breaking up with me?"

My mouth fell open. "Are you crazy? No, of course not. I've told you before that you're stuck with me until I die or you get sick of me, whichever comes first."

His lip pulled up, and his teasing eyes shimmered. "Okay, then, what's wrong? I know you well enough to know when you're holding something back that you don't want to say."

"I can never hide anything from you." Grabbing the soap off the shower stand, I squirted more than I needed in my hand and began cleaning Jace's body.

Jace gripped my chin, his eyes commanding the answer.

"I'm scared to ask this of you," I said honestly.

"Scared? What the hell would you have to be scared of?" His brow furrowed with confusion.

"That you'll say we're over. You'll say I'm breaking one of our rules and decide that life with me is no longer what you want."

Jace stepped back but placed both palms on the wall by my head. His muscles flexed, and he looked exactly like the dominating ass he could be. I'd seen this look more than once, especially when he thought I was being stupid about something.

If there was one thing Jace was not known for, it was tact. He had none, not even a tiny bit. If he thought you were an asshole, he told you to your face, just like that. If something tasted bad, sounded horrible, or in this case, was stupid, he told you. He would never make it as a politician, so it was a good thing he preferred singing.

"Did you get hit in the head?" I smirked and snorted. "Seriously, Avro. I've been in love with you since we were ten. Do you really think I'm just going to walk away now because you asked for a favor?"

"You haven't heard the favor," I countered.

"All right, what is it? What is so terrible that you think I would want to end us?" He crossed his arms over his chest and leaned back. I licked my lips. Damn, he was sexier every time I saw him.

I took a deep breath and jumped off the proverbial diving board into the deep end. "I want us to go exclusive with Raine," I blurted out. "And I may have already told her that you'd be exclusive with us," I finished in a rush and then waited for the explosion.

"I'm sorry, you want what?"

Sighing, I rolled out my shoulders and stood up straight. "Jace, I'm tired of the different partners coming in and out of our lives. I'm tired of seeing you all over the world with people other than me or someone of our choosing on your arm at parties. I'm simply tired of seeing you a grand total of twenty-five days a year."

I ran my hand through my hair. "I love you. I love you with everything I have, but I want more, and I'm lonely all the time without you. I know that I promised we wouldn't have this discussion until you were done with tour commitment, but...." I held out my arms. "It's how I feel, and I don't know what to do. I wasn't searching for Raine, but she's everything we ever wanted, and I fell in love with her."

Jace held up his finger, his eyes hard as he stared at me, which did nothing to comfort me. "Let me get this straight. You not only want to add a permanent third person—someone you decided on before speaking with me or letting me meet her any of the other times I was in town, to our relationship—but now you want me to travel the world alone without any form of physical interaction with anyone at all."

"Jace...."

"No, I'm not done. While I'm doing that, which you already know is supposed to be for another two years, you are back here playing house with Raine, and I get zoom calls. To make this worse, you already promised her, someone not even in our relationship, before speaking to me. You do see what an asshole move this is?"

When he said it, it sounded like I was being a selfish jerk. In my head, it hadn't sounded the same way at all. Leaning back against the tile, I crossed my arms and stared down at his thigh, tattooed with our names in the intricate artwork.

"Fuck, I screwed up. I'm sorry." I shook my head. "I don't know what to do. I don't know if I can last another two years like this. It feels like getting stabbed every time you have to leave."

"Is that what this whole thing with Raine is? If so, then just come with me. You don't have to be in the spotlight, but we can spend every night together," he said, reaching out and placing his hands on my shoulders.

"No, my feelings for Raine are real." Taking a chance, I gripped his waist, and that fact he didn't immediately jerk away from my touch gave me hope.

"You know I've dated, done the one-night stands, and all the other hollow, empty things we said we would do to experience life. I may sound like I'm being a selfish asshole, but I've never lied to you, and I'm not going to start now."

Jace looked away, and panic pierced my heart. "I don't know if I can do what you're asking, and it really burns my ass that you made all these plans, like my opinion no longer matters to you. Like I don't matter to you." His voice broke like he might cry, and the sound gripped my heart. I never meant for him to feel like he didn't matter.

"It wasn't like that. I swear, Jace. I love you more now than I ever have, and of course, your opinion matters." I took a deep breath. "I just sort of blurted it out when I was talking to her last night, and I couldn't take it back. Now that I said it, I don't know if I want to." Placing my hand on his cheek, I forced him to look at me. "I shouldn't have excluded you from any of these decisions. For that, I'm so, so sorry."

"But you want things to change, right?"

I bit my lip and nodded.

"Fuck, Avro. I don't want to promise you something I don't know if I can keep," Jace said, backing up to the other side of the shower stall. The water was cooling off and mirrored the chill running through my body.

"Are you saying I'm not worth it? You don't want to be with just me or me and Raine?"

His eyes narrowed as his anger flared, and I felt it coming before Jace opened his mouth.

"Don't you dare turn this around on me. You know I have no problem being exclusive. We've been exclusive before, and if you remember, we chose to have this open relationship together when I signed the contract to go on tour. Do you remember that conversation? The one where I spoke to you before making a decision," he growled as he narrowed his eyes and clenched his teeth like he was chewing on glass.

He put his hands on his hips, and I knew what was coming. I'd set myself up for this. "In fact, I'm pretty fucking sure it was your idea to have an open relationship. You even set our timeline to settle down and find a third person after my contract ended. Is any of this ringing a bell?"

"Yeah," I said.

There was nothing else to say. He was right. I was the one going back on the carefully thought-out rules and plans we had put in place so that we didn't end up in an argument just like this.

But that was before Raine came into my life, back when I was supposed to travel just as much as he was. I talked to Jace as much as possible, but he was still only here two days a month. What the hell was that? It was nothing, a speck of time. I stayed in bed, staring at the ceiling, dreaming about his touch, and holding a pillow, wishing he was with me. It wasn't his fault I'd found our third, but I hadn't planned any of this. I didn't know if you could plan when to fall in love with someone. Raine and my feelings for her had snuck up on me.

"Fuck." Jace grabbed the soap bottle and scrubbed down like he was as pissed with the soap as he was with me.

I could only watch him. I knew if I tried to touch him while he was this angry, it would only escalate the situation. We'd been there before.

"Fuck." He rinsed off and stepped out of the shower, pulling a towel from the pile. "Fuck!"

I lifted my eyes to look at him as he whirled around to face me. "I guess... see if Raine will come over again tonight, but Avro, what you're asking is a fucking piece of shit move. I need to think." He yanked on his clothes and left, the door slamming behind him. I slowly sank down against the wall.

Had I just ruined us for good? For nearly seventeen years, we'd been together in some form of relationship, and suddenly it felt like I couldn't breathe. I loved Raine, and I loved Jace. What the hell have I done?

Snake

16

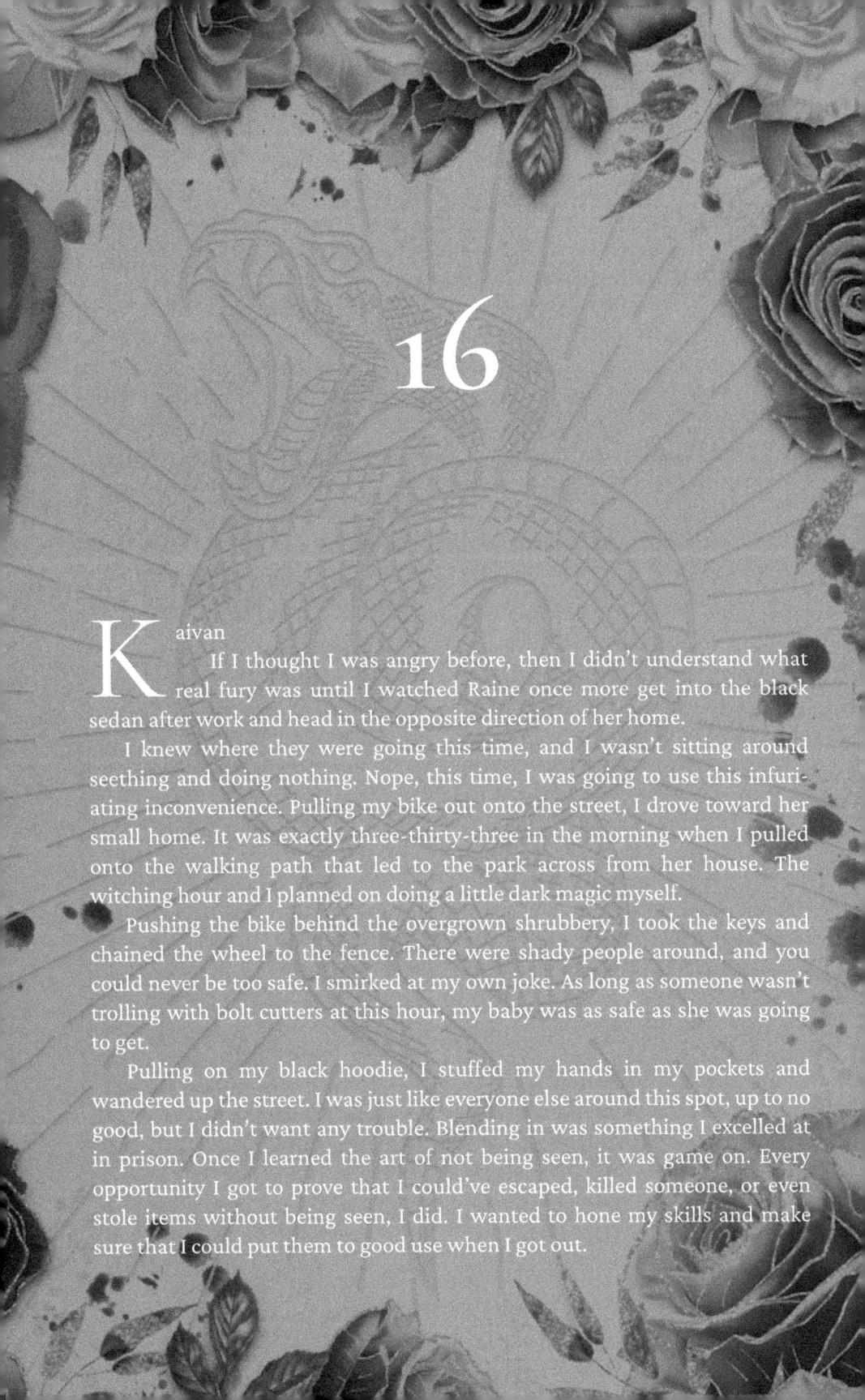

Kaivan

If I thought I was angry before, then I didn't understand what real fury was until I watched Raine once more get into the black sedan after work and head in the opposite direction of her home.

I knew where they were going this time, and I wasn't sitting around seething and doing nothing. Nope, this time, I was going to use this infuriating inconvenience. Pulling my bike out onto the street, I drove toward her small home. It was exactly three-thirty-three in the morning when I pulled onto the walking path that led to the park across from her house. The witching hour and I planned on doing a little dark magic myself.

Pushing the bike behind the overgrown shrubbery, I took the keys and chained the wheel to the fence. There were shady people around, and you could never be too safe. I smirked at my own joke. As long as someone wasn't trolling with bolt cutters at this hour, my baby was as safe as she was going to get.

Pulling on my black hoodie, I stuffed my hands in my pockets and wandered up the street. I was just like everyone else around this spot, up to no good, but I didn't want any trouble. Blending in was something I excelled at in prison. Once I learned the art of not being seen, it was game on. Every opportunity I got to prove that I could've escaped, killed someone, or even stole items without being seen, I did. I wanted to hone my skills and make sure that I could put them to good use when I got out.

That was the thing about prison. It didn't really help to set anyone on the right path. It simply gave us more skills and contacts. By the time we got out, we were pissed off enough that we didn't care if we ended up back inside. Besides, who the hell is hiring a guy fresh out of prison for rape? Not many, which is why meeting Mannix and him induct me into the MC had meant so much. I wouldn't have had a pot to piss in if not for him.

Glancing around to make sure that no one was peeking through a drape or walking down the street, I turned to follow the path to Raine's backyard. I had no idea if she lived alone, but the house was dark, so it was worth the risk.

The backyard was similar to the front. Overgrown with weeds, but not a blade of grass could be found in the dirt. A single chair was on the cracked and weathered patio, but aside from that, there was absolutely nothing. I pulled my small bag of tricks from my pocket and turned on the miniature flashlight. Holding it between my teeth, I worked at the lock. It was surprisingly sturdy for a shitty little house.

It took a lot more time than I anticipated, but I finally got the door unlocked. I hadn't met a lock yet that I couldn't pick. Reaching out with my gloved hand, I slowly opened the door and looked around for an alarm system. I didn't think she had one. No little sticker in the window acting as a ward or any extra wires, cameras, or lights, but it was always best to be safe.

Moving to the front door, I also checked there for a security panel before relaxing. It felt strange to be inside Raine's personal space again. The last time was when I kissed her, setting off a chain of events I never saw coming.

I knocked on Raine's door, and she looked up from the book she was reading. Fuck, she was pretty. I hated that I thought my best friend, who was off-limits, was hot. It was a blessing and curse that we lived in the same house.

My birthday was yesterday, and it was bittersweet. I was now an adult, and I would be heading out into the world to forge my own path, as the lame-ass Mr. Wright would say. But it meant I was leaving Raine, and she was still considered a teen for two-years, two-weeks, and one day. So it was a good thing I was going to be moving out, because every day was a temptation. She was who I dreamed about at night. Raine was also the star of my dirty fantasies, and I knew I'd break if I stayed. I would end up doing something that would get us both in deep shit.

"Hey, Tink, can I come in?" I held out the last piece of my cake and two forks. "I bring a halfway decent cake with way-too-sweet icing but a surprisingly decent jam filling."

Raine laughed, and it made me smile. No matter what, she could always make me smile. "That was a heck of a sales pitch. Not sure you're going to make it as a used car salesman, but I'm sold on the okay-but-not-so-great cake."

Walking in, I paused to close the door most of the way. I didn't dare close it fully, just in case we were found in here alone. My unusual meetings with Mrs. Collins had become more frequent the last month, and she insisted I see her at midnight. I had to refuse because of my fight later. She looked pissed at me, and I wanted to stop, but I felt trapped between a bad spot and a fucking worse one.

If I told someone what was happening, there was a good chance they would think I was just some horny teen who took advantage of Mrs. Collins. If she told her husband, I was a dead man. My best option was to move out, go to school, and never look back.

"You okay?"

I lifted my head from the heavy thoughts and winked at Raine. "Yeah, of course. Why wouldn't I be?"

One adorable shoulder lifted and fell. "I don't know, but you haven't seemed very happy lately. I miss my teasing Kai, who would make fun of the fact I have my hair in pigtails and call me his Tink."

I laughed. "They do look dorky," I teased. "Just a lot on my mind, I guess," I lied. I hated lying to Raine, but I couldn't tell her what was really going on in my head. I stuffed a forkful of the cake in my mouth and chewed, not really tasting it.

I couldn't help staring at her. She was lying on her stomach, feet swaying back and forth in the air. Raine was small for her age, which made her look younger than she was. She was obsessed with pink. I hated the color, but of course, it looked amazing on her. Today she had on a cotton candy-colored tank top and shorts, showing way more skin than I should notice.

"You going to eat any more?" Raine asked, breaking me out of my thoughts.

"Naw, you go ahead. I have a fight later. That much sugar will make me feel sick," I said.

"I don't think you should go," Raine said softly before polishing off the last of the cake.

She pushed herself up and maneuvered so she was sitting beside me but facing the opposite direction. Wrapping her arms around her knees, she nudged me, and my heart jumped around in my chest as she stared into my eyes.

"Tell me you won't go, at least this once. I didn't mean to, but I saw your side earlier when you were changing." Her eyes flicked down, and her cheeks pinked. "You had your door open. I wasn't spying or anything, but I saw the bruises."

Her eyes lifted to mine, and I don't know what came over me, but I leaned in and kissed her softly. Raine's eyes went wide, but she didn't pull away, and before I knew it, I was cupping her face and kissing her hard. God, she tasted so sweet, so perfect, exactly how I imagined.

A strange desperation had taken hold of me, and I didn't want to let her go. I didn't want to leave her here in this house while I went off to school. She was the only thing that made me feel like I wasn't just the kid who watched his mother die or had his father carted off to prison for murder. When I was with her, I wasn't the asshole that got into fights at school, and I wasn't the guy everyone thought wouldn't go anywhere. She made me want to be better just by being her.

"Stop, stop," Raine said.

Hands hit my chest, and my eyes snapped open. I stared down into Raine's eyes in confusion, trying to remember when I pushed her down onto her back or how I ended up lying on top of her while we kissed.

"Shit," I swore and pushed myself onto my knees.

As soon as I did, Raine jumped up, tears in her eyes. "I'm sorry, I'm not ready."

She bolted out of the room and down the stairs so fast that I didn't even have time to form a sentence.

"Son of a bitch," I growled out and punched the floor as hard as I could. What the fuck had I just done?

My hands touched every surface. From the top of the television to the soft grey pillows on the couch. I looked at the small framed pictures she had, but there were none of Mr. and Mrs. Collins or anyone I recognized. I pulled the frame off the wall and opened the back to find nothing but the original image that it came with from the store. I looked at the photo of the fake smiling family, and my brow furrowed.

I couldn't say why this bothered me, but it didn't feel like the Raine I'd known. The girl who had made art out of rice and pop-top tabs and it still looked fantastic. She had posters on every wall and kept the most ridiculous pictures of us that I wanted to throw away. She kept everything and loved life. I looked around, and the room seemed empty and void of all emotion.

Putting the image back exactly how I found it, I went up the stairs. My heavy boots creaked on every step like I was in a haunted house. Well, if anyone else were home, they sure as fuck knew I was here now. The place was as tiny upstairs as it was down. There was a linen closet that looked like it could hold all of one set of sheets. A bathroom you could barely walk into and turn around without hitting your elbow on the shower stall, and two bedrooms, if you could call them that. I wasn't one for expensive things, but even I felt claustrophobic in this place. The roof was old, low, and angled, so I could only walk three-quarters of the way into the room before ducking or hitting my head.

Taking my time, I opened her nightstand drawers, but there wasn't much, other than a couple of magazines and a book. I was closing the drawer when I recognized the cover of the book. It was *Flowers in the Attic*, the same book that Raine had been reading the day that I kissed her. Lifting it from the drawer, I opened to the first page. I wasn't sure why, but I kept flipping pages, then turned the book to fan the pages toward the floor. A picture fluttered to the ground.

Dropping the book back into the drawer, I leaned down and picked up the photo. I didn't need the little flashlight to know what I was staring at, but I shined the light on it, anyway. There we were, two happy, smiling kids. This was Raine's fifteenth birthday, and I had taken her to the movies as her gift. Her arm was wrapped around my waist while mine was draped on her shoulder. I remember how it felt to have her pressed up against me. She smiled up at me, and my hands shook with the torrent of emotions the image dragged to the surface.

I sat on the bed and couldn't peel my eyes away. I ran my thumb over her face and remembered how excited she'd been when I grabbed a large popcorn and drink for us to share. It hadn't been a super scary movie, but Raine had always jumped at the tense spots, and more than once, she'd grabbed my hand until I linked our fingers together for the rest of the show.

Turning the picture over, I read the writing that simply said, Kai and me on my fifteenth, and there was a little heart drawn. How did we go from this to one kiss and one year later, Raine accusing me of rape?

I gripped the picture, ready to tear it in two, but my fingers trembled. I couldn't do it. It felt like I would be tearing apart the only good memories I did have. That thought hurt as much as her accusation. Instead, I put it into my pocket and stood from the bed.

Making my way over to her dresser, I opened every drawer, not sure what I was looking for, but I kept looking anyway. The next one I opened had a wide variety of black underwear. Picking up a pair, I held them up and groaned at the thought of seeing her in these.

Fuck, stop that shit.

I dropped it into the drawer and slammed it shut. Finished with the drawers, I moved on to the closet and still came up with nothing. She had like ten outfits to her name. I had more clothes in my closet.

"What the fuck, Tink?" I mumbled. "You have to be making coin at that place. What are you doing with it all?" My fingers played over the cheap metal hangers, bare except for a few sweatshirts and T-shirts.

Leaning over, I sniffed the black hoodie closest to me, and I could still smell the lingering scent of her body wash through the clothes detergent. I turned in a circle and spotted a backpack stuffed in the back corner of the closet. Pulling it out, I looked inside and whistled low. It was filled with money and rolled clothes. I knew a go bag when I saw one. Why the hell did she have this?

Putting it back, I marched out of the room and jogged down the stairs. There was only a single closet, two-piece bathroom, and a living room. The kitchen wasn't much bigger than those Easy-Bake oven things she used as a kid. Raine was always trying to talk me into sitting with her while she baked a cake. It was oddly sweet, and I could clearly remember her squeezing frosting out and swirling it around like a professional before she'd shake on sprinkles. I quickly wiped that memory from my mind, but they were never gone for good. She was always there in the back of my mind, the memories quick to surface.

Hiding the flashlight, I slipped out the backdoor and relocked it. I didn't know what I expected to find, but the sparse and impersonal home I'd just walked through was not it. It seemed like she was ready to pick up and run at any moment, and maybe she was. Maybe she only stayed in one spot so long before moving on to the next.

It wasn't a terrible way to live. I could picture having a big RV, cruising the countryside, and picking the next stop by closing our eyes and placing a finger on a map. I had no idea why I was getting all nostalgic about Raine, and that could've, should've, would've been crap.

At the end of the day, the past was what it was, and she did what she did, and I was now who I was. The guy she tossed into jail was dead. I was what had emerged from the cage, and I was a whole lot meaner, and a whole lot pissed off.

Raine

17

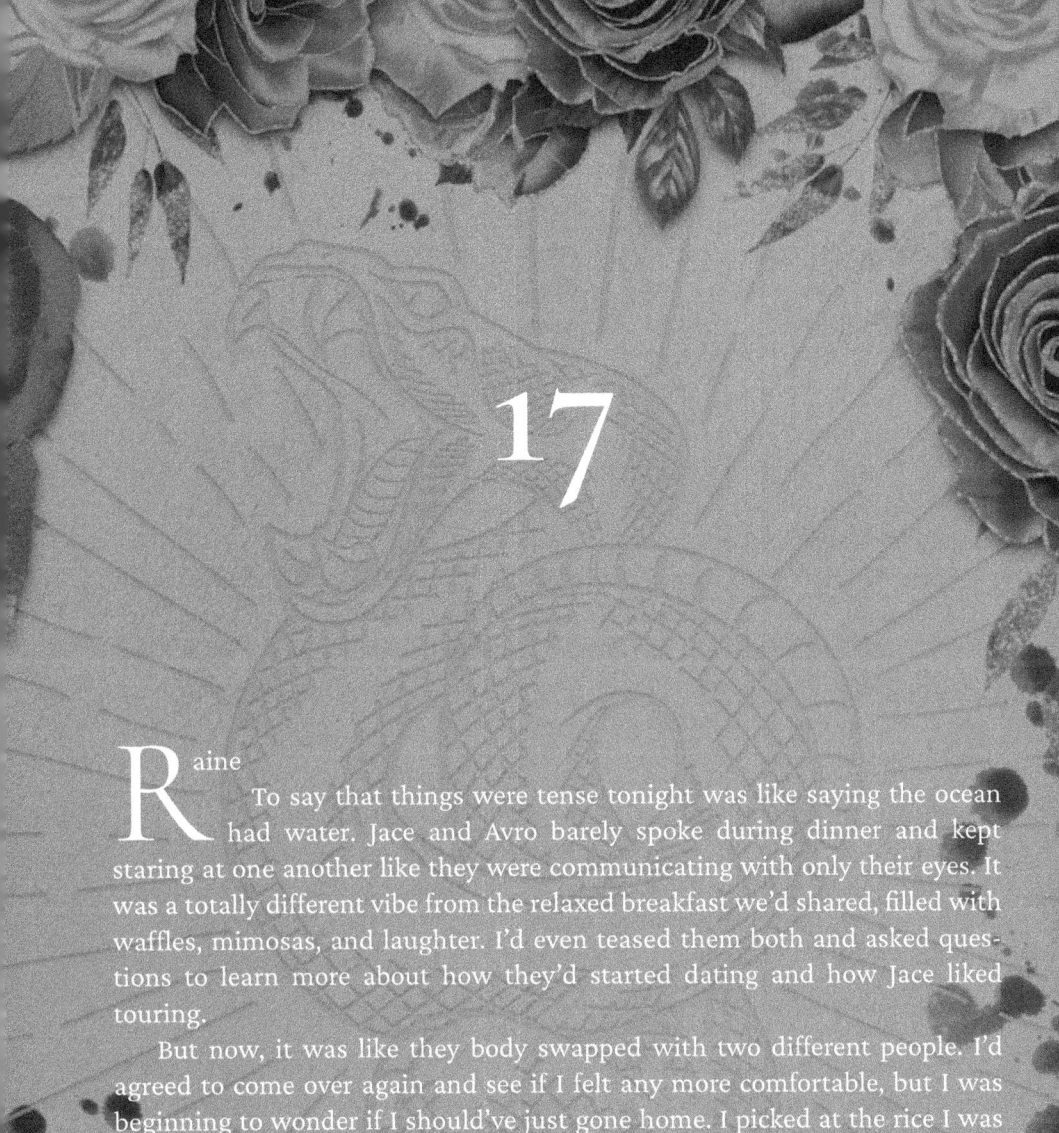

Raine

To say that things were tense tonight was like saying the ocean had water. Jace and Avro barely spoke during dinner and kept staring at one another like they were communicating with only their eyes. It was a totally different vibe from the relaxed breakfast we'd shared, filled with waffles, mimosas, and laughter. I'd even teased them both and asked questions to learn more about how they'd started dating and how Jace liked touring.

But now, it was like they body swapped with two different people. I'd agreed to come over again and see if I felt any more comfortable, but I was beginning to wonder if I should've just gone home. I picked at the rice I was eating and finally couldn't take it anymore.

"Can someone please tell me what's wrong? I can cut the tension between you two with a knife," I said.

Both men glanced my way and then went back to eating. Fed up, I stood, prepared to call an UBER to go home. I had no interest in staying around this all night long.

"Where are you going?" Avro asked as I went to the door to get my shoes.

"I'm going home. Whatever you two have going on isn't going to be solved with me here tonight," I said.

Avro met me at the door and held my hands to keep me from putting my shoes on.

"What do you think you're doing, Avro?"

"I'm sorry, and we don't mean to make you feel like you're stuck in the middle. We had a disagreement earlier, and..." He sighed. "We need to figure out the details, but we want you to stay. I'll put the argument aside if Jace is willing to do the same."

I looked between Avro and Jace, who lifted his head from staring at his equally barely touched food.

"Yeah, that's fine." Jace's eyes swung to mine. "I'm sorry," he said, but I couldn't tell how he actually felt.

Nodding, I dropped the shoes and walked back to the table to sit down. Avro seemed more like his normal self, but it was hard to tell with Jace. I didn't know him well enough.

"I found a new song for a new routine if you want to hear it," I asked Avro.

"Why don't you use one of mine?" Jace interjected before I could finish.

"We usually use something that is...." I started and looked to Avro for help.

"Silly, I guess, is the best word." Avro shrugged as he popped a strawberry in his mouth from the plate in the middle of the table.

"Yeah, silly. That's a good word. I mean, we can use one, but I didn't think you would want one of your songs turned into a drinking game," I said.

Jace shrugged. "That's fine, whatever. It was just a suggestion," he said in that same monotone voice. He seemed dejected and maybe hurt. I stared at him as he pushed his rice around. That was enough of whatever was going on.

"Okay, that's it. Tell me what the fight was about," I said.

Avro started to answer, but I stopped him with a hand on his arm. "No, I want to hear it from Jace."

Jace leaned back in his seat and crossed his arms. "You really want to know?"

"Jace, please," Avro pleaded, and I could tell he just wanted this whole topic to disappear, but we were past that, or at least I was.

"Let him speak, Avro, please."

Sighing, Avro stood and walked to the sink. Jace's eyes followed him with every stride. "Fine, you want to know, here it is. We're arguing over what gaming console to get."

"I'm sorry, what?" I asked, not sure if this was the truth but pretty sure it wasn't. I was positive it had something to do with me, and I had no intention of coming between them if that was the case, but a game console?

"Yeah, I want a PlayStation, but he wants an Xbox. You see, we play when I'm on the road, but we've only ever had one type, and now he wants to change it. I prefer to keep the same type for a couple more years, so I don't have to relearn all new games. Anyway, what do you think?"

I couldn't tell if this was some veiled argument, but the look on Jace's face was serious as he leaned on the table and stared at me.

"I'm not sure I'm qualified to answer this. I've never had either, but if the fight makes you this angry, then..." I glanced over at Avro, who was now leaning against the counter. "Maybe don't change," I said tentatively.

"Ha, don't change. Love that response," Jace said, and Avro rolled his eyes.

"Yes, but the old system sucks when you're on the road," Avro argued.

"Only for you," Jace countered.

"It's been three years of bad connection and terrible service. It's time to try something new," Avro argued.

"Wow, three years? Okay, I might have to agree with Avro. That's a long time to put up with a horrible system," I offered and then wondered why I'd asked in the first place. This was the strangest argument ever. Was this a guy thing?

"But I like my old system. It works well for me, for now," Jace said, leaning back in his chair. "I'm more than happy to learn any system you want once I'm home more."

"Maybe, but it feels like it is slowly killing me. Nothing ever feels right, and I'm always panicked for the few moments that there is...a stable connection," Avro said.

Jace groaned and pushed himself up from the table to pace the room. This all seemed very dramatic for a gaming system. I knew people got into it and chose sides and their favorites, but this was more intense than I'd ever pictured.

"Okay, new idea, hear me out," I said, and they looked at me. "Maybe it's time to try something completely new and go with a Nintendo Switch." I smiled. "You know, get some of those interactive games, and it would be new for both of you."

Avro and Jace looked at one another and laughed. Just like that, the tension evaporated.

It was the first laugh I'd heard from either of them all night. Avro walked over and held out his hand. "Who knows, maybe you're right, but I'm not sure arguing over it anymore tonight will make a positive decision."

Slipping my hand into Avro's, I stared at him and then looked over at Jace before standing. "For whatever it's worth, I don't think you two should argue over this."

My heart skipped a beat as Avro slid his arm around my waist. "Oh yeah, and why is that?"

"I haven't spent much time with the two of you together, but it's easy to see the love you have between you. One console or the other, it doesn't matter as long as you get to be with one another. Isn't that what's most important?"

"And you," Avro said.

"Me?"

"Yeah, I told you I want you to be with us long term, so the console decision includes you, too."

I lifted a shoulder in a shrug. "I can't make that decision. I've never played with any console."

Jace snickered and walked over to where we were standing, a smile pulling at the corner of his mouth.

"Well, that's going to change very soon," he said, his voice sounding like a soft growl and just as suggestive.

My heart went from sputtering to full-on freakout mode as Jace held out his hand for me to take as well.

"Come on. It's time for you to step out of your comfort zone." He tugged on my hand, and my feet felt like lead weights. Jace cocked one of those sexy eyebrows at me, and I shivered as he ran his thumb over my bottom lip. "I didn't take you for someone who backs down and gives in to her fears. Was I wrong?"

I swallowed around the throbbing worry in my chest. Stubbornly, I straightened my spine and rolled out my shoulders. "No, I'm not. At least not anymore. Lead the way."

Jace smiled, and Avro squeezed my hand. His pace was quick as he practically dragged me out of the room and up the stairs. With each step, my courage wavered, but I refused to give in to the anxiety that had repressed me for years. We barely made it over the threshold of the door to Avro's bedroom when Jace whirled around, and in a move that I hadn't been expecting, he gripped the back of my neck and dropped his lips to mine.

I sucked in a shuddering breath as the butterflies in my stomach exploded into fireworks. Everything with Avro was easy and calm. Even his kisses, which left me breathless and made me feel safe and warm. There was nothing safe about Jace. He demanded the kiss from me, taking over all my senses like they had forgotten how to function.

I realized I must have let go of his hand, as he was now cupping my face, and I was pushed backward. With a thud, I came into contact with the wall, and my adrenaline spiked, but instead of wanting to run, I moaned and allowed him to deepen the kiss. I felt something touch my tongue and realized that he had a stud in his that was textured with little rough spikes. It wasn't painful. If anything, it was turning me on more as my mind quickly imagined that tongue in other places.

Was I really kissing Jace Everly? *The* Jace Everly. Where had I made the wild left turn to get to this moment?

Jace released my face but didn't let up on the kiss igniting a fire within me. I jumped when his hands found my waist, and he pressed his body into mine, trapping me against the wall. The adrenaline coursing through my veins made me shake and want to run for the door or, hell, maybe run to the bed, but my decision was made when my body chose for me.

Wrapping my arms around his neck, I hung on through the storm he had created. His hands slid around my body to cup my ass, and with a small yelp, I was lifted up, and my legs wrapped around Jace's waist. I opened my eyes and didn't see Avro anywhere until Jace laid us down on the bed, and I realized he was already there waiting for us.

Jace released me from the intense kiss that had stolen my breath and left me speechless like my brain had completely misfired. Turning my head, I found Avro's heated stare, but Jace touched my cheek and forced me to look back into his silver eyes.

"You only look at me right now," Jace ordered.

I swallowed and nodded. He moved, and my body finally realized I was under his weight. He must have seen the spark of real fear within me. Jace waggled his finger back and forth in front of my face.

"There is no room for fear in here with us. It doesn't belong, and I won't tolerate it."

I arched an eyebrow at him.

"You won't tolerate it?"

"No, I won't. I wouldn't allow it with Avro, and I won't with you."

If there were ever a pair of eyes that could command you into agreeing, it was Jace's. I was tempted to quip back, and I didn't understand why, but the challenge in his eyes made me want to push back and agree at the same time. Dropping his lips to mine, he sucked my lower lip into his mouth, and the sassy comment on the tip of my tongue was lost to the taste of his mouth.

I moaned, gripping his shoulders as he writhed back and forth against me. Taking my hands in his, he moved them so they were above my head. The old vulnerable feeling was there, but it felt different this time. I was still standing on the edge of a cliff and could fall either way, but the choking sensation didn't take over. It felt more like I was riding a wave as he pressed his hips into me, and the friction hit all the right places.

"Do you know what I'm going to do to you?" Jace asked, his lips barely touching mine but still holding the same commanding air.

I shook my head. Words were lost to me. Jace smiled, and that only made me swallow harder. It did nothing to ease the tension.

"How about this? I'll tell you what I'm not going to do," he said, smirking, his lips flirting upward. "I'm not going to fuck you. Neither of us will fuck you, but you will watch us."

I licked my lips, and the sensation of wanting more and hating being told what to do pushed to the front of my mind.

"You're not going to fuck me, even if I wanted you to?"

"Not even if you begged on your knees with my cock in your mouth," Jace said. His voice was casual, and holy fuck, that was the hottest thing I'd ever heard. My breathing skyrocketed through the roof, making my nipples rub against Jace's chest.

"Are you sure you could hold off?" I asked, with the blooming urge to defy and push him.

Jace laughed, and I bit back the moan that wanted to escape with the movement of his body. "Peaches, I like your fire, but you don't have the skill to make me cave...yet."

It was a slap in the face, and worse because he was right. I was out of my league and treading water, my arms flailing about, but not really knowing how to swim. I was relying on water wings or maybe one of those floaty boards, but I definitely had no idea what the hell I was doing.

He dropped his lips to my ear and made a sound caught between a groan and a growl. "But that doesn't mean we don't plan to teach you, because I crave seeing that happen."

Shifting, Jace lay beside me, and like a dance that needed no words, Avro moved in close to my other side. My body came alive between one heartbeat to the next as both their hands touched me. Avro snaked his hand under my T-shirt, his fingers rolling my nipple between them and making me gasp.

His lips found mine when I turned my head. He was like taking a deep breath of fresh air after holding it for so long. I felt the flick of a button and heard the pull of my zipper. I broke the kiss with Avro, only to arch my back and whimper. Jace was quick to slip his hand down the front of my jeans and swirl his fingers against my clit.

Avro gripped my chin, and once more, I was kissing him. I so badly wanted to touch him, but Jace firmly held my hands above my head with his one hand.

"Oh fuck, you're wet," Jace whispered in my ear. "Are you hot for two hard cocks?" I'd never had anyone talk like this to me before. "You want to touch us, don't you? Your hands are itching to feel our skin, explore our bodies, and taste our cocks in your mouth. Am I wrong?"

His fingers were like magic as he moved my panties aside and slipped his finger inside my pussy as he nipped at my ear.

"Oh my god," I cried, my body demanding more now that they'd stirred something deep inside me.

"Answer me. Do you want to touch our hard cocks, Peaches?" He groaned as his finger pushed deeper. I was quickly coming undone at the seams. "You want to hold them in your hands, stroking us, making us cum all over you?"

Avro had somehow got my shirt up, and I opened my mouth to answer Jace when Avro's mouth found my nipple. The hot sucking with his unrelenting tongue sent another wave of ecstasy racing through my body. A pleasure that I'd never understood and had been too terrified to explore.

Gasping for air with all the sensations, I could feel my body rushing for orgasm. Then suddenly they stopped. They didn't just stop. Jace stood from the bed, released my hands, and Avro rolled off the other side.

I had no idea what they were up to now, but I rubbed my legs together, trying to relieve the ache throbbing between my thighs.

Jace's eyes found mine as Avro stepped up to him. They looked like a painting.

"And now you get to watch, Peaches, because naughty girls who don't answer my questions don't get to cum," Jace said, his eyes filling with a dark, erotic edge that made me shiver.

All I could think was, *oh my*.

Avro

18

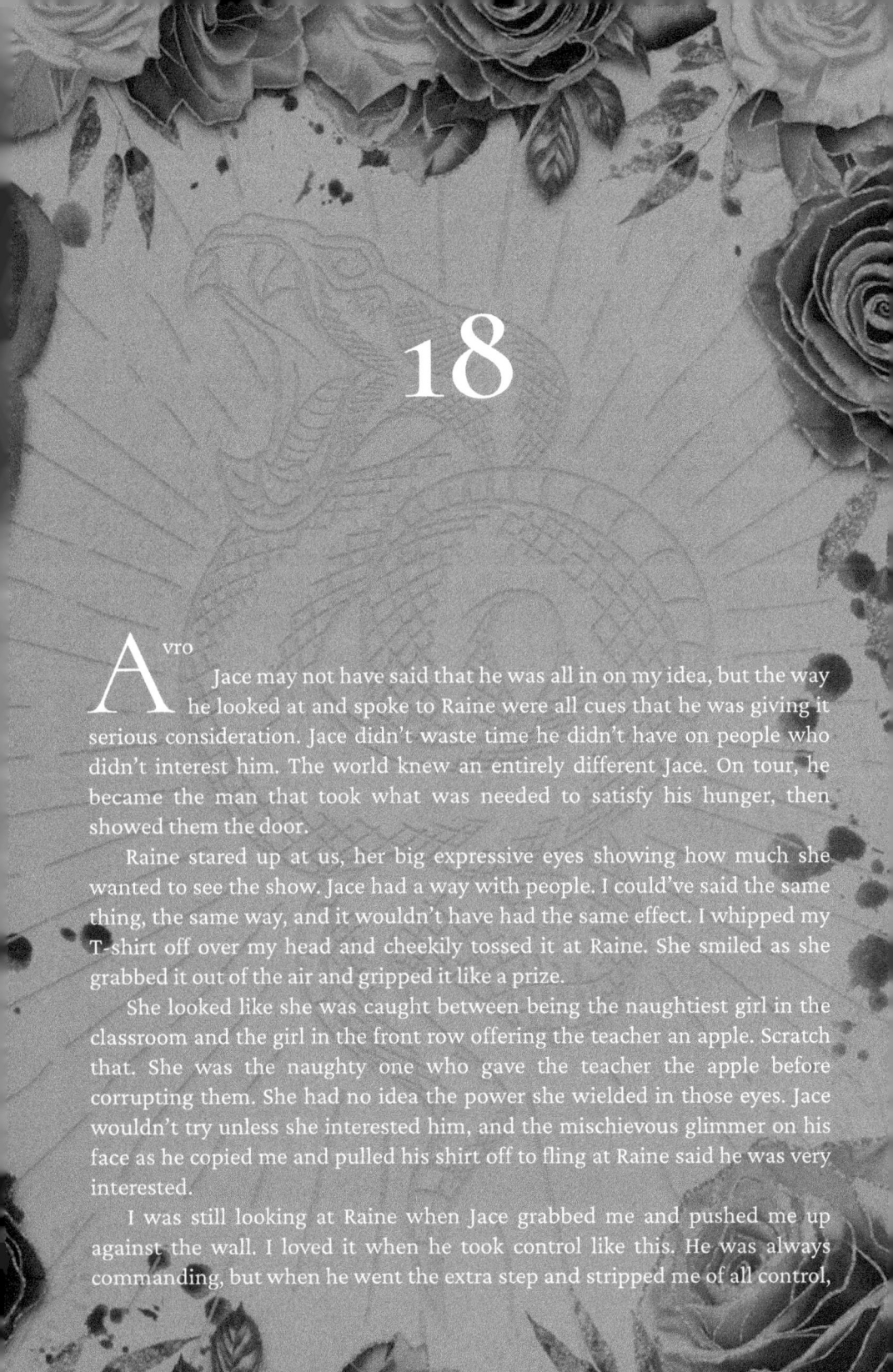

Avro

Jace may not have said that he was all in on my idea, but the way he looked at and spoke to Raine were all cues that he was giving it serious consideration. Jace didn't waste time he didn't have on people who didn't interest him. The world knew an entirely different Jace. On tour, he became the man that took what was needed to satisfy his hunger, then showed them the door.

Raine stared up at us, her big expressive eyes showing how much she wanted to see the show. Jace had a way with people. I could've said the same thing, the same way, and it wouldn't have had the same effect. I whipped my T-shirt off over my head and cheekily tossed it at Raine. She smiled as she grabbed it out of the air and gripped it like a prize.

She looked like she was caught between being the naughtiest girl in the classroom and the girl in the front row offering the teacher an apple. Scratch that. She was the naughty one who gave the teacher the apple before corrupting them. She had no idea the power she wielded in those eyes. Jace wouldn't try unless she interested him, and the mischievous glimmer on his face as he copied me and pulled his shirt off to fling at Raine said he was very interested.

I was still looking at Raine when Jace grabbed me and pushed me up against the wall. I loved it when he took control like this. He was always commanding, but when he went the extra step and stripped me of all control, it made me melt. I craved it from him. At one time, it scared me just like Raine, but now I couldn't imagine him any other way.

"Oh fuck." I groaned as his kiss went from hot to I'm-going-to-burn-you-up in the blink of an eye. My body was on fire, and as his hand cupped my cock through my jeans, I almost dropped to my knees.

Jace broke the kiss and stepped back, undoing my jeans before he grabbed for the button on his. It gave me enough time to lean over and use my tongue to play with the bar pierced through his nipple. I loved playing with his piercings and loved even more when he shuddered under my touch. There was nothing about him that I didn't love.

He'd started as my friend, then became my best friend, which slid into crush, then dating, and finally, what we were today. There were bumps and issues along the road as we navigated who we were and what we wanted, but we'd been inseparable for years. Jace knew all my secrets and deepest fears, and I knew his. I wanted more than anything to get to know Raine the same way, for her to look at us with the same love that I felt for her.

Abandoning the button on his jeans, he ran his fingers through my hair and gripped it between his fingers. I groaned and sucked harder, drawing an aggressive sound from Jace that rumbled in his chest.

The room swam as Jace's hand found my cock through my open zipper and stroked along the hard length. Lifting my head from my teasing, I glanced at Raine, still as a statue on the bed, but her eyes were pure desire. Jace quickly finished undoing his jeans and kicked them off, leaving him deliciously naked.

My eyes roamed over him like I was seeing his naked body for the very first time. Broad shoulders cut with muscle but not too bulky, chest and abs that were equally tight. His legs could've been used for any men's magazine, and finally, his cock, which was standing straight out from his body.

The artwork that spread out along his legs and arms stood out on his fair skin, but it was the glint of metal in his pierced cock that had me getting on my knees in front of him. A droplet of pre-cum sat on the tip of his cock, and with a quick swirl of my tongue, I licked him clean, taking my time to play with the piercing. Jace groaned as the tip of my tongue moved the ring back and forth slowly before sucking just his head into my mouth. I did it again and again, knowing that it drove him insane. It always did. This was his favorite tease. Feeling him shudder under my touch spread molten lava in my veins. Everything about him made me want to beg for more.

"Take your shirt off," Jace ordered, and I looked up at him, confused. His eyes were focused on Raine, and I slipped the tip of his cock back into my mouth. I could see Raine out of the corner of my eye, and she was slow to move. "Did you not hear me?" Jace asked, and I sucked him a little harder to keep him from leaping onto the bed. "I said take your shirt off."

His hand found the back of my head, but he didn't press, at least not yet. Raine moved on the bed, and I could see her hands shaking as she slowly pulled her T-shirt off over her head and set it aside.

"Good. Now the bra," Jace said.

It was such a fucking turn-on to hear him barking out orders like that. I rubbed his balls and then licked down his shaft until I could take one of them in my mouth, making Jace gasp.

"Oh fuck, that's good." He groaned and spread his legs wider for me.

"Come over here," I heard him say and knew it wasn't me he was talking to this time. I continued sucking on my prize before switching to the other one. "Don't look at me like that. I know how fucking wet you are and how much you want to touch me. So get over here, now."

Fuck, he was hot. This was what I was missing by not bringing Raine in sooner. Maybe she wouldn't have been ready, or maybe she would've been our third a long time ago, but the missing link was Jace. He pushed. He wasn't mean, but he wouldn't put up with not being listened to, and I was better at soothing.

"That's it. Good girl, Peaches," he said, his voice dripping with praise.

His fingers dug into my hair before he wrapped his hand around my neck to pull me closer. I closed my eyes and sucked harder on the sensitive area. Jace groaned and shivered, and the sound went straight to my aching cock.

I started to stroke my cock, but Jace snapped, "Avro, don't touch yourself. I didn't say you could."

My hand froze mid-stoke, and I ached so badly to be touched that it was a battle to force each finger to let go.

Raine gasped and then moaned. I couldn't see what was going on from this angle, so I quickly switched positions so I could watch the two of them as well. Licking Jace like he was my favorite treat, I watched the two of them kiss while his hands tweaked her nipples and cupped her tits in his large hands.

Breaking the kiss, Jace looked down at me. "Keep sucking. I didn't say you could stop."

My cock twitched, but I kept my hands on his thighs, so I wasn't tempted to disobey. Not that a punishment from Jace was ever a bad thing, but that was a game for another night. I moved my attention back to the tight balls and sensitive area right behind that I knew he loved to have licked.

"Touch me," Jace said, and my eyes flicked up. I smirked at the expression on Raine's face. She timidly reached out and placed her hands on his shoulders, and I snickered as Jace stared at her hands. "No, touch my cock," he said, and her face flamed a bright red.

"Oh...I...um...."

"What do you think it's going to bite you?"

"No, it's just that...."

"That what?" He waited for her to answer, but no words came out as she looked between the two of us. "You're touching me. I'm not touching you. You're the one in control. Now touch me." Raine licked her lips. "Do you want to leave?"

"No, I...."

"Then touch me," he said again, less aggressive this time but somehow sounding just as in control.

I held my breath as I waited to see what Raine would do, but just like every other time Jace challenged her, she met the challenge head-on. Reaching out, her hand wrapped around his shaft. I moved out of the way and slowly stood.

For someone who obviously didn't have much experience, she stroked Jace like she knew exactly what he liked.

"Fuck, that's good," he groaned. "Now him as well," Jace said, and I turned to make it easier for her. Before Jace could bother scolding me for helping, I kissed him hard and stole the complaint from his mouth.

I shivered as her small, cool hand touched my cock, which felt like it was on fire in comparison. Her stroke was soft at first, and I gripped her hand and applied more pressure, so she knew how much I liked.

"Holy hell, you two are hot," Raine said. We broke apart and stared down at her. Her hands stilled, and she swallowed hard.

"You think that's hot?" Jace stepped away from Raine and guided me to the bed. "You haven't seen anything yet."

Raine

I couldn't decide what was sexier, watching Avro work Jace over or watching the two of them kiss. They were perfect and better than anything I could've imagined. No amount of understanding or watching late-night movies for my own pleasure could ever prepare you for these two in person. I didn't know if all guys together were like this, but it was like watching a dance of dominance. The ebb and flow between them was so smooth and in sync that I felt like an outsider staring in on a private show.

Yet, the way Jace included me and how Avro looked at me made me feel that I could have this, too, if I wanted it. The only question was, did I want this? The only answer that came to mind was yes—a million times, yes.

The feel of their cocks in my hands was completely new, but I couldn't deny I loved the feeling. The look of pleasure on their faces was a drug, and I would never tire of the silky-smooth texture and the way they pulsed in my hands.

I licked my lips, dying to try them, to lick that pre-cum off their tips and play with the ring in the end of Jace's cock. I couldn't stop staring at it, and my tongue tingled with the need to lick and play with it and see what reaction I got from him when I sucked him hard.

"Holy hell, you two are hot." It was all my brain came up with, and I couldn't keep it to myself any longer. Had I ever seen myself as a two-man kind of girl? Hell no! I was scared to be with one, let alone two, but fuck, I would call anyone a liar if they said this was not fucking incredible.

"You think that's hot?" Jace stepped away from me and guided Avro to the bed. "You haven't seen anything yet."

I shivered, wanting to be close to them, and missed the heat, even if it was just in my hands.

"Come over here and get comfortable in the middle of the bed." Jace pointed to where he wanted me to go. I crawled onto the bed—which wouldn't even fit in my entire house—and lay down on my back. "Good, now take off your underwear."

I just stared at the thin lace material, and logic told me it offered zero protection. If they wanted to hurt me, then no little triangular piece of lace would stop them. Yet, my hands trembled, and my thumbs stayed firmly curled around the elastic top, not moving any further.

"Raine, look at me," Avro said, and I searched out his calm expression. "You can do this. Jace already said we're not having sex with you. We're not going to pressure you into it. Do you believe him?" I glanced between them and nodded. A smile played along his lips. "Then you need to trust us, and I know you don't know Jace as well as you do me, but I think I've done all I can to earn that trust from you."

He was right. Irritation burned inside of me. This anxiety I'd never been able to shake had controlled me long enough. I wasn't letting that one night over eleven years ago define me anymore. I was done having it taint all my actions and relationships.

Taking a deep breath, I lifted my hips, pushed the panties down, and tossed them aside, but Jace caught them out of the air. The dark look he gave me as he dangled them between his fingers made me flush hotter than if I'd stepped inside a burning building.

His eyes never wavered as he commanded my stare, and my mouth ran dry as he brought them to his nose. "Do you taste as sweet as you smell Peaches?"

There were some moments you could never prepare for, and this was one of them. Jace lowered the panties and licked his lips before running the small swath of material along the length of his cock. Jace growled as his amused gaze turned to Avro.

"I get your ass tonight, but she's all yours," Jace said, and I sat up a little straighter. Had they lied?

"Don't worry, it's not what it sounds like," Avro said as he slowly crawled onto the bed. It took a second for me to realize what Avro meant as he gripped my thighs and gently pried my knees apart. I could hardly breathe past the pounding of my pulse as he moved between my legs. "Do you trust me?"

Avro's voice was scarcely a whisper, but I heard him loud and clear and found myself nodding despite the old demons in my mind screaming for me to run away. He smiled when I yelped as he slid his hands under my ass, but any fear was swept to the far reaches of my mind as his tongue swirled around my clit.

I gasped as he did it again, and with a coy smile, he dropped his head completely. The pleasure could not be explained, and my back arched as he sucked hard like I'd just become dessert.

"Oh my god," I cried, grabbing his hair. The pleasure was so intense I couldn't decide whether to push him away or pull him deeper.

"That's it, Peaches. Let go and let Avro make you cum in his mouth. He's dying to taste you," Jace said, then groaned. I looked over and couldn't pry my eyes away from his hand, stroking his hard shaft.

Avro's tongue dipped deeper into my pussy, and I moaned, my body and mind finally coming together for the first time in my life. I pulled him harder into me. "Holy shit, don't stop."

Avro groaned, and as if that sound alone was the key to all my desires, I crested the peak of my orgasm. "Avro, oh fuck, yes."

"Now that was fucking hot," Jace said from where he was standing beside the bed. Avro lifted his head but continued to draw long wet lines along my pussy, making me shudder.

"Yeah, it really was," Avro answered, but he never stopped what he was doing.

Jace flicked open a bottle of clear liquid and poured it all over his cock before rubbing it in, and even in my passion-induced haze, I wanted to be his hand. He tossed the bottle onto the bed, and my head lolled to the side to read the words peach flavored. I smirked.

"I'm going to destroy this ass tonight, and you know you deserve it," Jace growled like he was part animal, as his hand cracked down hard on Avro's ass. "Lift this ass for me."

Avro shifted position enough to get his knees underneath him. "Oh, fuck me," he groaned into my pussy as Jace pushed forward.

I couldn't take my eyes off them. His muscles flexed, and all the cut lines became more defined. They froze in position, both breathing hard. Jace had his head back and his eyes closed. If I didn't know better, I would say he was in pain. He was so intense, and that look made me wiggle, wanting more.

"You ready?" Jace asked, but I had a feeling it wouldn't matter what Avro said. He would do what he wanted if Avro was ready or not. Avro nodded and then yelled as Jace slammed into him with no abandon. I watched Avro's face, those amber eyes hooded with pleasure from what Jace was doing.

I was so caught up in the show that Avro took me by surprise as his head dropped to my pussy once more and attacked it the same way that Jace was his ass. My knees fell open wider, and I gripped the blanket hard as his relentless tongue worked in and out of me. The last orgasm left me hyper-sensitive. I'd thought it was almost too much before, but now even my fingertips tingled, and my back arched as I yelled. Avro only sucked harder and swirled his tongue around my clit.

"Oh, fuck, that's it," Jace said through gritted teeth as he slammed into Avro harder, which pushed his face deeper.

I cried out as the second climax hit, and I couldn't help wondering if this was real or a dream that my mind had conjured. There was no way that the body could endure this over and over, and yet as the guys continued to fuck, their moans and groans getting louder and more desperate, I reached that sweet bliss for a second time and flopped back on the bed.

"Avro, yes, yes, fuck, I'm cumming," Jace grunted and drove into Avro hard. His body jerked the whole bed with a powerful thrust.

Avro suddenly rose to his knees, a hand wrapped around his throat and another on his cock as Jace pumped him hard and fast.

"Jace, I'm so close. Please, just like that," he groaned, but his yell was swallowed by Jace, who covered Avro's mouth with his own. Something hot hit my stomach, and I looked down as more of Avro's release landed on me.

It took a second to register what exactly had happened with my brain still doing the backstroke in endorphins. Swiping my finger through the cum on my stomach, I stared at it and then stuck my finger in my mouth.

"Oh fuck me, do that again," Avro said as he stared at my finger, his amber eyes dark with passion.

I drew another line through the cum and exaggeratedly sucked it off my finger. Both men groaned that time, and the sound made me shiver and want to puff out my chest with pride.

It was hot and salty—saltier than I'd been expecting—and I suddenly had the urge to do a tequila shot.

"You like that?" Jace asked as he stared at my fingers in my mouth.

"Would taste great with tequila and a lemon," I said, and both Jace and Avro burst out laughing.

The guys slowly stood and held out their hands to help me up. "Don't worry. We'll work up to you taking it all down the throat." Jace winked. "I have a feeling you're going to be a natural, but for now, we're going to shower."

"All together?"

"Peaches," Jace said, and cocked one of those arrogant brows. "On the bed, in a shower, on the floor, hell, outside in the backyard. Naked is naked. I won't randomly stuff my cock in you if you bend over in front of me. We do have control, you know?"

My cheeks burned with embarrassment for the completely irrational thought that Jace picked up on. Stepping close, he bent over, so his breath feathered my neck as he spoke. Goosebumps rose all over my body.

"Unless, of course, you ask me to," he growled softly, and my knees shook.

Jace stood up straight, and when he held out his hand, I felt confident in my decision for the first time. I'd never been one to fangirl over someone, but I understood what people saw in him. Maybe they only saw a small part, but I wanted more. Whatever it was that his aura held, it was addictive.

A couple of hours later, I was lying between them this time, and even though I was relaxed and content, I couldn't fall asleep. Avro's arm was wrapped snuggly around my waist as he cuddled me to his body. I felt his even breaths against my back, and his body twitched as he fell soundly asleep.

I was startled when Jace spoke, his voice soft in the dark room.

"I know you're still awake. Are you okay, Peaches?"

"Yeah, I'm great," I whispered back.

He shuffled down a little closer so we could stare into each other's eyes. "Can I ask you something?"

"Sure," he said.

"Were you really arguing about a game console?"

Even in the darkened room, I could see the smile pull up at the corner of Jace's mouth. "No, not really, but it was a good metaphor."

"It was about me, wasn't it? You don't really want me involved with you guys," I said, my heart sinking at the thought. A couple of days ago, I would've said that being disappointed to be left out of a threesome was ludicrous, but here I was, worried about his next words.

"Yes and no. Not you exactly, just the entire situation," Jace said as he ran his thumb over my cheek. It was nice to see this softer side of him. I'd seen him give Avro loving looks and soft touches, but he only had a firm hand with me so far. I wondered if that was by design. He understood I needed the push.

"What do you mean?"

"When I was offered a five-year contract to go on tour, we decided to have an open relationship, but only with people who didn't matter, and we would never get emotionally involved. We'd discussed and decided that, at some point, we would add a permanent third person to our relationship, but it had to be someone we both chose."

I sighed and looked away from his eyes. "And Avro wants me, who you'd never met, and he wants you to be exclusive," I whispered as all the pieces began fitting into place in my mind.

"Yes."

"And you don't want either."

"Don't go putting words in my mouth. I didn't say that. I'm not happy with how he thrust this on me. It's unfair, and I wouldn't have done it to him, but...I knew it would likely happen." I lifted my eyes to Jace's again. "This is not the first time we've tried the open relationship. Shared partners have never been an issue, but Avro has a huge jealous streak that he hides well. Most of the time." Jace smirked, but there was warmth in his eyes like he actually liked the jealousy.

"So what are you going to do? I guess I should ask if you'd like me to leave. I don't want to come between you two, and I'd never tell him why I'm not interested."

As the words came out, I knew I never wanted to go back to the girl who sat home alone with her pillow and the television.

"Are you interested?" Removing his hand from my cheek, Jace linked our hands together, and my heart soared. I felt like parts of the old me were learning to breathe again. They made me feel alive, and I didn't want this to end.

"Yes, I am. I didn't think I would be, but the answer is yes," I said. Even in the dark, his silver eyes seemed to penetrate my mind.

"Good. Then we will find a way to make it work." Leaning forward, Jace kissed me softly. The temptation to deepen the kiss was too much, and I licked at his bottom lip.

"Mmm, my sweet little Peaches, you're getting an appetite," he teased, but he wasn't off the mark. My body was already gearing up for another round. Jace opened his mouth and let me explore his as he shifted closer to my body. "Careful, or you may bite off more than you can handle," he whispered, breaking the kiss. "That's not a challenge, just a fact," he said, like he needed to make sure I understood the difference.

I'd gained a lot of courage, but he was right. I was playing with fire, and Jace was the type that was nice for only so long before he took what he wanted. I'd seen it in his eyes, and it made me hot, but it was also terrifying.

"Then again, what's one more time?" Jace said, and I shuddered as his fingers slipped between my thighs. "I want to feel you cum on my fingers, Peaches," he said, his voice deep and gravelly.

My entire being felt full. The shell I had been was cast aside and replaced with someone who wanted it all out of life and this potential relationship. I didn't even know what that meant, but I wanted it all the same. My heart was learning to beat all over again.

Snake

19

Kaivan

Leaning back in my chair, I crossed my arms and gazed around at the images on the wall. Most were old posters from a much earlier time for the club. There were a few framed cuts and patches, but everything in here honored the Lost Souls. Where they came from and all our leaders right up until today and our Grand Fucknut Mathers.

Usually, the church meetings didn't bother me. It was all just what you expected when you joined a motorcycle club, but that was when I wasn't in the middle of stalking Raine Eastman. We'd only had a dozen of these since my release. Most were to plan an attack or figure out a cleanup after the attack. So I was curious why one was called today, or I was until I realized Beast was just trying to keep the unrest at bay as Chase remained in Canada despite giving us no details other than he went to help his cousin.

I didn't want to hear any more of this garbage, so I hurried the meeting up. "Yo, Beast. Cut to it already. When are Mathers and the rest of them coming back?"

All thirty-one of the remaining members' heads turned in my direction. Thirty-two, if you counted the stray orange cat that decided this band of burly assholes was better than living on the streets. That said a lot about this part of the city if we were the preferred choice.

"I was getting to that," Beast barked, his voice rippling with annoyance.

"Not fast enough. I have things to do today, and listening to you kiss

Mather's ass even when he's not here is getting old. Either cut to the meat of the matter, or I'm out of here."

The room went dead silent. You could've heard a pin drop as the guys sitting around me held their breath. Beast slowly stood from his chair. He looked like a giant bear up on the small platform, but he didn't bother me.

None of them did except Mannix and, some of the time, Roach. If they came at me, I might pause, but if anyone else did, I would slit their throat and feed them to the gators. They all knew it too, which was also why they tended to keep their distance.

We had our honeymoon phase when I first got out. I mean, anyone would be happy to be out of prison. I was the first to grab a gun and yell, 'point me in the right direction.' Like any relationship, the longer you were there, the more you saw the bullshit people wanted to hide.

I'd only been on the outside one year, three months, twelve days, and eleven hours. That was enough time to realize that Chase never wanted to be our leader. I'd never spoken to the man before we went to Ashen Springs. As shocked as I was to learn that the leader I never knew existed was alive, I wanted to prove myself and fought as hard as any other member.

Once we got back, I spoke to Chase a handful of times about meaningless crap before he took off on a drinking and drug binge that left a trail of dead in his wake worse than Jack the Ripper. Now he was gone again, had been for weeks with no end in sight. Worse yet, he took two hundred and fifty of our men. We had no one left, and his parting words to me were, 'keep them safe.' Were you fucking kidding me? Me and what army was keeping the club safe from all the assholes that wanted our territory?

"If you walk out that door, then—"

"Then what?" I pulled a smoke from inside my jacket, lit it, and put it in my mouth to dangle between my lips. I rose to my feet as the two of us squared off.

"You're already down the majority of your men. You gonna cut your enforcer loose, too? Doesn't seem like a smart decision with three other gangs nipping at our heels 'cause they all fucking know that Chase is off gallivanting across Canada where they can't help us."

"He's up there helping family. That is what we do for family," Beast argued.

I snorted. "Aren't we his family?" I looked around at the down-turned heads and defeated looks. "Are you blind to what he is doing to this club? We can't sustain protecting our doors or turf for very long with ninety percent of our members gone with no return date." A few braver guards had been taking extra shifts and had been shot at more than once already.

"Tell me, Beast, why didn't Mathers leave us with an ally to have our back? Oh, that's right, he has none. He's either pissed them off or lost their respect. Why isn't he here earning the respect of the current members he claims he now wants to take care of?" I held out my arms. "That's right. His cousin called and said he needed help. A motorcycle club that isn't ours in a territory that isn't ours. He'll be lucky if he doesn't come back to find the Desert Vipers in his chair."

"He can't control how long it takes, and helping his cousin will give us an ally," Beast said.

Taking a puff of my smoke, I stuffed my hands into the pockets of my jeans.

"Great, so we could all be dead, but when they get back, they'll have earned an ally for some time in the future. Only three things are keeping the other gangs at bay. The first is the fence and the gators. It makes us harder to hit." I walked around to the back of my chair and leaned on the old leather. "The second is the amusement park next door that everyone is convinced is haunted. People go in and never come out."

If they only knew the reason they didn't come out. To the best of my knowledge, only a small handful, including Chase and me knew Wilder even existed.

I glared daggers at Beast. I had no problem with him, really. What I hated was his devotion to a man who had yet to prove he had the stones to be our leader and not a knock-off of his father's legacy.

As the story goes, Mathers senior handed the club's reins to Chase. Chase's brother got pissed and killed his family, but instead of exacting revenge and taking down the Reapers then, he pretended to be dead and hid for ten years while Beast and Mannix tried to hold the club together from constant attacks. In the meantime, Chase didn't care that his members were killed by his brother and only came out of hiding when he needed us—some leader.

"Lastly, but certainly not least, is me." I placed my hands on my chest, knowing that I was being a dramatic asshole. "All those fuckers out there know that if my bell is rung to go and kill them, they better be prepared, or it will be their souls that are lost." I gripped the chair. "So go ahead and kick me out. What the fuck do I care at this point? But don't expect me to cry or be held responsible for other clubs spitting on our sign and pissing on your corpses when they come knocking."

I looked around the room.

"Orrrr, you could shut the fuck up about Chase and his lack of accomplishments and tell us when they'll be back. That's really all we give a fuck about. They may not be asshole enough to say it, but we're all wondering. How long do we need to try and keep this place safe from the hundreds of men who want it?"

Beast looked like he was gearing up to charge across the room and toss me out, and I was almost hoping he would. I wasn't just angry at Raine. I realized that I was angry at the world. I was so fucking pissed off with the hand that I'd been dealt and the never-ending run on a treadmill that pointed up.

Was it really too much to ask to have a couple of things go right in this life? Or was it set in stone the day we were born that some people would get it all while the rest of us poor saps got the scraps? I was already neck-deep in the shit that had been sent my way, and if any more was added, I might as well let myself drown because I was sick of treading this disgusting water.

Mannix stood from his seat but didn't say anything. He didn't need to. He was silently telling Beast to back off and me to calm down. He showed no sign of aggression, and I knew he wouldn't. Mannix was the eye of the storm.

From where I stood, I could tell Beast was grinding his teeth as the muscles strained in his neck with the effort of holding himself back.

"Fine, they're running behind, and I don't know," Beast said.

I sneered and shook my head in disgust. "So I have to ask, does Mathers actually plan on coming back, or is he searching for another hole to rot in and expects us to do his work for him?" I shrugged. "I mean, it's a fair question. He's up in the fucking Great White North, doing what? We don't know, and now what? Are they planning on taking a scenic tour on the way back? Maybe stop in Frontenac and get a steamy as they lick their wounds."

Beast's eyes narrowed as he squared his shoulders. "You have no idea what it's like to go through what he's had to. We all process loss differently, and you need to give him a break and show some respect."

A snort left my mouth. Sighing, I pulled the smoke from my mouth and butted it on the bottom of my boot.

"Beast, we all have our crosses to bear. Do you think Mathers and I should sit down and compare notes? Maybe sip some tea and talk about how we overcame the pain of our woes, scars, and evil deeds?" I asked, my voice laced with sarcasm. I crossed my arms over my chest.

"Not going to fucking happen. Yeah, his family died horribly, and it sucks. I get that. But who in here hasn't lost someone they love? Or have no family at all? Or had their entire fucking lives destroyed for no good reason? Fuck, the whole reason your old lady is dead is that Chase couldn't kill his brother, or am I wrong about that too?"

Beast's face morphed from anger to pain, and I knew that the blow of my words was low and hitting hard with the loss of Jaz. It was a jerk thing to say, but I was sick of the rose-colored glasses routine. I'd liked Jaz. She'd treated me decent and hadn't deserved to die, and she wouldn't have if Chase had done his job. Just another soul lost in his wake.

"The point I'm trying to make is that you're still here working, I'm still here working, everyone is still here working but...Chase Mathers is the one person who is supposed to be making the decisions and taking care of the duties of this place. But no, it's more important to help his 'blood' family. Shows how much he gives a fuck about us. How many years have you given up to cover his ass?" I growled. "I won't do it, and I won't follow him blindly. If he doesn't come back soon and prove to be a worthwhile leader, you won't have to worry about kicking me out, Beast, 'cause I'll already be gone."

"Are you suggesting we get rid of our leader?" Beast asked.

Pushing away from the chair, all the guys looked at the floor like I'd just beaten them all with a stick, and I shook my head.

"No. I would have no problem with the guy if he did his job and looked out for us the same way we've been covering his ass. That's really not too much to ask. It shocks me every day that out of all of us, you, who had to take over and man up to run this club, is still the one who paints him as a fucking messiah." I tossed my hands up when no one said anything. "I'm done. You want to kick me out for being the only one brave enough to speak up, then go for it, but I have important things on my list, and I'm going to go take care of them."

I marched for the door and flung it open, leaving it that way in my wake. If they all wanted to show undying loyalty to Chase, then they could. I was more of the show me with actions to prove it type because words were fucking cheap, and so far, all I'd seen was a bunch of lip service.

"Snake," Mannix's voice stopped me in my tracks.

I slowly turned around to see him coming out the door and closing it behind him. Internally groaning, I remained where I was until he reached me.

"Follow me," Mannix said, and I followed along the hall to the far end, away from the church door. "Look, I know you have many very valid reasons as to why you're angry with Chase," he said.

"If you're going to tell me that I need to show him respect..."

Mannix shook his head. "No, I won't say that. In fact, I think you're right, and Chase would tell you that same thing. He doesn't deny fucking up and knows he needs to make amends."

"Then why isn't he here?" I countered. "Why is he in another country fighting for an MC that has nothing to do with us?"

"It's complicated. The thing is, you're not wrong with anything you said in there, but I'm going to ask you to tone it down. The aggression, although justified, isn't helping, and it has nothing to do with Chase's ego. We can't afford to lose anyone else. We already had one member pack their shit and leave in the night. The club can't sustain any more losses, and as angry as you are right now, I know you don't want to see this place fall apart."

I sucked in a deep breath. "Fine, that's a fair point. Do you need me to kill whoever left?"

Mannix laughed. His mouth turned into a lopsided smile. "Best enforcer ever. No, it's all good. I made sure he won't cross us."

"So, is that it?"

"Naw, man, I'm going to ask you to lay off until Chase is back and proves one way or the other that he's a leader, and I'm asking this as a favor to me."

"Fuck," I swore under my breath. He knew I would never say no to a personal favor. This was a sneaky tactic, but I wouldn't be alive without Mannix, and I respected the fuck out of him. "Fine, but know this. I will follow you wherever you need me to go, but if Chase gets back and it continues to be this dog and pony show, I'm done. You can beat the shit out of me and break both my legs. I don't give a fuck. I refuse to follow someone as spineless as my father was."

Mannix nodded, and I turned and stomped down the hall, so absorbed with my thoughts that it took a moment to register the yelling. The shrill sound out in the main club room nearly had me turning around and going the other way.

Almost anything was better than dealing with Naomi. Now that she was pregnant, she was more annoying than ever. At least before, her rants were just irritating. Now they ended in tears and her rubbing her belly as she demanded things like cocoa butter. It was 'cringe worthy', as she would say.

All the sweetbutts were gathered like they'd been herded, and Naomi screamed at the top of her lungs as she pointed at them.

"What the fuck is going on here? You sound like you've been possessed by Satan." I stared at her red face and messy blonde hair, which was normally neat and perfect. "You kinda look it, too. Are you sure it was Chase that knocked you up?"

A few of the girls appreciated my sense of humor and smirked or laughed, earning a glare that could've shattered glass from Naomi.

"And what fucking part of no drama by the old ladies do you not understand? Do you need it read slower to you?"

Her face turned a fiery shade of red. "I'm not an old lady!" she wailed, and I cringed. "I'm in my prime. I'm too young for this," Naomi said and looked like she was about to burst into tears when her face shifted as fast as a transformer, and she stomped in my direction.

"You, it was probably you," Naomi said, and just like that, the finger swung in my direction.

"Be careful where you point that thing. Something may bite it off," I growled and stepped farther into the room.

I had zero intention of hurting her shrieking ass. As far as I was concerned, old ladies, even ones causing drama, were the responsibility of their man. Chase wasn't here, but if Beast were reporting back, he knew what was going on, including any of the shit Naomi pulled.

She tried to give Chase's office a freshening-up paint job a week ago with a color called wheat fairy. She said the simple, grey walls were depressing and looked dirty. I left when Beast finally called Chase to talk her down.

But I also didn't have to put up with her antics. She wasn't my old lady. We had one sexual interaction when she gave me a blowjob to piss off Chase, and I honestly have had better from my bike.

Three things kept her breathing and acting like a raving lunatic. The first was that she was shacking up with Chase. I may not be happy with his leadership qualities, but to kill his old lady, fuck no.

The second was that she was pregnant. Only a real piece of shit killed a woman while pregnant. I was a grade-A asshole and had killed a long list of women on missions for the club, but only a man with no morals would do that crap.

The last was that as much as I didn't like her ninety-nine percent of the time, the one percent was mad respect. I'd watched her step off a boat onto a dock and do the thing that Chase needed to do and couldn't. Killed his brother. Point blank range, she walked up and pulled the trigger like she was swiping her credit card at Versace. That right there earned her a free pass for life unless she came at me for some reason. Any bitch who could do that was a bitch worth keeping.

She looked at her finger and then up into my face. "Whatever," she said but put her arm down. "Just tell me where she is."

My brow furrowed. "Who the hell are you talking about?"

"Don't play stupid with me. I know you know where she is." She crossed her arms over her chest and glared at her blood-red nails. Had the pregnancy hormones gone to her head? A voice in my mind warned me to keep that thought to myself unless I wanted her to go all banshee again.

"The only girls I know of are in this room and Raine," I said.

"Who's Raine?"

"My point exactly." I mirrored her pose and even added the foot tap she had going on just so she knew how ridiculous she looked.

Naomi looked me up and down and huffed out a sound that sounded more like a rabid squirrel, but I was sure it was her version of annoyance. "I'm talking about Bailey. She's missing, and I know one of you assholes took her."

I held my hands out. "Who the fuck is Bailey? And why the hell would we want her?"

Naomi chewed on her lower lip. "Bailey is my roommate."

"The blonde? I thought her name was Ava," I said and wondered if I'd been calling that girl the wrong name all this time.

"No, not her. My other roommate."

I shook my head and stomped toward the exit. "I have no idea who the hell you're talking about, but maybe you should visit the amusement park next door."

"What? Why?" Naomi gasped, her face horrified.

"I don't know, but maybe your crazy ass will get lost in the house of mirrors, and we won't have to listen to you wail in here." I paused at the top of the stairs and looked back at her. "At least if you're over there, people are already used to the haunting shrieks of insanity coming from inside."

"Funny, Snake. Ha, ha," I heard her yell as I jogged down the stairs. The others could try to pry her crazy ass out of here. I wasn't spending another second more than I had to. There were some things that even I, as the enforcer, refused to do.

Heading to my bike, I paused and looked over at the amusement park as an idea came to me. I walked over to the fence and tried to spot Wilder among the piles of broken things. He was always out here somewhere. It amazed me that the other guys hadn't seen the man lurking on the property. Then again, maybe they had but were too drunk to register that the walking pile of garbage was more than the booze talking.

"Wilder, man, you out here?" I called out and heard a hushed, "Shhh, this way."

I looked around for the source of the voice and spotted a pile of mangled rides near the fence. A head slowly rose from inside one of the rollercoaster cars. *This guy is fucking crazy. What are you doing?* Walking along the edge of the fence, I ran my fingers along the chain link, making little thudding noises as I went.

"Hey, man," I said once I reached the spot I'd seen Wilder appear. I stared inside the car that was at eye level, searching for the man himself.

"Shhhh, I'm down here. I don't want them to know where I am."

My eyes dropped, and there he was, lying on the ground, staring up at me from under the massive pile. Wilder had painted himself today, the same mishmash of colors as the cars. *How the hell had he done that?* Nope, wasn't asking.

"Do you want me to look somewhere else?" I asked.

"Naw, man, no need to be paranoid. What's up?"

I let that comment sink in and couldn't help wondering if he saw the irony in that statement. In the last ten minutes, I'd dealt with three levels of insanity, but Wilder and his ridiculous behavior were at least humorous.

"How easy would it be to get a tracker?" I asked.

"That's all you want?" He scoffed like I was the one being ridiculous and then shuffled back under the pile. I heard him inside, rooting around like a massive rat. Then again, the only difference separating him from a rat at this point was that Wilder could talk.

A moment later, I heard an "ah ha," and the man reappeared, but this time from inside the car. What the hell? Did he have an entire fucking system of tunnels? Wilder reached out and stuck his fingers through the links, and I took the small black square from his fingers.

"You just happen to have a tracker in here with you?"

"Yeah, of course. You never know when you're going to need one."

I licked my lips and swallowed as I wondered how many of us had trackers on us already. Did he watch us all day? Nope, not going there either. If he did, he did. I didn't want to know about it.

"So, how does it work?"

"Turn it on, sync it to your phone, and put it on the person you want to track. Easy," Wilder said, moving back into the center of the blue and yellow car. "Can I ask you a question?" he asked before I could make my escape.

"Sure," I said, not really sure I wanted to know after the last question.

"Chase told me that girls like flowers, but it doesn't seem to be working," he said, and my eyebrow rose. When the hell had Wilder talked to Chase? And why about flowers?

"Well, that was your first mistake. Chase ended up with Naomi. Does that seem like the right person to ask?" It was a low blow, but it made me feel better.

Wilder stared at me as if contemplating the joke as a real moment of understanding. "No, it does not. Good point, no flowers."

"Okay," I said, not sure what else to say at this point.

"I need another idea," he said. "I'm unskilled in the ways of creating affection."

I wanted to yell *shocking* but kept it to myself. "Do you know what her interests are? Does she like sailing or biking or books? Maybe she likes art or animals."

"No, why would I need to know that?" he asked, and my brain started to fry.

I could only handle so much insanity in a day before my meter was completely full, and it was getting pretty fucking close to full now.

"Alright, forget knowing her interests. Girls love it when you spend time with them. Take her out, make her a part of your day, and show her that you care about her interests. They also like a good meal," I said, hoping that I didn't just sentence some random girl to death.

"Fuck, you're good. I'm coming to you from now on," Wilder said.

"Oh, that's great," I mumbled under my breath.

"Thanks, man." Wilder dropped down into his maze, and a second later, he sprinted across the open lot to the center of his chaos.

"I should've just used the black market," I grumbled and stomped toward my bike. This was turning out to be a weird fucking day, and I didn't see it getting any better from here.

Raine

20

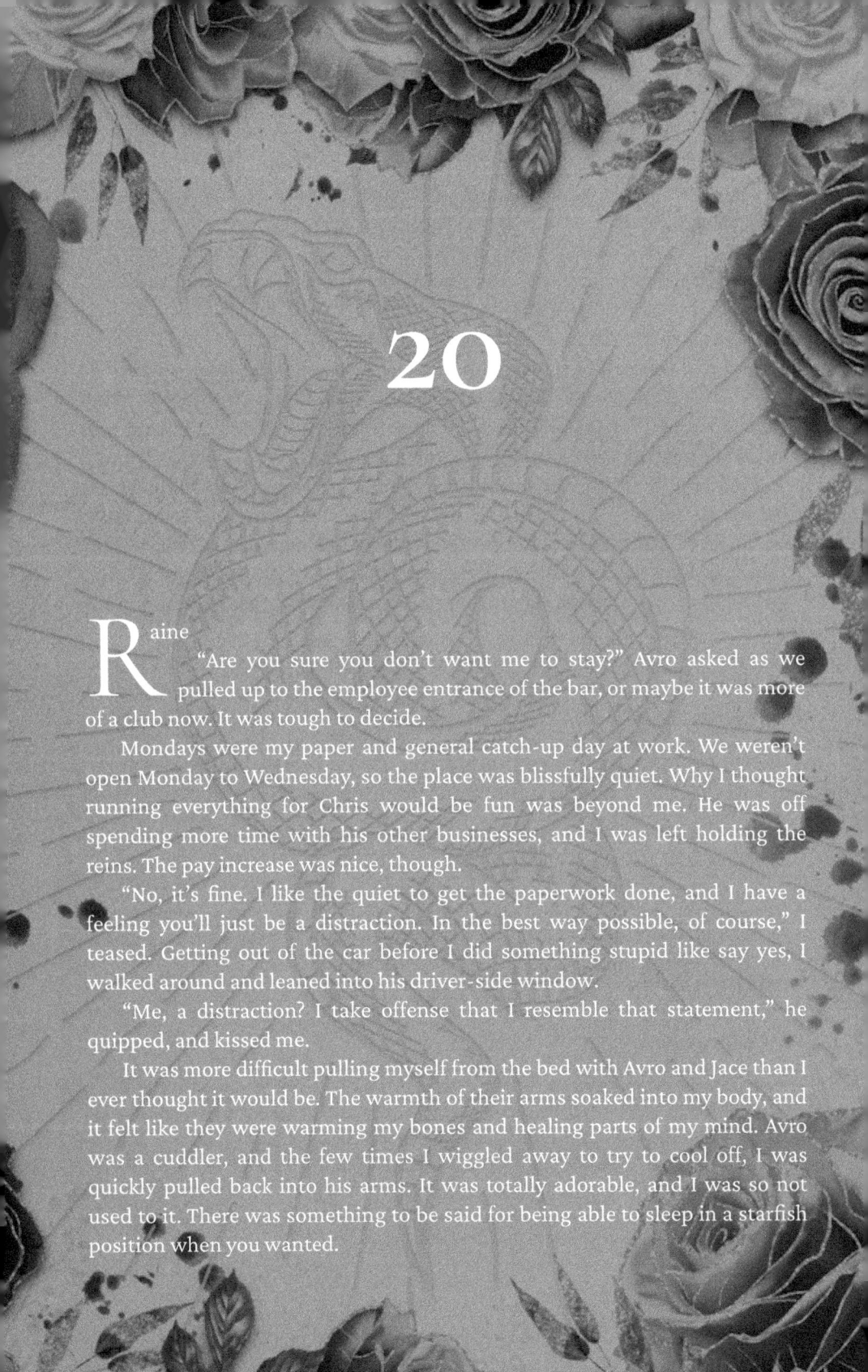

Raine

"Are you sure you don't want me to stay?" Avro asked as we pulled up to the employee entrance of the bar, or maybe it was more of a club now. It was tough to decide.

Mondays were my paper and general catch-up day at work. We weren't open Monday to Wednesday, so the place was blissfully quiet. Why I thought running everything for Chris would be fun was beyond me. He was off spending more time with his other businesses, and I was left holding the reins. The pay increase was nice, though.

"No, it's fine. I like the quiet to get the paperwork done, and I have a feeling you'll just be a distraction. In the best way possible, of course," I teased. Getting out of the car before I did something stupid like say yes, I walked around and leaned into his driver-side window.

"Me, a distraction? I take offense that I resemble that statement," he quipped, and kissed me.

It was more difficult pulling myself from the bed with Avro and Jace than I ever thought it would be. The warmth of their arms soaked into my body, and it felt like they were warming my bones and healing parts of my mind. Avro was a cuddler, and the few times I wiggled away to try to cool off, I was quickly pulled back into his arms. It was totally adorable, and I was so not used to it. There was something to be said for being able to sleep in a starfish position when you wanted.

"Try not to have too much fun going to the airport," I said, hitching my backpack higher.

"The drive there won't be much fun, but once we get there, I plan on molesting Jace one more time before he gets on the plane."

I couldn't tell if he was joking, but knowing Avro, he fully intended to take his fill of Jace Everly. Jace still made me as nervous as a cat on a hot tin roof, and I found myself talking too much or stumbling over my answers when he looked in my direction. He was amused, and I was not.

"I'm sure you will." I smiled, and he smiled back. The expression lit up the whole car. "I'll talk to you later," I said and waved as I flicked through my keys to find the one that opened the back door. Avro waited until the door was open, and I gave him the thumbs up before he drove off.

Jace's regular driver was sick, so everyone from the band was finding their own way to the private airfield. The drive took a couple of hours, and his flight didn't take off until eight, so long as the weather held out. They'd both offered to stay and keep me company until they needed to leave, but that was all sorts of a bad idea, and I needed time to unpack everything floating around in my head.

Grabbing the remote, I turned on the television as soon as I walked into the office. I loved that the place was quiet, but sometimes it really freaked me out. Every shadowy corner felt like someone was hiding. I was starting to realize that the thought was very conceited. The very idea that every guy was looking at me, hiding to attack me or whatever else my brain conjured, was irrational.

The channel was on the local news station, and I watched as the reporter pointed to the large screens showing the coming storm. By the look of it, there was a good chance that Jace's flight wouldn't get off the ground.

Sitting down, I booted up the computer and laid my hands on the desk. My emotions swirled as much as the colorful clouds on the news screen as I tried to digest the last two days. Closing my eyes, I played over the conversation from last night and the feel of their touch. But all that did was make me wiggle in my seat.

"Okay, you came here to work. You can wonder about your rapidly changing personal life later." I looked at the 'In' basket on my desk and groaned.

"Darryl," I grumbled, not seeing the final inventory boards from the alcohol storage. That was the one spot I hated to go, even when people were in the building. When the bar was empty, I avoided it like it held the plague.

"Shit, shit, shit!" I was tempted to go home and get Avro to go down with me tomorrow. "That is the most chicken-shit thing you've considered doing yet," I scolded myself as I pushed to my feet. "You're trying to be braver, remember?"

Squaring my shoulders, I stomped out the door and down the hallway that led to the storage area, like the stomping would somehow make the images of ghosts in my mind go away. I whipped open the door and swallowed hard as I stared at the black hole. It was only six stairs down, and technically it was still above ground, and yet it felt like a bottomless pit that disappeared into a cavernous void.

"You got this. You now have a wicked right hook," I encouraged myself, reaching for the light switch. Why were these storage areas so scary? Was it because from the time we were children, there were a million movies with things sneaking in or crawling out of these things? Or was it because we intuitively realized this was the closest we came to being in a windowless coffin while still alive? I paused with my foot hovering over the first stair. Unless, of course, you were buried alive in a coffin.

Okay, enough of that.

I trotted down the wooden stairs and decided to start at the farthest spot and make my way forward. That seemed logical, and then each aisle I completed was a reward, getting a little closer to the exit.

Walking down the last row, I swallowed hard and picked up the clipboard. I suddenly wished I'd turned on some music. At least then, it wouldn't be so quiet. I jotted down the remaining wine on the chart and grabbed the paper. When I stepped out of the row to move to the next, I heard a scraping sound. I froze as my eyes searched the rows of bottles and boxes, but with the product on the shelves, I could only partially see to the end.

My heart pounded hard as my fear spiked, and every muscle shook as I put one foot in front of the other. I moved toward the spot where I'd heard the sound. It seemed way too loud to be a mouse. Gripping the pen like a weapon, I glanced down each row I passed. I looked up the stairs as I stepped in front of them and once more contemplated saying fuck it and getting the hell out of here, but I was determined to stare fear in the face and defeat it. Too many years, too many ghosts, too many demons of my own making, and I was done.

Everything seemed to be heightened, the smell of the cardboard, the faint scent of mildew from the dampness that permeated everything, and the stale aroma of old alcohol from broken or spilled bottles. The scraping sound was louder now that I was closer, and one of the boxes moved slightly. My nostrils flared, eyes wide, and pen at the ready as I counted down each remaining row. As I reached the last row, a rumble of thunder echoed down the stairs, and the lights shut off, plunging the room into complete darkness.

Terror gripped my throat, and I slammed against the wall as the memory I tried so hard to forget stormed to the front of my mind.

"Shit," I mumbled as I jogged down the street.

It was late, and this was a terrible part of town, but I had to speak to Kai. I just couldn't leave things the way that I had. I couldn't believe he kissed me, and instead of hanging on forever, I freaked out. It was my first kiss, my first real kiss, from the guy I always wanted it to be, and I pushed him off me and ran from the room like a loser.

I'd paced the school yard until dark, and when I got home, Kai was already gone. Crawling into bed, I tried to sleep and told myself that I would catch him in the morning, but with each minute that ticked on the clock, my anxiety grew until I wanted to throw up. I wanted to see him—no, I had to see him. He was my friend, but I'd been secretly crushing on Kai from the moment he showed up at the Collins house.

I'd seen too many dead people in my short time alive. I'd stared into my parents' unseeing eyes and known they were dead. I didn't really know what to call it other than with the angels. Were there really angels, though? I didn't know anymore. I certainly didn't think so.

I'd also watched a man choke on his own puke and another suffocate to death while others convulsed on the floor. It was confusing at the age of six. I was unsure what was going on, but scared out of my mind. I didn't want to get anyone in trouble, but maybe if I hadn't cared about that, my parents or even one of their friends would still be alive today. I couldn't be expected to save them, yet their deaths weighed on my mind.

I glanced at the scar on my hand, the white line across my palm where I'd cut myself on glass that night. It was a constant reminder that my parents didn't give a fuck about me. The police came to the shitty little apartment, and I was hauled away.

I'd stared out the window for days, hoping that it was all dream and my parents would come for me. Like a television show where they showed up at the house, and we would run to one another and hug. The television lied, books lied, and people lied.

All but one. Kai told me the truth, no matter what I asked. He'd never treated me like a kid, and it seemed like, overnight, I couldn't help thinking about what would happen if I snuck into his room. Would he hold me all night? Would we talk and laugh as we tried not to get caught? I snuck in once and claimed that I had a terrible dream, but Kai said we couldn't stay in his room, and we ended up sitting outside. It was still nice, and he hadn't yelled or told me to fuck off, but I realized he didn't see me as anything more than a friend and foster sister.

At least, that was what I thought until earlier tonight. That kiss had been made for books. I could still feel the warmth against my lips and the sweet taste of the icing on my tongue from Kai's cake. The way his hand touched my cheek and the scent of his body wash had made me lightheaded. My heart had jumped around inside my chest like an animal looking to escape, and the feelings that came over me had me bolting for the door.

I pulled my hood down lower and stuffed my hands in my pockets to make myself look intimidating. That was not easy to do. At five feet four inches, I wasn't tall and was slim in all the wrong places. My pants drooped on my hips, and I had very little in the way of boobs. At fifteen, I looked more like a boy, except for my long hair.

Some guys stumbled past and laughed as they talked about the fight where they'd just won money. The strong scent of beer and cigarettes made my nose curl. I had to be close. Daring to lift my head from watching my sneakers, I looked around for anything that would give away where the street fights were. Across the road was another large group of people standing around outside a building. They were smoking and talking on phones or with each other, but not one of them looked like anyone I would want to ask for information.

Slipping into the alley, I watched the group and peeked up and down the street. The glass doors behind them opened, and loud shouting caught my attention. I watched as three men came out, pissed off. I had no idea what they were screaming about, but they were yelling at the massive guys dressed all in black blocking their way.

"They must be guards. That's got to be the spot," I mumbled.

My eyes traced up the front of the building, and a smile tugged at the corner of my mouth as I spotted the large eye with an 'O' and other fonts surrounding it. The paint job was faded, but it was definitely an eye, and Kai was always talking to the other guys who fought about the place being called the Oracle. While the argument continued and everyone was distracted, I ran across the street and slipped down the alley beside the building. I pulled on each door I came to, but they were all locked.

Walking around to the back of the building, I spotted one more door but only took a couple of steps when the door opened, and I darted behind the stacks of boxes and garbage cans.

"Fuck off, Joe. I'm tellin' ya, and I'm not lying. I have the perfect match for your guy. Big money fight. The spectators will go crazy for the match-up. Yeah, I know. The kid's name is Snake."

Daring to peek, I lifted my eyes above the garbage, but the guy had walked in the other direction as he spoke. They were definitely talking about Kai. That was the name he made everyone but me call him. He tried to get me to call him that stupid name, but I wasn't hearing it. I wasn't calling him a reptile just because he thought it was cool.

Light shone out the crack in the door, and I realized this guy had left the door open a little. Taking the risk, I moved like a cat on a tightrope and ran to the stairs, then tiptoed up to the door as quickly as possible without giving myself away.

The door was open just enough that someone tiny like me could slip in. I ended up in a stairwell with two options...up or down. It wasn't that loud in this back hallway, but I could feel the vibration from loud music through my feet and decided that I'd go down and quickly sprinted down the stairs, taking two at a time.

With my small size, blond hair, and always being light on my feet, Kai dubbed me Tink. I hated that he saw me as this cute little thing, but I would take him calling me that over never speaking to me again.

Reaching the bottom floor, I stared at the black door with the dents like someone had punched it hard a thousand times. Licking my lips, I slowly reached for the handle and pulled it open, only to be abused by the loud cheering and even louder rock music. I kept my hood firmly in place but stood up straight and tossed a bit of swagger into my walk, just like I saw the guys on my street do. It annoyed me how they would walk like they owned the road, but watching them strut around like a bunch of birds in a mating dance helped me now.

I moved through the crowd until I was positioned close enough to see who was fighting, and my heart soared and then sank when I realized it wasn't Kai. I didn't want him to fight, but did this mean he'd already fought, or was he next?

A hard bump from the guy beside me had me stepping sideways, and I glared at him out of the corner of my eye, but he didn't notice me. My foot slipped a little, and when I looked down, I spotted a program under my foot. I picked it up and stared at the list of names that were supposed to fight tonight. There were no times.

Dammit.

My eyes lifted to the cage when the crowd erupted in loud applause. One guy was pressed up against the chain link cage while the other guy repeatedly punched him. I didn't like watching this, and I couldn't believe that Kai subjected himself to this just so he could pay for school. There had to be a better way.

A buzzer went off like a fire alarm, and the guy left standing in the cage threw his hands up and cheered. I guess he was the winner.

"Winner, The Void!" the man acting as the announcer called into the microphone he was holding, and I glanced down at the form to see that they were the second last fight, which meant that Kai was next. I was jostled to the side again as more people pushed into the already packed room.

Bang

I ducked at the sound. It took an extra second for everyone else to register the sound of the gun. In a blink, everyone turned to run away from the cage area. I was dragged along, and my chest hurt as the crowd pushed and shoved hard. A hand hit the side of my head, and the hood I'd kept in place slipped down, but I couldn't worry about it as I tried to stay on my feet so that I wasn't trampled.

Bang

The group that was practically carrying me with them was diverted, and we ended up running back the way we came. Slipping through the small cracks that the stinking, sweating bodies left, I managed to get to the wall and pressed myself against it as hard as I could. My heart was pounding so hard that I thought I might pass out, and my lip hurt. Touching my mouth, I realized that it was bleeding.

Bang, Bang

A light smashed, sending little shards flying, and I covered my head as the pieces rained down. Some of the guys dressed in black pushed their way through the throngs of people still shoving their way out of the exits. They held up guns, and at that moment, the fear that had remained dormant due to shock took hold. Pushing away from the wall, I slipped under arms and dodged around the next group of people. Spotting the door I came through, which wasn't marked with a big red Exit sign, I peeled away from the group and ran for it.

When I pulled it open, and the light from the stairwell poured in, I could see people turn my way and break away from the group.

Where the hell was Kai in all this? Was he okay? Did he already get out? Please don't let him be one of the people being shot at.

I pushed away from the door and darted up the stairs, breathing hard as I took them two at a time. A hand landed on the rail beside me, and my heart leaped as I stared at the same tattoo Kai had gotten just a few weeks ago. Looking back, I stared up at the tall figure wearing a black hoodie. I couldn't see his face, and there was no time. It could wait until we were outside.

The door slammed open as I hit it, and as soon as we were outside, I turned to speak to Kai, but he was running along the back of the buildings away from Oracle.

"Kai!" I yelled and ran after him. "Kai, it's me. Wait up." I could hear sirens in the distance and pushed my tired legs harder.

Rounding the corner to the dark shadows where I'd seen Kai turn, I called out again. "Kai, stop! It's me."

I hadn't gone very far when someone in a hood stepped out of the shadows. I tried to stop, but it did no good as I ran straight into them. Bouncing back, I landed hard on my ass and stared up at the person I'd hit. I tried to see inside the dark hood, but the thumb hooked into the pocket showed off the back of his hand, and there was the tattoo.

"Kai, thank God. It's me," I said, looking around as two more people stepped into the alley. I couldn't tell what they looked like with the only light at their backs. I swallowed hard as I stared up at the three men. None of them spoke.

"Get her up," a gruff voice barked out.

"No, don't touch me." I tried to jerk away from the vise grip that wrapped around my biceps. "Ow! Let go," I yelled and tugged on my arm.

"Shut her up."

A hard hit to my stomach came out of nowhere, and I doubled over. Tears sprang to my eyes, and my knees buckled as I tried to breathe past the sharp pain.

"Better than nothing. Actually, this may work out even better." The same man sneered. He stepped in close and bent low to my side, but I still couldn't see his face in the dark. I caught the strong stench of alcohol and cigarettes. My foster dad smoked all the time, and it reminded me of that scent. "Bag her."

Black material was placed over my head by the second guy who had stepped into the alley, and everything in me screamed that I needed to fight or I was going to die. I had no idea why Kai was doing this and listening to this jerk, but how he'd said it "may work out better" sent a cold dread racing down my back. Kicking out hard, I didn't care what I hit as long as they let me go. I opened my mouth to scream at the top of my lungs when something hard hit my face. Then all I saw was black and little dots behind my eyelids.

The lights came back on, and as they did, my mind was pulled back to the present. I screamed and jumped back as a cat darted toward me and hit the stack of boxes at the end of the row. The boxes swayed dangerously.

I watched the grey cat disappear up the stairs and slumped against the wall, laying a hand over my eyes.

"Fuck," I swore and pulled at my shirt as my heart fluttered so hard that I thought I would pass out. "You know what? Screw this. Inventory can wait until tomorrow," I mumbled, every part of my body shaking with the adrenaline and lingering fear that always accompanied the memory.

I raced up the stairs and closed the door, so my furry little intruder couldn't run back down. I needed to finish up a few odds and ends, and then I was getting the hell out of here. Rome wasn't built in a day, and my fear wasn't going to disappear overnight.

I rarely asked for anything, but I would happily trade my tattered soul to be rid of the memory of Kai and his friends.

Raine

21

Raine

Damn this storm. I tried waiting it out, but instead of getting better, it only got worse. Digging around in my wallet, I pulled out the money to give to the nice lady who had risked life and limb to drive in the torrential downpour to bring me home.

"Thanks again. Here, take this for your trouble," I said, handing over double the Uber fee.

"You don't have to do that," she said, smiling, but still took the money and stuffed it into her pocket.

I'd been very frugal over the years and had money put away in case I needed it, for what, I had no idea. It wasn't like I spent money on lavish items, clothes, or even had a car, but you just never knew what was around the next corner.

Grabbing my bag, I jumped out of the Uber and sprinted for the front door. I was used to Avro driving me home and waiting till I got inside, but not this woman. She was gone before I reached the bottom step.

"I should've just taken today off," I mumbled as I tried to get my key into the door, but it wouldn't go in. "Why the hell is it so dark?"

Reaching over, I tapped my outside light, but it wouldn't turn on. Great, just great. Digging my phone out of my pocket, I tucked myself close to the door to keep it from getting wet and hit the flashlight option. Of course, I'd been trying the wrong key. It really had been one of those days. I got the stray cat out of the club, but in the process, it knocked over five hundred dollars' worth of bottles in the main bar, and I had to clean all that up. Then once I managed to get a hold of him, my arm got scratched up for my effort. I made it to the hospital to have it cleaned and wrapped and get a tetanus shot. All in all, it had been a day I wished I'd just stayed in bed.

Picking out the right key, I slipped it into the lock and pushed open the door as the thunder rumbled outside. I'd lived here my whole life and had never gotten used to the way the storms hit, and even though it wasn't a hurricane, it still felt like one.

I was soaked to the bone and shivering, as if the water had seeped right into my marrow. Locking the door behind me, I dropped my bag and hit the light switch, but it didn't want to turn on either. Glancing out the window, I saw the house across the street had light peeking through the closed drapes. It must be the breaker.

"Of course, why would anything want to go right?"

I stomped down the hallway toward the kitchen to grab a flashlight, so I didn't get my phone all wet. I glanced back at the wet prints and trail of water I'd left and groaned. I would clean that up after. The stupid fuse box was outside, and if my night hadn't been bad enough, I wouldn't be surprised to come face-to-face with a gator in my backyard.

"Fucking shit luck today. My stars must be out of alignment," I mumbled, holding up the phone as my guide. The lightning flashed outside, making me shudder a moment before the thunder boomed so loudly that I jumped and then ducked, covering my head. It sounded like it was right above my house as the walls shook. I didn't see myself getting any sleep tonight.

My luck, the house would catch fire. Seriously, could anything else go wrong?

Another shiver ran up my spine when I marched past the closet. My foot faulted as the little light on my phone reflected off the glass of the kitchen window. It wasn't my reflection that made me pause, my mind slowing to a crawl. It was the closet door opening silently behind me. As if I were dumped into the middle of a horror movie, I was suddenly staring at the monster I'd been hiding from all these years. I blinked, not sure this was real or if I was conjuring it in my terror-riddled mind. Goosebumps rose on my body, and my pulse tripled as my adrenaline soared through the roof.

Run.

My feet didn't listen to what my mind screamed to do. They seemed to be rooted to the spot.

Run.

Something large stepped out of the closet and turned in my direction. It was a man. My breath caught in my throat as the shock transformed into dread.

Thump, thump, thump. My heart pounded viciously behind my ribcage.

Run.

I couldn't breathe as the lightning flashed again and illuminated a pair of blue eyes I would never forget. Those eyes were burned into the deepest recesses of my brain like they'd been branded. Forever marked.

"Hey there, Tink," Kai said. His voice was much deeper and rough, but everything that I remembered. The same shot of excitement punched me in the stomach that I always had whenever I saw him. But this time, the thrill was quickly followed by terror.

My feet finally listened to the warning, and I lunged toward the kitchen. I barely made it a stride before I screamed. Hands much larger than I remembered grabbed me by the back of my neck and my sopping-wet sweatshirt. It didn't even register that I'd been jerked off my feet until I sailed through the air and crashed into the coffee table.

The sharp pain was instant as my elbow and shoulder slammed into the hard edge, before sliding across the top and landing on my shoulder hard. My phone was knocked from my hand and slid under the recliner.

"No, no, no," I whispered.

Fear roared through my body. I thought I knew what it was to be scared, but I was wrong. I clawed at the ground, trying to get my feet under me, but my wet sneakers slipped on the laminate floor. A massive boot slammed down in the center of the coffee table. I cried out with the loud crack that mirrored the echo of thunder, announcing that the table had snapped in two. I was being pursued by a monster and not a man.

"Kai, no," I cried out and scrambled to get away and reach my phone. Glancing over my shoulder, I couldn't see him clearly in the dark, but I felt his eyes boring into me with so much hate and anger. I knew he would come. I had always known he would come for me.

This was the nightmare that played on a loop in my mind.

Gripping the arm of the chair, I stuck my hand under to try to grab my phone, which softly glowed like my only beacon for help. My fingers grazed the edge when those strong hands yanked me back by my hoodie and choked off my air supply. A scream ripped from my throat as he picked me up like I weighed nothing, and once more, I was thrown through the air.

"Ah!" I cried out, my ribs taking the impact as I hit the partially open closet door and slammed it closed. "Get off me," I yelled as he grabbed me again.

Words I'd said so many times before and it hadn't worked then. I don't know why I thought they might work now. Tears burned my eyes as I battled my panic to think straight.

The fight was slowly returning to my brain. If I didn't fight, he was going to kill me. *Fight, damn you, fight.*

When he pulled me to my feet, I used all my strength and brought my elbow up like I was trying to perform a finishing move in a video game. The blow wasn't true and glanced off the side of his chin, but it was enough that he swore and stepped back.

Only a tiny bit of space separated us, but I let my right fist fly and caught him squarely across the cheek. The crack of my knuckles told me I definitely made good contact, but I'd hit him all wrong, and I cried out with the pain in my wrist. His head snapped to the side, a small cut opening up on his cheek from the little silver band on my middle finger. Ironically, it was the ring he'd given me the night before he attacked me. I didn't know why I kept it, why I couldn't throw it away, or why I wore it, but it never left my finger.

My victory was short-lived as his head slowly turned toward me. Blue eyes burning with malice glared into my soul, and I shuddered in his hold.

Not wasting a second, I grabbed the front of the leather jacket he was wearing in my fists and pulled in while I brought my knee up, but I only hit his hands. He shoved me hard, and I winced as the back of my head cracked off the hollow wooden door with a thud.

"Kai, stop, please," I cried out as he reached for me again, but he didn't stop.

His fist curled around the front of my sweatshirt, and I struck out with my left hand, smacking him as hard as I could from the awkward angle. The sting in my hand burned like it was on fire, but he didn't even flinch. My mind was unraveling, and instead of precise movements with strategic hits, I began lashing out like I was feral. I knew what I needed to do. I knew I couldn't act like I had last time, but I realized now the pathetic amount of training I'd done was nothing more than a mental bandage.

Kai was far stronger than I remembered, and it was like he was made of stone and didn't feel anything as my fists, feet, and knees struck out at him. I was nothing more than a tiny kitten in the jaws of a giant predator. I was the tiny Tink he called me.

Tears spilled over and trailed down my cheeks. Nothing moved him.

Nothing lessened his strong grip or wavered that unnerving stare. I tried to claw at his face, aiming for his eyes, but he kept himself just out of my reach.

His lip pulled up at the corner in a smirk that was once so sexy but now only sent cold dread racing along my spine.

"You having fun, Tink?"

He yanked me towards him and spun my body around. I cried out as I was smashed into the door, my cheek and already sore ribs taking most of the blow. Pinning me against the wood like an insect on a board, Kai got close to my ear, and all I felt was the heat radiating off his body.

I closed my eyes, and my body shook uncontrollably in his hold. Kai ran his nose up the side of my neck.

"You smell so good, Tink. You smell exactly how I imagined you would."

"Get off of me, you asshole," I growled and kicked backward, trying to find any soft spot or even a knee, but he must have been expecting that, and I didn't hit anything.

"Keep it up, Tink. I like hearing your screams."

"Oh, I know you do." Gathering all my strength, I pushed with all my might against the door and swung backward as hard as I could with my elbow.

"Fucking bitch," Kai yelled as my elbow made contact. I felt his grip loosen on my sweatshirt and spun around. I broke his hold and bolted for the front door.

The house that had always seemed so small now felt like a marathon run to the door. My legs pumped hard, my lungs burned, and my head felt light with my erratic breaths. I knew I might pass out with this much adrenaline pumping, but I couldn't stop it, no more than I could stop the hand from grabbing hold of the hood on my sweatshirt. The cool touch of the door handle grazed the tips of my fingers, and just like that, I was wrenched off my feet and crashed to the floor.

Everything went numb. The air was forced out of my lungs, my fingers and toes tingled, while my head spun.

I cried out but could only wheeze as a heavy weight pressed into the middle of my chest. The lightning flashed, and the thunder rumbled like the sky was as angry as the man that held me. Kai's knee was on my chest, but the hand wrapped around my throat, and the fingers that steadily pressed in until I couldn't breathe told me that I was going to die.

I grabbed at Kai's arm, begging with my eyes to let go. I locked eyes with him, and there wasn't anything left of the boy I remembered. The boy I'd fallen in love with, the boy who broke my heart, stole my virginity, and now was going to take my life.

How I wished I'd just gone to the airport.

He raised his fist, and I glanced at those large knuckles and then back up into his eyes.

"P...l...ease," I pushed past my constricted windpipe. "Kai..."

His arm shook as the fist hovered, but it didn't matter now. Black dots exploded behind my eyes, and I tried but couldn't get a breath into my burning lungs. Hot tears slid down my cheeks and were the last thing I felt before the world went dark.

Snake

22

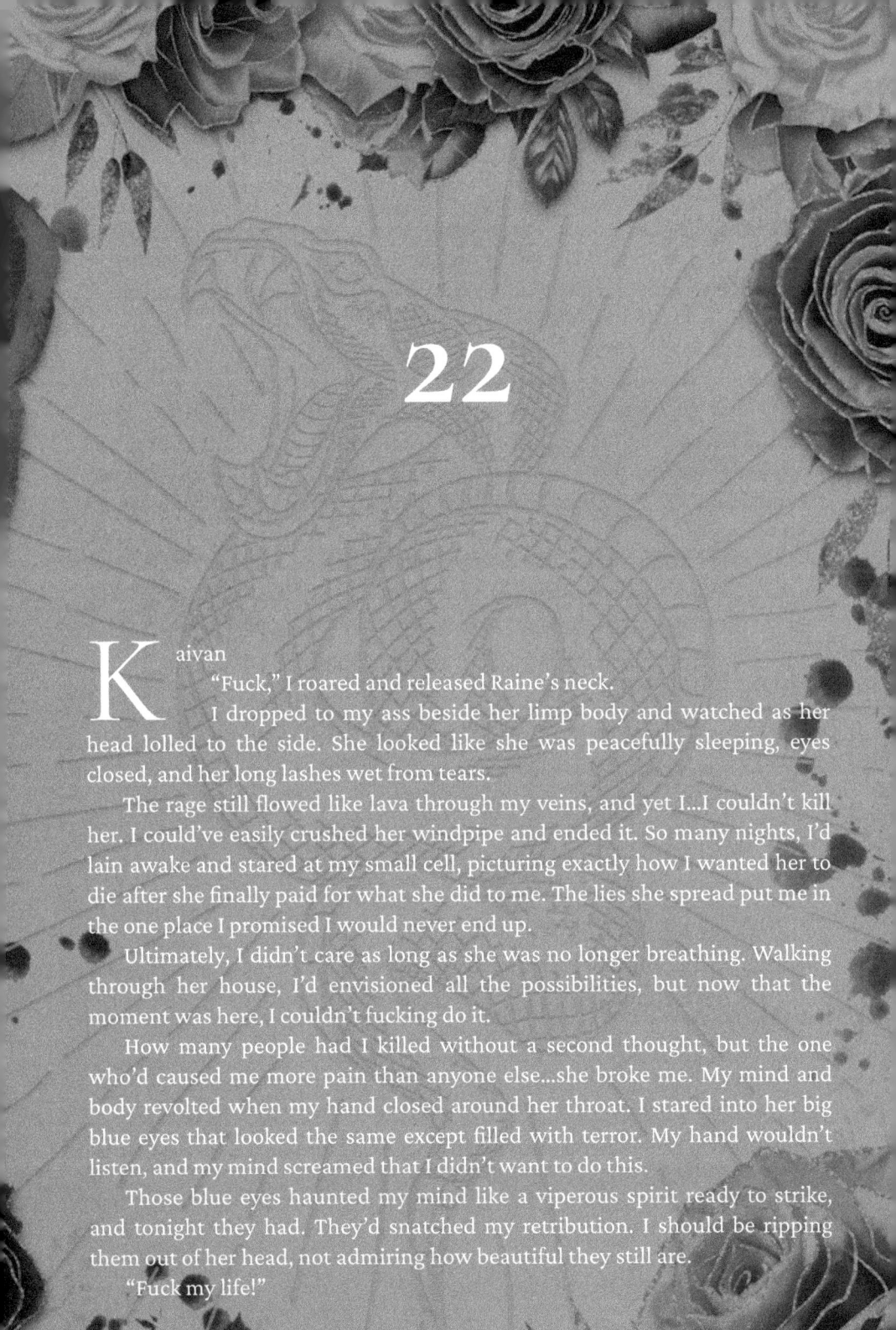

Kaivan

"Fuck," I roared and released Raine's neck.

I dropped to my ass beside her limp body and watched as her head lolled to the side. She looked like she was peacefully sleeping, eyes closed, and her long lashes wet from tears.

The rage still flowed like lava through my veins, and yet I…I couldn't kill her. I could've easily crushed her windpipe and ended it. So many nights, I'd lain awake and stared at my small cell, picturing exactly how I wanted her to die after she finally paid for what she did to me. The lies she spread put me in the one place I promised I would never end up.

Ultimately, I didn't care as long as she was no longer breathing. Walking through her house, I'd envisioned all the possibilities, but now that the moment was here, I couldn't fucking do it.

How many people had I killed without a second thought, but the one who'd caused me more pain than anyone else…she broke me. My mind and body revolted when my hand closed around her throat. I stared into her big blue eyes that looked the same except filled with terror. My hand wouldn't listen, and my mind screamed that I didn't want to do this.

Those blue eyes haunted my mind like a viperous spirit ready to strike, and tonight they had. They'd snatched my retribution. I should be ripping them out of her head, not admiring how beautiful they still are.

"Fuck my life!"

She made me no better than my old man, and now, after everything I'd done...I was worse.

"Fuck you, Raine! Fuck you!"

Memories of her smiling and laughing as she wore her little pink outfits raced through my mind. The feel of her touch lingered as she hugged me and told me she would miss me when I left for college. Her lips on mine as I kissed her, and for those few brief seconds, my life had been perfect.

Why? I needed to know why.

Fuck this. She would pay another way.

My body shook with anger so potent I could taste it as I pushed to my feet. I bent down, picked her up, and held her in my arms as she draped across them like a doll. Her breathing was subtle, but it was there, her chest slowly rising and falling. I was thankful I hadn't killed her, which just confused me more.

Stomping up the stairs, I shouldered her bedroom door open with a bang and laid Raine out on the bed. My eyes raked over her face and then slowly trailed down her body. I pulled my knife out of my pocket and flicked it open. The front of her wet, black sweatshirt split in two with a quick slice. She was wearing a plain black tank top, and that was next to go. I groaned as the damp material pulled away, leaving her braless tits exposed to my hungry stare.

She shuddered as the cool air hit her damp skin, and her nipples formed hard little peaks. My cock twitched and came to life. Raine was still just as beautiful as I remembered, more so now that she'd lost that teenage softness. The only difference was the pixie-cut hairdo, which didn't detract from her beauty. She just looked different. I couldn't help wondering why she cut it off when she'd made such a big deal about growing it to her waist.

"Avro," she murmured, and the rage that had quieted to a simmer flared again. Oh no, she didn't just say some other guy's name.

Grabbing the front of her jeans, I cut off the decorative belt just as her eyes snapped open, and her fist flew at my face. I shifted and blocked the second shot, swatting her hand away.

"Really? We gonna do this again, Tink? It is entertaining, but I thought you might have had enough," I sneered, and spun the blade in my hand.

"Fuck you," she snarled.

She was quick, I gave her that, and she still had all the fight I'd see burning in her eyes as a teen. Rolling off the bed, she ran for the bathroom, the door slamming behind her. Sighing, I closed the switchblade and stuffed it into my pocket before shrugging off my leather jacket. Tossing it on her dresser, I walked over to the bathroom door. There wasn't even a moment of hesitation as I hauled off and kicked the door as hard as I could. My shitkicker hit dead center and broke that cheap door right off the hinges as it crashed inward.

Raine screamed and covered her head from her perch on the toilet.

"You know, Tink, I'm having way too much fun chasing you around the house. I wish it were bigger. It would make this game so much more thrilling."

I reached into the bathroom, and she yelled again. The sound went straight between my legs as she tried to kick at me and hold her ripped top closed over her tits. Damn, she looked sexy all fired up like that, and fuck, she smelled even better. All the anger and hurt I'd been carrying was suddenly channeled into something far more carnal.

Getting a hold of her flailing legs, I yanked her hard, and to her credit, she flipped over as she fell and gripped the toilet seat. Any other time, I may have laughed at the ridiculous sight we made, but right now, there was only one thing on my mind. Taking what I was owed.

There was a squeaking sound when her hands slid off the seat, and she wiggled and fought as I dragged her back into her room. I bent over and pushed her legs aside—they were more of an annoyance than an actual threat—and tossed her on the bed. Raine bounced and tried to scoot off the other side like a little rabbit, but she wasn't quick enough.

Using her legs as leverage, I yanked her back onto the bed and pinned her on her back with my larger frame. My hand wrapped around her delicate neck once more, and those big blue eyes filled with the same fear as downstairs, but something else burned underneath. It was just a flicker, but I saw it. There was lust in her eyes.

"Get off of me, Kai," she yelled, and tried to push my arm away from her neck. I was so fucking hard as she wiggled under me that I groaned, and she paused in her struggle. "This is what you want? To rape me again?" she snarled, her eyes snapping at me as fiercely as her tongue.

"I didn't fucking rape you!" I roared, and my free fist punched right through the cheap drywall, leaving a huge hole behind. "Stop fucking saying that."

Raine shook under me. Her eyes closed tight. I stared down at her terrified face and loved it and hated it at the same time. The wild and toxic mix of emotions was quickly becoming addictive. I wanted to taste that fear. I wanted to fuck her hard until she admitted it hadn't been me.

"Just go away, Kai. Please, just leave me alone," she said, her eyes fluttering open to stare at me. Tears trailed down her cheeks, but I couldn't just go. "Why do you want to torture me like this?"

A growl rumbled in my chest, and my hand tightened a little more. Her nails clawed at my bare forearm, and every red line formed made my cock harder. I pulled my knife from my back pocket and hit the release. The sharp blade glinted in the flashes of lightning from outside.

Raine sucked in a sharp breath and froze as she stared at my hand. I felt her pulse spike under my fingers, and I groaned again.

"Hands above your head, now."

She swallowed hard, the trembling in her body getting worse as she slowly let go of my arm and laid her arms on her pillow. Pressing the blade against her delicate skin, I lowered my head, drew my tongue along her cheek, and licked up every one of her tears.

"These are mine, Tink. They're my payment for your deceitful tongue." She pressed her lips together like she was going to say something, and I arched my brow at her. "You got something to say?" Her nostrils flared, and there was again the flash of something more than fear in her eyes.

My lip curled up. "Undo your jeans."

"No."

"Do it, Tink."

"I'm not helping you. You want it, then take it," Raine said, her voice laced with anger, but it was her eyes that intrigued me. They told another story than the one spilling from her lips.

"You want me, don't you, Tink? You want me to fuck you."

She narrowed her eyes. "You're insane."

"Admit it," I growled.

"Fuck. You."

I shook my head slowly back and forth at her. "Fine, you want to play it that way? I can play."

Raine watched my hand as I slammed my knife down hard into the nightstand, so it stood up straight.

"Just remember, this could've been better for you. What happens next is all on you."

Raine opened her mouth, but before she could get a single word out, I flipped her body over and yanked her arms hard so I could kneel on them and keep her from being a pain in my ass.

"Kai! No, get off me!" she wailed and thrashed, but all she did was rub her ass against my cock.

"Yeah, rub against me just like that."

Raine froze, and I smiled. I grabbed my knife off the nightstand, yanked up hard on the back of her jeans, and stabbed into the material, stripping them down to expose her ass. "Unless you want a knife in your back, I would remain still."

She turned her head and glared over her shoulder at me as I slit the sexy little thong she was wearing and ripped it away. Locking the knife, I put it back in my pocket, just in case she managed to free her hands. She was pesky enough that I could see her going for it.

Fuck, that was hot.

I hadn't been this hard since I was seventeen and wanted to fuck anything with a hole. Not a single piece of clothing or a shower was safe in those later teenage years. Raine made me lose my mind, and I was so into this.

Reluctantly, I lifted myself away from her ass, and with one hand on her back, I quickly undid my leather belt. Raine jerked at the jingle my belt made as it dropped.

"Please, Kai...fuck, please don't do this ag—" She stopped before she said the word, but I knew she was going to say, *again*.

"I'm really sick of hearing you say that. If you're smart, you'll keep those words out of your mouth. Don't tempt me to cut out your tongue," I snarled.

Raine whimpered as I grabbed her hands in one of mine and pinned them behind her back. Unzipping my jeans, I slipped my hand inside and released my cock.

"Goddammit," I groaned, stroking my shaft, and watched as a clear drop of pre-cum dripped from the tip and landed on her sexy little ass. I shivered at the sight, and I pictured getting inside of her. With a hard crack, my hand landed on her ass, and Raine cried out. Her body jerked, and she began to fight all over again.

"Oh, you don't like that? Or do you, and you don't want to admit it?" I smacked that tight little ass again.

"Go screw yourself," Raine bit back as she tried to twist herself enough to look at me.

One eye glittered in the lightning flashing through the clouds outside. It lit up the room like a strobe light in a club. The snarl that pulled up her lip was as much of a turn-on as anything else. I smacked her again and again, her screams getting louder until my hand stung and Raine was reduced to sobbing. Her whole body shook as the tears fell in a steady stream.

"Let's see, shall we?" I mocked and slid my hand between her legs. She tried hard to close her legs to keep me from invading her pussy, but she couldn't with me kneeling between them.

We were long past that. Every cell in my body screamed to fuck her. My finger slipped between her folds, and a jolt flowed throughout my body as I came into contact with her wet little cunt.

"Fuck, Tink. You are kinky. Do you feel that? Feel how wet you are?" I stroked her soft pussy lips and let them slide between my fingers. She didn't answer me, but her rapid breathing told me she was fighting off her enjoyment. "You're a sick little fuck, Tink. You accused me of assaulting you, and now you're wet for me. Not just wet, you're dripping down the inside of your legs wet." I continued to bait her and was mildly impressed when she managed to keep quiet.

On my next downward pass, I slipped my finger into her. Fuck, I was gonna cum all over her ass without getting inside of her. My cock kicked and jerked, the head throbbing for the release that I had neglected for days now. I was too busy between Souls work and stalking Raine to fuck anyone, and my balls were begging for it now.

I stroked my finger in and out of her pussy. Raine turned her head into the pillow and tried to hide her face, but the muscles squeezing around my finger said it all.

Rubbing the wet from my finger all over my cock head, I couldn't wait any longer. My body weight pressed down on Raine as I took her arms and forced them over her head. She struggled but only helped my cock slip off her ass where it had been trapped to nudge her wet pussy entrance.

"I'm going to take from you what you made me pay for," I growled in her ear. Raine sucked in a gasp, her words reduced to an incoherent mumble as she begged me to stop. "You told the world I raped you and then tossed my ass in jail for a decade. This is what you get. I might as well do the crime, right, Tink?"

Grabbing my cock, I slipped the head between her pussy lips and groaned as I thrust balls deep inside her. Her screams and tears only made me want her more.

"Oh, fuck me." I clenched my teeth as her tight walls squeezed around the intrusion. She wiggled from side to side like she was trying to dislodge me as a high-pitched squeal escaped her mouth, but all that did was push me deeper into her body. "Fuck, you feel incredible. So tight, hot, and wet."

"Get. Off. Of. Me," she said, but each word was a pant and ended in a moan.

"You can't fool me, Tink. You're enjoying yourself too much to lie to me," I growled.

Keeping my hands firmly on hers, I bit hard into the soft area at the base of her neck and let loose. Raine screamed and bucked up hard. It was useless to fight me, but I loved that she tried. She pressed her ass up into me and twisted her body. I smirked at her wild horse routine.

"Not happening, Tink. You're not getting away from what you did to me."

Each stroke felt better than the one before. The only thing louder than the slapping of skin as my cock slammed home was her begging me to stop.

Both drove me crazy. The intense pleasure was amplified when I felt her body quake and shudder around my cock. She moaned and buried her face in the pillow. I smirked and let go of her neck, bruised from where I bit her.

"You come for me, you dirty slut? You're so fucking nasty, Tink. There is no way to deny the wetness flooding my cock." I slowed my pace just enough to emphasize my point as I slid almost all the way out and then slipped back into her pussy that, despite the orgasm, was still tight, as if this was her first time. "Mmm," I moaned in her ear. "You make me so hard, Tink. I could get used to fucking your tight hole."

Raine moaned softly, so low that I almost didn't catch it. I knew I could make her cum again. Forcing her to cum for the man she charged with rape seemed like fucking great payback. I closed my eyes and fucked her as hard as I could, with the bed banging into the wall rhythmically.

"I'm never cumming for you again," Raine yelled, but her breathy voice contradicted her words.

I stared at the side of her face as she sucked her lower lip into her mouth. I wanted to taste her but figured that might be too dangerous to attempt. At least right now.

"We'll see about that." I smiled, knowing that she was going to cum again.

I slid my free hand under her body, and she yelped, but I ignored her and found her clit. Picking up my rhythm, I rubbed that little bundle of nerves, and Raine made a noise that had me chuckling as she fought to keep from having the second orgasm.

"Oh, that's it," I said and fucked her in time to my rubbing fingers, and sure enough, her walls quivered around my cock as it slid in and out of her wet heat. "You smell like spring rain and tequila. That's fucking hot, Tink. Were you day drinking at work?"

"Come on," I cooed in her ear as she trembled under me. "Cum again. Show me how much you hate my cock inside of you. How much you hate my big cock filling you up."

"I hate you," she growled.

"You may, but trust me, Tink, when you cum for me again, you're going to hate yourself more than you ever could hate me."

She was right on the edge, and I felt her breath quicken as her walls did their little clenching thing. Raine yelled as she came this time, harder than before, and she arched against my hold as the pleasure gripped her body. I relished how much she would hate herself with each passing second.

"Yeah, that's it. Give it all to me. I want you to remember that no matter what, I can make you cum all over my cock. Doesn't matter that you hate me. I can still make you cum, because you're mine. You always have been." I breathed in her scent, and a shiver raced down my spine.

Picking up my pace, I grunted as her body relaxed and became soft in my hold. Her breathing was heavy, and her face was the picture-perfect snapshot of pure, quenched desire. I pulled out, slid my cock between her ass cheeks, and humped her as my load sprayed from my cock with an intense force that stole my breath. I growled as the first stream landed on her back.

"Ah, fuck," I shouted when the second one found its mark, but I managed to keep myself from letting my entire release spill.

Dipping my cock back into her pussy to get it good and wet, I slipped out and quickly lined up with her ass.

"No! Kai! No!" Raine's panicked yell only made me more determined to fuck her tight little ass.

My cock begged for the rest of its release, like a dog begging for a treat. She was my treat, this ass, her screams. They were all her fucking penance. She wiggled hard, but I pressed into the tight rosebud and moaned as the sensitive head of my cock slowly slipped into her ass.

She wailed, her body tense, as one slow inch at a time, I pushed deeper into her body. She was so fucking tight that I could hardly move, and by the time my pelvis touched her ass, I was sweating. I held still, or I would only get a single thrust in before I exploded.

Raine was crying fresh tears, her body trembling with quiet sobs.

"Holy fuck me, Tink. You have the sweetest ass." I groaned and took a steadying breath, but my cool didn't last. "What were you thinking? That I'd settle for just a single shot at your pussy. No, no, no," I tsked. "That isn't punishment enough for what you did. The pain you caused me, the fear, the betrayal of your words. My life was stripped from me all because of you."

Releasing her hands, I gripped her hips and pulled Raine up until she had her ass in the air at the perfect angle. She cried out as I moved her, but I'd been kind up until now, and I was taking what I wanted. I thrust into her ass hard and shivered with every scream. My cock swelled as I hammered her hard as I could and quickly pulled out.

"Fuck! Yes!" I yelled as my hand slid up and down my cock at a blinding pace. The rest of my climax I'd held off thundered up from my balls, and I came with the same ferocity as the storm that raged outside. Every last drop was squeezed out of my cock before I grabbed her tear-stained cheeks and forced her to look at me.

She whimpered something and then began sobbing hard.

"What did you just say?" I asked, holding her face firm as she tried to pull her chin away. "Say it again," I growled.

"It wasn't you," she cried.

"I fucking know that," I said, stuffing my cock back in my jeans. "I. Fucking. Know. That."

Raine

23

Raine

I blinked, not sure what had happened, but realized that the nightmare was real. Panic gripped me as I heard the rumble of men's voices, but I couldn't make out a single word or who the guys were.

Why had they taken me? Why was Kai letting them take me?

This was how girls ended up sold and overseas as sex slaves. I'd learned about it from the crime shows I liked to watch and, until tonight, had been so careful not to end up in a dangerous position.

Even though the bag was still over my head, I could see through it, but everything was blurry and shadowed, even with the bright lights. Where were we? I tried to move, but my body screamed as the pain of the hits I'd taken registered. My jaw ached, and my side felt like something was broken. The pain was sharp and made it hard to breathe. I was lying on something soft, but it stank like it was old and dusty. My nose wiggled as I held back a sneeze.

Pushing myself up with my arms, I tried to get the stupid material off my head, but it was tied too tight at the back. I could breathe okay, but the fear and the tug around my neck made it feel impossible. Holding my hands close to my face, I saw that my wrists had those awful white zip ties. They were cutting into my wrists and hurt every time I moved. Looking around, I tried to figure out where I was, but nothing seemed even familiar, and everything was shadow blobs through the stupid thing on my head.

The muffled voices were getting louder. "I don't fucking care! Someone needs to *pay, and you need to learn to take control. You're a sap, a doormat, and it's time you were a man."*

That was the man with the disgusting breath. Jerking upright, I didn't care if I could see well or not. I tried to run but screamed as I stepped and realized my legs were tied together. I landed hard on the floor. It was hard and cold and looked all grey, like a factory floor.

"Did you hear that?"

Oh shit! They heard me. I rolled over and sat up, hoping to get back onto what I now realized was a couch, but the door slammed open with a bang.

"Think you're going somewhere?" the man said as he stepped into the room. I couldn't see his features, but the shadow of him with the light at his back told me he was a large man.

Two more men stepped into the room, but they were both wearing black and maybe animal masks. It was hard to tell between the material on my face and the terror trying to take control. What the hell did they want from me?

"Let me go, and I won't tell anyone. I just want to go home," I said, and the man in front of me laughed. "I mean it, I promise."

"Oh, the word of a teenage girl, such a reliable source. How old are you? Fifteen, maybe sixteen? What are you doing in this area, anyway?"

"I came to see Kai fight." I looked at the other two hooded figures and couldn't tell if either was him, but the chances were good. "Kai, tell them we're friends," I said, still hoping he would step in and stop whatever the hell was going on.

The man in the middle bent over, and I could partially see his features. He had a long beard and dark eyes. He smiled, and I shivered. "Oh, that is very good news for me and very bad news for you."

My forehead crinkled in confusion, but it didn't last long as he stepped forward and ordered the other two men to grab me.

"Get off of me! Don't fucking touch me," I yelled, trying to yank my arms and feet away. "Kai, why are you doing this?"

I lifted my eyes to the man stuffing his arms into a leather jacket, and the sobs that overcame me wracked my body. What he just did was...I couldn't even comprehend how I felt about it yet. It was the knowledge that it hadn't been him. I'd sent him to prison, and it hadn't been him.

The men who did this to me were free all this time. I knew two weren't caught, but I never understood why Kai wouldn't name his accomplices. Now I knew. He had no names to give.

Grabbing my pillow, I gripped it to my chest and rocked as I cried. They were the soul-shattering tears that only accompanied having your heart ripped out. I'd cried like this only once before, and it was the day my foster mother told me Kai had taken the deal and was going to prison. It had been the final confirmation that it was him. He didn't try to fight it, didn't say it wasn't him, and didn't want to look me in the eye. I thought he was guilty and too ashamed.

"Why?" I managed to get past my closed-off throat.

"Why what?" His face was hard as he looked at me. Those light blue eyes had always been cool with his bad-boy demeanor, but now they were ice. Nothing of the guy I remembered stared back at me.

"Why did you take the deal? Why didn't you fight the charges? Why didn't you force me to go to court and make this go away?"

Kai stomped toward me, and I instinctively backed up until I hit the wall and had nowhere else to go. I clung to the pillow like a shield, my fingers digging into the softness.

"Why? You want to know why?" he barked out, stopping at the side of the bed, his hands going to his hips.

He looked so different. Even in the poor light, the sweetness was all gone. Tattoos covered his neck, and even more were on his face. He was muscled and looked like he could snap my neck with a flick of his wrist. Yet, I still found myself cataloging every feature. He was still just as sexy, and even though it was crazy after what he'd just done to me, my heart fluttered with him here. I'd never stopped loving him. It was insanity and a loop of self-loathing mixed with the sense of loss and love that had my emotions trapped in a vortex of fucked up.

"Fuck, Tink. I had no money, a stupid public defender who could barely stay awake any time we spoke and who acted like I was lucky not to get life, and then on top of that, the Collinses abandoned me. Me and what army was going up against you in court?" He held his hands out to the side as the thunder rumbled again. The weather seemed to mirror the storm that had just gone through here.

"I could picture it playing out. You on the stand crying about how I molested you in your room, and you ran off to get away, only to have me attack you later and take what I wanted. Are you fucking kidding me? The judge or jury or whoever the fuck was listening was never going to believe me. I was the asshole that came from a bad family. My father was already doing time. I got into fights at school and fought illegally. I had no backup, no support, and no decent character witnesses. You were the only real thing in my life, the only one I trusted, and it was you I would've been fighting."

He leaned against the nightstand and crossed his arms. "The guy representing me told me that you pointed me out dead to rights in a lineup, and I could get twice as long if I didn't take the deal."

I covered my mouth, remembering the day he was talking about so clearly. He'd walked into the room with the two-way glass. I was in a wheelchair and didn't want to but pointed at Kai. He looked confused and scared, like he didn't know why he was there, yet I never saw that as a clue that it wasn't him. All I remembered was the feel of him forcing me face down on that couch as he stole my soul, and all I saw was his tattooed hand holding mine in place. Inches from my eyes, it was burned into my memory. I stared at that bird and cried. The tears made my vision blurry, but I could see it clearly in my mind.

"Why did you lie? Why did you say it was me?" he growled, and I felt the anger building inside of him again. He filled the room with his presence. He always had, but now he didn't just turn heads. I was sure people jumped out of the way when they saw him coming.

"I didn't lie," I said.

He moved so quickly I barely registered it until he had me by the jaw, his fingers once more digging into the sensitive skin. My heart rate tripled in time as he stared me in the eyes.

"It. Was. A. Lie," he growled. "I never fucking touched you, and I will cut your fucking tongue out if you say it one more time."

I swallowed hard as I tried to choose my words. "I didn't think it was a lie." His fingers softened. "I was raped, Kai. That wasn't a lie."

His brow knit together, and his hand dropped away from my jaw. With shaking hands, I moved the pillow and slowly opened the front of my ruined jeans. I pointed to the scars on my stomach and looked away to compose myself as more emotion bubbled to the surface.

"What the fuck?" Kai said.

I jumped like he'd electrocuted me when his finger touched my skin and traced the six distinct lines and the scar from surgery that would never fade. I was stuck with them as a reminder for the rest of my life. A warning that you were never safe and couldn't trust anyone.

I couldn't look at him as I spoke, or I would break down all over again, but I needed to get this out. "I went to the fights to see you. I was upset that I ran out after you kissed me. I had all this shit in my head, stupid teenage crap, but mostly I was upset that I realized you might like me, and I'd ruined it. I thought you only saw me as your foster sister, a kid." I wiped the tears off my face. "I thought you were happy to go off to college and be rid of me. So I had to talk to you. Why it couldn't wait till morning, I don't know. I just needed to see you."

I licked my lips and closed my eyes, hating having to relive this. "When I got there, I snuck in the back, and I'd only been there a few minutes when the shooting started, and everyone was running. I was crushed between bodies; there were so many people, but I managed to get to the stairs that led out. The man behind me had your tattoo. The flower with the bird."

Kai finished tracing the last scar, and I couldn't sit still. Rolling from the bed, I marched over to my closet, peeled off what was left of my clothes, and tossed them aside. Pulling on track pants and a sweatshirt, I knew that no amount of clothes would stop him, but at least I felt better. I needed a shower, but I had to finish this first.

Kai stared at me from the other side of the bed, but I couldn't read the expression on his face. It was too dark, but it felt like his stare penetrated my soul.

Crossing my arms, I tentatively stepped out of the closet, but he said nothing. In fact, he was eerily quiet.

"When I got outside, I saw the man I thought was you running away from all the commotion. He had on a simple black hoodie like you always wore and was around your height, but it was dark, and I was alone and scared. All I could think about was getting to you, my safe person, so I chased after him. He turned down an alley, and when I went down it..." I stopped and pulled the thick sweatshirt tighter like that would keep all the terrible things that had already happened from happening again.

"There were three of them. They all wore hooded sweatshirts, so I never saw their faces clearly, but he had your tattoo and was where you said you would be. I...I'm sorry," I said and covered my mouth, stifling the sob.

"What happened?" he asked, his voice as cold as his eyes. I looked at the bed.

"They put a black bag on my head, one of those ones you see in movies. I could sort of see, but not well, and they hit me until I passed out. I regained consciousness in some office. I don't know where. I hurt everywhere, and my hands and ankles were tied. They...um...they took turns with me until..." I cleared my throat. "Until they couldn't get it up anymore." My body trembled, and I wanted to yell and scream and tell myself to stop it. Instead, I paced across my small bedroom.

"The one I thought was you held his hands in front of my face when he was holding me." I stopped pacing to demonstrate what I meant. "My face was pressed down, and the only thing I could see the entire time was his right hand. When they were through, the leader did this." I pointed to my stomach. "They had to do two surgeries to fix the damage. The doctor said he didn't know how I survived and made it clear I probably should've bled out." My eyes flicked up to his. "I didn't want to live, though. He kept saying I was lucky. I didn't feel lucky. I felt anything but lucky." My eyes pleaded with him for forgiveness.

"Kai, I thought my best friend, the one person in this world I loved with my whole heart, did the unthinkable and left me for dead." I gave up on trying to hold back the tears. It was impossible as they traveled in streams down my cheeks.

His face seemed just as fierce as I walked around the bed, but I didn't feel the same explosive anger. Like a balloon letting out air, it had simply floated away. Reaching out, I took his hands and stared down at the tattoos that now lined them.

"If all this happened, why are you so certain it wasn't me?"

I looked into his eyes and silently begged for forgiveness.

"Wrong hand," I said, looking down at the back of his left hand and the tattoo. I tapped the bird and flower image that I'd never forget. "Wrong hand," I said again and choked back a sob. "Wrong fucking hand," I yelled and dropped to the floor. I screamed like I was possessed as I slammed my fist down on the old floorboards.

Looking up at Kai, I didn't know what I expected to see, but that eyebrow lift and the contempt in his eyes was not it. My heart was breaking in two, and he seemed completely unaffected.

"So what you're telling me is that you put me away for ten years based on a tattoo," Kai said.

My mouth fell open, and I searched for the words to defend myself, but my mind was stuck in neutral and spinning its wheels.

"Kai I...."

He squatted down so he could stare me in the eye. I felt like we'd traveled back in time. The way he looked at me right now was the same look he gave me when I said something he considered stupid. I tried to turn away from that intense stare.

"Don't you dare look away from me," he said calmly, but it felt like he was screaming in my ear. "Five years. I'd known you for five years. In all that time, did I strike you as a rapist?" I opened my mouth, but he held up a finger. "That was a fucking rhetorical question. No, I know I didn't. I also don't remember ever hurting you. In fact, I always stuck up for you and beat the shit out of bullies for you. I remember bringing you cake, taking you to the movies, and making you smile when you got a bad grade. I held you when you cried or had a bad dream. I played board games with you, and we made plans to see the world." He paused, and the look he gave me lanced my heart with more precision than any weapon.

"What I know is that you were my best friend, and you didn't stop for even a moment to consider that it wasn't me. I would've thought you, out of anyone, knew me." He stood, and my eyes followed him, unable to look away.

"I guess I was wrong," he said softly and veered around me to march out the door.

I heard the heavy thump of his boots on my stairs and then the slamming of the front door. I didn't think that I could hurt any more than I already did. I didn't know there was another level to the torture that attacked me all these years and made my body tremble, but I was wrong. Something far more powerful now gripped me in its clutches as it tried to rip out my soul.

I now understood guilt.

Snake

24

Kaivan

My bike roared to life, and I sat there, letting the unrelenting rain crash down on me as if it would somehow wash away or roll back time. Pulling onto the road, I flew through the rising water that no one else would be stupid enough to drive a motorcycle in. It didn't matter that I could hardly see where I was going. As if I was on autopilot, I found myself pulling into the Lost Souls parking lot.

My hands gripped the handles so hard that they shook, and my knuckles cracked. I stared at the chain-link fence, water running into my eyes, and I felt nothing and everything. My life was one big game of fucked. There wasn't a single thing that I could remember that hadn't been painted with a toxic brush.

A terrifying rage was consuming my body and spreading at a rapid pace. The temptation to get drunk, pull my gun, and go on a rampage was erotic and enticing to my battered heart. I would never admit this out loud, but for the first time, I understood Chase Mathers and his streak of destruction.

It was only as I stared into Raine's heartbroken eyes that I realized I'd been living with no real emotion in my soul. My heart had blackened with my time in prison until I was numb, and nothing bothered me. My only real emotion had been anger, but now...now I was fucking feeling them all, and all at once. Shock, sadness, loss, betrayal, love...fuck, I still loved her.

I fucking hated to look into her face, knowing that she didn't have enough faith in me to at least speak to me before she accused me of a crime I didn't commit. But the thought of her being assaulted like that and left for dead enraged me even more. The terror in her eyes when she stared at my knife was real. The image of someone stabbing her six times made my blood run cold, and it had nothing to do with the cold water soaking me.

There was only so much you could take before you snapped, and tonight Raine filled my cup until it spilled over the edge. She'd inadvertently opened all the floodgates in my soul, and I didn't like any of the emotions pouring out.

"Hey, man, what are you doing?"

I jumped and almost fell off my bike as Wilder spoke from right beside me. "Geez-us fucking shit balls, man."

I glared at the guy as my heart restarted. What the hell was he wearing? Wilder looked ready to go deep-sea diving to attack a submarine. He was wearing a solid black outfit that was molded to every part of his body. There was more of Wilder's cock outlined than I'd ever wanted to see. He had weapons strapped to every inch of his body and was sporting night vision goggles on his face. He looked ridiculous and terrifying at the same time.

"Do you think you could give a guy a little warning instead of sneaking up on him in the dark when it's pouring rain?" I growled.

He tilted his head as if he were thinking about the concept before lifting a shoulder in a casual shrug. "But then you'd know I was coming."

"Kind of the point," I mumbled. "Is there a reason for you coming over here and giving me a heart attack?" I looked around the lot and then back to Wilder. "How did you get over here?"

"Oh, I just jumped the fence. I do it all the time," he said like that was the most normal thing in the world.

I turned to look up at the tall ass fence with the barbwire on top and shook my head. I suddenly had the urge to put this guy in a max security prison just to see how long it took before he was sitting on their front lawn doing yoga.

"I was wanting to know if you had any other tips to woo a girl?"

My brow rose. To woo a girl? Did he really just ask me that? At the moment, I was the worst person in the world to ask. He could pick the homeless guy on the street and get a better response than I could muster.

"I'm afraid to ask this, but what do you mean by woo?"

The rain suddenly stopped as if God or whoever was up there decided to flip the switch. I wiped my face off and wasn't sure if being able to see Wilder better was a good idea.

"I would prefer for the female of my interest not to scream and cry hysterically in my presence."

I bit my lip as I wondered what the fuck he was doing to some poor girl and then decided I really didn't want to know. Not my circus or, in this case, not my amusement park.

"I suggested that we watch television, but she didn't seem interested in watching anything."

"What did you put on for the two of you to watch?" I asked.

"Her friends," he said, and the corner of his mouth tugged up. That was as much of a smile as I'd ever seen on his face.

"Okay, well..." My brain screeched to a halt. "Did you just say watch her friends? Do you mean the show *Friends*?"

"No, her actual friends. You know, the ones from the sorority." I stared at him, not saying anything as I tried to piece together what code he was speaking. "See," Wilder said.

He pulled his phone out of somewhere extremely too close to his cock, which was disturbingly long as it traveled down his leg. Shit, man, wrap that around your leg or something.

Reluctantly, I took the phone from his hand and almost dropped it. One of the girls on the many little screens stripped and shook her tits for one of the other girls as they laughed and then started to make out.

"What the fuck?" I whispered, looking over all the small images of people. I found Naomi in her sorority room and held back a laugh, watching her. She was sitting cross-legged on the floor with a bag of potato chips in one hand, a jar of pickles in the other, and a massive container of peanut butter between her legs. The food was odd enough, but the bawling, like she was horrified by what she was eating, was classic.

Her friend Ava chatted enthusiastically and laughed like she was oblivious to Naomi's troubles, which made my night just a little bit better.

"Why do you have surveillance on the girls at the sorority," I asked, spotting the blonde, Lane, that Roach was obsessing over. She was brushing out her long hair as she sat on her bed with nothing more than a sports bra, flowy shorts, and bunny slippers on.

Oh fuck. Roach would be stealing Wilder's phone and jerking off to her every five seconds if he knew about this. My lip curled up. I so wasn't telling him. Fucking with the guy was going to be so much sweeter.

"I'm not really supposed to say, but I like you, Snake. You're my only friend," he said.

I was oddly torn between yelling what the fuck, driving away, and never returning or wanting to say aw. Yup, I'd definitely been hanging around the insanity too long, and here I thought prison was bad.

"Chase asked me to keep an eye on them and make sure that they were safe from Jax," he whispered, and looked around at the empty parking lot. Of course, I had to look as well, just to be sure.

"But Jax is dead. He has been for months," I said.

"I have not been told to cease my surveillance, so I will continue until told otherwise. It is my duty as a soldier."

So he really was a soldier. I mean, I figured, but that was the first time he'd said it out loud. I shook my head in wonder and tried to imagine what it was like inside Wilder's mind. Was it all just him? Was it PTSD? Was it both?

"Do you have anyone else you're watching?" I asked, wishing I could see his eyes instead of staring at the large goggles on his face that made him look like an alien.

"No."

I nodded.

"Well...no, unless you consider tracking people watching."

Reaching over, he touched the screen, and the next thing to appear was a bunch of little dots in an array of colors. Some were labeled as important buildings and landmarks, but it was the little floating bubbles with names in them that made me want to laugh. It was terrifying that I'd already wondered if he was keeping an eye on us.

All the Lost Souls members were red. There was a pin for Roach, Beast, Mannix, Tanner, and Chase. There was a pin for almost all the Lost Souls members, but there were others. A half dozen people that I didn't know were labeled in different colors.

Chase was definitely still in Canada, so we weren't going to see the fucker for a while. At least he hadn't lied to Beast. I had my doubts and couldn't bring myself to trust him.

"I don't see a pin for me," I commented, and he smiled.

"I removed your tracker. We're friends, and I don't track friends."

I decided to get the conversation back on the rails. "So other than her friends, what else did you show your love interest to watch?" Wilder screwed up his face. "Love?" he scoffed. "I do not love. She is merely interesting, and I enjoy observing her. Much how one enjoys watching animals at the zoo."

I bit my lip. Such a way with words he had. No wonder this poor girl was screaming. "I have a number of mission videos, but she didn't seem to like those, and the only other thing I have is a snuff video. That also didn't make her smile."

I needed a fucking Academy Award for being able to keep my face straight. I really wanted to know why he had a snuff film. The question was on the tip of my tongue, but I swallowed it down. That seemed like a very dangerous question.

I cleared my throat. "Well, it has been my experience that it's best to ask her what she would enjoy watching. She may like romantic comedies or action films, or straight-up horror. I also suggest offering her favorite snack and drink while you watch the movie." He opened his mouth, and I just knew what he was going to ask and cut him off. "Just ask her. She will tell you what she likes, and if she doesn't, you can grab snacks for her, like popcorn or chocolate-covered peanuts," I clarified. I could suddenly picture him offering her army rations or something.

Wilder rubbed his chin. "Once again, you have offered me good advice. I enjoy these chats." Wilder reached out and grabbed my shoulder, and I stared at his hand, trying to decide whether this newfound friendship was a good thing or not. "I'm learning so many new things from you."

Wilder turned toward the fence, and before he could do whatever acrobatics he planned to scale back over, I called out to him.

"Hey, Wilder?"

He looked over his shoulder. "What happened to all your other friends?"

"Oh, they died."

"Well, if that wasn't the most comforting thought," I mumbled as Wilder leaped onto an old crate and flipped over the top of the fence, landing without a sound. He stood and sprinted off into the dark. Great, I lived beside Batman.

I needed a new fucking life.

I'se The B'y that builds the boat and
I'se The B'y that sails her and
I'se The B'y that catches the fish and
Brings 'em home to Liza

I belted at the top of my lungs and held the round of...whatever in the air. Some liquid sloshed out and soaked my hand, but caring about shit like that was beyond me. Getting shit-faced was the most logical thing to do in my predicament.

Hip-yer-partner Sally Tibbo
Hip-yer-partner Sally Brown
Fogo, Twillingate, Morton's Harbour,
All around the circle

What else does one do when one found out that you spent ten years in prison for no good reason? I mean, I always knew that I'd been in prison for no reason. It wasn't like my cock had jumped off my body and fucked Raine before reattaching itself. The thing was, when I thought she was being vindictive and hateful like we'd been at war, I could accept that. Two enemies were facing off, but the reality was worse. Raine sent me to jail based on a tattoo—a tattoo on a board on the wall of my foster father's friend's tattoo parlor.

Sods and rinds to cover your flake,
Cake and tea for supper
Cod fish in the spring of the year,
Fried in maggoty butter

I looked down at my hand and the bird and flower tattoo and thought about cutting my hand off. Would it help? No, but maybe I could burn the thing off or slice it off. Glancing out at the room of bikers keeping their distance from me, I smiled and then yelled.

"Come on fuckers! Sing with me." I managed to pull myself up onto the bar, and the bartender ran for cover as I continued to sing and kick the glasses off the top.

Hip-yer-partner Sally Tibbo
Hip-yer-partner Sally Brown

Crash. The first glass hit the wall and shattered into a million little pieces. Why was it that everyone else could let loose and party and act like an asshole, but when I did, they stared at me like I'd sprouted horns on my head? Then again, maybe I had. I turned to look in the large mirror behind the bar, and the image was fuzzy, but there were no horns.

Fogo, Twillingate, Morton's Harbour,
All around the circle
I don't want your maggoty fish
They're no good for winter

Crash. Another glass shattered, and two guys standing around dove away from the airborne projectile. Laughing hard, I raised my glass, toasting those in the room, and then took a big swig and decided to chug the rest of it down. It burned on the way down like it was trying to burn the sin right out of me, but there was no hope of that.

I'd been born and bathed in the blood of sin. I was created by assholes, fucked over by assholes, and now I was the biggest asshole of the bunch.

Well, I can buy as good as that,
Way down in Bonavista!

I paused in my rendition of the song as the rest of the lyrics were lost to my fuzzy brain, so I just started over. Pulling my gun, I held it over the tattoo on my hand, and everyone scattered.

I'se The B'y that builds the boat and
I'se The B'y that sails her and
I'se The B'y that catches the fish and
Brings 'em home to Liza

"Whoa, there, Snake!" I stared down at Roach. His eyes were wide, his hands up in the air like he was surrendering.

"Where be da po po?" I asked and struck what I thought was a damn good gun slinger pose with my legs spread and the gun out in front of me.

"Get him off of there," one of the guys yelled.

"Fuck off, man, can't you see I'm singing here?" I yelled and turned in his direction.

"Shut up, Sparky, unless you want a hole in the head," Roach yelled.

"Yeah, a fuckin' hole in the head. What he said." I looked back to where Roach had been standing, and he was gone. "Where did he go?" I asked, amazed that Roach had leaned to disappear.

"I'm right here, bud," Roach said from my other side. He was now on the bar with me. I looked between him and the place he'd just been.

"How'd you do that?" I smiled. "Teach me. I'd like to learn how to disappear."

"Sure, once you give me the gun, and we get down." Roach held out his hand, and I stared at it with wide eyes as it went in and out of focus.

"Dude, ya need to stop moving it first," I grumbled.

"For fuck's sake." Roach touched my arm and slid his hand all the way down until he reached my hand.

"You just wanted to feel my muscles, perv," I said to Roach.

"Yup, that is definitely what I was doing," he agreed as he took the gun from my hand. "All right, let's get down."

"But I was singing for the audience. They loved my song," I said. "I was just about to dance. Wanna see me do the moon?"

"Okay, you're cut off. We don't need to see your ass. Come on down, and we can dance all the way to your house." Roach jumped to the ground, which seemed really far away.

"What does my ass have to do with a moon?" I asked, confused. "Look, I'll show ya." I went to walk backward like Michael Jackson, but Roach grabbed my leg.

"Down! Right the fuck now," he ordered.

"Guess I found the po po," I mumbled and decided to sit down before making the final daredevil leap off the bar. "Rawr!" I yelled as I landed and lifted my arms like I was going to attack him.

"What the fuck was that?" Roach asked.

"I'm a monster," I said. "Isn't it obvious?" I turned to the sitting area of the clubhouse. "Fuck, man, why are all you fuckers running in circ…"

Avro

25

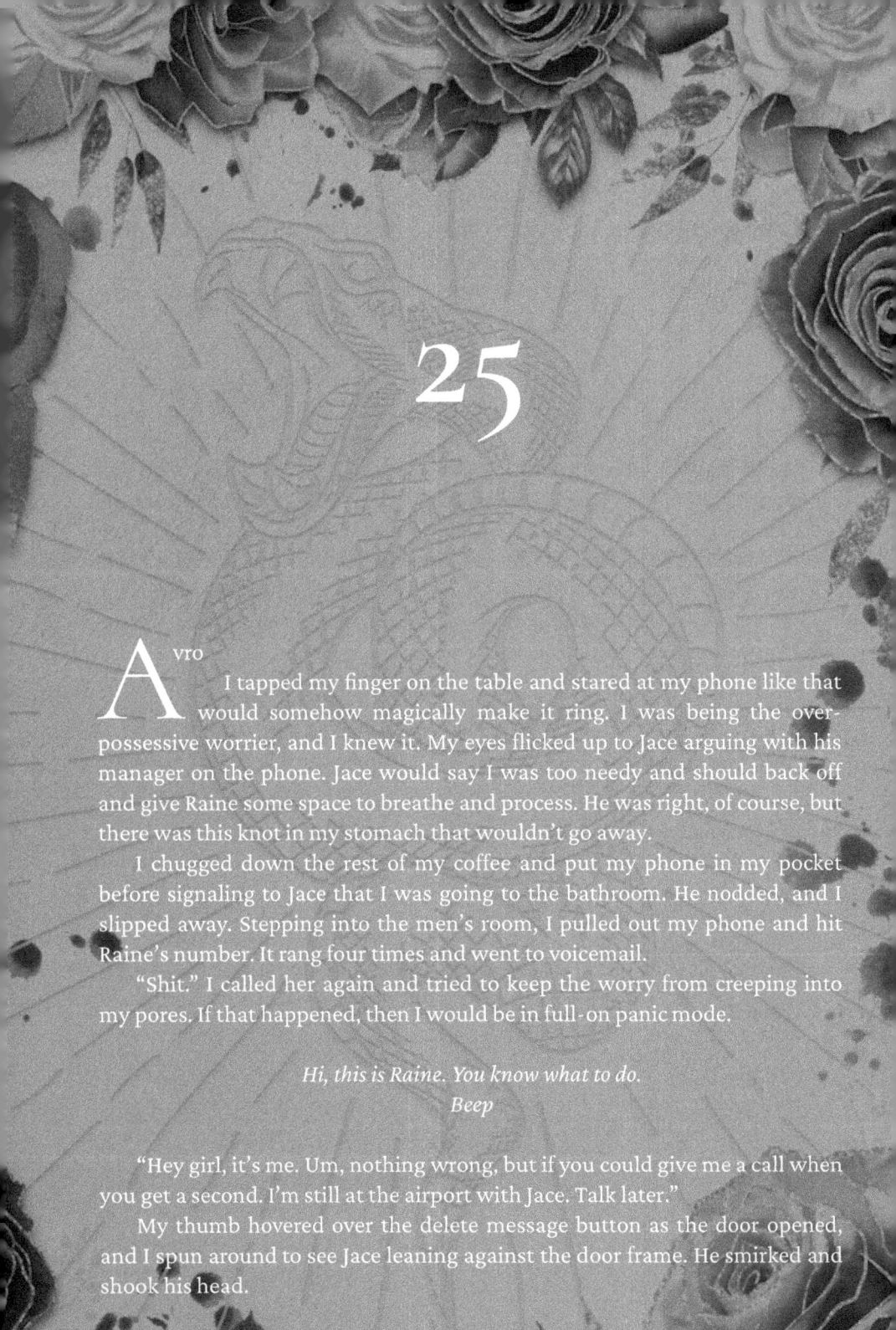

Avro

I tapped my finger on the table and stared at my phone like that would somehow magically make it ring. I was being the over-possessive worrier, and I knew it. My eyes flicked up to Jace arguing with his manager on the phone. Jace would say I was too needy and should back off and give Raine some space to breathe and process. He was right, of course, but there was this knot in my stomach that wouldn't go away.

I chugged down the rest of my coffee and put my phone in my pocket before signaling to Jace that I was going to the bathroom. He nodded, and I slipped away. Stepping into the men's room, I pulled out my phone and hit Raine's number. It rang four times and went to voicemail.

"Shit." I called her again and tried to keep the worry from creeping into my pores. If that happened, then I would be in full-on panic mode.

Hi, this is Raine. You know what to do.
Beep

"Hey girl, it's me. Um, nothing wrong, but if you could give me a call when you get a second. I'm still at the airport with Jace. Talk later."

My thumb hovered over the delete message button as the door opened, and I spun around to see Jace leaning against the door frame. He smirked and shook his head.

"You just couldn't resist, could you?"

I opened my mouth and looked at the phone, my brain scrambling to find some excuse that wouldn't make me sound like a total loser.

"Don't bother lying. I know you tried calling her. The stench of guilt is wafting off you."

"Shit, I just...fuck, I have a bad feeling. I can't explain it," I said as Jace walked toward me.

"How is it that someone so fucking sexy is so insecure?" My face heated with the compliment that also happened to be an insult. Jace wrapped his arm around my shoulder and forced me to turn and look into the mirror. "Look at yourself. You're lickable."

I smiled and shook my head. "You're also crazy. I'm not worried about her not wanting to be with us." Jace lifted his eyebrows. "Okay, I may be a little worried about that, but I don't know...I just have a bad feeling. Like one of those nervous, I can't explain it, feelings."

Jace didn't say anything as he walked over to the urinal, relieved himself, and washed his hands with the overly orange-smelling soap. I knew he was thinking. He got all introverted when he was deep in thought.

"Could it be the storm," Jace finally said. He tossed the paper towel into the air and made a little swooshing sound as it sank into the garbage. "Still got it." His eyes turned back to mine, and I shrugged.

"I don't know. Maybe, I guess."

"Avro, at some point, you'll have to find a way to stop letting your uncle control you. The man is dead, and he's not coming back from the grave to attack you. If he does, I'll be fucking running right beside you. That's straight-up *Walking Dead* territory."

I rolled my eyes at Jace. "I don't think he's springing from the grave. I just still get edgy about storms." I crossed my arms. "Besides, trauma is different for everyone, Jace. I don't choose to be like this."

Those silver eyes met mine, and I knew the rant was coming. "Avro, are you really wanting to start the laundry list argument? I may not have had a shitty uncle, but I fucking know pain and fear."

"Oh my god. You are so different from me. You're pedal to the floor, no looking back, take on the world, nothing bothers you for long," I said and then looked at the door as someone opened it.

The orderly with his bucket and mop stopped and stared between us, looking like we were ready to come to blows. Without a word, he backed out, and the door closed behind him.

"The point is, I'm not like you. I'm never going to be like you, and as much as I would love for storms not to bother me, they may always bother me. Are you going to call me out on it for the next fifty years?"

Jace took a deep breath, and the sound seemed so loud in the quiet bathroom. "I'm like that because I have to be." He paced away from me.

"What are you saying, Jace?" He didn't say anything as he stared at the door. "Jace?"

Jace whipped around, and his eyes narrowed in anger. "I'm like this because I'm always the rock. I have been since we were eight years old, and except for...well, you know the shit, I've always had your back and taken on the world for both of us." His words were a punch to the gut, and I took a step back. "Now, I know that I chose to be, just how I chose to be there when shit went sideways at school or home or with your uncle or afterward and then every night since."

"So you're saying I'm a burden?" My anger dangerously mixed like a cocktail in my system.

"No, never a burden, but Avro, let's be real for a moment. From the day we met until today, when have you been the rock in our relationship? Forget my family shit." He held up his hands. "Aside from those few months where I will admit that you and my music were the only things that got me through. Aside from that, when? Did you comfort me when we did what we did with your uncle? Have you spent any time since wondering how that night affected me?"

I hated that he was calling me out like this. Our life had felt perfect for so long, a fairy tale that others never got to live. Now Jace was poking at that image in my mind. Water was leaking out, and it was supposed to be my fault? It was true that I'd never spoken of that night again or asked him how he was, but we'd promised not to mention it. I thought I'd been there for him as much as he was for me, like we balanced one another out.

"Fine, don't say anything. I'm going to go sleep on the plane." Jace had the door open and was gone before I even got my stubborn lips to move.

I followed him out into the small area before the glass doors and the private jet sitting in the hangar. I could see Jace marching for the plane, but I needed a moment. Sitting at the table, I stared at the phone that refused to ring and ease my worry. As the rumble of thunder outside grew louder, the memories of that night came back to me.

"Mom, you know I hate camping. Why are you forcing me to go?" I asked, dragging my back duffel behind me like a ball and chain.

Camping felt like a death sentence. It had been the same way my entire life, yet every year my mom made the same plans with the same people to do the same things I hated. It took us forever to get there, and everyone wanted to sing and play games that made me want to cry. I was thirteen. Singing "Ninety-Nine Bottles of Beer on the Wall" or playing Eye Spy was no longer fun.

I just wasn't the type who liked to be out in the wilderness with bugs, snakes, and whatever else. I hated that there was no good way to charge my phone unless my Uncle Martin and Aunt Tilly let me use their truck. I hated that the only way to bathe for the entire week was in the little springs. Most of all, I hated leaving Jace behind, but my mom insisted that this was strictly family time.

"Alex, you're going to be going off to college in a few years, and you will have these memories with your family for the rest of your life," Mom said, her face glowing as she smiled.

As I suspected, it was seventeen hours of hell before we reached the campsite.

"Alex, help your cousin set up her tent," Mom said, but Courtney glared at me. You couldn't find two more opposite people, and for reasons I'd never figured out, Courtney hated me.

Doing as I was asked, I wandered over to Courtney. "Hey, did you want help with your tent?"

"If I wanted help, I would ask for it," she bit back.

I went to turn away but stopped and instead took a step closer. My voice lowered so only she could hear. "What the hell is your problem with me? I rarely see you, and I've never done anything to you, so why the fuck are you like this?"

Courtney looked around, making sure that the adults were engrossed in their own conversation. "I may only see you three times a year, but I can't get out from under your shadow. When we were little, all my parents talked about was you and how much they wished they had a boy, a boy just like Alex. Then it was how academically smart you are and how you'll get a full scholarship to whatever school you want. You couldn't stop there, though. Nope, the one thing I had was soccer, and I was amazing, but the moment you picked up a basketball and made the senior team, I lost that too." Courtney took a step closer. "How many games do you think my dad made after that? None. Why? 'Cause he was too busy going to your games to support you."

She put her hands on her hips and glared at me, her eyes narrowed into slits. "All I hear is how amazing you are and how they wished I could be more like you. If he weren't my dad, I'd say he fucking likes you."

"First, how is any of that my fault? Second, that's fucking disgusting, like I'd want to fuck your dad, and lastly, all it says is your parents are jerks," I said and

realized that it was louder than I intended. I looked over my shoulder, and four sets of eyes stared at us. Shit.

"Huh, looks like you might have just dropped down a peg there, Alex. Thanks," Courtney whispered and walked away.

The rest of the week was awkward. It was obvious that everyone had heard, and yet in our family, you didn't 'air your grievances,' as my mother would say. My aunt and uncle took turns glaring at me, but Courtney was miraculously much nicer. Fuck, I hated camping.

Thankfully, we'd reached the last day, and because it was storming so hard, it gave me the perfect excuse to remain in my tent while the others took turns hanging out. The storm was getting nasty, and my tent blew around me like a tarp. The rain that drowned out everything continued without any end in sight. We would've floated away by now if we'd still been back home.

J: You back tomorrow?

A: Yeah, thank god.

J: You wanna hang out when you get back?

A: Not sure what time I'll be back, but I'll text you.

J: Cool. Check ya later.

A: Night.

I turned off the phone and placed it in my bag for safekeeping and realized just how dark it had gotten. I didn't know what time it was when I was woken up. It was still dark outside, and the thunder rumbled with the driving rain.

I hadn't heard my tent flap opening or registered the blanket disappearing until hands gripped my sleeping pants and tugged them down. My half-asleep, muddled mind made me think it was Jace until a hand gripped the back of my neck.

All the sleepy fuzz dissipated, and my eyes snapped open, but I couldn't see who had me.

"Get off me," I said and tried to push myself up off the ground.

A heavy weight pressed down on my back, and hot breath fanned my ear. I was fit for my age, but as hard as I tried, I couldn't move. My heart was racing wildly, and I wanted to yell for help, but something was stuffed into my mouth when I opened it to scream.

"You're a disrespectful little prick." I froze at the sound of my uncle's voice. This wasn't some stranger that had wandered into our campsite. This was someone I knew.

"I'm sorry," I mumbled, but he didn't listen. "Courtney made me angry. I didn't mean to..."

"Shut the fuck up, and before you go squealing to your parents, they'll never *believe you. They'll throw you out of the house, disown you for making trouble, and make sure that all your friends and family know exactly what you are...a cock lover."*

I gulped down the panic of what his words meant, and my body trembled with the spike of adrenaline. He held me down harder, my face painfully pressing into the pillow so that I could feel the rough ground beneath the thin tarp bottom. I struggled to breathe and kicked out, thrashing around, trying to break free of his grip. At six-five, he was a big man, but I'd never seen my uncle as a threat until this moment. As he forced my legs apart, all I could see was his glare from earlier in the day.

How had I missed the malice in his eyes?

I whimpered as his naked cock pressed down on my ass. I knew what was coming. My brain had revolted against the idea that this could happen, but it was hard to deny when you felt the reality against your skin.

The reality was that someone I loved and trusted could do this to me. That someone I thought was family would hurt me like this. But as he took what he wanted, and the tears fell, I didn't know if I could ever trust anyone again.

Thunder crashed and made me jump from my seat. I looked down at my shaking hands and then toward the plane as the lights flashed. There was only one person I learned to trust with my whole being after that day. Well, now two, but only one of them was here.

Marching across the small terminal, I pushed open the doors to the private jet and jogged up the stairs. I expected Jace to be asleep, but he was lying in bed writing in his songbook.

As soon as he looked over, I knew that he was right. I'd leaned on him from the moment I got back from that camping trip and never stopped.

"I'm sorry." Jace lowered the book. "You're right. I never asked you if you were okay. I figured you'd tell me if you weren't, and it was selfish of me to think that just because you were the rock I needed, you weren't suffering."

"Pfft, he got what he deserved," Jace said, pointing to the other side of the bed. I smirked.

"True, but still." I sat down and kicked off my sneakers before stretching out.

"You're not the only one that needs to apologize. I don't do the sharing thing well, and I find it easier to let you lean on me than share, but I can't get mad when you did exactly what I expected you to do."

We stared at the ceiling as I tried to picture living like this all the time, traveling the world and sleeping in the jet with him. The moment I thought about it, Raine's face floated into my mind, and my chest ached. No, I didn't want to leave her, but I didn't want Jace to go without me, either. I felt like I was in a trap of my own making.

"What were you writing?" I asked.

"New ballad. Was kinda thinking of doing a love song about being torn between two people," Jace said, turning his head to look at me.

"Is the song for me or about me?" I smiled, feeling like he'd hit way too close to the mark.

"I guess we will have to see once it's done," Jace said.

I pushed myself up and stared down into his eyes. "You know I love you, right? Don't ever think that has changed."

"What happens if I say I have my doubts?" Jace ran his tongue along his lip, and that one little act had my blood heating and my cock twitching.

"You may need to be reassured that I do still love you. I wouldn't want you flying off and having any reservations," I said, laying my hand on his stomach. His abs flexed under my touch.

"Is that so?" Jace wrapped his hand around the back of my neck. "Then I think I have many, many doubts."

I leaned down, and our lips met, as potent as the first time we kissed. I really did love make-up sex.

Snake

26

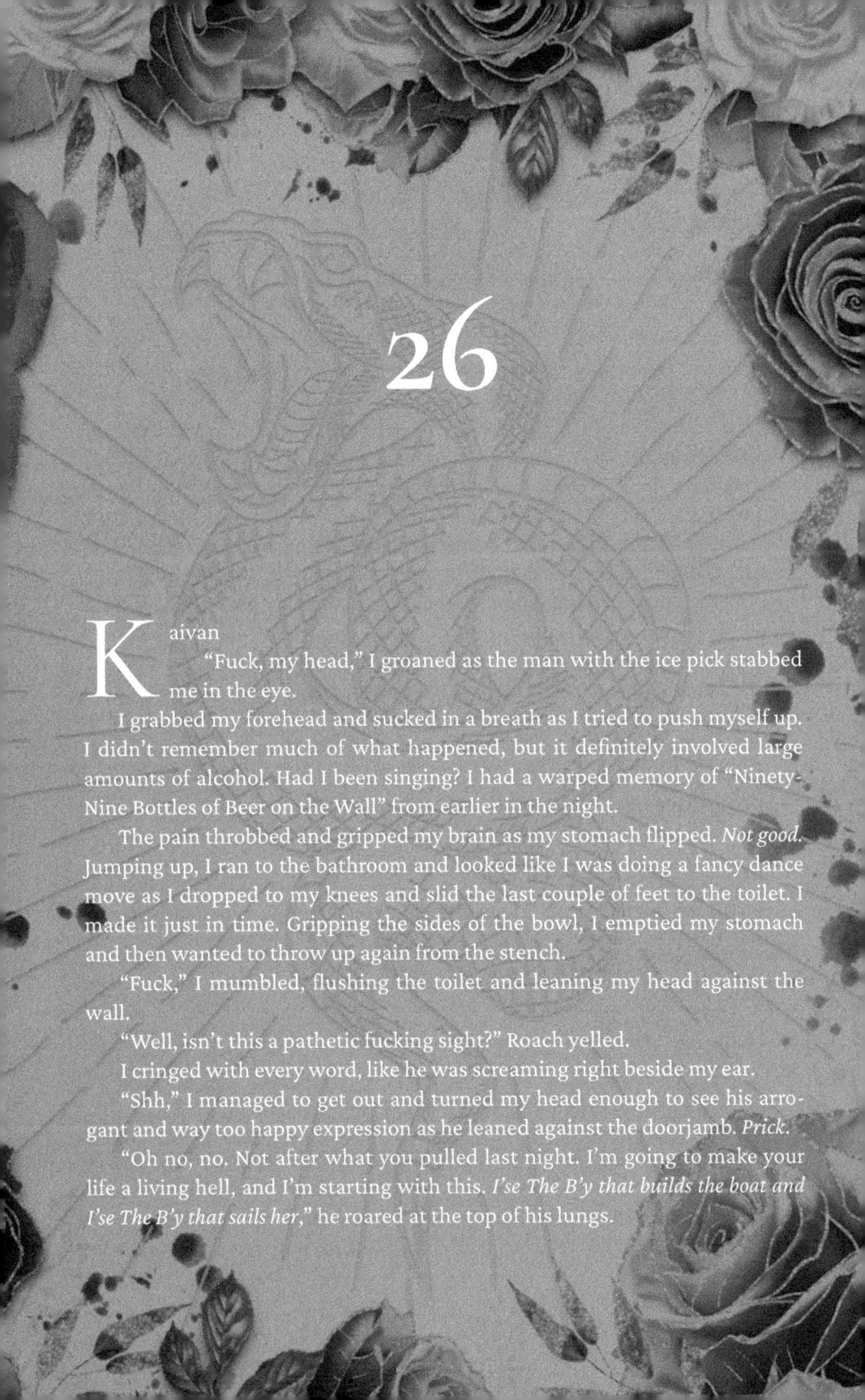

Kaivan

"Fuck, my head," I groaned as the man with the ice pick stabbed me in the eye.

I grabbed my forehead and sucked in a breath as I tried to push myself up. I didn't remember much of what happened, but it definitely involved large amounts of alcohol. Had I been singing? I had a warped memory of "Ninety-Nine Bottles of Beer on the Wall" from earlier in the night.

The pain throbbed and gripped my brain as my stomach flipped. *Not good.* Jumping up, I ran to the bathroom and looked like I was doing a fancy dance move as I dropped to my knees and slid the last couple of feet to the toilet. I made it just in time. Gripping the sides of the bowl, I emptied my stomach and then wanted to throw up again from the stench.

"Fuck," I mumbled, flushing the toilet and leaning my head against the wall.

"Well, isn't this a pathetic fucking sight?" Roach yelled.

I cringed with every word, like he was screaming right beside my ear.

"Shh," I managed to get out and turned my head enough to see his arrogant and way too happy expression as he leaned against the doorjamb. *Prick.*

"Oh no, no. Not after what you pulled last night. I'm going to make your life a living hell, and I'm starting with this. *I'se The B'y that builds the boat and I'se The B'y that sails her,*" he roared at the top of his lungs.

I groaned and cowered away from the noise, praying that the wall would swallow me.

"I'm going to kill you when I can stand," I said, slowly pushing myself to my feet.

Roach laughed. He turned on the water faucet, and like a homing beacon, I followed the noise and braced my hands against the counter as I let my stomach settle.

"How much did I drink? Feels like I tried to chug everything in the clubhouse," I said, splashing my face with some water and rinsing my mouth out before that felt like too much exercise.

"You drank more than I've ever seen you drink, and there was no sipping. You started the night drinking from a bottle of whiskey, and things didn't improve from there," Roach said as he slipped an arm around my waist and helped me back out of the bathroom.

I would never tell the guy this, but I'd always appreciated Roach's friendship. He could be as annoying as the bug he was nicknamed after, but I always knew he had my back, and in this world, that went a long way. He helped me sit, and I realized it was my living room couch. I had no memory of making it home and hated that sensation. I'd lost control of so many things in my life that I refused to put myself in a position where I had to rely on others. I did that last night—just another thing I could blame on Raine.

"Here," Roach said and held out a bag and coffee. I peered into the greasy bag, and my stomach rolled as if telling me to go fuck myself. "Eat one. You need something to sop up the shit in your stomach."

Even though I didn't want to, I pulled one of the breakfast burritos out of the bag and slowly unwrapped it. I stared at it, and it stared back. I think we were officially in a standoff.

"All right, spill." Roach flopped down on my powder blue recliner. He looked ridiculous, and I wondered if I looked just as strange when I sat there. As if reading my mind, Roach stared down at the chair. "Huh, surprisingly comfortable."

"You want to analyze anything else while you're in here? How about the position of the television, perhaps?" I took a bite of the burrito and swallowed, and when it didn't hit an immediate ejection button, I kept eating.

"Nope. All I want to know is why you've been an asshole for days. What, or should I say, who has got you acting like an asshole dipped in something sour and rolled in shit? You've been practically hostile, so I'm not leaving until you talk." He crossed his arms, and I wanted to punch his annoying face.

"I'm fine," I said. Stubbornly, I tried to push myself to my feet, but that wasn't happening. The room spun, and the band began to play in my brain again.

"Oh yeah, you look real fine." Roach leaned forward and hit me with a hard stare. "Talk, or I'm going to sing the Barney song at the top of my lungs, over and over." His lips curled up.

"That is the stupidest and most horrifying threat I've ever heard," I said, and we both smirked.

The coffee was from the shop I liked. I popped the lid off and took a huge gulp before meeting Roach's gaze.

"You're not going to leave, are you?"

"Not a fucking chance. I've given you space to deal with your shit, but instead of getting over whatever crawled up your ass, you're getting worse." He dug around in his pocket and pulled out his phone. I heard my voice and cringed before I took the phone from his hands. I watched myself standing on a bar waving a gun and singing a song I didn't even know I knew.

Hitting stop, then delete, I tossed the phone back.

"Asshole, don't fuck with my video. I'm pulling that out of the trash. It's my blackmail." Roach smiled and spun the phone in his fingers. "Now talk."

"You remember how I ended up in prison?" Roach lifted a brow and stared at me like I was a fucking idiot. "Okay, fine, you remember. The point is, I found her."

"Damn, no way." A smile broke out on Roach's face as he leaned forward. "Where's the bitch's body, and do I need to cover anything up?"

A flare of anger ignited in my chest. "Don't fucking call her that." I knew it was a mistake to say anything as soon as the words were out of my mouth.

Roach smacked a hand off his knee and began to laugh. "You still like her!" He laughed as I glared. His face sobered. "Oh shit, you really do," he said, his voice losing all the humor. "Fuck, I was only joking. How the hell is that possible?" he yelled.

His annoyingly loud enthusiasm was splitting my head in two.

"Shh, man. Fuck." I groaned and rubbed at my forehead.

"All right, tell me everything. I need to know how you can still like her after everything."

"I'm not your personal soap opera," I said. "Fine, whatever," I grumbled when he just stared. "She didn't send me to prison out of spite. She actually thought it was me."

Roach screwed up his face. "But I thought you didn't do it?"

"I didn't."

"Okay, then why the hell would she pick you, of all people? I mean, weren't the two of you friends or some shit?"

I sighed as I thought over what all Raine had told me. If I hadn't been so furious, I might have asked a couple more questions, but last night I needed to get as far away from her as possible. I yanked another breakfast burrito out of the bag and tore into it.

"She went down to the fights where I was supposed to be—don't ask me why, but I wasn't there. I was too banged up to go but didn't want to be around the house. Anyway, she was attacked by three men, and one of them had the same tattoo as this." I held up my hand and pointed to it.

"That still doesn't make sense. How did she not see his face? Are you sure she's telling you the truth and not something to keep you from hurting her?"

"Too late for that. I messed her up and may have done what I was in jail for," I said. My cock twitched at the thought of being inside her. Feeling her come all over me. The smell of her skin.

Fuck! Enough of that.

"Damn, and people call me the asshole." Roach held out his hand. "Gimmie one of those."

I tossed a burrito at him and chugged the rest of my coffee before continuing. I hated to admit it, but my stomach seemed pleased with the addition of solid food, and my head hurt less.

"Point is, I don't know what to do with this. She should've at least spoken to me before she named me as her attacker, but she was fifteen, terrified, stabbed, and left for dead. So...there's that. Before you ask, I don't know why I only got ten years. I'm thinking Raine had something to do with that, but I was too pissed to ask last night."

We ate in silence, and I stared out the window. The sun shone like mother nature hadn't just tried to kill us yesterday.

"Don't get pissed with me for asking this..." He shrugged. "But do you still have a thing for her? Like not of the obsessive hate variety?"

I laid my head back on the couch. My first instinct was to yell no and tell him to fuck off, but the reality was, I didn't know. No, that wasn't true. The ache in my chest and the pounding of my heart at the thought of her told me I was trying to lie to myself.

"I think so," I admitted. "But the hate for what she did to me, regardless of why, is as strong as any other emotion."

"Oh, I love hate-sex. I'm in."

I lifted my head to glare at Roach.

"I didn't mean with her. I just meant that it's one of the best ball-boiling, euphoric experiences," Roach said, his lip curling up.

"That's a mighty big word to be coming out of you," I teased.

"Shut the fuck up," Roach said and then looked out the window. The sound of a vehicle had him standing and pulling his gun as he did. "You know anyone with a little red car?"

"Nope."

I managed to get to my feet and hobbled over to the window. Fuck, my head didn't like that, and I had to grab at the wall.

"Damn, she's hot. Who the fuck is that? Someone looking for directions, or is she lost? I would give her directions right into my bedroom," Roach said, sticking his gun in the back of his jeans.

I reached the window and saw Raine bent over, talking to the driver. A moment later, the car backed out and disappeared. My heart stumbled in my chest at the sight of her. The sunshine bathed her like a little fairy in my yard.

"Fuck, that girl is fine. I'll be right back," Roach said, and I snatched his arm.

"That's Raine. You go anywhere near her with your cock, and I'll kill you," I growled.

"That's her? No wonder you have it bad. How the hell did she find you?" Roach asked as a soft knock echoed through the house.

"I don't know," I mumbled, releasing Roach's arm. Roach walked to the front door. "Where the hell do you think you're going?"

"Oh, I'm not staying here for this. I need plausible deniability." He smirked as he whipped open the door dramatically. I saw Raine jump back like she'd just been hit. I couldn't blame her.

"Um, hi. I was told Kai is here," she said, and my traitorous cock stood at the sound of her voice. I couldn't get my head to stop spinning, but my cock worked fine. Figures.

Roach stepped onto the porch, and Raine's eyes swung from him to me.

"Hunt me down when you're done. I have an errand I need you for," Roach said as he looked over his shoulder at me. His look said it all. He would fuck her if I gave him even a sniff of an opportunity.

His eyes were filled with mischief as he stood beside Raine, and I realized just how small she was. The anger that started last night over her attack flared in my gut. In a flash, I pictured her at fifteen, lucky to weigh eighty pounds soaking wet, trying to fight off three grown men. My teeth ground together until my jaw cracked.

"Don't have too much fun," Roach said, smiling as he jogged down the stairs.

Prick.

I pushed the pain in my skull aside and stepped up to the door, and as I looked into her big blue eyes, I knew it didn't matter why she was here. My fucking heart was in trouble.

She had her hands stuffed inside her sweatshirt pocket, but her back was straight as she stared at me.

"What are you doing here?" I looked around outside. "And how the hell did you find me?" It was a little annoying that she'd found me in less than twenty-four hours.

"I noticed your patch last night." She lifted a shoulder and let it drop. "A girl that worked at my club used to hook up with one of the members. She used to talk about this place and where it was." Raine pointed to the fence and the guards keeping watch. "I asked for you, and they pointed me here."

I was going to have to have a chat with those fuckers. I didn't care who it was. They shouldn't tell anyone where the fuck I am.

"Fine. Why are you here?"

Pulling her hands out of the pocket, she played with the cuffs of her hoodie, a nervous habit she had even back when I met her. She'd ruined more sweatshirts than I could count when the threads would finally give up and the cuff would fall off. I always loved to see her in mine when she stole them, but I would scold her for trying to ruin them.

"May I come in? I promise I won't stay too long. I just need to speak to you." She met my stare, and I cocked a brow at her as I ignored the steadily growing interest in my jeans that very much wanted her to come inside.

"You trust coming in here and being alone with me after last night?"

She crossed her arms and looked away.

"You proved that you will find me and take what you want anyway, so what does it really matter if I'm here or somewhere else?" she asked, and my back bristled. She wasn't wrong, but I still didn't like being called out like I was the bad guy.

"Whatever."

I stepped out of the way, letting her walk past me, and closed the door. She jumped but tried to hide it. Once again, I was conflicted by her presence. I loved that she jumped, and my cock stirred more with her reaction, but the reason she was so scared bothered me. A psychiatrist wouldn't even be able to wade through the confusing shit floating around in my head.

"Alright then, speak," I said and went to sit on the couch.

Raine looked like a cat, wary of its surroundings, as she slipped across the living room and sat in the chair Roach had occupied not long before. I watched her carefully and took in every bit of her body language. Raine rubbed her hands on her legs and then sat on her hands. Again, something she'd always done.

"I came to say I'm sorry." She paused and looked at me, and I shrugged.

"That's it? That's all you got?"

Her eyes narrowed before she took a deep breath. "All night, I thought about what you said, and you're right. I should've talked to you before I gave the police your name." She turned her head to look out the window, and I could see the stress in her eyes. I had the urge to wrap her in a hug like I would've done before all this shit went down, but now I stayed put.

"What is this? Do you feel guilty or some shit now? Little too late for that, don't you think?" I leaned forward, and her heated glare met my own. "Look at me. You ruined my life. Your guilt is not my problem. That's a you problem."

Her eyes filled with tears, but her jaw tightened, and I could see her fighting not to let them fall.

"You're right. It's not your problem." She bolted to her feet. "Forget it, Kai. I just wanted you to know that I'm going to speak to a lawyer about the steps to retract my statement and have the charges removed from your record. I'll pay for it, of course."

"What fucking good is that going to do? I already did ten years."

"Well, at least this way, you won't have to worry about police seeing that you're a parolee or have a record for rape. I'll have it all removed, and I'm going to have it sealed. I'll probably need you to sign paperwork, but it's the only thing I can think of to apologize for what I did."

A wiped record? I actually liked the idea, but instead of saying that, I stood and stared down at her. I liked that she stood tall and held my gaze.

"It will never make up for what I went through."

"Maybe, maybe not, but I haven't learned how to build a time machine, so it's all I've got," she snipped back, and my lips curled up. Fuck, she was hot when she was scared and sexy as fuck, riled up. My eyes went to the bruise, peeking through the makeup on her neck before I stared her down.

"Okay. Thanks."

Nodding, she turned to walk away, and I called out to her, unsure why I asked.

"Tink, before you go. Tell me something. Who found you, and why did Dave and Irene never come to see me?"

She turned to look at me, and her face was twisted in confusion. "I don't know."

"What do you mean?"

"I mean, I was in an old industrial building and didn't make it to a phone." She held up her wrists and walked close enough that I could see the scars I hadn't been able to see in the dark last night. "My wrists and ankles were bound with zip ties. As for the Collinses..." She shrugged. "I don't know. As soon as I mentioned the tattoo to the officer, Dave ranted about how he always knew that under all of the trying to get good grades, you were a fuck up. Then Irene chimed in and said you'd propositioned her. She started crying and said she could've prevented this from happening."

"She said what?" I barked out, and Raine took a step back. Her eyes went to my hands, clenched into fists.

"That you asked her to have sex with you. She said that you pushed her up against the freezer and said that you could fuck her better than her husband. She said it wasn't the first time you'd gotten aggressive with her, and she'd feared for her life but was too embarrassed to say anything."

"Son of a bitch," I growled and marched away. I spun around and faced Raine. "Let me guess, you heard that, and on top of the tattoo, all you could picture was me attacking you?" Her eyes flicked away, but she didn't need to say it. I saw it in her eyes. "You know what the irony is?" She shook her head. "I was fucking Irene." Raine's mouth dropped open, and her hands fell to her sides. "The bitch hit on me watching a movie and then cornered me in the garage and threatened to have me kicked out if I didn't fuck her. Don't get me wrong. I was seventeen and horny. The idea of sex with anyone interested me, but I didn't force her. Not even once."

Raine put her hands on her hips. "Let me get this straight. We were hanging out all the time, and you kissed me, but you were fucking our foster mother?"

I ran my hand through my hair. "As I said, she threatened to toss me out. Besides, I was young, dumb, and horny, and you were off limits, anyway."

Raine tilted her head to the side as she scrutinized me with her stare. "Doesn't look like much has changed in the dumb and horny department."

I growled and was on the move before I realized I was even walking. Raine squealed as I grabbed her and pushed her up against the wall.

"You're pretty mouthy for being inside my home," I said as she glared at me. I was tempted to kiss her. She licked her lips, and it was all I could think about, but I pushed away from her instead.

"Get out. I don't want to see you again."

"I need to ask you something," she said as I marched away from her and went to the kitchen to make another coffee.

"Yeah, well, I'm done talking to you," I snarled as she followed me.

"This is important," she said and leaned against the doorjamb. She looked way too sexy and adorable. I wanted to crush her and eat her up all at the same time.

"Will it get you out of my house if I answer?" I asked and busied my hands, making the pot of coffee.

"Yes. I just need to know if you're clean," she said, and my hand stilled as I was about to dump the little grounds into the filter.

"What the fuck did you just ask me?" I turned my head and stared at her.

"Don't do that, Kai. Don't act like I don't have a right to know," she said, her voice inching up a few octaves with her anger. "You attacked me last night, and I haven't seen you in over eleven years. Most of that was spent in prison, and I have no idea what you've done since you got out. You could've screwed your way around the world and back again for all I know."

My teeth ground together, and I wanted to tell her to fuck off and take her chances. Just looking at her brought up the memories of last night and what it felt like being inside her. I needed to calm the fuck down, or I was going to take her right there against my wall. I might've contemplated it longer if my hangover didn't choose that moment to bite like it was trying to rip out my brain.

"You okay?" Raine asked as I squinted and sucked in a breath. She took a step toward me, and I hated that she still acted the exact fucking same. Worrying, checking up on me, and showing affection when I didn't deserve it.

"Stay away from me, Tink, unless you want more of last night." She froze, her eyes going wide. Fuck, that was hot. "Haven't you learned your lesson by now? Don't put your arm inside the dangerous animal's cage." Raine swallowed and backed up to the doorway again.

Stomping over to the black organizer in the corner by the old landline, I thumbed through the paperwork until I found my last test results. I tested all the time. I wasn't unsafe, but I wasn't exactly celibate, and prison can make you a little paranoid. Yanking the sheet out, I walked over to Raine and tossed the paper at her.

"In case you're wondering, I only got tapped once in prison. Luckily, the guy was clean, but he had an unfortunate accident a few days later." Raine's mouth dropped open. If she only knew the body count, I had in my wake. "And other than you, your royal highness, I have always used protection and get tested every six months. So yeah, I'm fucking clean."

I turned back to the counter as Raine unfolded the page and began to read. "Maybe I should be asking for one. Who knows where your pussy has been?" I growled.

"Fuck you, Kai." Tossing the paper on the floor, she turned and marched for the door.

My body shook as I held myself in place and didn't chase her swaying ass down. Fuck, she made me hard and hot, and I wanted to put my fist through another wall and fuck her until she was screaming my name.

"Show yourself out," I yelled. She didn't say a word or look back, which pissed me off even more.

I leaned against the counter and slumped at the sound of the front door slamming. Fuck, why didn't that feel right? I should never want to see her or her big blue eyes again, but...

"Fuck!" I slammed my fist on the counter. She was making me crazy all over again.

Raine

27

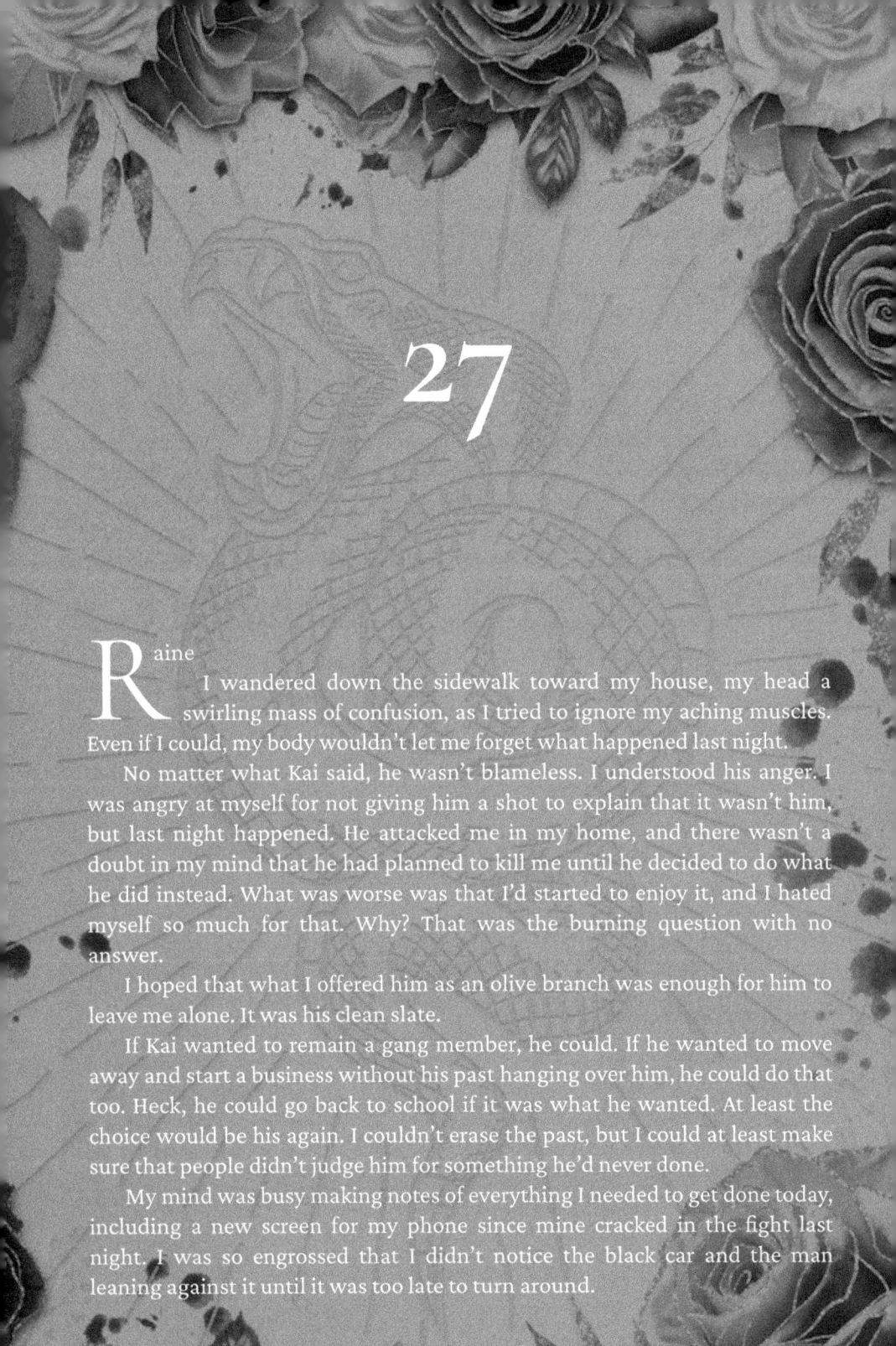

Raine

I wandered down the sidewalk toward my house, my head a swirling mass of confusion, as I tried to ignore my aching muscles. Even if I could, my body wouldn't let me forget what happened last night.

No matter what Kai said, he wasn't blameless. I understood his anger. I was angry at myself for not giving him a shot to explain that it wasn't him, but last night happened. He attacked me in my home, and there wasn't a doubt in my mind that he had planned to kill me until he decided to do what he did instead. What was worse was that I'd started to enjoy it, and I hated myself so much for that. Why? That was the burning question with no answer.

I hoped that what I offered him as an olive branch was enough for him to leave me alone. It was his clean slate.

If Kai wanted to remain a gang member, he could. If he wanted to move away and start a business without his past hanging over him, he could do that too. Heck, he could go back to school if it was what he wanted. At least the choice would be his again. I couldn't erase the past, but I could at least make sure that people didn't judge him for something he'd never done.

My mind was busy making notes of everything I needed to get done today, including a new screen for my phone since mine cracked in the fight last night. I was so engrossed that I didn't notice the black car and the man leaning against it until it was too late to turn around.

A warmth spread throughout my body at the sight of Avro, and I suddenly wished I wore a turtleneck even though it was eighty-five outside. I hadn't even begun to contemplate how to explain Kai or the attack to Avro and Jace, or if I should just keep my mouth shut. Shit...

"Hey, what are you doing here?" I smiled as I turned, so the bruised side of my neck was away from him.

Avro didn't answer. He just reached out and grabbed me, pulling me into a hug. Why I wanted to cry suddenly was beyond me, but as I wrapped my arms around him and took in the sweet comfort he offered, I could feel the tears prick at the back of my eyes.

He kissed the top of my head and didn't say anything for a long time. "Why didn't you answer my calls last night? I was worried when I couldn't reach you," he said.

"Yesterday was very strange, and I don't want to talk about it right now." I forced the words past my constricted airway. I could feel where Kai choked me as if he was still gripping my throat. "Did Jace get away okay?"

"No, he's here for a couple more days. Not that I'm complaining. The next two concerts couldn't be rescheduled, so the rest of the band left for San Francisco. He didn't have to leave yet and opted to stay and spend more time with us."

I held him a little tighter. Avro was like bathing in a warm, sensual bath of muscle. I opened my mouth to tell him about last night, but I just couldn't. The words wouldn't form. How did you say, 'I was raped again, but it was okay this time because I felt like I deserved it?'

The next issue was that I didn't know how to hide the bruises all over my body or spend time with them and not stay the night. My life had suddenly gotten much more complicated in the blink of an eye.

"That's great," I said, unsure what else to say.

"You heading into work?" Avro asked. "I noticed that the inventory isn't done. I stopped there on my way here to find you."

Stepping back, I rubbed at my face. "Yeah, I'll have to go in. I spent most of yesterday chasing a stray cat all around the bar. It broke a bunch of full bottles, and I got scratched and had to go to the hospital. It was a really weird ass day."

"Okay, let's go. I'll help you. Jace is busy working out the melody to the new song he wrote, and when he's in that headspace, you don't go near him. Not unless you want your head bit off." Avro winked. "I still like to entice him from time to time, just to make sure my ability to corrupt is still aces."

"I'm pretty sure he always has a hard time saying no to you." I smiled back and vividly remembered how sexy the two men were together.

"Let's just say it is one challenge I thoroughly enjoy winning, and I have a feeling that you will find it just as entertaining." The sexy look that lifted the corners of his mouth made me blush.

I cleared my throat. "I'm sure you're right. I guess we better go. Too much to do and not enough hours."

I wasn't sure this was a great idea, but I couldn't think of a single excuse he would actually believe. I got in the passenger seat, and while he walked around the car, I bunched my hood a little more around my neck.

Avro slipped into the driver's seat and looked over at me. "You sure you're okay? You seem...distant. Not your normal self."

"I'm fine."

"Which is code for you're really not. Did you decide that Jace and I aren't what you want? If you're not interested, then please tell me." He looked down at our hands as I linked our fingers together.

"No, it's nothing like that. I'm more committed than ever to a relationship with you both. I didn't sleep well. I never have during storms," I said, and he squeezed my hand before lifting it to look at my knuckles.

"How did you bruise all of your knuckles? And your hand seems a swollen."

I swallowed hard. Why did he have to be so observant? "The cat. I tripped and fell, then cracked my hand off the bar multiple times while trying to catch him. The power flickered at one point, and I walked into a wall," I said. It wasn't a complete lie. Those things sorta happened but didn't cause the marks on my body.

Holy shit, how many other lies would I have to tell to cover up what happened? This felt so familiar. The night of my attack, I started making excuses for why I was in that dangerous area. I said I was meeting a friend, but the lies quickly unraveled the more I was questioned. The problem was, I didn't even know what the hell the truth was anymore. Kai asked a question I'd never analyzed too much, but now I couldn't stop thinking about it. Who found me? How long was it before the ambulance arrived? I had snippets after I was stabbed, but not much. It was mostly a blur or nothing at all.

Had some homeless person wandered in because the door was open? Had the door been left open? I briefly remembered keys. Had one of my attackers worked there? My heart began to pound hard as little things that had never occurred to me before as significant were suddenly a lot more important. All this time, the three men who'd attacked me were still out there and never got punished. I hated to think about what they were doing out there, what they could've done to someone else. Maybe I'd passed them in the grocery store and never knew.

I shivered and cuddled into my sweatshirt as if it would help. Now more than ever, I couldn't help wondering why me? Was I a random choice, or had they set out for someone else, and I'd run into their trap? Was my attack meant for another girl? If so, then who?

As Avro drove, I watched everyone we passed and felt so detached, like I no longer belonged in this world. A woman jogged with her dog by her side and pushed one of those running strollers. People played frisbee on the beach while others drove by wearing suits in fancy sports cars. So many lives and variations, and not one of them worried about a girl left for dead in a building years ago. Not one of them cared that I was driving by now, watching them, and wondering if they were the person who'd attacked me. None of them knew that I sat here wishing I could've had a normal childhood, but when you watched your parents die, nothing is normal after that. It was an omen that followed me with its taint ever since.

"I watched my parents die," I blurted out into the silent car. I didn't look at Avro, but I could feel his eyes on my face.

"What?"

"My parents died when I was six. I shouldn't be able to remember it so clearly. I mean... I was six. Who remembers what happened to them at that age?" I asked, not expecting a response.

"What happened?" Avro asked, his voice full of concern.

"They were addicts. As far as I know, my mom got clean long enough to have me but couldn't stay off them once I was born. I remember going to the hospital once, not long before they died. She'd been locked up in this special wing that made me uncomfortable." I stopped and licked my lips as I gathered myself.

"I was terrified of being there, but didn't know how to say it, so my dad held me in his arms, and I just hid my face in his neck."

I put my hands in my lap and looked down at them as I played with Kai's ring. Even after last night, I still haven't taken it off.

"It wasn't until years later that I understood she'd tried to get clean again. It was some sort of a rehab facility, but I'm pretty sure she left before it was finished." I shook my head. "I wish I'd been old enough to help her. It may not have worked, but I would've tried."

"So where did she pass away?" Avro asked.

"At home. It was like any other Friday. I was picked up from the babysitter's house, and we ate dinner like a normal family. We even played a few hands of Go Fish. It was bedtime when their friends started to arrive. I recognized the other faces. They'd been over before, but just like all the other nights, I never spoke to them."

I took a deep breath as I remembered my mom and dad tucking me in and kissing me goodnight, saying I needed to stay in bed. It was far too late for little girls to be awake. I bit my lower lip as the images of that night flashed before my eyes as clearly as if it had just happened.

"I'd fallen asleep, but I woke up and needed to pee and get a drink. When I called out, no one came. I could hear music playing and crawled out of my bed with my blue bear tucked under my arm."

I lifted my head and realized Avro was parked at work, and I hadn't even noticed we'd stopped moving. "The party was them all getting high. All six of them were lying on the furniture and the floor and were very still. I remember thinking how strange that was. My parents were near a large chair I used to sit in to watch cartoons, and I tip-toed closer. I didn't want to wake anyone else, but I didn't have to worry about that."

"They all died?"

I nodded. "Tainted drugs. All six of them were gone or in the process of dying. I don't really know. I reached out and nudged my mom's arm, but she wouldn't wake up, so I went into the kitchen and got myself a glass of water." I licked my parched lips. "Being brave, I decided to use an adult glass, but once I filled it with water, it was too heavy and slipped through my hands and smashed on the floor." The glass had seemed to fall in slow motion, and when it hit, little pieces went everywhere. "I thought for sure that my mom or dad were going to wake up and come storming in, but they didn't."

"Holy shit, Raine. I'm so sorry. So then, what happened?"

I shrugged. "I tried to clean up the mess but cut myself on my hands and feet, and I was crying. I went to my parents again, and they still wouldn't wake up." As I recalled that night, I put a hand over my mouth, feeling a small pang of emotion for the first time. "I was bleeding and scared, so I took my mom's phone, and I remember fumbling, trying to get it to work, but finally I got it open, and I called my babysitter. I was crying so hard that she could barely understand me and said she was on her way over."

I leaned on the door and stared up at the club. "I don't know why, but I've never felt anything until now. It was all just this blank void in my heart. I've rarely even thought about it. Does that make me a bad person?"

"No, Raine, you're not a bad person. Do you mean you don't feel bad that they died?"

I locked eyes with Avro. "Sorta. I just don't really feel anything. Don't get me wrong, I understand now that they were addicts, but they were both good to me when they weren't getting high. I can't say they were terrible people and mistreated me or left me places." I sighed, trying to collect my thoughts.

"The thing is, when I think of them, I see their dead faces looking so peaceful, their heads touching like they'd fallen asleep resting on one another. I feel like they died doing the one thing they loved more than anything. Loved more than me. Is that the whole truth of the situation? Maybe not, but it's still how I feel." I lifted my shoulders and let them drop.

Avro reached out and grabbed my hand again. This time, he brought my cut knuckles to his lips and kissed each one.

"I worry, Avro. I worry that I'm always going to be damaged and broken. Something is wrong with me inside, and I can't put my finger on how to explain it to anyone." I turned my head to look him in the eyes. "I'm terrified that I will always feel hollow, and nothing will ever fix it. I've spent my entire life expecting the worst to happen, and I can feel it coming for me like I'm running along tracks and a train is barreling down on me. I've become desensitized to everything other than the crippling fear."

Reaching out, I touched his cheek. "You are the first person in a very long time to make me feel anything, but that scares the fuck out of me. I don't even know what to do with the emotions or how to navigate the new waters."

Avro didn't say anything as I stared into his amber eyes. I wanted to feel everything with him. I wanted to feel sad and disappointed. Laugh at his jokes and keep a tight grip on the butterflies I felt with him and Jace the other night. I wanted to know what it was like to love and be intimate without the touch of fear clouding every waking moment. Fuck, I wanted to try skydiving and scale a mountain. I wanted to run a marathon and travel to a different country. I'd never been outside of Florida, and my view of the world was on my phone and television.

"I feel so little, Avro." I sniffed and closed my eyes as the tears formed and slowly dripped down my cheeks. "I feel like this tiny shell of a person waiting to be crushed. I know it and know I need to fix it, but I don't know how. Most days, I'm filled with terror and an ache of loneliness that never wants to leave."

"Raine, you're so far from empty inside. Yes, you're struggling. I can see it, but you just said you felt something with me, right? And you felt something with Jace and me the other night?"

"I do and did, but how can I trust my feelings? What if all those emotions, hope, excitement, and passion all disappear once the hollow feeling catches back up? It always catches up with me. I feel like Artreyu, trapped in that desolate place with the sphinx in the movie *Neverending Story*. You know the part where he thinks he's getting somewhere, but then his heart betrays him, and the sphinx fires, and he narrowly escapes being killed?" Avro smiled at me. "Okay, maybe not the best analogy."

"Actually, it works perfectly, but remember that he made it through that test and the ones after that. That was the point. He kept pushing on and proving to himself that he could do it, and so will you. Every day you wake up, brush your teeth, and look in the mirror, you are staring the world and all the terrible shit in the face and saying that you won't quit. You will run the gauntlet of terror, and no matter how scared you are, you still do, and each day is a day to heal."

I wiped at the tears sliding down my cheek. "How did you get to be so smart?"

"Blame Jace. He's the insightful one, believe it or not." He smiled, and we both laughed. Avro sobered and wrapped my hand up in both of his. "We'll get through this together. The three of us will figure out how to make sure that each day is a step forward."

"What if some days there are steps back?"

"Well, we'll remind you that you're stronger for going through the pain rather than avoiding it."

I'd certainly gone through the pain last night. It was sad, or maybe pathetic, but I knew I would never get Kai out of my head. The feel of his rough touch and his glowing eyes were forever tattooed on my brain. How do I get over the boy I loved and lost and now the man that I realized a part of me still loved?

The heart was one map I couldn't figure out, but I wished I could. I really wished that I could.

Snake

28

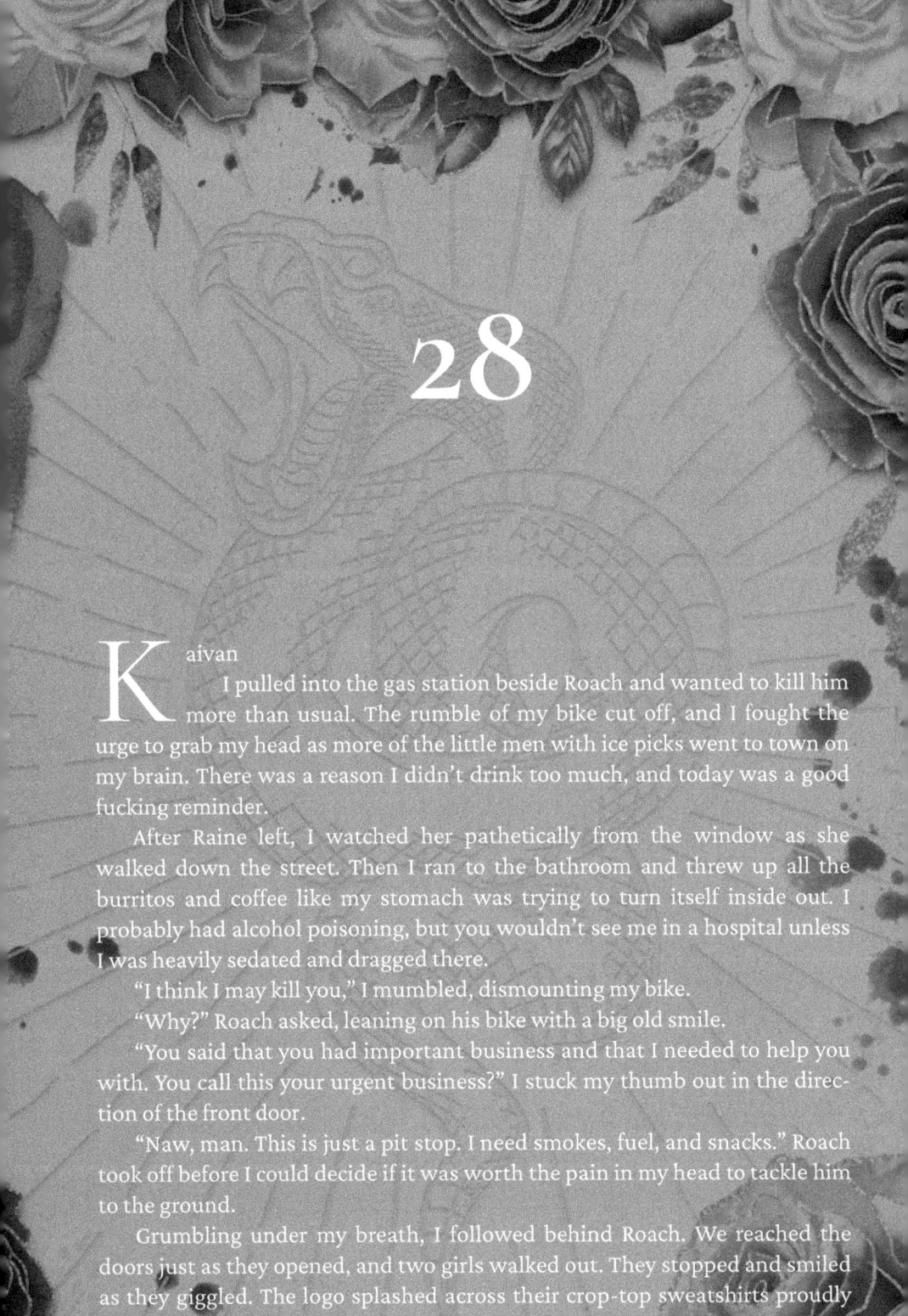

Kaivan

I pulled into the gas station beside Roach and wanted to kill him more than usual. The rumble of my bike cut off, and I fought the urge to grab my head as more of the little men with ice picks went to town on my brain. There was a reason I didn't drink too much, and today was a good fucking reminder.

After Raine left, I watched her pathetically from the window as she walked down the street. Then I ran to the bathroom and threw up all the burritos and coffee like my stomach was trying to turn itself inside out. I probably had alcohol poisoning, but you wouldn't see me in a hospital unless I was heavily sedated and dragged there.

"I think I may kill you," I mumbled, dismounting my bike.

"Why?" Roach asked, leaning on his bike with a big old smile.

"You said that you had important business and that I needed to help you with. You call this your urgent business?" I stuck my thumb out in the direction of the front door.

"Naw, man. This is just a pit stop. I need smokes, fuel, and snacks." Roach took off before I could decide if it was worth the pain in my head to tackle him to the ground.

Grumbling under my breath, I followed behind Roach. We reached the doors just as they opened, and two girls walked out. They stopped and smiled as they giggled. The logo splashed across their crop-top sweatshirts proudly announced they went to the university. They were nowhere near campus, the dorms, or the beach, which meant they were in this shit part of the city looking for trouble—drugs, sex, maybe both.

Any other time, I would tap that. Ride them hard and fast and boot them out the door just as quickly, but at the moment, no part of me wanted anything to do with them.

"Hi," the girl with dark hair said.

Roach opened his mouth to answer, and I cut in. Grabbing the door, I leaned in close to the girls. "I'd fucking break you," I growled low enough that only they could hear. The smiles slipped from their faces. "And if you were lucky, I'd bury your bodies deep enough that the animals didn't dig you back up." Standing up straight, I glared down at them through my dark glasses. "Get the fuck out of here."

Removing my arm, the girls dashed away, and Roach glared at me. "What the fuck? I could've had some fun. Why are you such a dick?"

"We are supposed to be on a super important mission. I was just doing you a favor." I smirked. "Wouldn't want you to get distracted or anything. Besides, what if they are Lane's friends and tell her you fucked them?"

"Once upon a time, I thought we were friends. Fucker," Roach mumbled under his breath as he stomped into the store ahead of me. "I need to take a piss."

Wandering the store portion, I was very aware of the guy at the counter staring at me like I was gonna run at him with a gun. Not that I blamed him. That had happened more than once in this area. Yanking open the fridge, I grabbed a large container of chocolate milk and the biggest energy drink I could find. It wasn't exactly the healthiest hangover drink, but it fucking worked.

The bell on the door chimed as I was staring at the chips, and I froze when I heard a familiar voice.

"Well, fuck me. Is that you, Kaivan?" Turning my head, I stared into the piggish eyes of Dave Collins. "As I live and fucking breathe. I thought you were dead or rotted away in prison," he said, smiling. Another guy walked around the corner with him, and neither of the men looked to be having the best of days.

I gave Dave the once over and took in the man who used to be my foster father. He looked like he'd just crawled out of a dumpster. His shirt was stained and untucked over his beer belly. He was wearing grey sweatpants that he should never have wiggled his ass into and had on running shoes that were on their last go around. He was sporting a beard now but was bald except for a thin ring of hair.

"I'd say it was good to see you again, but I'd be lying," I drawled. "You look like you've seen better days yourself. Did the old bitch finally toss your useless ass out on the street?"

His eyes narrowed into thin slits, adding to the pig look he had going on.

"Still have that smart mouth on you. That didn't get solved while you were locked up," Dave said. He stepped closer, and I smelled the alcohol wafting off his body like a bad cologne.

"Naw, it didn't. No thanks to you or Irene. I really appreciated all the support the two of you showed me by not showing up for...well, anything."

Dave took another step, the fake-ass smile completely slipping from his face.

"Dave, don't do it," Dave's buddy said.

"I'd listen to your friend Dave. He gives sound advice." I looked at my nails, flashing the fist full of rings that would knock his ass out if he tried anything.

"You got what you deserved—manipulating my wife and raping poor sweet Raine the way you did. You should've gotten life," he growled. "And you better watch out, or I'll send you back there," he threatened.

"Oh really? And on what charge would you have me go to prison for this time?" I asked as Roach reappeared from the bathroom. He gave me a look over the top of the two guys, and I gave him a subtle nod that I was okay.

"That fancy crest you have on your back. I'm pretty sure your parole officer would love to know that you've been hanging out with a motorcycle gang." He thought he was invincible. That much was clear as he took another step forward. "I'm pretty sure they would send you back to where you belong, with the rest of the animals."

"Ironic coming from you," I said, and purposely stared at what was most likely a cheese stick imprint on his shirt. Before Dave could say anything else, I smiled and continued. "I guess you're not in the family loop anymore. Did poor, sweet Raine not tell you? I'm shocked you weren't the first call she made," I drawled and leaned against the freezer door.

I suddenly wondered what Raine's relationship was with the Collinses. Did she still speak to them, or had she left them behind and never looked back?

"What the hell are you spouting off about?"

"Raine went and had my name cleared. She remembered a lot more pieces from the night of her attack and realized it wasn't me." Dave stepped back like

I slapped him, and I watched him carefully. He was actually shocked, which meant that Raine made the decision and either didn't call them or didn't speak to the Collinses at all. Then again, maybe she planned on sharing the news when Christmas came around. There was something else under the shock, though…fear…maybe, it was hard to tell.

"You're lying," Dave growled, his hands balling into fists. At one point in my life, if he'd done that, I would have immediately gotten up in his face, but I was older and wiser now. I also had no idea how long it took for charges to be cleared, but I doubted it was the same day. It wasn't like a fast-food drive-thru, so it was best to mind my P's and Q's.

"Not at all." I opened my cell phone to show Raine's name on my contacts list. Courtesy of my stalking, but again, Dave was on a need-to-know basis. "Did you want to talk to her and ask her yourself?"

I could see Roach milling about on the other side of the store, making sure that the guy at the counter didn't get too antsy or Dave didn't try anything stupid.

"I don't need to talk to her. I fucking know you did those things. I just wonder what you did to her to make her recant her story." Dave pointed a finger at me.

His buddy must have seen the look on my face as I wondered about cutting it off Dave's body here in the store. His friend didn't look as smug as Dave and grabbed his shoulder. Probably a smart move. It had been a few days since I killed anyone, and I felt the weight of my blade strapped to my back.

A grin pulled up the corner of my mouth. "Oh, come now, Dave. I didn't say anything about Irene. In fact, I don't deny fucking your wife. She did have a fine wet hole."

Dave's face turned a violent shade of red that made him look like a cartoon character, and his friend took a firmer hold.

"But manipulating Irene into it, that's a no. She was quite the needy cougar," I said, unable to help myself.

Roach slowly moved closer until I could feel him standing behind me. Dave may have been oblivious to the danger he was in, but his buddy looked like he was going to shit his pants.

"The truth is, Dave, she threatened to kick me out if I didn't 'service her,'" I said, making little air quotes with my fingers. "Apparently, your limp dick didn't stack up to a hard eighteen-year-old cock. That's pretty sad, man, but at least now you know your wife is a cheating whore and wasn't pressured into anything. Better to know late than not at all, I guess. Now Raine, on the other hand...naw, I never touched her, and now she knows it, too." I rubbed at my chin. "In fact, she says she has a few theories on who the three attackers were," I lied, but it made me look like I knew a lot more than I did. I also didn't think Dave was on the up and up. There was something about the uneasy look in his eyes that said he knew something.

I could see the muscle twitching in his jaw as he ground his teeth together. I sighed and shook my head. "You should be more concerned that Raine's attackers were never found. That's disturbing, isn't it?" I asked, and the weight of that statement firmly planted itself in my brain as the scars she showed me danced behind my eyes.

I sucked in a steadying breath as I pushed my shoulder away from the freezer. "Well, Dave, this has been a wonderful reunion. I can't wait for the next one. I hope the two of you have a pleasant day. I know I will."

Smiling wide as much for his benefit as the store cameras, I stepped around Roach and let him have the final stare-down as I made my way to the register. The guy behind the counter looked relieved when I pulled out my wallet. The bell rang, announcing that Dave and his friend had decided to move along.

"I'll also pre-pay forty on each of the two bikes out there," I nodded outside.

"That was intense," Roach commented, dropping some chip bags and candy on the counter.

"Yeah, but there was something weird about it." I pulled out two hundred in cash and dropped it on the counter as the guy put our stuff in bags. "Keep the change," I said, grabbing my stuff.

"How so?" Roach asked as we made our way outside.

"Did you see how he reacted to hearing that Raine had dropped the charges? I mean, he seemed shocked, but not about that. I don't know. The whole thing is strange as fuck. My gut is saying he knows something."

"Are you sure that's not just your hangover talking?"

I glared at Roach as I straddled my bike. I twisted the milk lid off and drank enough to pour the energy drink inside.

"Dude, you are fucking disgusting," Roach said as he stared at my concoction.

"Says the guy eating onion rings with sour candies. That's fucking weird, and I'm concerned you're pregnant."

I rested on my seat, staring at nothing, and let the conversation with Dave replay. The fact that the three men who hurt Raine were walking around scot-free while I went away for ten years pissed me the fuck off. I tried hard to ignore the anger that had nothing to do with prison and everything to do with Raine being hurt.

I'd loved her then. I loved her now, and they almost took her from me forever. If she'd died...I shook my head to rid the thought. No matter what words I said to Raine, she was mine. She always had been, and I was going to find the fuckers and give them the justice they deserved. It wouldn't be in a six-by-six with three square meals a day. No, that was too good for them.

Their blood was already running red in my mind.

Avro

29

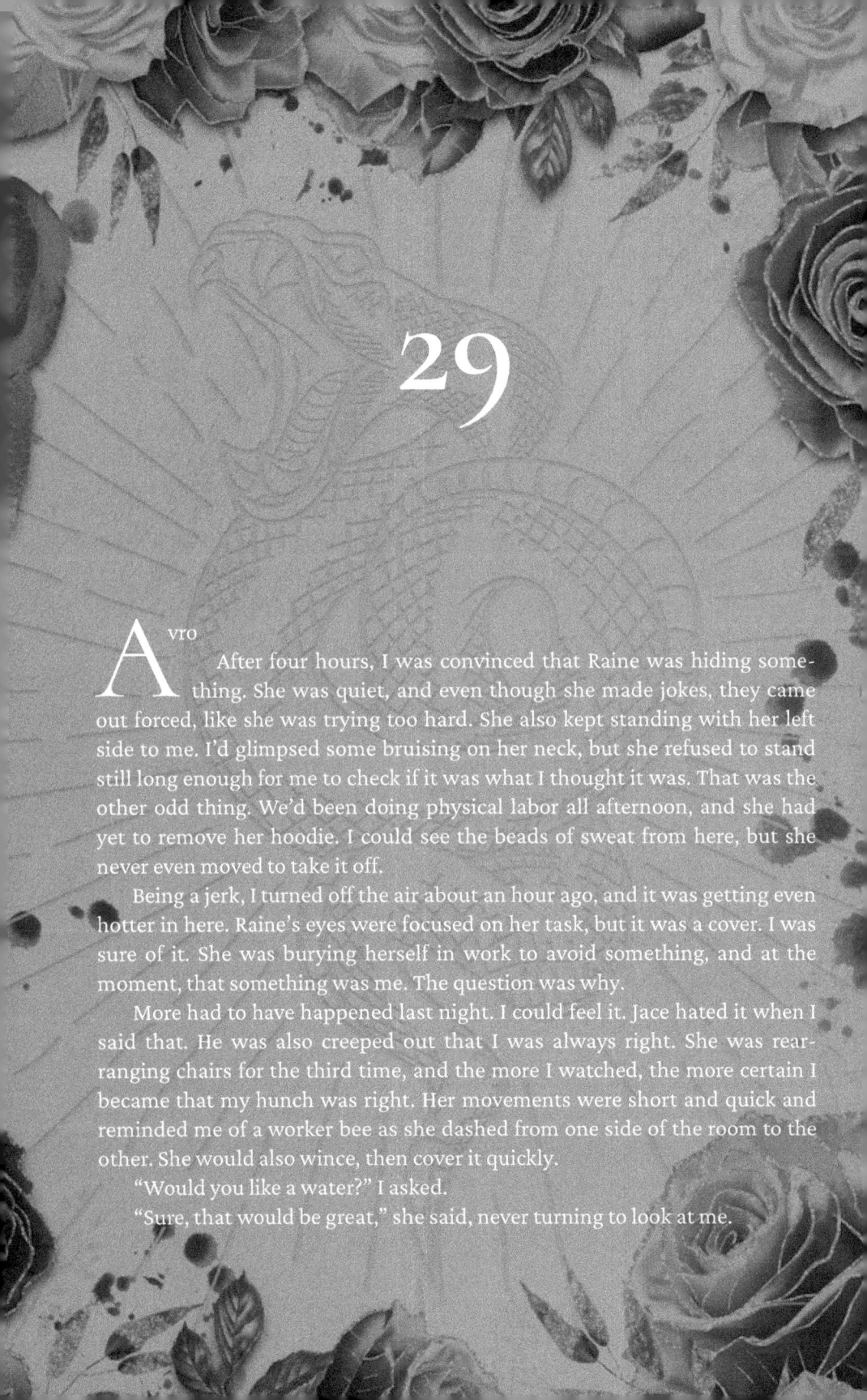

Avro

After four hours, I was convinced that Raine was hiding something. She was quiet, and even though she made jokes, they came out forced, like she was trying too hard. She also kept standing with her left side to me. I'd glimpsed some bruising on her neck, but she refused to stand still long enough for me to check if it was what I thought it was. That was the other odd thing. We'd been doing physical labor all afternoon, and she had yet to remove her hoodie. I could see the beads of sweat from here, but she never even moved to take it off.

Being a jerk, I turned off the air about an hour ago, and it was getting even hotter in here. Raine's eyes were focused on her task, but it was a cover. I was sure of it. She was burying herself in work to avoid something, and at the moment, that something was me. The question was why.

More had to have happened last night. I could feel it. Jace hated it when I said that. He was also creeped out that I was always right. She was rearranging chairs for the third time, and the more I watched, the more certain I became that my hunch was right. Her movements were short and quick and reminded me of a worker bee as she dashed from one side of the room to the other. She would also wince, then cover it quickly.

"Would you like a water?" I asked.

"Sure, that would be great," she said, never turning to look at me.

Pushing away from the bar, I grabbed two bottles and called out, tossing one her way. "Thanks."

"I'll be right back," I said, wandering down the hallway to the offices and bathrooms.

I slipped into her office after checking that she wasn't following or watching me. Luckily, the computer was still on, and I quickly clicked on the security footage and pulled up yesterday. I fast-forwarded to when Raine arrived, and I watched her walk to the storage room door. I knew she hated going down there. Watching her now, I half expected the eerie horror movie sounds to start playing.

About thirty minutes later, a cat did run out the door, and Raine wasn't far behind, closing the door behind her. I clicked on another camera and held back a laugh as I watched Raine dash around the bar. The cat made a huge mess as she chased it. She stopped in the middle of the dance floor and walked toward the patio, opening the doors wide. It was storming hard enough that the rain was driving in. The cat seemed distracted by the wind, rain, and the blowing blackout blinds, then Raine made her move and captured it. I watched as she took the cat outside, then stomped back in, looking like a drowned rat, as she closed and locked the doors.

Everything was as she said, except for the falling or running into walls. I'd been fed a half-truth—a cover story for what really happened.

"What are you doing?" Raine asked from the doorway.

I turned and leaned against her desk to stare at her. "I wanted to check your story," I said.

Her eyes narrowed into slits. "So what, you're going to be one of those overly controlling boyfriends now? Or whatever you want to call us," Raine bit out, her tone laced with the same venom that was in her eyes.

"Nope, I'm nothing like that," I said. "But I also know when I'm being lied to." It was subtle, but her face shifted just enough that I knew I was right. "You see, Raine, I know you. I know you so well that I have your routine memorized and how you like to do things. I also know that you would've tossed that hoodie off two hours ago, and you would've let me kiss you when I reached for you earlier." I lifted my fingers as I counted off all the oddities in her story.

"You've been tense, which could've been from our conversation on the way here, but you would normally put that behind you to work. You also aren't listening to your favorite soundtrack. You haven't put on any music at all. Lastly, your eyes are cagey, like you want to tell me something, but you're fucking avoiding the topic."

"Oh my god! You should be a damn detective," she fumed and marched into the room but still didn't come near me. Instead, she paced the floor, her hands pulled inside the long sleeves of the hoodie like she wanted to go full turtle and disappear.

"You want to know what else I know now?" I asked, keeping my voice even.

"I'm scared to ask. You may tell me what I ate for breakfast or how often I've used the bathroom today."

"See, that right there. That was also not you, but what really sealed the deal was looking at the footage from yesterday. You know what it showed me?"

Raine stopped pacing and looked at the door like she wanted to bolt. To prevent that, I walked over, closed the office door, and leaned against it. I was getting answers.

"Avro, please."

"Please, what? Don't tell you I saw your cat, but you never fell. Or, how about I don't tell you that you never ran into the bar or smacked into it or any wall? You know what that tells me?"

She swallowed and bit her lip. "Please stop."

"No, Raine, I won't let you cover for someone hurting you. I know that was what happened, and if it wasn't here, it happened during your ride to or from the hospital or at your house. So which is it? And more importantly, why don't you want to tell me?"

When she didn't say anything but stood in the middle of the room looking more defeated than I'd ever seen, I couldn't stop myself from going to her. Raine tilted her head up when I stopped in front of her, and her eyes glistened with tears.

Gripping her chin, I forced her to turn her head to the side, and using my thumb, I wiped at the makeup hiding long purple fingerprints. Fingerprints that belonged to a man or woman in the WNBA, but whoever it was, intended to hurt her. Maybe kill her. My blood ran like ice in my veins at the thought.

"Raine, what the hell happened?" I asked, my stomach dropping. I'd never hoped so much in my life that I was wrong about something.

"I can't tell you," she said.

I lifted my head and stared into her eyes. "Why?"

"Because it's a long and very complicated story, and if I tell you, then I know what you will want to do, and I can't go to the police. Not with this, not this time."

Moving my hands to Raine's shoulders, I tried to understand what she was saying, but it sounded like a riddle. "Tell me what happened."

"Avro, I can't. I want to. I do, but...I should just go home. I'm sorry," she said and tried to pull away, but I wasn't letting her take off like that.

"No," I said and held her in place. "Look at me. You can't cover or hide whatever this is. Whoever left those marks at the very least wanted to hurt you badly, or worse, they wanted to kill you. What if they come back?"

"They won't," she said.

"How are you so certain?" I pushed.

Raine jerked away from my touch, and my heart raced with panic. "I said just leave it alone."

I turned and went to stand in front of the door, then locked it. "You want to beat the shit out of me to get me to move, then so be it. I'll take whatever punch or kick you want to dish out, but I'm not moving until you tell me what the hell happened to you." I held out my hands as I pleaded with her. "I know you're getting used to the idea of us together, but to me, you're already part of my life in every way and have been for years. That means if someone hurts you, they hurt me. If they make you smile, they make me smile. You see how that works?"

She resumed pacing but didn't attack or tell me she never wanted to see me again, so it was a win.

"Tell me, Raine. Tell me, or I'll call the cops right now and say you were attacked. Even if you say nothing, they will have to drive out here and will want to interview you. Is that what you want?"

"Avro!" she yelled. "Fuck, why can't you just leave this alone?"

"Because I love you!" I yelled back and then snapped my mouth shut. Shit, this was not how that was supposed to go.

Raine stilled, her eyes finding mine as her arms dropped to her sides. "You love me?"

"Worst way for it to come out, but yes. I love you. I've been in love with you for so long, and not saying something has been one of the hardest things I've ever done. I can't tell you how many times I've almost slipped up while dropping you off or saying goodnight."

She looked shell-shocked, and I was terrified for a whole new reason.

"I'm not looking for you to say it back, but you asked why. That's why. I love you. That means I'm not letting you leave this room until you come clean. The whole story and why you don't want me to say anything. Please, Raine."

Raine walked toward me, and I could tell she was searching my face, but for what, I didn't know. "All this time, you've loved me?"

I reached out and ran my thumbs over her cheeks, then cupped her face.

"Yes. All this time."

"What about Jace?"

"What about him? He knows how I feel. We don't hide anything from each other. He loves me, and I love him too, and I hope that with time you two will fall in love as well," I said, tracing her bottom lip.

"I don't understand this, but it feels...."

"Right," we said at the same time and smiled.

My fingers trailed down her shoulders and arms until I could hold her hands. I looked at the marks from her punching something or someone. I wanted to pull her into my arms and protect her forever from whoever this was.

"Please tell me," I said softly.

"I will, but not yet."

My brows drew together, and confusion must have shown in my eyes because Raine touched a finger to my lips. Taking the hint, I kept my mouth closed while she stepped back and pulled the hoodie off. The tank top was next, and my mouth dropped as I stared at not only how beautiful she was but the marks and bruises all over her body.

"Don't stare at the bruises, just tell me...would you make love to me?"

My eyes snapped to hers. "What?" My mouth was suddenly parched.

Reaching behind her back, she undid the clasp for her bra and let it fall to the ground, and all I could do was groan as my cock came alive.

"You heard me. You say you love me. Will you make love to me before I tell you?" she asked, her big blue eyes pleading with me.

"Why do you want me to make love to you first?"

Raine licked her lips, and I followed the movement.

"Because when I tell you the entire story, you may never want to see me again, and I want to know your touch. I want this moment to hang on to if you decide to leave and never look back."

"Raine, nothing you could say would ever make me want to leave," I said, and my heart broke that she thought that.

"Then this should be an easy deal. I promise to tell you the whole sordid tale, but this is what I want first." She pushed the yoga pants down and stepped out, leaving her in only a sexy black thong.

I wrapped her in my arms and dropped my lips to hers. This wasn't how I saw our first time happening, but I would show her how much I loved her. Then I was getting the answers I was after and killing the man who did this to her.

Raine

30

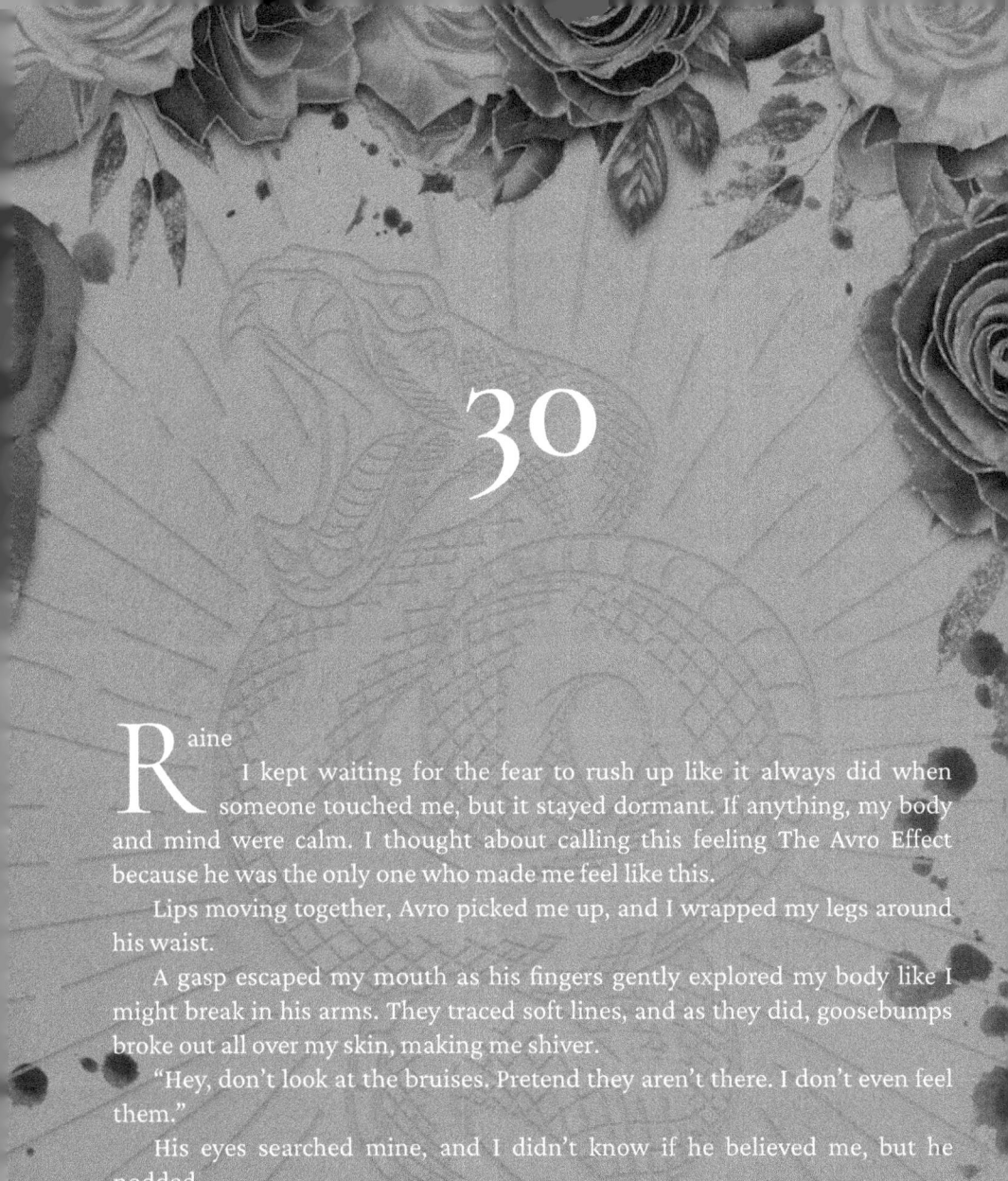

Raine

I kept waiting for the fear to rush up like it always did when someone touched me, but it stayed dormant. If anything, my body and mind were calm. I thought about calling this feeling The Avro Effect because he was the only one who made me feel like this.

Lips moving together, Avro picked me up, and I wrapped my legs around his waist.

A gasp escaped my mouth as his fingers gently explored my body like I might break in his arms. They traced soft lines, and as they did, goosebumps broke out all over my skin, making me shiver.

"Hey, don't look at the bruises. Pretend they aren't there. I don't even feel them."

His eyes searched mine, and I didn't know if he believed me, but he nodded.

Avro smiled against my lips. "I like it when you shiver," he said and ran fingers down the middle of my back.

I arched with the sensation that lit up all my nerve endings. His hands gripped my ass and squeezed, making me moan.

Everything about him was sensual and fluid. Nothing was rushed or overdone. Avro seemed to know exactly what my body wanted, and it didn't take long before I was a panting mess. I wiggled in his hold, and he broke off the kiss with a smirk.

"Lean back and close your eyes. Don't worry. I've got you," he said. I tentatively unlocked my fingers from around his neck. He smiled. "You do remember what I was training to do? I can hold my entire body sideways on a pole. Holding you is a breeze," he said, and I knew it was the truth. I'd seen him do it, and it always amazed me.

I did as he asked but yelped and jerked up straight again. I would've sworn I was falling and about to crack my head off the floor.

"Stop worrying. Let me take care of you." I licked my lips. "Close your eyes and trust."

Closing my eyes, I tried again and leaned back until I felt the firm press of his fingers holding my lower back.

"Oh," I moaned as the tip of his tongue ran little trails along my skin.

Warmth spread as I leaned more into his hold, and his finger pressed into my skin. I felt secure in his arms. Avro had always made me feel safe, and I could be myself.

His wandering tongue drew circles around my nipple before moving on to the next. With my eyes closed, the world was dark, yet I saw more than ever before. The tenderness in how he touched me and the whispers he placed on my skin were all I needed between us. Every caress made my heart pound harder, and the passion I'd been hiding from came alive and coursed through my system.

"God, Avro, please."

"Please, what?" he asked, his voice filled with a deviousness that I'd always known he had, but this was new.

He wasn't holding back or hinting at the mischievousness that lived inside of him. His teeth grazed along my ribs, and I fought the urge to open my eyes and watch as I shuddered in his hold. I let my arms drape back over my head, and it felt so freeing to be like this, trusting him a hundred percent to hold me and not let me fall.

"More," I managed to say, my mind nothing but a muddled mess.

"More of this?" Avro asked.

Warm hands slid up my back and forced me to sit up a little, and I sucked in a shuddering breath as he sucked my nipple into his mouth. There was no swirling or teasing this time, and the sensation of his insistent mouth had me gripping his hair and pulling him closer.

"Yes, more, please," I mumbled between the ragged breathing.

Releasing my nipple, Avro kissed me again, and I wanted everything he had to give right this second. I wanted the release. I wanted to feel him inside of me. I wanted to push away what happened to me years ago, and a part of me wanted to forget last night—not all of me but a part. I wanted to start clean, with a fresh slate, and fill my mind with new and better memories. Memories that would make me wet and crave the touch of another. Memories that would make me feel like I'm a woman to be desired, not damaged and broken inside.

I hadn't noticed us walking until Avro sat down, and my knees touched the cool leather surface of the couch. The shock had my eyes fluttering open, and I was greeted by the warmth of Avro's amber eyes. I had to take a moment to stare into them and make sure he was real.

"I love you looking at me like that," he said, nipping at my bottom lip.

"Oh yeah, and how is it that I'm looking at you?" I smiled and settled into his lap.

"Like I hung the moon for you. Whether I did or not doesn't matter. That's what it feels like when I look into your eyes."

My face heated, and I wanted to fan myself. "Have you always been this romantic, and I'm just now seeing it? Have I really been that oblivious?"

"I may have been hiding it, just a little." He smirked as he slowly leaned us over until my back touched the couch. I hissed. "Too cold?"

"No, just need a second," I said.

Avro pulled away and stood up. I shivered as I frowned at him, hating to lose the feel of his body. He laughed and peeled his T-shirt off before tossing it at me. I snatched it out of the air and felt like Jace from the other night as I brought it to my nose to breathe in his scent. He always smelled so damn good.

His hands went to undo the button on his jeans, and my body jerked like we were connected. With each agonizingly slow click of the zipper, my body temperature rose until it felt like I was melting as his cock came into view.

"Do you want me to use protection?"

Avro slid his jeans down his legs and stepped out of them. Licking my lips, I tried to form words as he stood tall before me. Avro snickered, but it sounded sexy. He turned and walked over to the large shelf that held the refilled jars of condoms that we placed around the bar for patrons.

"How about I do until you tell me not to? Deal?"

I nodded, still no sensible words coming to mind as I feasted on the sight of his muscled back and tight ass. I could just make out the scars, a lighter shade than his tanned skin, on the outside of his knee.

Avro turned around and held up a condom as he walked closer.

"I got peach," he said, his lip curling up. "I find that very fitting." He held out the shiny little packet to me, and my hands shook as I took it from him. "I want you to put it on." Bending over, he placed his fingers under my chin and lifted my head, so I had to stare into his eyes as he spoke. "You're in control here, Raine. I'm yours to do with as you wish." His lips brushed mine, the slight contact sending a charge through my system that spiked the scorching desire to a whole new level.

Avro stood straight, and I was left staring at the long cock directly before me. A tiny glistening droplet of pre-cum formed, then dripped down the head, and I suddenly wanted to taste him. Leaning in, I tentatively traced my tongue along the line the little droplet had traveled. Avro groaned, and it felt like that sound was directly connected to my own desires. I felt myself getting wetter, and the ache building between my legs had me wiggling on the leather.

"Fuck yes," Avro groaned.

Wrapping my hand around him, I did what I'd always fantasized about and slipped his cock into my mouth.

"Damn, Raine, you have a hot mouth."

I was quickly learning that I liked the praise. It wasn't something I'd ever thought about, but every word, groan, or touch of encouragement increased my desire. Closing my eyes, I let go and allowed myself to be in the moment and enjoy this time with Avro, letting the weight of his hand resting on my head and the noises he made fuel me.

"Fuck, I need you to stop." Blinking, I looked up at Avro. His eyes seemed darker, with his black hair falling forward, shadowing his eyes. I really loved this color on him.

"I want you now," Avro said, and I shivered with anticipation.

I struggled to open the packaging, and as soon as I did, I smiled at the scent of peach hitting me in the face.

"This is really going to be my nickname forever," I asked, pulling the condom out.

"Yeah, good luck getting Jace to change it, and the more you don't like it, the more he will purposely use it." Avro smirked.

"Good to know." I stared at the condom and realized that I probably should've practiced this at some point. I wasn't even sure which way it went.

Seeing my dilemma, Avro gently plucked it from my fingers. Turning it the right way, he sat it on the tip of his cock the proper way and I placed my hand in his. There was something incredibly erotic about doing this with him. Our hands worked the latex into place, and his eyes never left mine. As bold as I had been the last few minutes, it became clear that I was in control.

Avro had given me power, and this was my consent. It felt strange, like an out-of-body experience, as I lay back on the couch, and Avro gripped my panties, skimming them down my legs. An old nagging memory tried to form, but I crushed it as I pictured stepping on it in my mind and kicking it away. Nothing was ruining this moment for me.

I couldn't take my eyes off his as he moved over me, and his weight blanketed me in warmth. I wrapped my arms around his body, soaking in the feel of him and savoring this quiet moment between us. No walls. No boundaries. No fear.

"Is this what you want?" He baited me as he wiggled his body back and forth. The tip of his cock brushed against me.

"Yes."

He kissed me again, still just as controlled, while I felt frantic for him to continue. My body was singing with need and screaming with sensitivity at the same time.

"Then put me in," he said against my lips. The command was soft, but it was clear that Avro wasn't giving it to me unless I took what I wanted.

I slid my hand down, and he lifted his hips, so I could wrap my hand around his cock, doing as he told me. I took control. I rubbed him all over my clit and moaned from the teasing before lining him up. I was so wet, and the throbbing in my pussy was almost painful.

"You ready?" Avro whispered in my ear, and all I managed was a nod. My mouth was dry, and my brain was misfiring.

"You sure?" he said again, urging me to use my words.

"Yes, please," I panted.

I sucked in a deep breath with the feel of his body flexing and his cock easing inside me. My back arched off the couch as he pressed forward until I was sure he couldn't all fit.

"Wrap your legs around my waist," Avro said, and as soon as I did, he sank deeper. I yelled out with pleasure that was verging on pain as he bottomed out. "Oh fuck, Raine. I want to be gentle with you, but I'm already so close. I need to calm down," Avro groaned.

I didn't want him to be calm. I wanted him to feel as insanely wild as I felt. I clenched my thighs around him, and he shuddered in my hold. Gripping his shoulders, I bucked up into him and cried out with the delicious sensation.

"Fuck, Raine, you need to stop that, or...." He sucked in a ragged breath, his large body shuddering as my hips became more insistent. "Fuck it," he growled out and rose on his arms.

I hated to lose his heat but didn't care about anything as he pulled out and thrust in so hard that my mouth was forced open in a scream of pure pleasure.

My nails ran down his muscled arms as he picked up the pace, and I could feel the climax coming.

"Touch yourself," Avro said, and I opened my eyes, confused by the order. "Rub yourself, Raine. Cum all over me," he said through clenched teeth.

I had a brief moment of insecurity as I slid my hand between our bodies and felt his hard abs brushing the back of my hand, but it dissolved, and he thrust into me faster until I was a moaning mess.

My fingers rubbed my clit tentatively at first, but the sensation was too delicious, and I picked up the pace. Avro groaned loudly, and even though he didn't say it, I just knew he was close. His eyes were clenched shut, and every muscle was flexed. I slipped my fingers down lower and marveled at the feel of him disappearing inside of me and wanted to see what he looked like so badly. I wished I had a mirror so I could watch.

"Come on, Raine, do it. Slip over the edge. Cum on me and just let go," Avro said, his voice strained.

I rubbed my wet fingers over my clit and let go of the tightly wound stress that felt like it was sitting on my chest.

"Yeah, that's it, right there." Avro encouraged me as I moaned and pushed up to meet his powerful thrusts.

"Fuck me. Take what you need," he growled.

My climax hit, and I cried out as waves of pleasure washed over my body. I dug my nails into Avro's shoulders, and his unrelenting pounding became frantic.

"Yes! Oh fuck. You feel incredible," he said, the sound of our bodies coming together loud in the quiet room.

"Avro, yes, please don't stop," I yelled and begged as my orgasm kept going.

My arm muscles were tired from the workout, yet the continuous wave was building toward a second orgasm, and I could feel myself tumbling toward it. I never wanted this feeling to end.

"Oh god, yes!" I screamed as I reached the peak, and the wild noises he was making only added to the moment. "Fuck, Avro," I cried as the second climax hit me. I froze like it had physically gripped me and held me arched off the couch as the pleasure slammed into my body and flowed out to the tips of my fingers and toes.

"Oh fuck, Raine." Avro's movements were desperate and choppy as he slammed into me and stilled. His muscles bulged as his cock kicked and twitched inside of me with his release.

What would it be like to feel that release deep in my body as he came? I shuddered, thinking about Avro fucking me without protection.

Avro slumped on top of me, both of us panting hard.

"You all good?" Avro asked softly against my neck, and I shivered as he swirled his tongue in little circles and nipped at my ear.

"Yeah, I'm better than all right," I said, and a tear trickled down my cheek. Not because I was sad or scared but because I wasn't. I'd had sex for the first time and felt only pleasure. Smiling, I realized I wanted to do it again, but I wanted to ride him this time. "How long until you can go another round?"

Avro chuckled and slowly pushed himself up to stare down at me. "Give me five," he said and then narrowed his eyes. "This isn't getting us out of our talk."

"I know." I clenched hard around his still-firm cock, and he groaned. I loved that reaction. "I just really want to ride you first."

His lip curled up. "Who am I to deny you that?" he said, kissing me soft and sweet before pulling out of my body.

My mind filled with images of having him and Jace together, and my fingers slipped between my legs. What had changed inside of me, I couldn't say, but I was different. I felt the shift, and hiding underneath was an appetite for more. Much more.

Snake

31

Kaivan

After Roach dragged my ass around town all day on a mission of doing nothing but annoying the fuck out of me. I drove home and collapsed on the couch, staring at the ceiling. Images of Raine were stuck in my head on a loop, and nothing I tried got her out.

Then I realized my sneaky hand had slipped inside my unzipped jeans. Instead of pushing her out of my mind like I should've, I only wanted another taste. Her screaming my name played like a broken record, and I could feel her pussy cumming all over my cock.

I sat up in a rush. "Fuck," I growled.

I stared down at my cock, which had a damn mind of its own lately. I'd even invited one of the sweetbutts over, and I've never been so fucking annoyed as when the thing twitched, got a semi, but that was it. I had no interest. I even pulled all her blonde hair back into my hand so she'd look similar and still nothing as she dutifully bobbed her head. I sent her on her way when it became obvious it was a fruitless effort. Yet here I was with a steel rod and only one person to blame.

There was a lot of shit I was piling on the Raine train, and each time I tossed another layer on top, I should've wanted her less, but nope, I wanted her more.

I swore a blue streak as I stood and marched toward the bathroom, pulling my cell out of my jeans. I hit Roach's number as I pushed them down.

"What the fuck?" Roach answered the phone on the fourth ring.

"You asleep?"

"It's four in the morning. What the fuck do you think?" Roach barked back.

"It's three-fifty-seven, to be precise," I mumbled, reaching into the shower to turn on the water.

"Whatever, close enough. Hang on." I could hear sheets moving, and a rustling sound before Roach came back on the line. "Okay, I'm back."

"You're getting a blowjob, aren't you?" I asked and wished my cock was nice and let me have one earlier.

"Of course I am. You wake me up, and I'm hard. What do you think is going to happen?"

I shook my head. "I don't know. Maybe wait till I'm off the phone. Just a thought."

Roach groaned, and the phone was muffled as he covered it again, but I could still clearly hear him giving directions.

"Yo, can you knock it off so I can get this out?" I yelled.

"Fuck, no need to yell, man. I'm not deaf."

Before I reached through the phone and killed him, I took a deep breath.

"I need you here at eight," I said.

"Like tonight, right?"

I stared at my phone, tempted to call him an idiot.

"Why the hell would I call you at three-fifty-now-nine in the morning and wake you up if I didn't need you until tonight?" I asked, my voice thick with sarcasm.

"Dude, we are night owls. I'm not sure if you understand the term, but it means my ass doesn't roll out of bed until eleven in the morning if you're lucky," he bitched and then groaned.

"Just fucking be here at eight, bring your truck, and stop getting sucked off in my ear," I yelled. Roach laughed as he hung up.

I finished stripping and got into the warm water, letting it beat down on me. The water didn't do anything to cool the churning rage in my gut that, for whatever screwed-up reason, was making me so hard my balls ached.

"I give up. It's not like anyone is in here," I mumbled.

It was just me, myself, and my mind calling me out on my feelings. Pushing the annoying voice aside, I grabbed the soap and lathered up my cock. A deep groan rumbled from my mouth as I stroked my shaft. Closing my eyes, I shuddered as blue eyes danced with pleasure and fear in front of my face, and I let myself remember exactly how Raine felt.

I squeezed my cock a little tighter as I let the memories flick from one image to the next like an old projector. I could picture her riding me, her tits bouncing as I sucked on them. I vividly remembered how tight and wet her pussy was and how she tried to deny that her body wanted me, yet she came all over my cock.

"Fuck," I murmured and pressed my free hand on the tile for support. I could hear her yelling my name. The sound echoed around in my mind like a ping-pong ball with nowhere to go.

My hand moved faster along my aching cock. I wanted to taste her for real. No little peck as teens, but an all-consuming kiss that would steal the air from her lungs. Then run my tongue in a line down her body, making her squirm under my touch until I reached that sweet little pussy and ate my fill of her.

I wanted to sit her on my lap in the clubhouse and let all those fuckers see her body bounce as she rode my cock in front of them. They would be hands-off, or I'd cut theirs off, but fuck that image. They'd all want her, but none would dare touch her because she was mine.

"Oh, fuck me," I said, my teeth clenching as my jaw snapped tight. The sound of the soap and my hand helped me visualize my cock slamming into her body. "Shit!" I yelled and came hard. I watched the shot hit the wall, closely followed by more than I'd ever cum before.

Draining the rest of my release, I swore a streak that would impress a sailor. The girl was fucking with my head. Not just my damn emotions. No, she had to go for the gusto and take it all. My mind, my heart, my cock...the next thing she would be after is my soul.

I quickly finished my shower and hated and loved the euphoric feeling that imagining Raine gave me.

"What the fuck?" I yelled as I whipped open the curtain and found Wilder sitting on the counter by my sink. Grabbing my towel, I tied it around my waist as I glared at the guy trying to give me another fucking heart attack.

"Wilder, what the hell, man?"

"What?" he asked and then sucked on a purple slushie.

"How long have you been in here?" I wasn't shy about whacking off or having sex in front of others, but it was usually something I chose to do, and a lot of alcohol was involved.

"A while. I didn't want to interrupt you jerking off. I figured that was rude."

He figured that was rude. I couldn't stop staring at him.

"You really should get a clear shower curtain. It would make it harder for people to come in without you knowing, if that's what's upsetting you." He shrugged. "It would upset me. Anyone coming into my bathroom would be there to kill me. You're lucky it was just me."

"Have you ever heard of boundaries, Wilder? This scenario, for example, didn't strike you as an inappropriate moment to visit with me. Especially since you didn't plan on killing me."

Wilder twisted his head like he was thinking. Why I found that particular look as creepy as I did, I couldn't say, but the guy genuinely made me wonder what the fuck they were feeding the soldiers overseas.

"So tell me then...." He pulled a small black book and pen from inside his black jacket. "When would be a good time to drop in?"

"Gee, I don't know. Maybe when I'm taking a shit." I lifted my eyebrow as he jotted that down.

"And when exactly would those times be?" Wilder asked.

Was he serious? Did he actually think I scheduled my shits? And was he planning on dropping in for them? Maybe he would hide up in my fan next, a single eye peering down at me.

"Um...it was a joke."

"You shouldn't joke about bowel movements. You need to keep a tight rein on them, so you never need to use the bathroom unexpectedly. That works unless you have water that you shouldn't. Very unfortunate things happen when you jump out of an armored vehicle to use the bathroom. Don't shit on a landmine. It doesn't end well."

I couldn't tell if he was joking or not. With Wilder, anything was possible.

"Riiiight," I drawled out as I waited for the punchline.

Gathering my clothes, I walked out of the bathroom, not surprised to find him hot on my heels. Once more, my creep factor rose as I looked over my shoulder to see him slinking from one spot to the next, as if he'd memorized all the boards that made any noise. Who was I fucking kidding? That was exactly what he did.

"Okay, I'm going to go with the obvious question here. Why the hell are you in my home at—" I looked at my phone. "Four-thirty-one in the morning?"

I tossed my phone on the dresser and let the towel fall to the floor. I figured Wilder had already gotten a close-up view. What the hell did it matter now? Images of having sex in my bed and Wilder slinking out from underneath to ask a question suddenly popped into my head. I felt him staring at me while he took notes in his little black book. I needed to fucking move. That was the only answer, and even then, I didn't think the other side of the world would be far enough for this level of insanity.

"I wanted to let you know that the male fucking your girl has a very unusual past."

My hand clenched as Wilder mentioned the guy I'd seen leaving the bar with Raine. Why was Wilder following him around? That was the question that led to more questions. Was he really following me around, so he was technically following them around? Was I being stalked while stalking? Fuck, my head hurt.

"Why are you following Raine and the bartender around?" I asked, praying he didn't say he was following me. I pulled on a pair of black sleep pants. I still had the goal of getting a few hours of sleep tonight if I could get Wilder out of my house.

"I can't tell you that. It is on a need-to-know basis, and you are not yet needing to know," Wilder said.

I pulled on a T-shirt and turned to face him. Wilder had made himself comfortable. He was sprawled out on my bed, with his arms behind his head, like it was his bed, not mine. Why the fuck not? At this rate, I should just let him fuck me. He'd invaded every other part of my life. Why not my ass?

"Fine. What can you tell me?" I leaned against the dresser and tried hard to be interested in what he was saying. I expected him to say something like the guy used to run with squirrels and dance in a circus.

"I can tell you that he has a checkered past and one that should be looked into. There are some questions that should be answered."

"How very cryptic of you," I drawled.

"Thank you." He smiled as if I meant it as a compliment.

I'd learned over the last few months that common sense and sarcasm were lost on Wilder. He took everything as a literal fact that couldn't be changed. If I said I loved toast for breakfast, he questioned why I switched from toast to cereal one morning. Then wouldn't understand why I wanted variety. He reminded me a little of Sheldon Cooper from *The Big Bang Theory*.

"Why exactly don't you have him under surveillance?" Wilder asked.

I shrugged. "Why would I? Raine isn't my girl, and she's free to fuck whoever she wants," I said, but I wasn't fooling myself. The thought of her not being mine was equivalent to tossing gasoline on the flames of fury in my gut. The earlier rage that had died down was waiting to re-ignite.

"But you like her, yes?"

"I feel something," I said, not wanting to admit that I may still like her.

Fuck, I couldn't even think that without calling myself a liar. I fucking loved her.

I had zero interest in sharing that piece of information with Wilder, though. We'd be here the next two days as I tried to explain emotions I didn't fully understand.

"I know this sensation. I feel something too for the object of my interest." He tapped the pen off his lower lip. "Sometimes I like to watch her, sometimes I want to kill her, and many times I like to fuck her. That is proving to be fun when she stops screaming. Well, I better get going. I need to get some rest."

Oh fuck, he really did have someone he was torturing. I pressed my lips together and beat back the urge to ask who the lucky girl was.

"Such a novel fucking idea," I said instead.

He jumped from the bed and was already marching out the bedroom door. He was still as light as a cat, and I reached the bedroom door just in time to see him make the last few strategic steps to the top of the stairs.

"I'll follow you down and lock the door." I stepped into the hallway to follow Wilder, but he held up his hand.

"No need, I have my key," he said and smiled. "I find that easier than breaking in all the time."

I opened my mouth to ask, 'why the fuck are you breaking into my house all the time?' and, more importantly, 'where the fuck did you get a key?' Then I realized it didn't matter. I had visions of the guy going all *Mission Impossible* on my ass. I actually pictured waking up in the night to find him hanging over me like a giant spider on a string as he waited to ask his next ridiculous question.

Crawling into my bed, I set the alarm, knowing I would feel like a bag of smashed assholes with so little sleep. But I was after answers, and I knew exactly where to start.

Snake

AVRO

Jace

Raine

Wilder

"What the fuck?"
I yelled as I whipped open the curtain
and found Wilder sitting on the counter by my sink.
Grabbing my towel, I tied it around my waist
as I glared at the guy trying to give me another
fucking heart attack.
"Wilder, what the hell, man?"
"What?"
he asked and then sucked on a purple slushie.
"How long have you been in here?"
I wasn't shy about whacking off or having sex
in front of others, but it was usually something
I chose to do,
and a lot of alcohol was involved.
"A while.
I didn't want to interrupt you jerking off. I figured that was rude."

Snake

32

Kaivan

Roach's munching made me want to pull a gun and splatter his brains all over the window. I watched as another large and overly crunchy triangle was plucked from the bag and went into his gob of a mouth. Unable to take it anymore, I put my window down before snatching the bag from his hands.

"Hey, that's my breakfast," he complained, but I only smiled as I stuck my arm out the window and dumped the rest of the bag on the ground.

"It was either that or I shoot you. Since I actually like you, I decided this was better," I said, tossing the empty bag on the floor of the truck as Roach glared.

"Dude, you dragged my ass out of bed at the ass crack of dawn, and we've been sitting here staring at this stupid shop for over an hour. Other than a coffee, I haven't had anything to eat. You need to find new friends to hang out with that can put up with your sour attitude." Roach crossed his arms like he was a sulking child.

"Oh, really? And you've never yanked me out of bed, ordered me to get dressed, and forced me to stalk a certain girl with you?" I tapped my chin. "Now that I fucking think about it. This is all your fault, so you have no one to blame but yourself."

"How the hell do you figure that?"

"Well, you befriended me in prison. That was your first mistake. Then, when your ass was getting out early, you agreed to look out for Hollywood's sister. Now you've taken stalker to all new levels, and lastly, if you'd never taken my ass to that bar, Eclipse, I still would've been completely oblivious about where Raine was." I shrugged. "See, this is all your fault."

"If only I could go back in time," Roach mumbled, but he didn't know how true that statement was. There were a shit ton of things in my life that I would've done differently if I could go back. "So what do you want to do? It doesn't look like this shithole is planning on opening up."

"Well, the car registered to his name is around back, so he's got to be in there," I said.

"You do know this is the Mamba's territory? If they think we are down here working, they won't be too happy," Roach said, his eyes following every car that drove past.

"It's not for work. This is personal."

"Yes, I'm sure that will look wonderful etched into our tombstones." He shook his head. "Might as well pay the guy a visit."

Roach hopped out, and I followed. I hadn't planned on this stakeout becoming any more than a watch-and-learn, but Roach was right. The fastest way to get what I wanted was to kick some doors down.

We casually walked across the road and stepped into the shade of the alley. It felt like the temp dropped ten degrees, not that it helped the wet and sticky feel from the humidity.

Roach was already pulling his lock-picking kit from his pocket as we rounded the backside of the building.

"Not exactly the Ritz," Roach said as something furry scurried into the large pile of garbage.

It could've been a cat, rat or maybe a possum, but whatever it was, it was butt-ass ugly and moved fast. This entire neighborhood was one of those that should be burned to the ground so a developer could start over. I was sure that Derek would do it if Chase asked. The reality was the people that lived down here were exactly like my parents had been. School dropouts with too much time and too little skill. They were the product of the generation before them and the one before that. That mentality was learned. It was passed on like a hereditary disease that spread with each newborn. There were always exceptions to the rule, like I'd been or tried to be.

I didn't want to live in a one-bedroom place, one cigarette away from burning down around you, if you weren't shot by a stray bullet coming through your window first. I hadn't wanted to live in a spot like this where I worried about my girl traveling at night, and you had roaches for neighbors.

My brow furrowed, and I glanced at my friend picking the lock. Okay, I still had a roach, but still.

I became what my parents had brought me up to be. A prison rat who ended up bringing home the biggest fucking roach of them all.

The door clicked, and Roach pushed open the door. The smell of mold and stale cigarettes was the first to assault me. Stepping inside, Roach closed and re-locked the door. We stood there and stared at one another.

"Do you hear that?" He asked.

"Yeah, I do." There was the soft sound of rhythmical thumping and groaning from above our heads. Someone was getting lucky. No wonder he was late opening the shop. I nodded toward a door at the far right-hand side of the small building. "That way."

We walked through the tattoo parlor that had certainly seen brighter days. The leather chair was ripped to the point that it looked like a rat had tried to eat it, and only with the help of the magic silver tape was it not in pieces on the floor. Boards hung on the walls with pictures of people that had come in over the years sporting ink.

"Hold up a sec," I whispered.

Stepping around a few boxes, I reached the front of the shop where once upon a time, I'd spotted the tattoo that was now on my hand. My eyes bounced from one image to the other until I found it. Yanking the old and now faded photograph from the board, I stared at the artwork, the anger beginning to rise. It was just a hand image, and I needed to know who it belonged to.

"Let's go," I snarled as I marched for the stairs. The headboard was banging so loud that it masked the sound of our boots on the rickety wooden stairs. I thought my place was bad, but this place was falling apart at the seams. There were a few closed doors, but there was only one that was slightly open and sounded like a porno was being filmed.

Was it sick of me to like that I was catching this guy with his pants down physically and figuratively speaking? Maybe, but I didn't give a fuck. Pulling my gun, I lifted my foot and kicked the door. There was enough force that when it smashed open, the handle stuck into the shitty drywall.

A woman's scream echoed in the practically empty room as the man of the hour unceremoniously pulled the sheet up to his own chin, leaving her exposed. So much for chivalry, I guess.

"Well, isn't this cozy," I growled as Nick cowered. My eyes fixed on the woman's face, and low and behold, there was Mrs. Collins. In a blink, I was transported back in time, and my stomach rolled a little, thinking about my time between her legs.

"Long time no see, Irene. Seems your habits of fucking around on your husband haven't changed."

"Get the fuck out of my place, man," Nick yelled, sounding way too much like he'd just stepped out of the sixties and reefed one too many times. "I was kinda busy here."

"I noticed. We're not deaf," I drawled. "The difference is, I don't give a fuck."

"Kai, is that you?" Irene asked, her eyes blinking quickly. What the fuck was up with that? Was she trying to wish me away?

"No, it's Santa Claus, and he's the Easter Bunny," I nodded toward Roach.

Nick's face paled a little, and I could tell the lightbulb had just switched on in his brain. He stupidly reached for his cell phone, and I pointed my gun at him.

"I wouldn't do that if I were you. I have amazing aim, and I will blow your cock off." Nick's hand froze, and then he slowly pulled it back. "Smart choice."

"What are you doing here, Kai? I didn't even know you were out of prison," Irene said, then shrank back into the bed as I glared at her.

"Yeah, no thanks to you, I hear," I said, propping my boot on the bed to lean on my knee.

Nick's eyes went to my boot and then up to my face, and I looked away from Irene long enough to see if Nick was going to be stupid enough to say something. Her eyes grew wide, and she swallowed hard.

"I don't know what you're talking about," she said right on cue.

I didn't actually expect her to be honest with me. Liars didn't know how to be honest until their backs were against the wall. Roach paced around the room, and I knew that Nick was thinking of making a run for it.

"You know, Nick, your skill for making smart decisions has certainly diminished. If you bolt for the door, you'll end up with two in the back and one in the head for good measure." Flicking my gaze away from the shifty man, I gave Irene my best don't-fuck-with-me look. "Then I will assume you haven't spoken to your husband?"

"We aren't together anymore," she said.

"Shocking. The point is, I've had some very interesting conversations in the last couple of days. The first one was with Raine," I said, and let that piece of knowledge seep into her brain. I tapped the gun off my knee. "It was amazing what she told me. How the police were told I'd threatened you to have sex with me." I raised my eyebrows at her. "And how you were the one who said it. Didn't exactly paint me in the best light, now did it?"

"I don't know how she got that mistaken. I...ah..." She licked her lips. "I mean, can you really believe anything that little bitch says?" she said.

A growl left me, and I stomped the short distance around to her side of the bed and grabbed her as she tried to scamper over Nick to get away.

Hand wrapped firmly around her neck, I shoved her down onto the mattress and stuffed the barrel of my gun into her screaming mouth. "First, don't ever call Raine a bitch unless you want me to cut out your tongue. Second, don't fucking lie to me."

I got low to her face, so our noses were almost touching. She shivered in my hold. Roach moved close to Nick's side of the bed, so he couldn't take off without me even asking. I appreciated that.

"Third, and this one is the most important. My patience after spending ten fucking years in prison is really like skating on thin ice with hungry alligators waiting underneath. So, here is what's going to happen... I want to know why you said the shit you did. I want to know now, and if you lie, I will kill you nice and slow. Understood?"

Irene nodded slightly.

"Perfect." Pulling the gun from her mouth, I laid it against her cheek. "Start talking."

"Dave found out about us. He'd put one of those nanny cams in the bedroom and caught us on camera. I didn't want to lose my relationship, so I told him that you threatened me to have sex with you," she spit out in a single breath.

"So you decided to tell the cops when I was arrested?" I asked, the gun pushing a little harder into her cheek.

Nick chose that moment to make a run for it, and a child-like screech could be heard as Roach clothes-lined him. Coughing ensued, and Nick let out a loud breath as Roach slammed his foot down onto the guy's stomach.

Roach waggled his finger at Nick. "Tut tut, Nick. Now I get to cut off a finger for fun." Roach pulled a switchblade from his back pocket. He began to scream as Roach stepped on his hand with his other boot.

"Hold up. If Nick here can provide good information, I'll let him keep his fingers. See Nick, I'm a generous guy, but don't try anything that stupid again."

He shook his head hard, and Roach released the parasite from under his boots.

"Dave was more pissed than I thought and ordered me to do it, or he'd divorce me and leave me penniless without a home. I'd committed adultery, and he had it on film. What else was I supposed to do?"

"Exactly how pissed off was Dave?" I asked.

"Oh, livid. He stomped out of the house, swearing and spouting off that he was going to kill you."

A shiver traveled down my spine.

"What did he do?"

Irene shrugged.

"Don't fucking lie to me, Irene."

"I'm not, I swear. He stormed off and was back a few hours later and was calmer, but said he wanted you to move out. That he couldn't live under the same roof as you."

"When did the cops arrive?"

Irene screwed up her face as she thought. "I don't know. I was asleep by then and was groggy, but say, two hours. I don't know, Kai. It was a long time ago."

"Funny how prison will make it feel like it was just yesterday," I drawled. "Anything else you think I should know?"

"The only other thing I can think of is that when the cops came, Dave was all too happy to start telling them how terrible you were to me and how he was planning on throwing you out."

I stood up straight and fixed my gaze on Nick. "Your turn."

I walked over to where Nick was pathetically cowering against the bed. I stuffed my hand in my jacket pocket and pulled out the old image. I held it up to show Irene and Nick, who was whimpering more than Irene. This guy was a putz, and I'd quickly figured out there was no way he was one of the guys who raped Raine unless he had an entire personality overhaul in ten years. A guy who could rape a teenage girl was a different kind of animal than the piece of shit cowering in a ball in front of me.

Nick's eyes were shifty as he looked at the image and then away again. "You know what I want to know, don't you? That's why you're so scared."

A sheen of sweat broke out on Nick's forehead that had nothing to do with the workout he'd been getting a few minutes earlier.

"Before you try to lie, let me ask you a question. Between whoever you are covering for and me, who do you think will mess you up more? Who do you think will make your death more painful?"

Nick rubbed at his eyes, the quaking in his muscles making it very obvious just how terrified he was. "Fine, yeah, I know."

"Nick..." Irene started to say but shut her mouth when I looked her way.

"Keep going, Nick, or I'm going to let Roach here slowly saw off each one of your fingers and toes, one at a time, and if you pass out from the pain, we'll just wait until you wake up to continue."

"I only ever sold two more of those other than yours." He held up his hand. "And mine." He ran his hand through his hair. "The one dude was some random guy traveling through Florida and stopped at my tattoo shop on a whim. I never saw the guy again."

"And the other?" I prompted.

"The other is a guy named Frank, but he goes by Father Frank. He's a real whack job and has his own cult or something. Anyway, he is a friend of Dave's." My lip pulled up in a snarl, and Nick stumbled through the rest of his words. "That's his hand in the photo. He was the first one that chose that image, maybe a month before you came into the shop," Nick managed to stammer out. I looked at the artwork on the guy's right hand and knew this had to be the fucker I was after. Why couldn't I have chosen something like a fucking unicorn?

"How exactly does Dave know this Father Frank?"

"I don't know, man. Some bar, some random conversation, and the next thing you know, Dave is talking about him like he's the next messiah."

"You seem like a man who's in the know, Nick. One of those, like the local barber shop where everyone comes in and tells you their secrets." I squatted down to stare Nick in the eyes. "Tell me, Nick, did anyone happen to wander through your doors and spout off about who all put me in jail or, better yet, who raped Raine Eastman?"

Nick looked down at the floor. "Fuck, man. Yeah, someone might have come in and bragged a little."

"You're going to get us killed," Irene yelled at Nick.

"Well, I'll certainly kill you, and I'm in the same room." I smiled at Irene, but it didn't reach my eyes.

"Talk, Nick."

The man reminded me of a ferret with his narrow features and how he scrunched up his nose and wiggled it.

"His name is Jim, but everyone calls him Jumbo 'cause he always eats those massive hotdogs."

I knew exactly who Nick meant. I'd sat in the garage and chatted with Jim all the time. He might have been Dave's trucking friend, but he was around so much that he felt like family. The betrayal was thick as I thought about what had happened to Raine. About how many times she'd brought him a beer or his dinner when he was over. The more I thought, the angrier I became, until my knuckles cracked. I now understood the looks he'd given Raine and how his eyes would linger on her ass when she walked away.

I was pretty sure Raine had been collateral damage because I hadn't shown up at the fights that night. The fact that I had anything to do with what happened sat like acid in my stomach and burned the back of my throat.

My eyes slowly rose to meet Roach's, and he pulled his gun from the back of his jeans.

"What the hell? What is he doing?" Nick and Irene asked as Roach screwed on the silencer. Nick crawled onto the bed and jumped off the other side as if he could feel the walls closing in.

"We told you everything we know," Irene blubbered.

"I know. Kill them," I said and marched for the door as the sound of soft popping was accompanied by short-lived screams.

I was going to find those three men, and I was going to kill them. They'd signed their death warrants the night they attacked Raine. No one hurt Raine but me. She was Mine.

Raine

33

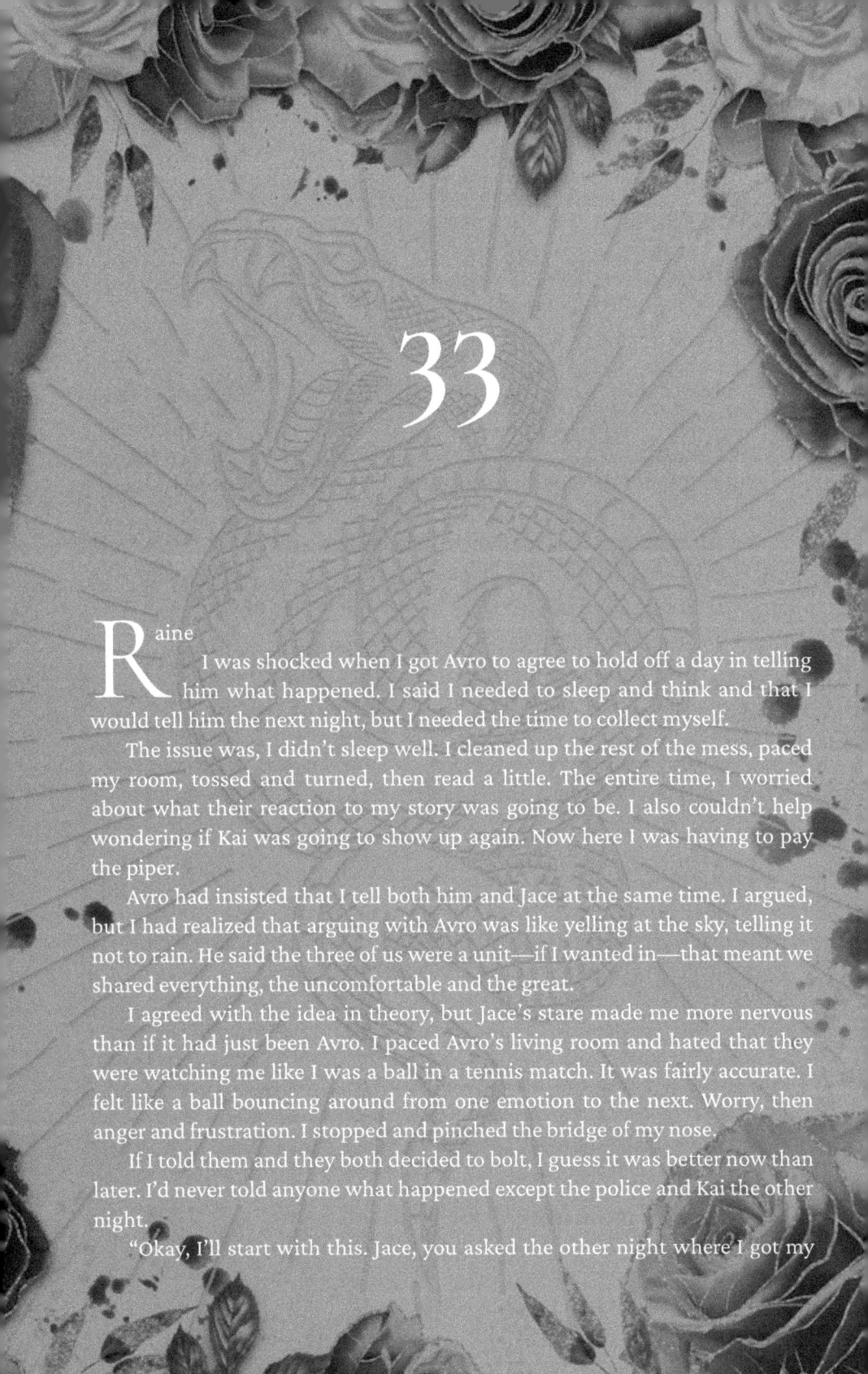

Raine

I was shocked when I got Avro to agree to hold off a day in telling him what happened. I said I needed to sleep and think and that I would tell him the next night, but I needed the time to collect myself.

The issue was, I didn't sleep well. I cleaned up the rest of the mess, paced my room, tossed and turned, then read a little. The entire time, I worried about what their reaction to my story was going to be. I also couldn't help wondering if Kai was going to show up again. Now here I was having to pay the piper.

Avro had insisted that I tell both him and Jace at the same time. I argued, but I had realized that arguing with Avro was like yelling at the sky, telling it not to rain. He said the three of us were a unit—if I wanted in—that meant we shared everything, the uncomfortable and the great.

I agreed with the idea in theory, but Jace's stare made me more nervous than if it had just been Avro. I paced Avro's living room and hated that they were watching me like I was a ball in a tennis match. It was fairly accurate. I felt like a ball bouncing around from one emotion to the next. Worry, then anger and frustration. I stopped and pinched the bridge of my nose.

If I told them and they both decided to bolt, I guess it was better now than later. I'd never told anyone what happened except the police and Kai the other night.

"Okay, I'll start with this. Jace, you asked the other night where I got my scars. I said it was a long story and didn't want to talk about it." The two of them nodded in unison. "I got them the night I was…." I licked my lips and stared at the ocean picture above the couch. "I got them the night I was raped," I said, and my shoulders slumped. It was like a fifty-pound weight lifted from my chest to get the words out.

The guys didn't move or even blink, which was eerie.

"Why are you staring at me like that?"

"Just didn't want to interrupt you. I know that took a lot to get out," Avro said. "I know it was like that for me, anyway."

I nodded and took a steadying breath. "I was just shy of sixteen. My friend and I have birthdays a week and two days apart, which made him eighteen. Anyway, I was attacked at this place that had underground fights." I waved my hand to dismiss that part. "The point is, I was attacked in an alley, and I thought that it was my friend who attacked me."

"Shit friend, if that was your first thought. But that doesn't explain the bruises now," Jace said, his eyebrow shooting up.

I chewed on my lip, angry at myself for wanting to defend Kai.

"I'm getting to that." I wet my lips to get some moisture into my dry mouth. "The friend that I went to see was supposed to be fighting at this club thing. When I was attacked, I mistakenly thought the attacker was my friend."

Avro crossed his arms. "Jace is right. That was some friend, if you thought that about him."

I glared at Avro. "Please don't interject like that. You have no idea what we went through together that led to that moment."

They looked at one another, silently communicating, before turning to stare at me. "You're right. I'm sorry," Avro said.

"The point is I was wrong, but I didn't think I was wrong, and he got a raw deal and was sent to prison for ten years." I sighed and looked up at the ceiling. "I sent my best friend to prison for something he didn't do." The words sunk in more now than the night I realized my error, and I fought back the tears forming all over again. I needed to keep myself together to get through this. "I have all this guilt over it, and I should. It was a shit thing to do to someone I cared about."

They shifted closer to the edge of the couch at the same time.

"Okay, stop doing that. It's weird."

"Doing what?" they asked together.

"That. Stop being so in sync. It's creepy."

They smiled at the exact same time, which I was sure they did to freak me out. Giving up, I started pacing again. The nervous energy was still thrumming through my body, and it didn't seem to want to let up any time soon.

"Okay, we will try to tone down the creep factor. So, tell us exactly what happened?" Avro asked.

This part was the worst. I knew what they would want to do, and I didn't know how to stop them. "My friend...he got out of prison a little while ago and...um. Well, he found me, and he was pretty pissed off about having to go to jail for something he didn't do and that I was the one who put him there for ten years."

Jace's eyes went wide. "So he beat the shit out of you?" His voice was a deep growl that made me shiver.

He leaned back, a scowl on his face as he crossed his arms over his chest. I could leave out what really happened, but with my luck, that would blow up in my face. I figured this entire thing would blow up in my face, anyway. Why the hell would they want to stay with me and the truckload of baggage I dragged around? If I were caught lying by omission, that would make it worse. At least this way, it was all out there, and if they kicked me out of the relationship, they did. Yeah, it was better to know now than months from now.

"He did more than that. He kind of...did what he was put into jail for," I said, and the room went silent.

I stopped near the window and stared out at the ocean across the road, but I could see their reflections in the glass. They looked like they'd been frozen between shocked and furious and couldn't decide which they wanted to be. I turned and leaned against the wall, crossing my arms over my chest as I waited for them to say something.

"I just want to make sure I heard you right," Jace said, slowly standing from the couch. I swallowed hard at the dark look in his eyes and was terrified to see what would happen with him and Kai in the same room. "This guy, this supposed friend, showed up at your house, assaulted you physically, and then raped you?"

"When you say it like that, it sounds really bad," I said.

Avro stood and placed a hand on his shoulder. Jace looked like he was getting ready to have a meltdown. His silver eyes bored holes into mine.

"Raine, that's because it is bad. I mean, who does that to someone who was once a friend? And you said he was in prison. Do you even know what he's been doing or has done? Could he be putting us all at risk?"

"I'd never let that happen," I said.

"How can you be so sure?" Jace asked, his eyes narrowing.

I swallowed hard. "Because I tracked him down and spoke to him first thing yesterday morning."

"That's where you were coming from? You went to go visit your rapist alone?" Avro asked, then shook his head and walked over to the bar. He poured himself a drink and chugged it back. My heart pounded harder at the thought of them wanting to end things. It would be exactly what I deserved.

"Yes, I needed to speak with him for a couple of reasons, and to make sure he was clean was one of them." Avro rubbed at his eyes as Jace paced the floor. "Guys, I need you to understand that I deserved it."

That was the wrong thing to say. Both of them whipped around to face me so fast that I wished I hadn't opened my mouth at all.

"Don't fucking say that," Jace growled. "No one deserves that. We're calling the cops," he said, taking out his phone.

Panic gripped my throat, and I pushed away from the wall. "No. No cops."

"What do you mean, no cops? He fucking assaulted you. Have you seen yourself? Go look in a mirror. You look like you were used as a human punching bag," Jace fumed and unlocked his phone.

I walked over and grabbed the phone out of his hand, glaring at Jace.

"I said no, Jace. This is my life, and if you do call, I'll deny everything," I said, then held the phone out to him. As he took his phone back, I realized he was shaking. "Just listen to me. I put him in prison. I did that. He did nothing wrong and was sent to a place with terrible people for ten years." I put a hand on my chest. "I named him and swore up and down that it was him. We were foster kids with no real family for help. He'd just turned eighteen and ended up spending all that time behind bars with only my face to blame. The one face he trusted most."

"That still doesn't give him the right to do what he did," Jace argued.

I could see Avro moving closer like he was worried Jace was going to Hulk out.

"You're right, it was an asshole thing to do, and I'm not denying that, but I also get it. I was his best friend, and he was mine, and I never even spoke to him after the attack to find out for sure that it was him. I was fifteen, scared, and felt betrayed. Between my foster father and the police, I felt pressured into naming him, so I did. What would you be like if Avro sent you to prison for doing something you never did?"

They looked at one another, and the anger in the room simmered down but only slightly.

"Fine, I concede that maybe I'd be pissed. I can't say I would do what your 'friend' did, but I can at least say I'd be angry."

"Try furious. Your singing career—gone. Your name—tarnished and forever with the label of rapist of a minor hanging around your neck. I'm sure that you would've spent all that time fighting not to be assaulted in prison. Avro would become the object of all that rage. I was the object of all his rage." Jace still didn't look convinced. "This doesn't mean I forgive him. I'm just saying I understand his side."

I reached out to touch Jace, but he pulled his hands away as my fingers touched his. Turning around, he walked to the far side of the room like he needed space from me, and it hurt. I didn't think it would, with us barely knowing one another, but the sting was there.

Avro touched my shoulder, and I looked up into his eyes. "Tell me, how is it that after all this time, you're so certain it wasn't him?"

I nibbled my lip. "When he was...." I stopped, trying to frame my words, so they didn't sound any worse.

"Fucking you," Jace said from his spot, his eyes flashing with anger.

It was way too hot in here, and not for a good reason. My body temperature was going through the roof.

"Yes. When he was fucking me, he held me in a similar position, and I realized that the tattoo I'd seen on my attacker's hand was on the other hand. I also realized that the guy felt like a man, had man hands." Avro arched a brow at me. "I mean, when I was attacked, I realized it was all men, but as I said, my friend was eighteen, and I knew what his body looked like and felt like. From hugs and stuff, and it was no eighteen-year-old who had me. There were three of them, and I was scared with a cloth bag on my head, so I wasn't paying attention to details like that. The tattoo was all I could see well. It was what I remembered."

"And you're one hundred percent positive it was on the other hand," Avro asked.

"Yes, I'm more than a hundred percent positive. The memory of it is burned into my brain."

"I still don't like this. He should be punished for what he did, and how do we know he won't try it again?" Jace argued and shook his head.

Avro answered before I could. "None of us are innocent. We need to remember that."

"What do you mean?" I asked.

"That is a story for another time. Jace does make an excellent point, though. How do we know he's not going to keep coming back?"

"We don't, but I don't think he will. When I saw him this morning, he wanted me to leave him alone." I walked over to the couch and flopped down, suddenly exhausted.

"How did you find him? I'm sure he didn't leave behind a business card," Jace said, the sarcasm dripping from every word.

"Jace, I don't need your attitude. I spent most of my life since that moment living like a terrified hermit. Do you think I don't see that attack like it happened yesterday when I close my eyes? You think I can't feel their hands on my skin or the sharp blade piercing my skin? You think I don't still feel helpless all the damn time?" My anger was stirring, and I clutched my hands into fists on my knees. "It happened to me, not you. And you're not the one who thought for eleven years that your best friend turned on you, only to find out that you fucked up and sent the wrong person to prison. So now not just two of my attackers have been walking around free all this time, all of them have."

I stared at my hands and the faint scars lining my wrists, remembering the white zip ties cutting in and making me bleed. The way the blood ran down my arms.

"They've been dancing all this time, thinking they got away with what they did while my friend rotted in a cell. This is my pain and my cross to bear, and it is also my body and my choice. So, no cops, not ever. If you want me to stay in this relationship with you, no one can ever know what happened."

He ran a hand through his hair and looked down at the ground. I took it as a small victory that he didn't continue to argue.

"As for finding him...he happens to be part of one of the largest motorcycle clubs in the area. It was easy to hunt him down."

Jace threw his hands in the air.

"Oh, this just keeps getting better and better."

He stomped out of the room, and I heard his heavy footfalls on the stairs. I slumped into the couch as the defeated feeling washed over me. My head hurt. The headache that had threatened all day now took hold as the rest of my muscles screamed from everything that had happened.

Avro refilled his drink and wandered over to sit down beside me. He held the glass out for me to take some. It was probably the last thing I needed, but I sipped some of the concoction, anyway.

"Hmm, this one is different. I'm going to say crème de menthe, Kahlua, and coffee mixed with chocolate," I said and then peeked at the counter to see the chocolate milk sitting out. "Not bad."

Avro smirked and took his drink back. "Jace wants to protect everything, and the more he cares, the angrier he becomes. When I told him about my attack, I knew he'd lose his mind and want to protect me. It's who he is. He just needs a minute to calm down."

He picked up my hand and linked our fingers together. I leaned my head against his shoulder. "Does that mean you're not planning on tossing me out the door?"

"Are you crazy?" Avro tightened his grip on my hand and brought it to his lips. The fear I had bottled up inside my chest let go, and I whimpered, letting the tears fall.

"Shh, it's okay." He kissed my forehead, but that only made the crying worse. I didn't deserve his kindness. Chaos loved me, and I was worried that I would only ruin what they had built.

"I know you think I should turn him in, but I can't, not this time. I understand him. I always have. It's like how you and I became friends, that instant connection, and now we finish each other's sentences. I had that with him. I knew him. I knew his heart and his soul, and I never spoke to him, never gave him a chance." I covered my mouth as a sob wracked my body. "I did the same thing everyone else did when they looked at him. I thought the worst. That ache will stay with me forever, and I can't add him going back to prison to the list. The weight of that happening will crush my soul," I said.

"So you still care for him that much?" Avro asked, his voice soft and soothing.

I loved how warm he was. It was like I could curl up in his lap and go to sleep, and he'd make me feel better no matter what was wrong.

"Yeah, I do. I know I shouldn't, and it's stupid, but I do. I saw genuine hurt under the anger. No matter what he did, I can't turn him in."

We sat quietly for a long time before Avro sighed and stood, bringing me to my feet with him. "Then we will respect your wishes. But, Raine, he can't hurt you like that again. Forget Jace. I'll hunt him down and kill him first."

There was something oddly calming about that statement, and I wrapped my arms around Avro's waist and held on tight.

Raine

34

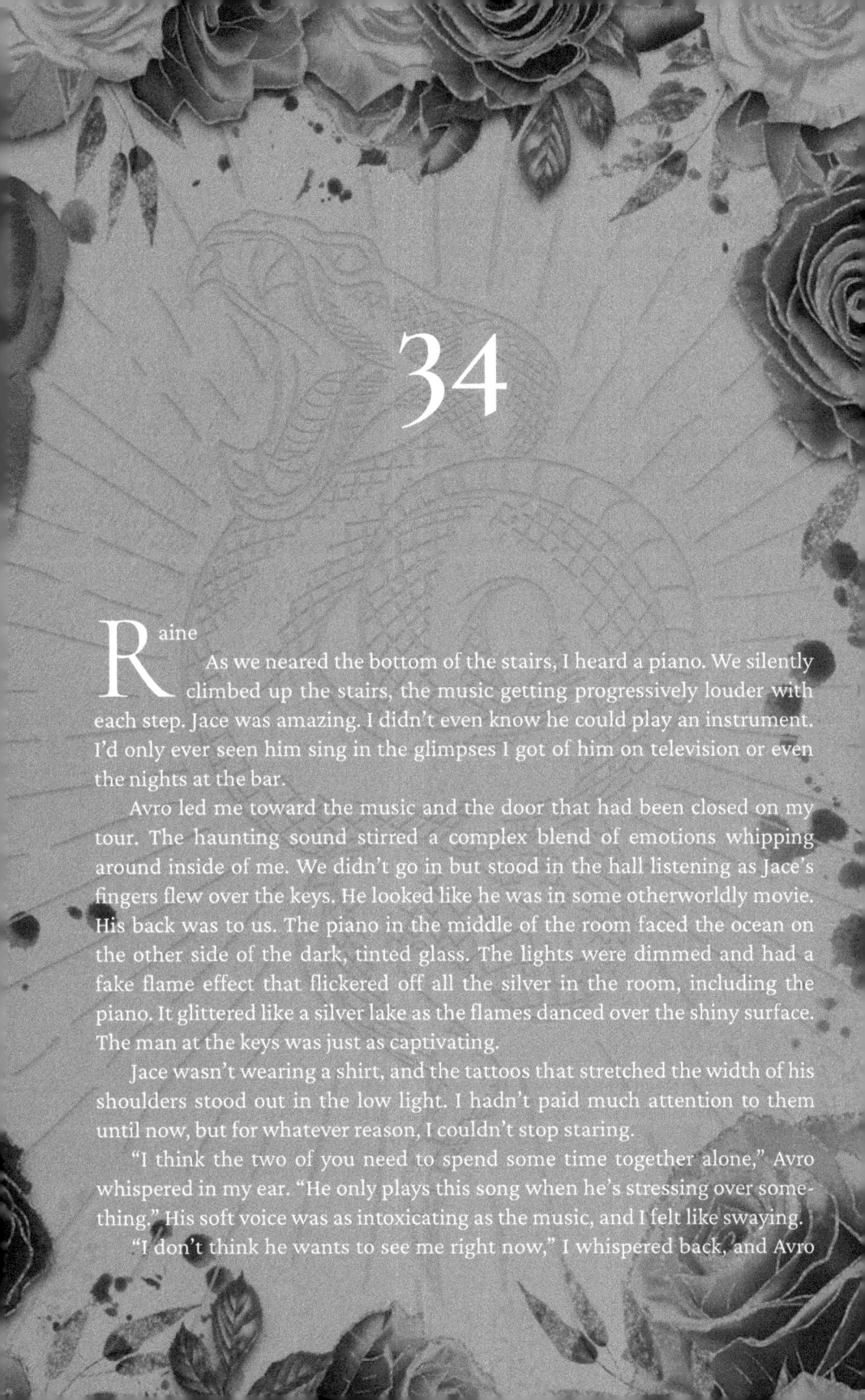

Raine

As we neared the bottom of the stairs, I heard a piano. We silently climbed up the stairs, the music getting progressively louder with each step. Jace was amazing. I didn't even know he could play an instrument. I'd only ever seen him sing in the glimpses I got of him on television or even the nights at the bar.

Avro led me toward the music and the door that had been closed on my tour. The haunting sound stirred a complex blend of emotions whipping around inside of me. We didn't go in but stood in the hall listening as Jace's fingers flew over the keys. He looked like he was in some otherworldly movie. His back was to us. The piano in the middle of the room faced the ocean on the other side of the dark, tinted glass. The lights were dimmed and had a fake flame effect that flickered off all the silver in the room, including the piano. It glittered like a silver lake as the flames danced over the shiny surface. The man at the keys was just as captivating.

Jace wasn't wearing a shirt, and the tattoos that stretched the width of his shoulders stood out in the low light. I hadn't paid much attention to them until now, but for whatever reason, I couldn't stop staring.

"I think the two of you need to spend some time together alone," Avro whispered in my ear. "He only plays this song when he's stressing over something." His soft voice was as intoxicating as the music, and I felt like swaying.

"I don't think he wants to see me right now," I whispered back, and Avro gave me a smile that warmed me to my toes. My eyes were drawn to his amber depths that always seemed to sparkle even in the dim light, like the mischief glowed from inside of him.

"Trust me. Do you think you're up for it, though?"

I peered through the gap in the partially open door and then back up at Avro. I knew what he meant. I nodded and bit my lip. "You don't want to join?"

He cupped my face, and we shared a kiss that was so light, yet held more weight than any other.

"No, you two need to find your path on your own. Besides, I think I had my fair share yesterday," he teased, and my cheeks warmed until I wanted to fan my face. The multiple rounds in the office had been incredible, but the shower afterward was hotter. Avro had some serious skills and played my body like he knew every button to push.

I had to admit that I was a little achy from all the new activities, but as my eyes drifted back to the man playing the piano like he was possessed, I didn't care. The old nervousness still hadn't surfaced, and I didn't know if it was gone forever or if it would suddenly come back, but I was taking all I could get while it lasted.

Avro kissed my hand, which he seemed to love doing, then turned and sauntered down the hall toward the bedroom.

I couldn't do anything but stare as I stepped into the room. Jace's fingers flew over keys, and his messy hair hung in his eyes as he hunched slightly over the piano. But it was the shirtless back and the tight muscles that had my mouth running completely dry.

Stepping up behind him, I tentatively reached for his shoulder. Jace stopped playing and spun around so quickly that I didn't even have time to react before his hand gripped my wrist. The soft silvery light in the room reflected off his eyes and made them look as liquid as the piano behind him. His eyes were hooded, and I held still as if caught in a trap.

He lifted one leg at a time over the bench he was sitting on as he turned fully in my direction. The walls in the room shrunk down around me as my pulse pounded hard in my veins. He pulled my wrist to his nose, and I shivered when he sniffed, as if scenting the blood underneath like a vampire. All he needed was a pair of fangs to complete the look.

"You always smell like peaches. Why is that?" Jace asked, his voice deep but smooth like an aged scotch.

"I don't know," I whispered.

"I like it," he said, and with a tug, I was standing between his legs.

His head was right at my breasts, and he playfully nipped at the zipper, but I couldn't take my eyes off the tongue ring that flicked out. I remembered all too well what his tongue could do and how that piercing felt. If Avro had been doing this, I would've said he looked cute, but there was nothing cute about Jace. He was sexy and rugged in a way that was more personality than his overall appearance, yet he oozed an intensity that reminded me of Kai before prison.

"Were you wanting something?" Jace asked, but as he stood, his body rubbed against mine, and all logical thoughts dove out the three-story window.

I squealed as he gripped my waist. With a single fluid movement, Jace lifted me and sat me down on top of the piano, the lid falling shut with a bang. His hands left my waist to grip the piano on either side of my legs like I was in a cage, and that was almost worse than if he'd touched me. I was suddenly terrified to move.

"I came in to see if you were okay and if we were going to find a way through this," I said.

He leaned in, and my heart sputtered with the sizzling energy he naturally ignited. I didn't know what he would do, and that was part of the thrill. He could kiss me or push me off the piano, and I could see both happening as surely as him fucking me on top of it. There was very little need for clothes in this house with these two around. All they had to do was look at me, and I turned into a puddle at their feet. My hand went to his chest, and he stared at it. I swallowed the lump in my throat as his silver orbs traced the line of my arm all the way up to my eyes. There was something so sexy and yet terrifying about the act.

"You planning on pushing me away, Peaches?" he asked, daring me to say no. I shook my head. "That's very good."

My heart stopped as his teeth nipped at my lower lip and sucked it into his mouth. The jitters in my stomach started, but they were different from before. I didn't fear him, but the anticipation of what he would do next and his ability to amp up every situation caused all my muscles to quake.

Fanning my fingers, I took in the feel of his hard chest and shuddered as Jace groaned when my pinkie finger ran over his nipple with the little bar.

"You seem different, Peaches," he said, and licked a line down the side of my neck.

"I feel different," I moaned, my voice no more than a whisper.

"Why?"

Jace pulled back, and I was forced to stare into those unnerving eyes. "I don't know. After what happened, I should feel worse, more scared maybe, but instead, I feel...calmer."

Jace lifted an eyebrow, and his lip curled up like he was laughing at me. "Interesting. Not the way I would've handled it, but it seems your friend did you a favor."

"I don't think it has anything to do with him," I said, not liking what he was insinuating.

"Oh, we may have already had you on the right path, but your friend literally forced you to relive and face your trauma in an almost identical fashion, I assume." I swallowed. "Not exactly a great recipe for therapy and could've gone wildly wrong, but then again, you're different. Aren't you, Peaches? You like it when Avro touches you with his sweet touch, but there is more to you."

I licked my lips, not wanting to hear what he would say next, and yet I knew he would say it, anyway.

Jace stepped in close to my body, and I shivered, but when he growled against my skin and nipped at my neck, I couldn't deny that I wanted him and was ready to strip my clothes off. Pulling back, he held my chin in his hand, and it felt like he was trying to look right through me with the intensity of his stare.

"You like it rough, Peaches. Whether it was always in you or caused by your first time being so traumatic, maybe. It's hard to say. This could simply be new, but you get off on the fear. I can see it in your eyes."

I looked away and clenched my jaw tight. "I do not," I said. Jace laughed.

"Oh, you can deny it all you want, but tell me something honestly. Did he make you cum?"

I wiggled on the piano, not wanting to answer this question.

"I'm going to guess more than once."

I knew my face was bright red as the tips of my ears burned. Jace moved enough that I was forced to look at him. Was closing my eyes an option?

"I'm going to go out on a limb and say that you screamed for him to stop, begged for it to be over, but there was a part of you that loved his hands holding you down, and that was even more terrifying to you than the sex. At least twice. But my guess is you came at least three times."

I crossed my arms over my chest. "Even if I did, it doesn't mean anything."

"See, I knew I was right 'cause I don't hear a denial." He smirked, and I wanted to smack the look off his face. "It's fine. I don't care that you got off. I probably would've while watching the show," he said, and my mouth fell open. "Don't look so shocked. There are a lot of kinks out there, Peaches, and we will explore them all until we find out what makes you so wet that you beg to be fucked. 'Cause you see, that is one of mine. I want to hear you beg for my cock from these sweet lips of yours."

I was fully clothed, yet I felt completely naked in front of him. He had just put his hand into my soul and ripped it open. I hadn't wanted to face my feelings about my time with Kai. Had I been scared? Hell yes. Had I not wanted it at first? Also, yes. But I couldn't deny that fighting with him in my bedroom had turned me on, and the fear of what I knew he would do intensified every touch. The moment Kai groaned in my ear and slipped into my body, something that I thought was disgusting took over inside of me—something that wanted the adrenaline and to feed off his anger and my terror.

"I don't want to talk about this," I said, and pulled my chin out of Jace's grasp.

"We don't need to talk about it, but it doesn't change facts, Peaches. You're fucked up, but in all the most delicious ways."

He smiled and stepped around the piano bench, out of my reach, which was good because I was liable to hit him. The voice inside my head warned that everything I said I didn't like or want would happen if I did it. My stomach tightened into knots as the thought had me squeezing my thighs together.

He was right. I really was messed in the head.

Jace grabbed his discarded T-shirt off the plush black chair in the corner and pulled it over his head. My eyes traced every movement of his reverse striptease, and even that was fucking hot.

"If you're done staring, I'd like to take you somewhere," he said with a teasing tint to his words.

"Where?" I asked, my eyes darting up to his.

"That's a surprise."

He walked toward me like a model as he ran his hands through his shock-white hair that, when you were up close, had strips of silver. I'd learned his hair color was similar to my platinum blonde, and I badly wanted to see his natural shade. My brain was still in a fog when he wrapped his arm around my waist, and as easily as he'd put me on the piano, he lifted me down.

"I could've gotten down," I said.

"Yes, but then I wouldn't have had your hard nipples pressing into my chest." Of course, I had to look down, and Jace snickered when I could see the evidence for myself. "Come on. I'll make this adventure worth your while."

"Wait a second." I tugged back on his hand as he grabbed mine. "That's it. You're no longer angry with me for not wanting to call the police?"

"Oh no. I'm still livid about that, but I want to show you something before we talk more."

I nibbled my bottom lip, and in the span of a breath, his lips were on mine. My head spun, and the earlier fog returned. Jace didn't just kiss me. He commanded my attention and took what he wanted, how he liked it. I gripped the white T-shirt and held on like it was the only thing holding me up.

Breaking away, Jace stared into my eyes. "Please," he whispered. A word I just knew he rarely ever said. I nodded, not trusting my voice.

Holding my hand, he marched out the door, and I was practically jogging to keep up with his long strides.

"Yo, Avro," Jace called out when we reached the top of the stairs.

"Yeah." Avro poked his head out of the bedroom door.

"I'm taking Peaches for a drive. We'll be back in a few hours," he said, and even though I knew they had a unique relationship, it wasn't until Avro smiled that I truly understood how complicated the layering was.

"Sounds good. I'm watching sappy rom coms, anyway," Avro said and laughed. "Are you going to be near Terri's Place?"

"Yeah, you want anything?"

"Couple pounds of spicy dill pickle and garlic wings with loaded fries and a banana milkshake."

"I swear to fuck you're pregnant, 'cause that is disgusting." Jace made a gagging face, and I laughed. It was pretty gross, but I'd seen Avro eat worse.

"If I am, it's yours, so we're fucked," Avro called back, making us laugh harder.

"Where are the keys?"

"Jacket pocket, and don't have too much fun without me," he called out as he disappeared into the bedroom.

"We're going to have all the fun without him, but don't tell him," Jace said, looking down at me.

"I fucking heard that," Avro yelled, making us both laugh as he jogged down the stairs.

When had I ever felt so free or at ease? Hell, I didn't even think feeling anything like this was possible. It was all fantasy and made up by those who wanted to convince little girls that there were perfect happily ever after stories out there. It was all bullshit, or at least I thought. Watching how Avro and Jace maneuvered through their conversations, the push and pull that was so natural, had my jaw dropping regularly. Score for communication. I'd never seen anything even close to the trust they shared, and it gave me so much hope.

Stopping at the door, Jace grabbed a baseball hat and pulled on a hoodie. "Don't you ever get sick of it?"

"What?"

"This." I held my hands out to what he was doing. "The constant hiding of your face and being unable to do normal things like go to a store in a mall or eat at a restaurant without a million pictures taken or people screaming and running up to you?"

Jace shrugged and put a pair of sunglasses on, even though it was dark outside. "It's part of the gig. If you don't want the success, don't fucking put yourself out there and act like you do."

"That's a pretty harsh way to look at it," I said.

"Not really. It's just the truth that no one wants to say out loud. We all grow up seeing what it is like to be in the spotlight. It's not like it's a shock that you're invited to fancy events and your moves are scrutinized, or your manager does shit to get your face in the news. It's all part of the game. Now if I'd been a kid, that's different, but I was twenty when my first video went viral, and two years later, I was offered a record deal and a five-year contract to travel."

We opened the back door, and Jace stepped out and looked up and down the street like we were getting ready to break into it, never mind leave the house. Convinced the way was clear, we walked to Avro's car and hopped in.

"The thing is, Peaches," Jace said as he removed the glasses and tossed the expensive rims in the cup holder like they were from a dollar store and didn't cost a fortune. "I never intended for the song to go viral. I was just having some fun and posted the videos on the right platform, at the right time. It was mostly luck." He started the car and backed out of the driveway. "And as much as I love to sing and, of course, the money, I prefer to be here with Avro writing songs. So that's my goal and dream once my contract is up."

We pulled out onto the main road, and I let what he said sink in. It was true. You didn't know what was going on inside someone. Because Jace Everly, the frontman for Grimhead Crew, wanting a simple life—I never would've guessed it.

Jace

35

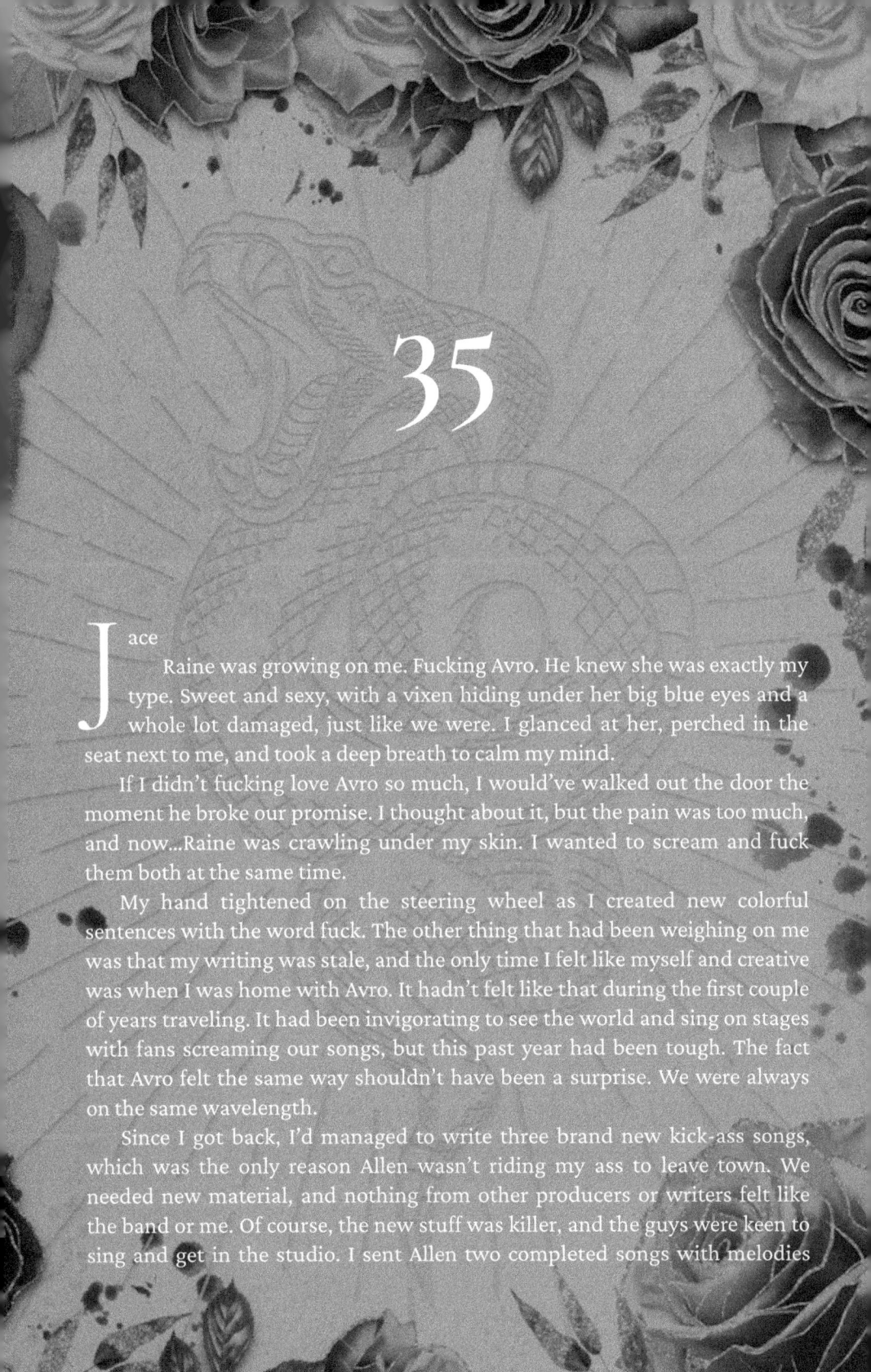

Jace

Raine was growing on me. Fucking Avro. He knew she was exactly my type. Sweet and sexy, with a vixen hiding under her big blue eyes and a whole lot damaged, just like we were. I glanced at her, perched in the seat next to me, and took a deep breath to calm my mind.

If I didn't fucking love Avro so much, I would've walked out the door the moment he broke our promise. I thought about it, but the pain was too much, and now…Raine was crawling under my skin. I wanted to scream and fuck them both at the same time.

My hand tightened on the steering wheel as I created new colorful sentences with the word fuck. The other thing that had been weighing on me was that my writing was stale, and the only time I felt like myself and creative was when I was home with Avro. It hadn't felt like that during the first couple of years traveling. It had been invigorating to see the world and sing on stages with fans screaming our songs, but this past year had been tough. The fact that Avro felt the same way shouldn't have been a surprise. We were always on the same wavelength.

Since I got back, I'd managed to write three brand new kick-ass songs, which was the only reason Allen wasn't riding my ass to leave town. We needed new material, and nothing from other producers or writers felt like the band or me. Of course, the new stuff was killer, and the guys were keen to sing and get in the studio. I sent Allen two completed songs with melodies this morning, and my phone had been blowing up with how much everyone loved them. He was tempted to cancel the next few concerts so I could finish a whole album. Maybe I would tell him I wanted to go country just to watch him faint.

Raine's hands were in her lap as she played with the cuffs of her hoodie, and I wondered if it was a nervous habit. I filed the information away.

I was going to ease her into the questions, but it wasn't my style. I tended to go for the jugular. So why stop now?

"Do you love Avro?" I asked. Raine's head snapped in my direction, eyes wide and mouth open. "You heard me. Do you love him?"

"I...I...I...."

I lifted my brows. "It's a simple yes or no question. No need to make it complicated," I said, and she fixed me with a glare that had my blood warming.

"I don't know," she said, and crossed her arms over her chest. She definitely didn't like talking about herself or her emotions, but that was going to fucking stop. There was a lot of shit that I wasn't good at, but my communication was A-1.

"Hiding behind indifference doesn't make emotions magically disappear," I drawled, knowing how much it would annoy her. "I mean, you've managed to get away with it for years, but that's why you were a fucking disaster when I met you."

"Wow, way to just toss that shit out there, Jace. I thought you said you were going to make this trip fun?"

"Hmm, did I, though? I said I'd make it worth your while, but that is completely different. It's your fault you didn't get clarification before we left." I smiled at her and loved that she pressed her lips together in a hard line as she shot daggers at me with her pretty blue eyes.

That's it, Peaches. Let the tiger out to play.

"Besides, what good does it do us if we sugar-coat shit? All it ever does is create half-truths, hurt feelings, or misunderstandings, and honestly, I don't have time for that shit. If I like you, I like you. If I don't, you fucking know it. So, I will ask you one more time. Do you love Avro?"

Raine licked her lips, and I was so fucking tempted to grab her face and scare the shit out of her as I kissed her while driving, but the highway was too busy to do that tonight. Scaring the shit out of her was one thing. Driving head-on into another car was not on my bucket list.

Raine sighed and leaned her elbow on the door as she rubbed at her forehead. "This is all new."

"But you've known him for four years. Are you saying you have no idea how you feel after all that time? I find that hard to believe. And if you're just leading him on, I will leave your ass right here on the side of the road," I growled.

Raine turned in her seat and hit me with a glare that went straight to my cock and had it swelling. The way her brows drew together and those bright blue eyes sparkled with anger...Even the way she bit her bottom lip like she was trying to bite it off rather than say what she really wanted. Fuck, that look was hot.

"You can't force me to say something I don't fully understand. Feelings don't exactly work that way, Jace," she said, her voice venomous as she said my name, and my cock twitched a little more. If she kept looking at me like that, I was going to pull over right here on the highway. It would make a great headline for the tabloids when the state police came knocking on the rocking car window.

"Tell me what you do feel. Spit it out, Peaches. Let go of all the doubt and wonder and worry and what ifs and just speak," I said, my voice holding as much heat as her gaze.

"Fuck, you're irritating," she groaned. I smirked. "I think so, but I'm not sure, and before you spout off again, I'll tell you why. I've spent our entire time together as friends. Did I want him? Sure, but I wasn't stupid enough to pine over something I thought would never happen. I shut down any inappropriate feelings before they got a chance to get rolling."

She held out her hands toward me. "You're asking me to describe how I feel when I've barely got my head wrapped around the ludicrous idea he even wants me. Then with the shit that happened with my ex-friend, I'm just not in the right head space to say yes, I love him, or no, I'm not as a definitive answer."

She moved her hands in two circles in front of her chest. "There is so much going on right now that I don't know which end is up, but if you are asking if I have strong feelings, then yes. He makes me smile and feel safe. He makes me feel things that I thought were only in fairy tales. So if you want to kick me out on the side of the road for that, go for it."

"Fine. Do you think you could?"

She nodded, but the softness in her eyes and the way her shoulders relaxed said she was all up in her feels, even if she didn't recognize it.

"Yeah, I do." She cocked her head. "Why aren't you asking about yourself?"

I tapped my finger on the top of the steering wheel and pulled out to pass a long line of cars that decided tonight was Sunday drive time. "Because I don't care if you love me or not." I gave her the full weight of my stare. "At least not yet."

"If you care so much about what Avro wants, why were you so upset when he wanted to change the arrangement you two have?" she asked.

"Had."

"What?"

"Had, as in past tense. Did you not pay attention in English class?" I snipped and bit the inside of my cheek to keep from laughing as she went as red as any cherry I'd ever seen. "Don't worry about answering. I don't really care. I grudgingly already agreed to his new idea, or I'm going to try for as long as I can." I shrugged, loving this game of poking at her way more than I should.

I still wasn't sure I could hold off having sex with anyone other than my hand for that long, but for Avro, I'd fucking give it my all. Not damaging our relationship was the most important thing to me. Not even my music career meant as much.

"So what does that mean? You just going to start cheating on him when you decide you've had enough?" Raine fumed, and my mouth curled up in a smile. Good, she was protective already, and that boded well for us.

"Do I strike you as an asshole?"

She turned her head like a bird as she stared at me with a 'are you fucking stupid' look on her face. "Is this a trick question?"

"Fine, I'm an asshole. Do I strike you as a cheating asshole?" I asked.

"How am I supposed to know that? We've spent less than a week together. I had a goldfish I knew better than you," she said.

I barked out a laugh and then smiled wide. "I like this side of you, Peaches. You have a fire that you've been keeping buried for far too long."

"Yeah, well, you seem to bring out the colorful side of me," Raine mumbled.

"To answer your question, no, I'm not a cheater. Despite whatever the tabloids, social media, or entertainment shows say, I don't do anything that is not a media stunt or is discussed and approved with Avro. I knew about you for a long time."

"You did?"

"Of course. Avro told me the moment he met you and felt a connection. I knew he'd want to bring you into the fold at some point. I was just sick of hearing him go on about you without meeting you, so I forced his hand. He needs that now and then."

"Oh," she said, and nibbled her lip. "So you actually do media stunts?"

"Yes, that happens. Not everyone does, but I find it works for me and what Avro and I wanted for our private life."

I ran my hand through my hair as I thought about the last time Allen made me do one of those fake shoots and play the role of the jerk boyfriend for ratings. He made a deal with the father of a Princess from some country I couldn't even pronounce. We made it look like we were living together in a fancy hotel suite in Paris.

We were in the same hotel for a month, but other than the staged photos, we never spoke or touched or anything else. The images circulating of us on a balcony, half-naked in a hot tub for the paparazzi went viral overnight. Fans started calling me Rock Prince, which I hated with a passion. I had no idea what she and her father got out of it, but I had a million more downloads than anticipated of the band's newest release in just two days.

"How does this work, then? You feel the urge to get yourself off with someone else and ask Avro for permission?"

"You and Avro," I stated. "If you're serious about being in this with us, then it's an 'us' thing. Not a 'you and him' thing, not a 'him and me' thing, an 'us' thing. Get it?" I pulled off the highway that led toward my old stomping grounds.

"I guess I get it," she said. "This is all very strange. I went from not having a boyfriend ever to two very different ones overnight." She made a little exasperated noise that was fucking adorable.

It made me so damn hard how she was sweet and naïve in many ways and yet so much more. I really wanted to draw that out of her, and the thought had my cock stirring again.

"Did you know Avro wants me to move in? I mean, isn't that a little soon? It seems a whole lot soon to me." She crossed her arms. "He blurted it out while we were at work today. Took me completely off guard."

I laughed hard. "Gee, I wonder what that feels like?" I said, and Raine blushed. "Look, Avro is an all-in kind of guy. He wants you to be with us, so he pushes all his chips to the center of the table. My suggestion is to compromise," I said.

"How?"

"What bothers you the most about moving in with us?" I asked, and she sucked in her bottom lip as she thought.

"I guess losing my own place," she said, her voice soft.

"Then don't. That's an easy fix." Putting on the turn signal, I pulled into the driveway of Terri's Place. This was the best chicken and pizza place for miles. It was a hidden gem far outside the city limits, but Avro and I used to come here at least once a week before I started to tour.

"You mean keep my house but still move in for now," Raine asked and tapped her chin.

"Why not? When Avro gets an idea in his head, he will chase that shit down and bug the fuck out of you until you agree, and good luck saying no. So you might as well give it a shot unless you want him harassing you every day." I swung my eyes to hers as I put the car in park. "And you know he will. Have you ever been able to say no to an idea of his?" I cocked an eyebrow and picked up my phone to put in my order. "Besides, you could rent it out after a couple of months of feeling comfortable and earn another income. If things go really well, you can then sell and put the money away or buy a different house when it's a good buying market. Many options."

Terri and the manager knew us by name and would bring the food out to the car, so I didn't run the risk of being spotted.

"Now that you mention it...No, I don't think I've ever said no to Avro. That's a little terrifying," she said, and I laughed.

"It's worth it, though. Trust me, he will fill you, and I don't mean with his cock, although that will happen too."

Raine laughed and gripped her stomach. The sound was as cute as she was.

"He does have a knack for making you feel like everything will be okay." Raine looked at me while I typed in the text message to Terri.

"Yeah, he really does." I held up the phone to show her the message. "Do you want anything, or would you like to share my pizza with me?"

"What are you getting on it?"

"Spicy buffalo chicken with barbecue sauce." Raine scrunched up her nose. "Trust me, you try it once, and you'll wonder how you ever lived without this in your life."

"Then sure, I'll share with you."

I finished typing in the message and waited for the thumbs up before setting the phone down. We lapsed into silence as we waited for the food. I took the time to gather my thoughts about what I was going to show her.

"How much farther do we have to go?" Raine asked as Terri pushed out the door with bags and a cooler. The man was always thinking.

"Not far," I said and then hit unlock on the car doors. Terri opened the back door, a dance we'd done many times in the last three years.

"Jace, it is good to see you," Terri said as he arranged the food that made my stomach growl. He still looked the same. Terri's dark hair was now going grey, but aside from that, the same smile was always on his face.

"You two, man. Terri, this is Raine." I nodded in her direction. "She is staying with Avro and me. So if you get a message from her, could you do the same thing?"

"For my best customer? Of course." He held out his hand for Raine to shake.

"Nice to meet you, Raine."

"Likewise." Raine shook his hand and offered a very business-like smile, and I picked up on the change even though most never would.

"Oh, Jace, I put the milkshakes in this cooler and packed it with ice for you."

"See, this is why I love you. Thanks, and the money is sent," I said.

"You're always way too generous, mon ami," Terri said, shaking his head as he backed away.

"To keep you in business, it's worth it. Who else is going to make my pizza the way you do and then deliver it to my car?"

Terri laughed. "Given how you're now a fancy rock star, I'm sure every restaurant in the state, but I appreciate your loyalty. Have a good night, and nice to meet you, Raine." Terri closed the door and was heading to the front doors before we could even say goodbye. He'd treated me in the same friendly and efficient manner the first time Avro and I walked through his doors.

"You're a conundrum to me, Jace," Raine said as I pulled out of the parking lot.

I smiled at the comment. "I like to keep you on your toes."

The last few miles felt like a chain slowly tightening around my throat. The memories flashing before my eyes had my heart pounding hard and my hands squeezing the life out of the steering wheel just so I didn't whip the car around and say fuck it.

Raine touched my shoulder, and I was startled by the soft contact.

"You okay?" she asked, her eyes filled with worry.

"Yeah, totally fine."

"Now who is lying?" she quipped.

"I'm so going to fuck that sauce right out of you later," I said, and I meant it.

If this unknown friend and Avro got a taste, then I sure as fuck wasn't standing on the sidelines with my cock in my hand like a good little boy. I'd never been one, so if the shoe fit, as they say.

She cleared her throat and mumbled something I was sure would've turned me on if I wasn't so distracted by the house we were approaching. I shut the car off on the quiet street, so we didn't draw attention, and I sat there trying to control my galloping pulse.

"Where are we?" Raine asked and looked out her window at the dark and boarded-up home. The caution tape was faded and torn but still hung on and flapped in the breeze like a warning sign that something evil had happened inside.

I wet my lips and looked straight ahead, not daring to glance at the house. "This was my home," I said. "Avro lived just down there, the second house on the left." I pointed to the house lit up with pretty little lights, the yellow garage door practically glowing in the dark. "His family is no longer there, though. They moved a while back and never gave us a forwarding address." I rolled my eyes. "We told them we were more than friends. Let's say it didn't go very well."

"Shit, poor Avro. I didn't know."

"He doesn't like to talk about it, but he will if you ask him to."

My leg started to bounce, and I couldn't sit there for another second. I started the car and pulled away from the curb. I could feel Raine's eyes as she silently asked what had happened.

"I just need a minute," I said through the pain constricting my throat.

In reality, I needed a lot more than a minute. It had been six years since my family was taken from me, and the only two things that got me through it were Avro and my music.

There were just some things you were never meant to forget.

Jace

36

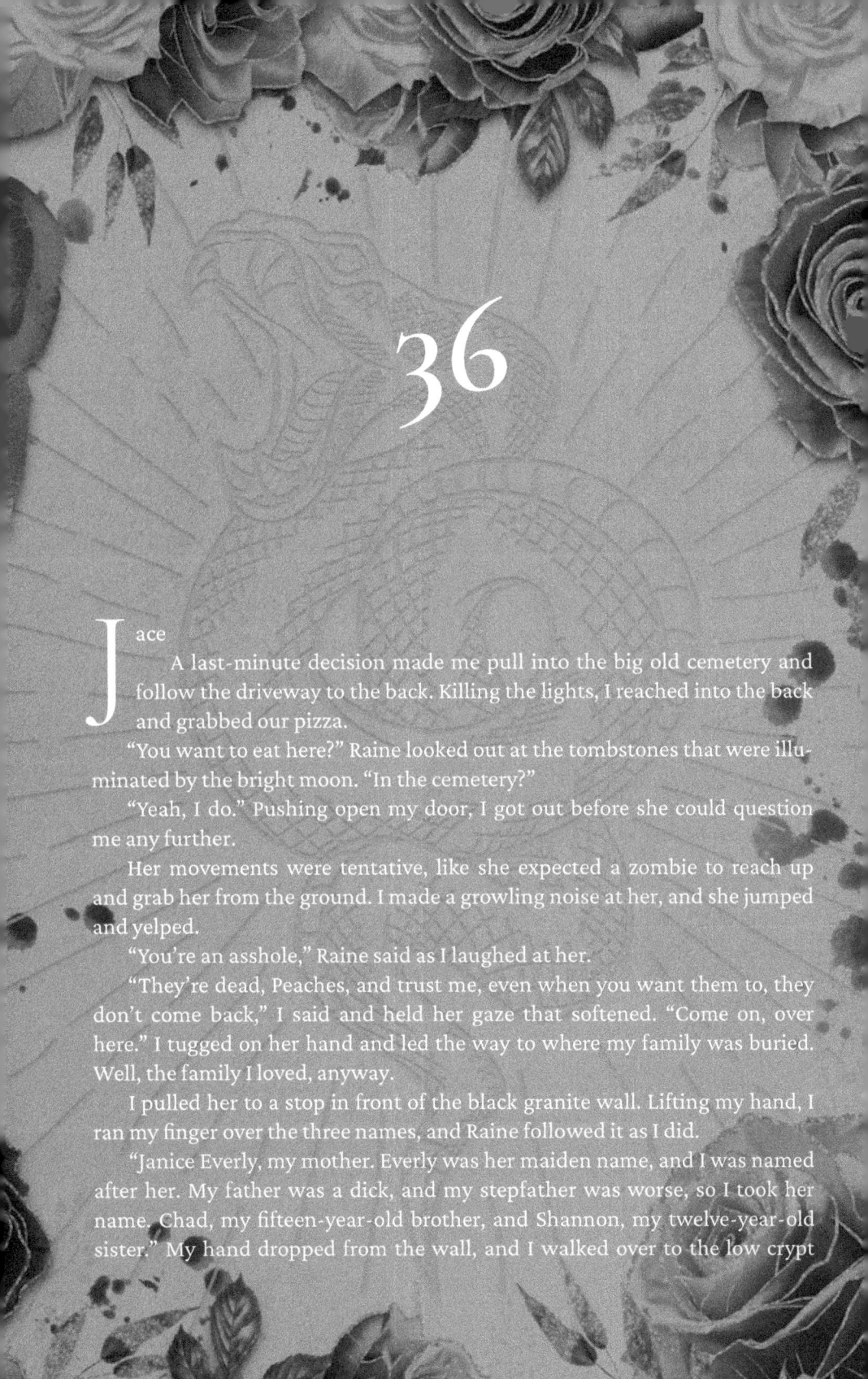

Jace

A last-minute decision made me pull into the big old cemetery and follow the driveway to the back. Killing the lights, I reached into the back and grabbed our pizza.

"You want to eat here?" Raine looked out at the tombstones that were illuminated by the bright moon. "In the cemetery?"

"Yeah, I do." Pushing open my door, I got out before she could question me any further.

Her movements were tentative, like she expected a zombie to reach up and grab her from the ground. I made a growling noise at her, and she jumped and yelped.

"You're an asshole," Raine said as I laughed at her.

"They're dead, Peaches, and trust me, even when you want them to, they don't come back," I said and held her gaze that softened. "Come on, over here." I tugged on her hand and led the way to where my family was buried. Well, the family I loved, anyway.

I pulled her to a stop in front of the black granite wall. Lifting my hand, I ran my finger over the three names, and Raine followed it as I did.

"Janice Everly, my mother. Everly was her maiden name, and I was named after her. My father was a dick, and my stepfather was worse, so I took her name. Chad, my fifteen-year-old brother, and Shannon, my twelve-year-old sister." My hand dropped from the wall, and I walked over to the low crypt beside it. I placed the pizza box on top before turning to Raine. "Do you need a hand to get up?"

"You want to sit on that?" she asked, her voice low and horrified.

"Do you really think whoever this dude was cares? Besides, I sit here all the time, and no one has struck me with lightning. Come on, up you go," I said and held out my hands like a step.

Raine stared around as if someone would come down the dark path screaming that we were going to hell. She tentatively stepped up and placed her hands on the top of the flat roof of the crypt. With a push, she jumped up and sat down with her legs swinging over the edge. I took a few steps back and jumped, using the tomb on the right to push off and up, and landed on the roof of the one Raine was sitting on.

"Holy shit! How did you do that?"

I laughed as I sat down beside her and flipped open the pizza box. It was so quiet here, and I loved coming and just letting my mind wander. I wrote two number-one hits in this cemetery.

"I used to dabble in parkour. I was pretty good, but Avro made it look easy." I nudged the box in her direction. "Try it."

She picked up a piece and stared at it like it might bite before taking a tiny little nibble off the end. I smirked as her features lifted into a smile, and she took another bite. Soon she was eating it and letting out little moans with each mouthful.

"Told ya. The man is a genius with his flavors."

"This is incredible," she smiled and then looked around. "Can I ask what exactly we are doing here, Jace?"

I ate another slice of pizza and stared at the lines of names I could no longer make out from here, but I knew exactly where my family's names were.

"I'm going to tell you why I was so angry earlier." I glanced at Raine from the corner of my eye. Taking a deep breath, I started telling the story that seemed so unbelievable that it had been aired across the country, so I relived it in every time zone.

"As I said, my dad was a dick—my biological father, I mean. He had a boatload of money but took off on my mom when I was seven with his secretary. Do you get any more cliché than that?"

"Oh wow. I'm sorry, Jace."

I smiled and looked over at Raine. "Oh, Peaches, that's not even the main course. That's the appetizer to the appetizer, so you may want to hold off on your sympathy until I'm done."

She bit into her slice of pizza and narrowed her eyes like she was tempted to say something but held her tongue. I was mentally daring her. Not that I needed a reason to fuck her right here on the crypt, but I should finish the story first. Then...we'd see.

"Anyway, it was just as well. He liked to smack us around when he was in one of his moods. It didn't happen all the time, but it happened, and my mom was terrified. He had her so scared that she breathed a sigh of relief when he took off and sent her divorce papers. She'd joke with her friends on the phone when she didn't know that I was listening that she'd never signed something so fast in her life."

A car driving past the cemetery blared its horn at someone else, but we couldn't see what was happening, just heard the loud, *fuck you*. That's kind of how I felt all the time, like I was trapped inside a large area while the rest of the world revolved around me, except with Avro.

"Sometimes I wonder if that prior relationship with my bio-dad tainted how she saw people. Like she couldn't judge who was good anymore, so she decided just to be really nice to everyone. She was always nice, but I think her asshole meter was broken. Then again, so was mine."

I closed my eyes and let the memories I never wanted to think about race to the surface.

"My mom was the best. She was this amazing, warm, caring person and just a little too good. She was the type who never missed helping with homework and would kiss 'booboos' better." I chuckled. "I can still hear her voice and how ridiculous she sounded when she'd say that. She made the best cookies and never made you feel bad for your dreams. She was always telling me I could be whatever I wanted, and she'd support me all the way. My mom meant it too. It wasn't lip service. She'd take extra shifts if it meant I could play sports and would go without new clothes or eating dinner." I paused and bit at my lip as I pictured her beautiful smile that lit up any room.

"She was the type of mom every kid dreams of having, and she saw the best in others, even when there was no good in them to see." Tossing the rest of my crust in the cardboard box, I leaned back on my hands and stared up at the night sky.

It was rare that it was so clear out. There wasn't a single cloud to block out the stars. I used to wish I could be one of those stars, and I ended up a rock star instead. The universe worked in weird ways.

"When I was eight, my mom started dating Lyle, and they decided to marry after she got pregnant with Chad, and then along came Shannon. My stepfather, Lyle, was fine enough, or I thought he was, but I never really saw him as a dad." I shrugged. "I can't say why. He didn't treat me any different from how he treated Chad or Shannon, but it never felt right."

I turned my head to look at Raine, and she looked like one of the statues placed around the cemetery. She wasn't moving or blinking, and for a moment, I wasn't even sure if she was breathing.

"You okay?"

"Yeah, I'm good." She shifted position, so she was staring directly at me, and I didn't know if that was better or if more of her intense focus was worse.

I pinched the bridge of my nose and swallowed as the pizza churned from the tension building in my gut.

"I don't know what I would've done without Avro. His real name is Alex, in case he never told you," I said and let my mind float back to the fight that I didn't know would be the beginning of the end of my family.

Alex and I wandered along the sidewalk toward my house. I didn't get home from Duke as much as I liked. Between the full course load, playing on the basketball team that had brought me there with a full scholarship, and trying to promote my music, it didn't leave much time for family visits.

I glanced at Alex and wished he'd change his mind and move to North Carolina with me. I knew he had dreams of his own, but I missed him. We went from spending every day together to swapping every other weekend. He made the twelve-hour drive two weekends ago and stayed with me from Thursday night until Sunday morning, and this was my weekend to drive back home. I loved the school, my team, and the entire experience, including meeting people to jam with, and yet it felt like something was always missing until Alex was there.

"What do you want to do tomorrow?" I asked and then froze. I grabbed Alex's arm as shouting from inside my house could be heard from where we were on the sidewalk.

"What the fuck?"

"Is that your parents?"

"Sounds like it." I jogged up the driveway with Alex beside me. My mom never fought with anyone, and I couldn't even remember her ever fighting with Lyle, but it was definitely his voice I heard as we neared the front door.

The door was locked, and I slammed into it as I tried to push it open. "Dammit."

Whipping my backpack off my shoulder, I rummaged around in my bag until I found my keys. My hand shook as I tried to get the key into the lock, then something inside smashed.

I looked at Alex, and he had the same horrified expression to match the anger and fear forcing me to break out in a sweat. Pushing open the door, I didn't understand what I was walking in on. My mother was sitting on the floor dabbing a tissue on Chad's head while Shannon stood in the archway to the kitchen, crying.

Lyle was pacing the living room, yelling about something to do with bills and money and where it was going. The sentences were choppy. As soon as he spotted us, he stopped and pointed at me.

"What the fuck are you staring at?" Lyle yelled. His hair was a mess, and his eyes were bloodshot with either lack of sleep or alcohol. I got my answer a moment later when he walked in my direction and looked like he was trying and failing a sobriety test.

"Lyle, did you fucking hit Chad?" I asked, my hands balling into fists.

I stepped toward him with my fists clenching tight and ready for a fight when my mom jumped in my way. She put her hand on my chest and shook her head no.

"Mom," I said, the anger over being held back clear in my voice. Before she could answer, a knock sounded on the open front door, and I looked over to see two officers standing in the doorway.

"You called the cops?" Lyle fumed at my mom.

"No. I did, Dad," Shannon said, the tears rolling down her face. "You're acting crazy," she said through her sobs. "You hit Chad and said you hate us," she wailed.

"You traitorous little bitch!" I pulled my mom into my side as the officers entered the room, their eyes focused on Lyle. My mom was liable to get in their way, but the fact he hit Chad and everyone else was in tears was enough for me to want to kick his ass.

"Sir, we're going to need you to come with us to give you time to calm down," the older of the two officers said.

"I don't need to fucking calm down," Lyle said, squaring off with the officers.

My mom covered her face and cried like I'd never seen before. I hugged her tight and watched Alex check in with Chad before wrapping Shannon in his arms. Chad seemed more pissed than hurt, but Shannon's heart looked like it was breaking. What the hell had caused this?

"Fucking little bitch!" Lyle yelled as the officers got the cuffs on him and escorted him out of the house.

"Mom, what the hell happened? I've never seen Lyle like that." I asked the moment the front door closed.

With Lyle gone, I realized I was breathing easier, and the room felt safer. His eyes held so much hatred, and I couldn't even imagine my mom doing anything to inspire that level of anger.

My mom waited until Alex had herded Shannon and Chad into the kitchen before answering.

"I'm sorry, Jace," she whispered. "I didn't want to tell you and have you worry while you were away at school, but I caught Lyle in a few lies and confronted him last month." She wrung her hands together. "There were these unexplained expenses from a city a couple of hours away when he said he was on the other side of the country for business. He was gone two weeks, got home, and acted like that was where he'd been the whole time." She took a shuddering breath, her lower lip trembling. I hated seeing her like this. "We fought, but I wasn't letting it go, and he finally blurted out that he has a whole other family." She broke down into full-on sobs, and I held her tight, not even sure I heard her correctly.

"I'm sorry, what? How is that even possible?"

She sniffed and pulled tissues out from the pocket of the knit sweater she was wearing. "He has two kids with her, Jace. They're eight and five. For more than eight years, he's been lying to us, all of us. Lyle came over because I had him served with divorce papers, and that was when Chad walked in. Lyle was going to hit me, and Chad took the swing." She wrung her hands. "I feel like such a fool. How often did I wonder why he didn't have the right amount of money going into the bank for me to pay bills?" She put a hand over her eyes. "How was I so stupid? How did I not see what was happening?"

I pulled her into another hug and held her until she said she was tired and needed to lie down.

When eleven o'clock came around, and everyone was asleep, I flopped down on the couch with Alex by my side. He picked up my hand and kissed my knuckles.

"What the hell am I supposed to do, Alex?" I looked over at the one person who had never changed and had always been the calm rock in my turbulent mind. "Mom said she's filed for divorce, and she wants me to go back to college, but how do I leave? I'm the man of the house now. Chad shouldn't have to take on the responsibility. And what about bills?"

"I don't know. Whether you decide to stay is not my call, but I think you need to do what will make everyone's life easier. If that's staying, see if you can get a temporary leave from the program. If your mom really doesn't want you to stay and ruin your scholarship, you need to decide how much you want to push back. One thing I can say is that if you drop out now, you'll never get the same ride, and if you got back, you could walk out of Duke with a six-figure job to help your family. Just things to consider, but I'm here no matter what you decide."

Laying my head back on the couch, I sighed. "Why is this so difficult?"

"Because you want to do the right thing, but you're not sure what that is."

Alex kissed me, his lips soft and warm, and I hung onto him like he was the only thing keeping me afloat.

"Lie down and rest. You can figure it out tomorrow," Alex said.

He gave my hand a gentle tug. I followed his lead and lay down on my side on the couch, facing him. Alex grabbed the blanket off the back and tossed it over us, and as he turned out the light, I shifted closer to the warmth of his body and the scent of the ocean that followed him around. Fuck, I missed that scent.

"Thank you," I said softly.

I hated to be weak. Maybe it was because my dad took off when I was so young, or perhaps it was always me, but I never showed any weakness to anyone other than Alex. He held me without judgment or pity and always made me feel better.

Mom refused to let me stay. She was in hysterical tears when I said I thought I should drop out to help the family until we could figure something out. Ultimately, I decided to go because it was causing her more stress, and that was the last thing I wanted.

"I hate this. I know she said it's what she wants, but why do I feel like such an asshole for leaving?" I growled and peeled my eyes away from the passing trees to look at Alex.

"Because you love your family."

"I can't even wrap my head around Lyle having another family. Mom blames herself, but I never had a clue that something was wrong. Was I the one that was blind?" Alex didn't say anything. He knew I just needed to vent everything I had going on in my head. "Lyle taught me how to ride a bike and helped me fix up my first car. We barbequed together, and he came to all my games. What the hell was I not seeing?"

"He's obviously a very good liar. You can't put this on yourself. I didn't see anything, and I was over all the time," Alex said.

"I guess you're right. What would that make him? A sociopath? A narcissist, maybe?" I turned my head to the scenery, and with each passing mile marker, I felt angrier about the entire situation. How dare he do this to my mom? He didn't want to be a dad to me, then fine, but don't hurt my mom. She didn't deserve that.

We pulled off the interstate at the service station. "You mind pumping the gas? I'll go in and prepay, but I need to take a piss, bad," Alex said as we hopped out.

"Sure."

"You want anything?"

"You know what I like. Just grab me something," I said.

I stared off into space, listening to the sound of the cars zipping along the highway when Alex came back out.

"You good?" I asked, taking in his ashen face and wide-eyed expression. He looked like he was in shock. He didn't say anything and climbed behind the wheel. Poking my head in the door, I stared at Alex. "Dude, what's up?"

"Get in," he ordered, his voice eerily calm and flat. He wouldn't even look at me. "Get in, Jace," he said again, completely freaked out.

I slipped into the passenger seat. I'd never seen him act like this before. He looked like he was in shock or frozen like a mannequin. I was worried something had happened inside the service station. Had someone done something to him? I'd fucking break their legs if they had.

"Okay, I'm in. Now tell me what the hell is going on," I said as Alex pulled out of the lot and onto the overpass. I looked back at the exit he was supposed to take and frowned as he pulled onto the interstate, going back the way we'd just come. He still hadn't said a word or looked over at me. "Dude, you're freaking me the fuck out."

He swallowed and didn't look over but gripped the steering wheel so hard that his knuckles were white and his hands shook.

"Alex, look at me," I said. He slowly turned his head, and it was like watching a horror movie where the person was possessed. "Answer me. What the fuck is going on?"

"Um..." I wanted to reach out and smack him out of it. "You, ah, need to open your phone." His voice was shaking as much as his hands.

"My phone?"

"Yeah."

"Okay, what for?" I asked, pulling the phone from my pocket.

"You need to find the news for our area. Like from home." Alex suddenly grabbed my arm, and I stared at his fingers as they gripped me hard. "Jace...I...Fuck, I'm sorry."

"For what? Besides freaking me the fuck out."

His bottom lip trembled, but he let go of my arm and gripped the steering wheel again.

Terrified now of what I would find, I unlocked my phone and scrolled to the news station from home. There was a live feed streaming. I turned it on and had no idea what I was watching. It was an aerial view from a helicopter as it hovered over a house I didn't recognize. The house was surrounded by police like in a movie.

"Turn on the volume," Alex said. I swallowed and wasn't sure I wanted to know what this was.

"The terrifying standoff is still underway.
Police have been trying to negotiate with the hostage taker for over thirty minutes.

The man, believed to be Lyle Winston, was tracked down here through a neighbor who saw his image on the news earlier today."

Lyle Winston? What was my stepfather doing at that house? Was this the other family's place? Was this the same Lyle Winston? It could be a coincidence.

My mind raced as my heart pounded out of my chest, but I couldn't look away. A cold dread seeped into every part of my body.

Suddenly, three pictures flashed across the screen, and I sucked in a strangled gasp as I stared at my mom's face and two blacked-out rectangles with my brother's and sister's names underneath. Under their names were the words deceased victim.

"No, this can't be real." My hand went to my throat as I tried to get air into my lungs, but I couldn't breathe.

*"Police say they have no motive at this time,
but our crews on the ground say that the three victims
he allegedly killed were his wife and two children.
Police are still trying to find the oldest son.
Bang, Bang, Bang...Bang
Four shots have been fired inside the home,
and as you can see, the police are storming the house now."*

I couldn't tear my eyes away. The world had become the small screen, the tiny thumbnail images of my family. Minutes ticked on, and the police slowly walked out of the house but didn't bring anyone with them. Switching the screen over to my cell, I tried my mom's phone, but no one answered.

"No, no, no." Hands shaking, I hung up and tried my brother. "Come on, Chad, pick up, pick up, dammit." Tears blurred my vision as I tried my sister.

"This is Shannon."

"Oh, thank god—" I started to say but was cut off.

"You know what to do." Beep.

My body trembled as I pulled the phone away from my ear and stared at the screen, counting down the seconds I had to leave a message.

"Shan, it's me. Um, I saw this thing on the news. Look, can you just call me? Please, it's important."

A pain-filled roar ripped from my body as the tears poured down my cheeks. Alex grabbed my hand as he sped down the Interstate, but it wouldn't matter. We'd always be too late.

I wiped away a tear and rubbed it into my jeans like that could scrub away the memories. Raine let out a soft sob, and my eyes flicked over to see her covering her mouth as tears streamed down her face.

"I told you. Look, the point is, I don't trust people often, and the only reason Lyle wasn't behind bars was that my mom dropped the charges. She felt bad. Why? I have no idea, but they should still be alive. Raine, I don't want to see you make the same mistake, and I definitely don't want Avro dragged into whatever you have going on."

She wiped at her eyes and shook her head. "It's not like that. I'm sorry for your loss, but this is completely different."

"Yeah, sure it is. Just another guy from prison assaulting his...what exactly were you before he went to jail? Friend, crush? Doesn't matter, he's a dick, and I don't want to see the same thing happen to you."

"Is this why you brought me out here, to see if you could convince me to turn my friend in? Unbelievable. I thought you wanted to connect. All you wanted to do was change my mind."

Raine jumped down from the crypt and began marching away. Fuck, that didn't go the way I hoped.

Raine

37

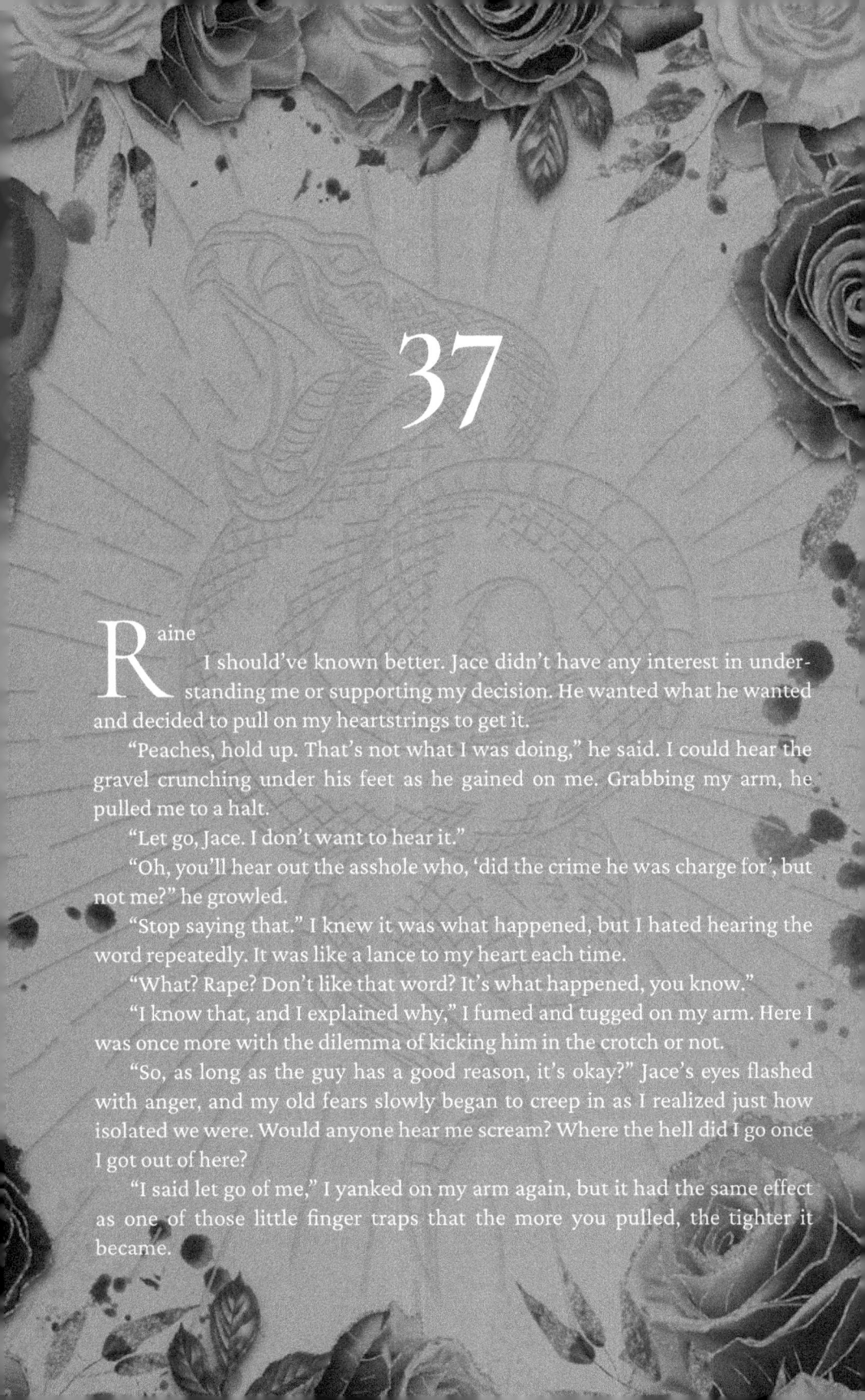

Raine

I should've known better. Jace didn't have any interest in understanding me or supporting my decision. He wanted what he wanted and decided to pull on my heartstrings to get it.

"Peaches, hold up. That's not what I was doing," he said. I could hear the gravel crunching under his feet as he gained on me. Grabbing my arm, he pulled me to a halt.

"Let go, Jace. I don't want to hear it."

"Oh, you'll hear out the asshole who, 'did the crime he was charge for', but not me?" he growled.

"Stop saying that." I knew it was what happened, but I hated hearing the word repeatedly. It was like a lance to my heart each time.

"What? Rape? Don't like that word? It's what happened, you know."

"I know that, and I explained why," I fumed and tugged on my arm. Here I was once more with the dilemma of kicking him in the crotch or not.

"So, as long as the guy has a good reason, it's okay?" Jace's eyes flashed with anger, and my old fears slowly began to creep in as I realized just how isolated we were. Would anyone hear me scream? Where the hell did I go once I got out of here?

"I said let go of me," I yanked on my arm again, but it had the same effect as one of those little finger traps that the more you pulled, the tighter it became.

Jace gripped both my arms as he glared down at me. "Why? This is what you like. You like it when a guy gets rough with you and terrifies you." His hands didn't hurt, but his words did.

"Jace, I'm warning you to back the hell off," I said, and pulled back hard. I didn't want to hurt him, but I was on the verge of a panic attack and needed him to let go of me.

"I said let go," I yelled and lashed out, catching him in the shin with my foot.

"Fuck," Jace said, and sucked in a deep breath.

I yanked away and stared at him, doubled over, rubbing his leg. His eyes flicked up to mine, and they were full of anger. Oh shit. With a burst of adrenaline, I turned and sprinted along the path to...I didn't know where. How the hell had I gotten so turned around?

"Not smart, Peaches," Jace called out. "Not smart at all."

Oh god, I could hear him coming. I looked over my shoulder, and even in the dark, the moonlight lit enough of the trail to see him chasing me down and gaining. A flutter of excitement had my stomach in knots, but I pushed it away. I hated that my body had that reaction at all.

Veering off the path, I weaved through the stones as I raced for the taller crypts, hoping to hide. I looked over my shoulder, but Jace was gone. Not seeing him was worse than knowing where he was.

"Ah," I cried out as my left knee clipped a tall tombstone. I sucked in a sharp breath as the pain lanced through my leg and hobbled my stride. A flicker of movement caught my eye, and I looked to my left, staring at the long shadows cast by the moon and the tall crypts.

"Oh fuck," I whispered as I spotted Jace's shadow and quickly looked up.

"Where do you think you're going, Peaches?" he asked, and even though I couldn't see his face, I could feel the smirk. A shiver shot down my spine while the rest of my body heated with words that weren't a threat but sounded like one.

"Leave me alone, Jace," I panted out and darted away from the shadow of the crypts.

I didn't make it three strides before I was hoisted off the ground like I weighed nothing. My back pressed into his hard chest, and my brain and body fought for control, each wanting very different things.

"Is that what you really want?" he growled in my ear as he hauled back into the dark shadows.

His arm felt like an iron vise squeezing the air out of my chest, and my brain screamed to fight, but the feeble smacks at his arm and wiggling were doing nothing. I needed to get mean if I wanted to get free. The question then became, why was I not fighting for my life?

With a spin and a hard shove, I was pressed against the cold wall of the crypt with my hands pinned above my head. Breathing heavily, I glared into Jace's silver, seductive, and terrifying eyes that glinted in the moonlight. His other hand clamped over my mouth when I opened it to scream, and he shook his head.

"I don't think you really want to do that, Peaches," he said, his body pressing into mine and setting it on fire. I nipped at his finger, fully intending to bite him hard, but only hung on as his teeth grazed the soft skin on my neck, and I quivered in his hold.

I reluctantly let go of the finger, and he removed his hand. His lips hovered over mine, and the heat of his body pressing into me was a stark contrast to the cool wall at my back.

"You going to bite me if I kiss you, Peaches?" The tip of his tongue flicked out and ran across my bottom lip, and my eyes narrowed.

"Try it and see what happens," I threatened.

His response was to rub his body against mine, and the desire I'd managed to kick down pushed my efforts aside. My eyes closed with a soft moan as he thrust forward with his hips, and I could feel the bulge of his cock pressing into me through his jeans. I knew exactly what he looked like with that silver ring pierced through the tip, and I still hadn't gotten a taste. I'd watched Avro play with it, and my mouth was once more watering with the thought.

What the hell was wrong with me?

I tried to pull my arms away again, but he didn't budge, and the only way out was to really hurt him.

"Fuck off, Jace."

Jace didn't even flinch as I tried again to free myself. Instead, he grabbed my lower lip with his teeth, and the aching between my thighs intensified.

"Let go, Jace," I mumbled, sounding pathetic even to my ears.

Releasing my lip, he smirked. "Oh no, Peaches. I know you don't really want that. You want me to rip these jeans off of you and fuck you right here. It's morbid and sick, and you fucking love it."

"No, I don't," I said, turning my head away so he couldn't see the truth of his words lying bare in my eyes. "You're the liar," I spit out, using the only bullet I had.

"Oh really, and why is that?" he asked, seeming genuinely amused.

"You say that you don't care about me, that you didn't want any of this, and Avro is forcing it on you." I turned my head to glare at him.

"That is what happened," Jace drawled, cocking his eyebrow.

"I call bullshit. I've only been around you a few days, and I can tell you don't want to go. You don't want to leave Avro, but more than that, you're different. Do you think I haven't done my research on you? I've watched you at these fancy award shows and the social media posts. I've listened to the last few songs you've released, and they all have one thing in common."

His eyes narrowed. "Oh, yeah, and what is that, Peaches?"

"They're uninspiring," I snarled. "They scream that you want out."

Jace's hands tightened on my wrists, and he made a growling sound that had a shudder ripping throughout my body.

"You don't know anything."

It was my turn to give him a cocky grin. "Oh, but I do. You're not the only one who people-watches, Jace. I've spent my entire life sitting away from others with my eyes and ears open. Everything you do when you're around Avro is different. You don't want to travel the world. Maybe you never did. Deep down, you knew that Avro would break away from you. You knew he would do exactly what you told him not to."

I paused and stared into his silver eyes, filling with rage, and he didn't look so confident now. "I'd go so far as to say that you hoped he would because then you'd have an excuse to stay. You want us to work. You want us to work, and you're terrified that if we don't, Avro will be devastated because we're already building a bond, and you can see it."

"Are you threatening to try to take Avro from me?" Jace asked, his voice low and sinister as his fingers dug painfully into my wrists. "Because I didn't get that vibe from you, but now I'm starting to wonder."

"No, don't be an idiot. Of course, I wouldn't do that. I'm saying that I'm not the only one hiding something, so stop acting like a paragon of fucking virtue."

"Oh, that's rich coming from you. Would you have even told Avro about your special friend if he hadn't seen the bruising? What was your plan, Peaches?"

I ground my teeth together as once more he pointed out how I wouldn't be truthful. Jace dropped his head, so our noses lightly touched, and my heart galloped hard in my chest. "Maybe you do see me, Peaches, but remember that I see you too."

Before I could think of something to say, he dropped his mouth to mine, and all the pent-up anger and desire erupted into something explosive. Hands ripped at my shirt as I yanked at his. We were like two animals that had been set loose, and in the back of my mind, there was a tiny little voice yelling that we shouldn't be doing this, but I already knew that I would. Nothing was stopping this now. I didn't want it to.

Jace

I hated that she saw through my act. No one did except for Avro, but he accepted it for what it needed to be. Raine didn't care about pointing out how unhappy I'd been, and I wanted to punish her for it.

Grabbing the zipper on the front of her hoodie, I yanked it down and pulled up the top she was wearing. I groaned as her perky tits came into view.

"No bra, you rebel. I fucking love it," I groaned.

Her nipples were already hard and begging to be sucked, further proof that she'd been lying about not wanting me or her dark needs. Needs she may not want to face, but I was about to prove to her once and for all that she was wrong.

Dropping my head, I sucked on her hard nipple and made her cry out as my teeth bit down enough to cause a touch of pain.

"Oh god," Raine moaned, her hands touching my hair.

I could still feel her trying to fight what her body craved. Switching to the other nipple, I ripped open the button and zipper on her jeans, confident I'd torn the material from the force.

Raine gasped and tried to wiggle away as she fought her mind, but I was quicker with my hand and slipped it down the front of her jeans to find her soaking wet.

"Oh fuck," I groaned as my fingers easily pushed the material aside and slid into her pussy.

"Ah, oh god," Raine cried as her body went limp in my hold like she'd finally given up the battle.

"Yeah, that's it, Peaches. Rub yourself on my fingers. You want to cum all over them." I left a wet trail along the side of her neck and sucked her earlobe into my mouth as Raine slowly moved her hips. "That's it. You're nasty, and you like it. Fuck my fingers. I'll even give you three," I cooed in her ear as I shoved a third finger inside her wet pussy.

My cock was so hard, it felt like I was about to cum in my jeans. I was so ready to bury myself deep inside of her. She'd been right about one thing. I'd hoped that Avro would pick well. I always knew it would be him to choose. My taste was whatever the fuck he wanted, and he hadn't disappointed.

"I'm going to fuck this tight pussy, Peaches. I'm going to cum in you and claim you as ours, and you'll let me, won't you?"

She bucked her hips harder, but only incoherent noises passed through her lips. The walls of her pussy tightened as she fucked herself harder. She was fucking sexy, and I couldn't get enough. I suddenly wanted to make her and Avro cum simultaneously. The thought was so potent that I groaned as my cock kicked behind the fly of my jeans. She was so close, but she wouldn't get to cum that easy.

I released Raine and took a step back. Her body slumped against the crypt wall as she panted hard. Her eyes filled with passion as she stared up at me. I could see her wondering what I would do next, but she wasn't asking, and I didn't plan on saying.

Lifting the fingers that had been buried inside of her, I stuck them in my mouth one at a time and cleaned them off. I groaned at her taste on my tongue and savored the look in her eyes. She was feral, alright. She'd starved her body for so long that now that she'd let the beast out to play, she couldn't get enough. Something else she tried to deny, but I could see it burning in her pretty blue eyes.

"Do you want me to fuck you, Peaches?"

She shook her head, but she avidly watched my hands as I undid the button on my jeans.

"Are you sure about that," I asked and slid the zipper down.

She licked her lips as my cock came into view, the silver ring glinting in the dull light.

"What's the matter, Peaches? I thought you didn't want my cock inside of you?" I spread my jeans open, and my cock was all too happy to be free of the confines.

I knew I was blessed and didn't take it for granted for even a single day. Gripping my shaft, I stroked my cock, groaning loud enough that Raine's eyes were trained on the head that now had multiple drops of precum sitting on the tip.

"Fuck, that feels good."

She shifted and rubbed her legs together as she stared at the prize.

"You don't want to taste it, do you?"

Her tongue ran across her lips.

"That's not something a good girl like you would want to do."

My hand picked up the pace, and I sucked in an exaggerated breath that ended with a moan. Raine shivered and took a small step forward.

"What are you, Peaches? Are you a good girl, or are you a nasty one who's going to let me fuck you right here so hard that you scream my name?"

Raine's eyes flicked up to mine. "I...."

"I, what?"

"I...." She wet her lips again. "I want you to fuck me," she said, and I was tempted to shove my cock back in my jeans and say I told you so, but even I wasn't that much of a fucking ass. At least not tonight.

"Then get over here and get on your knees. You're sucking my cock first for kicking me. That was a bitch move."

She nodded far more quickly than I thought she would, and I wondered if this was punishment at all with the way she dropped to her knees.

Her hand was cool as it wrapped around my heated cock, and I shivered as her soft fingers took the place of my hand. She was staring at it like it might bite, and I smirked because I planned on leaving my own mark. This ex-friend of hers had another thing coming if he thought he could swoop in and just take Raine. I had no doubt in my mind that this guy wouldn't be able to keep away, and as she drew her tongue along the underside of my sensitive head, I knew for sure that this time he was going to have to go through me.

My head fell back as she explored the ring and gently wiggled it with the tip of her tongue. Raine was tentative as she finally slipped my cock into her mouth, and I was nice enough to wait until she had a rhythm and a little bit of confidence before I grabbed her head and forced her to go deeper.

The shrill little noise of fear she made had a direct line to my cock as it vibrated up my shaft. I pushed my hips forward and forced it a little deeper before I released her head.

Raine pulled my cock out of her mouth and glared up at me. "What the hell?"

"What? It's a big cock, Peaches. You'll have to do better than that if you want to get me to come. Avro can take it all, and it would be pretty disappointing if you couldn't."

Her eyes flared as I cocked my brow at her, and I would've sworn she growled at me from under her breath. But it worked. She liked challenges.

A character trait that the two of us had in common. She sucked me into her mouth, taking a solid two inches more before she gagged and pulled out. She made another attempt and sucked hard while she did, and I had to force myself not to grab the back of her head and force the last few inches down her throat.

The temptation was real, and my fingers and cock both tingled with the thought, but I knew she wasn't ready.

"Fuck, Peaches, you know how to suck," I praised instead and was rewarded with it sliding a little deeper.

"Yeah, you like that?" she asked.

"It's what I said, isn't it?" As the words came out of my mouth, I knew that this would not end well, and a second later, I hissed as she gripped my cock ring in her teeth and tugged.

"Oh shit," I swore as the pain of the sharp jerk lanced down my cock. She continued to pull, and I was forced to take a step with her like I was a fucking bull with a nose ring. "Fuck, Peaches, that's not very nice."

"You're an asshole," she mumbled around the ring.

"You're right, I am," I agreed and bit my lip hard as she tugged again and hard enough that I worried she might actually pull it out. The combination of pain and anger was burning brighter than anything I'd experienced before, and I glared down at her, not even sure what I would do if she went that far.

"Are you going to stop?" she asked.

"Yes," I said through my clenched teeth.

She released the ring, and as soon as I was free, I snatched her by the neck and forced her to stand. Slamming her against the crypt, I glared into her wide, terrified eyes.

"Don't ask such stupid questions, Peaches. I'll never stop being an asshole. The nice part of me was sucked into the grave with my family when they were murdered, and it's never coming back."

Each breath I took hurt my chest, and my heart ached even after all this time, and I hated that Raine had forced me to look at it. We stared at one another, the tension still so thick in the air it felt like we were pulling on a rubber band, waiting for it to break.

"Fuck this. I'm out of here," I growled and pushed away from the crypt wall.

I didn't expect her to kiss me. The fear and anger in Raine's eyes fooled me. She wrapped her arms around my neck and crushed our lips together. My body reacted even if my brain was reeling. Nothing mattered other than getting inside of her now. All the different parts of my brain switched off as the need to take her overwhelmed my senses.

I realized there was so much more to Raine, and her ability to reach inside my chest and make my heart beat hard was just one of them. The way she looked at me was enough to make me shudder, but when her blue eyes burned with passion, I knew I was in trouble. Avro was right. She fit me as well as she did him, and I wanted her. I wanted all of her.

Deepening the kiss, I gripped her ass and lifted her so she could wrap her legs around my waist. I didn't need to see where I was going. The single light glowing on this side of the cemetery was all the beacon I needed to find the car. My strides ate up the ground, our lips never parting with the urgency that had broken free.

I dropped Raine to her feet, and she stumbled with the sudden change, but the car was behind her, and she leaned against the hood, looking like a sexy calendar model with her swollen lips and eyes hooded with desire.

Hooking my fingers into her jeans and thong, I pulled them down in a single hard tug and spun her around.

"You think you're ready for this?" I asked as I bit the side of her neck.

Her breath hissed out. "Would it matter?"

"Not really. Now bend over," I said, but she glared over her shoulder at me. Her elbow came for the side of my face. I snatched the arm out of the air and shoved her hard, forcing her to bend over. "You want to struggle, Peaches? Then you can do it with my cock in you."

Gripping her ass and holding her still, I lined up to her soaking wet pussy and thrust into her tight opening.

"Ahh," Raine screamed, her fingers clawing at the hood of the car as I forced the last inch into her body.

My cock was twitching and ready to cum already. Pulling almost all the way out, I thrust into Raine again, and I shuddered as she yelled again, but this time it was my name. It was as beautiful a sound as any song I'd ever written.

With each thrust, the little whimpering noises got louder. The sound traveled over my skin like a warm breeze.

"That's it. Scream for me," I said and picked up the pace.

I was lost to the pleasure flooding my system and was only vaguely aware of Raine cumming and soaking my cock with her release. Her body smacked into the car with each powerful thrust as I pushed us to the goal. Reaching around her body, my hand slipped to her clit. I pinched and felt it swell between my fingers.

"Scream for me, Peaches. Scream my name, or I'll stop fucking you right now," I growled. Lifting my foot up to the bumper, I changed positions, and Raine let out the first strangled yell with the new angle.

"Fuck, Jace!" she finally roared as I slammed my cock into her and pushed deeper than before. "Ahh."

"Do you want me to stop?" I asked, the sound of slapping skin and Raine's yells loud in my ears.

"No," she wailed, even as tears and sweat trickled down her cheeks.

"Rub your clit. Cum all over me again," I said, and watched her hand slip from the hood of the car to between her legs.

"Oh, fuck yes," I yelled, as I felt her hand rubbing vigorously at herself, and then she wrapped her fingers around my cock. They didn't even fit all the way, but it was still better than any fucking cock ring. "Fuck, Peaches, yes. You're going to make me cum."

"Jace," she screamed loudly.

Her body shuddered, and the walls of her sweet pussy gripped me hard as she came. There was no faking or denying it as she froze, and once more, my cock was flooded with the warmth of her orgasm. That was all it took, and a thrust later, my release gripped me in a chokehold. I opened my mouth to yell, but no sound came out. Pulling back, I slammed home hard, and more came out, so I did it again and again.

My breathing was ragged as I collapsed onto her body, and all I could hear was our panting and the drumming of my pulse inside my head.

Raine nodded, her eyes glazed over. "I really love the feel of that ring," she mumbled, making me smirk.

"That's good because as soon as I catch my breath, I'm fucking you again." The corner of her mouth pulled up in a grin, and my heart pounded a little harder for a totally different reason. Stretching my hands along her arms, I linked our fingers together. "You're ours now, Peaches, and no one is taking you away."

Snake

38

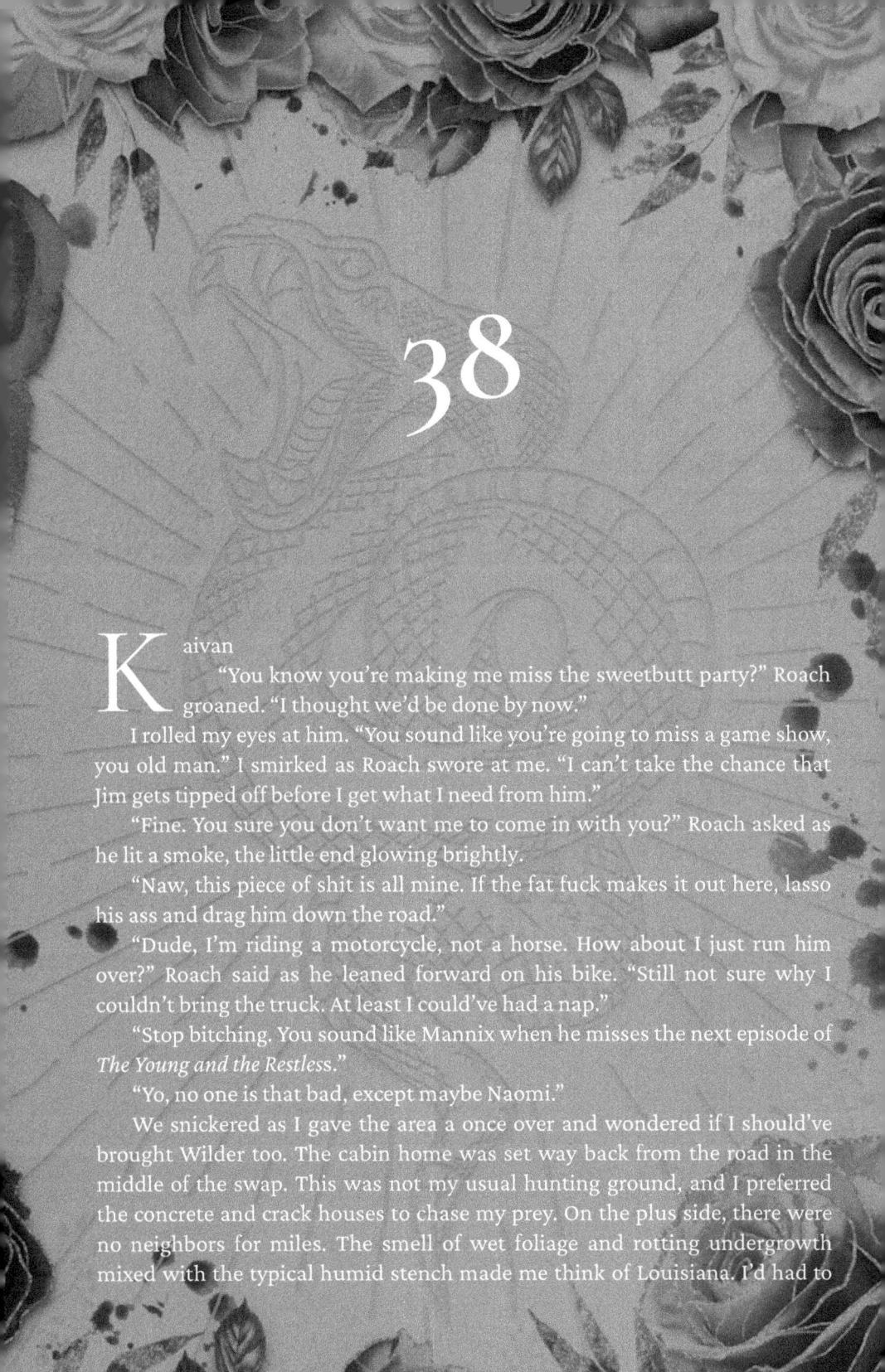

Kaivan

"You know you're making me miss the sweetbutt party?" Roach groaned. "I thought we'd be done by now."

I rolled my eyes at him. "You sound like you're going to miss a game show, you old man." I smirked as Roach swore at me. "I can't take the chance that Jim gets tipped off before I get what I need from him."

"Fine. You sure you don't want me to come in with you?" Roach asked as he lit a smoke, the little end glowing brightly.

"Naw, this piece of shit is all mine. If the fat fuck makes it out here, lasso his ass and drag him down the road."

"Dude, I'm riding a motorcycle, not a horse. How about I just run him over?" Roach said as he leaned forward on his bike. "Still not sure why I couldn't bring the truck. At least I could've had a nap."

"Stop bitching. You sound like Mannix when he misses the next episode of *The Young and the Restless*."

"Yo, no one is that bad, except maybe Naomi."

We snickered as I gave the area a once over and wondered if I should've brought Wilder too. The cabin home was set way back from the road in the middle of the swap. This was not my usual hunting ground, and I preferred the concrete and crack houses to chase my prey. On the plus side, there were no neighbors for miles. The smell of wet foliage and rotting undergrowth mixed with the typical humid stench made me think of Louisiana. I'd had to venture out that way a few times this past year on missions for Chase or Beast since I never saw our Prez. I just couldn't get used to the brackish smell that permeated everything around the Mancini Mansion. I had to give it to the Mafia family, though. They sure did know how to treat a guy right.

Cracking my neck, I revved my bike and wheeled into the driveway. I could have walked in, and that would've been a fuck load quieter, but I wanted to take him by surprise in a different way.

As I suspected, the sound of the bike drew Jim out of the house with a large rifle in hand. I pulled up beside his truck and cut the loud engine. My eyes skimmed over the shitty cottage-style home and any possible security system. There were no cameras that I could see and only a light on his porch.

"Who the fuck are you?" Jim called out as soon as the engine died.

A smile spread across my face. "Fuck, it is good to see your face, Jim. It's me, Kai," I said, leaning on the handlebars. I really could have a career in acting because all I could picture was ripping his balls off with my bare hands.

My gun was inches from my fingers, and they flexed and tingled, ready to grab it and shoot Jim where he stood. It would be quick, clean, and easy, but I wanted more than his death. I wanted answers. The rifle remained trained on me, but when I continued to smile, Jim turned the gun up.

"Kai? As in Kai, who used to be at Dave's?" he asked, a sheen of sweat breaking out on his forehead. His hands gripped the rifle tight enough to see the slight shaking from where I sat. The look of shock on his face told me he didn't know about Nick and Irene yet. That was good, very good.

You're going to be more than nervous before this night is through.

"Yeah, man. Took me forever to find you." I looked around at the surrounding trees and swamp. "No idea how you like to live out here with all these gators."

"What are you doing here?" Jim asked.

I let my smile fall and replaced the look on my face with shock.

"Jim, I came to have a beer like old times. It's been forever, but our talks in the garage are some of my best memories." Lifting my leg over the back of the bike, I kept my eyes trained on his hands. Walking over to the six stairs that led up to the porch, I stopped with my hand on the railing. "I can go if you want. I honestly thought you'd be happy to see me," I said and rounded my shoulders, hoping that I gave off a disappointed look.

The sound of the gun's safety being kicked into place was music to my ears, and the part of me that loved to kill smiled in the back of my mind.

"Wow, Kai. Sorry, man, I'm a little jumpy living out here. I don't get many visitors, and you're the last person I expected to see."

Jim smiled, and it was like being transported back in time. He had the same dopey expression that had always set everyone's mind at ease. It was the look that had sat in the garage, told stories, and let me have a beer even when I was underage. At the time, it felt like he was a cool uncle and the type of man I could've told anything, including my biggest fears. Ending up just like my father had always been at the top of my list.

I walked up the steps, and Jim did the same stupid dance he had when I was a teen. He got low and wiggled back and forth as he held his arms like a linebacker. The fucker wanted a hug, and I mirrored his pose and laughed as we embraced. The moment he touched me, the anger burning inside me rose, and I had to force myself to keep the smile on my face. My mind screamed that he'd touched Raine. He'd touched what was mine. He'd put his filthy cock in her. I planned to take it off.

"What the hell are you doing here?" Jim asked, pulling back and squeezing my arms as if he hadn't been involved in sending me to jail. Like he hadn't attacked Raine. My jaw twitched with the images my mind kept replaying on a loop, but I managed to hold the smile.

"I came to visit. I got out a little while ago, but it's been tough getting back on my feet," I lied and stuffed my hands in my jeans pockets. "I'm just getting around to reconnecting with the few people that I considered family," I said, laying it on thick.

He swallowed, and I saw a glimmer of something in his eyes. Regret, maybe. He could regret all he wanted, but it hadn't stopped him from doing what he'd done or ever coming forward to have my name cleared.

"Yeah, man...Listen, I'm really sorry I didn't visit you in prison," Jim said, rubbing the back of his neck.

"I won't lie. That hurt. Dave and Irene washed their hands of me, and I had no one. I thought you might visit, but I gave up hope after the first year," I said. That wasn't a lie. I hadn't known Jim was involved, and I'd kept hoping someone I thought was a friend would show up to see me.

Lifting a shoulder, I let it drop. "I'm hoping to reconnect, have a beer, and then head out. I'm leaving Florida. There are too many bad memories."

"Fuck, man. I'm so sorry. Come on in. Let's have a beer," Jim said, turning to the screen door and yanking it open.

I stalked him inside, my eyes searching every corner of the small home. There was a mounted gator head on one wall and pictures of Jim fishing and holding up a huge fish he'd caught. There was a particular picture that caught my eye as Jim stepped into the kitchen. The wall heading into the living room had a framed photo of Jim, Dave, and a guy I didn't know on a hunting excursion. It looked to be somewhere like Africa, based on how they were dressed and the boar at their feet. It wasn't the boar that held my attention. It was the face of the man with the same tattoo on his hand. There he was in a color photo, as he held a gun and smirked for the camera. This had to be Frank.

"Here you go," Jim said, handing me one of the bottles.

"Thanks. Cheers," I said, tapping his bottle as I pretended to take a swig. I didn't trust him any further than I could throw his ass. "This looks like an amazing trip," I said, pointing to the image. "I recognize Dave, but who's this?" I tapped the photo.

"It was a great time. That's Frank. I'm not sure if you ever met him."

I nodded and pretended to take another sip of my beer.

"Come on in and have a seat."

Jim flopped down in one of the two camo recliners facing the television. His taste in décor certainly was consistent. There wasn't a spot in the home that didn't have either a dead and very stuffed animal or pictures of killing them.

"I want to ask how things have been, but that seems like a terrible question to ask," Jim said, and had the decency to look a little remorseful.

"Yeah, what can I say? I went to prison for a crime I didn't commit, and it ruined my life. I planned on college and a good career, maybe one day having a family, and now I'm forever an outcast. A thug and ex-con. Just someone else for people to turn their nose up at. Getting a job was the hardest, and I had to stay at a men's shelter for a while." That was a load of lies, but I knew more than one guy who'd gotten out and that was their life.

"Sorry to hear all that. I wasn't sure what to think about the charges, and Dave talked like he was so sure it had been you who hurt Little Rainy. I was torn as to what the right thing was to do."

My hand twitched and flexed around the bottle at the mention of the nickname Jim had called Raine. I imagined wrapping my hand around his throat as I nodded and imitated taking another swig.

"You talk to Dave much?"

Jim squirmed in his seat, which told me he had.

"Not in some time," Jim said, and looked away. So Dave had warned him that I was out. Good to know. "You?"

"I saw him the other day. We ran into one another at a gas station. It was kinda fucked seeing him again. He was real aggressive. I mean, sure, I was fucking his wife, but it was over eleven years ago, man, and I paid my dues. Let it go already." I wanted to sound like I was being transparent, lull Jim in a little more. "He looked like shit. I would've placed a bet that he just crawled out of a dumpster. What the hell has he been up to?"

Jim's shoulders relaxed. He was obviously waiting to see if Dave had said anything about him. The more loose-lipped I could keep Jim, the better. I had no qualms about torture, and Jim would find that out, but I wanted him to have just enough rope to hang himself with first.

"His old lady left him a couple of years back, and she's been dragging him through the mud with the divorce."

I snickered, and Jim's brows rose in question. "I just find it funny. I mean, I was fucking Irene back in the day. You'd think that once Dave knew that, he would've left her long before now," I said, and Jim's hand stilled, the beer halfway to his mouth. I gave him a crooked smile. "What? Did you think I didn't know Dave found out and wanted to punish me?"

Jim swallowed hard, his Adam's apple bobbing as he did.

"Why do you look so freaked out, Jim? I mean, it's not like you had anything to do with me going to prison, right?" I drew out the last word and cocked my brow in his direction.

I loved this part of the game. I didn't get to do it often. Most of my interactions with those that I hunted were get in and get out, but make it as messy as possible. You'd think messy was easier than neat and clean, but that was a misconception. It was far harder to make things look like a slasher film and keep your DNA out of the shit. Knifes slipped, and blood was all over everything. It was actually a pain in my ass.

"No, no, of course not. I just thought you'd be a lot more pissed," Jim said, stumbling over his words.

He didn't know the half of it. Pissed was like saying I was mildly annoyed. I tilted my head and stared Jim in the eyes. "Why exactly would I be pissed, Jim? What did I have to be pissed about?" I asked, allowing my web to close around him.

"Um...I...ah...I just meant that..." Whatever Jim was about to say was interrupted by his phone ringing on the coffee table and making him jump.

We both looked at the phone and saw Dave's name. As Jim reached for the phone, I pulled my gun and pointed it at him.

"I wouldn't touch that if I were you." I allowed the full extent of my anger to shine through, and the man winced as I glared into his eyes. "Sit the fuck back."

Jim raised his hand in the air and slowly slid back into the recliner. "Kai, my man, I don't know what you've been told, but I swear to you on my mama's grave that I didn't have anything to do with you going to prison."

I smiled at him. "Splitting hairs, I see. How convenient that you can actually tell the truth and lie all at the same time."

"I don't know what you mean." He smiled, but the worry in his eyes was evident.

"Tell me, Jim. How does it feel to be invaded? To have the place you thought was safe turn into a jail? Or for the person you thought you knew to hurt you and rip your life away?" I leaned forward and let my forearms rest on my knees as the gun dangled between my legs.

Sweat was traveling in a steady stream down the side of Jim's face. The moisture showed on his upper lip as his body produced adrenaline and screamed to run, but he knew he couldn't.

"Tell me, Jim, was getting the chance to rape Raine worth your life," I asked, my voice coming out as a growl as I focused all my hatred on this man, someone I had trusted, someone Raine had trusted. Someone who was going to die. I'd trusted this man around Raine; a mistake I wouldn't make twice.

"He forced me to," Jim blurted, then bolted for the door and the rifle he had sitting beside it. He reminded me of a mouse that finally got its tail free from the trap, only to realize there was still a cat. Unfortunately for Jim, I was the cat waiting. Lifting my gun, I fired and got him in the back of the thigh. He yelled as he crashed to the floor in a blubbering heap.

Rolling out my shoulders, I slowly stood as Jim's phone rang again. "Apparently, Dave's worried about you. Isn't that sweet? Did you know your 'friend' had already given you up?"

Jim gripped his leg as he rolled around on the floor like a turtle on its back. His continuous begging for forgiveness was getting old quick.

Picking up his phone, I marched over, and before he knew what was happening, I held it in front of his face, and the thing unlocked. God bless modern technology.

"Please don't hurt me, please."

"Why shouldn't I? Dave already told me that you were the one who came up with the plan to get even with me. That it was all your idea to rape Raine," I said, once more lying my ass off.

"No, no, that's not true," he said as I flicked through his contacts and photos. I sent everything useful to the burner phone I'd purchased for this occasion and laid the phone on the tiny dining table. "I'll tell you what happened. Just please don't kill me."

I tapped my chin with the gun and watched the blood pool around Jim's leg. Walking into the kitchen, I grabbed a hand towel and tossed it at Jim. "Tie off your wound and tell me the truth. And, Jim, don't fucking lie to me, or I'll blow your kneecap off next."

He bellowed as I looked around for what I needed next and spotted his fishing equipment in the corner. That would work. Going over to Jim's boots by the door, I quickly pulled out the long black laces.

"What are you doing?" Jim asked, his eyes going wide.

"You said don't kill you. You didn't say don't secure you." His face relaxed. Such a stupid fuck. "Can't have you thinking you can grab your gun."

As soon as he had his leg tied off, so he didn't die before I wanted him to, I grabbed his wrists and tied them together, then dragged Jim across the floor to a crescendo of swearing.

"So nice of you to have this old-fashioned stove here," I drawled. I glanced at Jim's face, which was contorted in pain. "You better start talking before I even up your legs."

"It was all Frank," Jim said as I walked to the far side of the room and grabbed the tackle box I'd seen. That was not the answer I'd been expecting to hear.

"Why would your hunting buddy want me to go to prison?" I asked, pulling out the heavy fishing line. This shit was meant to hold a gator, so it would definitely hold Jim. Stuffing the gun in my jeans, I spun the round wire reel on my finger as I strolled toward my prey.

"He had Dave all fired up about you fucking his wife and how that was disrespectful and how you needed to be taught a lesson if he was a real man."

I lifted a brow at Jim as I squatted down and used the line to secure his hands to the heavy cast-iron stove. This was something you would see in a hunting camp way up north. Why the fuck he had one was beyond me, and I didn't care enough to ask.

"So you taught Raine a lesson instead?" I asked as I tied the knot in place and slit the line with my switchblade.

"Sorta. That wasn't part of the original deal, Kai. I swear to you. We were just supposed to rough you up a little. You know, teach you a lesson for messing around with another man's wife." He licked his lips as I moved to his feet and decided that the two recliners would have to do.

"Keep talking, Jim," I said, pushing the first chair across the floor.

"We went down to the fights and were going to wait for you to come out after you were done and jump you. Frank was the lookout guy. He was in the fights watching for you, but you never showed, and then there was a shootout."

My hands paused. I'd forgotten about the gunshots. What if she'd been shot that night? A cold dread spread throughout my body.

"Raine was there, and for whatever fucked up reason, she thought Frank was you and came racing down the alley where we were. Frank said this would be even better when Dave mentioned who Raine was. I swear to you. I didn't want to hurt her. Raine had always been nice to me," Jim said, lifting his head to look at me as I tied his first foot to the chair.

"So what you're saying is that you were forced to put your cock inside her and then frame me for it?" His chair scraped ominously across the floor as I pushed it toward Jim. "Or maybe you randomly ended up naked and fell on her, and then why not? You were already there."

"Man, look, I had sex with her, but you have to understand that Frank is scary. I didn't know what he would do if I refused."

I smiled wide as I tied Jim's second leg. "Psst, Jim," I whispered. "Guess who's scarier."

"Kai, believe me, I argued with them and begged them to let her go, but Frank wouldn't listen. He told Dave that this way, you'd be locked up for life."

"Oh, that must have been such a sad day when I took the plea deal for ten," I drawled, the sarcasm dripping off every word. Finished with my securing, I pulled out my knife, and Jim screeched like I'd already done something to him. Shaking my head, I slit the jeans on both legs and cut up the middle, so the material fell open.

"What the hell are you doing?" Jim cried, but I ignored him.

It figures this guy would be wearing tighty-whities. I really didn't want to see this, but I gripped the elastic band and pulled it up, so the knife slid through the material easily.

"I told you everything I know. I was scared, and that's the truth. I did what I was ordered to do," he said, his voice full of conviction.

"Did you come?" Walking to the gun case, I pulled out my leather gloves and stuffed my hands inside before gripping the rifle and fifty-caliber shells.

"What?"

"You heard me. Did you cum? Did you hate it so much that you were repulsed by her young ass, or did you cum?"

"Fuck, man...." Jim looked away from my hard gaze.

"Yeah, that's what I thought." Opening the ammunition box, I loaded the cartridge and marched toward Jim.

"What the hell are you doing with my gun?" He squirmed on the floor and pulled on his restraints, but everything held firm.

"Well, Jim, I believe in karma. That shit is my best friend, and today you're getting the chance to meet," I said and knelt between his legs. "Tell me something. Why the warehouse?"

"Frank busted open the door." His voice was shaking along with the rest of his body.

"Okay, one more question, and we're going to think of this as the bonus question. If you answer this one to my satisfaction, I'll let you go." Jim nodded. "Did she scream? Did she scream when you hurt her?" Tears filled Jim's eyes. "Did she?" I bellowed, and he jerked.

"Yes," Jim mumbled under his breath. "She kept begging for you to stop, but I swear I didn't want to hurt her."

I didn't think anything could infuriate me more, but I'd been wrong. To hear confirmation that Raine thought it was me. That she screamed and begged me to stop. That she was terrified out of her mind, snapped the last of my control.

"Well, tonight you're going to understand that pain, Jim. This is your night of reckoning," I said, and lined the end of the rifle up with Jim's asshole.

"No, no, no, please. Please don't do this!"

He fought the bindings, but he was already weak and secure, so all he was doing was wearing himself down further. The moment he stilled to catch his breath, I struck and shoved the end of the rifle up his ass to the sound of high-pitched shrieking. Jim's body bowed off the ground as the dry, cold metal penetrated farther up his shitter.

I held the gun still and let the wails die down to rambling that made no sense.

"You know, Jim, the sad thing is that I saw you as family. I thought of you as an uncle and one of the only people I could trust, but you destroyed that. So when you're on the slide down to meet the devil, I want you to remember that you would've been better off dying in that warehouse years ago."

"But you promised," he cried.

"So did you. You promised to always be there for me. Do you remember that?" I pulled on the gun until it was almost out of his ass and shoved it back inside. He screamed again, his wails mixed with tears and the stench of regret. "I want you to remember how you hit my knuckles and said I would always be family. How does it feel to be lied to?"

When no logical answer was forthcoming, I shook my head. "I'd say it was a pleasure, but that would be a lie. Thanks for the info, Jim."

"No, wait. I—"

Bang

The sound of the rifle rang out as I pulled the trigger, and I was shocked when the two recliners were dragged a few inches from the force of the shot before it blew off part of Jim's head. The bullet exploded out of his skull and hit the far wall. I smirked as I stared at the hair stuck to the shitty wood panel siding before it slid down, leaving a red streak in its wake. Smiling, I glanced at the half-missing face and the remaining eye staring back at me. I'd always wondered what would happen if I did this. This was definitely up there in my most favorites. Heck it might have even taken over the number one spot.

"That was fucking cool. Too bad I didn't have two of you. I'd love to have tried a different angle."

The door slammed open, and Roach stepped in, holding his gun out as his eyes searched for a threat before he looked down at the man on the floor. His brows knit together with a mix of disgust and horror in his eyes.

"Dude, that's fucked up. I'm never helping you again," Roach grumbled and left, the door slamming closed with a bang. Standing, I stared down at Jim to take in and appreciate this moment before I cleaned up anything I'd touched.

Jim's phone rang again as I stepped outside, and this time, I hit the answer button.

"Jim? Jim, you there?"

I breathed heavily into the phone.

"Man, seriously, you need to answer. This is no time for your stupid games."

A wicked grin pulled at my mouth. "I'm coming for you," I growled low into the phone and hit 'end.'

Snake

39

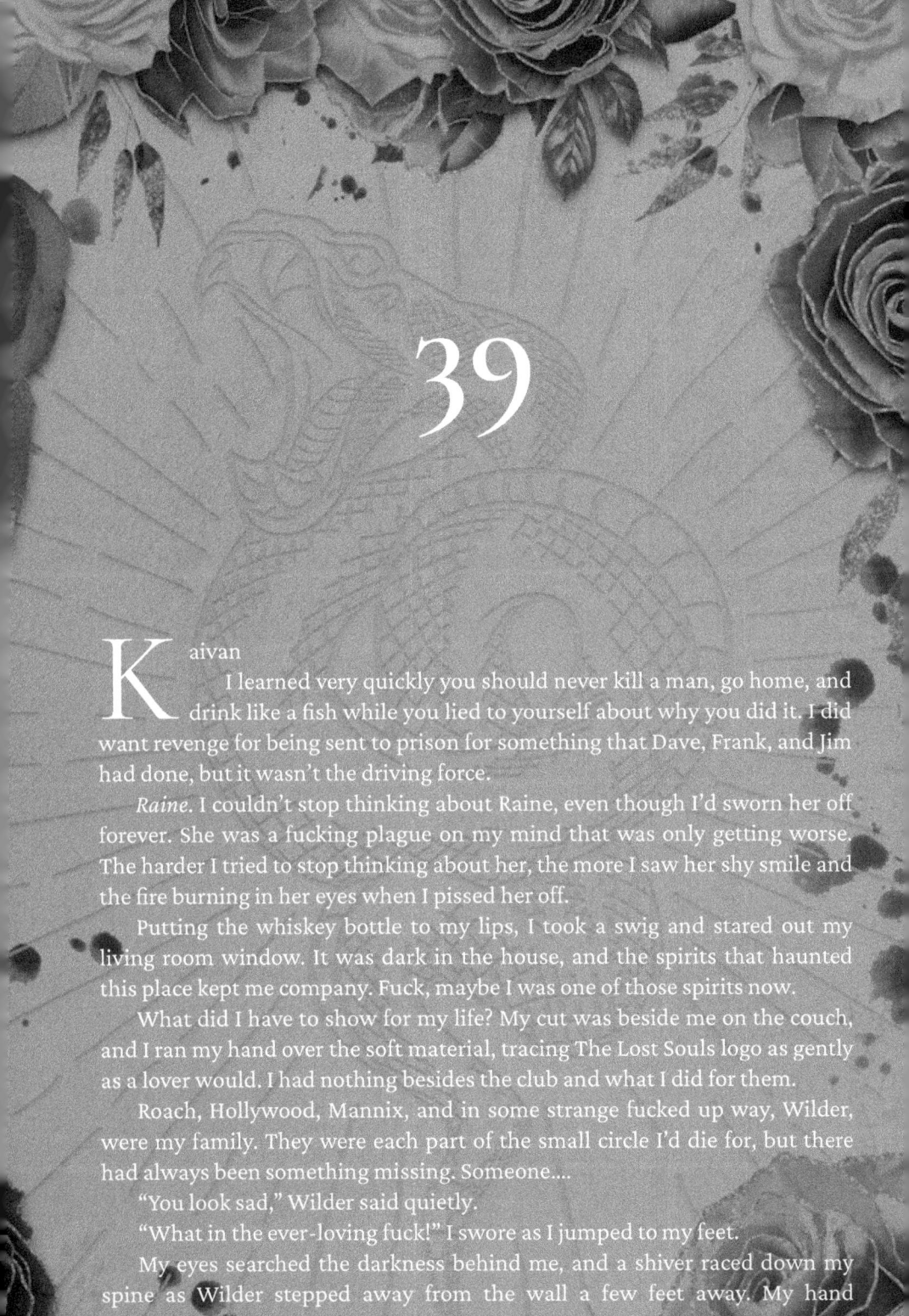

Kaivan

I learned very quickly you should never kill a man, go home, and drink like a fish while you lied to yourself about why you did it. I did want revenge for being sent to prison for something that Dave, Frank, and Jim had done, but it wasn't the driving force.

Raine. I couldn't stop thinking about Raine, even though I'd sworn her off forever. She was a fucking plague on my mind that was only getting worse. The harder I tried to stop thinking about her, the more I saw her shy smile and the fire burning in her eyes when I pissed her off.

Putting the whiskey bottle to my lips, I took a swig and stared out my living room window. It was dark in the house, and the spirits that haunted this place kept me company. Fuck, maybe I was one of those spirits now.

What did I have to show for my life? My cut was beside me on the couch, and I ran my hand over the soft material, tracing The Lost Souls logo as gently as a lover would. I had nothing besides the club and what I did for them.

Roach, Hollywood, Mannix, and in some strange fucked up way, Wilder, were my family. They were each part of the small circle I'd die for, but there had always been something missing. Someone....

"You look sad," Wilder said quietly.

"What in the ever-loving fuck!" I swore as I jumped to my feet.

My eyes searched the darkness behind me, and a shiver raced down my spine as Wilder stepped away from the wall a few feet away. My hand clenched into a fist on instinct before I could draw a decent breath. I grabbed at my chest.

"I swear your goal is to give me a fucking heart attack. You'd think I'd be used to this by now," I grumbled.

"Why would I want to give you a heart attack?" he asked as I stomped past him to the kitchen to clean off the whiskey that had spilled all over my hand and arm. "There are far easier ways to kill someone. I could've slit your throat or shot you in the head. I guess if I wanted it to be slow, I could poison you by slipping something in your drink," he said.

I stared at the bottle and then down the hall where I'd left Wilder.

"Yeah, definitely not finishing that now," I mumbled, and turned the bottle upside down in the sink before washing my hands.

I went back into the living room and used some rags to mop up what I'd spilled. Despite the house falling down around me, I liked to keep it neat and orderly. Some habits died harder than others, and the ones from prison hardly faded.

"What are you doing in here, Wilder?"

He didn't answer, just sat down in the recliner and stared out the window.

"Why are you sad?" he asked, and I glared at him. "You are sad, aren't you? Or do I have the emotion wrong?"

I cocked my head and stared into Wilder's eyes. Even though he had black and grey makeup on, like he was trying to blend in with the concrete and asphalt, I could see the confusion in his eyes. I'd always wondered why Wilder was so strange and why he asked the most fucked up questions, but a light had just gone on. He didn't have the same emotions as the rest of us. That was why he was always so curious. He was some kind of path. My best guess was psychopath, and I was suddenly more relieved than ever that Wilder didn't want to slit my throat, as he put it. He could've done it a hundred times by now, and I would never have felt a thing.

"Yes, the emotion was sorta sad," I said, flopping down on the couch. It was going to reek like whiskey in here for days.

"What do you mean by sorta?"

I rubbed my face and tried to put into words what I had going on inside of me. "It's hard to explain. There are things I wish for that can never be," I finally said. "Some of those things make me sad, others angry and frustrated."

Wilder rubbed at his chin. "Can you fix what is making you sad?"

"I don't know. Maybe, no, yes, it's hard to know. I kinda fucked up, and I'm not sure I want to fix it."

"But you can't stop thinking about it and wondering if you should fix it," Wilder asked.

"What the fuck, Wilder? Are you trying to be my shrink or what?" I growled and crossed my arms.

"Do you need a shrink?" he asked.

"I may need one shortly." His brow furrowed, and I knew he didn't understand my sarcasm. "Okay, yes. I may want to somehow repair what I fucked up," I said, hating that he'd gotten me to admit out loud that I still wanted Raine. Even after all these years of anger and hatred, she could stir up so much emotion with a single look. I wanted her. The thought of her moving on with the guy from the bar had my blood boiling.

"Then, if you want my opinion, you should fix it." Wilder nodded and resumed looking outside.

"Can I ask you a question?"

"Yeah, why couldn't you ask me a question?"

I wanted to smack my hand to my forehead. This guy made my brain feel like it was trying to walk along the floor of a fun house as it moved around.

"Why do you always dress like this?" I asked.

Wilder looked down at the matching black and grey camo fatigues he was wearing. "Why not?"

"'Cause it's not exactly normal. Do you see me or anyone else walking down the street dressed in camo or like a swamp thing or a garbage bin dude?" If he were going to kill me for insulting him, at least I'd see him coming.

"I don't wear this out," he finally said. "Well, I do, but only when I need to."

I wish I hadn't dumped out the rest of my whiskey. I'd rather take my chances with the possible poison. "Fine. Why are you wearing it now?"

Wilder leaned forward, his arms resting on his thighs. "To blend in. I thought that would be obvious."

Okay, forget the poison. I was going to pull my gun and shoot myself at this rate. "Wilder. Why do you want to blend in right now?"

Talking to him was like being at the top of a staircase with no recollection of how I got there. It felt like I needed to back up one step at a time until I figured out why I climbed them in the first place.

His steely gaze found mine, and I could feel him assessing me like I was one of the freak show exhibits from his dilapidated park.

"Can I trust you?" Wilder asked, his eyes narrowing and his voice dropping to a level that made the hair stand on the back of my neck.

"If you mean, will I tell anyone what you say? Then you can trust me to keep it to myself. I'll go to my grave with it," I said.

"Even if it puts you in danger?"

"Even better. I like living on the edge." I leaned forward. To finally learn the mysteries of Wilder was too good to pass up.

The corner of Wilder's mouth turned up as if what I'd said amused him. If he could be amused.

"I was ordered to do something but was set up, and now one particular person is after me, but they have the strength of many men like me looking for me." It was hard to tell if this was a wild truth or if this was just another twisted mess inside Wilder's mind. "That's why I was keeping tabs on your girl's fuck friend."

My nostrils flared at the mention of the bartender.

"Oh, really? And why is that?"

"He's related to the man who is after me. I keep an eye on all his family."

That had me sitting up straight. "Is she in danger? Are you planning something I should know about?"

I had no idea if I could get to my gun before Wilder killed me, but if he was planning to go after Raine, we were about to have an issue.

"No, the guy seems checkered for different reasons but has nothing to do with that side of his family. He seems to be estranged from most of his family. They don't like his life choices."

I had no idea what that meant, but I relaxed as Wilder said he had no intentions of attacking them.

"So these people who are after you, are you planning on eradicating them?" I asked.

"Killing them like rodents. I like that. Yes, if they come for me."

I leaned back and stared at Wilder. "I think you should take the fight to their door. Not that you don't look great in all your blending-in outfits, but wouldn't it be nice to be free of the worry?"

"I don't worry. There is no place for fear in my life." He turned his head and stared out the dark window. "But I do understand your meaning. Maybe you should take your advice as well. Better to know if you can fix what you fucked up than not try at all."

Crossing my arms, I stared at the side of his face and couldn't help wondering what it would've been like to have Wilder in prison with me. I had the protection of Mannix and the crew he'd gathered, and that was how I met Roach and Hollywood, but there was something about Wilder that made you want him on your team even if he made your brain do backward somersaults.

"Maybe I should. So, did you come over because you saw I was sad or to ask another question?"

"No, I just wanted to borrow some flour," Wilder said, and stood.

"Flour?"

"Yes, I'm baking cookies." He smiled, and I could only shake my head.

"Sure, I have a bag in the cupboard across from the stove. Help yourself."

"I know. You just purchased it last Tuesday." He walked out of the room like that wasn't the creepiest thing to date he'd said to me. I bet he also wrote down somewhere how many times I jerked off in a day. I didn't even want to fucking think about that.

Wisely or not, I decided to visit Raine. Pushing myself off the couch, I grabbed my leather jacket and called down the hall. "Hey, Wilder, I'm heading out. Can you lock up?"

"Yup, I always do." And there it was, the line that was creepier than the one before.

"How in the hell did I get talked into leaving the wet pussy I was fucking for this?" Roach grumbled as we pulled up to Raine's house.

"Because you still owe me," I said, eyes trained on the dark windows.

"For what?"

I turned my head to look at Roach. "You know for what."

He shook his head and lit up a smoke. "You're a prick. I paid that debt back a hundred times by now."

"Keep dreaming," I mumbled.

Hopping out of the truck, I jogged up the few steps and tried the door, but I wasn't surprised to find it locked. Now that I knew the locks in her home, I made quick work of it and stepped inside. Not much had changed. The coffee table was gone, but it hadn't been replaced. The closet door had a dent, and I could still feel her shoulders as I slammed her up against it. Running my fingers over the little mark, I felt a flicker of guilt.

Taking a deep breath, I walked away from the door and took the stairs two at a time. The room had been tidied just like downstairs. The bed was made and not slept in, and the door to the bathroom had been removed. Other than that, there was no sign of Raine or that she'd been here since that night.

My hand balled into a fist. There was a ninety-nine-point-nine percent chance that I knew exactly where she was, and I should stay away. I should head back to my house and let this be a fucking sign, but before I made it out the front door, I knew that wouldn't happen.

"Head to Eclipse. I'll give you directions from there," I barked out.

"Are we killing someone? I just need to know what we're getting into." Roach turned the truck around and pulled off the residential street and onto the main road that led to the beach. The place Raine worked was closed tonight, but as we got close, my eyes scanned the parking lot for the plain black sedan. Not seeing it only made the rage brewing in my gut rise to dangerous levels.

"That way," I said, pointing. The closer we got to the house I'd followed Raine to, the harder I ground my teeth. "Pull over here," I growled out. Roach did as I asked, and I stared at the three-story home. The lights were on, but I couldn't see anyone moving around inside, and that made me anxious and enraged.

When I grabbed the door handle, Roach gripped my biceps. "As your friend, you need to calm the fuck down before you go over there."

I glared at his hand, but he held firm. "I fucking mean it. This is not a job, and Raine and whoever she's in there with haven't done shit to anyone or anything to do with the club or you. Other than pissing you off by proximity to something you want. You've never been one to kill casually, but I know that look on your face, and you're close to murderous. Take a deep fucking breath, man. I mean it."

He let go of my arm, and I knew he was right. Every logical part of my being told me I should tell Roach to drive away, but I opened the door and got out. I wasn't letting Raine go without a fight.

Raine

40

Raine

"I still can't believe you got food first," Avro complained as he poured his once-upon-a-time milkshake into a glass. It looked like yellow milk, and I covered my mouth not to gag.

"You ordered more, and it will be here soon. What's the big deal?" Jace argued and earned an 'are you fucking kidding me?' glare.

I snickered as I watched the two of them together. It was easy to tell that they'd known one another for years. They were the embodiment of an old married couple, and it was hard to keep the smile off my face. Jace was still a total asshole, but we now had this weird connection, or maybe it was more of an understanding between us. It was a start. He certainly could make my blood race and made me squirm with just a look.

"And then you had hot sex without me in a cemetery. You know that's on my bucket list." Avro continued to sulk, but it seemed directed toward his now cold and melted food.

"Oh, my god. Do you want to go right now? I can fuck you in a cemetery on a tomb of your choice," Jace muttered, and rolled his eyes.

I couldn't hold back any longer and burst out laughing. Avro shot a glare my way.

"Sorry." I covered my mouth but bit my finger to avoid making noise.

"I thought you wanted Peaches and me to get closer," Jace asked.

He pulled a small dish of grapes from the refrigerator and popped one into his mouth. His eyes found mine, and the look he gave me made me warm all over as they danced with mischief that bordered on something darker. We hadn't been back very long, and the memories of what we'd done and the feel of his body were still very fresh in my mind. I'd officially decided I might be addicted to his piercings, because I could still feel them on my tongue and in other places.

"It is what I want." Avro leaned against the counter. "I'm just hangry. Ignore me."

"I need to hit the head. I'll be back." Jace left the kitchen, and I took the opportunity to go to Avro. He was quick to pull me close to his body.

"You sure you're okay with Jace and me…you know?"

Avro smiled widely. "Totally." He leaned in close to my ear. "I just love giving Jace a hard time. He gets extra spicy when he's riled up," he whispered, making me laugh. The doorbell rang, and Avro smiled even wider. "About time. I'm starved."

I was going to mention that the rest of the food was fine, and it was just a milkshake, but I figured that would set him off on another rant. I picked up the glass of liquid milkshake to try a sip as Avro opened the door. I looked up when Avro asked who the person at the door was, and the smile fell from my face.

"Fuck," Avro yelled as Kai punched him square in the face.

Blood thrummed through my veins, and the world slowed down as Avro stumbled back and Kai stepped into the house. I could hear the thump of his boots, and they echoed in my mind like a movie. I thought he'd leave me alone. I was so stupid.

My stomach flipped and then tied itself into knots at the sight of him with his hands clenched into fists, and his lip pulled up like he was snarling. My heart pounded harder with each step he took, but when those enraged eyes found mine, the world narrowed in on just him. I sucked in a shuddering breath and felt paralyzed, like his eyes alone could hold me in place.

Kai was almost at the kitchen doorway when Jace came out of nowhere and tackled Kai. I sucked in a breath as Kai and Jace disappeared. They crashed into the front sitting room so loudly that it jerked me out of my shocked state. The noise around me came crashing back as loudly as the sound of the two men swearing and growling like a pair of animals.

I forgot I was holding the glass until it slipped from my fingers and shattered on the tile floor, sending little shards and banana milkshake in all directions. I blinked as a flash of my childhood hit me. I could see the blood on my hands and remembered the feeling of the glass cutting my feet. I shook my head and closed my eyes to rid myself of the image.

Leaving the mess in my wake, I ran from the kitchen and rounded the corner to the sitting area. In those few seconds, it looked like a cyclone had taken the room in its grip. Kai and Jace rolled around on the floor, exchanging and taking blows with even measure. Neither seemed to have the upper hand, and I stood there feeling useless as I tried to figure out how to help.

"Kai!" I screamed, but he didn't glance my way.

If he heard, he ignored me, but it seemed more like he was so focused that a car could have driven through the window and he wouldn't have cared.

They rolled again, and this time Jace was on top, but Kai used his feet in a wrestling maneuver that tossed Jace over his head. Jace crashed down on top of the large glass coffee table, and it shattered on impact. He groaned, his face grimacing in pain.

"Kai!" I screamed again and ran at him as he lifted his arm to punch Jace. Slamming into his side only knocked him off balance. He glared but then looked away like I was a pesky insect.

Avro jumped into the fray as Kai got to his feet, blood dripping from his split lip. Avro wasn't as skilled as Jace, but he held his own as he and Kai took turns swiping at one another like a pair of boxers in a ring. They were saying something to one another, but I couldn't hear over the roaring in my head.

Darting around the two, I knelt by Jace, who rolled onto his side. "Are you okay?"

"Yeah, I will be. I'm going to kill this fucker." He shook off my hand as he stood up.

"Jace, don't. I'll get him to leave."

"Fuck that. This asshole is mine," Jace snarled, the glass shards falling off him as he stepped away from the table.

My heart leaped into my throat as Kai pulled a switchblade. I screamed like a banshee when he slashed at Avro. Jace charged, and as Kai turned to face the attack, he kicked the blade from Kai's hand with an impressive move and sent it spinning through the air until it stuck into the couch.

It was two-on-one, yet Kai looked like a feral dog in a fight to the death, and it terrified me. They all terrified me, and there was way too much testosterone and not enough brains between the three of them. I suddenly knew what it felt like to be the bone all the dogs were fighting over, and I didn't like it.

Avro gripped Kai from behind but got two hard elbows to the gut. The blows made him let go, and he was doubled over as he tried to breathe.

Jumping in, I tried once more to stop Kai. My hands gripped his leather jacket, but I was no more effective than a flea as he lunged for Jace, and the material was ripped from my hands.

The two men collided like bears. Kai and Jace gripped each other and pushed one other around the room. I had to dance out of the way as they ran sideways at me and crashed into the wall with a thud. A very sick and twisted part of me loved the ferocity of the moment and wished this was just for fun, but there was nothing fun or amusing about their intent.

"Enough!" I tried again and marched toward them, but Avro charged Kai again and gripped him around the waist before I got there. They managed to destroy everything they touched as it fell from the walls or clattered off tables. Avro and Jace picked Kai up and slammed him down hard on the floor like wrestlers I'd seen on television with a tag team maneuver.

Kai wouldn't stay down, and blood flew as his elbow cracked Avro across the jaw. Kai jumped up, but before he and Jace could go another round, he pulled a gun.

"I'm going to fucking kill you," Kai growled, his voice as threatening as the night he'd been in my home.

Jace gripped Avro's shoulder and pulled him back before holding his hands up.

"No, Kai, don't you dare!" I yelled, jumping in front of Jace and holding my arms out in my pathetic attempt to block the shot. "Kai."

"Get out of my way, Tink," he snarled, wiping at the blood trickling from his chin, his eyes focused on the men behind me.

I could see Jace in the glass, moving to grab me out of the way.

"Don't touch me, Jace," I said and glanced over my shoulder.

He was going to have a black eye. It was already swelling, and blood was flowing from his nose. My heart broke as our eyes locked. At that moment, I knew that Jace was right, Kai would always keep coming unless I locked him back up, and I couldn't do it.

Even now, I knew I couldn't put him back in the cage that had turned him into this. I loved Avro, and my feelings for Jace were wild and new and would eventually turn into love, and I couldn't put them at risk. This needed to end.

When I was sure Jace wouldn't try to yank me out of the way, I turned my head to look at Kai again.

"Don't you dare hurt them. They've never done anything to you. It's me you're after." I took a small step forward, and Kai's eyes flicked to mine. "Isn't that the truth? I'm the one who hurt you. I'm the one you hate. I'm the one you want to kill and end whatever fucked up war you have inside your mind," I said.

All the bubbling emotion was pushed aside with the urgency of the situation. There was time for fear later.

Kai licked the blood from his lip, but it was the slight tremor in his hand that told me he heard me.

"Look at me, Snake," I yelled, and he stepped back. I'd never used his fighting name, but I did now. It had divided us then and had the effect I was after now. Kai's eyes grew large as he stared at me. "You're not Kai, not right now, not like this. I don't even recognize you." I looked him up and down and tried hard not to remember the teen who had made my heart beat as if it would pound out of my ribcage.

"Don't call me that," he said, his voice soft and horrified.

"Why not? You want me dead anyway, right? That's what Snake wants. To destroy the person who made you this angry." I spoke like he was two different people. That was what it seemed like to me. Kai could be sweet, caring, and romantic, but then there was Snake, who was only out for blood and pain.

"Well, I'm right here. Do it. Take the shot and end this, because I'm not living in fear of you anymore." A tear slipped from my eye, and he watched it trickle down my cheek. "I know now that it wasn't you back then, but I've lived the last eleven years a shell of who I was because of what was done to me, and I won't hide in my closet anymore. I won't triple lock my door and stay up all night with a knife by my bed. I won't close my eyes and see your face hurting me." I shook my head. "Not anymore." I stepped forward as my anger rose higher.

"Raine, stay back," Avro said, but this was no longer about them.

Kai was here for me because of our past. I was the only one that could stop this.

Kai's eyes flicked to the ground. But I wasn't having any of that bullshit. He came here, and he was finishing it one way or another.

"Look at me," I growled. Marching the last few steps forward, I stopped when the barrel of his gun touched me, and I gripped the end so he couldn't simply pull away.

"Let go, Tink," he said. "I don't have a fucking safety. Let go." Kai's voice was panicked as I pushed the barrel, so it was over my heart.

"Do it."

"No."

"Do it!" I screamed at him, the tears breaking free and sliding down my face. "I've wasted so much of my life being scared. I can't be that person again. So do it, 'cause I'm done. My heart was ripped from my chest in that warehouse. You might as well destroy my soul too." Tears poured in a steady stream down my cheeks. "Do it," I whispered.

"No, Tink. Just let go. I won't shoot them," he said, but I didn't believe him.

The images of my attack flooded my mind. My hands clawed at the dusty old couch as my clothes were ripped from my body. My screams were never heard, and no one cared. The pain that they caused as they violated me over and over and shoved my face into the cushion so I couldn't breathe. My hand shook, and my body trembled. I wouldn't go back to being that girl, but I couldn't turn him in. I was fucked either way.

"I think everyone needs to take a breath," a new voice said.

I glanced over to see the man who was at Kai's house the day I went to speak to him.

He slowly stepped around the room, wisely keeping his distance with his hands in the air. "Neither of you wants to do this."

"And how would you know what I want?" I asked, never taking my eyes off Kai.

"Because you don't look like someone who wants to die. It's Raine, right?"

I looked at him but kept my hand clenched tight around the gun barrel.

"I'm Roach. Snake and I met in prison. Kai never stopped talking about you. He always loved you. He tried to convince me that he hated you, but no hate burns that bright."

"Shut up, man. You don't know what you're talking about," Kai said, but there was no conviction in his tone, and I hated that my chest clenched a little tighter for a man I should want to forget forever.

"Really? So you want to kill her? Then I'm with her. Do it. Get it over with. Otherwise, this is a lot of drama for nothing."

Kai turned his head and looked at Roach as he crossed his arms over his chest, possibly bored, I didn't know.

"Don't look at me like that. Do you want her dead or not?"

"No, of course, I fucking don't. Them, on the other hand..." Kai growled. "I'd happily see them bleeding all over the floor."

"For what?" I yelled, and my hand shook violently.

"Whoa, Tink, don't be doing that," Kai said like he was trying to soothe me, his eyes wide as he stared at the shaking barrel of the gun.

"Or what? It might go off. Let it. Avro and Jace are the first people to make me feel human and myself again in years. You want to come in here and destroy that, rip away the slice of happiness I've carved for myself? Fuck you, Snake." I pressed harder into the metal until it hurt. "I won't let you tear me down anymore, and I won't let you hurt them."

"Let go of the gun, Snake," Roach ordered, and Kai immediately let go.

My lower lip trembled as the last remaining bits of the girl I'd once been crumbled to dust around me. Flipping the gun around, I quickly popped the magazine, and it fell to the floor with a thud. I uncocked it, and the loaded bullet dropped to the floor. I tossed the gun at Kai, and he caught it. I'd never liked guns, but I'd gone to the range and learned how to use one. Fear makes you do things you never thought you would.

"Get out. I never want to see you again. If you ever loved me at all, leave me alone," I said, my heart breaking with each word.

"Tink...." I could see the remorse in his eyes now that he'd calmed down, but it didn't matter. The damage was done. In one single act of jealousy, he'd destroyed my life all over again.

"Don't call me that, and get out," I said, my chin held high.

"Come on. Let's go," Roach coaxed.

The way Kai hesitated, I wasn't sure if he would go. He looked at me, then glanced at Avro and Jace before letting Roach herd him out the door. I stood and watched from the window as the two of them got into a truck and drove away, and still, I didn't move.

As soon as I did, I knew what would happen. Encasing my heart in the walls it needed, I turned to face Jace and Avro. Jace was, of course, the first to speak.

He dabbed at his nose with the hoodie he was wearing. "Let me guess, that's your friend, and you still don't want me to call the fucking cops." I didn't say anything, and he shook his head. "Fuck me," he snarled and stomped off.

"I'll talk to him," Avro said, and I held up my hand.

"No, let him cool off." I lifted a shoulder. "He has every right to be angry, and so do you. I need to go home and spend the night there to clear my head." I took in the destroyed room. "I'm so sorry," I said. "I'll help with cleanup, but I just can't right now."

"Let me drive you home." He stepped toward me, and I held up my hand to stop him. I couldn't let him touch me, or I'd lose all the courage I needed for what was next.

I shook my head and grabbed my purse and hoodie. "I could use the fresh air. I'll be fine."

"But Snake could be waiting. I really should drive you."

I shook my head. "No, he won't stick around. He knows this was a huge fuck up. Trust me. I know that look in his eyes. He won't be back."

Avro's eyes held the same sad and hooded expression as my heart did. I stepped up to the front door and gave him a small smile as I tried to alleviate the worry I saw on his face.

"I'm so sorry for all of this. I really am. Can you tell Jace I'm sorry too?"

"You can tell him tomorrow. It will be better coming from you," he said, and I nodded. "You'll be at work tomorrow, won't you? Do you want me to pick you up? Jace flies out the following morning, so we can talk after work," Avro blurted out. He would make a terrible poker player. He was worried that this would drive a wedge between us, and he was right, which was why I couldn't let that happen.

"Yeah, that works. Pick me up at the normal time."

"You sure you're okay? It's no problem to take you home," he offered for the third time.

"No, I need the space at the moment." Swallowing down the emotions churning inside me, I sucked in a deep breath to help steady myself. "I love you, Avro," I said and heard him say it back as I closed the door. I couldn't stay for even another second, or he would tempt me to stay.

The walk was forty minutes to my house, and with each footstep, the tears fell a little more until there was nothing left to cry out. My life had been one blow after the other, and I wasn't sure how I was still standing, but I was, which meant that I was stronger than I'd realized.

Stepping into the little house I'd called home for the last six years, I ran up the stairs and didn't bother to look at my reflection in the mirror over my dresser. I knew I looked like hell warmed over. Stripping off the hoodie I had on, I tossed it into the pile of laundry that would never be washed and pulled on my favorite one and a jacket before grabbing my go bag. I swapped out my runners for the short leather boots and went to my nightstand to take the only other two personal items I had in the house: my journal and my V.C. Andrews book.

Tearing a page from the journal, I quickly wrote a note to Avro and Jace, and my lower lip quivered the entire time. Tears dripped onto the paper as I read it over, folded it, and put it in an envelope. Pushing the journal into the bag, I gave the room one more sweep before jogging down the stairs and locking the door.

There were some things in life you just couldn't fix, and this was one of them. Love or hate, Kai was filled with a toxic amount and would never be able to stay away. I'd seen it in his eyes tonight. That meant Avro and Jace would never be safe from his wrath. One of those rages would end up with me, or one of them killed, and I wouldn't have that. Avro had been my only friend for so long. He saw past the scars and cared enough to get to know me, and now he was the single piece of happiness and good in my life. If he died because of me...

I shook my head, unable to contemplate that thought. The look of fear and sadness on their faces was enough to crush me, but the dark bruises, blood, and cuts were just too much. This was for the best, and it was the only card I had left. The ace of spades was in my hand, and it was time to use it.

I put the envelope in my mailbox and walked to the bus stop. Pulling up the map on my phone, I thought about all the places I'd wanted to see in person. This wasn't how I thought it would happen, but it was time. The universe was giving me the boot like the Collinses had when I got out of the hospital. I had survived then, and I would survive now.

Avro

41

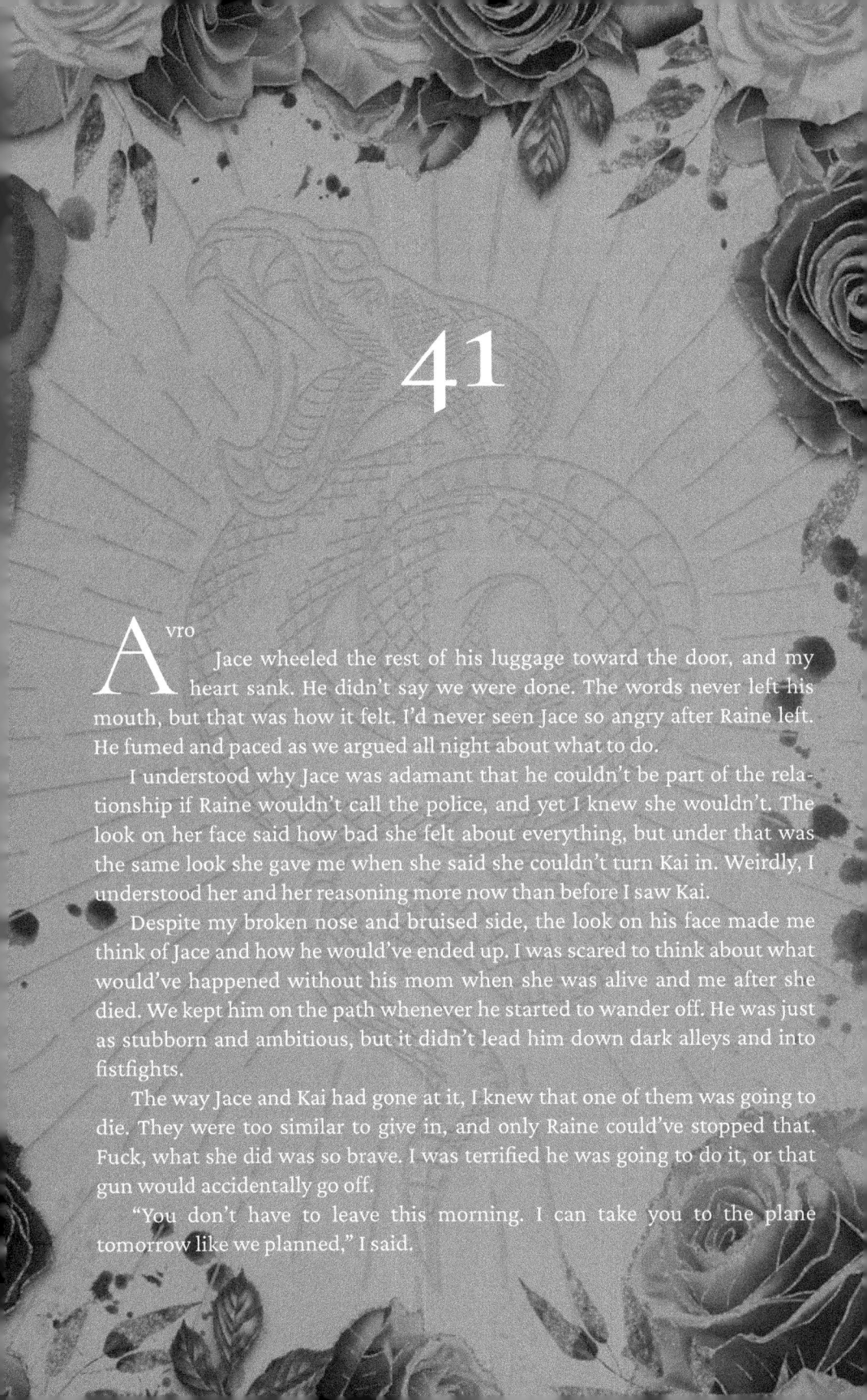

Avro

Jace wheeled the rest of his luggage toward the door, and my heart sank. He didn't say we were done. The words never left his mouth, but that was how it felt. I'd never seen Jace so angry after Raine left. He fumed and paced as we argued all night about what to do.

I understood why Jace was adamant that he couldn't be part of the relationship if Raine wouldn't call the police, and yet I knew she wouldn't. The look on her face said how bad she felt about everything, but under that was the same look she gave me when she said she couldn't turn Kai in. Weirdly, I understood her and her reasoning more now than before I saw Kai.

Despite my broken nose and bruised side, the look on his face made me think of Jace and how he would've ended up. I was scared to think about what would've happened without his mom when she was alive and me after she died. We kept him on the path whenever he started to wander off. He was just as stubborn and ambitious, but it didn't lead him down dark alleys and into fistfights.

The way Jace and Kai had gone at it, I knew that one of them was going to die. They were too similar to give in, and only Raine could've stopped that. Fuck, what she did was so brave. I was terrified he was going to do it, or that gun would accidentally go off.

"You don't have to leave this morning. I can take you to the plane tomorrow like we planned," I said.

"No, I need some space from all of this. I don't want to argue with you. I've always hated fighting with you, but I'm telling you, that guy will not stop. He is going to be back, and next time, he will probably pull the trigger the moment you open the door." Jace finished tying his boots and stood. "I'm surprised he didn't, and when I think about that." He shook his head. "I can't. I can't live through that again."

I pushed myself to my feet and faced the one person I'd loved almost my whole life, and it felt like I was being torn in two. Jace grabbed my face and kissed me hard. It was so Jace, so demanding, so all-consuming that I forgot he was leaving and this could be our last goodbye.

"I can't lose you that way, and if I spend any more time here, I'm going to fall in love with her 'cause the fucking tug is there already, and I can't. I just can't. Call me a fucking chicken all you want, but I already had to bury three people I loved because of an unhinged man." His hands dropped from my face. "I won't put myself in that position willingly again. If Raine won't do what she needs to, to make us all safe...." He grabbed the bomber jacket and shrugged it on. "If she calls the cops, then I'm all in. If you decide we find a different third, I'm all in." Jace paused in his rant and sighed. "But this? Always worrying when that fucker will come to the door with a gun? No. No. No. No."

"That's a lot of 'no's. Are you sure?" I teased and earned a glare. "Okay, bad timing. Look, Jace..." I grabbed his shoulders and searched his face. "Just give me time to get something worked out."

"I am. We're not done. I love you too fucking much, but you need to get Raine to see reason, and I can't be here for it 'cause I know that I'm just going to fight with her, and that will make it worse." A horn blew outside, and Jace walked over and opened the door to show off the long black limo. "I have three concerts over the next week, then three days off. I'll come home, and we can talk more."

"I hate this," I grumbled.

"So do I." He grabbed his bags and the suitcase and wheeled it to the open door before looking back at me. "I do want things to work out, Avro. You were right. She is unique and...I just wish it had worked out. Please be safe. That guy is not right. I saw it in his eyes."

With that, Jace walked out the door, and a minute later, the limo was gone. I stared at the living room, which was still a complete disaster, and knew it looked how I felt. My world had imploded. I had no one to blame but myself for falling in love with Raine, but I did and wouldn't change a moment.

Every touch, glance, and laugh we'd shared over the last five years were tiny building blocks in our relationship.

I couldn't wait until work tonight. I needed to see her now. Locking the front door, I grabbed my keys and ran to my car. My chest felt like it was being stepped on. Raine left, Jace left, and I was the ribbon in the middle of a game of tug-of-war.

Hitting Jace's number on my phone, I tried calling him, but as usual, when he was pissed and wanted space, he had it turned off. It was a habit I hated.

"Jace, it's me. Look, I'm sorry. I know we said we would talk soon, but I just...Fuck, I love you. Call me back."

Racing down the street, it didn't take long to reach Raine's house, and I jumped out and ran to the front door. I knocked, but no one answered, and I didn't hear anyone moving around inside. I knocked again when I spotted an envelope sticking out of the mailbox, and feeling compelled to do it, I grabbed it.

My hands shook as I stared at the name scrolled across the front.

Avro and Jace

I tore open the envelope and pulled out the small handwritten letter.

I don't even know what to say. I have all these emotions and thoughts, and they are all jumbled up and barely make sense to me.

Avro, I want you to know that I really do love you. You have a special heart, and you took the time that no one else did to understand me. You made me feel like I wasn't a walking scar that everyone would see and pity. I cannot even explain to you what that means to me.

And I'm sorry to go like this, but I had to. I just couldn't look you in the eye and do what I needed to.

Jace, I hate to say it, but you were right about one thing. Kai is never going to stop. I'm not sure what it would take to stop him, but no matter what, I would never put the two of you at risk. I did hear you. Please know our time, as short as it was, was very special to me.

I love you so much, Avro, and I know in time I would've loved you too, Jace.

The issue is that I still love Kai, even all these years later. I'm responsible for destroying his life and turning him into the enraged man who drove off the rails. He used to be so different and was someone the two of you would've liked. Now I don't recognize him, and that scares me.

It's time I start a new adventure, and maybe one day, our stars will realign.

Raine

I read the letter for a second time, my body shaking. No, this is not happening. I wasn't allowing that asshole to run her off. Letter in hand, I stomped down the steps to the car and flipped through the web search engine until I found what I needed—the dilapidated amusement park that sat next door to the motorcycle club.

Putting the car in gear, I drove to the old amusement park I'd been to many times as a kid. It used to be a huge attraction, and I had great memories of making out with Jace in a few dark corners. The top of the Ferris wheel had been highly entertaining. I felt free up there, with no one around to see or judge us.

I wasn't letting this guy destroy my life. I'd paid my dues on the wheel of fucked up. My hands clenched the steering wheel as I pushed the car much faster than I should on these streets, but I had one mission, and the blue-eyed motorcycle-riding fuckpot was it.

I pulled into the Lost Souls driveway as the gates were opening. Four bikes were getting ready to leave. They all had their hands behind their backs, waiting to see if the black car with tinted windows was a threat.

Putting my window down, I yelled. "Don't shoot. I'm just here to see Kai."

"Who the fuck is Kai?" one guy asked. I couldn't see who said it, but someone shouted back.

"Snake, you idiot. Get going. I'll meet you soon."

The three bikes peeled out. I took that as a good sign and slowly got out of the car.

"Roach, right?" I asked the guy as he cut the engine on his bike.

He leaned forward and looked me up and down. "Yeah, you got the name right. Are you fucking stupid, lost, or do you have a death wish?" Roach asked, and my back bristled.

"I need to speak to Kai."

Roach's eyebrow cocked upward. "Death wish, it is." Roach sat up and pointed toward the amusement park. "He has a house on the other side of that. Good luck. You're going to need it." Roach waited until I got back in my car and pulled out before starting his bike.

It was easy enough to find the long driveway with the weed-covered overgrowth he called a lawn.

Pulling up to the house, I got out and jogged up the porch. My fist banged hard on the door as I yelled Kai's name.

The door whipped open, and we glared at one another. He looked like he was ready for bed with jogging pants on. It was nice to see that his face looked as beat up as ours did.

"What the fuck do you want?" His hand flexed into a fist, and I pointedly looked at it.

"You gonna hit me?"

"Depends on why you're here," he said. "How exactly did you find my place?"

"Wouldn't you like to know?"

Kai's eyes narrowed as he glared.

"She's gone, and it's your fucking fault," I said before he could argue some more.

His eyebrows shot up. "What?"

I pulled the letter from my pocket and tossed it at Kai. He snatched it out of the air and slowly unfolded it. I waited until he had time to read it all before I spoke.

"She's gone, and it's your fault. What are you going to do about it?"

"Me? Why am I the one having to do something?" Kai asked and leaned against the doorjamb as he sneered at me. He looked me up and down like I wasn't worth his time, and I didn't like it. Like Raine, it took me a long time to figure out that I was worth someone's time, and my anger burned a little brighter.

"Are you hard of hearing? You and that fucking stunt last night chased her out of town. First, you almost killed her, then you assaulted her. As if that wasn't bad enough, you almost shot her after you tracked her down to my home. She was happy. We were fucking happy."

"Aw, did I ruin your little family?"

My fist flew before I had time to think about it. I gave him the same courtesy as he had with me last night and caught him in the middle of his face, completely off guard.

"Fuck," Kai yelled and stumbled backward. "I'm going to kill you."

"Then fucking kill me, but find her first, then fucking apologize and find a way to make her come back. I don't care what you have to do, but don't fuck this up. Remember, she's only gone because of you. So much for loving her." I shook my head as Snake's glare darkened. "Then if you want to kill me, you can, asshole." Snatching the letter from his hand, I marched down the stairs and got behind the wheel of my car.

There was no way he was going to be able to resist the thought of losing Raine. I'd seen it in his eyes just now when I said she was gone. His whole body twitched like he was ready to run out the door and find her that second. I would let him do the hard part. I was pretty sure he would find a way to hunt her down, and when he did, I would follow.

Everyone thought I was the nice guy, and most of the time, I was, but even nice guys could be pushed too far.

Jace

EPILOGUE

Jace

The plane's engine roared, and I sat back as the jet took off down the runway. I was able to get the pilot to come in early. I would've been too tempted to stay if I had to spend the night on the plane.

As the plane rose, I stared at the water and the state I called home. Even though I knew I was too far away, it didn't stop me from looking for Avro's house. My chest tightened with the thought of him. Then the memories of Raine and our time at the cemetery was like a movie behind my eyes.

"Fuck," I grumbled as we reached cruising altitude. The little light for the seatbelt turned off, and I connected my phone to the plane Wi-Fi. As soon as I did, it began to ding with notifications and messages.

I was going to ignore them, but I couldn't resist when I saw Avro as one of the callers. The first message was from Allen.

"Hey, I hear you're flying in early. That is great news. I'm going to set up an interview with the EN broadcast. They've been bugging me for months to have you come for an interview." I rubbed my forehead, not wanting to deal with all of this right now. "Also, things are too quiet lately. We need to stir up the hornet's nest, so think about what you want to do. All right, that's all I've got. See you in a few hours." Oh, I could give him a scandal.

I moved on to the next message.

"Jace, it's me. Look, I'm sorry. I know we said we would talk soon, but I just... Fuck, I love you. Call me back."

The phone beeped, and I saved the message. I saved as many messages as I could from Avro. It was silly, but I loved listening to his voice when we couldn't talk.

The next message clicked on.

"Jace...Shit, she's gone. Raine left. I couldn't resist and went to see her, and she was gone. This is all that guy Kai's fault. I need to go see him." The line clicked, and my heart pounded hard as I pulled the phone away from my ear. I stared at the screen expecting another message, but there wasn't one.

He couldn't see Kai alone. What the hell was he thinking? Did he have a death wish? I quickly hit redial on the phone, but it just rang and rang before clicking over to voicemail.

It's Avro. Leave a message unless you're selling something. Beep.

"Hey, it's me. What the hell are you doing going to see a motorcycle gang member on your own? Call me back." I tapped the phone off my bouncing knee. "Shit, shit, shit!" I tried Avro again, and it went straight to voicemail. Karma. It was fucking karma for turning off my phone.

Unable to sit still, I stood and paced. Raine was gone and probably in danger, since Avro was going to go tell Kai that she was missing. Avro would probably get himself shot in the head before Kai took off after Raine to finish killing her. All the worst scenarios raced around in my brain like a merry-go-round with no off switch. Meanwhile, the fear over them getting injured, or worse, gripped my throat.

Stop it. You're getting yourself worked up over nothing.

But it wasn't nothing. This was the same feeling I had when I left home and my family ended up dead. That wasn't happening again.

"Fuck this," I grumbled, and marched for the front of the plane and knocked on the door. "Marco?"

The door opened, and the co-pilot stared out at me.

"We need to turn around."

CLICK HERE TO READ BOOK 2 - SURRENDER

ARE YOU CRAVING MORE OF THE LOST SOULS THEN CHECK OUT CHASE'S DUET ADVERSARIES & FRENEMIES

SURRENDER

Do you feel that?
Do you feel how you're struggling to take a breath?
How every little gasping breath burns like acid in your lungs as you dream of death while you fight to survive?
That's how I've lived every day without you.
Never question my love for you again.

Surrender

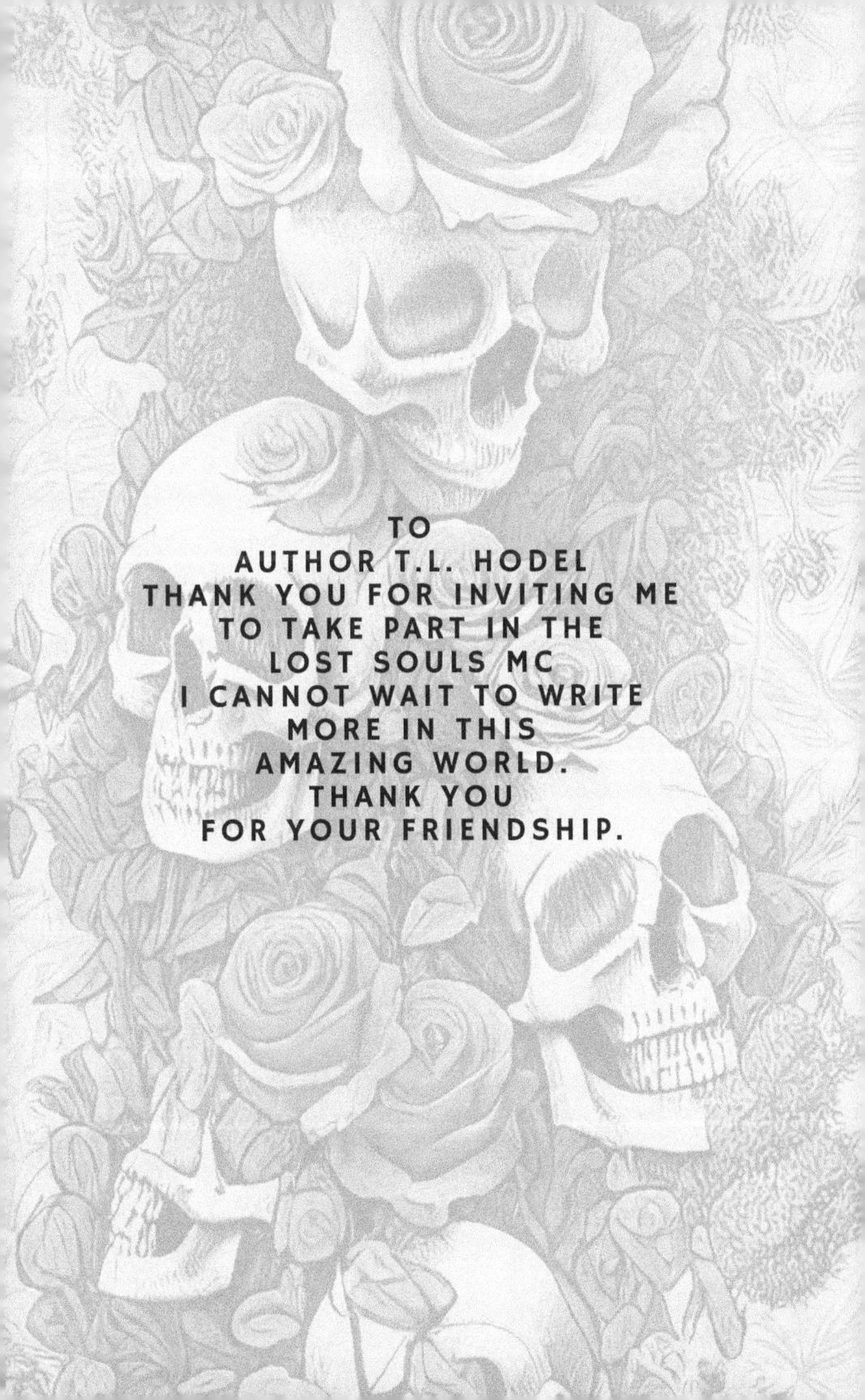

TO
AUTHOR T.L. HODEL
THANK YOU FOR INVITING ME
TO TAKE PART IN THE
LOST SOULS MC
I CANNOT WAIT TO WRITE
MORE IN THIS
AMAZING WORLD.
THANK YOU
FOR YOUR FRIENDSHIP.

Raine

1

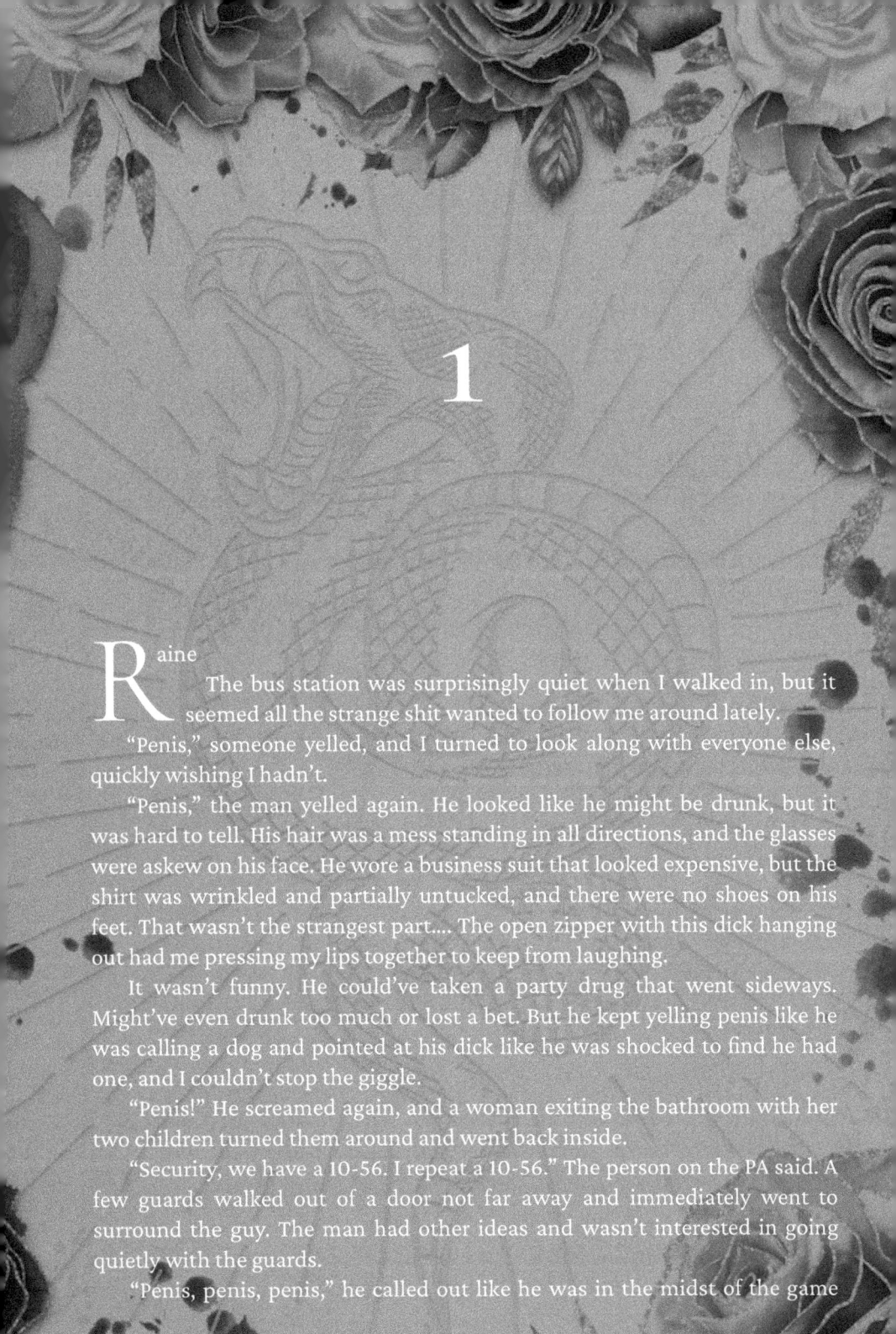

Raine

The bus station was surprisingly quiet when I walked in, but it seemed all the strange shit wanted to follow me around lately.

"Penis," someone yelled, and I turned to look along with everyone else, quickly wishing I hadn't.

"Penis," the man yelled again. He looked like he might be drunk, but it was hard to tell. His hair was a mess standing in all directions, and the glasses were askew on his face. He wore a business suit that looked expensive, but the shirt was wrinkled and partially untucked, and there were no shoes on his feet. That wasn't the strangest part.... The open zipper with this dick hanging out had me pressing my lips together to keep from laughing.

It wasn't funny. He could've taken a party drug that went sideways. Might've even drunk too much or lost a bet. But he kept yelling penis like he was calling a dog and pointed at his dick like he was shocked to find he had one, and I couldn't stop the giggle.

"Penis!" He screamed again, and a woman exiting the bathroom with her two children turned them around and went back inside.

"Security, we have a 10-56. I repeat a 10-56." The person on the PA said. A few guards walked out of a door not far away and immediately went to surround the guy. The man had other ideas and wasn't interested in going quietly with the guards.

"Penis, penis, penis," he called out like he was in the midst of the game

Marco Polo. It was like a train wreck I couldn't look away from as he took off in a run around the bus terminal. He hid behind shocked people, using them as shields and the large planters with small trees before sprinting toward the exit. "Penis," echoed back through the open door until it closed.

"I do hope he finds his pecker, terrible thing to lose it," the elderly man beside me said, and I couldn't hold back the laugh any longer. The man was dressed like an old English gentleman, from the wool cap on his head to the polished shoes on his feet and the wooden cane in his hand. He lifted a bushy white eyebrow and smiled before turning to face the front of the line once more.

"How can I help you?" The teller smiled as I stepped up to the glass.

"I need to get to Seattle," I said.

"We don't have a bus that takes a direct route, but there's a bus that goes from here to the Atlanta bus terminal. From there, you can take one bus the rest of the way or shorter distance ones if you want to stop along the way," she said.

"Sounds good. I always wanted to see Atlanta." I pulled out my wallet and was going to swipe my card but thought better of it and handed her cash. I had no idea what tricks Kai might have up his sleeve, but I wouldn't put it past him to track my cards.

I grabbed my ticket and wandered out to the bus idling on the curb. Seattle was the furthest place I could think of to put space between myself and all that had happened here and it was a spot I always wanted to see.

"Penis! No, you'll never take me alive." I looked toward the parking lot and saw security forcing Penis Man into the back of a police car. On the plus side, I wasn't starting my day in the back of a cruiser. I guess there was always a silver lining...

I hated this. I hated that once more, Kai found a way to terrify me. It didn't matter that it wasn't him that hurt me when I was fifteen. I'd still spent my whole life believing it. Then when he came back, it certainly wasn't to try and explain that it wasn't him. Then again, I don't know if I would've listened to him if he had knocked on my door. It was all so complicated.

No matter what I'd said to Kai, I was scared that my life would be forever living out of a backpack on the run from him and the rage that had built up like a volcano inside him. I realized that I could never be with anyone ever again. Whether it was five, ten, or even twenty years from now didn't matter. That shimmer in his eye had said it all—no one would ever be safe.

Maybe I just wanted to hurt, but I did what I ordered myself not to do and pulled out my burner phone. My finger hovered over the text message before giving in and tapping on the little dot. This would be my one guilty pleasure. I knew I wouldn't be able to resist when I sent myself the pictures. I had snapped some images of Avro and me at the beach and another that Avro insisted we take after Jace's concert with all three of us in it.

My heart ached for so many reasons, and I started questioning if I should be going.

"No, there is no point in dwelling on the 'what ifs,'" I mumbled.

Glancing at the time as a few people lined up, I realized I'd been staring at the photos for over half an hour. Stuffing the phone into my jeans pocket, I pushed away from the wall and made my way to the line of passengers slowly boarding the bus.

"Any big baggage needs to go around to the other side of the bus," the driver called out as the procession shuffled along.

The more I thought about it, the more it felt right to take the opportunity to spend a few days at each location the buses stopped to tour around. It would be my version of a hired bus tour. Besides, once I hit Seattle, I'd need to find a job and a place to stay. Who knew when I would get the chance to vacation again? I had enough money to keep me going for a while in my bag but not enough to live off of for a long time.

I handed my ticket to the man collecting at the door. My nose curled as I stepped inside, bombarded with the fake scent of coconut and pineapple. I normally didn't mind these particular flavors, but it was as if the smell had reached inside my nose and tried to choke me. Opting to sit as far away from the smell as possible, I wandered to the back of the bus and picked a spot with two empty seats.

Sitting by the window, I placed my bag in my lap and pulled out the pamphlets and maps I'd taken from the bus station. Of course, the first one I opened had an ad for Eclipse, and my heart fell.

My boss wasn't impressed with my impromptu departure. I told him it was an emergency that couldn't be avoided and recommended Avro take my place. He still grumbled and cursed into the phone about how no one could run the place as well as I had. It was a stupid statement, I hadn't been the manager for very long, but I promised that if I came back into town, I'd call.

My finger rubbed over the image, and I choked up. It felt like I was trying to contain the tide with my emotions raging and swaying one way and then the other. Never allowed to settle, never able to feel too safe before it all fell out from under me all over again. Like a bottle lost at sea forced away from shore only to tumble back and be yanked away once more, that was the story of my life.

. . .

I stared out the window, keeping my eyes on the butterfly floating around. Its brightly colored wings shimmered in the golden rays of the bright sun. A sun that had shined every day since my attack. A reminder that no matter what had happened to me, the girl in the bed beside me, or even the man in the room down the hall...the world continued to turn.

It was a terrible thing to realize that you were unimportant. I was nothing more than a blip on the radar or another grain of sand along the beach, blending in with all the others. I was no one special. The girl with cancer in the bed beside me was no one special. There wasn't a collective holding of breath to see if either of us survived. Only difference was, she had people that visited daily.

That reality was terrifying and freeing. I didn't matter, and no one cared, so I had no one to disappoint, but never being seen or understood and never being able to trust again was scary. I was now sixteen, having spent my birthday in the hospital, and it already felt like I'd lived three lifetimes and died twice along the way.

"Hi there, sweetie, are you all packed and ready to go?" The warm and cheery voice said from behind me. I smiled as I recognized Nurse Liz's voice. Pulling back on the wheels of the wheelchair, I slowly turned to face her. She always had the warmest smile. She nodded toward the wheelchair. "You're getting better," she said.

"Thanks. I'm still awkward, and I get mixed up on which way to pull and push to turn. It makes me feel stupid."

"Nonsense. A baby learns to crawl before it can stand and eventually walk and then run. You've only been able to get up and move around for a few days. You'll get used to it."

"Hopefully, I won't need it much longer. The doctor said that the wounds are healing well and the grafts are holding, so I can start walking around more."

Liz smiled and grabbed my packed bag, laying it on the bed. "You're not forgetting anything, are you?"

"I don't think so." I didn't have much, just a few changes of clothes and my journal. "Did my foster parents say when they would be coming to get me?" The bright smile slipped.

Liz looked away, and I knew something was wrong. "I thought you would've known," she said.

"Known what?" I wheeled myself a little closer, and Liz sat on the edge of the bed. She glanced out the door and lowered her voice as she spoke next.

"I guess I shouldn't be the one to tell you this, but it's Child and Family Services coming for you." My eyes went wide, and my heart tripled its pace.

"What? Why?"

I wouldn't say I loved the Collinses, they were both kinda cold and distant most of the time, but they were the only family I had left. I had loved Kai, or at least I thought I did, but he betrayed me and left me for dead. Now the Collinses weren't coming. What had I done to deserve this? Was I really that much trouble? Did everyone hate me so much that they wanted to hurt me?

"I don't know why, sweetie. I just heard that is who was coming to pick you up, so maybe they are just sending them to collect you or something," she offered, but I knew better.

I ignored Liz as she called my name when I wheeled out of the room and turned to roll down the hall. I didn't know where I was going. I didn't care as the tears hit and flowed down my cheeks. There was a small sitting room to my left, and I stopped the wheelchair and pulled into the small space, closing the door behind me. Breathing hard from the burst of exertion, I sat in the privacy of the four walls and covered my face to let the tears fall. Why did the world hate me so much?

It was then that I realized I was probably better off alone. No one could hurt me when I didn't let anyone in. I didn't need anyone anyway.

Snake

2

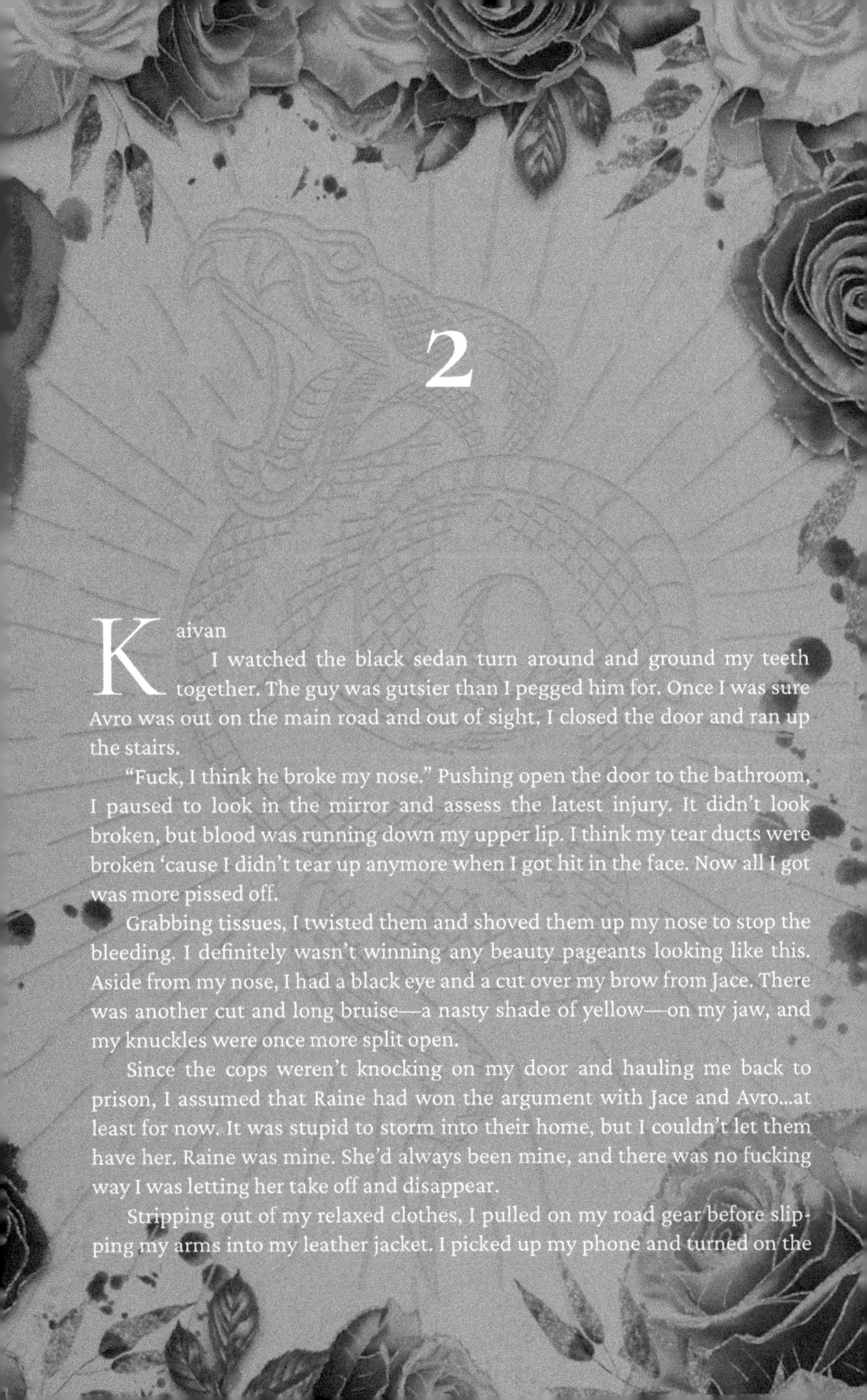

Kaivan

I watched the black sedan turn around and ground my teeth together. The guy was gutsier than I pegged him for. Once I was sure Avro was out on the main road and out of sight, I closed the door and ran up the stairs.

"Fuck, I think he broke my nose." Pushing open the door to the bathroom, I paused to look in the mirror and assess the latest injury. It didn't look broken, but blood was running down my upper lip. I think my tear ducts were broken 'cause I didn't tear up anymore when I got hit in the face. Now all I got was more pissed off.

Grabbing tissues, I twisted them and shoved them up my nose to stop the bleeding. I definitely wasn't winning any beauty pageants looking like this. Aside from my nose, I had a black eye and a cut over my brow from Jace. There was another cut and long bruise—a nasty shade of yellow—on my jaw, and my knuckles were once more split open.

Since the cops weren't knocking on my door and hauling me back to prison, I assumed that Raine had won the argument with Jace and Avro...at least for now. It was stupid to storm into their home, but I couldn't let them have her. Raine was mine. She'd always been mine, and there was no fucking way I was letting her take off and disappear.

Stripping out of my relaxed clothes, I pulled on my road gear before slipping my arms into my leather jacket. I picked up my phone and turned on the tracker app, smirking when I saw the little blinking dot. I knew it was smart to put that in her go bag. Wilder came through. Crazy fuck.

She was on the move, almost halfway to Atlanta, and a shit load further than I thought she'd be. With her headstart, she would be there by the time I caught up if that was where she stopped.

Sweat suddenly coated my body, and my gut churned as I pictured her hitchhiking her way there. She could be in some creepy trucker's cab right now. I knew she didn't have a car, and if Avro was here with his that left bus or putting her thumb out. If someone else hurt her, I'd kill them.

Grabbing my gun, I held it up, and what she'd said last night came rushing back.

"Look at me, Snake," Raine yelled. *She'd always refused to use the nickname given to me when I started fighting. She said it wasn't me, said that she could only see me as Kai and that Snake was some made-up character to scare people. She said she never wanted to see me like that or be scared of me. It had divided us then 'cause I thought it was cool, and it hurt now to hear her use it.*

"You're not Kai, not right now, not like this." Raine's eyes looked me up and down, and under the anger and fear was disgust and, deeper yet, disappointment. That look cut like a knife to my heart. I'd never wanted to hurt her, but the anger had been riding me for so long that it felt like it was a whole other person and all I had left, at least until now. "I don't even recognize you."

"Don't call me that," I said softly.

"Why not? You want me dead anyway, right? That's what Snake wants. To destroy the person that made you this angry." She spoke like I was two different people, and maybe I was. I felt as conflicted as two people inside of me.

"Well, I'm right here." She said, giving me a clear shot to do what I'd dreamed about in prison and to take my final revenge. "Do it. Take the shot and end this, because I'm not living in fear of you anymore." A tear slipped from her eye, and I watched it trickle down her cheek. Why that one tear punched so hard, I couldn't say, but a well of emotion was trying to break free of the cage it had been locked in for years.

"I know now that it wasn't you back then, but I've lived the last eleven years a shell of who I was because of what was done to me, and I won't hide in my closet anymore. I won't triple lock my door and stay up all night with a knife by my bed. I won't close my eyes and see your face hurting me." She shook her head, and my heart constricted in my chest. "Not anymore."

. . .

I stared at the gun in my hands. The same gun that had taken countless lives since I got out of prison and the same gun that could've easily gone off and killed the only person I'd ever loved on this shithole planet. She wasn't running. She was in protection mode. Protecting Avro and Jace and probably even me from myself. I pushed her to do that. I saw the look in her eyes last night. She knew I was on the line and would've killed them and had been willing to take the hit.

"Fuck!" I yelled. Self-loathing apparently had a lower level, and I had just reached the bottom floor. My hand began to shake, and I squashed the unease trying to take hold of my mind as old memories flooded to the surface.

"What the hell do you mean, Jack?" Mom yelled into the phone at my dad. She stomped across the living room and back again. I wasn't supposed to be listening, but I couldn't stay in my room when she started yelling.

Sitting on the stairs, I saw her shadow moving around with the light from the setting sun coming in the window at just the right angle.

"I told you I didn't want to deal with this shit anymore. We have a son, for fucks sake." I could hear the mouse-like sound of my dad yelling back as she stepped close to the stairs again.

"Yes, of course, I know he's your son too, but he doesn't want to be in the club. You were supposed to be done after the last job. I don't care! You promised you'd leave. No, no, Jack. I don't care." I'd never heard my mom this angry before. I knew why she was pissed off. They'd been arguing for months about my dad leaving the motorcycle club he belonged to. I wasn't really supposed to know much about what the club did, but I knew. Just like all the kids of the members knew, even though we were only allowed inside the clubhouse for special occasions or when my father needed to pick something up and I was with him.

When we'd all get together for parties and holidays and other shit like that, you could hear the men talking. Also, did they think we were all stupid and didn't watch television or the news? It wasn't normal for people to always wear leather jackets to weddings with a giant, snarling dog head on the back. They always assumed kids were stupid, but we picked up on a lot more than they knew.

Mom wanted him to be done. She said that he was too old for this shit and was always putting us in danger. She wasn't wrong, although I knew even without asking that no matter what my dad said, he was never leaving the club. He acted like that place was heaven. Maybe it was. How was I to know? Things had come to a head when three weeks and two days ago, our house was broken into, and everything was smashed. A warning, 'Stay out of our business,' was sprayed on the wall. Dad would only say that one of the girls that worked at the club was roughed up. That's when Mom got really intense and insisted that Dad leave and for us to move.

"Fuck you, Jack. I've given over the best part of my life to you and that club. Even with all the shit you've done and the women you've fucked while I sat home and looked after our son, I still stood by you, but I'm not sitting here like a target and just waiting for their next move. I'm taking Kai, and we're going to my sister's house in Connecticut. If you decide to leave the club, then you'll know where to find me."

The words had no sooner left my mom's mouth when there was a bang and glass shattered. I covered my head, not sure what was going on, and thought for just a minute that my mom had decided to break one of the glass tables in the living room. There was a loud roar that I knew was a motorcycle, and my hair rustled like a wind was lifting it.

Jumping up, I ran down the few stairs and rounded the corner to the living room.

"Mom!" She was lying on the floor, and blood was seeping into the carpet all around her. Running to her side, I dropped to my knees. Her eyes were wide and terrified.

"I don't know what to do," I said, my hands shaking as I stared at the wound in her chest. "What do I do?" She grabbed my hand in hers.

"Run," she said, her voice soft as she wheezed out the single word.

All I could feel was the pounding in my chest as my heart hammered, and I looked around for the phone. I needed to call for help. It was still in her other hand, and I realized Dad was still on the phone.

Leaning over Mom, I pulled the phone from her fingers that didn't want to let go. I could hear my dad yelling for my mom to answer him.

"Dad? Help, it's Mom, she's bleeding, and I don't know what to do."

"Okay, Kai, listen to me. Is anyone else still there?"

I looked around, confused by the question. We'd been alone the entire time. "No, it's just me and Mom."

"Good. Now, where is your mom hurt?" I could hear motorcycles revving, making it hard to hear my dad.

"Her chest," I said as something warm trailed down my cheeks. "Dad, there is so much blood."

"Hang up, Kai, and call nine-one-one."

"But dad...."

"No arguments Kai. Hang up the phone and call now." The phone clicked off in my ear.

"But I'm scared," I gasped as the asthma attack gripped me. Fear made me wheeze, and my eyes returned to my mom's face. Her eyes were still open, but she was looking right through me. "No, Mom, you need to stay with me," I said, gripping her shoulder to shake her. Mom's expression never changed as her head rocked with the movement.

Her hand was still wrapped around mine, but I pulled it free to stand and stumble into the kitchen. My mom always kept my puffers in the cupboard. It was getting harder to breathe with every passing second, and I knew that I couldn't pass out or I wouldn't be any help.

I shook the inhaler and got a puff into me before I dropped to my knees and fumbled with the phone to get those three simple numbers punched in. The phone slipped as I picked it up from the slick blood coating everything.

"Nine-one-one. What's your emergency?" The guy on the end of the line said.

"It's my mom, I think she's been shot, and I don't know what to do," I said, barely able to keep the phone to my ear as it kept trying to slip through my fingers.

"Are you in danger?"

"No, it's not me. It's my mom," I cried. I hated to cry. In this house, if you cried, you were not a man, but I couldn't hold the emotion back as Mom laid there. I'd never seen someone die, but I was sure my mom was dying now.

I couldn't remember what the man said to me. Everything had become a blur. From the police arriving and the paramedics to my dad showing up and yelling and crying like she meant everything to him. I stared up at him as they carried my mother's body out of the house, tears streaming down his face. All I could think was that he was a liar. I'd heard the fights and the names he called her. I heard the threats and the promises to kill her if she took off. That wasn't love, and if it was, then I never wanted to love someone.

I sat on the stairs, no one watching me or even looking my way because my dad was making so much noise. Trying for a part in a movie was my guess. The house became still after everyone was gone. My head lifted and my eyes locked on the front door and the bloody hand print smeared into the crisp white.

Rising to my feet, I slowly walked to the closet that held the cleaning supplies and pulled out a bucket and soap. Tossing in a sponge and the brush I used to get the dirt out from under my nails, I walked into the living room. The blood on the carpet was shaped like a person with a giant blob in the middle. It reminded me of the art projects from school when we would put a bunch of paint on paper and fold it in half.

Lowering myself to my knees, I grabbed the sponge and started to scrub, but the stain wouldn't go away. Instead, it got larger but faded to a terrible shade of pink, and no matter how hard I tried, I couldn't get the red out from under my nails.

I hated my dad from that moment on. My mom was scared. She'd been terrified that something was going to happen, and he chose to keep us in danger. Then he abandoned me. It was his fault, she died, and I prayed hard that he would die a terrible death.

. . .

The last word my mom said to me was 'run.' I didn't run, but I should've.

My father left on a Monday night at seven-thirty-one and never returned. By Friday, I'd eaten everything in the house that I knew how to make. I tried to call my dad, but he didn't answer. At the age of nine years, two months, and three days at exactly ten-fourteen on Saturday morning, the knock that would change my life forever sounded at the door.

Three months and six days after my mom died, I was hauled away by social workers to live with someone else because my dad was arrested for three murders. I never saw him again. I had the choice to visit but refused every time until they stopped asking. He meant nothing to me. He wasn't my dad, just a man who had given me some of his DNA, and if I could, I would give that back.

The first three homes I went to were all rich people with fancy homes, and not one of them had been a nice person. I quickly learned that just because people had money didn't make them any nicer or loving than my old man.

Then I ended up at the Collins home, and my world went from shit to amazing in a blink—only to end in a shitstorm. I figured it was karma for all the crap my father had done and for wishing a horrible death on him. Whether he was alive or not, I couldn't say, but I wanted him to suffer, and in the end, it was me that suffered.

I shook my head, trying to rid it of the image of Raine lying on the floor, bleeding out like my mom. I was worse than my dad. At least he hadn't pulled the trigger.

I almost did.

Raine

3

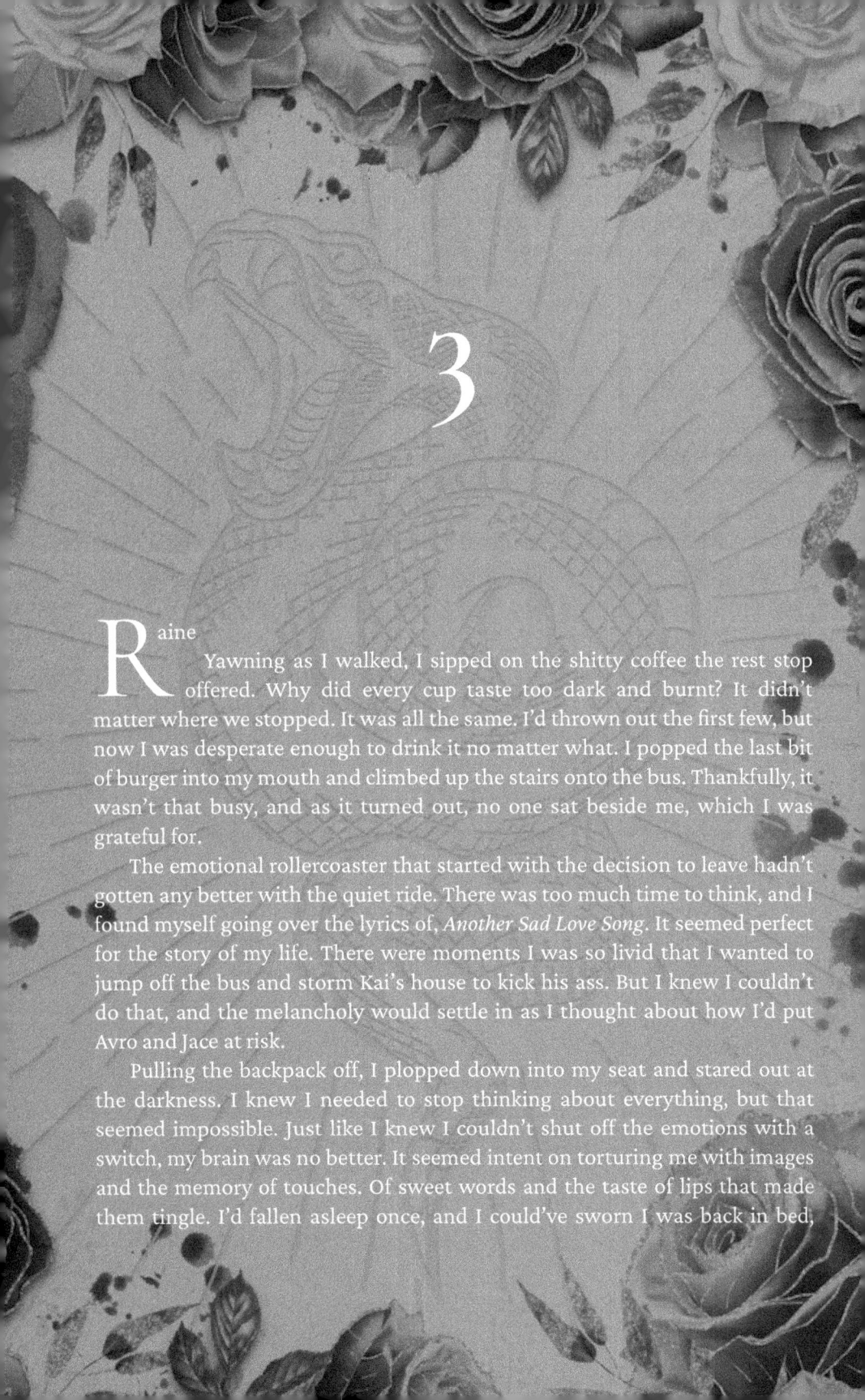

Raine

Yawning as I walked, I sipped on the shitty coffee the rest stop offered. Why did every cup taste too dark and burnt? It didn't matter where we stopped. It was all the same. I'd thrown out the first few, but now I was desperate enough to drink it no matter what. I popped the last bit of burger into my mouth and climbed up the stairs onto the bus. Thankfully, it wasn't that busy, and as it turned out, no one sat beside me, which I was grateful for.

The emotional rollercoaster that started with the decision to leave hadn't gotten any better with the quiet ride. There was too much time to think, and I found myself going over the lyrics of, *Another Sad Love Song*. It seemed perfect for the story of my life. There were moments I was so livid that I wanted to jump off the bus and storm Kai's house to kick his ass. But I knew I couldn't do that, and the melancholy would settle in as I thought about how I'd put Avro and Jace at risk.

Pulling the backpack off, I plopped down into my seat and stared out at the darkness. I knew I needed to stop thinking about everything, but that seemed impossible. Just like I knew I couldn't shut off the emotions with a switch, my brain was no better. It seemed intent on torturing me with images and the memory of touches. Of sweet words and the taste of lips that made them tingle. I'd fallen asleep once, and I could've sworn I was back in bed, cocooned in the warmth of Avro and Jace. I woke up with a smile on my face, only to have it slip as the bus bounced and jarred me back to reality.

I saw someone step onto the bus but didn't pay them any attention until they sat down beside me. Startled, I jumped and looked at the man I didn't recognize. I glanced around the bus at the four other people soundly sleeping.

"Um...can I help you," I asked, confused.

"Nope," he said and didn't look my way. It was hard to tell his age, but he had shoulder-length hair that ran into a scraggly beard. He was gripping a large book to his chest while his eyes searched the front of the bus.

"The seats across from me are empty," I offered, hoping I didn't sound too pushy and yet wanting him to take the hint.

"Oh, that's okay. Did you want to see my family?" He pulled the large book away from his chest to reveal a photo album. Before I could respond, he flipped open the cover. I looked down at the smiling images of people cut out from a magazine. "This is my son, Jeffery," he said, tapping an image of a boy doing a cannonball into a pool. It still had the for-sale banner from the pool installation at a twenty-five percent discount.

I wasn't sure what to do. I didn't want to upset him, but I wasn't sure it was healthy for me to play along with whatever delusion he had.

"Jeffery loves soccer, but his sister Leslie hates it." He shook his head, a scowl pulling at the corners of his mouth and wrinkling his brow. He flipped a few more pages and pointed out travel ads for Jamaica and Ireland, telling me how they'd all flown there as a family.

"Do you like this photo?" He tapped one of a large mountain with a sunset in the background and a vehicle set up like it was camping on the top of the tall peak.

I nodded. "It's stunning."

The man smiled and flipped a few more pages. My eyes went wide as he turned to a page littered with Polaroids. The people all looked dead. I swallowed hard as I stared into the sightless eyes. It was a crash scene with cars in the background and glowing lights from the emergency vehicles. I had no idea how someone would even get their hands on pictures like this.

He smiled at me. "They're not actually dead. This was for a movie. They are great actors," he said, but out of all the images, these were the ones that I believed were real. Glancing up from the book to his eyes, they were shimmering with happiness, and I swallowed hard. "Jeffery is going to be a famous actor one day. He keeps saying that he wants to be on a crime show."

The man pointed to a woman on her knees in the background. "This is my wife. Isn't she amazing? The kids get their acting skills from her." Her face was covered in blood, but it was the pain in her eyes as she wailed that had my chest aching for this man. I could almost hear her cries.

"She's incredible," I said softly, and his face lit up with emotion, but behind the smile were ghosts that I understood. I didn't know what else to say, but I could feel his sadness in my soul, and tears pricked at my eyes.

The bus shook, and I looked up as two police officers stepped onto the bus and walked down the aisle to where we were sitting.

"Come on, Luis, we need to get you back to your place," the first officer said. His name tag said, Dolson.

Luis looked up at them and then at me. The shadows in his eyes mirrored the scars in my mind. The smile on his face fell, and I suddenly wanted to stand up and yell at them to leave him alone.

"I don't want to go back there," Luis said and gripped the album to his chest like a shield.

I expected Dolson to grab Luis and drag him off the bus, but instead, he knelt down and reached out, laying a hand on his shoulder. "Where are you going to go, Luis? Your family is all here. If you leave, then how will you see them?"

Tears welled in Luis's eyes, and the pain was so raw that I felt the stab to my heart as if the loss was my own.

"I don't want to leave them," Luis said.

"I know you don't. That's why you need to come with us. This bus is going to take you far away from them, Luis. I know you don't want that."

He shook his head slowly as tears trickled down his cheeks. "But the doctors are mean. They say that my family is gone. I want them to stop that. They're not gone," Luis said. If I hadn't been watching Dolson so closely, I would've missed the sadness in his eyes, but he was quick to cover it and nodded and smiled for Luis.

"You're right. They need to stop saying that. Come on, I'll speak to them for you." Dolson stood and held out his hand.

"It was nice meeting you," Luis said as he took Dolson's hand and stood.

"Can you take him out to the car," Dolson said to the other officer, who had been quiet the entire time. Dolson turned to look at me as soon as they were down the steps and out of earshot. "I'm sorry about my Dad," he said.

"Your dad? But...."

"That was my sister and brother. They passed away in a crash with an impaired driver. My dad was the officer that arrived first on scene. He..." Dolson looked over his shoulder to the police car sitting outside. "He hasn't been the same since." The corner of his mouth turned up, and I had the urge to jump up and hug him. "Anyway, I'm sorry if he scared you." With a nod, Dolson walked away.

Pulling on my hood, I covered my head as I fought the sadness threatening to overtake me. How many days had I laid in bed, convinced that I wouldn't be able to get up and function ever again? How often had it been better to dream of what I wished my life was rather than dealing with the pain I slugged through? How many times had my mind sat on the edge of that very precipice? It would've been so easy to give up and let the imaginary world swallow me whole.

The reality of how close I'd come to that felt like a noose tightening around my neck. I was no longer that girl, but the pain stuck with me. The memories and dreams of someone with a future laid out felt like they belonged to someone else. Someone that had died in that warehouse. My body had been rescued, but my mind never recovered.

The bus hissed and lurched as we started moving, but I kept my face buried in my sweatshirt. I could run, but I could never hide from my demons. Those would stay with me forever.

Snake

4

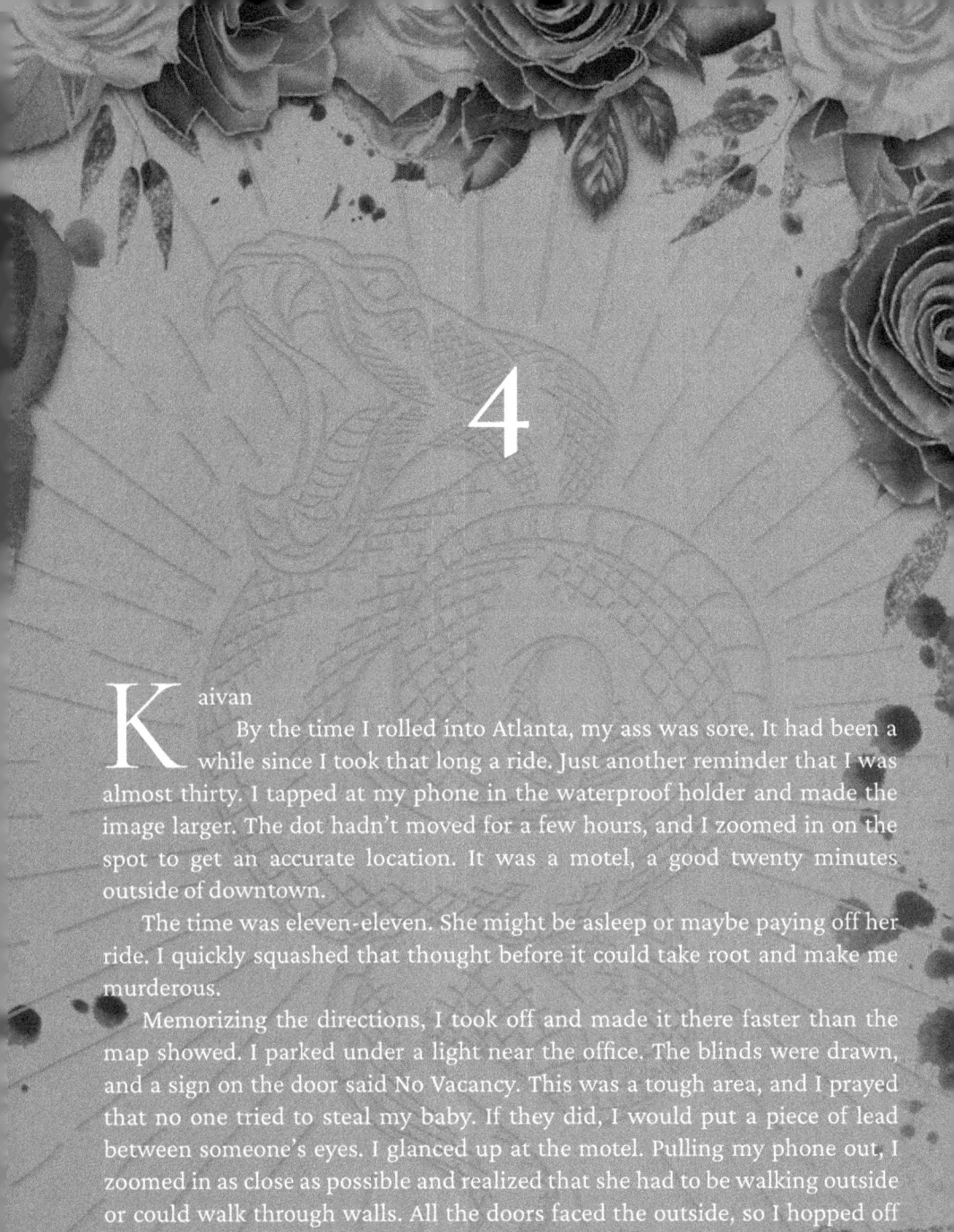

Kaivan

By the time I rolled into Atlanta, my ass was sore. It had been a while since I took that long a ride. Just another reminder that I was almost thirty. I tapped at my phone in the waterproof holder and made the image larger. The dot hadn't moved for a few hours, and I zoomed in on the spot to get an accurate location. It was a motel, a good twenty minutes outside of downtown.

The time was eleven-eleven. She might be asleep or maybe paying off her ride. I quickly squashed that thought before it could take root and make me murderous.

Memorizing the directions, I took off and made it there faster than the map showed. I parked under a light near the office. The blinds were drawn, and a sign on the door said No Vacancy. This was a tough area, and I prayed that no one tried to steal my baby. If they did, I would put a piece of lead between someone's eyes. I glanced up at the motel. Pulling my phone out, I zoomed in as close as possible and realized that she had to be walking outside or could walk through walls. All the doors faced the outside, so I hopped off the bike and began stalking my little dot to cut her off.

I still had no idea what the hell I was going to say to Raine. There really weren't words to describe what had gone on between us or how to apologize for acting out of my mind.

"What the fuck?" I heard Raine's distressed voice and grabbed the gun from the back of my jeans. "I said let go of me," she snarled. I rounded the corner to see her pushed up against the soda machine by some guy wearing a dark hoodie. I couldn't see his face, but I didn't need to. I knew what he wanted from her. Money or sex, and sometimes both—it was always the same.

My lip lifted in a snarl. No one hurt Raine. No one but me, anyway.

She was quick and broke the jerk's hold before rounding on him with a hard punch to the face. I smiled as she braced herself against the machine and kicked out with both feet. The guy grunted and stumbled back, almost landing on his ass. Raine glared at the guy, no one paying attention to the threat coming from the side.

"Bitch!"

"What the hell is wrong with the fucking male population?" She struck out and landed a couple more solid hits as he attempted to get close again. My heart soared with pride as the guy grabbed at his gut and narrowly missed the shot to his dick. That's my Tink. Feisty to the core. "Can't a girl just get a fucking drink without being harassed?"

"You fucking bitch!" The guy lunged at her, slamming her into the machine. She winced with the impact but snarled as she scratched at his face and kicked him in the gut.

"Fucking cunt," the guy yelled as Rained continued to strike at him like a feral cat. This was really fucking hot, and there was no denying it as I adjusted myself that it turned me on. I wanted to see her kick his ass, but hoodie guy wrapped his hand around her throat and lifted his fist to strike her.

I growled like a dog as I stepped up beside him and shoved the gun into the side of his head hard enough that he tilted it to the side and froze. "No one touches what's mine, but hit her and see what happens," I said, keeping my voice low and threatening.

Raine's eyes snapped to mine. Those beautiful blues looked worried—as worried as the guy at the end of my gun must look—but under that was shock.

"Let go of her now," I ordered. His hand dropped, and he slowly lifted them both up. "If I didn't already have an engagement tonight, I'd blow your fucking hand right off for touching her, so consider this your lucky night. Now turn toward the breezeway and run. Run like your ass is on fire before I change my mind and kill you anyway," I said, shoving the guy's head with the gun.

There was no hesitation as he turned toward the back of the motel and took off in a sprint through the gap separating the buildings, disappearing into the darkness. Dropping my gaze to Raine, her nostrils flared, and her eyes narrowed as she stared at me. She was pissed, and I was so here for it. God, I wanted her right there—looking at me just like that—up against the machine.

"What the hell are you doing here," Raine asked and then hit the button on the vending machine. She'd obviously already paid, or they liked giving away free beverages, as the bottle tumbled before it was spat out the bottom. Whenever I saw a soda machine work, all I could think of was The Matrix. I was forever ruined.

"I thought it would be pretty obvious that I came to see you. I don't make it a habit to wander around the seedy parts of Atlanta," I said.

"Why not? I'm sure you skulk around other seedy places," she quipped back as she bent over to grab her bottle.

"Ouch, you wound me," I drawled, and she glared over her shoulder as she fought with the machine. I never understood why they made the slot so awkward to get your hand in. Raine's ass was right in front of me, her hoodie riding up and showing off the string of her thong. Before I could stop myself, I reached out and grabbed her hip. My finger brushed against her bare skin, and all I could picture was ripping those jeans off her and fucking her just like that.

Spinning around, Raine smacked my hand, but all it did was encourage the fantasy playing out in my mind.

"Don't touch me." She glared, and I smiled.

Before I could get into more trouble, I stuffed the gun under my jacket to conceal it once more as Raine walked away.

"How the hell did you find me anyway," she asked as I fell in step beside her.

Lifting a shoulder, I let it drop. "I have my ways."

Banter should not make me this hot, but with each step she took, the harder I got.

"Go away, Kai, Snake, or whoever the hell you are tonight. I don't want to speak to you. I just want to be left alone. It's really not too much to ask."

"I need to speak to you," I said.

Right now, I wished everything was solved as easily as fucking it away. I knew it wasn't possible, but shit, she was tempting. Like a top-shelf scotch, she had my mouth watering.

We reached the corner room, and she pulled out the key from her pocket and unlocked the door. Stepping inside, she quickly turned and tried to push the door closed. I knew she would try and slam the door in my face, so I got my boot in the way. She made a little snarling noise at me, her nose scrunching up as she stared down at the boot.

"Fuck! Why are you so fucking annoying? Can't you just leave me alone?" She yelled and let go of the door, giving up. That was the question. Why couldn't I leave her to live her life, whatever that entailed?

Stepping into the small room, I closed and locked the door behind me. The fuzzy television was on low, showing some old sitcom. Raine opened the soda and took a swig like it was something much stronger. My lip curled up, figuring she wished it was.

"I told you we need to talk," I said.

She spun around, slammed the bottle down, and her hands balled into fists. "About what? How you decided to ruin my life? How I gave up the one piece of happiness that I'd finally managed to carve out for myself because you can't stand to see me happy?"

"It's not like that." She glared at me, her head twisting slightly as one of her eyebrows raised. It was her *you're a fucking liar* look. I'd seen it so many times when we were younger, but I didn't remember it being so damn sexy. I was having trouble concentrating, and my emotions couldn't keep up with the storm swiftly brewing inside of me. "I swear to you it's not. I mean, it was, but it's not anymore."

I ran my hand through my hair as she stomped in my direction, and my muscles tensed. The closer she got, the more charged the room became between us. By the time she was standing in front of me, I was breathing hard as I tried my best to keep my hands to myself.

Raine pushed on my chest, and my back hit the door.

"Oh really? Then tell me what the hell it's like, 'cause the guy that busted into my bubble of happiness last night didn't seem too concerned about what damage he caused. I'd say you got exactly what you wanted. Me on the run, scared to death of you all over again. Stripping me of all the hard work that I did to put myself back together again. I hate you, Kai." Her voice held so much venom that the poison seeped into my body.

"Don't say that. You don't mean that," I said, her words stopping my heart.

"I do. I hate you!" She swung for my face, and I grabbed her arm out of the air. But she was quick and landed a hard blow with her left fist that knocked my head to the side. Fuck she had a hook.

I saw her gearing up for another strike and snatched her wrist. Spinning us around, I pushed her back up against the door.

"Stop looking at me like that." She struggled in my hold and wouldn't look me in the eyes.

"Like what, Tink?"

"Please, this is me begging you to go away," she said, her voice breaking.

"No, tell me what you see." I felt the anger shifting to another level like a geyser getting ready to blow. Her body trembled, but it wasn't from fear. It was the same powerful connection I'd always felt between us.

"Stop looking at me like I actually mean something to you." Her eyes were as angry as I'd ever seen them and filled with tears.

All the layers of hurt, love, and memories piled onto me all at once, and my body mirrored hers, trembling while I held her. She pushed against my hold and growled, but that only made me want to lay her on the bed.

There was a good chance she was gonna bite my tongue off, but I didn't care and dropped my lips to hers before she could spew any more hate.

Her lips were firm and wouldn't grant me access. So I nipped at her bottom lip and sucked it into my mouth as I held her hands above her head. Even as she tried to twist her head away, I followed the movement.

"Please, Kai..." She got out, and I took advantage and deepened the kiss. The building energy in the room soared off the charts as she opened her mouth further to let me kiss her properly. It was our first real kiss since that fateful night years ago. Her lips were warm and so soft, but her mouth was hot, and I could taste the lingering sweetness of the soda. She felt perfect and exactly like I dreamed she would.

She stopped trying to fight me, and I let go of her hands to grip her hips. She was mine. She was made for me in every way, including our broken and damaged souls, which were twined together.

"I don't hate you, Tink. I wanted to so badly, but I don't hate you," I mumbled against her lips and then attacked her mouth again as she touched my chest. I felt each of her fingers as they fanned out like she was tentative to touch me, but couldn't resist.

She moaned as I explored what I'd wanted for so long. Years I'd craved and wanted her just like this, and then I ended up behind bars. I spent more years thinking she wanted to hurt me. In all that time, not once did I think she'd actually suffered. Why hadn't I thought more about it? I'd assumed so much because it was the easy answer. I was no better than her. If I'd known someone had hurt her...I shuddered with the thought. I would've found and killed them before they had the chance to lock me up, and I never would've signed off on a plea deal.

The raw pain of what she'd experienced was in her eyes last night. I saw the same trauma I shared shining back at me. She was willing to die at my hand to end the agony we'd caused one another. I loved her more now than I ever thought was humanly possible. I was obsessed. There was no other way to put it. Raine Eastman had always been the one consuming thought in my mind, but now she'd taken over my soul.

Cupping her ass, I pulled her up my body. She didn't fight me, wrapping her legs around my waist and her arms around my neck as she kissed me harder. "I'm sorry, Tink." I shook my head. "I...I don't know how to make up for what I did, but I want you. I've always wanted you."

"I don't know, Kai," she said.

"Yes, you do. You've always been mine. From the first day, we met, I knew we were meant to be together."

Breaking the kiss, she pulled back, and even though her eyes were still hostile, the edge was gone. Raine's eyes searched my face, and I wished I knew what she was looking for.

"You have a terrible way of showing it," she finally said, and I smiled. It felt like it had been forever since I smiled for real. "But, I'm not yours, at least not only yours," she said, and my smile turned into a snarl. "Be pissed all you want, but I had a life before you decided to blow it up."

"You can't mean those two assholes?" Her eyebrow lifted as she quietly sassed me. I let go of her ass, and her feet dropped to the floor. "You're serious? You want them?"

I backed away from her, needing to put space between us. I couldn't think straight when she was close to me. Reaching the furthest part of the small room, I turned to face Raine.

"But you said you loved me." I knew I sounded pitiful and was happy that none of the guys at the clubhouse could hear me. "In the letter you left for Avro. You said you still love me."

Her eyes got big and then narrowed as she crossed her arms. "How exactly did you end up reading a letter I left for Avro? You better not have fucking hurt him."

I rolled my eyes. "No, of course not, and I didn't raid your house if that's what you're thinking. The guy came to me and ordered me to find you. It was really stupid of him. But pretty brave. I'll give him that." Raine rubbed her face and sighed.

"Of course he did," Raine mumbled.

"How can you say you love me but want them and whatever you had going on?" I reached for my smokes and remembered I had already smoked the last one. Fuck, of all the times to be out.

"First, I know it's a stretch for you, but don't be an asshole," Raine sniped, making my lip curl up. Her face went bright red as she continued to fume. "And don't try to tell me that you haven't had more than one girl at a time before, or am I reading you all wrong?"

I swallowed hard as images of group sex with sweetbutts flashed behind my eyes. I stuffed my hands into my pockets.

"That's different."

"Oh, I see," Raine growled, and fuck, my body flushed hot. I could see the spark of anger and jealousy in her eyes, and my heart pounded hard for it. Why did she have this power over me? "Then please, by all means, explain to me how it's different. I'm really fucking curious to hear that answer."

I felt a trap coming. Licking my lips, I tried to find a way to back out of the pile of shit I was stepping in. Hopefully, there wasn't one of Wilder's landmines under it. "Cause...."

"Cause? Wow, I'm impressed with the overwhelming argument you pose. Good thing you didn't decide to be a lawyer. Your clients would be fucked."

My eyes narrowed into a glare, my neck cracking as I tilted it to the side. All I wanted to do was stomp across the room and force Raine to see I was the only one she wanted. Fuck those other two guys.

"Gimmie a second. I'm thinking how to word this."

"Well, you're doing a bang-up job so far. Go on. I'm waiting with bated breath."

"Damn, you still have that fucking sass. You make me want to fuck you stupid, Tink. Watch that mouth. I'm hanging by a thread here," I growled out, but it only made her angrier as her hands balled into fists. I didn't know what the fuck had happened on her trip to Atlanta, but this was not the same Raine that left Miami. Maybe it was the air, but I had a feeling it had to do with me pushing her over her breaking point last night. No longer fearing death changed a person.

Before I did exactly what I wanted to do and didn't get anything solved, I tried again.

"Fuck. It's just different, okay. The sweetbutts or any other girl don't mean anything to me. I fuck them and move on to the next. Doesn't matter if it's one or ten because there is nothing between us. They are there to be used, and that's what I do. Fuck 'em, use 'em, leave 'em, done."

It was like the air was sucked out of the room as the glacial glare she gave me somehow turned more lethal. She looked so badass, and all I could think about was ripping her clothes off. My head was fucked.

Raine whipped the door open, and I stared out at the poorly lit parking lot. The scent of stale air, loneliness, and regret wafted in at me. If I stepped through that door, that was it. I knew in my heart that as surely as the door would close behind me, so would the opportunity to make this right. I couldn't let that happen.

A mix of panic and rage burned in my gut. I didn't even know who the rage was pointed toward anymore, which added to the internal confusion. The only thing I was clear on was that I couldn't step one foot outside that door if I wanted Raine.

"You said you love him. How can you say you love him and me too? I don't get it. At least tell me that. Tell me why these other guys are so important when we can finally be together. As fucked up of a situation as it is, Tink, I want you. I've never stopped wanting you," I blurted out.

She slowly closed the door, and my heart rate slowed, but when she turned her head and looked at me, the pain in her eyes gripped my throat as surely as a hand would.

"You don't get it, do you," Raine asked, her voice soft. She let go of the handle, and I swallowed hard as she stepped toward me. "I've always loved you."

She gripped her shirt in her hand over her heart, and I swear I felt it as if she was squeezing the pounding organ in my chest. "Even when I thought you hurt me in the worst way possible, I never stopped loving you and mourning you like you'd died because, to me, that's what it was like. I'd stare at your photo and cry for hours, wondering why you did what you did, and I hated myself. I loathed every part of my being because I couldn't stop loving the guy who looked at me like I meant something. You made me feel like I was worth seeing, and then...." She snapped her fingers. "Just like that, you tore me down."

I opened my mouth, and she held up her hands to stop me. "I know it wasn't you, but I didn't know that then. I'd already lost so much, and at that moment, I became nothing." She walked closer, and my chest constricted a little more with each step. "I didn't want to live, I didn't want to wake up in the morning, and every day I fought to fix this." She tapped the side of her head. "You may have been locked away in a concrete cell, but my mind became my prison, and there was no escaping the torture it would inflict again and again."

Tears trailed down her cheeks, and for the first time since I found her, I truly understood that we'd both been caged that night. Our souls were tossed into a different hell of darkness, but both were just as lethal. The emotion was so raw on her face that when she reached me and smacked her hands off my chest, it felt like she'd hit me with a car and drove the air from my chest.

"Do I feel bad that you went to prison for something you didn't do...fuck, of course I do. I didn't think I could hate myself anymore, but I do. I sent the one person I loved and trusted in this world to prison, I...."

Her hands gripped my leather jacket into her fists. "You joke about having however many people a night and had the nerve to ask me where my pussy had been." I licked my lips as my throat went dry. "No one Kai. No one until Avro touched me. Eleven years I've had no contact with another living soul. Not to shake their hand or give them a hug."

The leather complained as her fists tightened. "It took Avro years to earn my trust. He was my only friend. I have no family. They were all dead, and the Collinses sent me packing the day I was released from the hospital. There were no nameless faces and wild orgies, no sweetbutts, as you put it, to satisfy bodily desires." She jerked on my jacket, and my stomach gripped in a tight ball. "I was terrified. Do you get that? My only experience was extreme pain that landed me with two operations and no idea if I can ever have children, and all that time, I thought you did that to me. I still see your face in my mind sneering at me. I couldn't see their faces, but it didn't matter. My mind conjured you. How you'd hold me down...."

Raine let go of my jacket and walked to the dresser. Her shoulders shook as she covered her mouth and cried, but I didn't move. I wasn't even sure what to say at this point. We had so much pain between us. So many memories and misinformation.

She choked back a sob and turned to face me again. I hated to see that pain. I thought for so long that it was all I wanted. I loved her pissed off and fired up, but this...I didn't want this anymore between us. It was toxic and destroying us both.

"So, to answer your question. Yes, after eleven years of knowing nothing but fear and loneliness, I finally let someone in. Someone that is wholly good and saw the scars on my soul and my damaged heart and didn't run. For the first time, I could breathe again because I realized I could trust. It was freeing to finally not see everyone as a hooded figure looking to hurt me, and I took it."

Her face fell. And I wanted to wrap her up in my arms. I had no idea that she'd lived like that. It made my rage toward Dave, Frank, and the now rotting-in-hell Jim burn that much brighter. I wanted to tell her about Jim and that I planned on making sure they all paid. But now I didn't know if it was worse for her to know that two different people she trusted did this. I didn't know, but I wasn't willing to set any progress back further.

"And then you come along, and just like that, you crush me and the sliver of happiness I was building," she growled and stomped the few steps to me and pushed my chest hard enough that I stumbled back and hit the wall. "You almost killed me, Kai, and then you almost killed them after you said you never wanted to see me again. I'm the problem? What the fuck?" She growled at me.

"And now what? You hunt me down. Say you want me and that I'm yours. Like you own me." She shook her head. "What's next? You planning on giving me a cut that says your property? Then the cycle will be complete. You can officially own my body and do whatever you want with whoever you want. That is how it works in an MC, right?" She shrugged, and I still couldn't figure out what to say.

"The old ladies...." Raine lifted her hands and made finger quotes in the air. "First off, a sign of respect or not, if you ever call me an old lady, I will rip your fucking balls right off your body."

I licked my lips, torn between impressed, a little terrified by the look in her eyes, and turned on so bad that I thought I might fucking cum in my jeans.

"But that is what they do, isn't it? They have to shut up and support their man, right? Let their man fuck who they choose and never cause drama, all for the privilege of sitting on the back of your fancy bike." Raine laughed and backed away. "No, I don't want to live like that. I've felt like I had a sign saying I was owned by you for far too long. You already took my body, have my heart and mind—hell, you fucking have my soul. I have nothing left to give you, Kai, and I don't want to be controlled by anyone, including my fear, any longer. I'm not that same girl you knew." She looked down at the ground and then squared her shoulders as she looked up and her eyes found mine. "That girl died." Turning around, Raine walked to the door. "I'm going to ask you again to please, just leave."

"It's not always like that." Her brow furrowed in confusion. "With the old...the wives, I mean. It's different for everyone. A lot of the guys are loyal to their other half." Her hand gripped the door handle but didn't turn it. "I'm here, Tink. I came because I want you, so tell me what you want?" I lifted my shoulders in a shrug. "I will listen."

Raine crossed her arms and leaned against the door as she stared at me.

"Just say what you want, Tink."

She smiled, but it was a sad smile as she wiped at the dampness on her cheeks. "I want to be selfish for the first time ever. I want it all. Call me greedy, or a slut, or whatever you want, but I want all of you, and no, that doesn't mean you can fuck whoever you want." It was my turn to cross my arms.

"You want all three of us exclusive to you and at the same time?" Rubbing my eyes, I ground my teeth together.

The thought of the bartender or rock star touching her had all the dark and dangerous parts of me coming to life. I needed to try and stay calm, or I would tear apart this room and then drive back to Miami and shoot those two fuckers in the head.

I knew she'd run, and I could let her. It would solve the issue. If she wasn't around, then maybe I could finally move on too. The small voice in the back of my head laughed hysterically. I'd been locked up for ten years and hadn't seen her a single day, and I wanted her more now than the day I was put away. It didn't seem like her leaving town would stop me from wanting her.

"I don't mean we all have to have sex together," she said, and a low growl rumbled in my chest. "I mean, if you all could and not kill each other, I'd be open to the idea," she said, and my eyes snapped up to hers. "That would be really fucking hot, actually," she mumbled and tapped her chin.

The murderous side of me wanted to rip them apart. Even though, by all accounts, it sounded like they were decent enough, I just couldn't wrap the possessive part of myself around the idea.

"Not fucking likely. Just thinking about them touching you makes me want to cut off their cocks and shove them down their throats."

"Well, you asked what I wanted. There it is. I want all of you." Raine laughed. "I don't want to deny myself anymore."

I looked up to the ceiling like, by some fucking miracle, I was going to find the answers written there. "Do you love them?"

"Avro, yes, but Jace is still new to me. They have been together along time so Jace is part of the package with Avro."

I shook my head, trying to wrap my head around this disaster. "So, you're in love with Avro, but not Jace, but Jace and Avro are together, so to have Avro, you need to fuck Jace?"

Raine's eyes turned murderous again as she glared at me from across the room. "Don't be an asshole Kai. You're the one that chased me down. You're the one standing in my motel room, and you're the one that just asked me what I want. You don't see me standing at your door, do you?"

I leaned against the wall and crossed my arms. "Fine, just explain to me why it is that I can't have you, Avro have Jace, and we go our merry fucking separate ways?"

"Because what I wanted for my life before you stormed back in and started pounding your chest was vastly different than becoming your leather-wearing, bike-riding side hustle."

"Fuck Raine! I don't want anyone else. I don't ever want to fuck anyone else again." I yelled, my body shaking as I tried to contain the rage that wanted blood. "You've been tattooed on my heart from the day we met." The admission had me sucking in a deep breath. She was the only good thing I'd ever had. Even when shit went sideways, it was still her face I dreamed about. It had always been her.

I ran my hand through my hair. "Now you're asking me to be okay with you sleeping with other guys, while we're together? I've never been okay with other guys around you. Fuck you must remember that. Tink, you're it for me."

She looked down at her boots, her arms crossed. The minutes ticked on, and I glanced at the clock. Sweat broke out on my brow when the number clicked over to exactly five minutes. It was the only thing moving in the room.

"I can't explain this any better to you, Kai," she finally said, her voice a whisper, yet I heard every word. "I have actively tried to push you from my mind and heart since the night I was attacked." Her eyes slowly lifted, and I knew she wouldn't give in. I felt the anger and panic building.

The one person, the one thing I wanted more than anything else in this world, was her. A family with her, and I couldn't find a way to make her see that we belonged together. I couldn't force her emotions away, couldn't buy them away, and couldn't scare them away. Raine would rather accept being alone or dead. I saw it behind the shimmering blue of her eyes. My heart pounded frantically, trying to figure out how to make this work and make her see things my way.

I'd always been able to sway Raine, always had the power to make her smile and talk her into whatever I wanted. I slumped against the wall as her words sank into the deep recesses of my brain. I wasn't the boy she swooned over anymore, who she dreamed of and would sneak into his room. I was who she saw when she was attacked, the embodiment of her worst nightmare.

I was the creature that lived under the bed, that made her run screaming or die trying. My body shook with the harsh reality of what Irene, Dave, and his friends had cost us. They stole my happy ending. Our happy ending.

"Kai, this is only going to work one of two ways. You can leave, and I will continue on my way, and none of you get me. Because I know you couldn't handle seeing me around town or know where I'm living with them without you having another meltdown like last night. I won't put them or myself at risk or even risk the possibility of you going back to jail."

"And the second option?"

"You can concede that I want Avro in my life, and with that comes Jace. This is your choice, but there is no third option. The one thing I'm not doing, is going half-measure on what I want. You asked. There is your answer."

"And I assume killing them is off the table?" I snickered as Raine gave me her best 'Are you fucking stupid look.' It was the same look she gave me when we were kids, and I'd say something to get under her skin. It made me smile.

"I don't know if I can do that and not kill them." I lifted my hands and let them drop. "I'm being honest. I don't want anyone else, so being faithful to you isn't the issue." I left out that I'd tried to get a blowjob, but my dick had been annoyingly uncooperative since I found her. "But adding two guys...Tink, you're like the blood in my veins. Sharing that, sharing you is...." I held my hands out as I thought of the right word.

"The reality is, Kai, that my heart shattered into a million little pieces the day those men took my innocence. I've spent the rest of my time slowly gluing the little shards back together. It finally started to beat again, but I'm changed," she said, her voice firm in her conviction.

Raine gripped the bottom of the hoodie she was wearing, and my throat stopped functioning as she peeled it off, leaving her in a black lace bra. "I'm no longer that innocent teen. I'm a woman exploring what I want and who I want, and I want it all. Please don't try to deny me that or control my heart with an iron fist and fear."

She tossed the sweatshirt aside, and my eyes roamed over her body. The bruises I'd left were green and yellow, and I hated seeing them. It was a visual confirmation that I'd tried to kill her and almost succeeded. That I had done what she feared the most. I really was the monster.

"Am I not worth trying for," Raine asked, her voice soft and silky. The sound made me shudder. She bent over and pulled the laces on her shitkickers, kicking them off along with her socks. Her toenails were painted black with one pink one, which made me smile—a tiny bit of the girl she had been wrapped up in this badass woman.

My cock strained under my pants as she bit her lip. I groaned as her hands unbuttoned the top of her jeans, and I heard each link of the zipper as she pulled it down.

"Am I not worth the effort?" Her voice sounded somehow both sad and alluring. "For us to still find a happy ending to the pain we were put through?"

"You're not playing fair," I said as her hands worked at pushing down the tight denim, her hips wiggling from side to side and making me groan as she stepped out of them. She was left in a mismatched set of lacey underwear, and I smirked at the look. The black bra and pink bottoms just did something to me. I was practically panting like a dog by the time she was within arms reach. All my muscles strained to remain still.

"Fuck me, Tink. It has nothing to do with your worth, I...I'm just not great at sharing anything, and you are the most prized piece of my heart. To share that...." Her cheeks pinked with a blush, but she didn't retract her request.

Her delicate hand reached out, and I watched it, knowing that she would seal my fate like her touch was magical, and yet I couldn't move away. I closed my eyes as her hand made contact with my chest and slid up to wrap around my neck. Her other devious hand slipped under the leather jacket and gripped my shoulder. I could feel the pulse pounding in my neck as I tried to draw a deep breath.

"You can have me, Kai," she whispered like a siren, and I shuddered. "You can have me whenever you want. However, you want." She stepped in close until her body was brushing against mine. Even through the T-shirt, I could feel the warmth of her body and wanted to blanket myself with her touch. "I'll try whatever you want and wherever you want. You want to put me on display, if you want to fuck me on your bike, then I'll do it, but Avro and Jace are my only condition. I'm worth the effort, or I'm not."

I stared down into her blue eyes that had always drawn me in like a whirlpool and threatened to whisk me away right now. She had power over me. Something I couldn't understand and never explained to anyone, but it had always been there. If she wanted the stars plucked from the sky, I would've found a way to make them hers. If she wanted me to kill someone, I wouldn't stop to ask why. She was my it, my forever, my all.

My hands had a mind of their own, and I sighed as I gripped her waist, finally touching her soft skin. She took that as a sign and pressed her body up tight against mine, and whatever brain power I had left to argue flew out of my head. Slipping my fingers under the lace, I gripped her ass, and a deep growl rumbled from my chest as her muscles flexed under my touch.

"You still love me," I asked.

"Yes, I always have. Not a day has gone by that I have stopped loving you," she said as her nails softly scraped along my neck, making me shiver. "And I will always love you. No matter what you decide, a piece of my heart will always be yours. No matter what has transpired between us, I would never change that."

"And this is the only way?" I licked my lips as she raised up on her toes and laid a soft kiss on the side of my mouth.

She nodded, and as her body pressed into mine, she could've asked me to do anything, and I would've agreed.

"Fuck me," I growled and dropped my head to her neck, breathing in her scent. She smelt sweet, like flowers and candy. I wanted to devour her. I opened my mouth again and knew that I'd at least try. If that meant I needed to do this, then that was what I'd do. Her leaving and never seeing her again wasn't an option.

Because fuck me, Raine was mine, and I needed her like I needed the fucking air to breathe.

Raine

5

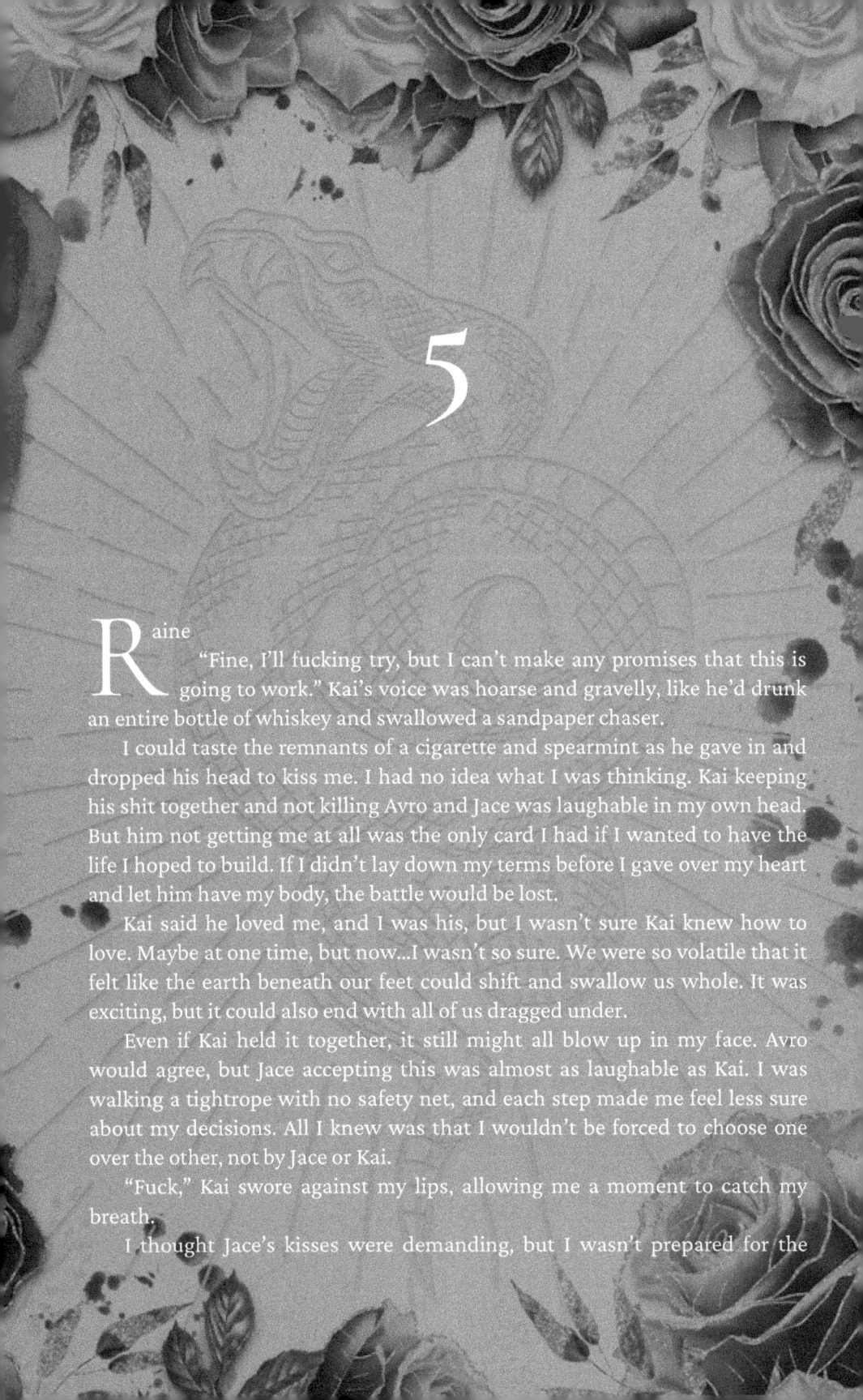

Raine

"Fine, I'll fucking try, but I can't make any promises that this is going to work." Kai's voice was hoarse and gravelly, like he'd drunk an entire bottle of whiskey and swallowed a sandpaper chaser.

I could taste the remnants of a cigarette and spearmint as he gave in and dropped his head to kiss me. I had no idea what I was thinking. Kai keeping his shit together and not killing Avro and Jace was laughable in my own head. But him not getting me at all was the only card I had if I wanted to have the life I hoped to build. If I didn't lay down my terms before I gave over my heart and let him have my body, the battle would be lost.

Kai said he loved me, and I was his, but I wasn't sure Kai knew how to love. Maybe at one time, but now…I wasn't so sure. We were so volatile that it felt like the earth beneath our feet could shift and swallow us whole. It was exciting, but it could also end with all of us dragged under.

Even if Kai held it together, it still might all blow up in my face. Avro would agree, but Jace accepting this was almost as laughable as Kai. I was walking a tightrope with no safety net, and each step made me feel less sure about my decisions. All I knew was that I wouldn't be forced to choose one over the other, not by Jace or Kai.

"Fuck," Kai swore against my lips, allowing me a moment to catch my breath.

I thought Jace's kisses were demanding, but I wasn't prepared for the ravenous and overwhelming kiss from Kai. He broke contact only long enough to peel off his leather jacket and toss it on the chair in the corner before he attacked my mouth again. His hands gripped my ass tighter, pulling me hard into him as he bowed my body back with his ferocity. Heat bloomed like my body was being licked by flames as it spread like wildfire.

"Fuck Tink, what are you doing to me," Kai asked, leaving me lightheaded and with swollen lips. He released his hold, his fingertips trailing gently over my skin, and everywhere he touched, goosebumps rose. My eyes fluttered open, and I couldn't look away from his blue eyes, so intense that they stole the air from my chest.

I gasped in a breath, my heart racing as hard as it ever had as he ran his thumb over the marks he'd made on my neck. They were fading now, but traces of his fingerprints were still visible without makeup. I didn't move as he stared at the imprints. His face was dark and so unreadable that he could've been thinking about fucking me hard or questioning why he hadn't already killed me.

"I was planning on killing you, you know," he said, and I shivered, my feet instinctively taking a step back, but his hands locked onto my shoulders, and I was once more trapped. "I meant that night. I'd dreamed about it for so long, but I couldn't."

His voice sounded wistful, like he craved to go back in time and finish what he had started. I swallowed the massive lump in my throat as my pulse pounded harder through my veins.

"Do you regret not killing me," I asked, and his eyes snapped from my neck to my eyes.

"No." Nothing sweet followed the single word, yet it held as much weight as if he'd gotten down and begged my forgiveness. "Stand on the bed," Kai ordered.

I shivered from the chill as I stepped away from the warmth of his body. Doing as he asked, I turned to face him just as he laid his cut down on the dresser. Unlike the jacket, he placed it as carefully as one would a child. I didn't know why his doing that touched me, but it did, and I felt tears prick the back of my eyes.

Under the gruff 'I don't care' exterior was the teen I knew, who wanted a family and to be accepted. It didn't surprise me that Kai had ended up in an MC. The little I knew of clubs was that even when at odds, they had one another's backs, and deep down, I knew that was something he always craved.

I was that person for him at one time, the person he could turn to and trust, and I destroyed that. I glanced at the club's name on the cut and then at Kai as he pulled his T-shirt off over his head.

"The name is fitting," I said. "We are definitely lost souls."

"Were," Kai said and kicked off his boots. He stomped toward me. Anyone else would think he was angry, but it was the desire in his eyes that drove him, not anger. Everything he did was with purpose and demand. "We were lost, but not anymore."

My lip curled up. "Speak for yourself. I don't know if I will ever be found," I said, letting him in on the fear that always gripped my heart.

His features darkened, and I sucked in a startled breath as he grabbed my waist and pulled me in close to him. "You are now. I see you, Tink. I've always seen you."

I stared into his eyes, tears threatening to spill once more, shuddering as his tongue flicked out and traced the first of six thin white scars. By the time he'd traced them all—never taking his eyes from mine—I was a mess and could barely see him through the blurriness.

"I will kill them for what they did to you. For what they did to us." His hands tightened on my waist. "That's a promise."

I knew he would and should be terrified, but I felt safer at that moment than I had at any time in my life. Unable to form words, I simply nodded.

Kai nipped at the lacey material of my underwear, and the feel of his teeth made me whimper in his hold. Drawing a line with his tongue down, he stopped on my clit, swirling and sucking until the material molded to my skin, making me moan.

"Fuck I want to devour you," Kai said, and my head fell back as he attacked my pussy with the same voraciousness as he had my mouth.

"Oh god, Kai,"

He yanked the lace aside and drove his tongue into me. My hands gripped his hair, pulling him harder into my body. The lingering doubts about whether this was a good idea were firmly pushed aside with each passing second.

"Cum in my mouth," he growled. I shook in his hold as he pushed my body toward the edge of a cliff with a drop that would have my body soaring. "Look at this fucking sexy pussy." His finger slipped inside of me as he continued his dirty talk. "I'm going to fuck this sweet hole all night, and you're going to scream my name until you can't scream at all."

"Oh god, yes," I moaned as another finger was added. My legs trembled and wanted to give out as he resumed sucking on my sensitive clit, but Kai held my hips up and pressed his face harder into pussy, making me yell.

"Don't stop. Please don't stop," I begged and pinched my nipples. The rough material of the bra only enhanced the sensation.

"Yeah, that's it, cum for me, cum all over my tongue Tink." Hearing my nickname on his lips seemed so dirty, and I loved it. All the time that had passed between us, all the hurt we'd caused one another disappeared, even if only for this moment in this small motel room with the squeaky bed.

"Oh fuck, Kai," My eyes closed as the climax hit and rocked my body. He made a sound that was more animal than man, and it vibrated through me. My fingers dug into his hair and held him tighter as I rode out the sensations.

"Fuck you taste like sweet sin," Kai said as the shuddering slowed. I couldn't stop the cheeky smile that pulled up the corner of my mouth as he licked the inside of my thighs. I was sure this was a kink, and if it was, I was into it. The way he slowly dragged his tongue up my leg like I was his meal with that feral look in his eyes was everything.

Hooking his fingers in the waistband of my thong, he pulled the little piece of material down.

"Turn around and get on your knees," Kai ordered as I stepped out of the underwear. Turning my back on Kai made me shiver. It was like turning your back on Satan himself, and yet I slowly turned around and lowered myself to my knees. He unclipped my bra, and I'd only gotten the material off my one arm when his hands slid around my body and cupped my breasts.

"Fuck, you're going to kill me with need. You're my poison and the antidote all wrapped into one. I can't not have you, and yet...." His teeth nipped almost painfully at my neck as his fingers tweaked my nipples until I cried out. "The idea of another cock but mine inside of you makes me see only red. Do you know what you're asking of me?" He growled into the side of my neck.

"To tame the devil," I whispered and panted out a breath as he pulled me back against his chest. He was so hot that it felt like maybe he had stepped out from hell itself, and yet all I wanted was for him to do what he wanted with my body.

He sucked my earlobe into his mouth, and even that was done as if he was going to bite it off. I realized then that the line between the man I knew and the man he'd become in prison was as narrow as the tightrope I felt like I'd been walking.

"That's right, Tink, and some things just can't be tamed," he said and wrapped his hand around my throat. The pressure of his fingers made my pulse spike, and a tremor of fear spread throughout my body.

"So, I want to make myself clear." Stepping back, he bowed my body with his movements until I had to put my hands on my ankles to keep from falling off the bed. I was left staring up at him, my chest heavy and pressing my sensitive nipples higher into the air. Kai's blue eyes seemed so dark as he leaned over me, his hand still around my throat as his lips hovered over mine. "I said that I will try, and I'm a man of my word, but I'm going to take all my aggression and anger about it out on your body. You will take the punishment for making me concede to this, do you understand?"

I knew that there was something different about me. Whether from birth or due to my trauma, no matter the reason, Kai's words only made me want him more. My pussy was wet and already aching, and the fear racing through my body heightened my senses. It all screamed the same thing. I wanted Kai, and if that meant he did things that others would call me crazy for allowing, I didn't care. I'd welcome every depraved thing he could think of.

"I understand," I whispered through his tight grip. My arms were starting to shake, and still, I held the position until a wicked smile curled up the corner of his mouth. It was the kind of look that told me just how much trouble I was in.

"I don't think you do, Tink, but you will. You were right. The devil does live under my skin, and you're the angel he wants to consume."

I expected his kiss to be as demanding as the first time, but he surprised me by kissing me sweetly as his fingers tortured my nipples. He rolled them around between his fingers and alternated which nipple he teased until I was trying to attack his mouth.

"What's the matter, Tink," he asked, breaking the kiss and running a soft line from my lips to my ear. "You seem pent up." I glared at him. He damn well knew exactly what he was doing to me. "Are you wanting my cock?" His voice was a whisper, yet I could still hear the taunting tone underneath.

I was tempted to be a smart ass but decided I should wait to push that button. "Yes," I said and nipped at his lip as he brought it close to my mouth again.

"Sit up," he ordered and let go of my neck. My muscles complained as I pulled myself up to kneel once more. "Now get on all fours."

My hands touched the bed, and I cried out and jumped forward as his hand cracked down on my ass. Kai gripped my hips and yanked me back. I could still feel the sting of his palm and wanted to jump away again as I looked over my shoulder and saw his hand raised again.

I closed my eyes and tensed for what I knew was coming, but I couldn't stop my body's reaction and leaped forward on the bed as that sharp slap hit my bare ass.

"Fuck," I yelled. "That fucking hurts." I rolled over to glare at Kai, welcoming the cool feel of the comforter against my heated cheeks.

"Oh, there she is," Kai said, a smile spreading across his face. "I was wondering when the angry sass would show up. That didn't take long." My eyes narrowed further as he undid the wide leather belt on his jeans and slowly pulled it out of the loops.

"Don't you dare," I said, backing up on the bed.

"Oh, I dare. Have I told you how much I love it when you look at me like that? How hard it makes me," he said, his voice strained, and my eyes immediately went to the large bulge that had formed behind his zipper. I licked my lips and squeezed my thighs tighter as the aching intensified. "Like what you see, Tink?"

I jerked my eyes away from his jeans and the outline of his cock, up to his face.

"I told you that you would be punished, and I meant it. So if this is really what you want and those two guys mean that much to you, you'll crawl over here and lay on my lap while I punish you."

I snarled at him, which only made him smirk. "It's your choice, Tink." He folded over the leather and smacked it off the palm of his hand, the sound loud in the otherwise quiet room. "I mean, if you can't handle this...." He lifted his shoulder. The look on his face made my blood boil but my pussy wetter. It was a potent combination.

"Oh, I can take it," I said, rolling over to crawl to him.

"Are you sure? Cause I'm going to make your ass good and sore," Kai said, his eyes glittering with dark desire.

"I'm fucking sure," I bit out, wanting to punch him and ride his body to the ground at the same time.

He sat down on the edge of the bed and patted his lap. "Then lay on my lap facing that way." He pointed toward the front of the bed, and I crawled around his body, making sure my eyes said 'asshole' as I positioned myself over his lap. I could feel his cock pressing into me through the rough denim and wanted to feel him against my skin, but I figured this was all by design. He wanted to torture me for asking him to bend his own possessive code. A sliver of doubt tried to worm into my brain, but I stomped on it. I could do this. I wanted to do this, and he could go fuck himself if he thought that I was going to back down.

"Yeah, that's it. Keep looking at me just like that," he said, laying the cool leather against my still-warm ass. His finger stroked between my thighs, and I shuddered as he rubbed my pussy lips. "Look at how wet you are, Tink.

You're going to leave a big wet spot on my leg by the time I'm through with you."

He wiggled his finger, and I bit my lower lip to keep from moaning. "You're wrong. I don't like it," I said, and he laughed. The movement jostled me on his lap and pressed his stiff cock into the softness of my belly.

"Oh, you're a sexy little liar." He dipped his finger inside my pussy, and my body writhed with the feel. "I bet you won't just cum all over me. You'll be gushing and embarrassed as your cum soaks my jeans." I turned my head to glare at him. "Just like the other night when you coated my cock."

I remembered clearly how hard I came for him despite the fear racing through my body and how the sheets were soaked from the mess I had made. As if to prove his point, his finger fucked me a little faster, and I clenched my teeth against the pleasurable sensation thrumming through my body.

"That's it, Tink, try and fight it. It just makes you all the sweeter to break."

I opened my mouth to swear at him when the leather smacked down on my ass. The sound was almost worse than the bite, but I cried out nonetheless. I jerked on his lap, and he groaned and shuddered under me.

"I hope you cum in your fucking jeans," I growled at him, and he laughed again as the leather found a fresh spot to hit.

"Not likely, Tink," he said.

"Ah," I yelled out and couldn't stop the moan that followed. He fucked me with his finger and only stopped to play with my clit. I could feel just how wet I was and hated that he was right. My body rocked against his hand, wanting more and purposely rubbing against the cock under me.

"That's it, fuck my hand," Kai said, and his voice was strained. Two more hard cracks of his belt hit my ass, and tears stung my eyes with the sharp bite. I yelled out, my hands gripping the comforter. This time as his finger slipped inside me, my legs opened, giving him better access. "Such a naughty girl liking to be punished."

Pushing back hard into his hand, I didn't even care who was winning the battle of wills. All I wanted was to cum. I could feel it building and was so close to the edge that the walls could have crumbled down around us, and I wouldn't have cared.

"Fuck, you're so hot." I picked a steady rhythm and rocked my hips down so my clit brushed his jeans with every little movement. "I can't wait to bury my cock into this wet pussy. Maybe I should stop this now and take what I want."

"No," I cried out, not wanting him to stop.

"You don't want me to stop," he asked and removed his finger to squeeze my ass. He pressed his fingers into the soft skin like he was massaging my tender cheeks.

"No, don't stop," I panted out, thrusting my ass up higher into the air to entice him to keep going.

"Whatever you say, Tink. Just remember I'm going to fuck you after this." I shuddered and moaned loud as his fingers pressed into me once again. "Oh, and talk dirty to me. I want to hear that sweet mouth of yours begging for it."

I looked at him, and as his eyes met mine, I knew he was serious. He'd leave me like this all night to prove his point. I licked my lips, and his eyes tracked the movement making me squirm.

"Well, Tink, I'm waiting."

"Yes, oh god, yes Kai, fuck," I said, giving in. "Yes, yes, fuck me with your fingers, make me cum."

"I love your dirty mouth. Say it again," he ordered, his fingers working faster and making my head spin.

"Make me cum. Make me cum all over you," I cried out and yelled his name as he shoved me over the edge, and the orgasm stormed through me. I could feel my body soaking his lap like he said I would, and I didn't care.

"Oh fuck, you're so fucking sexy. You almost made me cum in my jeans, Tink," Kai said as I collapsed onto his lap, panting hard. "I need to be in you. Now." Kai stood, and I was too relaxed to care that he took me with him and then laid me on my back in the center of the bed.

My head lulled to the side, and I smiled as I stared at the dark wet mark on his jeans that only accentuated the outline of his hard cock.

"Fuck me," Kai growled out as he undid his zipper, and his large cock sprang free from the confines of the denim. The head of his cock was shiny, and I didn't know if that was from me or his own precum, but I licked my lips, wanting a taste. "Sorry Tink, maybe later. Right now, I need in that pussy of yours."

Kai ripped his jeans off and tossed them across the room. "Get up," he ordered.

As I did, he grabbed the blankets from the foot of the bed, yanking on them like he was pissed off, and untucked them. He walked toward me, and the energy around us grew until it felt like electricity racing over my skin.

"Get in," he ordered, lifting the blankets so I could slip in. Confused as to why he'd bother. "I plan on fucking you until we pass out, but I'm going to stay buried inside of you where I belong, and every time I get hard, I'm going to fuck you all over again."

I shuddered as he answered the question in my mind and crawled between my legs. "Lift your hands over your head."

I lifted my hands and couldn't help jerking a little as he licked up my stomach to my nipple, stopping long enough to suck each one into a stiff peak and making me squirm from the overstimulation. As he settled between my legs, I could feel his cock pressing up against my opening.

Slipping a hand between our bodies, he lined up his cock, and I moaned as the thick head pressed into me. It didn't matter that I was soaking wet. He was thick enough that my body needed to adjust to his size, a luxury I wasn't given the first time we did this. I firmly slammed the door on that thought. If we were moving forward, I couldn't keep thinking about that night.

He sucked in a deep breath, pushed in a little further, and ran his hands along my arms until he could hold mine. This time as our lips met, it was with a tenderness I didn't know he was capable of until this moment. The kiss didn't command anything from me, and it didn't promise pain. Instead, the kiss spoke of deeper things, and my heart swelled as a tear fell from my eye.

"You're perfect," Kai whispered against my lips as he slid deeper into my body until he was fully inside me. "I plan on cumming in you all night. Are you on the pill?" I shook my head. There hadn't been the need until recently. "Good. If there is even a one percent chance that you can get pregnant, then I want the kid to be mine."

Tears clouded my eyes as he stared down at me, leaning in to kiss me again. I didn't think he could've said anything more endearing or that screamed how much he loved me. He began to move, but there was no urgency to his movements. It was like he was taking the time to enjoy what we'd missed all these years. We were quiet and let our bodies speak for us as he slowly picked up the pace. Our lips continued to touch, the kiss deepening as slowly as the way he was making love to me.

He'd said he loved me, but I didn't truly believe it until now. His eyes held all the emotions he'd been hiding underneath the rage. There was no anger or fury, and the walls that had been firmly in place were gone.

I wrapped my legs around his waist, and he sank deeper. He groaned as I moaned, but we both shuddered as he bottomed out. My heart, which had calmed from the intense orgasms, was once more pounding hard for him. I could feel the thump in his chest as easily as my own as he held me tighter.

"I've wanted this for so long," Kai said and broke the kiss to stare into my eyes. "I'd lay in my cell and dream of this moment, of what it would be like to be held by you. To no longer hate you. To go back in time and fix whatever I'd broken." Tears spilled over, blurring his image. "I'm sorry. I'm sorry I never gave it a single thought that you were actually attacked. That will haunt me for the rest of my life.

"I'm sorry too. I can never say sorry enough for not being stronger and listening to the voice that kept saying it couldn't be you. Maybe if I had...." My lower lip trembled as the complex emotions continued to rise. Kai dropped his head and stole the next apology from my mouth.

"I know," he said and laid his forehead against mine as his cock continued to slowly coax my body into reaching for a third orgasm. "I just wanted you to know that nothing I could ever have imagined compares to you. I love you, Raine, I always have."

My heart swelled and felt like it would burst right out of my chest. "I want to hold you," I said. There was no hesitation as Kai let go of my hands, and I wrapped my arms around his neck. He couldn't be close enough, and I held onto him like he would disappear as our breathing increased.

"Fuck, I can't hold back any longer," Kai said, breaking the kiss and burying his head into the crook of my neck. "Cum for me," he whispered in my ear, sending a shiver down my spine. "Fuck, you drive me crazy," he said and thrust into me harder with each word. His teeth nipped at the sensitive skin on my neck, and I turned my head to give him better access.

"Yes, Kai. Right there, please keep going," I begged as I reached the top and felt close to tumbling over the other side.

"You like it like that," he asked as he thrust into me hard.

"Yes. Don't stop, oh god Kai, I'm so close."

"Fuck." Kai reared up onto his arms, and all his muscles strained as he pounded into me hard, making the bed bang against the wall. "Cum for me, Tink, right now," he growled as he closed his eyes, his face tense as he tried to hold off for me.

"I'm. All. Most...ahh. Yes, Kai, I'm cumming," I screamed, my body arching off the bed as the most powerful orgasm gripped me in its hold. My nails dug into Kai's shoulders, and his rhythm picked up to a furious pace. I was still riding the high of my climax when Kai roared. His face contorted as he came. I could feel him filling me with each thrust. "Fuck me, Tink."

Kai collapsed on my body, both of us damp with sweat and panting to catch our breath.

"I love you," I whispered into his ear, and his arms tightened around me. I had to find a way to make this work because I never wanted to let him go again.

Avro

6

FOURTEEN HOURS EARLIER

Avro

Although I never wanted to take up stalking as a career, I had to admit I was pretty fucking good at it. Racing home, I grabbed my baby. I only took her out for special occasions. The fancy Mustang was my pride and joy, but only Jace knew I had it. I was going to show Camille off to Raine when the moment was right to introduce them, but Camille was the jealous type, so these things had to be handled delicately.

The only issue with a sexy ass muscle car was that it drew a shit load more attention than the sedan I normally drove.

I doubted Raine would head deeper into Florida. If I were going to run, I would find the furthest point I could get to and call that home, and since we were almost always on the same wavelength, I chose that as the most likely option. She didn't drive or have a car, so that left planes, buses, or hitchhiking. The last option I eliminated immediately.

Raine might be braver, but there was no way she was walking down the side of an interstate with her thumb sticking out. So here I was, sitting in the dark shadows of the overpass and the closest interstate on-ramp to where Kai and the Lost Souls were located. If he was heading out of town as fast as possible, this is where he would come.

Hopefully he didn't decide to go to Walmart for socks or some shit. That would screw up my perfectly thought-out plan. Luckily, I didn't have to wait very long to find out. The loud rumbling of the Indian motorcycle roared passed my hiding spot and shook my car as it went. I'd positioned myself perfectly and caught a glimpse of him as he rode by with the Lost Souls emblem on his back. I could admit that the motorcycle held a certain appeal. The shiny black paint job and glittering chrome looked sick.

"How did I fucking know you'd find a way?" I tried tracking her with all my tricks, but anything I had was no good when she left her phone behind.

Revving the Mustang, I pulled out as the motorcycle started up the ramp. I followed and spotted the red taillight of the motorcycle gaining distance. I didn't bring Camille out just so Kai wouldn't recognize me. She had a whole fuck ton more get up and go.

The car roared like a lion as I shifted into fifth, making me smile wide. "I know, girl, it's been a while since I opened you up, but don't worry, we have a bit of ground to cover." I wanted to ask her if I could make out with Raine in here one day, but I didn't need her having a fit and stranding me on the side of the road. Camille could be a petty bitch.

We flew down the outside lane, and once I was a comfortable distance away, I pulled in behind another car to follow. It was way too bright out to get close

I knew what Kai's plan would be. He didn't give a shit about Jace or me, so as soon as he found Raine, he'd try and convince her to only be with him. Kai didn't exactly strike me as the sharing type, but I had something that the other two guys involved didn't have, and that was faith.

I'd seen and felt Raine's heart, and I truly believed she wouldn't let Kai storm into her orbit and steal her away. She left for a reason, and it wasn't because she didn't love me. It also meant I needed to be smart. Kai would still try to talk her into only being with him, and if by some miracle she talked him into sharing, he would have demands. I needed them to work out whatever that was before I stormed the castle. If Jace were here, he'd say, 'Fuck that shit,' and bust the door down to get to Raine.

Of course, when we argued last night, his solution was to announce to the world that she was his girlfriend. He also suggested flying off and making some other place our home, like Venice, Paris, or maybe Ireland. It was great in theory if Raine wanted to do it, but I doubted it. That would only last so long if Kai saw Jace and Raine on the television. Then he would only become more obsessed and enraged. I knew my personality types, which was why I handled the talking and Jace did the stomping.

I smirked at the thought and picked up my phone, staring at the missed calls from Jace. I couldn't listen to these messages or answer them right now. If I did and told him what I was up to, he would have a meltdown of epic proportions. I loved him, but sometimes that overprotective side was a bit much.

We had been on the road for three hours when Kai pulled off for fuel. This was the tricky part. I should top off too, but the question was how to do it without being noticed. I pulled up to the furthest pump from Kai and lifted the hood on my sweatshirt to cover my face.

I looked over my shoulder and spotted the little sign on the pump, covering the credit card slot that said I had to pre-pay inside. Well, wasn't that just fucking perfect? I watched Kai go inside the store and head to the men's room. This was my opportunity. Jumping out, I made my way inside. The guy behind the counter gave me a once-over. I realized I must look like I was about to rob him with my hands stuffed inside the pocket.

"Hey, I need fifty on pump six, and I'll take these," I said, grabbing a handful of different candy packages. "Oh, and a bottle of water."

"Which one," the guy asked.

"Which one what?"

"Bottle of water?"

"I don't know your biggest, I guess." The guy looked at me like I had two heads. I tapped my foot, nervous about being found in here if Kai came back out. "I'll grab one," I said calmly while inside, I felt like screaming.

Marching over to the fridge, I opened the door and grabbed a large water. Of course, that was when I heard the men's room door's hinge squeaking open. Oh fuck, please let him have already paid, was all I could think as I walked back to the counter to pay. Of course, I didn't have that kind of luck and could hear his heavy boots on the cheap tile floor coming up behind me. The hair stood on the back of my neck, warning me of the danger.

It felt like the guy working the counter was moving as slowly as possible as he put my stuff in a bag and handed it over. I stepped sideways, pretending to look around, and then escaped to the bathroom and locked the door.

"Oh fuck. What am I doing," I asked my reflection. "I'm going to get myself killed." I gave myself a stern look. "No, I've got this."

Shaking off the building anxiety, I quickly took a piss and washed my hands, horrified that I would have to touch the handle.

The bike was still in the same spot when I got outside, but there was no sign of Kai. I was so busy staring at the black bike that I didn't notice him until I rounded the far pump and froze in my tracks. He was leaning up against my driver's side door, smoking a cigarette and looking as casual as could be, but as his eyes met mine, I knew he was contemplating murder.

"Hello, Avro," Kai said and took a drag off his smoke.

"You really shouldn't do that," I said, and he cocked an eyebrow at me. "Smoking at a gas station. There's a reason they have all those, do not smoke here, signs up."

Smirking, he took another pull and then dropped the cigarette to the ground stomping it out with his shitkicker. I was pretty sure he was going to try and shove the boot up my ass.

"Why are you following me?"

"Who says I was? Maybe I was just out for a nice drive in my sexy car."

Kai smiled. "She is a sexy car, I'll give you that, but the rest is bullshit. I spotted you an hour ago. So, I'll ask you again, why are you following me?"

Giving up the lie since I sucked at it anyway, I lifted my shoulder. "Well, I thought that would be obvious," I said, and Kai rolled his eyes and then rubbed at them as he swore something about a Wilder answer. I had no idea what that was supposed to mean.

"Look, if you know where Raine is, then I'm going to follow you. I know you don't like me, but I love her, so if that means you're going to shoot me for it, then so be it. I'm not letting her disappear."

Kai turned sideways and leaned against Camille, his eyes roaming over the shiny paint job. Internally I screamed don't scratch my baby, but managed not to say anything and give him the ammunition. I imagined him dragging the large silver rings on his hand along her side just to make me faint.

On a bright day like today, it was blue, but as soon as the shadow hit, it would look purple, then black at night. I spent a fortune for it to be done, but it was worth it. She was a beast and deserved the best.

"You played me." He smirked, but it wasn't a friendly look. "You figured I'd find a way to track her down, didn't you?" I shrugged, not agreeing or disagreeing. "You're braver than I thought, Avro. Stupid, maybe, but definitely braver. Go home. I'm not hunting down Raine. If she wants to take off and never come back, then so be it."

"Ha!" I barked out before I could stop myself. "Now, who's the terrible liar?" I dug around in my plastic bag and pulled out a couple of packages of candy. I tossed one at Kai, and he caught it. "Don't ever play poker. You'll lose."

"What's this for," he asked, staring at the gummies.

"People tend to eat them," I said, smiling as Kai glared. "I'm not sure what the wildlife does with them."

Kai made a snorting sound like he almost found my joking insult amusing. "And you have a sense of humor, good to know. One that is going to get you killed, but it makes me like you a little bit more," he said and tore open the package.

I glanced at the large window and the guy behind the cash register staring at us as if expecting things to turn into a shoot-out.

"Well, we seem to be at a stalemate because I'm not continuing with you following me," Kai said.

"Another asshole move. I shouldn't be surprised after you stormed my home, attacked Jace and me, destroyed my sitting room, and almost shot us all. For no reason, I might add."

"I had my reasons, just not ones you'd agree with," he said, and fuck, he sounded way too much like Jace. I just couldn't picture either of them sharing Raine with one another, but that was a problem for another day. One problem at a time.

"Fine. I'll make you a deal," I offered.

"I'm not really sure you're in a position to make deals," Kai said.

"Maybe not, but I will sit here and watch you like a fucking annoying ass fly and stick to you like glue until you either shoot me or lead me to Raine. So I'd take the deal."

Kai glared, and I was sure it scared a great many people, but this was Raine we were talking about, and I wasn't about to back down. He could fucking forget about it.

"I wouldn't tempt me with shooting you," he said and dumped the last of the candy in his mouth.

"I'm sure it is tempting for someone used to simply taking whatever they want. The thing is, I don't think that's the real you. At least not the you before prison, but what do I know?" I rubbed at my chin as I analyzed his glare. "Maybe you really are the type that if you want something, you just take it. You don't like someone. You shoot them in the face." Wisely or unwisely, I took a step toward Kai. "I honestly don't give a fuck what you do to me, but I've never done anything to you, and you're the one that will have to live with my death on your conscience." I took another step so that I was standing at the trunk of my car. "And if Raine ever finds out what you've done...well, you don't need to be a rocket scientist to know how well that will go over."

"Okay, it's official. You're fucking annoying me." Kai pushed away from my car and stood with his hands on his hips.

I shook my head and sighed. "I'm right, and you know it, Kai. From what Raine has told me about you, one thing was made very clear. She said that you had a good heart. She said that you stood up against bullies and that it was breaking her heart to see how much you've changed. How much she no longer recognized you. How much who you'd become scared her."

It was like I punched him in the stomach. All the anger fell from his face to be replaced with uncertainty. I had a feeling that people didn't call Kai out much. They probably weren't brave enough or didn't care.

"Raine still sees the good in you, and I think I see it too, but this....." I pointed my finger up and down his body. "This attitude and the threatening to kill me because I was Raine's friend and dared to look out for her when no one else did. Because I fell in love with her and her beautiful soul that was broken when we met. Because I would lay my life down for her. None of those are reasons." He licked his lips, and I could see him warring with his inner demons, whatever those were.

Kai cracked his neck and sucked in a deep breath. "What's this fucking deal?"

"Pull out your phone," I said, and he slowly reached inside his leather jacket. "Now go to text messages and send whatever message you want to this number." I held up my phone with my number glowing across the face. A moment later, *fuck off*, came in, and I smirked. "Perfect, now I will know it's you."

"What are you talking about?"

"I'm going to turn around and go home like you want. You want this time with Raine alone. You want to try and convince her to just be with you. Go for it. I won't stop you. What I want is to know she's alive and well. So as soon as you find her and know she's okay, you'll text me and let me know she's alright."

"And? What's the catch?"

"No catch. You try and convince her to come home and be with you or whatever you want, as long as you don't hurt her again. Then you will piss me off, and I may not look it, Kai, but I'm a lot smarter and more resourceful than you're giving me credit for." I smiled wide. "Just make sure she is doing well and stays that way and text me that she is, and I'll call it fair."

"I don't understand."

I smirked. "You wouldn't."

"What's that supposed to mean?" Kai growled, his hands immediately balling into fists. Okay, he was like Jace if he was on steroids. I wanted to shake my head but watched a few cars driving by, minding their own business, before I answered.

"It means that what you fail to realize is that at the end of the day, what happens from this moment onward has nothing to do with you, me, or Jace." I paused, and Kai cocked his head as he stared at me. "The decision is Raine's." I shrugged. "If you truly love her the way you seem to, then you'll eventually see that, and you'll have a choice to make."

I stepped up to Kai, and at first, he didn't back away from my door as I reached for the handle, but I waited patiently until he finally stepped away. Opening it halfway, I stopped before I got behind the wheel and looked at Kai.

"For the record. I don't see a monster when I look at you. I see who Jace and I would've become if we hadn't had each other. There's time to heal Kai if you let yourself. You just have to give yourself the space and stop telling yourself you're no longer worth the effort." I slipped behind the wheel, and Kai remained standing in the same spot as if I'd frozen him in place.

I went to start the car and then remembered I had prepaid for gas and never put any in Camille. Fuck. So much for a grand dramatic exit.

"Son of a bitch," I swore under my breath as I got back out.

Snake

7

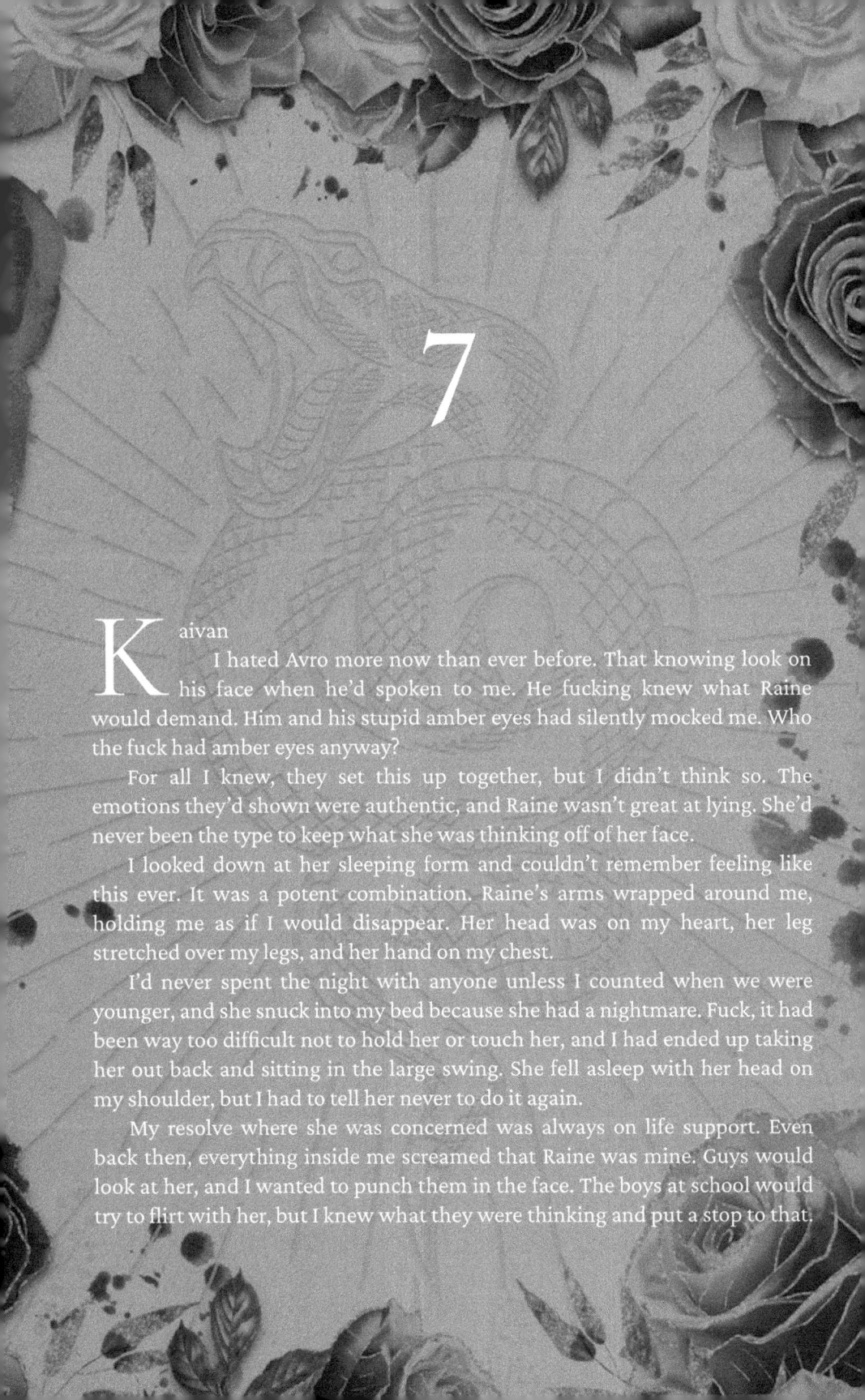

Kaivan

I hated Avro more now than ever before. That knowing look on his face when he'd spoken to me. He fucking knew what Raine would demand. Him and his stupid amber eyes had silently mocked me. Who the fuck had amber eyes anyway?

For all I knew, they set this up together, but I didn't think so. The emotions they'd shown were authentic, and Raine wasn't great at lying. She'd never been the type to keep what she was thinking off of her face.

I looked down at her sleeping form and couldn't remember feeling like this ever. It was a potent combination. Raine's arms wrapped around me, holding me as if I would disappear. Her head was on my heart, her leg stretched over my legs, and her hand on my chest.

I'd never spent the night with anyone unless I counted when we were younger, and she snuck into my bed because she had a nightmare. Fuck, it had been way too difficult not to hold her or touch her, and I had ended up taking her out back and sitting in the large swing. She fell asleep with her head on my shoulder, but I had to tell her never to do it again.

My resolve where she was concerned was always on life support. Even back then, everything inside me screamed that Raine was mine. Guys would look at her, and I wanted to punch them in the face. The boys at school would try to flirt with her, but I knew what they were thinking and put a stop to that.

No one touched her or went near her without my permission. If you had a dick attached to your body, your intentions better be pure.

She was so fucking innocent and sweet. A bright light in my dark world that made me smile just by looking my way. I didn't know what to do with the emotions then, and eleven years, three months, three weeks, and two days hadn't made it any easier to navigate.

Having sex with women was easy, but with Raine...she pulled me all over the place. One moment I was happy, then scared, horny as hell, pissed off, and finally confused. My head had been a mess for a long time, but this emotional shit had it all scrambled up like someone came along and swiped everything off my already disorganized desk into a heap on the floor.

I traced my finger along Raine's bare shoulder. She shivered and snuggled closer, right on cue, making me smile. Grabbing the blanket, I pulled it up to cover her. She sighed, and I knew I was seriously fucked. I couldn't picture my life without her. I didn't do fluffy shit, yet words like soulmate bounced around inside my skull. She made me crazy. That was all there was to it. Raine had stolen the heart from my chest and refused to give it back.

Her fingers twitched on my chest, and a glint caught my eye. I hadn't noticed the ring before but stared at it now. Without even trying, she had me wanting to cry and fuck her into oblivion all over again.

The thin silver band was a gift I bought and gave to her the day before our worlds exploded. I had wanted to tell her it was a promise ring, but instead, I said it was an early birthday gift since we always celebrated our birthdays together. I loved that she was two years, two weeks, and two days younger. The little unity symbol on the top had felt so right to buy for her, and she'd smiled wider than I'd ever seen. She had practically jumped into my arms to hug me as she said thank you over and over again.

Sliding my hand under hers, I lifted her fingers enough to see the ring clearly, running my thumb over the symbol. She kept it. All this time, and she still wore it. My silent promise to her that I would forever be hers, and she was mine.

The anger that consumed me for so long was still there. I was annoyed as shit that what Raine wanted went against every one of my base instincts.

But I was more pissed off at those that manipulated a traumatized teen into thinking I'd hurt her and put us in this position in the first place out of spite. She told me more about what Dave had said to her. How the police caught me down near the fights, and my hoodie had her blood on it, how I'd admitted to being obsessed with her.

That last part was true, but no one knew that. I hadn't admitted it to myself, let alone a bunch of cops. Irene had put on quite the show. She cried and told her that I was so angry when I thought she went downtown to see another guy that I lost it and attacked her, and that was how she got the black eye. I'd bet money it was Dave that put it there when he found out about her fucking around on him with me.

Raine said she didn't have a reason to think they'd lie to her and didn't ask to see any of the evidence. She was in the hospital facing a second surgery, scared out of her mind. Every noise made her heart monitor leap, and they put a security guard at the door for a week so that she could get some sleep.

What hurt my heart the most was how she wished she had died. That last part killed me more than anything else. They almost succeeded and took any hope from my life with a single act. I don't know what I would've done if she had.

I shivered and wrapped my arms around Raine, linking my fingers together. She said that so many times during the investigation, she had doubts, but the response was always the same. She was making excuses for my actions because of her feelings for me.

Raine suddenly jerked, a whimper escaping her mouth. "Shh, it's okay, Tink, I've got you. I've always got you," I whispered, kissing the top of her head. "I'll never let anyone hurt you again."

Her body twitched a few more times before she settled again. "I love you," she slurred out in her dream state.

"I love you too," I said.

Yeah, there was no letting her go. But she was clear about what she wanted, including two other men. My nostrils flared with the thought of them touching her. I had to figure out a way to live with this if I wanted her in my life. Without her being chained to my fucking wall like a prisoner. Wilder came to mind, and I couldn't help wondering who he was keeping prisoner and what he was doing to them. Nope, don't wonder. You don't want to know. Plausible deniability was what I was going for. Hell, it wasn't like I was going to be turning his crazy ass in, so better off not to know.

Maybe I could talk Raine into hitting the road with me for a few weeks or months. Everyone else seemed to be able to take off whenever they wanted. Why the fuck shouldn't I have the opportunity?

Raine bolted upright from my hold, her hand clutching her chest as her wide eyes searched the room before finding my face.

"You okay," I asked, trying to pull her back into my arms, but she shook her head.

"I will be. I just need a few moments alone. I'm going to go shower."

Leaning down, she gave me a quick kiss, but I saw the shadows in her eyes. She didn't have to say it, I knew what haunted her dreams, and here she was, lying in the arms of the man she thought had hurt her. I guess there was going to be an adjustment for both of us.

"You sure you don't want me to join?"

Raine gave me a small smile as she stood from the bed. Fuck me. My eager cock stirred at her naked body and the faint outline of my handprint on her ass as she dug around in her small backpack.

"Thanks, but I just...." Raine ran her hand through her short hair as she clutched a T-shirt to her chest. "I just need a few minutes to...." She closed her eyes and covered her mouth. I watched her battle back the emotion like it was her enemy. "Just give me ten minutes and then join me," she said, walking into the bathroom as the first tears started to fall.

Murderous thoughts bounced around my mind as I pictured Dave's smug face. Swinging my legs out of bed, I stood and hunted for my jeans as a knock sounded at the door. I looked at the time as the clock clicked over to five-o-one in the morning. I grabbed the T-shirt and pulled it on as the knock came again.

"Hang on to yourself," I yelled, yanking my legs into my jeans but didn't bother doing them up. I grabbed my gun and stood to the side of the door. "Who the fuck is there?" I called out. "Answer me, or I shoot through the door and then find out who's on the other side."

"It's me."

Fucking Avro. I yanked open the door, my hand shaking on the gun as I stared at his calm face.

"What the fuck are you doing here?"

"You said you'd text when you found Raine." He held up his phone. "Oh, look at that, no text."

"So I lied. Sue me. You said you were heading home," I growled.

"So I lied, sue me," he mocked.

"I want to knock your teeth down your throat," I said, and he smirked. "I swear to god, wipe that look off your face before I do." Avro stopped smiling and crossed his arms over his chest.

"Are you going to let me in?"

"I'd prefer to punch you in the face." He glanced down at my shaking hand, gripping the gun.

"So we're back to you wanting to kill me?" Sighing, he leaned against the open archway of the door.

"Technically, I don't think I ever stopped," I said. His face was bruised with a cut along his jaw and tape on his nose. He still looked like a fucking model and far too perfect. That alone was enough to make me want to shoot him. Guys like him running around ruined shit for the rest of us.

"Well, I'm not leaving," he said. I chanted in my head that Raine would never speak to me again if I killed him. It was the only thing keeping me from snatching him by the neck, dragging him into the room, and putting my gun in his mouth.

"Avro?" I groaned at the sound of Raine's voice. No hiding the body now.

"Yeah, it's me." He leaned around me to look at Raine, smiling wide before pushing my arm out of the way and walking in.

"Come on in, why don't you? We weren't having a private moment or anything," I muttered under my breath. Closing the door, I turned and watched as Raine's face shifted. In a blink, she looked relaxed, like the guy had some superpower to make her feel okay. Yeah, I was gonna kill him.

"Did Kai call you?"

Like I'd actually call Avro. But the hopeful look in her eyes made me feel guilty that I hadn't. Fuck, fuck, fuck.

"No, but he was about to," Avro lied smoothly, and I raised an eyebrow.

Raine smiled and hugged Avro, her eyes closing. What the hell was it with this fucknut? I found him...creepy. He was too perfect. Just look at his hair and teeth and his bone structure. No one had that perfect of a jaw. Then there was the supernatural ability to soothe Raine. That really annoyed me. I needed to mess his pretty face up some more. He was unnatural.

"If Kai didn't call, what are you doing here?" Raine asked.

"I asked him the same question," I said and put the gun down. I didn't trust myself not to shoot him just because he was in the room. Raine only had the bath towel wrapped around her body, and I ground my teeth together as Avro's hand lingered on her shoulder.

Marching past them, I grabbed my jacket and swore for the second time. I still hadn't gotten more smokes. I sat down in the chair and played with my lighter instead. All I could think about was whether I should kill him or not. Maybe I should bring him to a field and pull the petals off a daisy to decide his fate.

"I came to make sure you're okay. I waited as long as I could, but it was terrible sleeping in a sports car. I don't recommend it," Avro said, and Raine's face scrunched up in confusion. "I need to use the bathroom. I'll be back."

Raine watched him disappear into the bathroom, and then her eyes found mine. She silently asked me if I was alright, but I didn't have an answer for her. Standing, I stuffed my arms into my jacket and pulled on my boots.

"Where are you going, Kai?"

"I need smokes, or I will shoot him." I looked up as I finished tying my laces, and Raine's lips pulled down in a frown. "Look, I said I'd try. I didn't fucking say I'd like it or that I would spend time with him in the same motel room. All I really want to do right now is shoot him in the head, so space is required." She crossed her arms and looked away. "And please have some clothes on when I return. I might not be so angry with him touching you if you weren't practically naked."

Raine sighed and pinched the bridge of her nose. "Are you coming back?"

Cupping her face, I kissed her hard, loving the fresh minty flavor of her mouth. Her hands went to my waist, and she gripped me tight. My lips lingered on hers, not wanting to leave her alone with Avro but knowing I needed to. Avro stepped out of the bathroom but stayed near the door.

"I'll be back," I said.

Grabbing the rest of my crap on the way, I stomped to the door. Flinging it open, I stopped dead as I almost ran into a raised fist about to knock. Jace lowered his arm as I glared.

"You have got to be fucking kidding me!" I growled at the sight of him. My body trembled with the burst of adrenaline. It took all my resolve not to tackle him out the door and continue what we started at the house. The dark glare in his eyes said he was thinking the same thing.

"Funny, I was just thinking the same thing," he said. My eyes flicked down to his hand. I thought he was holding a gun but realized it was a Taser and smirked.

"You brought a Taser with you?" My respect for him notched up slightly.

"You can never be too careful these days. Don't know what sort of asshole you'll run into anymore. I'm really hoping you try to hit me again, though, just so I have an excuse to use it. I've been dying to see what this can do when turned on high."

My eyes narrowed. "I'm flattered that you think you need that toy."

"Unlike you, who would jump straight to murder, I'd prefer to stop you, then throw you back into the cage where you belong. The one you never should've left," Jace said, and the curl of his lip had my fist clenching. I reminded myself that he was pushing me on purpose. He wanted me to make the first move.

"Jace? What are you doing here," Avro asked.

"Seems to be the question of the day," I muttered, stepping out of the way for Jace to enter. Why the fuck not at this point? My plan to whisk her away for a few days was officially ruined.

"If you bothered to check your messages and call me back, then I wouldn't have to track you down," Jace growled as he stepped inside but kept his eyes trained on me. The tension grew with his proximity. Our eyes locked on one another.

"I didn't want to worry you," Avro said.

"You didn't think that leaving me a message that you're going to go speak to him...." Jace pointed a thumb in my direction. "And then go radio silent, wasn't going to worry me?"

"He does have a point. I've thought about killing you multiple times already," I said, and all three sets of eyes turned in my direction. "What? I'm being honest. Jace has a valid point."

"See," Jace said, glaring at Avro.

"Don't get like that with me. You're the one that decided you were going to leave before anything was resolved," Avro shot back. My brow lifted as Jace's face went dark, his lip pulling up in a snarl. He would've held his own in lock up. I might've liked him if he didn't want to put his cock in my girl.

"Enough!" Raine shook her head. "Not that I'm not happy to see all of you, but I don't understand. Did I leave a fucking breadcrumb trail for you all to follow? And if you two are only here to fight with me about Kai, then don't bother."

I couldn't stop the smile that lifted the corner of my mouth. At least she was just as firm with them as with me. Good to know.

Jace crossed his arms over his chest. "I haven't decided why I'm here other than to make sure the two of you were alive. Obviously, that was a waste of time since Avro was actively dodging me."

"I was not," Avro said and stepped toward Jace.

"Don't fucking lie to me. You knew I didn't trust him and knew I'd worry when I couldn't reach you. Yet, you set out to see him alone and then disappeared. What the fuck was I going to think? I pictured you floating in some swamp as alligator bait."

"What, no love for me?" I drawled out and earned a glare. "I hate to admit it, but I do have alligators and have thought about it." It was fairly close to what I'd debated doing.

"Why do you have alligators," Raine asked, and I smirked.

"Would you believe me if I said they make great pets?" Before they could drag me into any more of this argument, I grabbed the door handle. "I'm out of here so you all can have your lovers quarrel," I said mockingly.

I slammed the door behind me. Closing my eyes, I took a slow deep breath. My heart was pounding hard while the anger tried to consume me. I sucked in the cool, early morning air and spotted Avro's car tucked in the corner of the lot. Was the asshole here all night? The fact that he kept an eye on the room was unnerving, but that also meant he let Raine and I have that time together. It was confusing. I wouldn't have been able to stay in the parking lot knowing that they were having sex inside.

The thought of the three of them alone had my blood pressure rising. My hand twitched as I mapped out all the areas I could dispose of their bodies. I needed to step away, or I really would lose control It wasn't just words. I felt myself stepping close to the line that always took over when I was sent to teach opposing club members a lesson.

Walking away from the room, I made it three doors down when a guy stepped out, lighting a smoke. Fucker.

"Hey buddy, do you have a smoke I can bum off ya?"

The guy turned his bloodshot eyes in my direction and snorted like I'd said something funny. The anger I was trying hard to control slipped a little more. I hated that look. I'd been stared at like I was worthless most of my life.

Before he even answered, I knew what words would come out of his mouth and pulled my gun.

"Go fuck yourself," he said and spat at my feet.

The gun was up and pressed into his forehead before my mind registered what my hand was doing. I glared into his terrified eyes that suddenly didn't look so smug.

"Do I look like someone you want to fuck with?" My voice dropped low as I growled the words. He shook his head slightly. The cigarette, long forgotten, was now dangling from his lips. "So, I'm going to ask you again, and I expect a different answer. Hey buddy, do you have a smoke I can bum?"

His hand shook as he pulled out the pack from inside his jacket, and I plucked it from his fingers. "Wow, thanks man. You're too nice," I drawled as I put the pack in my back pocket. Snatching the one from his mouth, I tossed it on the ground and stepped on it, crushing it so I didn't do the same to his face.

The guy's chest heaved as I lowered the gun, and he took a deep breath. "So generous of you to give me your whole pack," I drawled as I tapped the gun against my leg. His eyes followed the movement like a scared rat. "It's a nice day for a walk, you say? You want to get more smokes? What a fabulous fucking idea. Run along then," I said and watched as he slowly turned and walked away so fast he looked like he was in one of those weird walking races. He had decent form with his straight back and tight ass. Okay, it was official. I'd completely lost my mind.

Pulling out the pack of smokes, I lit one up and took the first sweet pull. Did Raine still hate that I smoke? Why the fuck did I care? Was this my new reality? Wondering what Raine liked and didn't like every time I did something. Who was I kidding? It was always my reality. I just couldn't admit it until now.

Shaking my head, I wandered back to the room and leaned against the wall outside, clearly able to hear them through the shitty door.

"No fucking way! I'm laying the law down right now. We are not getting into a relationship with that psychopath," Jace yelled. "The pair of you have lost your fucking minds."

"He's actually not a psychopath because he has emotions, and a lot of them, including regret," Avro said and the room went silent. I smirked as I pictured the look on Jace's face. Okay, I was man enough to admit this was entertaining shit. At least it wasn't just my nerves that Avro got on. I could picture him swinging off Jace's last nerve right now.

"I don't need you to be the Webster dictionary to know that man is unstable as fuck. By his own admission, he has thought about killing you and feeding you to alligators. He could decide today he is okay with this and tomorrow that he wants the two of us dead and do it." Again very accurate of Jace. Apparently, there was more to him than singing.

"He won't," Raine piped in.

"Oh yeah, and how can you be so sure about that? Let's not forget he's attacked you, raped you, and almost shot you the other night. Not exactly an outstanding track record," Jace growled.

I sucked in another drag of the smoke and hated Jace a little more for calling out all the shit I'd done to Raine in a very short time. I rubbed my eyes. He wasn't wrong. I was angry and had never stopped to think that she might actually believe I was the guy.

"I know because he made me a promise," Raine said, surprisingly calm. I loved the sound of her voice. She used to hum all the time, and I would sneak closer to whatever room she was in to listen. From the first moment we met, she calmed the storm of toxic waste that was my soul.

"A promise? That doesn't sound like much of a reassurance, no offense."

"Jace, I know you hardly know me, and the only thing you know of Kai is the anger and violence, but...he is to me who Avro is to you. I know Kai inside out. I never should let myself think for even a moment that it was Kai that hurt me all those years ago." Her voice was getting louder and I knew she was close to the door. "We have a complicated and sordid past that binds us in a way I can't explain, but I know his heart. Any doubt I had left about my attack is gone. I love him." I rubbed at the spot that had ached for Raine for so long. Hearing her talk about me like I was worth something made me warm all over. I didn't deserve it. I didn't deserve her, but I couldn't walk away.

"Fuck, Raine. I get that. I do, but...shit, this is so dangerous."

"Maybe, and I'm not going to force the two of you to be in a relationship with Kai if you don't want to be. It's what I've asked for from him and now from the two of you, and I will hold true to my choice. It's either all of you, or it's none of you. I'm not going back to live a half-life, and I'm not going to be forced to choose between one side of my heart an the other."

I wasn't sure what was worse at this point. Jace not agreeing and Raine taking off again, never seeing her again, or was it worse for him to agree? Forcing me to try and accept them. I felt physically torn, but I shocked myself when I realized I was rooting for him to say yes.

"You know what happened to my family," he said, his voice softer, and I perked up. For some reason, I suddenly wanted to know what had happened to his family. I pulled out my phone and began an internet search for his name.

"I know, and what happened to them was tragic, but Kai is not your stepfather. His heart is battered and bruised, but under that, he is still the man I remember, and his word is as solid as any contract." My lip curled up. "I can assure you that if Kai makes a promise, he will never break it unless you force him to. Despite what he did to me, he has honor in his soul."

Fuck, why did she have to make me sound like I was a decent human? I wasn't, not anymore. The part of me that had been decent died in prison, yet the emotion she evoked clogged my throat. I flicked the forgotten smoke down on the ground.

"Avro, what do you want," Jace asked, his voice sounding exasperated.

"You know that I want you and Raine in my life. I love you both, and if Raine loves Kai and wants him in her life, then I trust her judgment."

I heard a loud sigh and almost felt the frustration coming through the door. "Fuck! Fine, I'll try if he will, but I want it to be known right now that I don't like it. I don't trust him." Jace bit out, and I chuckled at the disdain in his tone.

You and me both, Jace Everly.

Snake

8

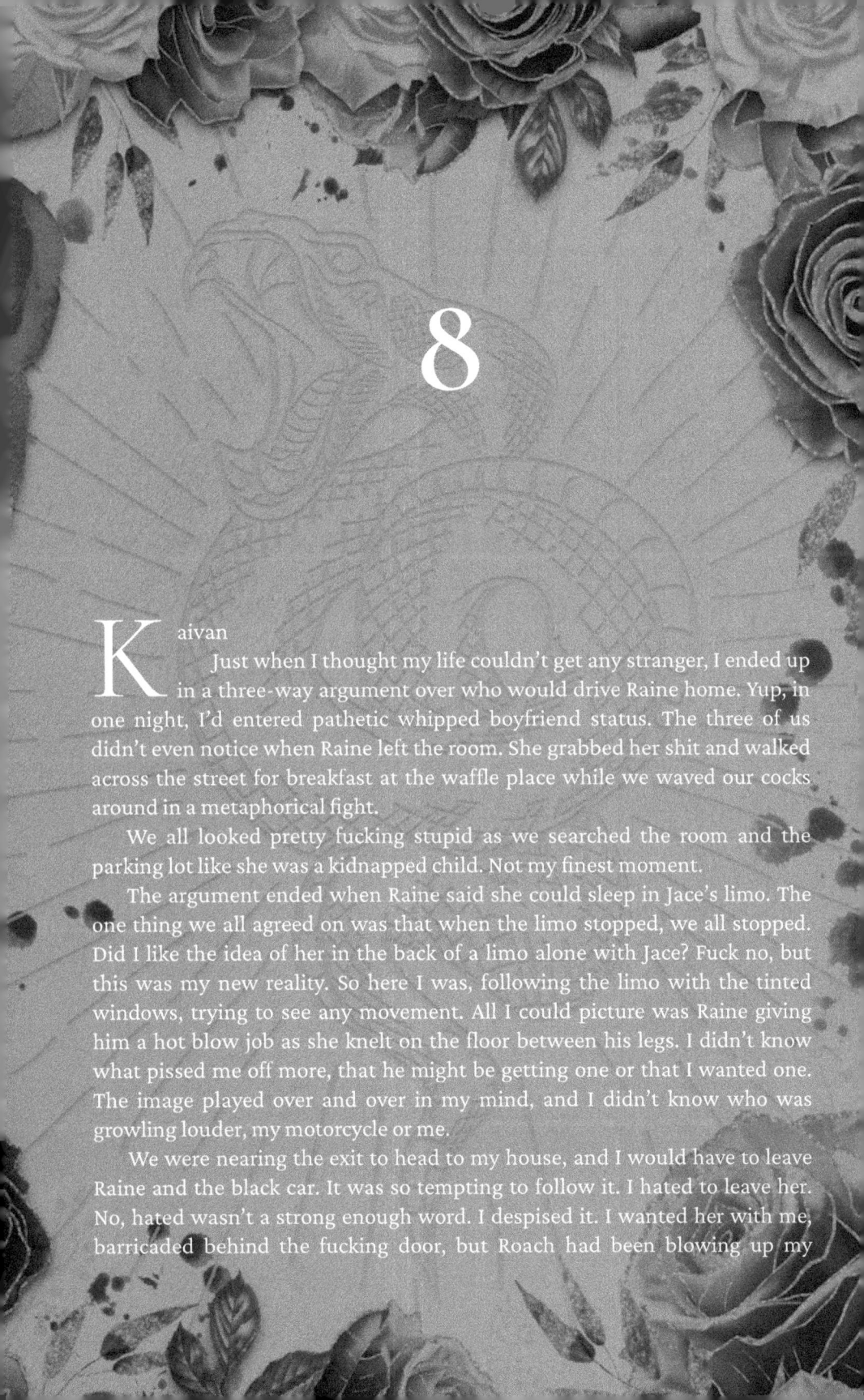

Kaivan

Just when I thought my life couldn't get any stranger, I ended up in a three-way argument over who would drive Raine home. Yup, in one night, I'd entered pathetic whipped boyfriend status. The three of us didn't even notice when Raine left the room. She grabbed her shit and walked across the street for breakfast at the waffle place while we waved our cocks around in a metaphorical fight.

We all looked pretty fucking stupid as we searched the room and the parking lot like she was a kidnapped child. Not my finest moment.

The argument ended when Raine said she could sleep in Jace's limo. The one thing we all agreed on was that when the limo stopped, we all stopped. Did I like the idea of her in the back of a limo alone with Jace? Fuck no, but this was my new reality. So here I was, following the limo with the tinted windows, trying to see any movement. All I could picture was Raine giving him a hot blow job as she knelt on the floor between his legs. I didn't know what pissed me off more, that he might be getting one or that I wanted one. The image played over and over in my mind, and I didn't know who was growling louder, my motorcycle or me.

We were nearing the exit to head to my house, and I would have to leave Raine and the black car. It was so tempting to follow it. I hated to leave her. No, hated wasn't a strong enough word. I despised it. I wanted her with me, barricaded behind the fucking door, but Roach had been blowing up my phone, and I refused to call him back. The fucker and his quest to stalk Lane could wait.

My hands ached, gripping the handlebars like I was trying to choke them to death as I forced myself to peel away from tailing the car. As soon as it was out of sight, my heart rate skyrocketed. This was insane. They were only going twenty minutes away, not taking off forever. Although I wouldn't put it passed Jace to drive to the airport and fucking take off. If I had a private jet, that's exactly what I'd be doing. I think I was going to need a few more trackers.

I rolled into the Lost Souls parking lot, and the gate rattled closed behind me. I glanced around for Wilder like he'd poke his head out of the grate or some shit but didn't see him in the bright afternoon sunshine.

"Snake," Mannix called out. I looked to the front door of the clubhouse as I dismounted the bike. "Where the fuck have you been?"

I ground my teeth together, annoyed with the interrogation. "Busy. What the fuck is up?"

"Roach has been trying to reach you. We're having an emergency meeting. Let's go." Mannix disappeared inside and I swore under my breath.

"Fuck, of course the one time I don't answer is the one time it's actually important," I grumbled, stomping to the door.

I yanked it open, letting it bang against the wall, and treated the stairs like they were my next victim. A few sweetbutts wandered around the lounge, which was odd for this time of day, as I made my way to the meeting room.

"Hey Snake, did you want me to help you get rid of that frown later?" I looked over at Dee. She smiled, but I didn't say anything. Dee was one of my regulars or had been. Not that I felt the urge to fuck her, but I didn't have time for sweetbutt shit right now.

I closed the door and pushed the thought out of my mind as the room bustled with activity. The secret door hidden behind a panel in the wall was open, and men were pulling out an assortment of guns and ammunition.

"What the hell is going on," I asked Roach as I stepped up beside him.

"Desert Vipers are on the move. May or may not be heading our way, but they are armed, and none of the old ladies are riding with them. Not a good sign."

"Fuck me. I knew this was going to happen sooner or later." I looked around the room at the men pulling on bulletproof vests and covering them with their T-shirts and leather jackets. This was bullshit. "How many of them are on the move?"

Roach slowly turned his head a looked at me, calm but worried. An emotion I didn't see on his face often. "All of them."

I shook my head and wanted to wrap my hands around Chase Mathers' throat and squeeze. I would say my piece if I lived. The satisfaction of punching Chase in the face was too tempting not to live. Stepping up to the open compartment, I grabbed a vest, and the noise slowly disappeared into the background.

"You love me?"

"I've always loved you."

The conversation with Raine played again in my mind.

"Hey man, you okay?" Roach gripped my shoulder, and I nodded, not bothering to say anything. What did you say when you realized that you actually gave a crap if you lived.

Quickly getting ready, I loaded my guns and made sure they were working well when an idea came to me.

"Be right back," I said to Roach and jogged out of the room.

"Is everything okay," Dee asked as I went through. All the girl's heads turned my way.

"I'd get a gun and a safe spot to hide. Kill anyone that is not one of us," I said and left them as they scattered. Jogging down the stairs, I pushed open the door and ran around the side of the large building. "Wilder? Hey man, are you here? Wilder?"

It would be my luck that the one time I actually wanted the guy to be stalking my ass, he wouldn't be anywhere in sight. A flash of light caught my eye, and I looked up toward the top platform of an old rollercoaster. I couldn't see anyone, but the reflection caught my eye again and it was too rhythmical to be anything but Morse code. I wasn't up on my code, so I lifted my hands in confusion, hoping Wilder understood I couldn't understand him. I got my answer as my phone rang a second later with an unknown number.

"Wilder?"

"Hey man, you should really get in a better spot than that if you're going to be fighting. You're out in the open."

I bit my lip. "Thanks for the tip," I drawled. "I take it you already know and are planning on helping?"

"Why else would I be on the top of a rollercoaster," he asked, and I'd never wanted to punch myself in the face so hard in my life.

"Okay, great." I pulled the phone away from my ear, but Wilder called my name. If it weren't for the fact I was pretty sure he had binoculars trained on me, I would've just hung up on him. "Yeah man?"

"I was thinking of getting her a friend to play with," he said. I waited to see if there was more to the random statement.

"I'm assuming you mean the girl you're interested in?"

"Who else would I be talking about." I turned away from him and bit my fist before I said what I really wanted to say. I needed his insane ass right now.

"Not sure, just felt it was best to clarify," I said.

"Good idea. It is always best to have a full understanding of any situation. Yes, the girl that fascinates me seems lonely."

Again with the veiled comments that had me picturing a girl trapped in a cell while he poked at her with a stick like she was an exhibit.

"So you want to get her a friend?"

"Yes, someone for her to play with and talk to," Wilder said.

"You sound like you're talking about a dog," I said.

"No, she is human."

Oh, for fucks sake, give me strength. "I assumed she was human, but it sounds like you're talking about a dog. Never mind. What do you mean by get her a friend? I'm pretty sure you can't just pick one of those up at the store unless you plan on choosing another of the sorority girls?"

"Hmm, I wish I could go to the store. That would make things easier."

"I have to head inside and finish getting ready for the fight, but if she seems lonely, then getting her a pet would be my suggestion. I'm not sure a random person will have the desired effect."

"A pet, now that is an interesting idea. What if I got her a friend that could also be her pet? That would serve two purposes in one." My hand stilled on the door to the front entrance of the club.

I really wanted to ask if he planned on dressing a person up like a dog or cat and telling them to pretend to be her pet. That was some kinky shit that I did not want to picture Wilder doing. Raine wearing a catsuit. Now that had fucking possibilities.

"You getting her a collar, too," I asked sarcastically.

"You think she'd like that?"

I smiled wide, the asshole in me needing this at the moment.

"Oh yes, I really do. Especially one that you can't get off and maybe some gemstones to make it look pretty," I said and chuckled to myself.

"See, this is why I keep coming to you for ideas. She is screaming less lately, and I owe that to you. Don't worry Snake, I have your back," Wilder said and then hung up.

I snorted and shook my head as I pictured what he was going to do to this poor girl, whoever she was. Why I didn't turn this into a game sooner was beyond me, but this was too good to pass up. Wilder never ceased to amaze and surprise me with his ability to confuse the fuck out of me and creep me out. Yet it was comforting to know that the crazy ass that was once a Green Beret would be watching my back.

Beast was coming down the stairs as I walked inside. "What's the latest," I asked.

"Nothing good. They divided into four groups and are coming at us from all different sides. I'm sending six guys to watch the back and the families, but...." He stopped, and I knew what he didn't want to say. It was what I'd been saying all along. Chase left us with our fucking pants down and no one to help.

"Doesn't matter now. What's the plan?"

Beast sighed, and for the first time, the mask he had worn for so long as the leader of this club slipped. Worry danced in his eyes.

"I think it's best to stay in here. This is our home, and we know all the hiding spots."

I rubbed my chin. "That's true. Are the cops staying away?"

Beast laughed. "Yeah. I heard from my friend at the department that they are telling their officers to let us fight it out and to stay out of the line of fire."

"Helpful," I said, rolling my eyes. "Of course, when we actually want the cops to come around, they are going to ghost."

Beast shrugged, his big shoulders dropping dramatically. "Makes it easier for us. At least this way, they're not on our doorstep, and we won't have to worry about them searching the premises."

I opened my mouth to answer when the sound of motorcycles could be heard a moment before the warning alarm went off. The red light and piercing siren sounded in the building.

"Inside it is," Beast said and ran up the stairs. "You coming," he asked when I didn't follow.

I shook my head no. "Can't have them trapping us and starting a fire," I yelled over the alarm. "I'm staying on this level."

"Fuck, why did you put that thought in my head," Beast said and took off as the roar of the motorcycles got louder until the entire building was shaking. The guards pulled open the doors a moment later, their eyes wide with fear.

"Head up to the roof with the M4s and stay low," I said, and they took off. I locked the door and brought the thick security bar down into place. It would hold for now. There were a few windows on this level that we never used, but if they got past those on the roof and couldn't get in the front door, this was their next point of entry.

I'd already walked the building a million times and found all the weak spots. It didn't matter if the rest of the club was here or not. We always ran the risk of being attacked. With them gone, I'd been extra diligent.

Marching into the back room we used for storage, I slipped through the piles of boxes and shelving units until I reached the three windows but stopped short when I felt a draft. Staring along the aisle, I spotted the open window and reached back for my gun. Movement caught the corner of my eye a moment before I was jumped.

The air was driven from my lungs as we collided with the unforgiving wall.

"Fuck," I growled and drove my knee up and my elbow down at the same time. The guy grunted as my knee connected with his stomach and yelled as I drove my elbow into his back three more times before he stumbled away. He came at me again, and we sailed past the first window and landed hard on the ground. I was really sick of being tackled. It had happened more than once in prison, then Jace, and now this guy.

I was all for ending up on my back, but not with this guy and not like this. There was no room to maneuver, but I managed to connect with the side of his face and ear before he could land a blow.

"Ah fuck," the guy yelled, and I recognized the voice as he rolled off, holding the side of his head.

"Sparky, what the fuck? Are you lost? I'm not a fucking intruder," I growled out and stood up, letting Sparky get to his feet.

Sparky was here when I got out of prison. He fixed all the bikes and did other mechanical work. I'd always known him as a fun, easygoing guy and one of the most loyal assholes in the group.

"Seriously, what the fuck?" I dabbed at the back of my head, but there was no blood.

"You should've left when you had the chance Snake," he said and held the side of his face as he stood up. I'd never seen him look so serious. If you wanted to laugh, you went to Sparky. "I actually liked you, but you should've just gone. I thought you had when you didn't come back last night."

"Leave the club? Why would I leave the club," I asked.

"You said it yourself. It was only a matter of time before another club knocked on our door to kill us, and here they are." He held his hand out toward the front of the building and the sound of gunfire. "I'm not dying like that. I know a losing side when I see one."

My eyebrows shot up, and you could've knocked me over with a feather. I was so shocked. Of all the members, he was the last I would've ever thought to go turncoat. "So, you planned to sneak out a window and slink to the other side like a fucking traitorous piece of shit?"

"No, not quite." Sparky pulled a gun and fired before I had time to flinch. The bullet hit center mass, and at this range, I flew off my feet and landed on the ground with a loud crash as I slammed into stacks of boxes. The contents went flying and littered the floor. My back arched up, and I gasped for air as I pulled at the front of my shirt. I couldn't get a grip on the vest to relieve some of the weight that felt like it was crushing me. I now knew what it felt like to be hit by a sledgehammer.

Sparky walked closer as I rolled onto my side and managed to take a wheezing breath. I knew this was it. I'd already used my nine lives, and it was time to pay up for all the shit I'd done.

"I really didn't want to kill anyone, and I liked you, Snake. I truly did."

I watched the arm holding the gun raise and stared down the barrel. "Don't do this, man." I coughed and managed to drag in another breath that felt like knives piercing my chest. "You're not a killer. It changes you," I managed to get out.

"You're leaving me no choice. I can't let you live. I'm sorry, Snake."

Taking a shuddering breath, I closed my eyes and pictured Raine's face. The way her eyes crinkled at the corners when she smiled and how her cheeks would pink slightly just from looking at me. I could feel her in my arms, and I couldn't get enough of the weight of her head lying on my chest as she held me tight. I wanted to take everything about her with me when my heart stopped beating. She was the only person I ever loved, and my only regret was that I wouldn't get more time with her.

"Fuck, I'm sorry, Snake."

Bang.

Snake

9

Kaivan

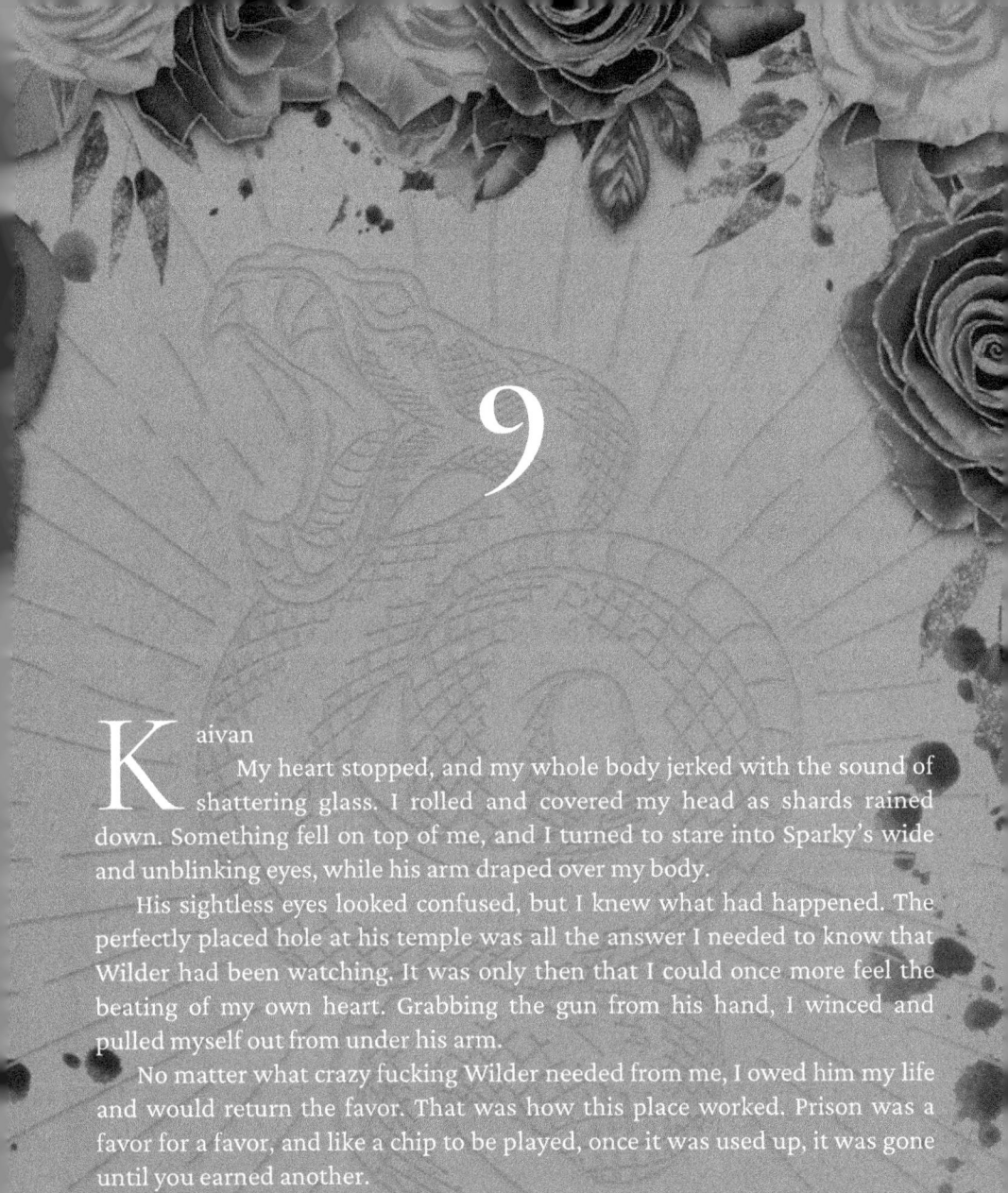

My heart stopped, and my whole body jerked with the sound of shattering glass. I rolled and covered my head as shards rained down. Something fell on top of me, and I turned to stare into Sparky's wide and unblinking eyes, while his arm draped over my body.

His sightless eyes looked confused, but I knew what had happened. The perfectly placed hole at his temple was all the answer I needed to know that Wilder had been watching. It was only then that I could once more feel the beating of my own heart. Grabbing the gun from his hand, I winced and pulled myself out from under his arm.

No matter what crazy fucking Wilder needed from me, I owed him my life and would return the favor. That was how this place worked. Prison was a favor for a favor, and like a chip to be played, once it was used up, it was gone until you earned another.

One thing that the MC had given me was a place where favors didn't come with an expiration date. I yanked my other leg out from under Sparky and got to my knees to pull at the Velcro sides of the bulletproof vest. Air was still hard to get in without the feeling of someone pressing on my chest, and I needed to take a moment to rest and assess the damage. The Desert Vipers had other ideas. Shadows could be seen passing the furthest window. I stayed low and crawled to the wall.

I couldn't hear any gunshots, but the yelling told me Wilder was picking guys off. The third window shattered with what sounded like an explosion, and I pulled up on my leather jacket to protect myself from the raining debris.

Guns were firing, and bullets were randomly sailing through the window, hitting boxes. Pieces of history and memories from members long past were torn apart with the rain of bullets.

A Viper jumped through the middle window. He landed and rolled before looking my way, and I sneered as I glared at my enemy. My hand moved fast, experience and instinct putting two bullets in the Viper before he got his gun up. Another member tried to jump through the window, but he wasn't as graceful. He screamed as he landed on the bottom portion of the shattered window piercing his stomach as he hung half in and half out. He fell back out a moment later, leaving a trail of blood sliding down the wall.

I knew they would keep trying to get in. This was the only decent access point, and we were so low on men that they would easily overwhelm us.

If I ever wanted to know what being on The Walking Dead was like, I'd just gotten my wish as more men tried to pile through the windows. Their moans and yells were loud as bullets hit them. The floor and the boxes were now coated in blood.

Sparky had planned on giving them an easy in, but I'd fucked with that. What started as five guys turned into ten. I fired as men yanked the dead out of the way and leaped through the frames to find me on the other side. My guns clipped empty, and I quickly reloaded one, but I didn't have the right size clip for Sparky's gun and dropped it to the ground. I fired faster than I could keep up with the sheer number of men crawling over one another to get into the windows. The pile of dead, dying, or groaning people on the floor was building up like a wall.

"What the fuck zombie movie did I wake up in?" I grumbled as one of the guys I shot pulled himself across the floor, leaving a blood trail in his wake. I quickly put a bullet in his head as he reached his hand out for me.

"Get the fuck in the window. We need to get in there." A loud voice boomed as my gun clicked empty for the second time. *Shit.* I reached for another clip, but it was missing. *Fuck.* It must have fallen out when Sparky shot me.

Dropping to my knees, I crawled to one of the dead Vipers. Each movement felt like being stabbed in my side. Grabbing the gun, I pried it out of his hands and checked the clip.

"Full, thank fuck."

The gunfire outside was getting louder. I wasn't surprised. We'd been sitting with a bleeding limb in a frenzy of sharks and no boat to save us.

Sliding across the floor to my vantage point, I caught my breath. I really needed to get this fucking vest off. Leaning against the wall, I managed to pull myself upright when the sound of heavy boots coming down the hall drew my attention. Gripping the gun tight, I shifted positions slightly to see who it was. The cool metal felt heavy in my hand, my finger rubbing over the trigger. Was this going to be it? I figured I would die like this at some point, but I didn't think today would be the day.

If it wasn't my guys, I would have a hell of a fight on my hands, but as the shadows stepped into the light, I sighed and slumped against the wall. It was fucking Tanner leading the charge. I'd never been so fucking happy to see his face.

"What the fuck took you so long?" I barked out as Tanner jogged the rest of the way to me and then shot a guy that stuck his head through the window.

"Traffic was a bitch. What the hell are you doing starting the festivities without me? You know I like to party."

I snorted. "Have at 'em," I said.

"You heard him. Let's have some fun! Yippie ki-yay mother fuckers!" Tanner did his Bruce Willis impression. I shook my head as he hooted and hollered, firing at the living and the already dead. More men piled through the door, and soon anyone outside the windows was retreating.

You needed to be careful when it came to Tanner. He had a knack for taking a shit storm and somehow turning it into a shit hurricane and not in your favor.

I let my leather jacket drop so I could peel my vest off and winced, reaching around to grab the velcro.

"Snake, fuck," Roach said as he joined the room now filled with Lost Souls members. "Shit, you okay." His worried eyes scanned me as I leaned, panting against the wall.

"I need help getting the vest off," I said. Roach grabbed the Velcro sides, pulled hard, and lifted it off over my head. He dropped it to the floor with a thud. Without the weight of the thirty-pound vest, I took a shuddering breath.

"I have no idea how cops wear those all the time, fuck, they're terrible," I said.

"Lift your shirt." My hands shook from the boost of adrenaline still coursing through my body, but I got the T-shirt lifted enough to show Roach.

"We need to have you looked at," Roach said, ignoring my cop joke. My eyes flicked to his as he pulled out his phone, and I knew he was calling the doc we always used for the club.

Reaching out, I squeezed his forearm as he spoke into the phone. His eyes found mine as he relayed the information and location. Roach said nothing as we stared at one another, but I knew what he was thinking. I was fucking lucky. We may not have been blood brothers or even childhood friends, but we had a friendship that had seen the worst and lived to tell the tale.

"Thanks," I said, as he hung up the phone.

That one word held so much weight for me. I didn't thank or rely on people, but Wilder had just saved my life, and I knew Roach would've jumped in the way of that bullet if given the chance. I was grateful for their friendship, something I hadn't fully realized until now.

Looking down, there was a black bruise already forming. I gently touched the spot and knew I had at least one cracked rib. I knew the feeling all too well, having had more than my fair share in life.

I was fucking lucky, though. If the bullet had been a couple of inches higher, it would've been a direct blow to my heart. From such a short distance, it could've stopped it for good.

I placed my hand over the beating organ. "I love you, Raine," I whispered as the gunfire dwindled and stopped.

"Fuck, they're retreating. Bunch of fucking dicks. I was having fun," Tanner said and ran out of the room.

"Let me help you get upstairs," Roach offered when everyone was gone.

"Naw, I need a moment alone." He nodded, turned, and disappeared down the hall.

Emotions locked up tight were set loose, and I covered my face and let a tear fall. I almost died the same way my mother had. Choking on blood with no one to help, and all I could think about was that I would never see Raine again.

The next breath I sucked into my lungs had never felt so sweet.

Jace

10

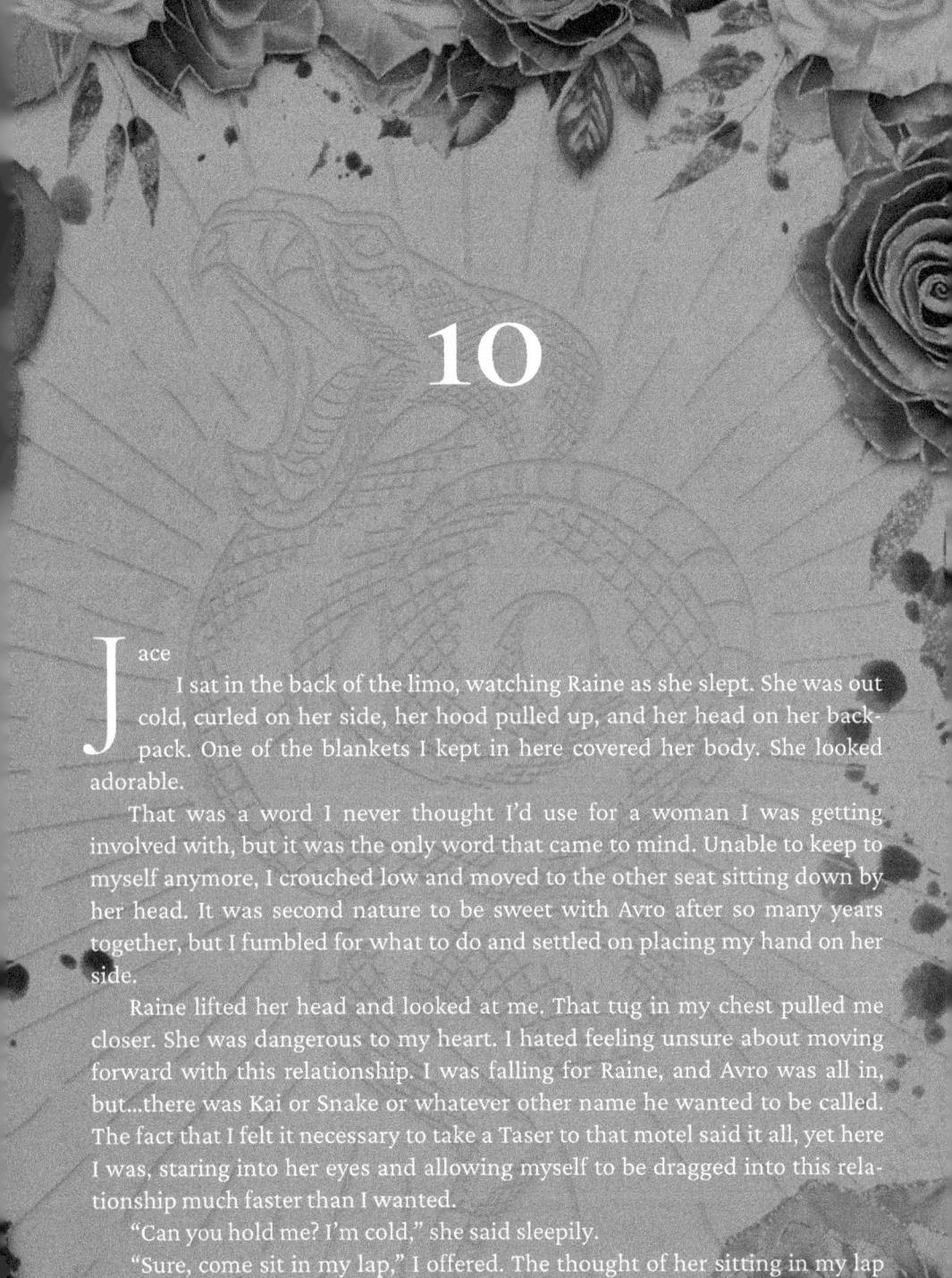

Jace

I sat in the back of the limo, watching Raine as she slept. She was out cold, curled on her side, her hood pulled up, and her head on her backpack. One of the blankets I kept in here covered her body. She looked adorable.

That was a word I never thought I'd use for a woman I was getting involved with, but it was the only word that came to mind. Unable to keep to myself anymore, I crouched low and moved to the other seat sitting down by her head. It was second nature to be sweet with Avro after so many years together, but I fumbled for what to do and settled on placing my hand on her side.

Raine lifted her head and looked at me. That tug in my chest pulled me closer. She was dangerous to my heart. I hated feeling unsure about moving forward with this relationship. I was falling for Raine, and Avro was all in, but...there was Kai or Snake or whatever other name he wanted to be called. The fact that I felt it necessary to take a Taser to that motel said it all, yet here I was, staring into her eyes and allowing myself to be dragged into this relationship much faster than I wanted.

"Can you hold me? I'm cold," she said sleepily.

"Sure, come sit in my lap," I offered. The thought of her sitting in my lap and having her all to myself was fucking enticing. As Raine sat up, I slid to the center of the seat and smirked as she crawled into my lap like a cat before sitting down and cuddling into my chest.

Fuck all that shit about it not being right to want to protect your girl. There was nothing that felt as good as this. Raine needed me, and it wasn't for something fancy or expensive or because I was Jace Everly. I was desired on a primal level that until you had it, you couldn't explain it, but we all craved it. Every person out there wanted to be needed like this. To feel vital to someone's existence.

I spent too much time warding myself against those who wanted to use me for something. It came with the territory, and some of it I genuinely didn't mind. Like helping a new and talented musician get started. But there was a lot of bad that came with the good. Those who just wanted my money or to be seen with me to enhance their careers. It made it tough to know who was legit and who wasn't.

Grabbing the edges of my jacket, I wrapped the bomber around her body and linked my fingers together. She sighed and wiggled closer, pressing right on my cock.

"Jace?"

"Yeah Peaches."

"Are you angry with me for wanting Kai to be part of us," she asked, and my immediate response was fuck yes. But that wasn't the whole truth.

I sighed, settling deeper into the seat, wishing I could see her face. "No, I'm not angry. I'm scared for all of us, and when I'm scared, I'm an even larger ornery asshole than normal." She chuckled, her body vibrating. I bit my lip to keep myself in check as her ass rubbed against me. "The problem is Peaches that you see who you want Kai to be, which is the person you knew. I see who he's become. I see him as clearly as I understand myself, and the dangerous edge is never far from the surface. He would snap my neck if given the opportunity, and right now, the only thing keeping him from doing that is the fear of losing you."

Raine turned her head, and for just a moment, I considered having the driver take us to the private jet and forcing her to get on. It was irrational, I didn't really want to kidnap her, but old fears that I'd managed to tame over the years were gripping me by the throat.

"You may be right for now, but Kai is as loyal as they come. If you two find common ground, it won't just be me that holds things together."

I rubbed my eyes. "I need to be careful, Peaches. I'm always in the spotlight. If I'm found hanging around with an MC member who is most likely a killer, it will make headlines worldwide, career-ending headlines. That doesn't just put me at risk. That puts all of us, including Kai, at risk. He will never be able to go anywhere without people filming him, and forget wiping his record if they start digging into what he's been doing for the club since he got out...."

"Oh shit," she said, sitting a little straighter in my arms. "I hadn't even thought about that. I mean, I knew you were always being watched, but it didn't dawn on me the implications with Kai." She paused, and her brow furrowed. "Do you really think he's killed people?"

"More than one, and I'm not saying that to scare you. I'm simply stating a fact. He's an enforcer. That's what they do. They ensure other groups don't want to mess with their club and teach a lesson to those that have. Besides, he has a look in his eye that tells me he's far more comfortable with death than most people."

Raine pulled down the hood on her sweatshirt and stared at me. "How would you know that?"

I swallowed and looked away from her. "Killing someone changes you. I mean, those in the military will tell you that, and police officers as well. He has that closed-off dead look," I said, covering up the real reason. I wasn't sure I was ready to share that particular secret with anyone. Some secrets were better left in the past and never spoken about again.

Raine looked around the car and then back up at me. "Why are you being so understanding and nice? Are we being recorded or something?"

I laughed and gripped her face with one hand, squeezing her cheeks enough that her lips puckered. "Do you like me being the asshole, Peaches?" She swallowed, the sound loud in the quiet car. "You want me to bring up that overnight you've turned into a cock slut?"

Raine's face flamed bright red, and she narrowed her eyes at me. "Nowhere to run off to in here," I said as she shifted like she was going to move away. I nipped at her bottom lip, which was begging to be kissed. "I'm always the asshole," I whispered in her ear. Raine rolled her eyes at me, making me smile, but I felt the slight wiggle of her ass on my cock.

"Tell me, Jace. Is this the real you, or is the sweet guy that wanted to keep me warm the real you?"

"Why can't they both be me? I'm not one-dimensional, but I do love getting you all fired up. I bet if I checked, you're already wet and ready for me."

She crossed her arms. "Don't you wish."

I chuckled again. "Should I check?"

"Okay, can I have nice Jace back? Is there like an off switch to this one or something?" I laughed hard, something that I didn't often do, and as hard as she tried to hold it back, Raine ended up laughing as well.

Sobering, I smirked at her. "Good luck. Avro has tried for years and still hasn't found one."

"How does he put up with you," Raine asked, yet the question hit close to things I didn't want to look at. I'd been lucky to call Avro my friend, and I won the lottery when it turned out his feelings for me were as strong as mine for him. How I'd managed to hang onto him this long was a mystery.

"I was joking," Raine said, her hand landing on my chest over my heart like she sensed the fear and sadness that filled me.

A smile tugged at the corner of my mouth as I traced my thumb across her lower lip. I wanted to lose myself in her. "I know, Peaches." An idea struck. "I have an awards show I need to attend coming up, and I want you to go with me."

Raine's mouth fell open before she started to laugh all over again. "You can't be serious?"

"Why not?" I shrugged. "I have to take someone. I've already been told that I can't attend alone. Which means I will end up at the mercy of Allen and what and who he decides. He wants drama, so lord knows what he has cooking."

"You're serious," she asked.

Picking her up, Raine wrapped her hands around my neck as she straddled my lap. I groaned as her ass settled into place. Sliding my hands under her hoodie, I sighed as my fingers came into contact with her smooth, warm skin.

"I'm very serious," I said as I unclipped her bra with one hand, the material springing apart. My cock thickened as she moaned under my touch. "I don't invite people to go with me, Peaches. I've always been assigned someone that will make me look good or start a conversation. You know what they say, 'No headline is a bad headline.' But, I'd like to have someone that I want by my side for once."

"I'm not sure I'm red carpet material," Raine said, her voice breathy as I pushed the sweatshirt up over her tits. Pulling her closer, I sucked the first nipple into my mouth and loved how it hardened as she squirmed in my lap.

"You're more red carpet material than I am," I said, then switched nipples to give the other one equal treatment. "Fuck you taste good." My tongue licked over the sensitive tip, and Raine moaned loudly. Nails seductively scraped the back of my neck as I teased her.

"Take off your hoodie and T-shirt," I ordered, my mouth finding her soft skin as soon as the material was out of the way.

"Oh fuck," Raine moaned. "I don't know if I'm ready for such a huge public event like that," she said.

"You never are." It was an honest answer. I'd thought I knew what I was getting into, but I had no idea. "I almost threw up when I stepped out of the limo, and all the lights started flashing."

"Not a selling point," Raine teased, and even though I couldn't see her face, I could picture the look she was giving me. I gently nipped at her nipple, and she yelped but wiggled closer.

"That's it. Keep wiggling on my cock like a good girl," I said, and let my tongue trail a line from her nipple all the way up to her collarbone. Gripping the back of her neck, I pulled her closer and growled against the soft skin under her ear. "Do you really want me to go with some random girl?"

She stiffened, and I smiled. "We'll have to hold hands and kiss for the cameras. I'll have to stare longingly into her eyes and answer questions like we're hot for each other." My breath fanned her skin, and goosebumps rose, making her shiver. "Maybe get caught coming out of one of the private areas with our hair a mess and cleaning lipstick off my face to get the rumors flying."

Raine made a little sound in her throat like she was growling. Fuck, that turned me on. I'd always played it off like Avro's jealousy was too much and over the top, but I secretly loved it, and it made me so hot for him. When I could, I would make a special trip home to surprise him after the event. It was always the same each time I had to go to one. Avro would text me every fifteen minutes, sending me dirty photos and videos that made it hard to focus on a single conversation, and insisted on having phone sex when I got back to the hotel. He may have said he was fine with our lifestyle, but he didn't like it splashed on television, especially when I needed to pretend to be in love with someone else.

Raine had the same jealous streak, she may not fully realize it yet, but I knew she would lose her mind if she saw girls hanging on me. The anger was vibrating off her now, making me so fucking hard.

"Is that what you want, Peaches? For me to pretend to be fucking another woman for all the cameras. Maybe have to pretend to live together for a while before it all falls apart?"

"I don't fucking care," she said, but her clenched jaw and tight, annoyed tone told an entirely different story.

"Okay then, I'll call Allen and set someone up. Maybe two this time," I said and pulled away from her neck as I reached for my cell. She grabbed my forearm, and her eyes were fierce as she stared into mine. "Something wrong? I thought you said you didn't care?"

"I thought you said you wouldn't be with anyone else?"

"Peaches, this is not cheating. This is part of my job. Just like a hooker offers sexual favors for money, this is something I must also do." It was a stretch, but the sparks of rage in her eyes were too much for me not to toy with a little longer.

"You're comparing yourself to a hooker," she asked, and I had to bite the inside of my cheek not to smirk.

"Like I said, just part of the job. Would be nice to have someone there that isn't just grabbing my ass and cock for the cameras," I said, pouring it on thick. I tried to move my arm, but she held it firm.

"I'll go," she said.

"Are you sure? You don't seem that interested. I really can just call Allen," I said. "I mean, Avro is used to it, and I don't want to force you to go if you'll be that uncomfortable?"

"Fuck you, Jace. I'm going," she growled.

"If you say so." Dropping my cell, I cupped her face. "You're so fucking hot, and I bet you'll look like a damn queen in a designer dress. Avro will be drooling back here."

"Why don't we take him too?"

"To the awards?" I bit my lip at the possible backlash and wondered if I really cared. I didn't. But as open and all-inclusive as things had become, that might create more of a stir than even Allen was ready for. I would do it in a heartbeat, but Avro hated the spotlight. Crazy considering what he'd planned on doing for a career before his knee surgeries. He kept telling me that was different. I didn't see the difference.

"No, he can stay at the hotel. I'm sure you're going to have a room, right?" She lifted a shoulder and let it drop. "He can be waiting for us there."

"I like that idea a lot." Gripping her ass harder, I pulled her tight against my body and stared up into her blue eyes. "You know what other idea I really like the thought of?" A coy smile played along her lips, but she devilishly shook her head. "Having you all to myself."

Raine's eyes held a mischievous glint, and as she opened her mouth, I wrapped my hand around her throat. "Don't bother lying to me, Peaches. I know your pussy is fucking wet for me." I gave her throat a little squeeze, and her hands tightened on my shoulders. "You want to wiggle right now. Rub yourself along my cock," I growled. "You can barely contain yourself."

She shuddered, her pulse jumping under my fingers. "Not a chance," she whispered.

The devil would've been impressed with the smile I gave her. "Then prove it, take your jeans off, and let's find out."

"I don't need to prove anything to you," she quipped.

"No, but you will."

"And why is that?"

"Because if you don't take them off," I said, pulling her close enough to attack her lips and leave her gasping for her next breath as I tasted every inch of her sweet mouth. "I'll rip them off your body and fuck you on the floor with the partition to my driver down, rather than here on the seat, without an audience. Your choice," I said and smirked. "Go ahead and call my bluff and find out if I care about being seen fucking you."

I released her body and let her decide. "What if I said I didn't want you at all?"

"You could. I'm not going to pull a Kai on you," I smirked, but her eyes flickered with the jab.

"Asshole," she said. Her tone was angry, but her eyes were sad, and even though I knew I may have pushed the line too far, I also didn't regret it. Why did Kai get a hall pass? She needed to treat us all the same if she was serious about us all being one.

"Yes, I am, but it only bothers you because I poke at things you don't want to look at. Go ahead and deny it, but I'd call you a liar."

I could see her wanting to argue. Her eyes said it all—if looks could kill, I'd already be dead—and that was the sexiest look ever. Raine's body tensed, and her hands balled into fists which made me smile wider. Her nostrils flared as she sucked in a deep breath.

"Do it, hit me. It won't change the fact you want to fuck me, and it won't stop me from being an asshole." Raising my hips as we went over a bump, Raine lost her balance. She gripped my shoulders, which put her nipple right in front of my mouth. Taking advantage of the angle, I flicked it with my tongue. "In fact, hitting me will only have the opposite effect. I like you all fired up."

"You and Kai both," she said, and I was sure that the comment was supposed to sting.

"Means he has good taste in at least one thing," I said. "Besides, if he wants to challenge me in the bedroom, he can come at me. I'd love nothing more than to play who can last longer and make you scream louder." Raine's eyes widened, and she swallowed hard. "Now, are you taking your jeans off, or am I taking them off for you?"

Her hands went to the button.

"Good choice, Peaches."

I shouldn't push her the way I did, it was bound to blow up in my face at some point, but I couldn't help it. There was something about Raine that made me want to push her to her limits. See just how much she would take before she snapped.

Slipping off my lap, she finished undoing her jeans, glaring at me the entire time she pulled them down her legs and set them aside.

"Come here," I ordered. My cock throbbed as I stared at her naked body and the wet patch on the hot as fuck, boy shorts she was wearing. There was something entirely too sexy about this look. My muscles tensed as she maneuvered so she was on her knees on the seat beside me, her tits swaying hypnotically with the movement of the car.

"Now mine," I said.

"I'm making a mental note never to ask about asshole Jace again," she said. Her blue eyes were full of the same fire as earlier. I wanted to shove her naughty mouth down on my cock until she was choking. My hand itched to teach her sexy ass a lesson. I wanted to leave bright pink handprints all over it but held myself in check.

"I bet you are," I drawled as she undid my belt and the buttons on my jeans. I liked the button-down style, less chance of zipping my cock or my piercings in the little metal teeth after I've had a few drinks. Been there and never want to do it again.

Lifting my ass up, Raine pulled down on my jeans, and my overly eager cock sprang from the confines. The silver ring was already shiny from my excitement. Raine's eyes tracked the movement of my cock, hypnotized by the sight.

"Don't worry, Peaches, I plan on having my cock down your throat soon enough, but I want you now, so those fun games will have to wait." Raine opened her mouth, a scowl drawing her eyebrows together. Reaching out, I put my finger on her lips. "Don't bother with the attitude." I wiped at the corner of her mouth and the imaginary drool. "I can already see how much you want my cock."

I stuck my thumb in my mouth and sucked as Raine's eyebrow arched up. Removing it, I held it out to her. She glared and opened her mouth. I hooked it over her bottom teeth, and she growled at me seductively as I pulled her closer like she was on the end of my line.

I forced her onto my lap so she was settled in place and resting on my hard cock that remembered all too well what it felt like to be inside her tight pussy.

"Suck it," I ordered, and groaned as she sucked my thumb and swirled her tongue around the tip. "Now raise your hips," I said and then flicked my gaze up to hers. "Did I say you could stop sucking?"

She bit down slightly, and I smirked, shifting under her. Using my free thumb, I rubbed at her clit as she moaned and shuddered for me.

"That's it, Peaches, give in to what you want. There is nothing wrong with wanting to be my slut. I will treat you like fucking gold, but I have some unusual tastes. Fucking you in public, for example, or chasing you down as you run away, both of which you already found out at the cemetery." Raine moved her hips back and forth, making me wet with each twitch of her sexy ass.

"What else?"

I groaned and watched my cock sliding between her legs. "I like to watch and to be in charge. Put them all together, and it's a potent cocktail I'll always be down for. Does that make you nervous?"

She shocked me when she shook her head no. "Good. Now lift your hips."

She didn't hesitate this time and braced herself on my shoulders as she lifted enough that I could straighten my cock and find that sweet entrance. As soon as I was in place, she sucked in a sexy ragged breath and slid all the way down as she threw her head back and moaned.

Fuck she was stunning. I clenched my jaw tight with her heat soaking into my cock, making it want to explode.

"You feel so fucking good, Peaches," I growled out and gripped her tits to fondle as I feasted on them. The little whimpers of pleasure were like the sweetest song to my ears. I could listen to her all day and never tire.

Taking me by surprise, she kissed me hard, her tongue slipping into my mouth, seeking out my tongue piercing like it was her toy.

"Fuck me, Peaches. Ride my cock," I managed to get out as she broke the kiss. Grabbing her ass tight, Raine rose up and back down. As she picked up the pace, I encouraged her faster, my fingers pressing into the soft skin.

"God, Jace," Raine moaned, then sucked my bottom lip into her mouth. Her hands ran all over my chest, slipping under the material to tweak my nipples and play with my piercings. "I love these," she said.

"Fuck," I groaned, with her endless exploring. She bounced faster and nipped at the side of my neck. The girl was making me wild. I was coming undone in the back of my limo, a completely new experience. Despite what the entertainment magazines thought, I had never held orgies in the back of this thing. In reality, it was my office away from my office. I never let anyone travel with me unless it was a scheduled appearance, and we would hardly speak, let alone fuck.

"You going to cum for me? You going to cum all over my cock?"

"Yes."

"You have no idea how badly I want to put down the windows so everyone can see me fucking you." I smirked. "But I won't, at least not today," I added as her mouth fell open. "Come on, Peaches. You want to let go. Do it. I want your cum. Give it to me. Soak my cock." I slapped her ass, and she moaned louder as she feverishly picked up the pace. My hips thrust up fast and hard as I drove into her at a blinding pace. "You're thinking about two cocks in you, aren't you, Peaches? Two of us filling your holes as we use you, and you want it. You want it so bad, don't you?"

"God, yes," Raine cried out as she wrapped her arms around my neck and hung on tight as the orgasm hit her body. She bit down hard on my neck and screamed. The sound muffled as I continued to hammer into her. I groaned at the feel of her marking me. It spoke to the monster that I kept buried deep inside of me. The monster that wanted to feel her struggle beneath me while she was unsure if she was screaming for me to stop or fuck her harder. I could feel the waves of her release coating me as the walls of her pussy clamped down around my cock.

"Peaches, you're so good, fuck you're amazing. I'm almost there." The sound of slapping skin was loud as my cock drilled deeper into her with each thrust and had Raine whimpering all over again. "Fuck yes, right there. Rub yourself, keep cumming for me." Her hand slipped between our bodies and rubbed her clit as she moaned out my name over and over, feeding my soul.

A thought came to me, and I stopped moving. I gripped Raine's chin hard and savored the worried look in her eyes. "Did he cum in you?"

Raine bit her lip. "I'll take that as a yes."

"Yes," she said, her voice wispy as she wiggled, trying to get me to continue.

"Well then, Peaches, I guess it's a race to see who can get you pregnant first." She opened her mouth, and I didn't wait to see if she would argue, fucking her harder than before.

"Ah! Jace!" Raine screamed, her head thrown back as the climax she was riding gripped her again. The sound of my name coming from her mouth like that was all I could handle. My back arched, and Raine hung on to me tighter as I came, the release so powerful that I felt frozen in place as she continued to bounce and drain my cock of all I had.

Panting, Raine draped herself over me, and I held her close. "So many fucking positions I want to fuck you in, Peaches."

"Is that so?"

"Yeah, and I can't wait to get back and gloat that I've had you twice to myself," I said and smiled as she leaned back and hit me with her patented glare.

"You really are an ass."

Cupping her face, I kissed her long and slow, allowing myself the luxury of her soft pillowy lips. "You'll fall in love with it. I can promise you that."

"Always so sure of yourself."

"I'm sure of you," I said, grabbing her discarded hoodie and wrapping it around her shoulders. "What you crave deep down is what I can give you. What I'm willing to give you. What I want to give you."

"And what exactly is it that you think I want?" Her voice was soft as she cuddled into me, seeking my warmth.

"You want to let yourself go and feel safe." Raine didn't say anything. "You're safe with me. I will protect you, Peaches. However I can, and I won't stop." She kissed my neck softly. "And you want to experience everything you've denied yourself for years. You want the three of us to give it to you. I don't like Kai, and I certainly don't trust him, but I get the appeal. I said I'd try with him, and that means I'm in until he gives me a reason not to be." She made a little sound, and I wasn't sure if she was crying, but she held me tighter. "And you love to be praised. I've figured out another one of your kinks, and I'm going to keep finding them, and I'm going to fuck you in all the ways you crave."

"You confuse me, Jace," she said softly, and I chuckled.

"I confuse myself, so we're even."

"I'll move." She went to get up, but I held her tight.

"Oh no, you don't. We have another hour left in this ride. That gives me lots of time to have you again, and this time, I'm going to tan your ass every time you disobey me."

I smiled as she shivered.

Oh yeah, I was falling for her, fast and hard, like I was jumping off the tall diving board. This was why I didn't stay. I knew myself too well. Avro and now Raine were filling up my heart. If Kai came at us again in any way, I'd be prepared, but I prayed that it never came to that.

Raine's body relaxed, and her breathing deepened as she napped. I really did have a thing for being needed and kissed the top of her head.

I grabbed my phone and found the latest text from Allen, who was still freaking out over me turning the plane around and missing the interview he'd set up. I was purposely ignoring my bandmates, who were just as pissed off. They were used to me going rogue, but even I didn't miss concerts or interviews. That was money out of our pockets and looked terrible without a good excuse. I had a great excuse, but they wouldn't see it that way. I did have an idea, though.

J: You said you wanted a good story to sell before the awards show. I have one for you.

A: I'm not speaking to you.

I smirked at his response. I could easily picture him pouting somewhere, half wasted, looking like he'd been drug in from a back alley by a tom cat.

J: I'll make the last concert on the list. Re-schedule the interview with my apologies that it was an emergency, and I have a date for the awards.

A: Please tell me it's Taylor Swift

I glared at my phone.

J: I've told you a million times we're just friends.

A: I can keep hoping. Fine, who is it, and don't say some cousin of yours. I can't spin that, no matter how hard I try.

My face screwed up as I stared at the message.

J: No, she's not a family member. What kind of fucked up question is that anyway? How much have you been drinking?

A: Lots, I deal with you daily. You're giving me a fucking ulcer Jace.

J: Her name is Raine Eastman, and she is not rich or famous or a princess, before you fucking ask.

A: You mean the manager from the bar? What good is she?

I ground my teeth together as I stared at the question. I couldn't tell if he was purposely trying to be a dick, but the implied tone was pissing me off.

> J: What do you mean?"

> A: I mean, if she has no pull, clout, or workable drama, then what good is she?

I squeezed my phone tight as I glared at the screen even though Allen couldn't see me. This was what I hated. I loved the music, I loved writing and recording and even singing for the fans, but this bullshit was what I was sick of. My fingers hovered over the keypad as I thought of what to say. How did I explain Raine to him and not mention Avro or Kai?

> J: She's the girl that I love.

Did I love her? I didn't know yet, but it felt like that was where we were heading and what I needed to say to shut Allen up. There was no immediate response. The little dots appeared and disappeared multiple times. I couldn't believe that I had just typed that to Allen. I couldn't believe I typed it at all. Raine sighed, and I could feel her breathing even out as she slept in my arms.

> A: I don't know what to say. I don't know how this happened, and I don't know if this is a good thing or not. I mean, I thought the show you did there was the first time you met.

> J: Of course, it's a fucking good thing. Raine is coming with me to the awards show, and I don't need to explain myself.

> A: Not to be a downer here, but you better have some answers prepared because there will be a ton of questions, and they won't just be coming for you. They'll go after her if they sense she's the weak link in the story.

Allen wasn't wrong about that. It meant I needed to prep Raine before she spoke to any reporter or interviewers without me by her side.

> J: I'll make sure she is prepared. I want the penthouse booked at the same hotel I stayed at last time. Put the room under Mr. Beck.

Allen knew that I liked to fuck Avro, but he didn't know just how close we were or what his last name was. This way, Avro could book in and get all the keys, and we'd never even have to put my name on a room.

> A: Who the hell is that? Do you suddenly have an alter ego?

> J: Just do it.

> A: Fine.

> J: Oh, and Allen. If you dig up shit on Raine and try to exploit it, I will fire you. Not even a moment of hesitation, I mean it.

I really wanted to say that I'd destroy him, and they'd never find his body, but you just didn't put shit like that in a text. At least not if you were smart.

> A: Why are you always making my life difficult, Jace?

> J: It's just my nature.

I quickly left the chat with Allen and found the group chat with the band that had completely blown up. Sighing, I started answering questions. Glancing down at Raine in my arms, I knew I'd do it all over again.

Snake

11

Kaivan

Holding my side, I stomped around the far corner of the clubhouse.

"What the fuck do you mean it's just you guys? Where the hell is Chase?" I looked around at the added fifty-two people and ground my teeth together. We were up to a whopping eighty-two since Sparky was now gator bait with the rest of the trash.

Tanner bit off another piece of the banana he was eating, and I was fucking tempted to jam the thing down his throat when he winked at one of the sweetbutts and shoved the entire thing in his mouth. Of course, now the guy chewed like a fucking cow with a mouthful of cud and gave me a view of the yellow mush moving around his open gob. He was giving me flashbacks to prison and making me want to vomit. If I did, I was aiming it at him.

"Just what I said, he didn't come back with us. Shit is pretty much wrapped up, but he still had some crap to sort out with Keenan." Tanner lifted his shoulders and let them drop.

"Hey sweetheart," Tanner yelled and pointed at the couch with every one of the sweetbutts occupying a lap. Both Mannix and I rolled our eyes when they all pointed at themselves. "Yeah, sure, any of you. Someone get me more food, and I want a bottle of whiskey. Oh! And one of you better be ready to fuck me soon."

My hand clenched as I fantasized about knocking this guy the fuck out.

Had I been this annoying at twenty-two? Naw, I was already four years into my sentence and a hardened, miserable prick by twenty-two.

"Can we focus," I asked, glaring at Tanner's smiling face. He'd already chugged a few drinks and was more annoying and immature than ever.

"I am. On my stomach. Next will be my cock, 'cause it's hungry too," Tanner said. He took a swig of the latest beer before letting out a loud belch that sounded like his name before pointing at one of the girls.

Luckily Mannix stepped in before I decided that a couple of cracked ribs were no big deal and beat the shit out of Tanner.

Mannix grabbed Tanner by the arm.

"Hey, what are you doing man?" Tanner whined as Mannix marched him off to the meeting room and away from the other guys. Roach and I followed.

I kept looking out of the corner of my eye to see if anyone was more interested than they should be, but I didn't see anything unusual. Didn't mean shit, as I found out, but I felt like I needed to interrogate all those left here while Chase was away. I bitched about Chase, fuck, I didn't even like the guy, but it took next-level scum to switch clubs and do what Sparky had planned. If I left, it would be to lay my pale white ass on a beach somewhere for the rest of my breathing days.

Once inside the meeting room reserved for church sessions, I closed the door so no one else could eavesdrop.

"Where the fuck is Beast? He wouldn't let you treat me like this," Tanner complained as Mannix released his arm.

"Beast had other things to take care of, and my guess would be that he didn't think you'd act like a newbie and force me to drag you in here," Mannix drawled, crossing his arms over his chest. I bit my tongue to keep from laughing. Being called a newbie or a bootlicker was a huge insult to anyone in the club once you'd been here for over a year.

Tanner had been a breath of fresh air after being in prison for ten years, but I quickly learned that the immature and fun side got old when that was all he ever did. He was always looking for trouble or getting drunk and doing shit that would normally get him punched in the face or a bullet between the eyes. Chase was the only reason the other members held back.

I was shocked that Chase hadn't given Tanner his one percenter patch regardless of how he acted. It gave me hope for our Prez.

Beast had gone home for the night. I couldn't blame him. All the dead lying around was bound to stir up memories of his wife. As tough as he showed himself to be, I knew he was still hurting. Raine had only been back in my life a short time, and I couldn't imagine losing her. After years of marriage and the kind of love Beast and Jaz had...the guy was lucky he could put a foot in front of the other.

Didn't mean I went any easier on him. Beast would've found that disrespectful, and someone needed to make decisions with Chase gone. Beast had volunteered himself, and that came with assholes like me pointing out shit, such as we were vulnerable. If I didn't point out the crap, people died. We got lucky tonight. I'd gotten lucky, but I didn't like luck. It tended to shit in your face and then drink your beer.

"Did I piss in your fucking beer, Mannix?"

"Tanner cut the attitude. There is no one in here for you to show off for. I need you to focus on the questions. What is the ETA for Chase and the rest of the crew? We now have multiple bodies to clean up, cops to keep away, and more than ever, we need to build an alliance with a local club. We have a huge target painted on our backs. So, tell me what you know," Mannix said, his voice as calm and firm as ever.

"Look, I don't know why you're all in such a twist. I'm back, and so are some of the men. Chase will be back soon enough," Tanner said, crossing his arms. "It's not like he gave me an itinerary."

"Tanner, for fucks sake. We're still breathing because you took them by surprise when you came back, and they thought the entire crew was home. The Vipers have ninety-seven members more than us at the best of times," I said.

"A few less now," Tanner mocked and sat down laughing.

"Do you ever take anything seriously?" I growled. I lifted my T-shirt to show off the bandages. "I almost fucking died. Does that not register with you?"

"Fuck Snake, you can remove that stick from your ass any time," Tanner said. "Maybe we need to get you laid."

I looked at Mannix. "I'm going to kill him." I reached for my gun, but Roach grabbed my arm.

"You could, but we all know I'm Chase's favorite. He'd send the whole club after you." Tanner smiled and reminded me way too much of the jerks I used to beat the shit out of in school. I was tempted to do it again now. Ribs be damned.

"The only reason you're his favorite is cause he sees you as a charity case. You're the piece of shit he pulled out of the garbage. Ever wonder why you need a babysitter Tanner? Why you never get sent on important jobs alone? Why do you think you don't have your patch yet?" I growled out. "Even the man you follow around like a pathetic dog knows you're not worthy."

"Fuck you, man!" Tanner burst from the seat like he'd been ejected and was in my face a moment later. Our noses touched as he tried to intimidate me.

Ten years in prison had done many things to me, but one thing it had done right was to teach me to shut off my humanity. That place and those that thought they could control me taught me how to kill without remorse. A deadly calm washed over my body, and I needed to get away from Tanner, or there was no telling what I'd do. It would certainly be something I couldn't come back from with Chase, even if the rest of the club would cheer. Roach touched my shoulder, and I remembered I had something else to live for. Someone else, and I took a deep breath.

"Both of you knock it off and sit down," Mannix ordered.

Tanner backed off first with Mannix's meaty hand firmly on his arm. "You too, Snake. Sit the fuck down."

"Sitting hurts," I said and wandered over to the wall to give myself space from Tanner. I didn't normally give a shit about whatever crazy antics he got up to, but this shit was getting annoying fast.

"Do you live in the real world, Tanner," I asked, and he crossed his arms and glared at me.

"What the fuck is that supposed to mean?"

"You lack the ability to understand what is real life and what is one of your video games. We lost people tonight. People that someone loved, people that Beast is planning a service for, and you're acting like this is all a big fucking party." I pointed out toward the clubhouse. "You're more worried about getting fucked."

"It's how we deal with shit. All those guys out there are acting the same way. I'm not doing anything different."

"But we're not out there. We are in here asking you a few simple questions, and you're being evasive." I shook my head. He just didn't get it. Then again, anyone that would light a Molotov cocktail and toss it in a room full of chemicals while we were all in there was a case in point that he couldn't see past the end of his nose. We were all fucking lucky he didn't kill us that day, and the fucker only laughed like we'd regenerate.

"I'm telling you, Snake, you're too tense. Just have a drink and relax."

"Don't bother wasting your breath," Roach whispered. He was right. There was no point trying to explain something to someone that had no interest in seeing the bigger picture.

Tanner was shrugging off the very real possibility of another attack and us losing more people, all while grabbing his cock and saying bring it on. It was a sure way to get us all killed. I did dangerous shit all the time, but this was different. I'd never been this cavalier with my attitude. I spent ten years in prison looking over my shoulder and protecting those that would protect me. I had looked out for Raine before that, and now I looked out for those in this MC. I would've thought that a kid that came from a shit start—like me—would have more respect for the home he'd found. It was obvious that he'd been spoiled, and I had no intention of feeding into that. I almost died tonight, and with that came clarity.

"Everyone take a fucking breath. We're all on the same side," Mannix said.

"Are we though," Roach asked, shocking me. He stood by my side, his arms crossed and his stare fixed on the two men. "Snake was almost killed by one of our own. Someone we thought we could trust." He pointed toward the door, the sound of music and laughter getting louder.

"We have no way of knowing how many more men were pulled into other clubs. Snake is right. We need order. We need our men and our prez back. We have no idea how many are sitting out there right now waiting like sleeper agents to be activated. What's next? Slit our throats in the night?"

Tanner rubbed at his chin, and I could tell by the smile on his face he was still thinking about the shootout and the fun he had killing the Vipers. Or the girls he was getting later. Tanner rolled his eyes and made a scoffing sound like Roach was overreacting.

"Give it up, Roach. No one wants to slit your useless throat," Tanner said. "And so what if we lost some people, we always do. It's just the way it is."

If I weren't leaning against the wall, I would've fallen over when Mannix punched Tanner so hard he flew off the chair he was sitting on and crashed to the floor in a heap.

"What the fuck? Why the hell did you do that?" Tanner growled as he rubbed his face.

"Do not disrespect our fallen members, not ever. They were part of this family, and they deserve to be remembered with honor." Mannix roared. I'd never seen the man so angry, and his presence filled the room as his stare stayed firmly on Tanner.

"Inside this room is all business Tanner and we are meeting about real issues. If you can't handle that or the responsibility that comes with your potential position in this club, I'll speak to Chase when he gets back about removing you for good." Mannix placed his hands on his hips. "I will not put up with any more of this crap from you," Mannix said.

"Chase wouldn't do that. We're family," Tanner argued. "And I've done things to help. I've done lots of things."

"Don't kid yourself, Tanner. You're no longer in Ashen Springs, fucking all the lonely, married housewives. The members of this club hardly know you, and they will vote you out if you keep this attitude up. Chase's hand will be forced, and I'll be the first to nominate you to leave." Mannix growled. He was fucking scary when angry. The fact we rarely ever saw him that way made it more impressive. "Are you listening now? If not, I'll happily knock your fucking teeth out of your head one at a time until you do."

"Fuck, you're all wound way too tight. I just wanted to party off this energy, and we could've talked tomorrow or something," Tanner grumbled.

"But I'm asking you now, and that's what matters. So, answer the question, or my next move will be to call Chase and settle this once and for all."

Words I never thought I'd hear.

"Fine, Chase said he'd be three to four days tops. Some of the men were wounded, and we lost a few. Chase is making arrangements to have their bodies brought home. Happy now," Tanner asked as he picked himself up off the floor. "And don't fucking hit me like that."

Mannix puffed out his chest, and his hands balled into fists as large and destructive as any sledgehammer. "Then stop acting like I need to tune you in. You might be the youngest member at twenty-two, but you're not a kid anymore. It's also not just you and Chase in Richie Rich world, where you can play all day without any cares. You might know Chase better than I do, but I've been helping run this club since before you were cum shot from your father's body. So don't think because Chase likes you that, you have an unlimited shield of protection." Mannix stepped up to Tanner and stared down at him. "This is a motorcycle club with real business and real family. This is not your personal playground. Do you hear me?"

I almost heard the balloon pop as his attitude fizzled. He stuffed his hands in his pockets and looked his age. "Yeah, fine, I get it. Can I get on with my night now? My ass is sore from the long ride, and I'm hungry," Tanner said, his voice missing all the earlier cockiness.

I still had a million questions, but Mannix nodded and stepped out of the way for Tanner to head to the door. He stopped with his hand on the handle and turned to look at the three of us.

"I am sorry you got shot, Snake, and if anyone is playing two sides, I'll find them," he said, walking out.

"I swear that guy makes me want to kill him some days," Mannix grumbled.

"Get in line," I said.

"At least we have an answer," Roach said, lighting a smoke. "The question is, can we keep shit together until the rest of the men are back."

"I'm just happy that at least the two of you see why I've been so fucking angry." I shook my head and went to cross my arms and thought better of it. "I'm heading home unless you need me for anything else?"

"Naw, whatever is going to happen isn't happening tonight," Mannix said and made his way to the door. Roach and I followed. I expected Roach to veer off and hang out with the group, but he stayed with me instead.

"What's going on," I asked as we reached the bottom stair.

"I may need you to help me check on Lane tonight. I haven't seen her in a couple of days and need to make sure she's okay. I think she found ways to avoid me following her around." Roach looked genuinely concerned, but it was never too early or too late to fuck with your best friend.

"Oh, I saw her," I said.

"You did?"

"Yeah, she was giving some frat guy a spit polish. She had good form too," I lied, keeping my face straight as Roach's eyes narrowed, his lip pulling up in a snarl.

"You better be fucking joking."

"Sorry man, wish I was. She was down by the beach where Raine's club is. You know, the one you forced me to go to? Anyway, I suspect she's back at the sorority now." I grabbed his shoulder. "You may need to consider that cage after all. She looked really into it. Not sure what she got up to after that, but...."

Roach yanked his shoulder away and swore as he stomped out the door. "I'm going to find this guy and kill him."

I smiled as I watched him get on his bike and ride away. And that was how you fucked with your best friend, who was totally in love and seemed completely oblivious. I could admit it was a little sadistic.

What I needed was a shower, a bite to eat, a pack of ice for my side, and... fuck. Raine was with Avro and Jace, but I wanted her with me. I ground my teeth together, already fucking hating this.

Raine

12

Raine

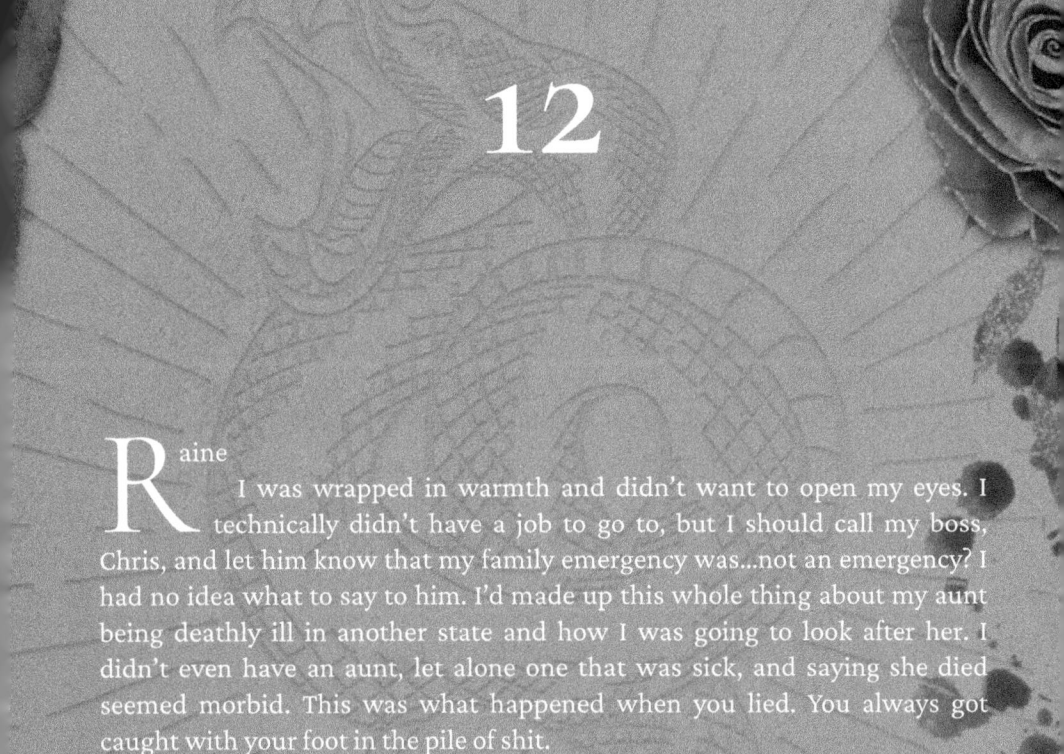

I was wrapped in warmth and didn't want to open my eyes. I technically didn't have a job to go to, but I should call my boss, Chris, and let him know that my family emergency was...not an emergency? I had no idea what to say to him. I'd made up this whole thing about my aunt being deathly ill in another state and how I was going to look after her. I didn't even have an aunt, let alone one that was sick, and saying she died seemed morbid. This was what happened when you lied. You always got caught with your foot in the pile of shit.

The room was bright. Blinking and rubbing my eyes, I found myself staring at Jace's sleeping face. He looked so sweet like this. Not the ass that he could be. His long lashes fanned his cheeks, and the messy hair that was almost hanging in his eyes looked like he'd gone to bed with it styled.

Avro's arm was wrapped snuggly around me. His body pressed tight like he wanted to make sure that I didn't run off. Glancing over my shoulder, I saw he was still very much asleep, and I desperately needed to use the bathroom. It took some wiggling, but I got myself out from underneath Avro's arm and down to the end of the bed.

Grabbing the closest T-shirt I could find, I pulled it on. It was a mini dress on me. Laundry was suddenly a necessity. I didn't have many clothes to begin with and hadn't done a wash in a few days. Quietly padding over to Avro's long dresser, I pulled open the drawer I'd seen him pull boxers out of and found a pair with yellow minions all over them. Smiling, I stole those and my phone from my bag before heading into the bathroom.

It looked like I had a million messages from Kai. Unlocking my phone, I started going through them.

> K: I hate this
>
> K: I want you
>
> K: Can I come get you?
>
> K: Tink, poke. Poke. Poke. Poke. You can't be asleep already. Actually, you better be asleep. I don't want to think about you fucking those two.
>
> K: Why did I type that? Now that image is stuck in my head. Fuck.

I shook my head as I scrolled through the messages that were basically Kai arguing with himself. It was stalker-level obsessive, and yet, I was smiling into the mirror like I was the one that needed help.

> R: Hey

The response took a few minutes, but soon the little bubbles appeared.

> K: Finally! I've been lying in bed thinking about you.

I bit my lip, and even though he wasn't in the room, I could feel my face going bright red. Glancing in the mirror confirmed my suspicions.

> R: Oh yeah? What exactly were you thinking about?
>
> K: How about I show you instead?

A video arrived before I could ask what he meant. Tapping play, the short clip caused my legs to rub together. I pressed play again when the clip ended and watched his hand travel up and down his hard cock. A second video came in, and I hit the play button immediately. This one had sound. He groaned as he worked his hand faster, and I had to lean against the counter.

> K: Do you want the ending?

> R: Is that a real question?

> K: Lmfao. Then you need to come see me. Today.

> R: Oh, that's just mean.

> K: Mean is my MO. Today, and I'll show you the ending you deserve, or…I can just finish now. Here. All alone. Fuck I'm hard.

> R: Okay, I'll come see you, but I have to go to work and sort some stuff out first, and there are errands I need to run. I'll have Avro drop me off after that.

> K: …Way to ruin my mood by mentioning his name.

I shook my head at the phone like Kai could see. My lip curled up, and a nervous energy washed over me as an idea came to me. Hitting the little camera, I lifted the T-shirt and struck a sexy pose. This felt ridiculous, but I gave him my best pout while my fingers splayed over my nipple like I'd been playing with them. Snapping the photo, I stared at my image and could admit it looked hot. I still felt silly, but before I lost my nerve, I pushed send.

> K: Oh fuck! Hello! Okay, I want those fucking sexy lips of yours wrapped around my cock.

> R: Will that hold you over until I get there?

> K: What? You're leaving me like this. You're terrible.

> R: Gotta keep you coming back somehow. LOL!

> K: I will take a dirty photo from you anytime, but Tink, I'll always come back to you, sexy photos or not. TTYL

> R: LV U

> K: LVU2

I had to blink back tears as I read those four little letters that gripped my throat. I couldn't stop staring at them. I felt each word like they were branded on my soul.

I turned on the taps and splashed cool water on my heated face before I finished up in the bathroom and tackled my main obstacle for the day. How do I get my job back and not sound like a flake or an asshole?

Opening the door, I screamed as Jace picked me up and sat me on the counter. "Geez us Jace, you scared the shit out of me," I said as he smiled and stood between my legs. "And get the smile off your face. I can't right now. I have things I need to do today."

"Yeah, like me," he said, kissing the side of my neck.

I glared at him as Avro laughed from somewhere in the bedroom. I peered around Jace to see Avro making the bed. I wish I had his affinity for neatness. Jace pressed forward, and no matter how hard I tried, I couldn't stop myself from looking down at the large tent in his boxers. My hands went to his waist, and he groaned. The sound made me squirm. It wasn't fair that they were so tempting. I mean, it wasn't really a hardship to stay in bed and fuck them all day.

"Fuck you smell good, and I love you in Avro's boxers." I laughed.

"Yes, super stylish of me," I said.

"I got them as a gift for him, but they look better on you."

"I heard that," Avro called out.

"I swear he has superhero hearing," Jace whispered, making me giggle as he tickled my ear with his breath.

"I need to get my job back before he hires another manager," I said.

"Too late," Avro said and came to stand in the doorway. Jace waved his hand in his direction.

"Go away. I'm trying to convince her to come back to bed," Jace said. I hadn't seen this lighthearted teasing much from Jace, and I really liked it. He was a very complex personality, but puzzles were something I always enjoyed playing with.

"Who did Chris hire?" Avro cocked an eyebrow. "Shit, I totally forgot that I told him to hire you. Sorry, I should've remembered that."

"Yes, and you have an interview for your new position today. I might even let you in my new office." Avro smiled as I swore under my breath.

"See, lots of time to come back to bed," Jace said. "Would it make a difference if I told you that I have to fly out tomorrow for a few days?"

"Ohhh laying it on thick with the guilt, are we?" I leaned back on the counter and braced myself on my hands.

"Fuck look at this," he said and slid his hands up the shorts. I smacked at his hands, but he continued until he could grip my hips, his thumbs tracing the inside of my thighs.

"Stop it you. Is he always like this," I asked Avro, who was smirking.

"Worse, actually. I kinda enjoy his trips for work, or I'd be stuck in bed all day with a sore ass."

Jace laughed and looked over his shoulder. "True story, but you love it."

"Also true," Avro said. "I have an idea. Why don't you go with Jace?"

"What?" Jace and I said together.

"I'm serious. You said you want to take Raine to the awards show, so why not start laying the groundwork now? It will be more believable if you're seen together sooner. You can catch the two concerts you need to do and fly back. It's what? Three days?"

"Oh, I don't know if that's a good idea." I nibbled my lip as I thought about Kai's reaction. Who was I fooling? He was going to lose his mind.

Jace turned his steely gaze on me. "Let me guess…Kai?" He shook his head. "Are you always going to walk on eggshells where he is concerned?" He stepped back and crossed his arms. I looked between him and Avro and wanted to be pissed off, yet I couldn't think of a good comeback. "I mean, if you start now, then he'll dictate everything you do. You realize that, right? Don't fool yourself, Kai may have agreed to, try, as you put it, but he's already formulating a plan to pry you away from us."

I narrowed my gaze at him. "And how can you be so sure?"

"Because it's what I would do if I were him." Walking over to the shower, he ran the water and turned around to face me. "I'd make sure that I was always in your face. Texts, phone calls, surprise visits. Then it would be jealousy. Have you see me with other women and make sure that you were good and pissed before I fucked you so good that you wouldn't be able to walk right for a week. Then I'd make you feel guilty for thinking that I'd actually ever fuck those girls. Then I'd mark you, something like a tattoo or fancy jewelry that screams you're mine and that the other guys can't compare. Last is undermine the other guys and find a way to make them look bad."

"Wow, you've put some thought into this," I said, glaring at him, yet I couldn't stop thinking about the text messages waiting for me.

"I don't need to think about it. It's classic alpha behavior." He held up a finger. "One treat you like a goddess." He lifted another. "Two make you jealous." He held up a third. "Three make you doubt yourself and your feelings." He lifted a fourth finger. "Mark you somehow so you feel labeled and owned." He held up his whole hand. "Lastly, separate you from the pack."

"But Kai is not like that," I said and realized as Avro and Jace laughed that either I was naive or they were right, and I didn't like either option.

"Oh yes, he is. Every man is capable of it, even if they don't mean to do it. Kai may not set out to complete the steps consciously, but unconsciously, his whole goal is still to make you solely his. He has no interest in sharing you with anyone. You wait and see."

"And that's not your goal. Right now, putting doubts in my head?"

"Wrong, I'm educating you. I'm used to having multiple people in a relationship and navigating the waters with different personalities that have their own agendas. Can you say the same for Kai?" Jace lifted his shoulders and let them drop. I wasn't sure what to believe. On the one hand, he had a point, but on the other, I saw Kai as more of a stomping around, beating his chest type rather than using mental manipulation. "Look, all I'm saying is stay watchful until things find a good groove. Just because you want this to happen doesn't mean it's magically going to be okay."

Jace pushed down the boxers he was wearing and smiled as my eyes fixed on his still, very hard cock, the argument I was about to make crashed into a wall.

"I'm going to shower. Anyone care to join," Jace asked.

"I'm in," Avro pushed his boxers down, and I was left staring at the two of them completely naked. I licked my lips as my eyes roamed over their bodies. They stepped in the shower but kept the door open. As their lips met and hands roamed over each other's bodies, I felt myself wanting to cave. What the hell had I done to myself?

Avro broke the heated kiss and turned his head my way. Water dripped off his chin and slid down his body in thin streams.

"Are you coming, or am I getting Jace all to myself?" He smiled at me, and my heart fluttered.

I had no idea what had gotten into me, but no one could say no to that eye candy.

Snake

13

Kaivan

Raine was late. She said that she was busy shopping with Avro. So, instead of sitting around the house like a sap, I came to the clubhouse for a drink. Now, I wasn't sure that sitting with the obnoxiously loud group of people was helping my state of mind.

My fingers tapped off the top of the bar while I stared at the television tuned to the latest horse race. I wasn't much for betting, I preferred certainties, but I could appreciate the rush of watching the powerful animals speed around the oval at a breakneck pace.

"Come on, Fartindawind," Brick yelled at the television. "Yes, that's it, Fartindawind, you can do it! Come on, girl. Push, push, push."

I snickered as I swallowed down the last of my drink. Did Brick even know that he was yelling?

"Yes!" Brick yelled, and I watched in the mirror behind the bar as Brick jumped up with a yell and brought the sweetbutt that was sitting on his lap with him. "Fuck yeah, what a fucking rush. The next round is on me!"

"Big talk since the drinks are free," Ink drawled.

"Shut the fuck up, man. It's the thought that counts."

As the two began to argue, I turned my attention back to my drink. I swirled the liquid around and watched it swirl up one side and then the other as if mirroring my own messed-up emotions.

"Hey there, Snake," Dee said and ran her arm over my shoulders. "Do you want to spend a little time relieving your stress," she asked, laying her other hand on my leg.

"We could make it a party," Crystal said as she pressed against my other side. She was so close that I would only have to turn my head, and her tit would be in my mouth. The small piece of leather she wore would easily pull off and leave her ready. Could I appreciate that both women were talented? Yes, I could, but shit was a lot more complicated now.

"I wouldn't touch me," I drawled. The two women must have thought I was joking, as they only laughed. "I have a girl," I said.

"Yeah, we know. Us," Crystal said next to my ear. The girls were hyped up with the extra guys and the excitement from yesterday, but I was shocked that they were approaching me. They normally flirted from across the room until I called them over, so I wasn't sure what was up. Did I have a new allure now that I was taken? Could they sniff that shit out like bloodhounds?

"I have to say. This is entertaining." Roach laughed. He was the only one I told about my new relationship, and even with him, I hadn't mentioned Avro or Jace. The guys here wouldn't get it, and as much as I didn't really give a shit what they thought, I wasn't in the mood to explain it either.

My eyes met Roach's in the mirror, and I shook my head in disbelief as he made a kissing face and then shook his finger at me like we were teens. At this point, I didn't think the guy would ever grow up.

"You could help here," I said to him.

Dee's hand slid up my leg, trying to palm my cock. Grabbing her wrist, I stopped her from reaching her goal. "I said I have a girl, and I wouldn't touch me." I turned my head to stare at Dee, her lips set in a pout as her eyes blinked back with confusion.

"You mean like a real girl?"

"What other kind is there," I asked, my brow furrowing.

She shrugged. "I don't know. It's you. Didn't really think that was a you thing," Dee said. "You don't have relationships with anyone, barely even the guys." She wasn't saying it to be mean. In fact, her tone was soft and unsure, but it felt like a smack all the same. I purposely distanced myself, which came with bonuses and the reality that I was isolated as much as Raine.

"I'd listen to him, ladies," Roach said. He was turned on his stool so that he was leaning against the bar but made no effort to peel Crystal off of me as she rubbed up on me like a cat in heat. "She's on her way, and she's going to be pissed if she sees this," Roach said.

An image of what that might look like crossed my mind, and my lip lifted. Would she be jealous? Would she get angry? I actually loved the idea, and my cock stirred with the fantasy playing out in my mind. I was so distracted by the sexy images of Raine fuming mad and fucking her hard that I didn't notice Crystal lift her leg to straddle me.

"We need to repay you." She rubbed her tits against my arm and giggled. Blinking and pulling myself out of the fog, I let go of Dee's wrist and looked up at Crystal.

"Whoa, Crystal, you need to get off of me," I said.

I felt the pull of Raine's arrival like she had some sort of magic. My eyes snapped up to Raine's reflection in the mirror behind the bar, and I sucked in a sharp breath. It felt like the oxygen was sucked out of the room as our eyes locked. If I thought I'd seen her angry before, I knew nothing as her face darkened. My cock jumped along with my heart, going from flaccid to hard in an instant. I licked at my suddenly dry lips. Fuck she was beautiful.

"Oh holy crap," Roach said the words that I was thinking. Raine marched across the floor, her eyes never leaving mine in the mirror. "Come on, Crystal. Get off, Snake," Roach said, trying to take control of the situation since I couldn't seem to move while locked in her stare.

"Now that's better," Crystal cooed as she gripped my hard cock through the jeans.

Oh, this was bad, like really bad. I could feel Raine's wrath the closer she got, the tension filling the room and making everyone look at the newcomer. I grabbed Crystal's hand to stop her. I'm dead was all I could think as Raine's lip pulled up in a snarl which only made me harder. I shuddered.

No one moved as they watched her, and I didn't blame them. The only one that was stupid enough to jump in the middle of a relationship issue was Tanner, and right now, I had money down on Raine to win. Besides, if anyone tried to touch her, I'd cut off their hand. Every bit of her jealous fury was mine. She was mine, but I couldn't seem to make my brain function properly to stop this from turning into a bloodbath.

"I'd intervene, but even I'm not that stupid," Roach said, sitting his drink on the bar and moving away.

Raine's eyes broke the stare first, and it felt like I'd been caught in a tractor beam from Star Trek. I hated the show, but Raine loved it. I'd lost count of how many nights we sat and watched a marathon of them.

"You need to get off me now," I said, grabbing Crystal's wrists. A sound rippled from Raine's mouth that was more animal than human.

Raine moved much faster than I thought she would ever be able to as she grabbed Crystal's arm and wrenched her off my lap in a single tug. Crystal's confused scream was short-lived as she landed on her ass with a crash.

The dark glare Raine gave me sent cold racing down my spine. She was blackout mad, I'd seen that look in my own eyes a time or two, and you did things you normally wouldn't when that happened.

"Raine, no."

I reached for her, but my mouth fell open as Crystal jumped up, and Raine went full MMA on Crystal's ass. Raine looked small next to Crystal, but that wasn't slowing her down. Crystal backed up and tried to block the hits as Raine advanced on her.

I should really stop this, but fuck, it was hot. Crystal yelled once before Raine's fist caught her across the jaw and sent her stumbling backward. Crystal hit a chair and flipped over it with a groan as she landed on the floor. Raine gripped the edge of the small card table and, with no effort at all, flipped it out of the way. It crashed near Roach's feet and rolled.

"Oh fuck, you're a dead man," Roach said, stepping further away. Fucking coward.

"Now, do you believe me?" I said to Dee, still standing very close with her mouth hanging open. Swiveling around on the stool, I jumped up as Crystal rolled over onto her back and screamed as another fist cracked down hard on her face. Raine's form was good, like she'd been professionally trained, as she knocked Crystal out cold with one shot.

Before she could think about doing more damage or attacking anyone else, I gripped her around the waist and picked her up. I backed away from Crystal as she flailed her arms and legs.

"Don't any of you ever fucking touch him again," Raine snarled and clawed at the air. Fuck she was making me hard, like bust a nut hard, as she thrashed in my hold. "I'll kill you." I shuddered at her words. Damn, I loved this side of her so much. It was always there, but she kept a tight hold on her emotions. She was the understanding one, the sympathetic one, but apparently, even Raine had a limit.

"Oh fuck," I growled as Raine's elbow caught me across the jaw hard enough to rattle the teeth in my head. I dropped her to her feet and rubbed at my jaw with one hand while I kept hold of her with my other.

She twisted out of my hold, leaving me holding a leather jacket. Spinning around, I managed to get a hold of her as she stomped toward the group of sweetbutts gathered together as they watched.

"You too, don't think I don't see all of you. If you fucking touch him...I will claw your fucking eyes out," Raine yelled, her body fighting mine as she wriggled in my hold. Holy fuck, I didn't think I could love this girl any harder, and she goes all Rhonda Rousey with jealousy. I mean, a guy could hope, but I never thought she'd actually do it.

"Tink, calm down."

"Don't you dare fucking tell me to calm down," she roared and caught me in the gut on the same side as my bruised ribs with her hard elbow.

"Ugh, fuck." My grip loosened, and I thought she was coming for me next as she turned to face me. Instead, she yanked the leather jacket I was still holding out of my hands and marched for the exit. "Fuck you, Kai."

My long strides ate up the ground, and I caught her before she could get out the door.

"Tink, stop," I said, gripping her shoulder, but when my hand touched her, she whipped around and caught me with another wild fist that knocked me back a step. Fuck, she could really hit when she wanted to. This was not the same scared kitten I found in her home. She was another animal altogether. This was the girl that was locked away, but she was free now, and I loved her so damn much it hurt.

"You can't even go a single day, and you have the nerve to talk about me," Raine said, her voice dripping with anger and jealousy. Raine's hands slammed into my chest with a hard shove. "Fuck you. I never want to see you again. We're done."

"Fucking hell we are," I growled, my temper flaring.

That was so not happening.

TWENTY MINUTES EARLIER

Raine

It was later than I had planned when Avro dropped me off at Kai's house, but I'd never traveled except for my bus ride to Atlanta. So I needed luggage, and I had very little clothing to my name. So after the rigorous yet enjoyable shower with Avro and Jace, I had a nap and some food, then went shopping with Avro.

It was official the man could shop. He knew all these great stores I'd never been to that had amazing clothes with even better deals. We were both loaded down like pack mules by the time we were done.

"Thanks for dropping me off. I guess one of these days I should learn to drive and get my license," I said.

"Well, if you want me to teach you, just say the word. I know many empty parking lots where you can't hit anything." He smiled.

"Such a vote of confidence." I looked down at the new leather jacket I wore, running my hands over the material, and couldn't stop wondering if Kai would like it. My stomach was all butterflies which was crazy considering what we'd already done, but I couldn't seem to get the jitters under control.

"Are you going to give me a kiss," Avro asked as my hand went to the door. Jace was right. I was worried about what Kai would think and how he would feel. I needed to stop that if this was going to be my reality from now on. Either he was in and okay with them in my life, or he wasn't, and we would have to part ways. I couldn't let his anger dictate what I did.

Leaning across the seat, I grabbed Avro's face and kissed him as if I didn't care if the whole world saw. "I love you," Avro said.

"I love you too." I opened the car door and stepped out, then leaned in and looked at him. "By the way, how did you find me and Kai?" He smiled wide and winked.

"A story for another night."

"I'm not going to forget if that's what you're hoping?"

"I'd never dream of such a thing," he said, laughing as I closed the door. Backpack in hand, I waved as he turned around and left. I waited until he was gone before I walked up the steps to the porch, knocking on the door to Kai's home.

Avro said Kai's motorcycle was an Indian, so he drove to the dealership and helped me buy a plain black jacket with the small emblem on the sleeve. It was so soft and way too hot, but I never wanted to take it off. There was something about slipping it on that made my heart pound hard. I thought about what it would be like to sit on the back of Kai's bike and hold him tight. It was a hot image that had me blushing.

"Why are you doing this," I asked Avro as we got back in the car from our last stop of the afternoon.

"Because I love you, and I want to see us all happy, and that's not going to happen unless Jace and Kai get on board. Don't kid yourself. They said they would try, but they're both making plans. Regardless of Jace's speech this morning about Kai, he is no better. He wants to cocoon us for himself," Avro said.

"And you don't?"

Avro lifted a shoulder and let it drop. "First, you must know by now how much you have me wrapped around your finger," he said, smiling as he linked our fingers together. He effortlessly set me at ease and made me smile. I squeezed his hand. "Second, I'm more pragmatic than either of them. I'm also more open with what I'm okay with in a relationship...the majority of the time."

I laughed at that statement. Based on what Jace said, you'd think that Avro was a raving jealous lover, but it seemed that Avro was good at playing up what Jace wanted. I smirked and leaned back to look his face over.

"What? Why are you staring at me like that," Avro asked.

"I'm just realizing for the first time what a chess player you are." His eyes darted away from mine, but I saw the truth before he looked away. "You manipulate Jace. Are you manipulating me too?"

"Whoa, manipulation is a strong word. I simply know what he likes and needs and mold myself, not because I have to, but because I like to."

"And you're doing the same with me and Kai?"

He lifted a shoulder and let it drop. "Again, I'm in love with you. If the only way to have you is with Kai, then I work within the parameters given to make things happen."

I wasn't sure what to make of that and then froze, my mouth falling open. "You really did ignore Jace's calls on purpose, didn't you?"

He laughed as he started the car. "Yeah, I definitely did that. I wanted him to turn around, and trust me, there is one thing that will always override his fears, and that is if he feels he needs to protect."

I couldn't help but laugh, it was wrong, yet I laughed. "And here I thought you were the nice one."

"Pfft, I am the nice one. Could you imagine those two lunatics left alone in a room together?"

"So me going with Jace to the concerts for three days? Let me guess. This is to solidify his feelings for me." Avro's eyes glittered with mischief. "Okay, you're a devil," I teased, but I felt like I'd just gained an ally as we pulled out onto the main street.

"Kai, I'm here." I knocked on the door again, louder this time. The sun was just starting to set, making it hard to see into the home, but I covered my eyes and peered through the small triangle piece of glass and didn't see or hear any movement. "Kai?"

"Are you looking for Snake?"

Screaming, I whipped around and then screamed again as I jumped back and slammed into the door. My gaze flicked up and down the man dressed up like a bush. He reminded me of those army guys in movies that would lay out in the open, and you'd never see them cause they dressed like a tumbleweed or a scraggly bush. His face was painted the same but with stripes, and he held what might actually be a sniper rifle in his hands.

"You're Raine, right? You're looking for Snake?"

I licked my lips. "Yeah, I am. Who are you?"

"I can't tell you that," he said.

"Oh...okay. Is it like you'd have to kill me sort of thing," I asked teasingly.

"Yes."

My face fell. I looked around for any sign of any other person, but no one was even walking along the sidewalk.

"You're a girl," he said before I could excuse myself and get the hell out of there.

"Last I checked."

He narrowed his eyes as he shifted his weight like he was intrigued. "Do you have to check often? Is this normal? Is it possible to wake up not being a girl?"

What the fuck? "Um, no. It's just a saying. It means yes, I am."

"Then why not just say, yes, I am?"

"Why are there sayings if we're not going to use them," I asked.

"Huh. That is a good point. Tell me, what is your favorite position to be fucked," Bush man asked.

I cleared my throat after I picked my jaw up off the porch. Did he really just ask me that? "I'm not sure."

He pulled a small book out of somewhere inside the bush garb and flipped open to a blank page. "Why don't you know?"

"I think I should go," I said and stepped to the side to try and get around the man, but he stepped in my way.

"Snake always answers my questions," he said. His voice didn't change, but there was a daring edge to the statement. Like if I walked away, I wasn't as good as Kai.

I crossed my arms over my chest. "Okay then. I don't know because I don't have a lot of experience to know. I don't have much experience because of something that happened to me when I was fifteen. No, I don't want to share what happened, but I can tell you that every girl is different, and what I like doesn't mean that the girl driving by would be the same. Does that help?"

He tapped the pen off his chin. "So how do I find out what a girl wants when she refuses to tell me?"

I wasn't sure I should answer this question, but I did anyway. "Why doesn't she want to tell you?"

"I have her locked up. I must think on this some more," he said, like he hadn't just admitted to kidnapping and possibly being a serial killer or something. "Snake is at the clubhouse. He usually goes there to fuck the sweetbutts. Have a good day." Bush man jogged down the stairs and then stopped. "Oh, by the way, Snake's favorite position is the reverse cowgirl."

Smiling, he jogged off around the corner of the house. It was official I was going to kill Snake. The initial shock of the strange encounter was quickly wiped away as his parting words registered in my brain. My fists clenched as I marched down the stairs and walked around to the clubhouse.

The gates were closed, but a guy was sitting in a small metal booth that looked like it had been shot at more than once. Not very comforting.

"Yes," he said.

"I'm here to see Snake. He was expecting me. I'm Raine," I said and planned on punching him in the face when he walked out thinking he was going to tell me to go away, but instead, the guy looked at a sheet and opened the gate for me to walk in.

"Front door and then up the stairs," the guard said and left me to find my own way.

Walking past the long line of motorcycles was intimidating as hell. It was the visual confirmation that Kai really was a badass in a motorcycle club. I mean, I knew it, but it was different knowing it and understanding it. Pulling open the door, I could hear the music and the sound of television as well as the yell of someone who was overly excited.

The smell of stale smoke wafted down at me, and I suddenly wasn't so sure I wanted to walk up those stairs and find out what he was doing. If I saw him with someone, it would break my heart. Nibbling my lip, I put one hand on the railing and closed my eyes for a moment to gather my courage. I needed to know. I couldn't leave without knowing, and I'd be pissed off with myself for not finding out the truth.

With each step, my blood pressure rose a little higher. Just as I got to the top step, I saw Kai sitting at a bar where two girls were openly flirting and touching him. He didn't push them away, he didn't stand up and yell I'm taken and my bottom lip trembled as I turned to walk away.

As I looked down the stairs, my body shook with a crippling sadness that quickly morphed into a wild rage. I'd never been this angry, but when I thought about all the pretty words and promises. The lies he said so easily in the motel and how he tried to convince me to just be with him. How he said how much he loved me. A fire erupted in my chest.

A fury stormed up from the depths where I kept all my pain and loss stored. I wasn't turning away again. My body shook as I turned around to step up the final few stairs into the clubhouse.

Kai's eyes locked with mine, and I wanted to destroy the world. I wanted to rip it apart with my bare hands. I was done being hurt.

Done.

Raine

14

Raine

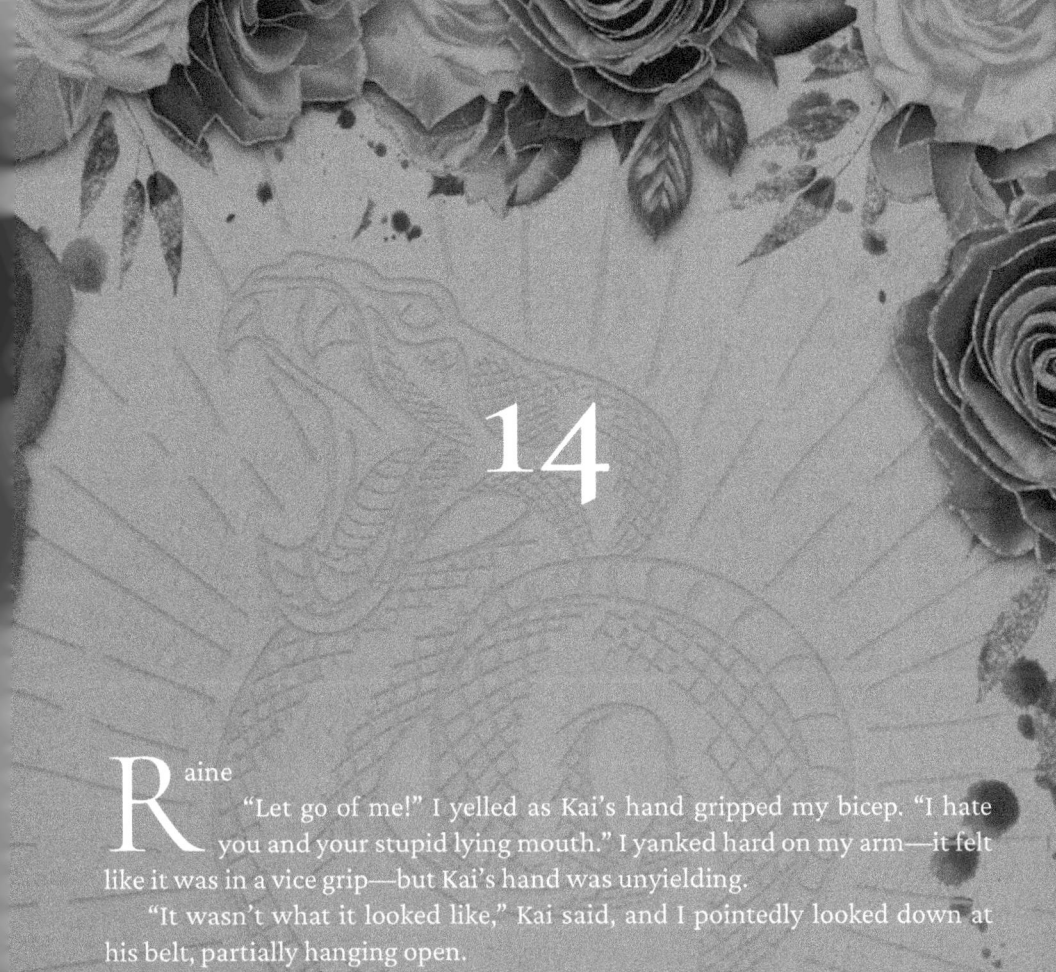

"Let go of me!" I yelled as Kai's hand gripped my bicep. "I hate you and your stupid lying mouth." I yanked hard on my arm—it felt like it was in a vice grip—but Kai's hand was unyielding.

"It wasn't what it looked like," Kai said, and I pointedly looked down at his belt, partially hanging open.

"Is that so? And just how stupid do you think I am?" I could feel all the eyes in the room silently watching us like we were the best soap opera in town. Some had glasses halfway to their mouths, while others sat wide-eyed like they were scared to move or breathe, but I didn't care. I didn't care if they saw me kick his ass, either.

"Okay, I know this looks bad, but I swear I wasn't going to fuck her. I was just telling her to get off me."

I shook my head.

"Excuse me if I don't believe you. Now let go of my fucking arm and stay away from me. I should've known this would never work, but I was stupid and fell for all the crap you spewed."

"Tink if you'd calm down for a second so I can explain," Kai said. I could tell he was getting angry, and a part of me wanted him to be as angry as he made me.

"Why so you can feed me more lies? I never should've trusted you. Jace said you'd pull some shit like this." Kai's lip pulled up in a snarl at the mention of Jace's name, and a thrill shot through my body as he jerked me close to him. "I guess I should've believed him instead of defending you." Part of me knew that I was poking at a bear, and yet...I couldn't stop myself.

"Fuck this," Kai said, his voice rough. He let go of my arm, and my heart stupidly sank, but it was short-lived as he grabbed me around the waist and tossed me over his shoulder.

As if on cue, people started taking bets on who would win. Money was passed around while odds were shouted. This was crazy.

"Let go of me, you asshole," I yelled and smacked his ass.

"We're done when I say we're done," he said. "All of you get the fuck out of my way," he growled. I couldn't see who he was talking to but knew it was whoever was on the couch as he unceremoniously dropped me on my back.

I should jump up and run for it, but instead, I stared up at him as he towered over me. My mind and body fought over what I wanted. Kai glared at all those watching the show. "Spread the word. If anyone ever touches Raine Eastman, I'll cut your fucking hands off. She is mine. If anyone ever touches me again, you'll have to deal with her, and next time I won't stop her. Understood?"

There was mumbling and nodding and a few cheers I didn't understand. This all seemed crazy. I should've just left and never looked back. The problem was that Kai was part of me. We were forever tied together, no matter how angry or hurt we got, and it felt like those wild and very turbulent emotions bound us tighter. Now he'd just claimed me, and my stupid heart swelled with a toxic joy.

"You think threatening people will make this all go away?"

Kai gripped the front of my shirt, and I sucked in a deep breath as he brought us nose-to-nose. "No, it's because I fucking love you, and I don't care who knows. You're mine, Tink, and I'm only letting go if I'm in a body bag."

My heart hammered fast inside my chest with his words. Why that turned me on and made me want him more was beyond me. My body was heating up for a totally different reason as the anger subsided a notch.

Kai's stare made it hard to draw a breath, but as he grabbed the jacket from my hold and tossed it on the table, I stopped breathing altogether.

"Take your shirt off," he ordered.

"No. Why?" I looked around at the dozens of eyes and wanted to sink into the couch and disappear.

"Because I'm going to fuck you right now, in front of them." He pointed to the crowd that hadn't dwindled at all. In fact, it seemed like more people were staring.

"Have you lost your mind?" I whispered harshly.

Kai leaned down and gripped my jaw in his hand, and I gasped in a sharp breath as he got right in my face. Our noses softly touched, and all I could feel was my pulse pounding in my neck.

"By your own words, I can have you anyplace, anytime, and any way that I want. Were you lying?"

I licked my lips. "No, but...."

"No buts. No one in here will touch me ever again, and now it's your turn to prove you meant what you said."

I'd said it, and I'd meant it, but I never thought in a million years he would want to fuck me in front of his club in the middle of the clubhouse. I turned my head and looked to the side, but Kai used his finger to turn my eyes back to his.

"You only look at me. I'm the only one that matters," he ordered, and I nodded. "Good. We have something to take care of first, though. Take your T-shirt and jeans off," he stood and looked around. "Leech, go get your kit," he said.

I wasn't sure what the hell he was up to, but my shaking hands went to the button on my jeans. Was I really going to do this? I'd never even kissed a guy in public until Avro.

"I said take them off, don't make me rip them off you. You know I'll do it," Kai commanded, and I glanced at the exit for just a moment as I contemplated bolting for the door and then wondered how far I'd get before he caught me.

Pushing the jeans down my legs, I balled them up on my lap, trying for a semblance of modesty. A man who reminded me of an old wizard dressed in biker gear pushed through the crowd so deep that I couldn't see the far side of the room. I spotted the girl I hadn't gotten a chance to hit standing in the inner ring of people, and the memory of the other girl on Kai's lap crossed my mind.

A steely resolve formed in my chest, along with the earlier burning jealousy. No, if Kai wanted to make a statement, I'd let him. I'd rip her hair out one handful at a time if she ever touched Kai again, and if this would stop that from happening, then I would do whatever he wanted.

"Stand up," Kai said. Pushing myself to my feet, I dropped the jeans on top of the jacket and peeled off my shirt. Kai groaned, and I looked up to see him staring at my body. He held out his arm and tapped on a tattoo that said, Lost Souls. "I want this font, and I want you to put her name right here."

Kai pulled his T-shirt up and over his head. My hands covered my mouth as I saw the bruising that lined the left side of his ribs. "Kai, what the hell happened?"

"We were attacked yesterday by another MC, and I got shot."

I thought I was going to faint, and grabbed his arm, my nails digging in.

"I don't understand."

"I'll explain later." He tossed the T-shirt on top of the growing pile of clothes. "Right here over my heart." The older guy opened what looked like a small toolbox and got everything set up.

"You want a tattoo of my name," I asked softly.

Kai didn't bother answering with words. He grabbed the back of my neck and dropped his mouth to mine. Any lingering voices of doubt were wiped away. He didn't stop kissing me as the buzzing of the tattoo artist's gun started up. Even the kiss was a demonstration or a message, maybe. He didn't let go of my neck or release me from the kiss until Leech finished his work. It looked amazing, and I felt myself getting all emotional and quickly reined it in.

"Now it's your turn. I want my name right here," Kai said, tapping the front of my leg right at the very top. This was just another thing I shouldn't want with all the uncertainty swirling around us, but I did. "Make it look sexy." Leech sat down on the low coffee table and was now right in front of me with his head at the same height as my pussy. My tiny thong was the only barrier between myself and this stranger.

Leech placed his hand on my leg, and Kai growled. "Leech, if you touch her more than you need to or in any way I don't like, I will cut your fingers off one at a time with a bolt cutter. And I'll make it nice and slow, so you feel it compressing the bone before it snaps."

My mouth fell open as I stared at the dark glare Kai gave the man in front of me. He was visibly shaking, and I didn't blame him.

"Kai," I whispered, and his eyes flicked to mine. "I really don't want a shaky tattoo. Maybe try not to glare at him like you're going to eat him."

A smirk pulled up the corner of his mouth. "Good point. I don't want it to look like Keven or something."

The buzz of the machine started up again, and I sucked in a sharp breath as the needle came into contact with my leg. I nibbled my lip and decided to ask the question that wouldn't stop nagging at the back of my mind.

"Were you going to push her away?"

"What do you mean?"

"When I came up the stairs, I saw that woman hanging on you, and you didn't push her away. What would've happened if I hadn't walked in when I did?"

Kai's hand was quick as he gripped me by the throat, instantly making it hard to breathe. I tried not to move, but as his lips grazed my ear, I couldn't help but shiver.

"Don't move, Tink," he said and nipped my earlobe. His hand squeezed a little tighter, and instinct had me gripping his forearm.

"Do you feel that? Do you feel how you're struggling to take a breath?" I could only stare into his commanding eyes as a trickle of fear traveled down my spine, and I wheezed out the air in my lungs. "How every little gasping breath burns like acid in your lungs as you dream of death while you fight to survive? That's how I've lived every day without you. Never question my love for you again." Kai released my throat, and I sucked in a deep breath, my mind reeling from what he'd just said. "Of course, I told them to fuck off. I made you a promise." He picked up my hand and ran his finger over the silver ring I'd never taken off. I hadn't known if he recognized it until this moment. I couldn't tear my eyes away from his penetrating stare that seemed to reach into my body and grip my soul.

"I'm done," Leech said, wiping my leg with something cool.

Gripping Kai's face, I kissed him hard, no longer caring who the hell was standing around. If they wanted to watch, they could watch. Kai groaned. Cupping my ass, he pulled me up against his body.

"I hear your favorite position is the reverse cowgirl." I smirked as his brow furrowed.

"Fucking Wilder," he mumbled. "I'll try and explain about him another time. Yes, I do enjoy it."

I undid the button and zipper on his jeans and was rewarded with a growl as I slipped my hand inside the open flaps to pull him free. His face contorted with a dark desire as I stroked his very hard cock.

"Then sit down," I ordered and gently pushed his chest.

Kai smiled, and the noise around us faded into the background. As soon as he was sitting, I went to push my thong down. He grabbed my hand and shook his head no.

"They get to have a show, but not that much of a show. Just pull it aside. As it is, I may have to rip all their eyes out of their heads for doing this," Kai said, his voice lethal, making me shiver.

Leaning over, I braced my hands on the couch on either side of his head. "We could just go to your house." I sucked his lower lip into my mouth.

"No." His hand slid around the back of my neck, and I captured his lips as his fingers tightened. He didn't say anymore, and I didn't push. If this was what he wanted, then I wanted it too. "Get on your knees, Tink and suck my cock," he ordered and ran his hand through my short hair. He managed to grip a handful and pull my head back, bowing my body away from his. I whimpered as his lips attacked the sensitive skin at the base of my neck and sucked.

"Now," he said as he let go of my hair. Kneeling, I slipped between his open legs. Wrapping my hand around his cock I opened my mouth, and Kai gripped my chin between his thumb and finger, forcing me to look up at him. "No hands, Tink. Put them behind your back. I want to see if you can take it all."

My mouth fell open as I stared at the long cock and then up at Kai's eyes. Did he think I was a fucking superhero? I was lucky it fit in my pussy let alone down my throat. My lips wrapped around the tip of his cock, and any tentativeness I had subsided when he groaned and shuddered as my mouth slid down. There was no greater aphrodisiac. Sucking hard, I bobbed my head, and it didn't take long for Kai's hands to grip my hair again.

"Fuck Tink, you've been holding out on me. Damn, that feels so fucking good," Kai said, his praise going through my body and ending between my legs. The desire that had been a steady roar since he picked me up was now throbbing steadily between my legs. Moaning, I bobbed faster, loving the feel of him sliding in and out of my mouth and the sounds of pleasure he made. The room had become a roar of sounds, but in the chaos, there was only an intense calm between us.

Kai groaned and pulled my hair harder. Before he could force my head down, I closed my eyes and sucked in a deep breath as I managed to swallow his cock down. The panic was there, but I fought it as Kai swore, his fingers tightened painfully, adding to the moment.

"Fuck Tink, shit," Kai said and pulled my head off his cock. I gasped in a breath, my lips swollen. I licked at the moisture around my mouth and savored the taste of him. "Where did you learn that," he asked, his face dark with threads of anger.

I cocked a brow and smirked. "Jace is a good teacher."

The words had the exact reaction I expected as he snarled like an animal and hauled me off the floor. "Is he now?"

"Apparently. You liked it," I said softly, purposely poking at him. It was like a matador waving something red in front of a bull. His eyes took on that murderous glare, a growl ripped from his chest, and I melted at the sound.

"You think you're being cute, Tink?" He turned me around and yanked my thong out of the way. "I'm going to fuck his name right out of your mouth."

Kai's voice was rough, and I could feel the anger rolling off of him. But where it scared me the first night he crashed back into my life, now I craved it. I wanted his love as much as his anger and jealousy. I hated to admit that Jace was right. He'd seen my dark desires, but I hadn't been ready to admit it to myself.

Now I fully understood what I wanted, and the crazier Kai became, the more I wanted him. It was toxic and completely unhealthy—a psychiatrist would have a field day with me—but I stopped caring somewhere between that first night and this moment. There were no sweet and kind words of love as he thrust into me, and the hands gripping my hips forced me down to meet him.

"Ahh," I screamed with intense pleasure and intoxicating pain. "Fuck, Kai," I yelled and fell back against his body as he pistoned in and out of me. I tried to help, but his pace was too quick, and the orgasm that was building now soared toward the cliff's edge.

I screamed loud as sharp teeth bit into the soft skin at the base of my neck. I gripped his legs as Kai slipped his hands around the front of my body and cupped my breasts. A whimper was forced from my mouth as he thrust into me and pinched my nipples hard. My eyes snapped open, and my mind registered a massive group of people, many half-naked and fucking or jerking off to our show.

The once sane part of my brain was in shock, but the rest of me only wanted more. More of him and more of this.

"Kai," I moaned as I was pushed over that edge and came hard in a rush, but he never let up or slowed down. If anything, he seemed more frantic.

"Get up," he growled, releasing my neck from his bite. I stood on wobbly legs. Kai grabbed my hand and dragged me around to the back of the couch. "Bend over," he ordered, pointing.

I was almost bent in half over the back, and I groaned as he slammed home in a single thrust. My hands clawed at the leather as his hips punished me.

"You're so fucking naughty, Tink," Kai said, his hand hitting my ass hard. "Play with your clit like the bad girl you are." My hand slipped between my legs, and I could feel him pushing into me. He felt so fucking good. There were no coherent words to describe the waves of pleasure washing over my body.

"I see you, Tink. Trying to make me jealous." Another smack. "Make me angry." The third smack had me teetering at the top of the climax peak all over again. "Make me want to hurt you."

"Yes, please Kai, hurt me," I cried out as he smacked my ass for the fourth time, this one the hardest of them all. The sharp sting made me jerk, and I rubbed furiously at my clit as desire shot between my legs.

"Such a naughty fucking girl, and I love you more for it," he said and then groaned as he slammed into me hard. The force of the thrust pushed me over the edge for the second time, but the orgasm was drawn out as Kai came. "Fuck, yes," he hollered. I could feel the powerful release that came with each stroke until he went still, buried deep in my body.

Slumping over on top of me, we were breathing hard and sweaty, but I still welcomed the heat of his skin pressing into my back.

Wrapping his hand around my throat, he pulled me up from the bent position until my head rested against his shoulder.

Kai's lips brushed my ear, and I trembled. "I love you, never doubt it." All I could do was nod. "Good, now get dressed. I want to take you home and fuck you again."

Raine

15

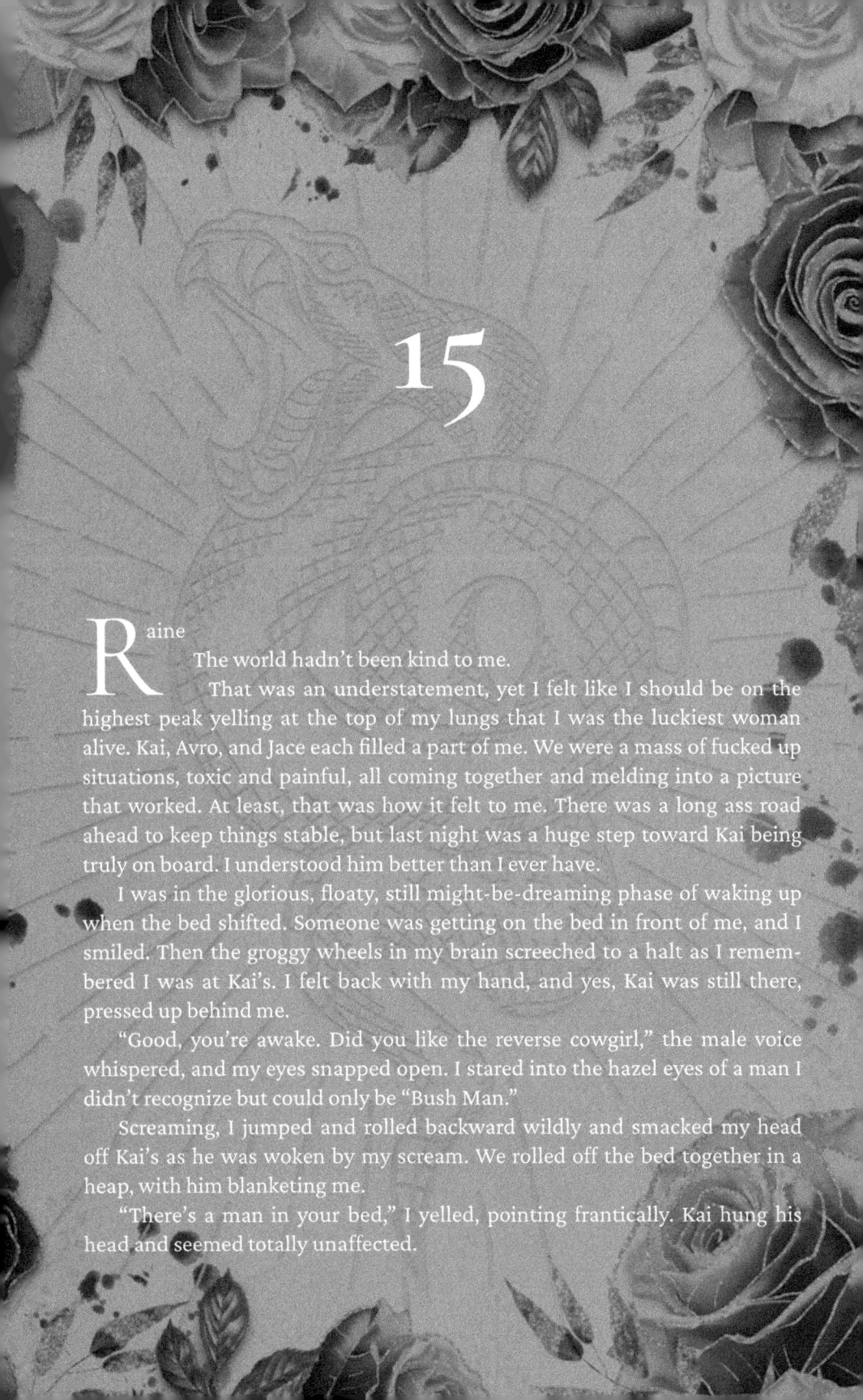

Raine

The world hadn't been kind to me.

That was an understatement, yet I felt like I should be on the highest peak yelling at the top of my lungs that I was the luckiest woman alive. Kai, Avro, and Jace each filled a part of me. We were a mass of fucked up situations, toxic and painful, all coming together and melding into a picture that worked. At least, that was how it felt to me. There was a long ass road ahead to keep things stable, but last night was a huge step toward Kai being truly on board. I understood him better than I ever have.

I was in the glorious, floaty, still might-be-dreaming phase of waking up when the bed shifted. Someone was getting on the bed in front of me, and I smiled. Then the groggy wheels in my brain screeched to a halt as I remembered I was at Kai's. I felt back with my hand, and yes, Kai was still there, pressed up behind me.

"Good, you're awake. Did you like the reverse cowgirl," the male voice whispered, and my eyes snapped open. I stared into the hazel eyes of a man I didn't recognize but could only be "Bush Man."

Screaming, I jumped and rolled backward wildly and smacked my head off Kai's as he was woken by my scream. We rolled off the bed together in a heap, with him blanketing me.

"There's a man in your bed," I yelled, pointing frantically. Kai hung his head and seemed totally unaffected.

"Wilder! Learn boundaries, man, get the fuck out," Kai yelled as he pulled the sheet to cover me more.

"But I wanted to ask a few questions of your female interest."

"I don't fucking care. Get out. Now." Kai glared at the man that came into view and walked to the door. All I could do was stare up at Wilder dressed in military fatigues. Once again, he looked like he'd just walked out of a movie. What the hell was this guy's problem? My heart, which had nearly jumped right out of my chest, was slowly calming to a normal pace.

"But...."

"Now." Kai bellowed so loud it felt like the floor shook.

Wilder walked out the door and closed it. Kai slumped before kissing my forehead, where we'd collided. "Sorry about that."

"Who the hell is this guy? Yesterday he scared the shit out of me on your porch. He was dressed up like part of the bushes and was carrying a sniper rifle. Is he sane?"

Kai snickered. "Well, that's debatable. Come on. We better get up. I can almost guarantee he's waiting downstairs." Kai groaned and gripped his side as he moved. I didn't like the look of the bruising, and after he told me how he got it, I wanted to bring this Sparky back to life so I could kill him all over again.

"Was he in the clubhouse watching us?"

"Knowing Wilder, it's a very distinct possibility. You don't want to know everything he knows about...well, probably everyone. I don't banish him because he's relatively harmless in his stalking and helped the club out. He also saved my life. He's the sniper who shot and killed the guy about to kill me. He's quirky as fuck, though, and has zero boundaries."

"Well then, it doesn't matter what weird stuff he does. I'll need to kiss him instead." Kai stopped moving as he pushed himself up and stared at me.

"I didn't mean actually kiss him. Relax. Are you sure you're okay," I asked as he grimaced. "You look like you're in a lot of pain."

"Yeah I'm fine. I've had worse, but I'll have it looked at later to be safe. The doc is coming by to check in on everyone that was injured." Kai untangled me from the blankets. I jumped to my feet and darted to my clothes. "What are you doing, Wilder won't come back up now, or at least I don't think he will."

"I know, but I think we should get you some ice and new bandages. I'm such an asshole. I never even thought about your ribs with...well, you know, all that we did," I said, clipping my bra into place. I pulled on my top but didn't get any further when Kai laid his hands on my shoulders.

"Stop and breathe," he said softly. Everyone liked to tell me that lately.

Kai's lips made me shiver as he placed a soft kiss on the side of my neck. "Everything we did yesterday is worth every bit of pain today." He ran his hand over the bruise from his bite mark.

I turned in his arms, my eyes flicking to the clear bandage over the tattoo of my name, and I smiled as happiness bubbled inside me. He seemed so different when we were alone like this. He was gentle and quiet, reflective. I'd never say it, but Avro was right. Kai and Jace seemed to have a lot in common. It was like they were completely different, yet cut from the same cloth.

"I love it when you look at me like that," Kai said, his lips soft as they touched mine.

"You may not say that when I tell you what I agreed to do tonight, and no, I'm not asking," I said. Kai froze, but his eyebrow arched up in question. And just like that, he went from sweet to intimidating with a single look. "Jace has two concerts over the next three days, and he invited me to go. Well, actually, Avro suggested that I go because I'm supposed to be going to some red carpet awards show, and going to the concerts will help sell us being a couple." I rambled out and then shifted back and forth as Kai continued to stare and not say anything. "In hindsight, I probably should have told you about the coming out as a couple part, but I was just so excited. How many people get to say that they walked the red carpet? I really want to go to this and stop staring at me like that."

I was getting ready for the explosion, planning my argument as to why I should go, and ready to race to the door and block it before he stomped out to find and kill Jace.

"Okay," Kai said.

I stared after him as he stood up straight and wandered over to his closet. He said nothing as he pulled on a black T-shirt, and I couldn't take it anymore.

"Okay? That's all you have to say?" I crossed my arms over my chest as I analyzed his body language. He didn't seem angry, but he could be faking it and waiting for me to let my guard down.

"Yeah, what else did you want me to say? You already made up your mind anyway, so what would it matter if I said no?" He slipped his leg into his jeans, and I still couldn't decide if he was masking a meltdown or was really okay with this.

I shook my head. "Something is not adding up here."

"What do you mean," he asked.

"I don't know, but...wait." I tapped my chin as I ran through all the possible scenarios in my mind. "What do you already have planned that you don't want me to know about?" I knew that look. His eyes shimmered with the truth. "That's it, isn't it? You have something going on and either didn't want me around or weren't going to have the time for me, and this helps you out?"

"You know, Tink, you always were the smartest in the room." He smiled as he did up the belt on his jeans. "First, yes, I have a few things that I need to take care of for the club, and I wasn't going to be around anyway, so yes, this helps me out." Kai walked toward me, and I couldn't decide if I should be happy that he was this calm and accepting or annoyed and worried. "Not that I don't want you around," he said, wrapping his arms around my waist. "But you'd be a sexy distraction, especially when you seem to like standing around half-naked." His eyes lingered on my lips. "I do get you wanting to attend a red carpet event. I mean, I'm not a heathen."

"Yeah...okay, I don't trust this attitude. I don't know if I should go."

Kai laughed and then grabbed his side. "Don't make me laugh. It hurts."

"I'm serious. You can't stand Jace. The fact that you're this calm has me worried about what you're planning on doing. I expected rage and a mantrum at the very least."

His face sobered, and he cupped my cheeks. "I promise I'm not doing anything that will hurt me, and no, I cannot tell you, so please don't ask." I nibbled on my bottom lip, the worry settling into my gut regardless of what he said. "Look as far as Jace and Avro go." Kai sighed. "Avro is okay. Jace...I don't like at all, but I don't have much of a choice and need to figure out how to deal. So this way, I'm busy, and if you're out of town, it makes it hard for me to just kick in a door and wave a gun around." Kai smiled.

"Not funny." I crossed my arms. "But I get your logic. You promise me that you're not going to get hurt?"

"I can't promise I'll never get hurt. It's the nature of who I am, my club, and what I do, but I'll always be as safe as I can."

"This feels exactly like when you used to go to the fights. I'd worry and pace my room until I heard you come home and knew you were alive. It made me sick to my stomach to see you all bruised up. You have no idea how many times I was tempted to try and lock you in your room."

"You paced your room?"

My cheeks warmed. "Yeah. I told you, I've always loved you."

Kai dropped his lips to mine and kissed me softly, making my head feel light. Breaking the kiss, he leaned his forehead against mine and linked our fingers together.

"No matter what, our souls are forever twined," he whispered, melting my heart as he kissed me again.

Snake

16

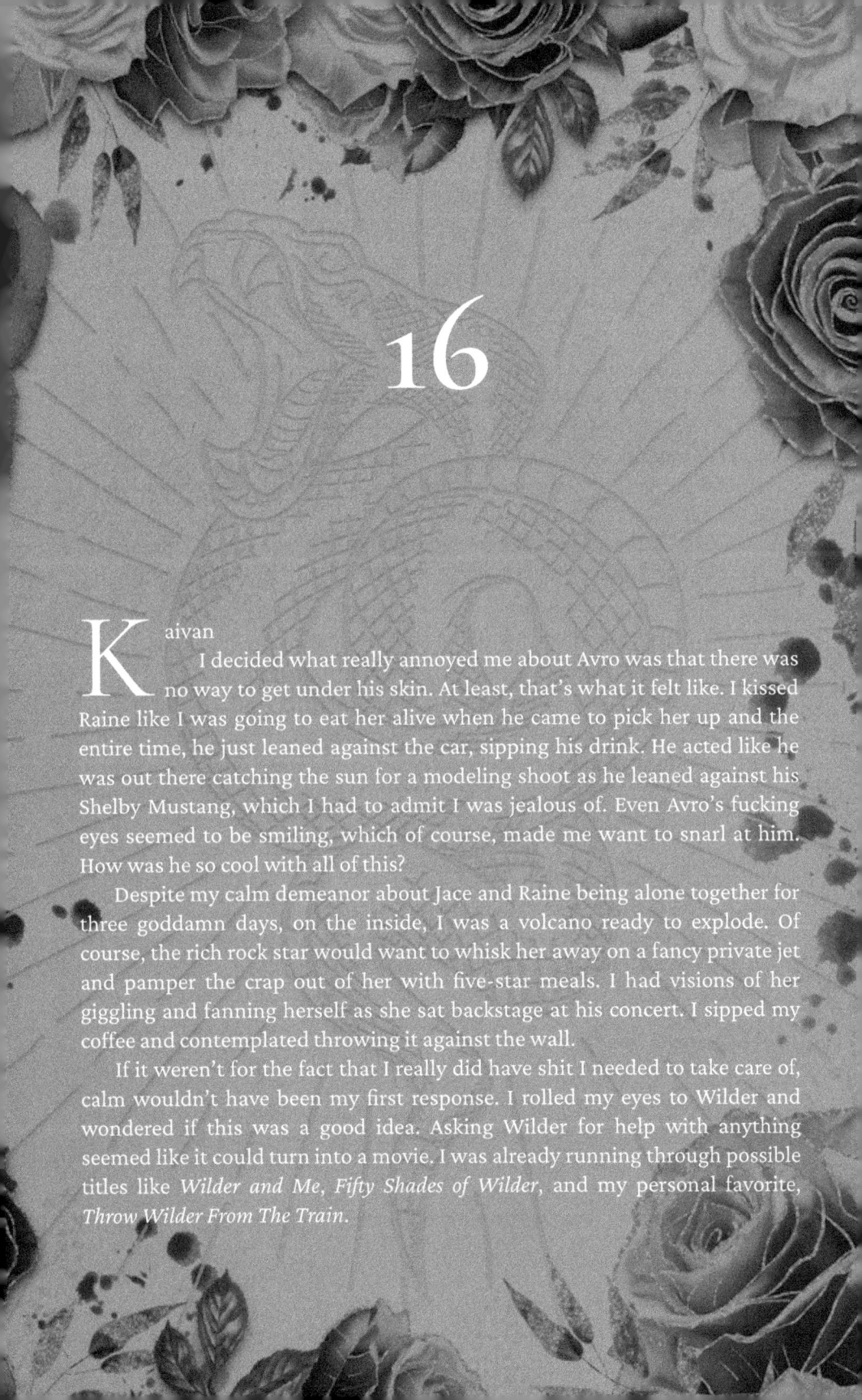

Kaivan

I decided what really annoyed me about Avro was that there was no way to get under his skin. At least, that's what it felt like. I kissed Raine like I was going to eat her alive when he came to pick her up and the entire time, he just leaned against the car, sipping his drink. He acted like he was out there catching the sun for a modeling shoot as he leaned against his Shelby Mustang, which I had to admit I was jealous of. Even Avro's fucking eyes seemed to be smiling, which of course, made me want to snarl at him. How was he so cool with all of this?

Despite my calm demeanor about Jace and Raine being alone together for three goddamn days, on the inside, I was a volcano ready to explode. Of course, the rich rock star would want to whisk her away on a fancy private jet and pamper the crap out of her with five-star meals. I had visions of her giggling and fanning herself as she sat backstage at his concert. I sipped my coffee and contemplated throwing it against the wall.

If it weren't for the fact that I really did have shit I needed to take care of, calm wouldn't have been my first response. I rolled my eyes to Wilder and wondered if this was a good idea. Asking Wilder for help with anything seemed like it could turn into a movie. I was already running through possible titles like *Wilder and Me*, *Fifty Shades of Wilder*, and my personal favorite, *Throw Wilder From The Train*.

"You sure you're good with Roach meeting you?" I looked out the window to see the man in question pulling into the driveway.

"Of course I am. You act like I'm paranoid." I wanted to yell you are paranoid as Wilder clamped a hand down on my shoulder. "A road trip with my friend and his friend. This will be fun."

"You do know this is not a road trip, right?"

"We will be in a vehicle and on the road. By definition alone, that is a road trip."

Shaking my head, I decided this was a terrible idea, but I couldn't back out of it now. The Wilder wheels were in motion, and that truck planned on rolling until it crashed. Grabbing my leather jacket off the hook, we walked to the door and stepped outside as Roach honked the horn.

"What the fuck, man? Are we in high school? You picking me up for a date?" I yelled at Roach's open window.

"Only if you plan on sucking my cock," Roach yelled. Roach's eyes darted to the man practically skipping beside me like a fucking golden retriever out for a walk.

"What are you doing?" I stared at Wilder in his black fatigues with a massive bag slung over his shoulder that I knew was loaded with every gun man had created. He smiled wide, the look so fake that it seemed painted on his face. He was only missing the clown nose and little car to ride in to complete the picture.

"I'm happy. Isn't this what people do when they are happy?"

"Sure, when you're five or if they've had too much LSD," I said.

"Oh. How do I show my enthusiasm properly?"

I stopped walking before we reached the truck. Taking a deep breath, I asked the question I'd been dying to ask since the first moment he decided I would be his ask-it-doll. "Wilder, you were in the military, so I need to fucking ask you. How the hell did you get by without being kicked out?"

"Because I was good at my job."

"I don't doubt that, but how do you have so little life experience to know what is proper? You were around other soldiers all the time and must have had to go to school and had parents." His face remained blank, like he didn't understand the question. I pinched the bridge of my nose and decided never to do this again. Dealing with robot Wilder was like a computer that kept putting up an error box without reason. "Dude, why are you so awkward? Emotions or not, you're older than me. How is it possible no one has taught you about emotions or proper reactions? Have you never asked these questions of anyone?"

"Are you two getting in or are you going to grab each other and make out?"

"Gimmie a minute," I chirped back at Roach.

"No, I did not ask these questions of anyone," Wilder answered, his voice softer like he might be able to experience sadness.

"Why?"

"I had no one to ask that I wanted to ask. My parents didn't want me after I stabbed a kid." My eyes went wide. And people thought I was the bad apple. "But the guy had it coming. I was placed in military school and excelled in the field, but the others avoided me until I became a Green Beret. I did ask some questions and learned to pleasure my body." Okay, that was a visual I never needed swimming around in my head.

"You've never dated, never had a friend?"

"My unit were my brothers, so you could call them friends, but we did not speak much, and when we did, it was about the missions we were assigned."

"And they are the ones that died?"

"Yes, they were all killed on a mission, and now you are my friend."

I wasn't sure how to feel about what he'd just told me. "Yes, I'm your friend, and I'll answer your question. We would give each other a fist bump, maybe smile a little more, and offer to buy a round of beers if we needed to stop. There is definitely no fucking skipping."

"I wasn't skipping. That was my happy walk."

"That's how you walk? Okay, never mind, whatever it was, don't do it." I grabbed his arm before he could skip off to the truck. "And Wilder, we need some fucking boundaries because that shit this morning was not right, and it can never happen again."

"You had a problem with your shit?"

My brow furrowed. "No, I mean with Raine."

"You had a problem with Raine's shit?"

"I swear to god...." I started and caught the slight lift of the corner of his mouth. "You're screwing with me right now, aren't you?"

"Yes, I like to pay attention to your jokes. I'm confident that soon I will be able to say sarcastic things and be funny, too," he smiled. "You're a really good teacher, and I enjoy watching you." Smiling, he walked away and left me staring after him. He always managed to answer a question and leave you wanting to ask a million more.

Wilder opened Roach's backdoor, tossed in the massive bag, and then proceeded to get into the front passenger seat, leaving me standing outside.

"Hey Roach, I'm Wilder," I heard him say as he closed the door.

What the fuck? Watching me? What the hell did that mean? And now I was going to wonder if he was playing me or if he was truly that fucking awkward. The possibility of him messing with me this entire time was terrifying, and now I didn't know which version of Wilder worried me more. Who the fuck was I kidding? They both scared the fuck out of me, and he just took my fucking seat. Asshole.

Roach looked back at me as I climbed into the back and smirked. "Shut the fuck up. I don't want to hear it," I grumbled as I crossed my arms.

"Are you okay back there, sweetheart?" I glared daggers at Roach in the rearview mirror. This was humiliating.

Wilder turned in the seat to look at me. "Do you like being called sweetheart?"

"No."

"Yes."

Roach and I answered together, and Roach laughed as I glared. I shouldn't have warned him about Wilder. That gave him too much time to prepare for this moment.

"Where are we heading first?" Roach put the truck into gear and pulled out of the driveway.

"The gas station where we saw Dave. I'm hoping Wilder here has some tricks in his bag to help us get the outside camera footage from that day. I want to see if Dave got into a car."

"You think that will help?" Roach asked.

"It's a start. Jim's phone had nothing. It was like he'd already wiped it clean or got a new one before I got to him, and the moment I answered that call, Dave disconnected his phone. Smarter than he looks."

"Your girl is obsessed with bunny slippers," Wilder interjected, and Roach and I both looked at him.

"Who, Raine?" I hadn't seen any in her room.

"No, his girl. She has them in every color." I bit back my laugh at the horrified and then enraged look on Roach's face.

"How the fuck do you know what slippers she likes?" Roach's voice was threatening, but the glare he gave Wilder was worse. Before Wilder could say something else that would end up with Roach crashing the truck, I interjected.

"Chase asked him to keep watch over the sorority house and all those that live there to keep them safe," I said, and Roach's shoulders relaxed.

"Yes, I watch them sleep at night. She tends to wear zoo animal pants and a cutoff top to bed or sometimes no top."

Roach's head whipped around again, the corner of his lip pulling up in a snarl as I pinched the bridge of my nose. This was going to be a long fucking day, and one of us may end up buried yet.

Jace

17

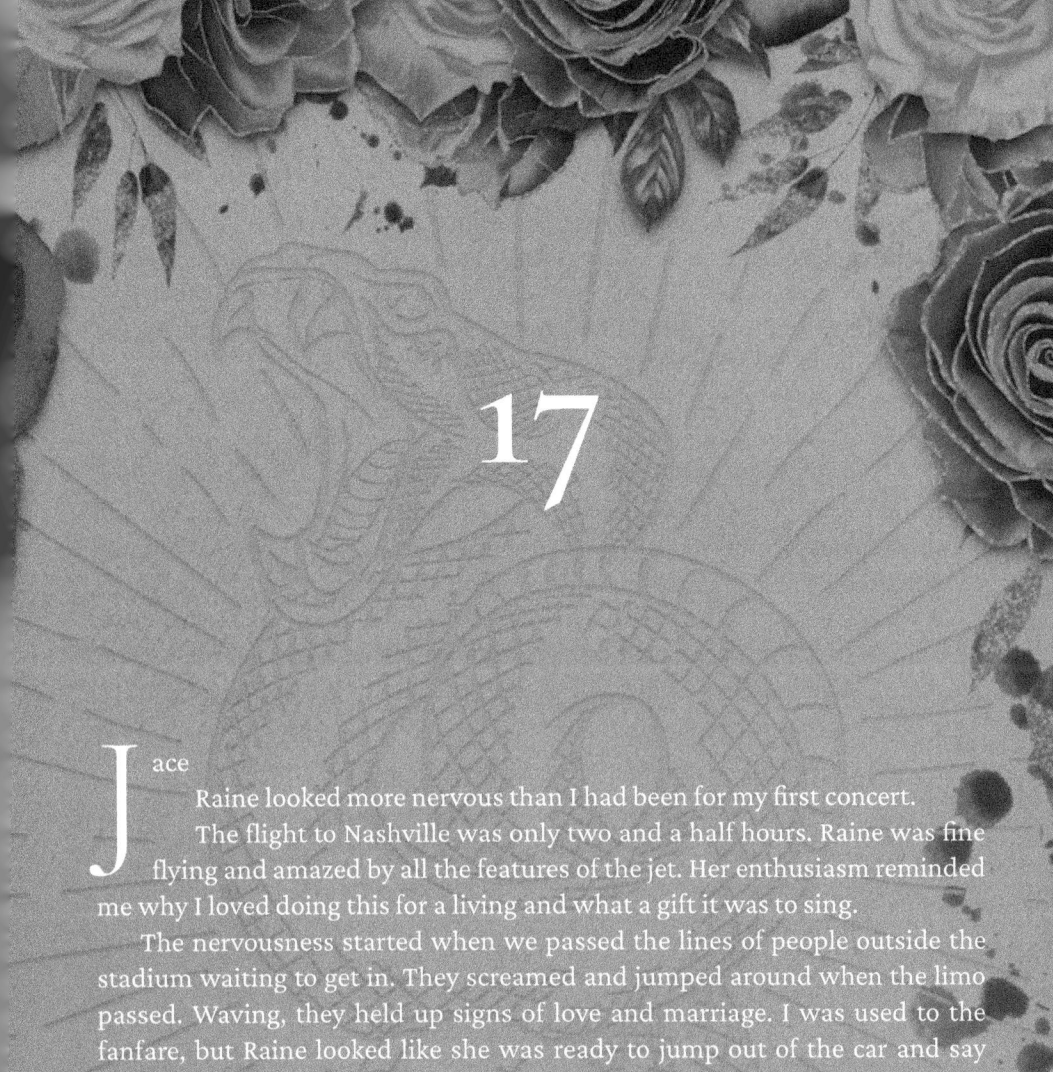

Jace

Raine looked more nervous than I had been for my first concert.

The flight to Nashville was only two and a half hours. Raine was fine flying and amazed by all the features of the jet. Her enthusiasm reminded me why I loved doing this for a living and what a gift it was to sing.

The nervousness started when we passed the lines of people outside the stadium waiting to get in. They screamed and jumped around when the limo passed. Waving, they held up signs of love and marriage. I was used to the fanfare, but Raine looked like she was ready to jump out of the car and say forget it as a more rambunctious group broke the line of guards running over to the limo as we parked. They banged on the glass and tried to peer inside. Raine jumped in my lap as she stared wide-eyed at the overly eager faces.

Since then, she'd been nothing but a ball of nervous energy threatening to make me the same way.

"Peaches?" Raine spun around to face me as Sherry, the hairdresser, put the final touches on my hair. "Sit the fuck down, or I'm going to find something to tie you down with."

"You wouldn't dare."

My eyes locked with hers in the mirror. The bright blue color looked fiery as she narrowed them to glare at me.

"Try me." My voice was husky, and I licked my lip, letting her see just how much I hoped she tried to test my patience.

Sherry stepped back like she expected me to leap up from the seat at any moment.

"I have a stress ball," Sherry said, her voice soft. She was always the same, sweet and helpful. The rest of the band thought I'd fucked her a million times, but we'd never touched. Other than for her to do my hair, of course. Just because the rest of them couldn't keep it in their pants, they thought I fucked everyone that walked into my dressing room. Idiots.

Raine was the first to break the staring contest, her eyes going to Sherry. "Good, I can hit him with it."

"Oh, I didn't mean...um...I'm done, so I'm going to go. If you change your mind, hunt me down," Sherry said. She gathered her array of sprays and muds, combs and brushes, and stuffed them all in her bag before making her mad escape.

I leaned forward to inspect the job that Lori, my makeup artist, had done. Other than the slight swelling around my left eye—that no amount of ice was getting rid of until it was good and ready—the rest of the bruising from the fight with Kai was covered.

"I can't believe you just said that in front of someone that works with you."

Turning in my chair to face Raine, I gave her a hard stare. "Yeah, 'cause that is the worst public embarrassment you've had in the last twenty-four hours," I said.

The moment I saw the bite mark—hidden by the sexy outfit Raine was wearing—and the tattoo of Kai's name, I almost lost my mind. He moved fast. I didn't think he would work so quickly to try and tear us apart, but I'd underestimated him and would use these three days to my advantage. Fuck Kai and his marking. If he could do it, then so could I.

Raine's face became a vibrant shade of red as she blinked and looked away.

"Fair enough."

"So, we are going somewhere after the concert, and I don't want any arguments."

Standing, I stretched and peeled off the T-shirt I wore to put on the one chosen for tonight.

"You're really fucking bossy. Has anyone ever told you that?" Raine crossed her arms over her chest, pushing her sexy tits up in the low-cut top.

I sauntered across the room, and the closer I got, the more she looked around like she was trying to find an exit. She was fucking adorable.

"I'm very bossy, but you also like it." Stopping in front of her, I glanced down at her cleavage. It was making my mouth water. "I'm going to enjoy getting you out of this later."

Raine pulled down on the short skirt that would've shown off her ass if it hadn't been for the leggings she was wearing underneath. I was tempted to cut the leggings off her body, but I figured I'd kill one of my bandmates for staring at her ass if I did that. They wouldn't be able to resist. Marcus was the worst. He had a sex drive like I'd never seen. While performing a concert in the Bahamas, I walked in on him fucking an entire watermelon. The guy had it on his makeup table going to town while red juice sprayed everywhere.

He didn't bat an eye as he looked over and said he still preferred coconuts. That was the last time I walked into his dressing room without knocking and asking if he was decent. That was also key since he really didn't care if the world knew the crazy shit he did. It was also why I never questioned the exorbitant cleaning bills that always came from his room. I never wanted to fucking know.

Draping my arms over Raine's shoulders, I leaned on her. She scowled, but under the annoyed façade, she was already picturing me stripping her later. I could see it in her eyes.

"Don't you trust me to make it worth your while?" I stuck out my bottom lip, purposely wetting it with my tongue.

"The last time you said that, I ended up being chased through a cemetery," she said, making me smirk.

"Yes, and if I remember correctly, you came multiple times." Dipping my head to hers, I nipped at her bottom lip until she opened her mouth so I could kiss her. Our tongues lashed as the kiss went from sweet to intense and all-consuming. It was tempting me to say fuck it to the concert, so I broke away. I looked down into her face, loving the hooded eyes and swollen lips. I moved closer to her ear.

"You screamed my name so loud they heard you cumming in the next town." Raine shivered, and my cock rose. I pictured being inside her and planned on bending her over every piece of furniture in the hotel room.

I sucked in a deep breath before I was late for my own concert. It wouldn't be the first time, but it would be when I was already on site and because I was fucking someone.

Bang, bang, bang

Raine let out a yip at the loud knock. "Yo man! It's time," Damon called out.

"That's my cue. You ready?" Raine smiled and nodded even though I could see her shaking. "You'll be fine. You get the best seat in the house."

Linking my hand with hers, we walked for the door. The guys all wore the same creepy stare as I swung the door open. They didn't even blink as they looked Raine—in her sexy outfit—up and down. Even used to them, I found it annoying after the first five seconds.

"You can stop staring now. Yes, you know her, yes, it's serious, and no, you can't fuck her."

"Dammit," Marcus said, unsurprisingly.

"Peaches, this is the band. You saw them in passing, but let's make this official. This smiling asshat is Marcus, the walking hardon." I pointed at my drummer.

"Hey! Okay yeah, that's fair," he said, making Raine laugh.

"Damon, my bass guitarist. Stone is all over the electric and steel guitar, and lastly, Owen plays the piano, keyboard, and really anything else we need. He's like a freaking wizard." I pointed out the guys one at a time.

"Owen is just an overachiever," Damon teased.

"You're just jealous that all the girls want me instead," Owen shot back.

"Eat shit," Damon said, punching Owen in the arm.

Stone didn't say anything. He was also the only one who wouldn't shake Raine's hand when she offered it. I glared at him, then he at least nodded and said hi. Raine looked up at me as the group moved on, and I knew she was confused by his reaction to her.

Turning for the stage, I held Raine back, walking slower until the guys were out of earshot. "Don't mind, Stone. He takes time to warm up to anyone new. We've had our share of crazy ass groupies that attach themselves to the guys. He's making sure we stick before he bothers getting to know you."

"Oh, okay. I get that, but he seemed angry." Raine hesitated, and I watched her while she stared through the slim crack in the stage wall.

"No, just an ass. He's like that with pretty much everyone other than the band."

The roar of the crowd was extra loud tonight inside the football stadium. These were my favorite venues. They always got my heart racing and the adrenaline pumping. Raine's eyes were wide, and her mouth was hanging open.

"That's a lot of people. Like a lot, a lot. It's one thing to see it on television...."

"But a totally different experience in person." I smiled wide and glanced through the crack. "Yeah, sometimes I can't believe this is actually my life. Even after three years, it blows my mind that this is real." I gave her hand a gentle tug. "Come on. The announcer is getting everyone hyped for us to go on."

After squeezing her hand and giving her a quick kiss, I ran out in front of the insane crowd. The stage vibrated with the stomping of feet and screaming fans. I glanced over to where I'd left Raine at stage left and winked. This was the first time someone that meant something to me was at my concert. Avro never wanted to take the chance on his identity being discovered, so he had never come. I didn't like admitting it, but it hurt.

He would be devastated to know he hurt me, which was why I never said anything. I knew he thought he was doing something to help us, but seeing Raine smiling off to the side of the stage made me warm all over, and for the first time in a really long time, my stomach flipped.

Raine

This was incredible. It took a few songs to stop being nervous about the thousands of people singing, screaming, and waving their hands in the air, but once I did, I fell in love with the entire experience. The energy in the building made it impossible not to fall in love with every second.

I never saw this happening. I wasn't the kid that dreamed about being famous or meeting someone famous. I had dreamed about my parents being alive or playing a school sport. Making a team without worrying about moving to a different school cause I was shipped to a new home.

I'd listened to Jace's songs many times. He really did have an amazing voice with smooth, sultry tones that broke at just the right times to make you want to wiggle in your seat in all the best ways. He was in his element, the cockiness and arrogance coming off as captivating on stage. I still couldn't wrap my head around how this all happened, but I wasn't going to let go now. I was all in on this entirely new me.

"Are you enjoying the show?" I yelped and jumped as Allen yelled in my ear. "Sorry, didn't mean to scare you," he said.

He reminded me of an accountant who, at one time, was a bad-boy rocker himself. His hands and forearms were covered in tattoos, but he wore a tidy suit with glasses, and his hair was styled messy. He had a clipboard in hand, a pen behind his ear, and rings on every finger. It didn't feel put together like some people pulled off. It was almost as if he couldn't make up his mind who he wanted to be. It was the same when he was at Eclipse, but I noticed it more now, not in business mode.

"Yeah, the show is amazing." I had to yell for him to hear.

"This thing with you and Jace, is this for real," Allen asked out of nowhere. His eyes searched my face, and I didn't like it. It felt like he was analyzing or maybe judging me. It was hard to tell.

"Yes."

"How?"

"What do you mean?" I crossed my arms over my chest.

"I'm just trying to figure out when this sudden love of his life situation started. I mean, I'd never heard your name until I had to make arrangements for the band at the bar. When have you been spending time together? Did you sit out in the audience at other concerts? How did you sneak into the hotels without me knowing? When exactly did the two of you fall in love?" He yelled, and I swallowed.

I looked around at those behind the scenes working, and a few sets of eyes flicked my way. My brain raced, and then it hit what he'd said about Jace being in love with me.

"Fall in love?"

"Yeah, that was what Jace said, is that not how you feel?"

My gut told me not to give him any ammunition. He could simply be looking out for Jace since he was his manager and agent, but I had an uneasy feeling in my stomach. Had Jace really told him that he loved me? Do I confirm it?

The song Jace was singing ended, and both Allen and I clapped. Putting two fingers in my mouth, I blew hard, making a loud shrill whistle. Jace turned, looking at me, and I smiled. He was infectious. Avro's description of him was very accurate. Butterflies took flight in my stomach as my body warmed, and it had nothing to do with the huge crowd.

Jace had a way of penetrating your senses. His touch lingered long after he let you go. If I didn't know better, I would think the man was a walking morning glory flower. Jace and all of this felt like an illusion.

"So, do you have an answer," Allen said, and I wanted to punch him in the face.

Even though I didn't want to, I smiled.

"Honestly, I'm just surprised he told you at all. We were keeping the news quiet, but I guess taking me to the awards show derailed any plans you were making, and it forced his hand," I said, as if I had a hell of a lot more knowledge than I did.

I lifted a shoulder and let it drop casually. "As for how that's not really any of your business unless Jace wants to tell you." I looked away from his expression, which was darkening by the second. "Since it's obvious you don't know, it's not my place to say."

I could feel him ready to explode beside me. He was like a volcano about to erupt, and I felt tremors. My hands twitched in my lap as my heart rate spiked. Jace was well into the next song when Allen spoke again.

"I will find out if you're just here to use Jace to climb out of that shithole bar." He bent over so his face was near mine. "Even if it means digging up everything in your life to do it. There will be nothing that is not out there for public consumption."

The pounding of my heart got worse as I pictured my childhood, my parents, the assault, the depression I suffered, and the anxiety meds I took. Then finally, my involvement with Kai splashed over every social media site. My painful and sordid story would be out there for anyone to read and judge. I could picture the twisted tales now.

Abused drug addict using Jace Everly to climb the social ladder while she continues to have relations with a known criminal and MC enforcer. The same man was charged with her assault. Does this girl just like trouble? What are her real intentions with Jace Everly?

Allen's glare told me he was going to do just that. He would have someone look into me and leak it, regardless of what Jace wanted. That thought made my throat close up.

"Do we have a problem here?" Jace's voice made me jump, and I jerked away from Allen.

"No, of course not," Allen interjected. "I was just getting to know the love of your life a little better. Considering you never mentioned her until the other day, I was curious about her." Allen smiled like a snake oil salesman and clapped Jace on the shoulder. "Great concert as always."

The crowd was cheering for an encore, but Jace didn't budge as he stared Allen down. Without batting an eye, Allen turned and walked away. I watched Jace as his eyes tracked Allen.

"What did he really want," Jace asked his voice on the verge of seething. I looked over my shoulder to where Allen was now talking to one of the crew. If I said what happened, I knew Jace would do something that neither of us could come back from. Visions of Jace punching Allen in the face flooded my mind, so I decided to keep my mouth shut, at least for now.

"He seems overly concerned and confused as to where our relationship began. He was asking some questions about how we met." I shrugged. "You know, he's the person that looks out for you. If I were him, I'd have questions too."

Jace's silver eyes were drilling holes into mine, making me so hot that I wanted to rip my clothes off. He was acting more intense than normal, so I slipped off the stool and stood not to feel quite so small as he towered over me.

"So he didn't threaten you?" He glared, his jaw twitching as his eyes flicked to Allen and back to me. "Cause if he threatened you…so help me god…" Jace growled, and a shiver raced down my spine. This was exactly what I was worried about, and quickly shook my head. Wrapping my arms around his waist, I rose up on my toes and kissed him.

"All is well. Now come on, you need a shower. I thought only athletes got this sweaty." I stepped back and held my arms out as if disgusted, making Jace laugh.

I squealed as he picked me up, and I was forced to wrap my arm around his neck. "Jace, put me down."

"Nope, I intend on making it so that you have to shower with me." Smirking, he kissed me hard and wiggled his chest against me.

"That's disgusting," I said, laughing.

"Maybe, but I plan on having you sweaty very soon." Jace had a way of deepening his voice at just the right moments that made you shiver, and I did now, which only pulled up the corner of his mouth in an arrogant smirk. "Three whole nights of me, all alone. You think you can handle it?" We turned the corner to the dressing rooms.

"Can you," I asked as he walked to his room and closed the door with a kick.

Jace buried his head in my neck, his lips brushing against my skin. "Oh Peaches, the little bit I've done with you is only the tip of the iceberg. You'll scream until you pass out. That's a promise."

Jace's voice was husky, and there was not a doubt in my mind that he wouldn't follow through on his promise or threat, depending on how you looked at it. The old me would've jumped out of his arms and ran screaming. But that girl, scared of new emotions and experiences, had packed her bags and disappeared. I never wanted to see her face again.

Jace walked us right into the shower with all our clothes on and hit the water, making me squeal with the sudden burst of cold. We laughed hard until our lips met again, and Jace pulled my shirt off over my head.

I was a whole new me. I was going to live life and experience what it had to offer, and right now, that was Jace Everly, the rock star with a commanding personality. Life was way too short to do anything else.

Grimhead Crew set playlist

DROWN OUT THE SOUND

THE DAY I FELL

LOVERS IN THE DARK

FRESH

TIL THE DAY YOU LOVE ME

LIE TO ME

HALF BAKED

FEARLESS

WHEN TOMORROW COMES

STOP ME BEFORE I FALL

SLOW LOVE

I'M A MONSTER

I'LL COME FOR YOU

Grimhead Crew

Rock On

Avro

18

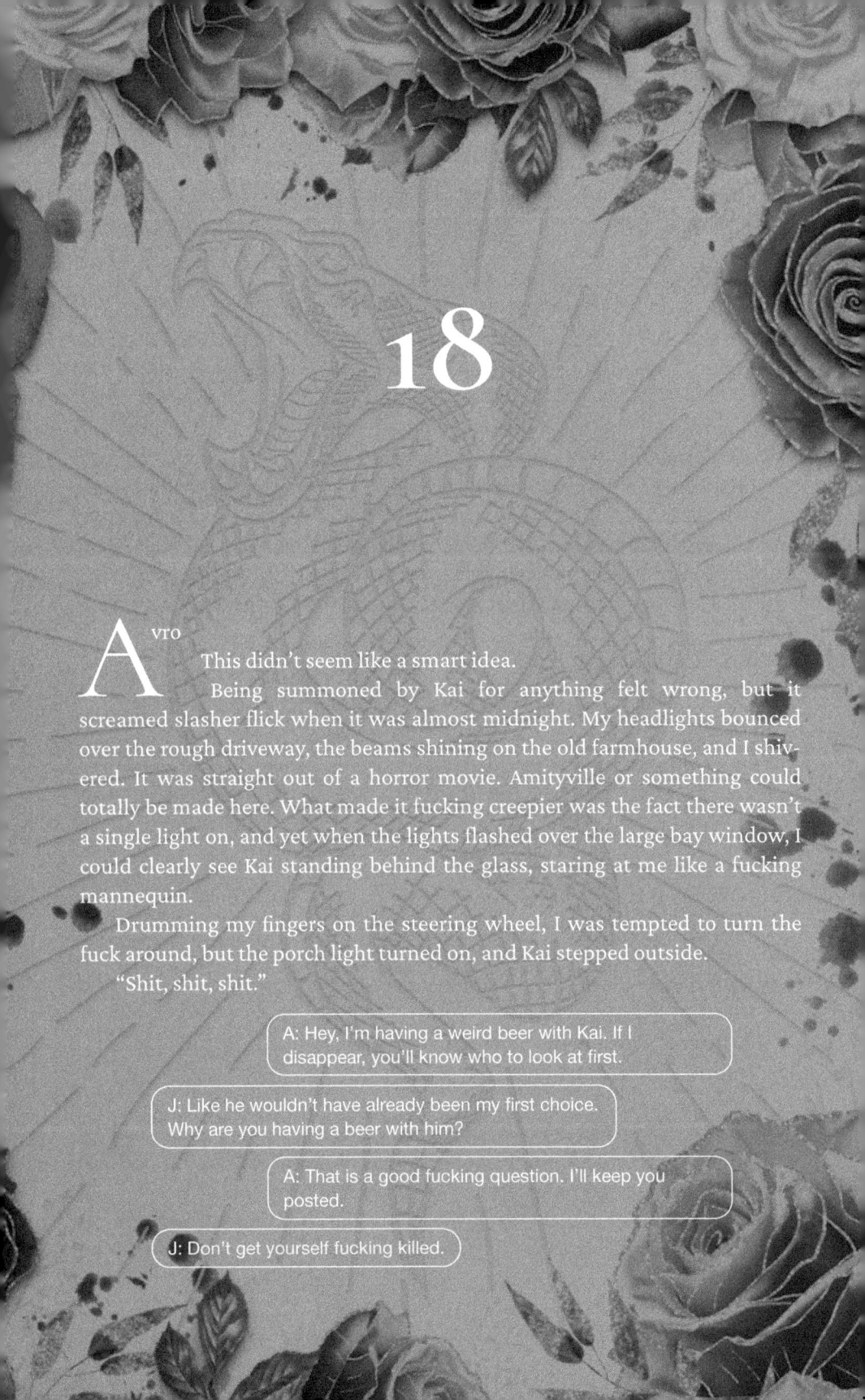

A^(vro)

This didn't seem like a smart idea.

Being summoned by Kai for anything felt wrong, but it screamed slasher flick when it was almost midnight. My headlights bounced over the rough driveway, the beams shining on the old farmhouse, and I shivered. It was straight out of a horror movie. Amityville or something could totally be made here. What made it fucking creepier was the fact there wasn't a single light on, and yet when the lights flashed over the large bay window, I could clearly see Kai standing behind the glass, staring at me like a fucking mannequin.

Drumming my fingers on the steering wheel, I was tempted to turn the fuck around, but the porch light turned on, and Kai stepped outside.

"Shit, shit, shit."

> A: Hey, I'm having a weird beer with Kai. If I disappear, you'll know who to look at first.

> J: Like he wouldn't have already been my first choice. Why are you having a beer with him?

> A: That is a good fucking question. I'll keep you posted.

> J: Don't get yourself fucking killed.

> A: Thanks, I'll try not to.

Stuffing the phone in my pocket, I got out, and Kai smirked at me as he leaned against the support beam. Not walking any closer, I leaned against my car and crossed my arms.

"Making sure someone knows where you are?"

"You know what they say. Someone should know where you are at all times." My eyes darted to the darkness beyond the pathetic glow of the lone light. "Especially when visiting a gang member in the middle of the night."

"I'm not sure I'm the most dangerous thing out here, but I do like that you're smart and think ahead. You do that a lot, don't you, Avro?"

Kai lit up a smoke, the little flame of the lighter glowing brighter than anything else. I didn't bother to say anything and watched him calmly as I thought about the baseball bat in the back seat and how I left the keys in the ignition for a quick escape. I might love Raine enough to accept this situation, but I was no one's fool, and trusting Kai blindly was a sure way to get myself killed.

"You not planning to answer?"

"Didn't know I needed to. You seem to have me figured out," I said.

Kai snorted, and I couldn't tell if he was amused or annoyed, but he sat down on the top step of the porch and opened the small cooler waiting for him. It was as if he knew I wouldn't go inside the house alone and had anticipated that. He pulled out a beer and tossed the can for me to catch. When he said, 'Have a beer,' this was not what I had in mind, but it worked. Holding the can away from my body, I opened it and let the fizz bubble out onto the ground before taking a sip.

"Decent. At least you have good taste in more than a particular woman," I said. It was a brand I'd never seen before.

"It's from Canada, just had a shipment arrive."

"Huh."

"So tell me, Avro, how do you see all this ending?"

"Is this a serious question?"

"Yes."

I took another sip of the beer as I thought about the question and the best way to answer it. "Well, I see this ending in one of two ways. You and Jace find common ground, or everything explodes, and we all lose Raine."

Kai took another drag on the cigarette, the light scent of it floating in my direction. He leaned back on the wooden porch reminding me of one of the deadly snakes that liked to lounge in the shade. They were fine as long as you didn't disturb them, but watch out if you did.

"What if I told you that I thought it would be in your best interest to make sure Jace doesn't try anything stupid."

I narrowed my eyes. "What exactly does that mean?"

"Don't act stupid, Avro. You know as well as I do that Jace would love to persuade the two of you to fly off into the sunset with him. I can picture him convincing Raine that she wants to be his traveling groupie and forget all about me."

I tilted my head and snorted. "Pot, I'd like you to meet kettle," I said, holding out my hands. Kai just laughed. "Well, if you think that Jace has that kind of power, then you're not giving Raine very much credit. Are you that insecure?"

"I love your mind, Avro. This is exactly what I'm talking about. You see all the pieces and how they are moving and what you should say and do next. It took me a bit to figure you out, but it hit me when you showed up at the motel and said exactly what each of us needed, wanted, or expected to hear. Well, that and you're really good at hiding secrets. Secrets I'm sure you don't want the world to know."

My heart jumped in my chest, but I forced myself to keep the surprise off my face. "I will admit that I'm strategic, but not to be harmful. I know what Raine wants, and that is all three of us. I'm simply trying to make sure that happens."

"Come now, Avro. You're being modest," Kai said, and I gulped down the rest of the beer as I thought about what Kai might be referring to.

"What the hell is that supposed to mean?"

Kai stood and slowly walked down the stairs. There was something far more lethal about the stroll than if he ran at me. Stuffing his hands in his pockets, he stopped a few feet away. My body tensed as I readied myself for a physical or verbal attack.

"I have to say, Alex, I'm impressed. I didn't think you had it in you to kill someone, let alone cover it up and get away with it for this long," Kai said, his voice low, yet I sucked in a breath like he'd punched me in the gut. He knew my real name, and how he found out about something that Jace and I refused to speak about to anyone was beyond me, but the pounding in my ears made it hard to hear his next words.

"You and Jace did a great job covering your tracks. Don't worry, your secret is safe with me, or it will be if you can make sure that Jace doesn't play dirty," Kai said, his eyes filled with dark humor that only he found amusing.

"You'd get bonus points if you walked away and took Jace with you, but I'm not going to push that button...yet."

"So you're threatening me?" I shook my head and glared at Kai.

"I wouldn't say I'm threatening. I'd say I'm being strategic," Kai said.

"You're an asshole." I didn't care if he hit me. Let him attack me at this point. He was digging at the wound I'd tried to heal from most of my life. "Do you even know what happened or why?"

Kai smiled, and there in his eyes was the man that had attacked us at my house. The man that wanted to rip me in two and would happily do it if it wasn't for Raine. A cold shiver raced down my spine as I stared into his cold, blue eyes.

"I don't care about the why—the exact how is also lost on me. I just know that your uncle is dead and that you and Jace are the prime suspects. It was so long ago, and you were both minors, that it has gotten swept under the rug. But I'm sure some poking around would cause a new stir, especially with your other uncle being a general. How long do you think it would remain buried what the two of you did? How do you think that would affect Jace's singing career? You might even do jail time since you're now adults."

"Why are you doing this to me? I've done nothing to you, Kai. I'm the one trying to make sure we all get along for Raine's sake."

Kai stepped forward, but I didn't flinch. At this point, I'd rather him kill me than force me to relive what happened in a court, or worse, drag Jace down for his part.

"I'm doing this for that exact reason, Avro or Alex, whatever you want to call yourself. You are the lynchpin to this fucked up relationship. Raine loves you, although I'm still baffled as to why. You obviously love her, or you would be helping Jace undermine me, but I don't see you doing that. At least, I don't unless Jace wants you to, and I'm stopping it before it ever happens. I will keep your secret, but in return, you keep your rock star boy toy in line. I need you to understand that Raine was mine. If it hadn't been for a tragic situation that drove us apart, we'd be living our life without the two of you. I need her and will do whatever is necessary to keep her."

I could feel the anger radiating off his body. "If Jace tries to sweep her off her feet and whisk her away, then I'll make sure you're the collateral damage. Before you ask, I don't care about what happens to you. You and Jace are not in my bubble of give-a-shit, but Raine is my heart. If you or Jace try to rip it out of my chest, I will take you down with me. Do I make myself clear?"

Swallowing, I nodded. "Crystal."

"Excellent. I'm so happy we had this little chat to clear the air between us." The sarcasm was obvious and dripped off every word.

Kai stepped back, and I pushed away from the car to walk around to the other side. Opening the driver's door, I stopped and glared at Kai.

"You know, I didn't need to be threatened to keep Raine happy, but thank you for showing me your true nature. It's eye-opening to what a fucking piece of shit you really are. Too bad Raine didn't see this side of you, maybe she'd think twice, and it would have nothing to do with Jace or me if she ran in the other direction. Sleep well, Kai."

His face darkened, and his hands clenched into fists, but nothing was worse than what he'd already threatened.

Slipping into the car, I quickly started it and drove out of the driveway, caught between fuming mad and terrified. My hands squeezed the steering wheel, and it complained with a squeak.

"Fuck," I swore and slammed my hand off the top of the wheel as if that would somehow help.

"Dude, for fucks sake, what the hell happened," Jace asked as he gripped my arm and yanked me into an empty classroom.

I jerked my arm away. "Nothing is wrong."

"Yeah, not buying it. You've been weird ever since you got home from that camping trip. You won't look me in the eye, you refuse to hangout, and you're dodging my texts and calls. Now you refuse to turn around when I call your name in the hall? What the fuck?"

"Nothing happened. I'm fine. You're just imagining it." I went to walk around Jace and out the door, but he grabbed my arm again, and this time when I tried to jerk away, he wouldn't let go.

"Let go."

"No." He closed the door and leaned against it before letting go of my arm.

"Fuck off, Jace, just let me leave. This has nothing to do with you," I said, anger and fear bubbling to the surface. I couldn't sleep, and I had to have the lights on all the time. The sound of light rain sent me into a panic attack that I couldn't explain to my mother, and the last thing I needed was to share what had happened with Jace.

"Alex, you're my best friend. You know you mean more to me than that." His voice softened. "If you met someone else and you know...don't wanna...hangout anymore, then just tell me."

Hangout was code for us. It was simple, mundane, and all the other kids used it, but for us, it meant exploring our interest in one another.

"It's not that." I ran my hand through my hair and turned my back on him. I jumped and yelped as his hand touched my shoulder. When I turned to look at him, I lost it, and tears broke free—tears I'd refused to cry for almost two weeks. My lip trembled, and Jace stared at my face, worry evident in his eyes.

The door opened, and Jace looked over his shoulder at the math teacher about to walk in. No words were exchanged, but Mr. Mattacini backed out and closed the door.

"Great, now we're in trouble," I groaned.

"No, we're not. I caught him and the new art teacher doing it in the storage room, and I made sure they both knew it," Jace said and lifted his shoulders, which didn't help him look more innocent.

"Caught as in by accident or followed them?"

"Does it really matter? Knowing is knowing, and with that comes power. He won't say shit to us, and I'm no longer failing math." He smiled, and I shook my head. "What? It's not my fault he decided to fuck someone at work. He's a cheating dick, and as far as I'm concerned, he's getting what he deserves. He's just lucky I don't leave a note for his wife."

I wiped away the wetness on my face, annoyed that I was crying at all. "Whatever. Can I go now?"

"Fuck no. Not until you tell me what happened," Jace said.

"I don't want to talk about it here." I crossed my arms and looked down at my new sneakers. "After basketball practice."

"Fine, but I will find out, and I want you to be the one to tell me. Don't force me to go all undercover P.I. on you."

True to his word, as soon as practice was over and everyone had left, Jace called his mom and asked if I could stay the night to work on a school project. He amazed me with how easily he could lie.

I was never that good. It was why I tried so hard never to give my parents any reason to question my sexuality. It was safer to pretend everything was fine, and I'd gone along with it since I started to see Jace as more than my friend. I figured if they didn't ask if I liked guys, I wouldn't have to answer, and they wouldn't be faced with kicking me out. They'd both made it very clear that no son of theirs would fuck another guy.

I guess my uncle didn't get that memo.

My mom only agreed to the sleepover when I said it was for school. I thought I heard relief in her voice. They hadn't said much to me since the camping trip. It was what Courtney said and had nothing to do with my Uncle Martin. I didn't think they knew what he did. If they did and were protecting him...no, I couldn't think about that.

"Okay, we're alone. I even double-checked the locker rooms and got rid of Matt and Lacey making out under the bleachers," Jace said as he dropped down beside me. In his very Jace way, he sprawled out on the bleachers. The giant Gator logo stared at us from across the gym. "Spill, what's going on?"

I ran my backpack straps through my fingers, my body shaking as I thought about what had happened. Jace moved, and although I knew he'd touch me, I still couldn't stop myself from jumping as his arm wrapped around my shoulders. Instead of pulling away, he gripped me tighter, hugging me.

"Alex, what the hell is going on?"

"Jace...I don't want to say it out loud. It feels like it will make it worse somehow, or I don't know, but...." I stammered out quickly, my chest heaving. I wiped my hands on my jeans over and over like that would wipe away the stain of what had happened.

"Okay, slow your roll. You're gonna make yourself pass out," Jace mumbled as he held me tighter. "Whatever happened has happened, and nothing you say will make it worse."

"I know, but I can't help feeling like this."

"No, but it's true." Jace pulled back, and I didn't want him to let me go. For those few short seconds, I felt safe. Jace always made me feel safe. "And no matter what you tell me, I'm here. You know that."

"You may not be. You may decide to fuck off," I said, and Jace's brow furrowed, his eyebrows pressing so close together that they almost touched. I knew what was coming before he opened his mouth.

"Are you fucking stupid?"

I smiled, but the happiness faded as I blurted it out. "My uncle hurt me, Jace. After I texted you and fell asleep, he snuck into my tent."

"Hurt you? You mean like hit you? For what?"

I shook my head no. I wished he'd hit me. I'd take a thousand punches over what he'd done to me.

"Did he say mean shit?"

It was my turn to stare at Jace. He just wasn't clued in, and I didn't want to say it. His eyes remained confused a moment longer and then went wide. "He...he hurt you like...touched you...like not hitting?" I nodded, and once more, the fucking tears filled my eyes. "Like just hand or more?"

"More," I choked out. "Like everything."

Jace grew really still and quiet, and I dared to look up. He seemed frozen. My stomach dropped as his eyes went wide. Was this the moment he was going to shove me away? Panic gripped my heart, and a moment later, it tried to jump out of my chest as Jace leaped to his feet.

"I'm going to fucking kill him," Jace growled. He turned and stomped down the bleachers.

I believed him. I could picture Jace running to my Uncle's house to do it, and then he'd be in jail.

My brain registered what was about to happen, and I jumped up, chasing Jace down before he could leave the gym. His lip pulled up in a snarl when I got in his way. He looked terrifying with his fists balled and muscles flexing. We might have only been thirteen, but we were both almost six feet, which was part of the reason we were so good at basketball. Jace had been working out hard since he turned twelve, and he looked it.

"Stop, Jace. Please, you can't make this worse."

"Worse? Alex, he not only hurt you, but he is family. I watched that prick sit in the stands and cheer our team on last night and act like he's not a fucking piece of shit. I wondered why your shots were so terrible. I just thought you were having an off night." Jace tried to walk around me, and I fisted his T-shirt.

"Please, Jace. I'm begging you. I can't deal with whatever happens if my parents find out. At least not yet. I'm not ready. Besides, I can't lose you."

"Oh, for fucks sake." I let go of his shirt as he began to pace. "Aren't you supposed to go there next week, with your parents going on that second honeymoon cruise or some shit?" I nodded, already terrified to go. I'd been dreading it since the moment we got back.

"So, you have to stay with your uncle for a week and don't want me to do anything?" I nodded. "Not happening. You can stay with me."

"I already thought of that. I asked my mom, and she said it was too much to ask of your mom with the two young kids. She's made the arrangements. If I push, they'll start to ask questions."

"Fuck that," he yelled, his voice echoing in the empty gym. I jumped.

"Jace...."

"No, Alex. He doesn't get away with this. Give me a couple of days to come up with an idea that doesn't let your family know what happened and ensures he won't touch you again. Okay?"

I sucked in a deep breath, knowing I could scream from the top of my lungs that I didn't want him to get involved, but it wouldn't matter. Nothing stood in Jace's way when it came to what he wanted.

Jace

19

Jace

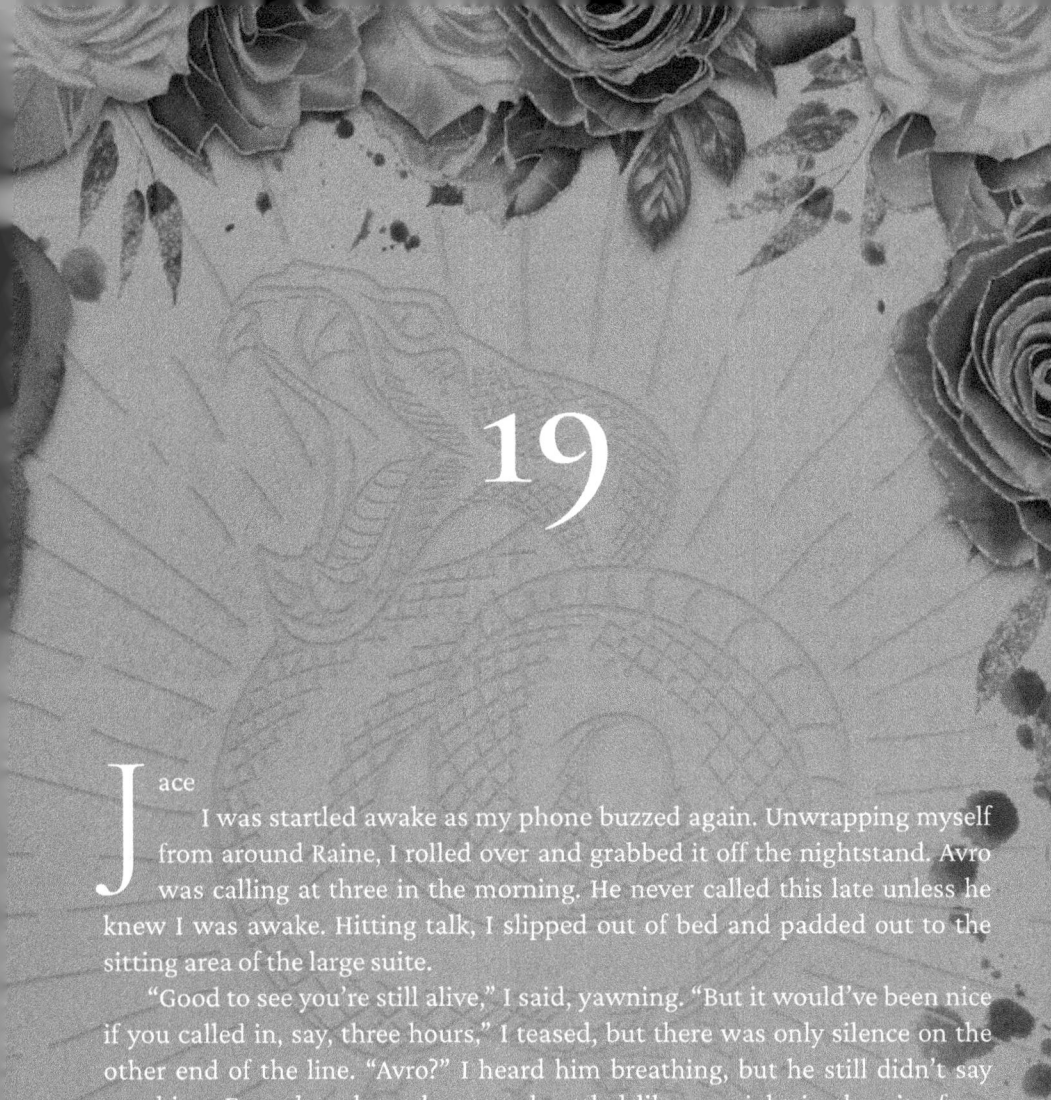

I was startled awake as my phone buzzed again. Unwrapping myself from around Raine, I rolled over and grabbed it off the nightstand. Avro was calling at three in the morning. He never called this late unless he knew I was awake. Hitting talk, I slipped out of bed and padded out to the sitting area of the large suite.

"Good to see you're still alive," I said, yawning. "But it would've been nice if you called in, say, three hours," I teased, but there was only silence on the other end of the line. "Avro?" I heard him breathing, but he still didn't say anything. Fear shot through me and settled like a weight in the pit of my stomach. "What the fuck is wrong?"

"He knows," Avro said, his words slurred like he'd been drinking. Avro rarely ever got drunk, and the fact that he'd clearly had more than normal worried me.

"Who knows what?" I walked over to the large window and stared out at the city and the lights of cars moving steadily along the interstate.

"Kai. He knows about us."

My brain whirred, but Avro wasn't making sense. Of course, Kai knew about us. He fucking came over to our house with a gun. Just how much had Avro drunk?

"Dude, you okay? Of course, he knows we're together. Did you hit your head tonight?"

"For fucks sake!" Avro swore, and I had to move the phone away from my ear.

"Geez us, Avro. What the fuck is up with you? Just spit it out," I grumbled, annoyed now.

"He knows about us at thirteen. He knows about things we swore we'd never talk about again," he said, and I stopped breathing.

"What?" I growled into the phone as my mind caught up. "How? And what the fuck does he plan on doing with the information?"

"How? I don't know. I mean, he has connections with some seedy people, so who the fuck knows, but as of right now, he doesn't plan on doing anything with it." My hand tightened on the phone while I ran the other through my hair.

"I don't believe that," I said, the initial shock turning into anger. Hadn't this guy done enough already? He had to go and dig up dirt on us?

"Well, he did have one request," Avro said, and a low growl left my mouth.

"I'm not giving Peaches up 'cause he's threatening us. I won't be scared off Avro. That's an asshole move, and if he wants to play that way, so can I. I'm pretty sure I can find a long list of dead in his wake."

"Stop! Just listen, for once, please just listen to me before you react."

My teeth ground together, but I sucked in the rage and tried to push it down. "Fine, what is his demand?"

"That you don't try to tear him and Raine apart," Avro said.

"I hadn't planned on it, but now he makes me want to fucking try. Fucking dick. Have I told you I don't trust him? And I really don't like him."

Avro groaned on the other end of the line, which turned into a mumbled litany of swear words.

"Jace, you know I love you, but let's be real for just a moment. The two of you don't like each other cause you're cut from the same fucking cloth. He knows you'd try, just like you knew he would. I'm telling you right now, Raine will split and tell us all to fuck off if we start playing that game."

Even though he couldn't see it, I tossed my hand in the air in frustration. "Dude, I'm not the one that started this."

"I know, but you're always the one to end it, and I'm asking you, no...I'm begging you and calling in every favor I have. Do not do whatever you have cooking up in your head," Avro said, his voice pleading with me through the phone.

Fuck I hated not having the upper hand. I needed something on Kai. Even if I didn't use it, I needed to have the shield to block his attack. No matter what Avro said or thought, Kai would push later on. I knew it cause Avro was right about one thing, the two of us thought alike, and I would use it when needed. Maybe even when I didn't if I thought I could get away with it.

"Fine, I won't do anything, but if he makes even one move to release or leak anything he knows, someone better be watching out for his soul because I will take him down with us."

I could picture Avro's face on the other end of the line as he rolled his eyes at me. "I worried you might say that."

"I promise to be good as long as he does. There is that better?"

"Jace?" I turned at the sound of Raine's voice. She looked adorable in my band T-shirt that stopped mid-thigh. Oh, I was sending her home with a fucking case of those. Petty? Most definitely, but it made me smirk as I pictured the look on Kai's face when she wore one for him.

"Hey Peaches, you okay?"

"Yeah, I just woke up, and you were gone." She padded across the floor, her footfalls quiet on the fancy tile.

"Just talking to Avro. Do you want to say hi?"

Raine shivered and tucked herself under my arm. Why was it that girls were always so much cooler to the touch? I handed her the phone and went back to staring out the window as my mind traveled back in time.

"I'm telling you Alex, this will work. We just need to get him on film, and he'll never want the video released. He'd never dare touch you again," I said, laying my hands on Alex's shoulders. He still looked unsure as he chewed on his lip.

"But it means I have to get him in the car, and I'll be alone with him until we get to the park. What if he decides to stop somewhere else, and you're not there, and I'm stuck in the car with him?"

They were valid concerns, and I didn't have an answer for any of them, but I knew he could pull this off. It was the only reasonable plan, and there was no way I was letting Alex stay even a single night without blackmail.

"You've got this. Nothing is going to go wrong. Just think about how well you did when auditioning for the school play. Pretend you're doing that again," I said.

"Fine, I'll do it, but you better be there," Alex said.

"Well duh. The whole thing hinges on me being there. I've got you."

When it got dark outside—and my mom and Lyle were watching a movie—I told my mom I was heading to bed early since I had practice the next day. She kissed me on the cheek and wished me a good sleep. I felt bad lying to her, but it needed to be done. No one else could know about this.

I stuffed the small video camera in my backpack, put all the pillows under my blanket, and turned off the light. We were screwed if she came in to check on me, but it was worth the risk.

Climbing out the window, I closed it softly behind me, moved to the end of the low eaves, and jumped. It wasn't far, ten feet at most. I wondered what Alex would say to lure his uncle out of the house. Would he tell him that he wanted to be alone with him or that he wanted to talk? I didn't know, but the longer I thought about Avro alone with Martin, the more worried I got.

Hopping on my mountain bike, I peddled hard and soon traveled almost as fast as the cars on the main street. I weaved through the subdivisions and then onto the road that led to the state park. It was where I'd told Alex to lure Martin. There was a huge parking lot, no cameras, and lots of places to hide so I could film.

Wheeling my bike into the entrance, I kept an eye out for gators. Not that they wandered away from the water too much, but I really didn't feel like getting bit or worse.

I'd come prepared and pulled a flashlight from the pack. Something glinted in the distance when the light hit it, and I pushed the bike in that direction. It was a spade shovel left behind by the maintenance crew, but it was a perfect weapon, just in case.

Hiding my bike behind the map of walking trails, I got the camera ready and crouched down to wait. The wind picked up, bringing with it the smell of rain. You could feel the moisture in the air and hear the rumbling of thunder in the distance.

My watch said it was almost eleven-thirty. I flipped open my phone to see if Alex had texted me, but there was no new message, and I didn't dare text, just in case. I was just stuffing the phone into my pocket when bright lights turned into the long driveway and closed in on the parking lot. I stayed completely hidden as the car parked.

"Come on, Alex, get out of the car," I whispered as I stared at the side of Alex's face through the passenger side window. I could hear the muffled yelling from my hiding spot, which made me antsy. I was about to stand up when Alex's door swung open, and he jumped out.

"Get the hell back here," Martin yelled.

I turned the camera on and set the small camcorder on the large rock near the sign. I could see the car and everything clearly now. Alex marched away from the car, straightened his spine, and turned to wait for Martin as he got out of the driver's side.

"No, I wanted you to know I'm never letting you touch me again," Alex yelled, the shadows from the parking lot light making him look fierce. He was so hot.

Martin stomped around the car, looking like a bear. Alex's entire family was tall, but it wasn't his height that made him look big. It was his college football build. He was still all muscle with his large hands balled into fists.

"Is this a joke? You got me to come all the way out here for this?"

"It's not a chat we could have at the house, but I wanted you to know that if you touch me again, I'm going to go to the cops, and I'm going to tell my parents," Alex said.

"Oh no you won't."

Martin stepped closer to Alex until he was towering over him. I could see him beginning to shake, and his fear had my blood boiling. I hated bullies and especially hated someone picking on Alex. I'd bloodied more than one guy who thought they could say mean shit.

My hand tightened around the handle of the shovel as Martin reached out and snatched Alex by the front of his shirt. "I will. I'll tell them what you did on the camping trip, and I'll tell them about tonight. The police will drag you off to jail."

"For what? You wanted it."

"Let go of me," Alex said, grabbing Martin's forearm.

"You're an ungrateful shit. How do you think your parents can afford to keep you in the fancy basketball academy to train? They don't have that kind of money. I pay for it. You owe me, and you're lucky I waited this long to collect."

My mouth dropped open at the same time Alex's did. This man was crazy. Donations for us came in from the entire neighborhood. Did he think we were supposed to fuck everyone as payment?

"I said get off of me," Alex said. I could hear the wavering in his voice and knew he was close to losing it.

"And I say get on your knees," Martin growled. His hand went to the belt on his pants, and Alex swung at his face. His fist connected hard, and Martin looked rattled as he shook his head but didn't let go of Alex. If anything, his fist twisted tighter in the material.

"No. Get the fuck off of me, you perv."

Martin hit Alex hard in the stomach, and he doubled over, coughing. A growl ripped from my chest, but Martin didn't hear it or see me stand as he dragged Alex toward the car. His back was to me, and all I saw was red.

"You dare threaten me. I'll ruin you. You can kiss any chance at basketball in high school or college goodbye. No one will want to take you after they hear what I have to say. You're nothing." I squeezed the shovel and gripped it like a baseball bat. "You'll regret ever messing with me."

Martin pulled his arm back to punch Alex again, and I swung. I didn't care how hard I hit him. I didn't bother to aim or think about the angle of the shovel. All that mattered was that he let Alex go. That he never hurt him again. No one hurt Alex, not ever.

I heard him yell, and a thrill traveled through my body. I swung again, and this time Alex screamed. I froze mid-swing. I wasn't sure what happened until Martin fell to his knees at my feet with his hands covering a massive wound on the side of his neck. Blood poured through his fingers and down his arm, and I stepped back, eyes wide.

I expected to be horrified, but instead, I watched him choke as his eyes flicked up to mine, and his mouth moved as he begged for help. Alex whipped off his T-shirt and pushed it against Martin's neck.

"Jace, you were only supposed to scare him," Alex said, his hands shaking. "I need to call for help. Do you have your phone?" I shook my head no, even though it was a lie. Martin gripped Alex's arm, fear glittering in the depths, and all I could think was it was time he met his end.

"No, no, no," Alex said. He continued to press on the wound as Martin tipped over sideways and landed on the ground. His mouth opened and closed, and I stood there silently watching. I was the monster tonight. I'd swung my weapon and taken the life that needed to be sent to hell. Not an ounce of guilt filled me.

"Jace do something. Why are you just standing there?"

"Because he deserves to die."

"No, he was supposed to go to prison," Alex said, his body shaking as he looked up at me from his knees. The blood seeped into the ground around Martin, and it felt right that this was how he died.

Then it was over as quickly as it started, and Martin lay staring at nothing. I'd never seen someone die, and I wasn't sure what I was expecting, but the quiet nothing that followed hadn't been what my mind conjured. I wasn't struck down by lightning, and there were no sirens as if the police would know what I'd just done.

I waited a few more moments, my eyes trained on Martin's lax face and blank stare, my heart pounding hard. Was I going to feel anything more than happiness? Maybe, but I didn't right now. The one thing that was there was relief. I didn't have to worry about him hurting Alex again.

Alex stood, his arms covered in blood, shaking. "Oh my god, oh my god, he's dead. Jace, he's really dead. What the hell are we going to do?" He was a wreck, sweat dripping off his forehead and mingling with the wetness already on his face. I didn't know if it was sweat or tears.

"We need to call the cops. We can explain that it was self-defense," Alex said, his voice shaking as much as his body.

I stabbed the shovel into the ground and gripped Alex's shoulders. "Look at me." His eyes found mine. "No cops. He got what he deserved."

"Jace...."

"No. He was never going to stop. Watching Martin with you, I'm surprised he didn't attack you before the camping trip. He was sick, Alex. He needed to die."

Alex pulled away and stepped around Martin's body. He paced in front of the car and jumped at the sound of a semi's engine brake. I sighed and knelt down to stare into Martin's eyes. Shaking my head, I decided what we needed to do.

"Alex, come here and help me." Pulling the shirt away from his neck, I left it on the ground and picked up one of his arms.

"What are you doing?"

"I'm fixing the problem. From this moment on, we will never speak of this again. Now pick up his other arm and help me drag him to the water."

"What? I can't do that. Jace, please, we need to call the cops. We're only thirteen, they'll let us go, but if they find out we hid a body, we could go to jail for the rest of our lives," Alex begged.

"The cops aren't going to believe us. Look, I know you're scared, but this is what we need to do. I have your back, always." My adrenaline was pumping hard. I wasn't as sure about this plan as I made it seem, but it was our best shot. I had a bad feeling about calling the police.

Alex sighed. "This doesn't feel right. My Aunt Tilly and Courtney will be worried about him." He held his hand out toward Martin.

"He's dead, Alex, not sick. They can worry all they want. He's never coming back. Now are you going to help me or not?"

"Fine." As Alex bent over, I thought he would lose his nerve, but he grabbed Martin's arm, and one slow step at a time, we dragged his body to the calm, black water. Daring to wade in up to my knees, I pulled Martin into the water, then pushed his body away from the shore. Pulling off my T-shirt, I looked at Alex, whose eyes were trained on the floating man.

"Quickly before a gator thinks we're fair game. Soak your arms." I snapped my fingers in front of his face. "Alex, do it now."

He blinked as if I'd just appeared in front of him and then did as I asked. Forcing him to step away from the water's edge, I used my T-shirt to wipe off the remaining blood, grabbed his arm, and marched us back to the car.

"Stand here." I opened the car door and found the gym bag I'd seen Martin toss in here a few times. Unzipping the top, I found a couple of rolled white T-shirts. I tossed the bag back on the floor and closed the door. "Here put this on."

"You want me to wear my dead uncle's shirt?"

"He's dead. It's the least of his worries at this point." We both turned at the sound of splashing, and I looked over to see a tail flick above the shimmering water bathed in moonlight.

"I think I'm gonna be sick." Alex closed his eyes, his hand covering his mouth again.

"No, you can't. Look at me. He deserved what he got, now focus."

I ran over to the camera and stopped the recording. It felt like it took forever for the cassette to release. Picking up the bloody T-shirts on the way, I went to the garbage can and tossed everything in.

"What are you doing?"

"Destroying the evidence, do you not watch any crime shows? We can't just leave it like this."

"Shouldn't we do that somewhere else," Alex asked.

"No time." Running back to the car, I pushed in the lighter and waited for it to pop before jogging back to the can. It didn't take long for the shirts and other garbage to ignite, and soon the barrel was engulfed in flames.

"Bring me the shovel."

Alex handed me the shovel, and I threw it in handle first.

"Okay, now for the car," I mumbled.

"What are we doing here, Jace? Alligators just ate my uncle."

"Again, he's beyond caring. Now you need to care about yourself. So stop worrying about him and worry about us." I stared at Alex's face and wondered if we would be okay after this. I couldn't think about that right now. "This is what we're going to do."

"Jace?" I jerked and sucked in a deep breath. "Are you okay? You were shaking," Raine said.

My heart warmed, looking down at her bright blue eyes. "Yeah, I'm good. I think I was dozing, and I'm chilled. Let's go back to bed."

Nodding, Raine wrapped her arm around my waist. One thing was very fucking clear. If Kai wanted to play games, I would play and win. He wasn't stealing anything from Avro or me. Not now, not ever.

Snake

20

Kaivan

I glared at the television, the beer bottle touching my lips, but I had yet to take a sip. Raine had been gone two nights. She texted and called, sent photographs, and…she looked fucking happy. Not just happy, she was practically glowing in the selfies she sent. Even the cute little kissy faces and suggestive lip bites couldn't do anything to cool down the steadily building unrest flowing through my body.

Of course, because this world fucking hated me, the news—usually filled with shit like war and people dying—tossed up glimpses of Jace's concert like a fucking entertainment show. I didn't see Raine on the stage or in the audience with the quick pan, but it didn't matter. I knew she was there.

"You plan on drinking that or kissing it all night," Roach asked.

I side-eyed him as he put his glass down. "Why are you in such a bad mood anyway? I mean, some of the guys are back, all is quiet with the other clubs, and you have a fucking hot ass old lady that anyone here would die to have."

Sitting the beer down, I contemplated telling him the situation, but with Roach, there was a fifty-fifty chance he would be understanding or stand up and yell out that he had just heard the funniest shit ever. I wasn't taking that chance. The last thing I needed or wanted was for every fucking asshole in here to know I let my woman fuck other men, but I needed to stay faithful.

"I just have a lot on my mind. Consider this my resting bitch face."

"Oh, it's hard to tell since your 'I sucked on a whole lemon while I killed your dog' look you have going seems to be the norm lately."

"Fuck off," I grumbled. I wasn't upset about not fucking anyone else. I wasn't even sure I was pissed off at her fucking Avro and Jace...no, that bothered me. But that wasn't what turned my stomach.

The more time she spent around them, the more she would realize I was nothing but a worthless piece of shit criminal. I was a killer and couldn't say I didn't enjoy it. I did my share of drinking, fucking, and drugs and watched more people die than I could remember. I'd become the monster she thought I was.

If she saw me, really saw me for what I was, why wouldn't Raine feel she was better off with just Avro and Jace and fucking disappear into the night. Avro had cut a sore spot open. I'd called him over to get the upper hand, and now it felt like he had it instead. Would he dare tell her? What would she do? Shit.

I rubbed my chest and tried to focus on anything other than Jace as he was interviewed on television. His smiling face practically yelled 'Fuck you, Kai,' through the television screen.

"Can we turn to something else? There's got to be something other than fucking news on," I barked. One of the newer sweetbutts jumped and ran for the remote.

I glanced around the room, and my eyes stopped on the couch. Not very long ago, I had Raine bent over right there. The thought made my cock stir.

"Okay, fine, don't tell me. Do you think the shit that Wilder guy knew about what Lane sleeps in was true?"

I smirked. It had taken longer than I suspected before he asked, but it was the burning question in Roach's mind. Had someone else seen Lane's tits before him.

"With Wilder, anything is possible. He takes his job seriously," I said. Roach's face darkened as he polished off his drink.

"If he does anything to her, I'm going to kill him...."

"He won't," I said.

"How can you be so sure?"

Whatever pile of bullshit I was about to hand, Roach was squashed at the sound of the main door opening. Chase's voice boomed up the stairwell as he laughed while Beast talked. All the anger I'd contained curdled in my gut, and a growl ripped from my throat.

Then like some grand magician making his entrance Chase stepped into the clubhouse smiling.

"Hey!" Cheers went up as the men sitting around spotted the prez, returned from his Canadian tour. He was back earlier than Tanner said, which made me wonder if the asshole was lying to us all along.

I slipped off the bar stool and walked across the floor, fully intending to welcome Chase home. But as he shook hands with those he couldn't care less about, my fury rose to new heights.

"Fuck, it is good to be back! Someone grab me a celebratory drink," Chase called out.

"I have your drink right here," I said. Chase turned in my direction, and a moment before my fist connected with his jaw, I saw the confusion in his eyes.

"Fuck," Chase said, holding his jaw as he stumbled backward. I was impressed he didn't end up on his ass.

Before I could land another hit, someone grabbed me from behind. I knew it was Beast without having to look. Only two people would dare grab me like this, and Mannix wasn't here tonight, leaving one person.

"Get the fuck off me," I snarled over my shoulder.

"No fucking way. You need to calm your ass down," Beast said.

Like fuck I did.

"Let him go, Beast. If Snake has an issue with me, we'll sort it out between the two of us."

"Are you sure?"

"Yes, I'm sure. Let him go," Chase said, dabbing at the blood on the corner of his mouth. Beast's python-like arms released me, and I was tempted to lunge for Chase again but kept myself rooted to the floor. "I take it you'd like to have a meeting?"

"I'd rather continue punching you."

Chase smirked. "I deserve that," he said, the anger diffusing, which pissed me off more than if he had yelled back. I wanted him to fight me, and all he did was fucking agree? Fuck him!

Beast stayed close like a looming giant as I stomped up the metal steps behind Chase to his office.

"It's fine, Beast. Go back downstairs, I think Snake and I need a moment."

"I don't think that's a good idea," Beast said like I wasn't standing two feet away.

"Fuck you," I growled at Beast, but he ignored me. What was it with everyone? Had I lost my touch?

"Yeah, I'm sure. I don't need a bodyguard." Chase pulled a bottle of whiskey and a pair of glasses from the bottom drawer of his desk.

"Whatever, but if he tries to kill you, don't say I didn't warn you." Beast slammed the door to the office on his way out. The Harley picture on the wall rattled and tipped sideways. I stared at it until I couldn't take it any longer and straightened the frame.

"Here." Chase held out the full glass of whiskey, and I grudgingly took it from his hand.

"You can't placate me with alcohol," I said. Taking a sip and flopping into the leather chair as Chase sat down on the couch. I wondered how often that couch had been slept on over the years. How many times had Beast slept there trying to hold this place together?

"I know I can't. I like you, Snake. You're loyal but not afraid to speak your mind. Too many yes men in this place." Chase rubbed at his jaw, a bruise forming already.

"You calling Beast a 'yes man?'"

A deep chuckle filled the room as Chase shook his head no. "Beast speaks his mind, just not openly. Look, the point is I owe you and the club an apology. I haven't been the prez you all deserved."

I glanced around the office. "Is this a joke? Am I being punked?"

Chase smiled and then took a sip of his drink. "No. I know it may seem like I'm an oblivious asshole—"

"No, just an asshole," I said, cutting Chase off.

He laughed and nodded. "Fair enough." Chase leaned forward so the drink dangled from his fingers between his knees. His eyes were fixed on the floor for a long time, and I wondered if that was the end of the conversation.

Music and laughter could be heard through the two-way window as the other members were welcomed home. I wouldn't be participating in the festivities tonight. I had a lead on Dave and planned on looking into it before the slippery slug could vanish into another hole.

"Look, I'm gonna be straight with you, Snake," Chase said, and I jerked out of my fantasies of killing Dave. "We don't know each other well, but I never wanted to run an MC. I'm sure that's not a surprise to you. This place was my father's legacy, my grandfather's, and so on. I always thought my brother would get the gig. He was older, and it made logical sense."

Chase shrugged as if he still couldn't believe that this had happened. This wasn't news. He was given the MC before I was sent to prison and had hidden, pretending to be dead the entire time I was locked up.

"When my father handed the Lost Souls to me instead and started the war between my brother and me...." Chase's eyes turned to look out the window. It was like he was watching a movie play out on the glass that only he could see. The sound of a crash was followed by loud laughter from the clubhouse below.

"Let's just say that if I could go back, there are a lot of things I would've done differently, but that's the fucked up thing about time. It only travels in one direction, and all we can do is move forward." He held up his finger as I opened my mouth. "Fuck time zones and the clocks moving an hour," he said. I smirked. "Stupid forward, backward shit. You know what I mean."

"Yeah, I do," I said, tapping my finger on the glass. I wanted to hate Chase, maybe pick him up and toss him through the glass, or I thought I did. Seeing him as a decent man wasn't something I wanted, but he made it very fucking difficult.

"Don't kill him, but Mannix filled me in on your old man a while back," Chase said, and my eyes snapped to his. Just the thought of my father made me want to put my fist through the wall. "I knew him or knew of him. Jackson McMillan, otherwise known as Razor, was an enforcer for the Wild Dogs. Not many of them around anymore."

My hand tightened on the glass as I glared at Chase. The anger that had simmered was beginning to rise. Why the hell was he telling me this?

"Oh yeah, I wouldn't know. After he got my mother killed and I watched her bleed out on my living room floor, he got himself tossed in prison for life. That was about when I stopped giving a shit."

Chase rubbed at his eyes. "Listen, man, I'm no shrink, and I wouldn't even profess to be highly intelligent most days, but I've done some shit that has paralleled your past."

"What the fuck are you trying to say that I think of you as my Daddy? That's why you being an asshole burns my ass so much? Cause I can tell you right now, I'm never fucking calling you Daddy Chase."

Chase laughed hard, the sound coming out like a bark as he started to cough. He sat the drink down and continued to laugh hysterically. Fucking idiot. I smirked and then chuckled. Okay, it was kind of funny.

"Oh shit, please, for the love of God, never say that around Tanner. He'll fucking start calling me that out of spite," Chase said, and I sobered with the mention of Tanner.

"We need to talk about him," I said. "The guy has no loyalty to the club. To you, yes. The club, he would watch burn for all he cared. I don't really feel like having to kill one of our own again anytime soon, so could you talk to him or beat the shit out of him? I'm not picky as long as he stops acting like he's a fucking eighteen-year-old punk."

"I fucked up with Tanner. He had his run of Ashen Springs. He fucked every housewife there, partied hard, and was never locked up for any of the shit he did. I made him untouchable, and now he's...."

"A fucking immature punk. Despite his eagerness to help kill, he's a wild-card in any situation which will get someone killed. His open lack of respect is rubbing more than just me the wrong way, and that is not doing him any favors." I sighed. "Look, I like the kid, but he needs to grow the fuck up. Chase, he will get kicked out or a bullet between his eyes. If you want to stay in control, then take my advice, don't give him the one percenter until he proves he won't abuse the power that comes with it."

He grated on my nerves and used this place, the people, and his friendship with Chase like a get-out-of-jail-free card. If I had to kill him, I would, but I didn't want to. Chase nodded but didn't say any more on the subject, and I was done talking about Tanner.

"I'm sorry for what happened with your mother," Chase blurted, dumping cold water on my head all over again.

I gulped down the whiskey, loving the burn on the way down. That sensation told me I was still alive. The only other time I felt that way was holding Raine. She made me feel grounded and worth something. "Let's not talk about my mother, okay?"

"Fine, but I need to tell you something because I owe you. It's the least I can do for everything you've done to hold this place together and keeping my ass from being tossed in jail for the shit I did." He rubbed his forehead and gulped his drink. Chase looked me in the eyes, and I knew I wouldn't like what he said.

"It was my father that ordered the hit on your mother," Chase said, and it was like the air was sucked out of my chest. I didn't move or blink. There was only the pounding of my heart loud in my ears.

"What the fuck did you just say?" My voice was low and lethal as my muscles shook.

"Snake, you know how this shit goes. People on both sides make decisions for their clubs, and there is always collateral damage. From what I know The Wild Dogs sent your father to kill my brother, but he wasn't killed, and my father retaliated. The Lost Souls enforcer at the time did the job, and my brother rode shotgun on the back of the bike."

"You fucking knew this MC killed my mother, and you let me join?" I burst from my seat, and my hands clenched as I pictured slitting Chase's throat. "You let me stay for a year and never opened your fucking mouth," I yelled. "I must really look like a sucker to you." I held my hand out toward the desk.

"Did you sit up here laughing at me as you sent me to clean up your fucking mess?"

Every part of me was ready to kill, all I saw was red, and it was taking every bit of self-control I had not to jump on Chase.

"Whoa. Whoa, no. It wasn't like that. Let me explain before you try to kill me." Chase held up his hands. "And before you ask, no one else knows. Not Beast, Mannix, Roach, or anyone else." Chase glanced at my hand, and I realized that I'd pulled my knife. I was still tempted to use it but eased myself down into the chair. I wanted answers before I decided if I was going to kill him. His eyes told me he wasn't lying, which was why I hadn't already slit his throat.

"I only started to look into your family history after I learned they were MC legacy. I asked Mannix a few questions about you, and he told me what happened with your mother, but it didn't click right away." He rubbed the back of his neck. "This all fell in my lap just before I left for Canada, and I've warred with telling you the entire time I was gone. Some shit is better off being left buried."

"Then why the fuck are you telling me now? Why take that chance?" I growled.

"Because I thought you deserved to know. This way, at least you got to see my brother killed. It's a small thing, but in life, the little moments help us move forward," Chase said calmly.

"What did you smoke a bunch of that strong Canadian weed while you were up there? What's up with the introspective, laid-back act? Where the fuck is the Chase that was snorting coke like it was going out of style, burning the world down, and leaving me to clean up your mess?"

The corner of Chase's lip curled up before he polished off his drink. "All I can say is I have a second chance at life. The baby coming helped me pull my head out of my ass. That version of me is not who I want my child to have as a father."

"I'm not sure I'm buying this act. It's easy enough to say you want to do better, but it's a whole other thing to keep it together long-term. What assurance do we have that you won't disappear again at the first sign of trouble? Spend another ten years hiding in a small town or go on a drug-induced rampage?"

"There is nothing I can say to convince you. I can only show you with time. And, for the record, I'm not saying me or your father are saints, but he tried to do right by your mother when it came to revenge. He stormed our clubhouse and shot it up good, killed three members before he ran for it and got caught by the cops."

"I'm confused now. Are you saying you're going to do better by the club or running?" I smirked as I sat back in the worn chair. At one time, I would've wished it swallowed me whole, but not anymore. Raine coming back into my life changed all of that.

"Always the sarcastic jackass, but I guess I deserve it. I'm going to prove myself to you and the rest of the club. I need to earn respect. I fucked up. I ran off and haven't been the Prez or the leader I need to be. I'm just asking you to give me the opportunity to make good on my word."

I stared at the man that sadly did remind me of my father. Until Chase said the words, I hadn't seen the similarities, but I couldn't unsee it now.

"I should still kill you," I said.

"Normally, I'd expect you to try."

Our eyes locked, and I couldn't do it. It would be like someone trying to kill me for the shit my father did. I had no control over that any more than Chase had control over what happened with my mother. He could've easily kept it bottled up, and I would never have known the truth.

"Before I can agree to let this drop between us, I need to know one thing. What happened to the old enforcer? Did he die?"

"I don't know. He was with my brother at the docks but disappeared during the fighting. His body was never recovered, so I don't know if he's dead, caught by the cops, or...." Chase shrugged.

"Or out there living his best life," I finished. "You gonna try and stop me if I decide to find him?"

Chase smiled. "You'd be doing me a fucking favor. Skin him alive for all I care. He goes by Happy Harris, which is ironic cause he was the most miserable fucker you'd ever meet."

"Well, I can drink to skinning him alive," I said. Chase smiled and stood when the door banged open, making us both jump. The knife I'd never put away sliced the arm of the leather chair as I stood and spun around.

"You fucking get home after weeks away, and this is the first place you go? Do you even know what I've had to deal with?" Naomi seethed. She didn't look much better than the last time I saw her. She'd tried to put her hair up in a bun, but it looked more like a bird's nest. Her makeup—which at one time was always perfect—ran in streaks down her face along with the tears.

"I had to come and...."

Naomi pointed her finger at Chase, and I strategically moved out of the line of fire. "Look at me! I'm a horse! No, I'm a fucking walrus! This kid is ruining my perfect body. I have stretch marks, you asshole," Naomi cried, then broke down into hysterical sobbing.

    I glanced at Chase's horrified face, his eyes pleading with me not to leave him alone, but this was sweet payback. Mouthing good luck, I snuck past Naomi, who began to shriek a long line of profanities, and closed the door.

Raine

21

Raine

"Did you get everything that you need," Jace asked as I got back into the limo. The lawyer was very helpful, and I now had a copy of the papers I filed to have Kai's charges removed. Jace had been surprisingly on board when I told him I wanted Kai's record expunged. He said it was better for all of us if that happened, and although I agreed with him, I couldn't help wondering what else was going on. As with Kai, I worried there was an ulterior motive for their actions.

The plane landed much earlier than expected, so he had the driver bring us straight to the lawyer's office. How he got an appointment for me so quickly was another Jace mystery.

"Yeah, they printed off all the paperwork and had me sign it but said it could take some time to get through the system and that I might need to speak to a Judge, but the ball is rolling."

Settling beside him in the back of the limo, he tapped on the divider, and we pulled away. Jace wrapped an arm around my shoulders but kept typing on his phone.

"Thanks for bringing me here and helping when I know you're not Kai's biggest fan."

"What gave it away?" He teased. "But you're welcome. I've dealt with a few lawyers over the last few years. You get to know the good ones." His eyes lifted to mine and then went back to his screen.

His jaw was tight, and he was glaring at his screen. "Everything okay?"

"Just typical disagreement stuff with Allen, our tour dates and locations. I only agreed to do certain countries and dates, but now he wants us to go to Southeast Asia for six months. I'm not doing that. I strategically planned everything so I could come home at least a couple of days a month."

"What do the other guys want to do?"

"They don't care and will follow my lead on this," Jace said.

"Then stick to what you have. He can't change it if you don't agree. Offer to do three weeks and no more."

"Yeah, I think this is going to be a phone call argument," he said, turning off his phone as more conversation bubbles popped up. "Now he can't annoy me for a few minutes."

Jace laid his head back on the seat, and I cuddled into his side. The short trip had been a whirlwind of excitement, and I was still processing all that had happened.

"Is it normal for the two of you to fight this much? It seems to be all you do." I asked, my voice soft. Something was off about him, but I couldn't put my finger on what it was that bothered me. Allen had well-laid plans for Jace's career, and he always found a way to let me know I was messing with them when no one else could see or hear him.

"Things have changed. I can't even explain it. I don't know if it's cause we made such a quick rise to the top or if it's something else, but he's been strange recently," Jace said.

"Could it be that he senses you're not as happy as you were before and is worried you'll quit?"

"I guess anything is possible."

Jace fell silent, and I chose not to press anymore. He seemed stressed enough. I pulled out my phone and brought up a group text, smirking as I pictured Avro and Kai's faces when they received the message and saw who was in the chat. They had to get along at some point, and Jace's phone was off, so I knew it wouldn't bother him right now.

> R: Hey guys, we're back and about an hour away from the house.

> K: Which house?

> A: Mine and Jace's house, obviously.

> K: What the hell are you doing in here?

> A: That's a dumb question. Raine sent out a group text.

> R: I did. It's much easier to let you both know where I am.

> K: I don't like it.

> A: Of course you don't. Why would you like anything that makes Raine's life easy?

> K: I swear you make me want to kill you a little more each day.

I rolled my eyes at that. Well, if nothing else, this provided an outlet to bitch at one another. Did everyone with multiple partners have this issue? I really wanted to know because I often felt like hitting them all.

> A: I'm shocked. Your threats are getting old, Kai. Maybe try something really shocking and be nice. That will confuse everyone.

> R: Okay, that's enough from both of you. I just wanted you to know that I'm back safely. Isn't that what's most important?

I felt like I was wrangling children and not men.

> A: Yes, you're right, it is. I'm happy you're back safely.

> K: Suck up.

> R: Kai!

> K: Yes, of course I'm happy you're back. Now I don't have to hunt Jace and his fancy jet down.

I smirked but wanted to hit my forehead at the same time. Kai was impossible, yet I couldn't help the butterflies fluttering around at the thought of him moving heaven and earth to find me.

> R: See you soon.

Shifting on the seat, I curled into Jace's warm body and closed my eyes. I had to admit that a private jet was pretty badass. I mean, I wasn't one to be wowed by the glitz, but we had the entire thing to ourselves for the short flight, and Jace made the most of the alone time. I was officially a member of the mile-high club.

My lip curled up as I replayed how voracious he could be and how much I enjoyed myself. For the first time, my heart felt full, and my body relaxed. I didn't have to talk to myself to stay calm and didn't jerk at someone brushing by me.

The jumpiness over loud sounds was still there, but I no longer searched every shadow and craved to learn and experience more. I wanted to ride on the back of Kai's motorcycle and have Avro teach me how to surf.

I couldn't help wondering what my parents would've thought of my choices if they'd lived. Then again, I probably wouldn't have met Kai if they had, and the thought of that hurt more than their loss. It was a sad truth, but I'd technically spent more time with him than with them. He was my rock and my shoulder to cry on and so much more. The time apart had done nothing to lessen the feelings he stirred.

I heard the lyrics of Jace's songs in a whole new way while away. Sitting at the side of the stage, humming along while tapping my foot, it felt like the words were written for me. Now I found myself singing all his songs in my head, the words on a loop and each one cutting or healing my soul.

> *My heart won't stop bleeding*
> *The final curtain is calling*
> *I have hurt you, and you have hurt me*
> *Gripping your heart and my four-leaf clover*
> *I'm only human, my heart won't stop bleeding*
> *Can't you feel my pain?*
> *I can feel yours, but you break my heart in two*
> *Yet, I still love you*
> *I'm only human, my heart won't stop bleeding*
> *The bite of the wind hits my face*
> *The rain drenches me to the bone*
> *I can't give up on you*
> *I can't give up on you, so don't you dare walk away*
> *I'm only human, my heart won't stop bleeding*
> *You promised you'd never leave me*
> *That we'd be together til the bitter end*

You promised not to let me fall
I'm only human, my heart won't stop bleeding
Don't leave
Don't leave
Don't Leave Me
You promised not to leave
I can't stop the memories
Times of better days
Baby, please, don't you want to stay
But final curtain is calling, your hands barely keep you from falling
I'll be damned if I don't fight
Until I take the final flight
I will never change, but you're always my light
I'm only human, my heart won't stop bleeding
I'm only human, my heart won't stop bleeding

Why I'd never seen the pain in the words before, I couldn't say. I loved the song as much as the next person, but it was more personal now. It gave me insight into the man. For all of Jace's bravado, I could feel so much of him locked away, and I wanted to find the key.

Closing my eyes, I snuggled closer, loving when he kissed the top of my head before I fell asleep.

Raine

22

Raine

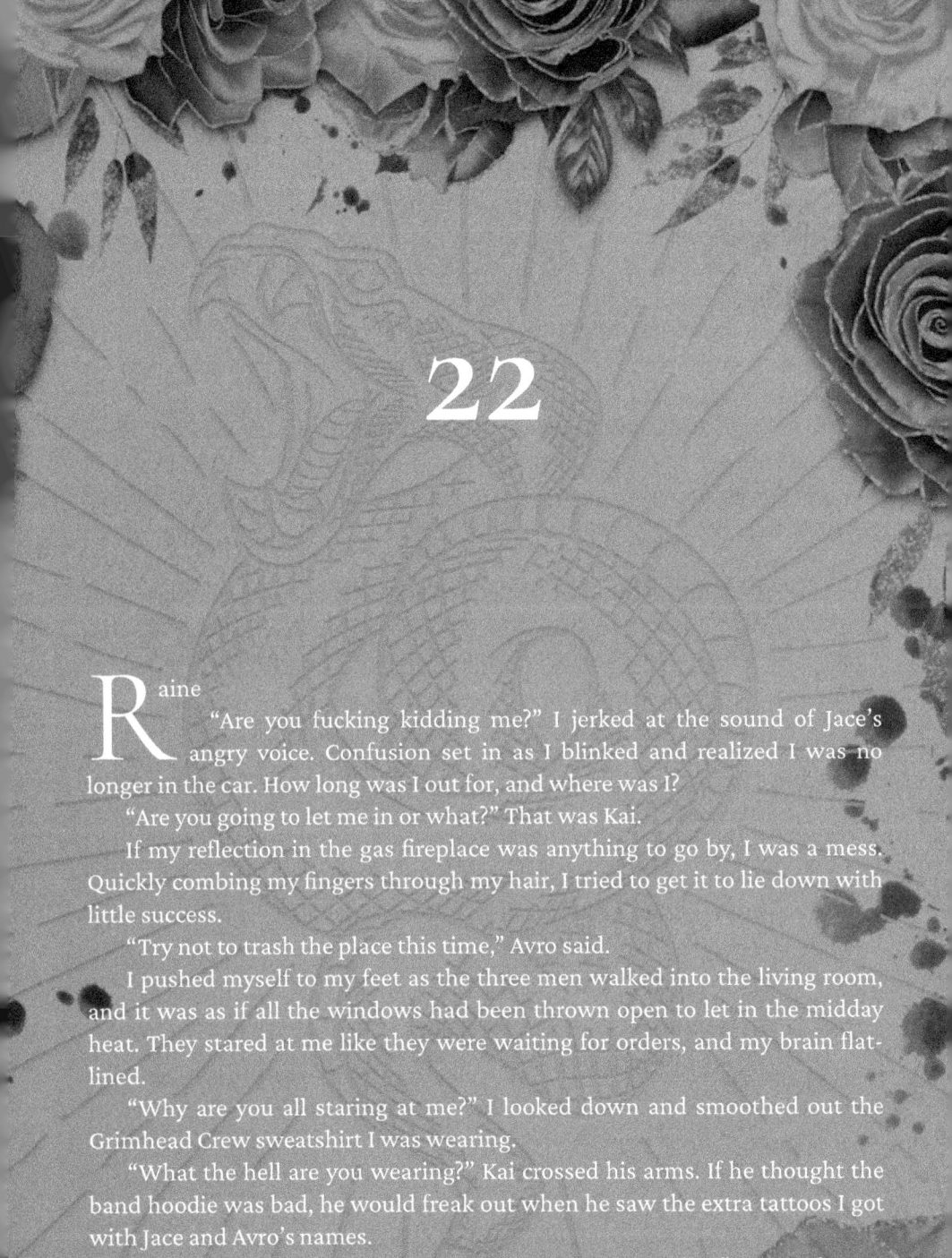

"Are you fucking kidding me?" I jerked at the sound of Jace's angry voice. Confusion set in as I blinked and realized I was no longer in the car. How long was I out for, and where was I?

"Are you going to let me in or what?" That was Kai.

If my reflection in the gas fireplace was anything to go by, I was a mess. Quickly combing my fingers through my hair, I tried to get it to lie down with little success.

"Try not to trash the place this time," Avro said.

I pushed myself to my feet as the three men walked into the living room, and it was as if all the windows had been thrown open to let in the midday heat. They stared at me like they were waiting for orders, and my brain flatlined.

"Why are you all staring at me?" I looked down and smoothed out the Grimhead Crew sweatshirt I was wearing.

"What the hell are you wearing?" Kai crossed his arms. If he thought the band hoodie was bad, he would freak out when he saw the extra tattoos I got with Jace and Avro's names.

"It's my band hoodie, and it looks fucking amazing on her," Jace said.

Kai glared, and the tension in the room tripled. I couldn't deny I loved it. There was something far too sexy about the three of them in the same room together. The problem was I wasn't sure how to approach this. Who did I go to first? Did it matter? Should it matter?

Kai made the decision for me when he stomped around the coffee table. My heart hammered hard as I stared into his blue eyes. A deep rumble rippled from his throat when he growled and wrapped his arms around my waist, dropping his lips to mine.

Our tongues battled as the burn in my stomach erupted into an inferno. Kissing Kai felt like drinking a sweet poison. So potent it could kill you, yet you could never get enough.

"Yeah, yeah, you made your point," Jace drawled, and my cheeks flushed as I remembered we were being watched. This was more awkward than I thought it would be. Kai broke the kiss but kept his hand on my waist like I would try and run. "Don't need to eat her alive."

"Jealous rock star?"

Jace scoffed and crossed his arms over his chest. "After that plane ride home, not likely." I felt Kai tense. "Nice tattoo, by the way. Such a great idea. So great I couldn't resist adding my name. I took the prime spot between her legs too."

Avro pinched the bridge of his nose as he swore under his breath, and I felt like doing the same as Kai made a deep primal noise.

"You think you're smart, do you?" Kai let go of my waist and got in Jace's face.

"Smart enough to have had cameras installed in all the rooms of the house, so if you're planning on pulling a gun again, I'd think twice, asshole," Jace said, his lip pulled up in a smirk. "Unless, of course, you liked prison enough to want to go back there for life."

I didn't know if Jace was telling the truth, this was news to me, but I looked around the room the same way Kai did.

"I really don't like you," Kai said.

"Aw, my heart is breaking," Jace made a sniffling noise. I knew he was purposely trying to get under Kai's skin now. That glimmer he got when he was enjoying himself way too much was back in his eye, and all I wanted to do was knock their heads together. "And here I thought we were going to be besties and braid each other's hair."

"I'm going to knock your teeth out of your fucking head," Kai growled.

"I'd like to see you try," Jace said, stepping closer to Kai.

"Can you two not have a single, civil conversation," I asked, and they both looked at me.

"No," they said in unison.

"Wow, the first thing you can agree on. At least it's a start." I wandered to the bar and grabbed two bottles of wine from the selection and a pair of glasses. Holding up my hands, I motioned to Avro while the other two just stared. "Avro, why don't we go upstairs and let these two work out their differences?" Avro smiled wide.

"I won't say no to that. Less chance I get a fist in the face too," he said, and stepped around Jace and Kai to meet me.

"You're really going to leave us alone," Kai asked.

"Why not? You're both adults. At least, I think you are. You need to work this shit out so we can get on with an actual relationship. I don't want to tippy-toe around the two of you. So say what you need to say to one another and be done with it already." Avro took the wine from my hand and linked our arms together. "At least one of you thinks with more than the little head between your legs."

"My cock is not little," they said in unison again and then glared at one another.

Shaking my head, I did the only thing I could think of and left them alone. They could both end up dead, but they were grown-ass men, and I didn't feel like playing ref for the rest of my life.

"Are we really leaving them alone?" Avro whispered as we walked up the stairs.

"Yup. Want to have a shower?"

"You never need to ask me that. The answer is always yes." Avro chuckled.

They would tear the entire house apart as they tried to kill one another, or they'd figure shit out—either way, I wasn't giving them more fuel by being in the same room. I refused to be the flag they fought over in their tug-o-war match.

Jace

"I can't believe she actually left us alone together," I said. "But I'm happy she did."

I cracked my neck and rolled my shoulders as Kai smirked, his eyes going from cold to lethal. I should be scared, I knew he was a great fighter, but there was something open about his aggression. He didn't keep it hidden like Lyle did. There was no doubt in my mind he'd kill me if given the opportunity and motive, but he'd make sure I saw it coming. There was no hidden agenda, sneak attacks, or shooting me in my sleep.

My hand clenched as the memory of my family's murder flashed behind my eyes. The pain gripped my chest as it had that day. It never stopped aching, and the what-ifs never stopped flowing, but I hid it well because no one really wanted to hear about your pain. They asked how you were but only wanted an 'I'm fine.' The moment you started to open up, their eyes got squirrely, and they shifted in their seat, uncomfortable with the sudden heavy reality. So I kept my crap locked up tight.

Except with Avro and now Raine. Avro lived it all with me, and Raine held onto every word I shared. After the wild night in the cemetery, she'd hugged me tight and whispered how sorry she was. They mattered. No one else did.

"Oh yeah, and why is that? If you're thinking of going round two, I'm more than happy."

I snapped back to the present as we glared at each other.

I felt the same rage in me rolling off of Kai and knew we were too similar for my liking. Avro and I were balanced. It wasn't that Avro didn't get a say—he usually made all the decisions—but I made the final call when it came to certain shit. Kai was just as demanding, and I saw him wanting to yank that away from me. There wouldn't be any sharing or negotiating with Kai unless we had an understanding.

"I don't like being threatened," I said, and as I suspected, Kai's lips curled up, obviously pleased with himself. I was about to wipe that smile away. "You think I don't have resources just because I'm in a rock band, didn't go to prison or spend my time with shady people?"

"I'm surprised that Avro told you. I really thought he'd keep that to himself."

"Then you don't understand what we share because we don't hide anything from one another. Then again, I'm not sure you'd ever understand the concept of real trust, not with how you live and what you do," I said, picking at the wounds I knew we shared.

"It's unwise to trust that much, then the other person holds the cards," Kai said.

I smiled wide, a low chuckle escaping my mouth. "And that's why you'll never really have all of Raine, because you won't give all of yourself."

"You don't know anything about us," Kai snarled as I hit the right chords. His hands gripped the front of my shirt, and I cocked a brow at him but didn't move to further the fight. If he hit me, it was on camera, and I warned him, so he couldn't say I tricked him.

"I know enough, and I know your type. You'll fuck up, and this will all fall down around you because you can't hold your shit together." I glanced down at the fists holding my shirt. "Case in point," I said, my voice as cool as a spring rain. "Do it, Snake," I growled low, accentuating his name. "Hit me. I dare you."

One finger at a time, his fists uncurled like he had to order his hands to let go of me. I smoothed out the wrinkles, just to be annoying as fuck before continuing.

"I know what you're trying to do, and you're not fucking worth it," Kai said, his hands going to his side.

"Calling Avro out in the middle of the night to threaten him...." I shook my head. "Not a smart move. It's a good thing you don't play poker. All you did was piss me off, and when I'm pissed, I stop playing nice. The things that I found about you...."

"I don't give a fuck what you have. I have no problem making a few calls and ruining you if you ever try to run off with Raine and think you can cut me out." Kai stepped in close again so our noses were almost touching. "I will do anything to keep her. Do you understand that? She is mine."

"Ours," I growled back, and his body shook with the building tension. "There are three of us now, in case you didn't learn to count past one."

"I swear I'm going to kill you. One of these days, you're going to push me too far. I can already see it."

I smiled wide but knew that my eyes held as much hatred as the blue ones staring back at me.

"You don't scare me, Kai, which is what I know really bites your ass. You're used to intimidating everyone wherever you go and it almost worked when you came here waving your gun the first time. But, I see you now. I see you for who you really are. I'll never let you intimidate me again, and you're already toeing my give a fuck limit." He took a deep breath, and we were so close his chest pressed into mine. "I've been blackmailed by much worse than you. And, here is the funny thing about blackmailers, they always have shit in their past that they don't want anyone knowing about." I narrowed my eyes at Kai. I'd only scratched the surface and found more dead bodies than he would ever want to be shared.

"Isn't that right, Kaivan McMillan? Son of Jackson and April McMillan. It's incredible what you can find when digging through the graves of someone else's life."

Kai's nostrils flared, and the excitement grew in my body, making my heart pound as uncertainty flashed behind those cold, blue eyes.

"What the fuck do you think you know?"

"I know enough. And as we speak, I have more being dug up on you. Not just one, but four private investigators I use regularly have all been sent to dig up everything on you they can find."

Kai stepped back, his eyes searching my face. I assumed to see if I was joking. "Does the name Keith Moore mean anything to you? You would've called him Red. Don't bother answering. I already know you do. He was the first man you killed and got away with it. Or you have up until now, that is. It's amazing what can be pried away from a prison guard for the right price." The cocky expression on Kai's face fell, but I had to give him credit. He didn't back down.

"I know you stood over his dying body with a bloody shank in your hand. I also know a guard covered it up because he owed you a favor and because of what Red did to you first. I bet the warden and the parole board don't know that, though, do they? A new murder charge on your list of offenses, and I'm certain that by the time my investigators are through, I'll have a deep pile of bones to shake from your tree. More than enough to bury you forever and send you away for life this time."

Purposely turning my back on him, I wandered over to the bar, readying for any move he made. Pulling out the bottle of rum and a coke, I poured two drinks and sat down with mine.

"For you, if you want it," I pointed to the glass and sipped my drink.

Kai made his way to the bar but kept his eyes on me the entire time. He picked up the drink and sat in the seat across the way. As soon as he was settled, I continued.

"I'm also sure that all those you call friends would be at risk. That Roach guy, and how about your friend Hollywood who's still in prison? Then there is a Mannix...."

"This better not be recorded." Kai looked around the room.

"I'm not that stupid. There's no sound," I said.

He glanced around the room again before his eyes settled on me. "You think your expensive shit and piles of money will keep you safe?"

Kai might not have realized it, but he just told me how he saw me. I was a walking moneybag of annoyance. Someone or multiple someones with money had done him dirty, and I tucked that knowledge away for another time.

"I'd spend every last cent I have to keep those I care about safe. So yeah, in this case, I do."

"Your money won't stop me from putting a bullet through your eyes," Kai said.

"Not much is going to stop that if you don't care about hurting Raine, or going back to prison, but I don't think you want either of those things."

His eyes narrowed into slits. "What the fuck do you want," Kai asked.

I tapped my finger on the top of my glass. "The same fucking thing you do, for you to fuck off and never come back, but I also know that's not what Raine wants, and unlike you, I plan to respect that. So all I want is for you to stop digging, and so will I. What you learned is burned, and I'll do the same."

As his glare darkened, my muscles tensed, hoping he'd jump across the space and attack me, but I knew he wouldn't. We were at an impasse, and the next move could tilt the entire board, and everyone would lose. Kai wasn't stupid and didn't want that to happen anymore than I did.

But he was unpredictable, so it was better to be safe. I was sure of one thing…how much he cared for Raine. It was in everything he did and said, and even if he didn't admit it to himself, he was scared. Kai didn't strike me as the kind of person to handle fear well. I also knew what that was like. Some ran when they were scared, but with Kai and I, the monster that lived inside of us came out, and we were more dangerous backed into a corner than ever before.

"But I want to make myself really fucking clear. If you threaten Avro and me again, I'll burn you to the ground."

Kai shocked me when he smiled and rubbed at his bottom lip. "You have balls Jace. I didn't think you had it in you." I didn't say anything and just waited for him to speak. "Fine, it seems we're at a stalemate, but if I catch wind you're trying anything stupid, then all bets are off, and I won't use money to solve my problems."

"Same goes for you," I said. We stared at one another for a long time, like two animals in the same cage sizing one another up. "I'm going to take a chance and tell you something."

"You going to admit that you killed someone," Kai asked.

I smiled, sipped my drink, and let the fizz and alcohol soothe my nerves.

"You're funny, Kai. I won't confirm or deny any such thing, but I will tell you this as a show of good faith. The man that Avro and I allegedly had something to do with his disappearance and untimely demise pulled a Red on him when he was thirteen. I'm sure you can understand why something may or may not have been done."

I watched Kai's face closely, and other than the subtle tick of the muscle in his jaw, no other emotions showed, but the hard lines of his scowl lessened.

"I just thought you should know that, and I'd do it all over again if given the chance," I said, lifting my glass and tipping it in his direction like I was offering a toast. Kai surprisingly did the same.

"Then I guess it's a good thing we're determined to keep both situations buried," he said and downed the rest of his drink. "Do you really think they are having sex without us?"

I burst out laughing. "Oh guaran-fuckin-teed. Avro wouldn't waste an opportunity like that." I could hear his teeth grinding, and right on cue, the sounds of wild sex echoed down the stairs. Kai shot to his feet, gripping the glass so tight he could crush it.

His leather jacket was squeaking as his body vibrated with pent-up rage. "Did you want to join?"

Kai's eyes narrowed as he glared at me. "Fuck no."

"Sure, I believe that." I stood and stretched.

"Get that smug fucking look off your face," Kai growled as the sounds got louder. He took a step in the direction of the stairs and stopped as if he couldn't help himself. Kai slammed the glass down on the table before balling his hands into fists. It was easy to tell it was taking everything in him not to get involved. Trying to kill Avro was also possible.

"Sorry, no can do. I've been told that I have a resting asshole face." Kai crossed his arms over his chest but didn't move further for the door or the stairs. "I guess make yourself at home. You can sit here and listen, leave, or join, I don't care, but I'm not missing out," I said.

"Oh, like hell you are leaving me down here alone," he growled as he stomped along like an elephant behind me. I wasn't sure if he was making sure they knew we were coming, but the stairs shook with each step. If Avro saw that, he'd lose his mind, but I didn't think this was the best time to mention it. Score one for me on not being a total asshole.

As soon as we rounded the corner to the bedroom, I knew we were the butt of a joke. They were jumping around and making noises as they tossed pillows at one another.

Raine stopped first. "Yes, I win. Pay up," she said, laughing.

"What the fuck is happening right now?" Kai tentatively stepped over the threshold like it might swallow him whole.

"They're jerks, is what's happening. Got me all hard for nothing." Leaning against the door frame, I couldn't be angry even if I wanted to.

"Who said it was for nothing," Avro asked.

His amber eyes practically glowed with the sun's rays pouring through the window. He whipped off his T-shirt and threw it at me. I caught it a second before Avro pushed me against the wall and captured my lips. Whatever else was happening was forgotten as his body pressed into mine.

I had no idea if this would ever work, but a part of me felt that Kai and I had at least come to a truce. Don't fuck with me, and I won't fuck with you. It was simple, and yet I could only hope it held. I didn't give a fuck about me, but the idea of Avro behind bars for something I did, lanced my heart. I'd never let that happen. I'd kill Kai first or die trying.

Snake

23

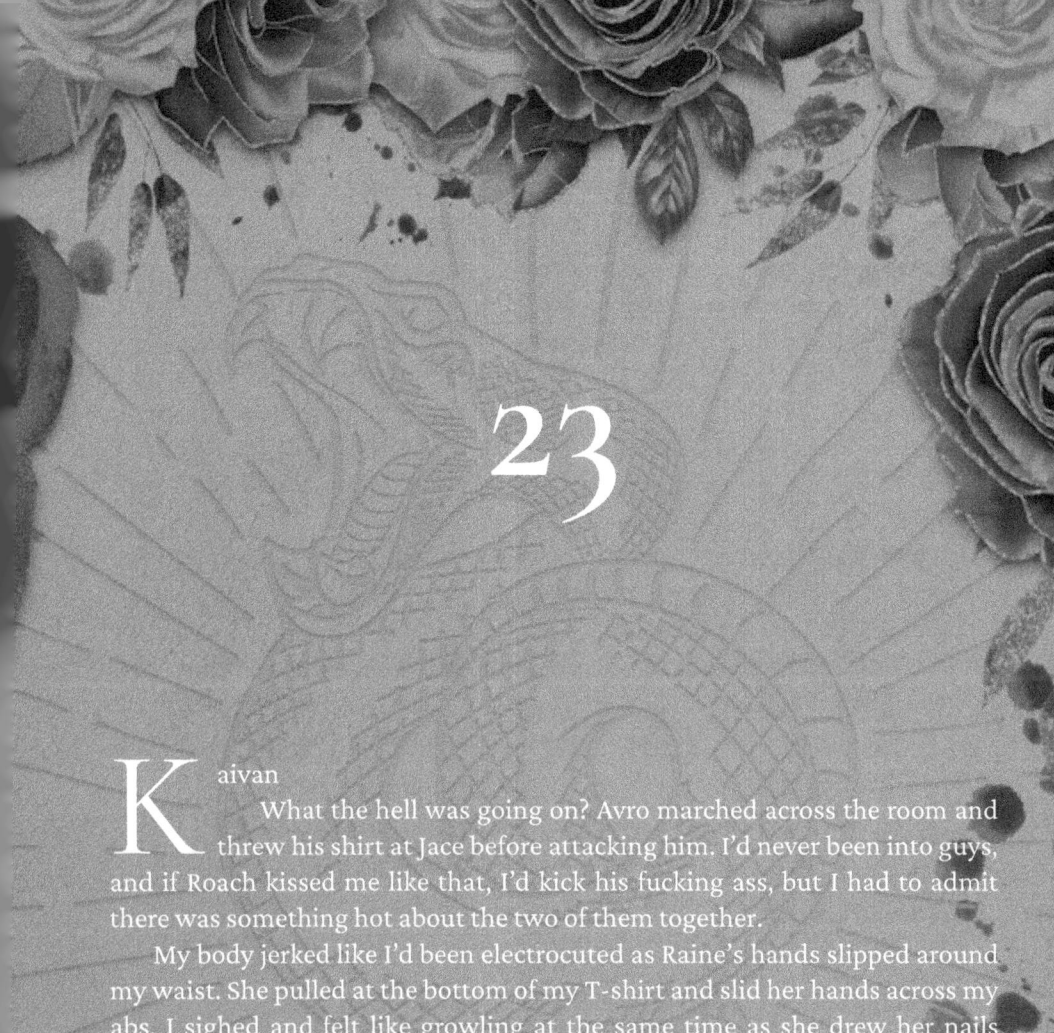

Kaivan

What the hell was going on? Avro marched across the room and threw his shirt at Jace before attacking him. I'd never been into guys, and if Roach kissed me like that, I'd kick his fucking ass, but I had to admit there was something hot about the two of them together.

My body jerked like I'd been electrocuted as Raine's hands slipped around my waist. She pulled at the bottom of my T-shirt and slid her hands across my abs. I sighed and felt like growling at the same time as she drew her nails along my skin. Fuck, that alone had me hard.

Grabbing her arm, I pulled her around so she was in front of me. "Not very nice to trick me." I loved the devious glint that was staring back at me.

The girl I knew was still in there. She'd been buried and hidden, but the more time we spent together, the more of her I saw. She didn't bother to cover the faint bruise where I'd bit her days before. My thumb rubbed over the mark, and she shivered under my touch, biting her bottom lip.

"We had to get the two of you up here somehow," Raine whispered, and my heart pounded so hard that I needed to take a moment just to admire her.

"I fucking missed you." I needed to taste her and wasn't waiting a second longer. Dropping my lips to hers, I kissed her hard. She gripped the front of my jacket and moaned as I bent her body backward. Our tongues fought a battle that neither of us backed down from.

"Oh fuck," Jace yelled. Breaking the kiss, my hand went to my gun, but as my eyes found him, he was definitely not in any position to attack me. He leaned against the dresser with his jeans around his ankles while Avro went to town on his cock.

"Never mind them right now. Just keep looking at me." Raine's voice was soft as a whisper, her breath fanning my neck just before she pressed her lips against my skin. "This is no different than the clubhouse," she said, but it was different.

I'd made a statement, a proclamation to everyone there that she was mine and I was hers. This felt very different. Even if Raine and Avro hadn't been up here having sex, they'd been together and would be again. The rage that stirred was dangerous and explosive, and it scared me how much I wanted to kill them and fuck Raine between their dead bodies.

"Please, Kai." I looked down and met Raine's pleading look. Her eyes were the only thing pulling me back from the edge of insanity. She pushed the leather jacket off my shoulders, and it fell with a thud to the floor. "This is for us. Don't think about the time we've lost, but what we can have. You know I love you." Raising up on her toes, she nipped at my ear, and my hands gripped her ass, pulling her flush against my body. "Are you really going to let Jace and Avro have all the fun? Are you going to let them show us up?"

"I know what you're doing, Tink, and you're not playing fair." She knew I loved a challenge. The harder, the better. I'd always been that way, and she was poking at me, but it worked. My cock was hard and begging to be buried inside her. To make her scream where they could see it and know that no matter how many times they fucked her, her heart was mine first.

"Maybe, but it's the truth. I missed you too."

Tilting Raine's head up with my finger under her chin, I stared into the eyes that had gripped my heart like barbed wire and never let go. "Did he really tattoo you?"

Raine's face flushed a bright red, and she licked her lips. "Yes."

"I swear to fuck, I'm going to bury his body somewhere no one is going to find it," I growled, my head snapping back to the two men that had changed positions. Jace didn't glance my way, yet it still felt like he was laughing at me.

"Kai, I let him, he didn't force me, but you'll always be on the front where everyone will see it first. It was only fair. There are three of you, and I can't play favorites as much as each of you would like that."

"I don't like this fair crap. I don't like any of this," I said and grabbed her hand, pulling her over to the large seat in the corner of the room. "Take your jeans off. I need to see this."

Her hands went to the top of her jeans and unfastened them in record time. I smirked as she wiggled them down her body. Standing straight, she stretched her leg to show off her new ink. I glared at the signature on the inside of her thigh. Then she turned to show me the outside of her leg and Avro's name. I should've fucking had a ring of my name done all the way around, but the prick would've just picked another spot. Tattooing her whole body with my name suddenly didn't sound crazy.

"Now mine."

Raine tilted her head and smiled as her eyes snapped like she was telling me to fuck off. There wasn't a world in which I'd be okay walking away from her, no matter the dangers to my soul.

Reaching out, I gripped her face and forced her to step forward. "Take. My. Jeans. Off. Now," I groaned, needing her.

She actually fluttered her eyes at me—which was fucking sexy as hell—before smirking as best she could in my grip.

"No."

"Fuck you make me so hot," I said, holding her face tighter. "And you know it too, don't you?" She made to nip at my hand, but it was a playful, half-hearted effort, and I wanted her spitting mad. When she was that angry, she couldn't see straight, and fuck, that got me so hard I didn't care who was around. Maybe that was her goal, or maybe this was just us. Either way, I wanted her on my lap and her ass tanned red.

I stared at the band T-shirt and the rock logo splashed across the front with team Jace in the corner. This guy knew how to get under my skin, and it pissed me the fuck off. He was worse than Roach. At least Roach was an asshole that didn't want to steal my girl.

Growling, I grabbed the material by the front and pulled hard. Raine squealed, and the loud tearing sound was sweet music to my ears. Fucking Jace and his fucking band. I didn't have any Lost Souls T-shirts, but I suddenly wanted a box of them made up just for her to wear instead.

Of course, she wasn't wearing a bra.

I swear she walked around like this on purpose, so I'd always have a permanent hard-on thinking about her tits brushing against the material. How it made her nipples hard, and all I had to do was slip my hand under whatever she was wearing to get a feel.

Yanking her close, I buried my head in the crook of her neck and breathed deeply. The sweet scent of her body wash calmed the darker side of me that wanted to toss her over my shoulder and take her from the house like a fucking caveman while I shot the other two men in the head. With each breath, her hard nipples rubbed against my chest, driving me insane, yet I never wanted to release her from this position.

"I can't decide if I want to eat or fuck you." Raine shivered in my hold but pressed her body closer, and my mind snapped like a brittle stick. The remnants of her shirt and mine disappeared in a flurry. I set my gun on the table as Raine pulled at the button on my jeans. When the material was pulled down to my knees, she caught me off guard and pushed me.

The jeans locked my legs together, making me stumble back, and my ass landed hard on the large chair behind me.

"Oops." The sexiest curve of her lips pulled up as she pretended to be sorry. I fucking loved everything about her. The sweet and sexy side, the innocent and timid parts that warmed my heart, the wild fury and jealousy that made my cock rock hard, and even the mischievous games she liked to play. I was all in on all of it.

"Oh fuck." My voice strained as she bent over before me and grabbed her ankles. Inches away were her soft, lush ass and her already glistening pussy. Torn, I gave in to both desires, cracking my hand down hard on her soft skin, then burying my tongue into her delicate folds.

The yell that accompanied the smack ended with a moan as my tongue swirled over her sensitive clit. Clamping my lips around the little ball of nerves, I sucked hard as my hand cracked down hard enough to sting my palm.

"Ah! Fuck, yes," Raine cried, and I growled. The vibrations had her pushing back harder into my mouth. As much as I wanted to continue punishing her, I gripped her hips instead, pulling her back so my tongue could get as deep as possible. She tasted so fucking good, I was addicted, and the whimpering noises were like ringing a dinner bell. My cock ached and begged to be buried deep inside her, the agony building as the delicious flavor of Raine coated my tongue.

"Keep your legs straight," I ordered as they shook in my hold.

"Oh god," she moaned.

"There is no God in this room. You only say my name when I'm touching you." I looked down to where she was peering around her leg and waited until she nodded. Her short blonde hair waving from the upside-down position she was in. "Are you going to cum on my tongue?"

"Yes."

"Are you sure?" I teased and swirled my tongue around, not staying on any one area too long. Raine moaned, desperate, and stepped back until the back of her legs touched the edge of the chair, forcing her to stop. I moved my head back so the contact never got any deeper.

"Yes," she panted out.

"Say it louder."

"Yes," she yelled.

"Yes, who?" I sucked on her clit hard, and her legs trembled, the small panting breaths going straight to the tip of my cock and making my racing heart pound faster.

"Yes, Kai," she yelled.

It still needed some work, but my needs clouded my judgment, and I wanted her to cum in my mouth before anything else. Spreading her cheeks further, I got as deep as I could and licked from her clit to her adorable little rosebud before doing it again and again. Raine was leaning most of her weight into my hands as her panting became more insistent.

"Fuck Jace, yes, fuck, fuck, fuck." Avro's scream was jarring and pulled me back from the edge for just a moment. I glanced over Raine's ass to see Jace on his knees and Avro sitting on the bed. I knew what a man's face looked like as they came, and Avro was doing so now. Why it pissed me off that Jace was able to get Avro off before I could get Raine to cum was not something that I could logically explain, but as soon as I started to suck again, I did so with urgency.

"Yes, right there," Raine moaned a moment before she came on a yell that made me proud. I sucked harder, forcing little whimpers from her, and drank down every last drop she gave. There wasn't a spot my tongue didn't lick, and as I drew lines over the tempting globe of her ass cheek, I couldn't resist and nipped at her.

With the most adorable fucking sound, she leaped forward and went to her knees. The dark glare she gave me over her shoulder was so sexy that my throat went dry, and I couldn't think of a single word to say.

"Not cool, Kai," Raine purred as she turned around to face me. "Maybe I should return the favor and bite you." I was paralyzed as she crawled the short distance to me and settled between my legs.

"Do it. Bite me. I want your teeth marks on me forever." The words tumbled out, but my cock kicked hard, and my heart hammered at the thought of her marking me.

A wicked grin pulled at the corner of her mouth as she leaned in close enough that her warm breath fanned my cock. I was so turned on that the precum looked like my cock was drooling as it dribbled down the side.

"I have a better idea, and before you say anything, hear me out." Oh god, if she said anything to do with Jace, then I was going to have to grab my gun and shoot him. Raine placed a finger over my lips like she knew I would protest, but it brought me back to her and her tits brushing against my cock. "Why don't we tattoo your cock with my name? You already have one over your heart, but this would make a real statement."

Not what I thought she was going to say, but as her tongue swirled along the top of my cock and her eyes stared at me with that much lust, I would agree to any fucking thing she wanted.

"You want a little property of Tink on my cock?" I sucked in a sharp breath as she sucked the tip into her hot mouth. "Fuck me," I groaned.

"I think it's only fair. You did start the tattoo idea, and this way, if another girl decides to try and take liberties...it's my name staring back at her if she gets it out of your jeans."

Grabbing her wrists, I pinned them to the arms of the chair, and her eyes locked with mine. "I will tattoo my cock with whatever you want, it is yours forever, but no one will ever touch me again. If they're stupid enough to try, I meant what I said at the club. I'll cut every finger off their hand." Raine's eyes were wide, but she licked her lips like she wasn't sure if she was horrified or turned on.

"I shouldn't, but I love that," she said, her voice soft and soothing and not at all like she was instantly condemning anyone who ever touched me. I would do it and wear the fingers as a necklace for her. My hands locked her wrists to the chair like iron shackles.

"You've always been my forever." Her cheeks flushed a bright red. "Now, before I cause a fight by tackling you to the floor, suck my fucking cock."

Raine's eyes flared with dark passion. She loved the dirty talk, and I smirked as she once more sucked my cock into her mouth. I shuddered, the pleasure so close to pain as she hollowed out her cheeks.

"Yeah, that's it bitch. Keep sucking just like that." Raine's body stilled, her eyes rolling up to mine. "No bitch?" She cocked a brow, and even though she didn't say a word, I knew she was daring me to say it again. Then I would really find out what it was like to have her teeth leave marks. I was tempted, fuck, I was so tempted as her blue eyes glared daggers at me. Any sane man wouldn't want to piss off the person with his cock in their mouth, but the angrier she got, the harder I got. I was fucked. "Okay, I won't say it again unless you want me to."

Appeased, she bobbed her head with renewed vigor, and my hands gripped her wrists and the chair harder as my body soaked up the intense pleasure. Fuck she was good.

"Ah fuck," I cried out as she licked down my shaft and sucked on my ready-to-explode balls, taking me by surprise. Every muscle strained, and my back arched away from the seat as her mouth and tongue worked magic, leaving me gasping for my next breath. Like a master, she divided her time. I tried to hold back the urge, not wanting to release yet, but as she slid her mouth over my cock and I felt her swallow me down her throat, I lost all control.

"Fuck. I'm going to cum. Oh fuck me!" I roared, but Raine removed her mouth at the last second, and the release landed all over my chest in long lines. "Fuck!" I released her hands with the full intention of jerking the last bit out, wanting so badly to be touched. But Raine had other ideas, and this time she grabbed my wrists and pinned them down.

She stood and leaned over me, my eyes fixed on her like a wild animal as my cock continued to kick, my body begging for more. I'd never seen a more beautiful sight as the wicked grin that played across her lips a moment before she dropped her head and began to clean my chest.

"Oh dear god," I grumbled as she lifted her mouth and showed me my cum on her tongue before swallowing it down.

"There is no god in here, remember?" She quipped before licking another line off.

"Tink, you are fucking incredible," I said, smiling as she finished her work and stood straight, licking her lips. She reminded me of a cat that had just lapped up a bowl of milk, and I wanted to see her do it all over again. I'd be her fucking bowl any damn day of the week.

"Shit," Jace said, drawing our attention. He was in a similar position to me, and the look on his smug ass face—this time, he lasted longer—pissed me off to the core of my dark heart.

"Hey, Peaches, you want more?"

Before I could snatch Raine's wrist, she was out of reach.

Jumping from the chair was a lesson in always removing your boots and jeans. I fell to the floor and landed in a push-up position. Oh, this was not happening.

I glanced up at the sound of Raine giggling, her eyes filled with humor that I wanted to tan her ass for.

"You think this is funny?"

"Do I get spanked again if I say yes," she asked.

"I'm going to fucking spank you no matter what, but you're going to get extra for laughing at me," I growled.

"Then what do I get if I do this?" Bending over, she kept her eyes locked with mine but joined Avro in cleaning Jace's chest. A snarl rippled from my throat, but she didn't stop.

Rolling over, I grabbed at the laces of my one boot and fought with the knot. Jace groaned, and I looked over to see Raine running her tongue along his cock and then playing with the cock ring on the tip. Of course, he had a cock ring. Why wouldn't he have something that cool? I didn't think I could hate Jace more than I already did, yet he somehow found a way to make me want to throw him out the window.

"Fuck that feels good," he said, and I ground my teeth together, but I couldn't peel my eyes away from her mouth.

"Are you going to join or just stare all night," Jace asked.

"I'm going to rip your fucking balls off," I said.

"You can try, but you'd have to get your other boot off first. That seems to be a real battle you have going on." Jace smirked, and two things hit me. I wasn't sure which was more unsettling. The first was that Jace's antics were similar to Roach and the banter I enjoyed. The second was that watching Raine lick his cock was turning me on. Neither sat well.

Focusing on my stupid boot, I got the second one off and my jeans. I'd never live it down if Roach ever heard about this. Pushing myself to my feet, I marched for the bed and froze, almost tripping again. Raine knelt on the floor in front of Jace and Avro. Her hands were wrapped around their cocks as her mouth swapped back and forth between the two.

There were no words to describe the sexiness of the image and the rage that overcame me in a single shuddering breath.

"He looks like he's going to cum and blow a gasket at the same time," Jace said.

My eyes flicked up to his, and my hands clenched. There was a good chance I would've jumped over Raine and tackled him if she hadn't picked that exact moment to stand up in front of me in all her naked glory.

"Come here," she said, and my feet moved as if she held a remote to my body. My hands wrapped around her waist, and my body tingled with the feel of her skin. "Wanna play a game?"

"What kind of game?" The sound was rough as my body continued to tremble. Raine bit her lip, and some of the control I'd managed to lock into place slipped. My body sang with the silky soft feel of her skin as I slid my hand up between her tits. I couldn't explain what she was doing to me even if I wanted to.

Wrapping my hand around her throat, I glanced over her shoulder to see Avro and Jace watching but not moving. There was an ethereal quality about

Raine that had always been there for me. She'd called to my senses when we were young and made them sing now, but my heart had grown so dark that everything was twisted like a patch of thorns.

"Jace said it would be fun to see who could last longer. Him with Avro, of course," she whispered, and I shivered. Raine squeaked like a terrified mouse as I turned her and forced her to walk backward until the wall stopped us. My hand tightened ever so slightly around her throat, and I could feel her pulse jumping under my fingertips.

"Did he now," I asked so only she could hear.

"Yes." She trembled under my hold, and her hands went to my arm. I could see her fighting her instincts. Everything in her was telling her to fight. The flash of fear, anger, and dark desire, was conflicting. I brushed my cheek against hers, and she sucked in a sharp breath, her pulse pounding harder with each passing second.

"You make me want to do dark things, Tink. You make me want to watch the light fade in your eyes just so they can never touch you again." She swallowed hard as goosebumps rose on her body. "You see it, don't you? You see the edge of insanity in my eyes. It's you that makes me this way. It's always been you."

I sucked her delicate little earlobe into my mouth and bit down enough to make her gasp and whimper. My cock throbbed at the sound, and I took a moment to close my eyes and breathe in her scent as the fantasy of either her or them dying played out behind my eyes.

"Are you going to hurt me," she asked, her voice far too sweet for the moment.

Leaning back, I once more stared into the pools of blue that swallowed my soul and refused to give it back.

"No, Tink. But you need to understand that you're fully in the driver's seat of every dark and depraved desire I have. I want their blood to run red as we fuck between their cold bodies. I want to throw us off a tall bridge and die clutching your hand in mine. Images of blood and pain are like a vivid painting in my mind, and you are the muse in all of them."

Releasing her neck, she sucked in a deep breath, and even that made me shudder with a need that coursed through my body. I ran my thumb over her bottom lip and wanted to bite that soft skin until she screamed.

"I said I'd try this Tink, but be very careful what buttons you push. The trapdoor to my sanity is hidden under one of them." She nodded, her eyes never leaving mine. "Yes, I will accept Jace's challenge, but I doubt he's going to win," I said, loud enough for him to hear, and smirked when he scoffed.

"I wasn't even trying earlier, and I beat you," Jace said. Over my shoulder, I looked at the cocky grin. So he was paying attention. That told me he was a good actor and wasn't as secure as he liked to let on. That thought simmered the wild static in my mind.

"Who says that I was," I said.

"Well then, by all means, let's see what you've got." Jace held his hand out toward the bed.

Was I really going to do this? Like Raine said, was it that much different than the clubhouse? I was about to find out.

"I have a feeling my ass is going to get punished, and I wasn't even a jerk tonight," Avro said, crawling onto the bed.

"You tricked us into coming up here together. That's worth at least one blackout fucking," Jace said, and as hard as I tried, I couldn't stop the corner of my mouth from pulling up. So the gauntlet was tossed down. Fuck them until they blacked out.

Now that was a challenge I could get behind.

Raine

24

Raine

Why I thought Kai would take it easy on me the first round, I didn't know. I screamed as he thrust himself into me, his cock filling me and shooting intense pleasure and pain throughout my body.

He growled something at Jace that I didn't catch over Avro's yell and knew he wasn't getting it any easier. What was I thinking when I decided it was a good idea to have not just one but three men and then have them all in the same room?

Kai's hands gripped my hips hard as he stayed pressed fully inside me, allowing me to catch my breath and adjust.

"Go," I heard Jace say, and a shiver raced down my spine. Were they actually going to race? My question was answered a moment later when Kai pulled out and slammed into my body so hard that my hand shifted on the bed, and another scream lodged in my throat.

"Fuck Tink, why are you so fucking tight? You're making me want to cum already."

I dared to glance over my shoulder. The stereo sound of groaning and slapping skin was intense from both Kai and Jace. A dark passion masked their faces. They didn't look at Avro or me but shot menacing daggers at one another. Apparently, staring at each other proved something I couldn't understand.

Sweat dripped off my forehead, and with each powerful thrust, my nipples ached as the breeze brushed against the sensitive tips. I bit my lip hard, my arms burning from the strain of remaining on all fours and meeting his strokes with an even pace.

I felt the orgasm building, the steady pleasure hitting all the right places, and I lost my ability to focus on anything else.

"Oh," I moaned and closed my eyes as I reached the amazing cliff. "Yes, Kai, please," I begged, not wanting him to stop.

"Touch yourself, Tink. Cum for me, cum all over me," Kai growled, his fingers pressing harder into my hips.

"I...yes, I can't," I breathed out with a gasp.

I shuddered, unable to stop myself, as Kai slipped his fingers around my throat and pulled me up until my back was against his chest. Somehow his pace remained the same. His arm snaked around my waist as the other tightened on my neck. As he whispered into my ear, the dark edge of his voice had my body trembling.

"Do it now. Cum now."

My hand slipped between my legs, and it didn't take long with all the buildup and teasing. I screamed as I came, so hard that my legs quaked, and my body arched and froze in his hold. Kai was relentless. He never slowed or allowed me to catch my breath. The iron-like grip around my waist only loosened so he could pinch one of my hypersensitive nipples.

"Oh fuck," I yelped.

"I'm going to fuck you until you pass out or Jace gives up." The words should've seemed sexy, but they were slightly terrifying. How long could he go? How long would I last before my body was too worn out to go any longer?

Avro yelled, and I watched him as his hands gripped the bed hard, balling the sheets into his fists.

"Please, Jace let me touch myself," he begged. It was easy to tell he was on edge and just needed a little push.

"Are you aching yet?"

"Yes."

"Is your cock brushing against the bed and driving you crazy?"

"Fuck, yes," Avro groaned.

The loud crack of a hand meeting skin had me lurching forward in Kai's hold, even though I knew it wasn't me that received the smack.

"Jace, fuck. Please."

"Only because you begged. Go ahead," Jace said, and within seconds Avro was yelling as he came.

"You like that," Kai asked against my neck. His hot tongue drew little designs, driving me wild. "You like watching them? I can feel you squeezing my cock tighter, and your breathing gets faster." I licked my lips. This felt like a trap. "Do you?" He asked firmer this time and then nipped at my neck.

"Yes," I breathed out and expected his hand to tighten around my throat, but instead, he picked me up with his cock still deep inside me. I had to wrap my legs around him and didn't know my back could bend back that far. I gasped with the added pressure from the unusual position. Walking around the bed, he placed me down, and I unlocked my legs.

"Roll onto your side, but you better make sure I don't fall out," Kai ordered, and I gripped him as I made the turn to make sure. "Good, now lift your leg onto my shoulder." He tapped my left leg, and I put it straight up in the air, leaning it against him like he told me to.

"Oh fuck!" I slapped a hand over my mouth as he thrust harder than before. He was getting so much deeper as he hammered into me. The volatile mix of pleasure and pain made black dots dance across my vision. My eyes rolled to look at Avro's face, and he wasn't in any better shape. His face was contorted like he was trying to scream but instead groaned with pleasure.

"You going to cum for me, Tink?" I could barely think straight, let alone answer, and that was before his thumb started furiously rubbing my clit in circles. Just when I thought I couldn't take anymore, he slipped his thumb in with his cock.

"Fuck that feels good," Kai groaned, his body shuddering.

My hands reached out, nails clawing at the blanket when my fingers linked with Avro. I knew Kai noticed, his rhythm changing ever so slightly, but that was all the indication I got other than the furious pounding my body took as he pushed me at full speed toward the next climax.

As if we'd timed it, Avro and I yelled at the same time. Our hands tightened, lending each other support.

"Oh fuck, no, not again. I can't yet. I'm tapping out," Avro moaned.

"What? How am I supposed to finish the challenge?" Jace complained.

"I don't know, but I need a cold shower and a few minutes to recoup." Avro looked at me. "Sorry."

He rolled off the bed, and even though Jace had acted annoyed, he stopped and kissed him tenderly, asking if he was okay. Avro spoke so quietly you couldn't hear him, but I knew what he said. Working at Eclipse helped with lip reading.

"I'm good. I just need some ice and painkillers. I'm done for the night. Sorry." Avro said as he limped to the bathroom.

"Don't be sorry. I'll come with you." Turning to us, Jace said, "I'm out, Kai. You win."

"No, you stay."

"No, don't argue with me," Jace ordered.

Kai stopped moving, and I looked up at him, silently wondering what was happening, but he wasn't looking at me. I held perfectly still and allowed my body to rest up.

"You'd hand over victory just like that," Kai asked. "Did you cum? Is that what's going on here?"

Jace crossed his arms, and I nibbled on my cheek to stop laughing as he gave Kai the 'Don't be stupid' look.

"Does it look like I came?" He pointed to his cock, which was still standing perfectly upright. "I do anything for those I love, and beating you is not as important as making sure Avro's knee is okay. I'm done. Take the win," Jace said and turned to head into the bathroom to join Avro.

"Hold up. I don't do winning by default," Kai growled. "You got me to agree to this. You can't just back out now."

"I'm not sure what you expect me to do. I won't force Avro to be in pain for us to play a game," Jace said.

Kai's eyes narrowed, and with a creepy slowness, he turned his head and looked down at me.

"What?" I couldn't help but ask, my already racing heart tripling in time with the dark look. He didn't say anything for what felt like an eternity.

"I don't know what you're doing, but you two have fun," Jace said, getting a few strides away when Kai growled.

"Stop. Fuck, what the hell am I thinking?" He roared and pulled out of my body. I moaned and slumped on the bed, my body tingled, and all my limbs felt heavy. "Fuck, fuck, fuck," Kai growled and turned in a circle. Jace seemed just as confused as me and cautiously watched Kai and his strange outburst.

I stared wide-eyed as he cracked his neck, his muscles flexing like he was getting ready for a fight, before he took a deep breath and locked eyes with me once more.

"Could you do a third round?"

"Yeah, I'm okay," I said. I knew I'd ache all over, but it was worth it.

"Fine, let's do this. I can't believe what you have me doing, Tink. I swear to God or the Devil, whoever reigns over my soul...." I had no idea what he was going on about as he sat down beside me with his legs over the edge. "You want both of us?"

My eyes went wide, and my mouth dropped open. "Like at the same time?" Kai nodded. "I mean, it's something I've thought about trying, but I never thought you'd be interested...."

"Good, then it's settled. Get on me, and you better hold my wrists over my head."

"Are you serious?" Jace asked the question that was on the tip of my tongue.

"Yes, don't ask any more fucking questions. Let's just do this," Kai growled, turning to look at Jace.

"Alright, give me a minute to clean up and get more lube," he said and marched to the bathroom.

I turned my attention to Kai as I pushed myself off the bed and straddled him. I sucked in a breath as I slid down on his cock, my body already telling me off.

"You feel so fucking good," Kai groaned. Leaning down. I kissed him slowly, pouring everything I was feeling into the kiss. He moaned softly, his arms wrapping around my body, and I pressed myself into his warmth.

"Thank you." My voice was breathy and filled with hope. My lips brushed against his as I took advantage of this sweeter moment between us. "You don't know what this means to me," I said, and his arms tightened.

"I love you, Tink. One thing Jace and I have in common is that I will also do anything for those I love, and that is you." Smiling, I used my fingers to turn Kai's head to the side. "What are you doing?"

"I'm marking what's mine," I said and loved how Kai shivered as my lips touched his neck and I began to suck. I was so engrossed in what I was doing that I didn't know Jace was back until a cool liquid was poured onto my ass. I moaned as Jace used one of his fingers and slipped it into my ass.

I couldn't believe I was attempting this. My first time wasn't exactly pleasant, but nothing about my reunion with Kai had been. I'd grown so much since that moment, and Jace's finger was magic. I found myself wiggling and moving as I moaned into Kai's mouth.

"Hold my wrists, Tink."

"I have leather cuffs," Jace said. I looked over my shoulder at him. "What? They're fun."

"Yes, get me those. Where are your hooks," Kai asked. Was it wrong that I thought Kai tied up with leather was sexy as hell?

"Head of the bed, you'll have to move if you want the tie-downs."

"Sure," Kai answered. I didn't know what they meant, but I got the picture as Jace wandered back with leather cuffs and a black rope. I couldn't help but laugh as Kai pushed his body up, keeping me firmly with him as he repositioned and laid his arms once more above his head.

Jace tossed the cuffs by my hand, and I smiled. "You don't have to look so happy about this," Kai said, but there was no anger in his voice.

"Oh, but I do. I really, really do." Teasing Kai was fun, and I was nearing giddy as I buckled the first cuff and then the second around his wrists.

Jace was bent down beside the bed and stood holding the rope. "I'm making this simple with a quick-release knot, so if you want to, all you have to do is roll off the bed and pull the second line," Jace said as he slipped the rope through the rings on the cuffs and then squatted down once more. "I won't bother with the other side."

"Do you really want it to be that easy for me to get up and untie myself," Kai asked. "Not scared that I'm going to kill you?"

Jace chuckled as he stood. "Try the tension," Jace said. Kai tugged and couldn't move his arms. "I'd be stupid if I thought there was no chance of you trying to kill me. But the fact that you initiated this and want something to keep you from killing me tells me it's not what you want. You're worried about your snapping point. Consider this a trust exercise given the circumstances."

I grabbed Kai's face as Jace got on the bed behind me and resumed his playing, prepping, or whatever it was he was doing.

"Just kiss me and look at me," I murmured against Kai's lips.

"I'll go slow," Jace said.

I tried to keep a straight face for Kai, but fuck, the feel of Jace stretching me was intense on its own, let alone with Kai already inside of me.

"Oh shit, oh wow," I moaned with each inch he pushed deeper. I could feel them filling me up to levels I didn't think possible, and the pleasure stole the air from my lungs. My mouth opened to scream, but nothing came out. It was too much, and my heart was beating so fast that I thought I would pass out. At least they wouldn't have to worry about sharing for long.

"Bite my chest," Kai growled low against my cheek. "Breathe, Tink. The tension will make it worse."

"I'm trying," I gasped, tears forming as the pain and pleasure brought back memories. I blinked, trying to force them away as the sounds and smells of that night and those men flooded my senses. As if sensing things were at a breaking point, Jace stopped moving altogether.

"Look at me," Kai whispered. "You're not there." I nodded as a tear escaped and dripped onto his chin.

"I know," I breathed out but couldn't look him in the eyes. The embarrassment over what happened and the guilt of what I did to Kai...what I did to us, bounced around inside my brain. It couldn't have picked a worse time to race to the front of my mind.

"We can stop Peaches. This doesn't need to happen if it's too much too soon," Jace said, his voice smooth. Them both being so nice was freaking me out more. That wasn't like either of them.

"Do you still want to do this," Kai asked.

I was tempted to say no, that I couldn't handle it. But if I stopped now, I'd hate myself later for being weak and letting the past sneak up and grip me. This might be the only time Kai and Jace let this happen. And I walked away? No, I couldn't stop now.

"Yeah, I do." I took a deep breath and ordered my body to relax, not that it did much good. So much for the yoga classes. They don't prepare you for two cocks inside of you.

"Okay, then bite my chest as hard as you want. I fucking love the pain when it comes from you. Give me all you've got, Tink. I want your mark on me forever."

I bushed my lips against his chin, and his eyes softened briefly. These glimpses of Kai under the mask of an MC enforcer gave me hope for us...for all of us. I licked at the area I was going to bite down on and reminded myself he wanted this. My teeth just touched his skin when Jace thrust the rest of the way in, his body hitting mine.

"Ah!" I screamed as I bit down hard. Kai growled and arched up into my mouth.

"Fuck yes! Harder!" Kai said, mixing with my screams.

Jace held off moving to let me adjust, but once he started, there was no holding back. He was as voracious as ever, and then Kai thrust his hips, mirroring Jace.

"Damn, Peaches, you have a sweet, tight little hole. You're making me want to cum already," he said, his pace quickening.

I unlocked my jaw and released Kai's chest as the sharp, burning pain shifted into passion. Desire erupted in my stomach. No logical thoughts or words would've come from my mouth as I closed my eyes and let my body soak all this in. Kai's muscular chest beneath my fingers, and the dueling cocks determined to tear me apart with pleasure.

"Holy fuck Tink, you're so tight," Kai said through clenched teeth.

"Please don't stop," I mumbled as the tremors started in my body. Kai sucked my lower lip into his mouth. "Right there, oh fuck." The thrusting increased, yet they managed to stay in rhythm while I was reduced to a drooling mess and laid my head on Kai's chest.

Their primal grunting and groans were sensory overload to my system, and I screamed their names as I came. The orgasm was so powerful that the black dots once more formed behind my eyes, and still, they pumped on.

"You want me to cum, Peaches? You want me to cum in your tight little ass?" I didn't answer, and he smacked my ass hard.

"Ah!" I screamed, but the sting only drew out the climax that my body was riding.

"Answer me, or you get another one," he said.

"Yes, yes, I want you to cum," I wailed.

"What about me, Tink? You don't want me to cum," Kai asked, and I felt like hitting him for asking such a stupid question.

"Yes, I want you to cum too."

"Then say it like you mean it. That was weak," Kai bucked up harder, and I cried out as my body revolted against the possibility of cumming again, and yet I could feel it in the distance like a slow-moving train that was picking up steam.

"Fuck, Kai! Yes, I want you to cum in me, cum for me."

"Where do you want me to cum?"

"In my pussy. Please, please," I begged, my muscles losing the ability to hold myself any longer.

"Here I come," Jace groaned, his body slamming into me hard and holding still.

"Fuck! Yes, Tink!" Kai growled. He pushed up and froze.

I could feel them both filling me, and I fucking loved it. It was the last thing I remembered before I passed out, my head over Kai's pounding heart.

Snake

25

Kaivan

Things I never thought I'd be doing, spooning Raine in a California king bed with her sound asleep while I stared into Jace's eyes. More like glared, but it was close enough. He was in the same position holding Avro, and we were left wide awake, making sure the other didn't move or try anything.

"You can go to sleep, you know," I said quietly.

"Like I'm going to close my eyes with you in the house," Jace countered.

"What the hell do you think I'm going to do? Slit your throat or something?"

Jace's eyebrow arched, and I smirked. "See, I wasn't thinking that, but then you go and put that thought in my head, and I'm definitely not closing my eyes now. So you go right ahead."

"Not a fucking chance," I said.

We were quiet for a long time, and I could just make out the digital clock glowing behind Jace. It was two-twenty-three and counting.

"Aren't you getting sleepy," Jace asked.

I snorted. "You trying to hypnotize me now?" Raine mumbled something and wiggled closer in my hold. I would've been tempted to slip between her legs again. Toss her leg over mine and fuck her while she slept until she woke up, but I knew she was tender. So I adjusted myself, my cock already thickening with the image and feel of her body pressed up against mine.

Lifting my arm off Raine, I eased out from under the covers. I hated to admit it, but the stupid bed was comfortable, and I loved holding Raine. I'd missed her way too much the three days she was gone, and she was leaving again for a night. I didn't like this at all.

"Where are you going?"

"Drink. You want anything," I asked, being nice instead of being my usual sarcastic self. It felt weird not instantly wanting to go another round of who could sling the better pile of shit.

"Bottle of water. Thanks."

"You better not switch spots while I'm gone. I'm not cuddling Avro," I said, and Jace chuckled.

"No promises. Peaches has a nicer ass to cuddle."

I glared, and he laughed a little harder.

"Too soon?"

"Fuck you," I mumbled and padded out into the hall and down the stairs. I wanted to tour the rest of this house. I always liked to know every inch of any place I stayed for more than a single night. Even in a shitty motel room, I checked under the bed, the windows, door locks, and the best place to store my weapon. Fun little habits you pick up locked away.

"What the fuck? Who the hell is this organized?" The impeccable organization that I found when I opened the fridge was intense. It looked like a showroom model fridge with fake and perfectly aligned food. Reaching in, I grabbed two waters from the stocked door.

I was just about to close it when a small container caught my attention. The label read: homemade lasagna, single piece, made Sunday at 6:00 pm. This had to be Avro. I couldn't see Jace labeling anything like this. I grabbed the container, my stomach growling as I lifted the lid and took a sniff. Fuck that smelled good.

"Fuck it." I tossed the container in the microwave and fumbled through the drawers to find a fork. "Holy shit," I mumbled as I stared at the built-in trays and the technically redundant labels. I liked it. No one I knew appreciated organization. I didn't do it with my cutlery: dessert forks, salad forks, dinner forks, butter knives, and steak knives, soup spoon and so on. I mean, could he not see what the items were? This was next level, leaving me wondering why go to all the trouble. If I wanted to get all introspective, I would say it made him feel like he had control, something leftover from whatever trauma he suffered at the hands of his uncle.

I did kinda hate that I threatened him with that information. If I'd known what happened and hadn't been so focused on getting at Jace, I wouldn't have done it. I still would've held onto it for insurance. I wasn't an idiot, but calling him out could've been avoided. The look of terror in his eyes...shit, it didn't feel right. Fuck I was going soft.

The microwave dinged, and I grabbed a *dinner fork* before re-closing the drawer and claiming my meal. Leaning against the counter, I peeled off the lid and had to admit it smelt a little like heaven. The first bite told me all I needed to know. Whoever made it could really cook. It was rich and bold with flavor and had the perfect combination of meat, sauce, noodles, and cheese. I had no idea when I became a food connoisseur. Move over, Gordon Ramsay.

I put my dish in the sink, disappointed that there wasn't an entire pan to eat 'cause I would've been all over that. Grabbing the two bottles of water, I cracked my lid and was taking a big gulp when I stepped out of the kitchen. Something caught my peripheral vision, and I stopped moving, my eyes searching the darkness. The hair stood on the back of my neck, letting me know someone was there. I'd learned the hard way to always trust my senses. Of course, I didn't have a weapon on me.

A car drove by. the bright lights flashing in the living room, and—even though I should be used to the unusual visits by now—I jumped at the sight of Wilder. My open water bottle squirted from the top and landed all over my chest.

"Geez us, fuck!" I hissed and glared at the man who was worse than a flea on a dog's ass. "Wilder, what the hell are you doing here?"

Stepping into the room, I hit the light switch closest to me. It turned on four small ceiling lights around the room to show Wilder casually stretched out with his hands resting behind his head. He looked like he didn't have a care in the world with his boots on the new coffee table. All I could think was Avro would faint at the sight.

"Sitting," Wilder said in his standard monotone way that told me nothing and only confused me more.

"Fuck. I mean, why are you sitting in this house? Why are you here at all, and how the hell did you get in?" I took a step back, just enough to glance at the door with the security panel. It still had a bright red light announcing it was armed.

"Because it was late, and you weren't home. I was concerned, so I decided to ensure you were alright," he said. Stuffing his hand into his pocket, he pulled out a handful of almonds and tossed a few into his mouth. "I tracked you down here."

"I didn't realize I needed a curfew at twenty-nine years, seven months, and thirteen days old, but heck, why not start now?" Wilder's eyes found mine, and his head turned slightly as he fixed me with a stare right out of *The Exorcist*.

"I like that you do that. Why do you do that?"

"Do what," I asked, exasperated.

"Count time so specifically. I do that."

Great, something we had in common. I shrugged and drank some water, glaring at what was still trailing down my chest.

"I don't know why. I just do. So, are you still concerned for me, or are we good, and you're going home?" When had Wilder stepped things up from the odd, weird questions to a personal stalker?

"No, I'm no longer concerned. You seem to be in perfect health. Your stamina while fucking is very impressive. You would do well with the *Art of Kamasutra*. At least that's what I've been told." Wilder said and casually closed his eyes.

"First, why the hell were you spying on me having sex...again? Second, why are you still here if you see I'm alright?" I leaned against the wall. I was pretty certain that I would need the support after whatever 'What the fuck' answer he gave me next.

"I always take notes of everything. It's much easier to refer to my books when I want to look something up." He pulled a little black book out of someplace and held it up for me to see. "And I'm still here because this couch is comfortable."

Great so he was making notes of me fucking. I pinched the bridge of my nose. I shouldn't have asked. This man was going to drive me to drink. Well drink more than I already did.

He wiggled a little deeper and sighed. Such a strange combination of personalities, this guy was. I had visions of the egg he was made from trying to swim away from the sperm like it knew they weren't a great match, but the sperm tied the egg up until it submitted. I was fucking tired. That was the only reason for that random thought

"Don't you have a bed?"

"I have a cot, and most of it is taken up with the object of my affection. She steals the blankets and wraps them around her like a cocoon. Is this a girl trait? I find it much harder to fuck her like that. We usually have a rumble session over the blankets first. She's very possessive of them."

"You don't say," I drawled out and covered my eyes as I pictured what he was putting this girl through.

Wilder sat up and produced a pen from thin air like he performed a magic trick. I felt like asking what was next, a rabbit? My luck, that would be exactly what Wilder pulled out of his cargo pants. That, of course, would lead to more questions I didn't want to know the answers to. Like, 'Why the fuck is there a rabbit in your pants?'

"I don't know if it's a girl trait. The only girl that has stayed the night with me is Raine, and she didn't steal them, but she may now, after waking up to a strange man in our bed."

"I'm not a stranger," he said, his brow knitting together.

"To her, you were. She doesn't know you, Wilder. You scared the shit out of her. Not literal shit, I don't mean she shit the bed, although I'm sure she felt like it." The fact I had to explain this boggled my mind.

"Hmm." Wilder rubbed at his chin. "I see."

"I'm going to bed. Do you need me to let you out?" I asked and then realized I didn't have the alarm code.

"No, I have a key." Of course, you do. "And I have the code, so no worries, the place will be secure once more." Except from you, was all I could think.

Creepy fucker.

When Wilder continued to sit and stare at me, I gave up and hit the light switch, plunging us into darkness as I turned to leave.

"Snake?"

I was so close to escaping, so, so close. He saved my life. I repeated that in my head as I turned to face him once more.

"Yes, Wilder," I said, hoping my voice didn't sound as annoyed as I felt.

"Why do you choose to sleep with your enemy?"

There was a movie title in there somewhere. "I'm not. They're not my enemy." I really hated that—of all people—it was fucking Wilder that made me say that out loud.

"Avro did sucker punch you in the face. You don't consider that an enemy?"

Of course, he saw that humiliating moment, the guy sees everything. "No, it was payback for doing it to him."

"Is that how you and your friends like to treat each other? I would think punching someone in the face and then, have them punch you back would not make them your friend."

How did I say Avro wasn't exactly my friend, but also not my enemy. "No, I...forget it. It's too hard to explain. The point is he's not my enemy." Twice he made me say it, twice. Fucking guy. "And I'm technically not sleeping with them. Well, I'm sleeping with them if I ever get back to bed, but I'm not fucking them. Do you see the difference?"

"You lay with them but are not sticking your cock in them. Yeah, I get it."

Wilder leaned back on the couch once more, his eyes closing. "I don't know if I could share the object of my affection, but maybe I should try. Do you think maybe she needs more cocks to make her happy?"

I opened my mouth to say that probably wasn't the problem but then decided, nope, I wasn't getting involved. I didn't know who this girl was, and the last thing I needed was to get involved with Wilder's drama, kidnapping, or whatever he had going on. For all I knew, the guy had a Stockholm syndrome fantasy he was playing out. Who was I to stand in the way of a good fantasy coming true?

"I can't answer that question. Shouldn't you get going? What if this object of your affection needs you, and you're not there?"

He shrugged and then smiled. "She won't. I got her watered, fed, and changed her piss pot. She was curled up on the cot and asleep before I left. Plus, I can watch her at any time. See."

He pulled his cell from his pocket and held it up for me. I couldn't see who was in the image from this far away, but the security camera clearly showed someone curled up on their side on a low cot. It was barely big enough for one person, let alone two.

I couldn't believe I was going to ask this and knew I'd probably regret it, but I found my mouth open. "Wilder, have you considered unchaining her?"

"You mean like let her roam around?"

Or run away as fast as she can.

"Yes, that's what I meant."

He lifted his shoulders and let them drop dramatically. "I can't. I keep her chained for her own safety."

That was an answer I didn't see coming. If I'd been a betting man, I would've said he took this girl because she caught his eye. He didn't understand it, so he had to find a way to make it make sense.

"So, someone is after her?"

"No."

"But she's in danger?"

"No."

For fucks sake, I knew this was another rabbit hole of insanity.

"Okay then." This was a redundant conversation, and my brain was screaming it would rather fuck Jace than spend one more second in this conversation. That said it all.

"Night Wilder." I went to turn and then held up a finger. "Oh, and no coming into the bedroom. I don't care about the reason...unless someone is dying, the place is on fire, or you see people breaking in. But those are the only reasons you step foot in the bedroom, especially when I'm having sex." Like it wasn't weird enough that he was sitting listening, I didn't need him propped up in the corner scribbling in his book. "Got it?"

"Sure, but why would I want to?" He screwed up his face, his eyebrows raising like I was the one saying something crazy.

I bit my lip to keep from freaking out. "Just don't." I turned and stomped away. "Fuck, fuck, fuck," I mumbled under my breath and jogged up the stairs. Maybe there was such a thing as Wilder repellent. If not, there should be, and the first can I'd hand out was to the girl he had locked up.

Avro

26

Avro

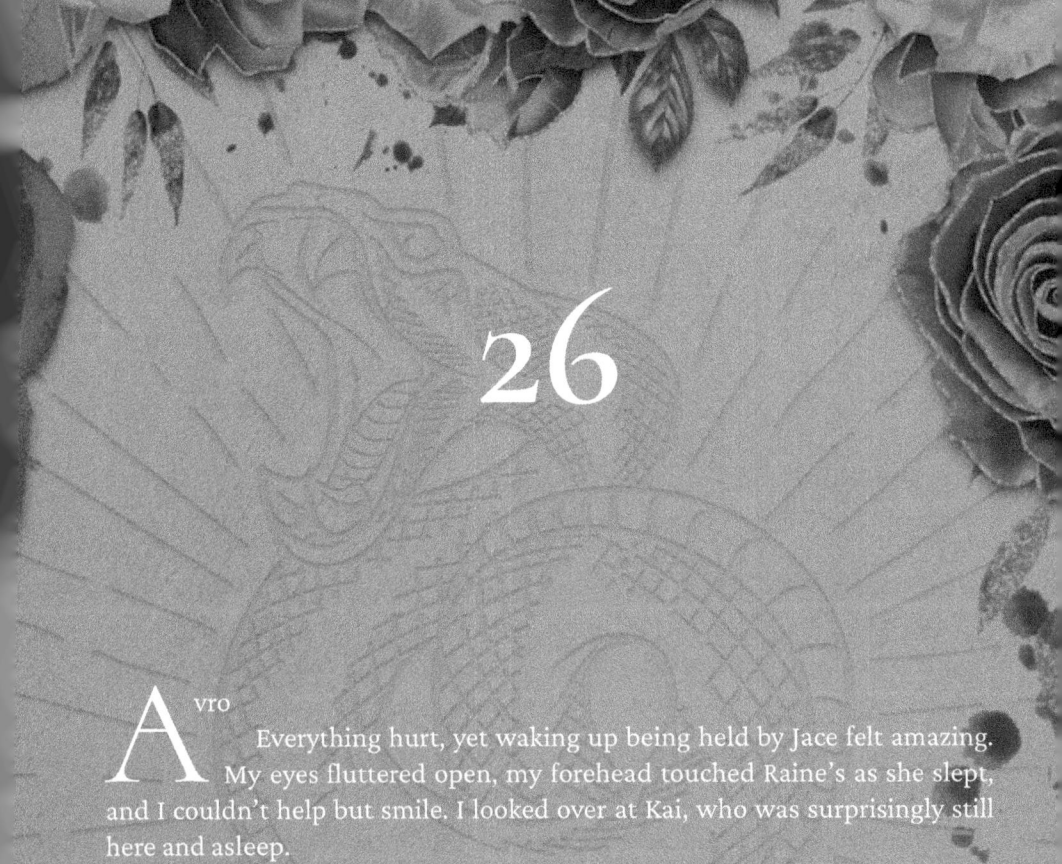

Everything hurt, yet waking up being held by Jace felt amazing. My eyes fluttered open, my forehead touched Raine's as she slept, and I couldn't help but smile. I looked over at Kai, who was surprisingly still here and asleep.

I was still pissed at him for threatening Jace and me, but Jace said he had the situation handled and for me not to worry. How was I not supposed to worry? We were talking about our lives. We could be sent to prison for the rest of what was left of them.

"You're awake," Jace's soft breath made me shiver as he whispered against my neck. "You okay?"

"Yeah, I'm good."

"I'm sorry again about last night. I wasn't thinking," Jace said, his arm tightening around me.

"I'm good, really, don't worry about it. If I didn't think I could handle it, I would've spoken up," I said, and he scoffed.

"No, you wouldn't," Jace said. My mouth turned up in a smile.

"You're right. I like to push too much."

"Did you tell Raine you need another surgery?"

I stared at her peacefully sleeping face and so badly wanted to touch her but didn't dare with Kai holding her. Last night was a massive breakthrough, but no one knew what today would bring after he woke up in this bed.

"No, not yet. I will. It's not that important," I said. "We've had a lot going on. I just didn't want to...."

"Burden anyone," Jace finished for me.

"You know me too well." I shuffled around and tried not to wince as I rolled over to face Jace. The first rays of the sun peeking through the blackout curtains reflected the silver in his eyes. They were always so intense but held a softness as he stared at me.

"You're not a burden. Why do you even think like that?" Jace cupped my cheek, and I soaked in his warmth.

"I don't know, you know me. I'm a cancer sign. It's in our nature to be emotional," I teased, but Jace didn't smile.

"Tell her. She's not going to care. It's not a big deal."

"I will, I promise. But right now, I'm going to get up, do my stretches, and then make waffles for breakfast. I even got fresh cream to make whipped cream."

"And now I'm picturing licking that off of you. Thanks for that," Jace smirked before gently kissing me. He rolled over and stood to let me up, holding out his hand so I didn't struggle. I tried not to think about being laid up from surgery all over again. It took a huge mental and physical toll last time. It was the reason I hadn't told Raine. It was better not to think about it and put it out of my mind until I had a surgery date. "I'm going to sleep a bit longer while he's still asleep." Jace pointed his thumb at Kai, making me smile. Apparently, Jace didn't trust Kai any more than I did.

Jace grabbed my hand as I turned to walk away. "You sure you're okay?"

"Yeah, why?"

Sometimes I hated that he knew me so well. I was the overthinker, the worrier, and the one who stressed over everything from bills to what to eat. It was rare for someone to notice as I liked to keep that part of me buried. I was so depressed and worried after the last time I went under the knife that Jace had pretended to be sick for three weeks to come home from tour and help me feel like myself again. I didn't want to go through it again.

I fought the depression every day, battling to get out of bed. I hated it so much. I was scared to end up in that same mental state. The worst was when I overheard someone say, 'Just get over it.' They didn't get it. You didn't just get over it. If they'd really suffered, they would understand that I chose not to let it keep me down, but the pull to hide in my room and never leave was there and poked at me as it taunted my mind every moment of the day. I'd felt like an addict, and the overwhelming sadness was my drug.

"It's not going to be like last time," Jace said as if able to pluck the fears from my mind.

"I know," I said and squeezed his hand. "I'll let you know when breakfast is ready." I walked into the closet and threw on some comfortable clothes before I broke down and poured all my fears at Jace's feet. I hated doing that. It felt like I did it all the time, and as many times as he said he didn't mind, it still bothered me.

Walking down the stairs, I turned toward the workout room I'd set up. It wasn't huge, but large enough for a couple of mats on the floor, a treadmill, and a universal weight machine. Jace liked his free weights, so we made space for a rack of those, and I had wall-to-wall mirrors installed. Grabbing a set of weights, I wandered over to the bench and sat them down to start my arm workout when the white scar on my knee caught my attention.

It seemed glaring to my eye against my tanned skin. I didn't care about the imperfection. It was just another reminder that no matter how well you planned your life, shit always crept up and punched you in the face.

I couldn't believe how nervous I was. Stopping at the large doors of the theatre, I stared at the posters that lined every door. They were all the same. An image of me flying through the air or posing for the camera. I still couldn't believe I'd been chosen to be the headliner. It was my first big gig, and to be the star was crazy to me.

Reaching out, I touched the poster of the death-defying leap I'd practiced for months. I loved flying through the air. This particular show wanted to incorporate traditional circus trapeze, an acrobat routine, and unique dances, as well as the unusual acts of athleticism that a Cirque du Soleil performance was known for. The entire thing piqued my interest from day one.

It was more like a play, the story of a boy dreaming of working in a big top, but his family didn't understand or support him. It followed the boy's life from when he was young and the challenges along the road to following his dreams. It was as if the story had been designed for me. More than once during practice, I'd been moved to tears by the emotion the entire show evoked. I was so proud to open the show in two days, but I wished Jace could be here to see this.

He was, unfortunately, in Germany at his first massive venue. It was a sold-out show, so this was an important week for both of us. He promised we'd talk after, no matter how late it was.

Yanking open the door, I watched as everyone stretched and got warmed up for practice. The sessions were long and grueling, and I'd never been happier. Basketball was never really my thing. I played to do a sport, and Jace was good at it, so it gave us something to do together that our parents had approved of.

Now that my parents had disowned me for 'daring to be bisexual,' I was free to do what I wanted, and I did feel free. If I'd known that the weight that always hung around my neck would be lifted once they knew, I would've done it a lot sooner.

"Hey Avro, you're going to be partnering with Julian today. Maurice is off sick, and we need him well-rested for opening night," Coach yelled when he saw me.

I looked to where Julian was already on the large stage warming up. He was basically my understudy and knew the main parts of the show. He was nice enough, and we got along fine, but I always felt like he was jealous that I hadn't 'paid my dues' in the industry to earn a headliner position.

I may not have been in the industry long, but I was a natural and trained every spare moment. I'd been training from the time I could walk and would practice everything I thought would help me improve my strength, flexibility, and skill. The best was when I talked Jace into doing parkour with me. He wasn't a huge fan of heights, but within a month, I could scale a building. I knew then this was my calling. I wasn't some sloth that had wandered in and got the job cause I knew a producer or something. Normally I was the first to arrive and the last to leave. I'd sit in my small apartment going over what I needed to do and when throughout the night. The only time I took a break was to speak to Jace and catch up.

"Okay, no problem," I yelled and went backstage to get changed. Jogging out, I warmed up with everyone as I reviewed the opening sequence in my head.

"Hey, you good that I'm working with you today," Julian asked as he stepped up beside me.

I gave him a smile that I hoped came off warm and genuine. "Yes, of course, you're a fantastic partner. I've seen you working with everyone."

"True, I am gifted," Julian said and then chuckled, but I didn't get the feeling he meant it as a joke.

"Alright, places, everyone. We are going to run through with lighting and sound all day. I want this to feel like the real thing," Coach said.

By the time the first half of the performance was done, my uncertainty about working with Julian had eased. He was not only a great partner, but we were completely in sync with every movement, a perfect mirror of one another, and Coach was calling out how beautiful everything looked. I wondered if Maurice would have a spot to come back to.

My adrenaline spiked as I climbed the tall ladder to the top of the platform, where I would perform the trick that was being advertised all around Vegas. It was what was on the posters. The timing had to be perfect, or I would plunge to the stage below. There was a net lying on the floor that the audience couldn't see. It had an emergency pull in it that if something went wrong, it would snap up and into position to catch me. The first test run to make sure it was working had been terrifying.

Reaching the top, I waved to the fake crowd and smiled before grabbing the fly bar. I knew the movements in my sleep. Julian signaled that he was ready, and we were off. The amount and type of flips before I caught Julian's arms were what made the sequence so dangerous. We took the theme of 'death defying' to a whole new level, and the platform sat twice as high as any other show in the world.

Performers used the ladder and bars on either side to continue to perform as I flew, their vibrant costumes shining under the bright lights. The first release and catch went off without a hitch, and Julian smiled and counted down the release to return to my bar. The next two were equally smooth. I was tight and on point.

We pretended to smile at the crowd again as we caught our breath, and the performer acting as Ringmaster called for silence. We took our cue and once more sailed through the air. I released my bar and did the tight twists that made me look like a spinning bullet before stretching my arms wide in a Superman pose.

Julian was right on cue, and I locked my eyes on his arms, but in the split second, before he caught me, he moved his arms just enough that I missed my grab. One hand missed completely, but the other managed to link the tips of our fingers.

I lifted my gaze to his eyes, and he smirked subtly as his eyes remained wide like he was surprised, "Oops."

There was this moment of hesitation as his finger relaxed, and I began to fall. Julian watched as I plunged to the floor, and the voice in my head screamed that this couldn't be happening.

A burst of fear had adrenaline pumping through my system, and my arms and legs pinwheeled like that would somehow make me fly. I remembered the safety net and relaxed into the position to land safely. I saw the worried faces of the other performers as I dropped like a stone.

Sure enough, I hit the net and bounced high into the air. Like we were taught, I stood up to land on my feet for the second bounce, ready to scream at the top of my lungs what Julian had just done. As my feet touched the net the second time, one side snapped, and that was all it took. The momentum of a twenty-foot bounce and the odd jerk as the safety line broke dropped me at an odd angle onto my left leg.

There was no pain at first, just the sound of a pop and then tearing as my knee bent one way but my body the other as I landed in a heap. I could hear people screaming and shouting and one of the paramedics that we always had on hand telling me not to move. Unable to help myself, I looked down and didn't understand what I saw. Why could I see my heel? Either my leg or spine was backward, and I knew I was in bad shape.

Out of the corner of my eye, I saw Julian running over as if he was concerned, and I screamed and pointed at him.

"You did this. You're evil," I hollered as loud as I could.

Fake tears trailed from his eyes. "I'm so sorry, Avro. It was an accident, I swear," he professed over and over, but I knew better.

That one day, that one man, and that one decision had changed the course of my life forever.

Bending over, I touched the half-moon line and winced. Sometimes I wished I'd told Jace the truth, told him it wasn't an accident, but I knew what he would do. I'd seen him do it to my uncle, and there wasn't a doubt in my mind he would kill for me again, and I didn't want that for him, me, or our souls. No, it was better this way.

I wanted Julian to pay, but the dark hatred I felt for the man scared me, and I decided to move forward with my life rather than live in the past. As it turned out, I could've gotten a position with the same group but a different show when my knee was healed, but by then, I'd met Raine.

Laying down on the bench, I went through the first half of my arm workout and then sat up and finished it off. I felt better by the time I was done and was tempted to do more, but the others would be up soon, and I wanted breakfast well underway or done. I hated people staring over my shoulder while I cooked, and Jace loved to do it because he knew it would annoy the shit out of me.

Wandering down the hall, I turned into the kitchen and stopped walking as I tried to process what I'd just seen. Taking a step back, then another, I stared into the living room, my eyes searching the corners like this was a great prank. But, it wasn't hiding in any of the corners.

"Jace," I called out. "Jace, can you come here?" I yelled and could hear more than just one set of footsteps running down the stairs.

"What is it? What's wrong? Is it your knee," Jace asked as he looked me over like a worried hen. Raine was next as she stared at my face and then down at my body. They were acting as if I'd just been shot.

"Stop, both of you." I pointed into the living room. "Where the fuck is the couch?"

"Un-fucking-believable." We all looked at Kai, who shrugged as he ran his hand through his hair. "Fucking aliens."

What did one do with that answer other than blink?

Snake

27

Kaivan

Killing Wilder wasn't an option, but fuck me, I wanted to.

Avro had a meltdown like I didn't think he was even capable of. He searched outside and in the garage, thinking this had to be a practical joke, and of course, I was the top suspect.

I lost track of how many times I said, 'I didn't touch your couch,' and 'What the hell would I even do with it?' Jace checked the cameras, and I covered my eyes, thinking for sure they would see me talking to a random guy in their home and just letting him stay. That would take some explaining. I mean, how the hell did you explain Wilder?

But Wilder had a camera scrambler or some other weird government tech shit on him. Or he scrubbed the three hours and seven minutes he was here because it was nothing but white snow, which set Jace off. I had to admit. It was nice not being the one freaking out for a change.

Just when we thought Avro was calming down, he noticed the container in the sink and went off, thinking whoever took the couch also ate his food. *How rude.*

"Okay, that's my cue to get going," I said to Raine. She was leaning against me as we stood in the kitchen. We both watched as Jace paced while he was on the phone. Avro was off cleaning every inch of the house, which apparently was his way of calming down.

It was driving me crazy that I felt bad for Avro. I should be laughing and joining Wilder as we sat on it and drank a beer. I should be rejoicing that he managed to piss the guy off, but once the initial anger wore off, Avro seemed beaten down. I could see it in his eyes as clearly as I could see my own reflection in a mirror.

"I'm going to go clean," Avro said, pulling supplies from a walk-in cupboard.

"Do you want me to help," Raine asked.

Avro shook his head and smiled at her, but it didn't reach his eyes. "No, I just need to do this on my own," he said and hugged Raine before disappearing.

"I'm really worried about him," Raine whispered. "What's going on, Jace? I know it's his couch, but it seems like so much more."

Jace poked his head out of the kitchen, making sure Avro was gone before turning to face us. He crossed his arms over his chest and rubbed his bottom lip with his thumb.

"Avro has some control issues if you haven't picked up on it. It comes out in mostly harmless ways, but it started after what happened to him. I've been able to help him through most things, but it got really bad again after his accident, and he refuses to talk about it," Jace said. "He saved for months to get that set and was so proud of it, but it's not just the couch. This made him feel violated." Jace shook his head.

"So, not to be the asshole in the room, but why don't you just buy him a new one? I'm sure you have the money," I said, earning myself a punch in the arm and a hard glare from Raine. Man, she had hard little fists.

"What? It's a good question. He's a rock star, for fucks sake."

"I could, but Avro won't let me. I haven't spent a dime on this house except for my music room. I refused to let him buy anything in there and had a huge fight about that. He wants to do shit on his own. He hates leaning on me, especially financially. I could buy him the whole fucking block if he wanted it. I could build a custom home, but nope. Anyway, I'm going to call the cops. This is the weirdest fucking break-in."

Jace paced the living room as he spoke to whoever picked up at a police station. I'd never called one to find out. We hadn't seen Avro since, and I felt like an asshole, even though I had nothing to do with the couch caper.

I wasn't worried for Wilder, anyone that could carry a freaking couch out by himself without making a noise or leaving a scratch didn't need it, but I had no interest in being interviewed by cops and my name popping up in the parole board system. That was a no-go for me.

"I don't understand this. It's crazy," Raine said, shaking her head as she turned to face me. "This place was supposed to be the safer option."

Leaning down, I whispered in her ear. "Wilder showed up last night, but I swear I didn't know he would take the couch."

When I stood straight, her mouth was hanging open, her eyes wide in obvious disbelief. "What the fuck? Why didn't you say anything?"

"How do I explain Wilder? My possibly unstable and delusional neighbor broke in to make sure I was okay because he was worried about me. He then randomly decided to steal a couch when I went back to bed. Oh, and he's like ex-military, ghost-level shit and already had your house code. But don't worry, he's harmless and thinks he's protecting me or maybe all of us."

"Yeah, okay, aliens seem more plausible."

"Thank you, but…I'll talk to him and see if I can get him to return it." I pinched the bridge of my nose, already picturing how that conversation would go.

"No, don't. That would just add another layer to the violated feeling Jace mentioned. I understand the need to feel safe and in control. I still check my locks multiple times a night when I'm at home. I barely slept, and I'd find a place to hide on really bad nights. I know it probably all sounds stupid to you," Raine said.

I cupped her face and forced her to look at me. "No, I don't think it's stupid," I said and then brushed her lips with mine, loving that she opened up and moaned softly.

Breaking the kiss, I laid my forehead against hers. "You think that if he knows it wasn't some random joke and 'whoever it was' can get back in, it will make the insecure feeling worse."

"Yes, exactly. I'll take him furniture shopping, make a day of it. I know his favorite lunch spot, and there is a sale at one of the stores he likes. I'm just going to spend the day with him."

I nodded in agreement, but I was still talking to Wilder. I had no idea how to get him to understand boundaries, but I obviously needed to make that happen.

"I have a few things that I need to get done today, and I don't know when I'll be finished, but I'll call," I said, grabbing my leather jacket off the kitchen chair and shrugging it on.

"Is that code for I'm going to be killing people today," Raine asked.

"Who says I would do that? Okay, maybe once or twice." I smirked before I sobered and walked back to where I'd left Raine standing. I couldn't tell if she was okay with what I did or not. It wasn't a conversation I ever planned on having with someone. "Are we okay? Are you good with what I do?"

My heart rate picked up as I waited for her to respond. What the hell was I going to do if she said no? Would I force her to be okay with it? Would I quit the MC? Shit...

"Am I okay with you breaking kneecaps and killing people?" She put her hands on her hips and stared at the floor as she nibbled her lip. I knew that look and held perfectly still as she thought.

"Honestly, Kai, I don't know how to feel. It's not like I know much about the inner workings of an MC. Like how do you choose who to go after? Is it you that chooses or someone else that chooses them?" She rubbed at her eyes and sighed. "I don't want to know anything about any of it and don't tell me when you're going because I'll worry myself sick. I want a backup number for someone you trust that I can call if you don't come home. Shit, I need to think about it more. It's not as if I woke up one day thinking this would be an issue and I should have a plan for how I would feel or react."

"That's fair," I said, but I was worrying now.

I didn't want to be like my father or force Raine to live as my mother had. She hated what my father did, and his cheating ate her alive. I watched it with my own eyes, and yet we were trapped. You don't just walk away from an MC. I understood that now, but he could've done things to make them better, and he chose not to. That wouldn't be me.

Other guys in the club had great home lives and still worked with the MC. That was what I needed to figure out how to do. Cause I wasn't letting Raine go, that wasn't even an option in my mind, but I wasn't cut out to work a nine-to-five in an office either.

I wrapped my hand around the back of her neck and drew her in close to my body. Raine's hands slipped around my waist and held me tight, instantly calming the storm that constantly raged in my body.

The scent of her body wash and shampoo drew me in, and I laid my lips against her forehead and closed my eyes. I took a deep breath and let her smell wash over me. The world disappeared when she touched me.

"I can't let you go, Tink," I whispered. "Not ever again, and that should scare you because it scares me. It terrifies me what I will do to keep you." She shivered in my arms, but instead of stepping away like a sane person, she hugged me tighter. Maybe we were both a little unhinged.

The anger simmering under the surface of my skin was ready to lash out at anyone or anything that tried to tear us apart. It didn't matter who it was. I'd rip their beating heart from their chest if they dared to come between us.

But what did you do when that person was yourself?

Snake

28

Kaivan

"That was fast," I mumbled as I stared at the number calling on my phone. "Mutt, what do you have?"

"So, just to be clear, we're even once I give you this info. Right?" Mutt said, and I wanted to punch him through the phone. He really was a weasel. It was appropriate that he was in the Weasel Legionnaires.

"Yes, we'll be even until your club fucks up again and thinks they are sharks in a pond when they're really only guppies. Just remember that it will be my face, you see. If you and that MC of yours crosses us again," I growled into the phone.

"We're not, I promise." Mutt's voice was shaky coming through the line.

"Good, now give me the info."

"I couldn't find anything on the Dave Collins guy you mentioned, but I found an address that will interest you. That Father Frank guy is a real nutjob. He started as a motivational speaker for men looking to improve their self-esteem, but it became much bigger. He is at full-blown cult status now, but no one knows where the compound is because either you never see the men that join again, or you do, and they are so brainwashed that they never give up its location."

Great, more good news. "How is this information helpful, Mutt? You mentioned an address."

"Hang on. I'm getting to that." I rolled my eyes.

I looked over to where Roach was freaking out. His angry tone carried on the breeze as he stomped around like a child having a tantrum. I couldn't hear what he and Wilder were saying, but only one topic made Roach that angry... Lane. Hopefully, Wilder wasn't sharing her showering habits, that would send Roach over the cliff.

There was a rattling paper on the other end of the line. "You have a pen?"

"Yeah, go ahead," I said, not bothering to write it down. Memorizing random crap was my specialty.

"It's 555 Catalina Court."

"So, what's this address?"

"When the guy decides to interview the men, he takes them to that house," Mutt said.

"How do you know this? You better not be playing with me, Mutt. I fucking swear, I don't want to have to kill you over this shit."

"Nooo, I promise. The info is legit. I know a couple of guys that, before they joined the club, had interviewed, thinking it was going to be this self-help workshop, but they were taken to this crappy house and videotaped as they answered questions for hours. They decided they didn't want anything to do with his crazy ass, but a lot of others love him."

"What does he want? Power, money...control of the world. What's driving this guy?" I said it out loud but more to myself.

"I don't know, but I do have one more piece of info that is fucked and going to blow your mind. Frank's real name is Francois Hanson, and he has a twin brother. Now get this, the brother was a fucking FBI agent and a serial killer called the Chameleon. He's got an undisclosed number of kills to his name and was like the FBI's most wanted. That right there is some fucked up shit. One brother is a cult leader, and the other a serial killer."

I didn't say anything as I processed the information. Was that why this Frank guy was so cocky?

"So did they catch this Chameleon, or is he still running around," I asked.

"I don't know, man. But that's one family I wouldn't want to be part of. Anyway, no idea when he'll be at the house next, but that was where both guys were taken."

"Thanks, Mutt."

"So listen, I scratched your back. Maybe you can scratch mine and put a good word in for me with your Prez?"

"Not a chance." I hit end on the phone and stuffed it in my pocket.

I was staring at complete opposites as I marched over to the truck. Wilder was leaning back on the truck, taking in the sun's rays, while Roach paced, his face red as he snarled like a dog and mumbled under his breath.

"Dude, calm down before you have a stroke."

"I can't! Do you know what he said to me?" Roach pointed at Wilder, and I shook my head. "That Lane has a boyfriend. A fucking boyfriend. When did she get a boyfriend, and how did she get one? This is not happening. I will cut his cock off with a butter knife if he touches one hair on her head."

"They've already kissed," Wilder said, and Roach went volcanic.

I stepped back as he shook like he was going to erupt. "He's a dead man. This fucking punk is mine."

"He's actually—" Wilder started, and I cut him off.

"That's quite enough info for today, Wilder. Thanks." I glared at him, hoping he would get the message and shut up.

I grabbed Roach's arms and forced him to look at me. "Bro, you know I love you like a brother, right?" He nodded, his nostrils flaring and muscles twitching under my hands. "Great, take this advice from someone who cares if you remain breathing. You need to calm the fuck down and back off Lane's doorstep."

"What? I'm not..."

"Yeah, you are. Keep denying it all you want, but the problem is Hollywood will castrate you if you go anywhere near his baby sister with anything but pure thoughts. She needs to live her life, and you're only supposed to be watching her to make sure she doesn't end up in a dangerous situation. She has your number to call if she gets into trouble."

His body slumped in my hold. "I'm so fucked." His worried eyes met mine. "I can't go near her again, can I?"

"I wouldn't, but I'm not the one with the best friend in jail who is counting on you to keep your cock to yourself. You need to reign this shit in." I shrugged. "Unless you don't give a shit about Hollywood and your friendship anymore."

"I've known that family my whole life. I was at the house playing video games with Hollywood when they brought her home from the hospital," he said. "How the hell did this happen?"

"I don't know, but that's even more reason to stay away. Roach, do you really think she won't see through your I don't like you act? Or Hollywood, for that matter? What if she gets freaked out and tells Hollywood? Just get control for your own sanity." I pulled out a smoke and lit it up, taking my usual two drags before putting it out. "Take it from someone that has been consumed by a woman for over a decade. The shit will not get better if you continue to stalk her ass."

"I wasn't stalking. I was dedicated to my promise." My brow arched at the perfectly worded statement only a stalker would use. "Okay, fine, I might have been taking it a little too seriously."

"Why are you watching this girl at the sorority when I already am," Wilder asked, and Roach glared at him.

Sometimes I really wish Wilder would learn to shut up. "Remember, Chase asked him to protect the sorority," I said before Roach tied himself into another knot.

"Well, I guess that settles it. I don't need to anymore," Roach said, stuffing his hands in his pockets.

"It's for the best." I laid my hand on his shoulder as he looked down, his face so miserable it was like I'd just told him he was dying.

"You get an address," Wilder asked, effectively ruining the moment. He was right, though. We needed to get going.

"Yeah, I do. Let's roll."

We found the place easily enough. It was a run-down shack on a cul-de-sac, surrounded by mostly abandoned homes and crack houses. Not exactly a warm and fuzzy kind of neighborhood for a man trying to convince people to better themselves. It made me wonder what the fuck this guy was really doing with his members.

"What do you think?" I asked.

We were currently parked across the road from our target. The driveway was in such bad repair that I thought it would swallow the truck when Roach parked. The house wasn't any better, and the badly damaged roof had collapsed. Anyone living inside wasn't gonna be a credible witness.

"Looks like an abandoned shithole. Are you sure this is the right spot," Roach asked.

"Mutt swears this is the joint." I peered up at the sky. It would be dark in about twenty minutes. "I don't think he'd lie, he has nothing to gain, but there is a good chance that Frank no longer uses this location."

"Only one way to find out," Wilder said and jumped out before I could stop him. I didn't even get the button pressed on the automatic windows when he ran across the street and disappeared behind the house.

"That guy is fucking crazy," Roach said, dumping the last of his chip bag into his mouth.

"You don't know the half of it, but I'd rather have him as a friend than an enemy." I pushed open the passenger side door. "I guess we better follow him."

"Oh, you mean you want me to get out and not just be the sexy getaway driver?"

"I think you need a new mirror. Yours is definitely broken." I closed the door as, *asshole*, was yelled loud and clear. I smirked as I pulled my knife and flicked it open. Switching the grip, I held it in my fist and let the flat of the blade lay along my arm.

Walking across the road, I kept my eyes and ears peeled for sirens or any sign of life. The whole street was eerily quiet, like nothing living wanted to stay here, and a shiver raced down my spine. I wasn't much for evil spirits and shit, but everything felt off.

"This place has a bad vibe, man," Roach said, echoing my thoughts. We'd been in some pretty hairy situations together, in places that most would never travel, and his feeling confirmed I wasn't going crazy.

"Agreed."

Wilder jogged around to the front of the house. "This is definitely the place you're looking for." Wilder nodded toward the back. "Follow me."

"Are we really going to follow him?" Roach whispered. The corner of my mouth pulled up in a lopsided grin.

"He grows on you, kinda like a barnacle that just sorta sticks and grows back if you scrap it off."

"That's a horrifying image, thanks," Roach said as he made a gagging face. We rounded the back of the house, but Wilder was nowhere to be seen.

"Over here," he said, waving his arm from inside a tool shed.

"Yeah, definitely not feeling any better about the situation now," Roach grumbled as he pulled his gun.

The shed looked like one you'd pick up at any hardware store for all your lawn crap. It was metal and rusted, with no windows and a single door. Scraggly trees had grown around the sides, and a few vines were growing along the top.

Reaching the door, I looked inside the small space expecting to see Wilder and maybe a pile of bones. Instead, a massive trap door was open with a soft glow coming from inside.

"Fuck my life. I said I wasn't helping you anymore. I should've stuck with that," Roach complained.

"Oh shut up, it's not that bad...." I said and then watched as a spider the size of my hand ran across the dirt and disappeared.

"Right...cause I didn't just see that rat-sized spider," Roach said.

I glanced over my shoulder at him. "You should feel right at home with your fellow insects." I smiled wide.

"I fucking hate you. You know that, right?"

"Are you two coming," Wilder asked as he poked his head out of the ground like a gofer.

"Coming." I waited until he jumped back down before stepping on the steel ladder and making my way down. Roach was close behind me. I looked around the tunnel that was over six feet tall and about the same width. "How is this even possible? I didn't think we could even dig this deep here in Miami?"

"He had the entire piece made from formed concrete, metal, and a silicone substance. Then he had it installed and sealed to keep water from penetrating the cavity. Quite smart, actually, but how all this got done without anyone knowing is the real mystery. This takes a backhoe to dig, a crane to install it, and a massive flatbed truck to move it. This is not a sneak in the night quietly sort of situation," Wilder explained.

"Why the fuck would someone go to all this effort," I asked, following Wilder and his flashlight.

"Not sure, but wait until you see this," Wilder said when we reached the end. All of this was boggling my brain. The door was sealed with a wheel like you'd see on a submarine, and when Wilder opened it to the space beyond, the stench hit us. Roach and I gagged while Wilder seemed completely unaffected.

The combination was similar to the prison laundry I used to wash, but on top of the shit and cum scents was old piss, mold, and something rotting. My nose was assaulted by the worst combination of smells someone could ever put together.

Covering my nose with my arm, I followed Wilder into the basement of a house and assumed it was the one we'd been watching. It was an open space with nothing but darkness. There were no windows, but as Wilder shined his light around, my eyes went wide. Chains and cuffs lined the walls, enough for a dozen people. We reached another hallway with a line of doors that reminded me of solitary confinement at the prison. They were solid metal with a small flap that could be slid open to look inside. The first one we looked in was empty except for a thin old mattress that had seen better days and more chains and cuffs.

There were six doors in total, all the same. The last one had fresh blood on the ground and a smear that couldn't have been more than a few days old.

"What the hell am I looking at here," Roach asked, his voice muffled behind his arm.

"Trafficking, I think, or torture and murder. Each room has a different feature." Wilder pointed to the corner of the room and the tiny camera I hadn't noticed. Then he pointed to the thin lines of wires pulled up like a beast ready to drop from the ceiling. "Those are for electrocution. They can drop and dangle a designated height off the floor. The person here has to stay flat or get zapped, but I'm sure there is more to it. If this were my torture room, I'd let loose a few of those massive spiders or a snake so the person wants to jump up."

I stared at the side of Wilder's face. "You're creepy, man. I like you, but you worry me."

Wilder turned his head to look at me. "Why?"

"Never mind, let's keep searching. I need some clue about where this asshole is hiding. I find him. I find Dave."

The door to go up was locked, but Wilder had it unlocked faster than I ever could. We walked up the stairs quietly, ready for anything.

"Is this the house we were watching?" I looked out a window between a crack in the wooden boards covering the glass.

"Nope, the one behind it. We traveled in the wrong direction, and I bet you won't see your truck if you look out the front."

"This is getting stranger by the second," I said. Doing as Wilder suggested, I looked out the front window. Sure enough, we were facing the wrong way. This was not what I expected.

The place was dated with peeling, floral wallpaper, and floors that were a mix of shag carpet and subflooring. No pictures anywhere, but a new roll of toilet paper was by the shitter, water was running through the taps, and the thermostat on the wall glowed with the temp.

"Hey, Snake, come see this." I left the back room I was looking through and found Wilder sitting at a computer with Roach standing behind him.

"Where did you find the laptop?" He pointed to an air exchange vent, and I shook my head. I would never have thought to look there. Wilder pulled something out of his pocket that looked like a memory stick. The screen glowed and then showed a lock screen. Before I could ask how he planned on getting past that lock, he shoved the stick in the side, and the computer dinged and opened.

"Government encryption decoder," Wilder offered, and Roach and I looked at one another and shrugged. I could kill people with no problem and even make it creative, but this was why I brought Wilder. "These are all files on people, women mostly." He pointed to the long list that went on forever. He opened a file, and even my eyebrow rose with the violent images. A woman's face was contorted in agony as spikes were shoved through her body while someone fucked her. This was a new level of fucked even for me. You couldn't see the attacker's face for the large hooded robe that covered his body, but each image Wilder clicked on was more disturbing than the next.

He went to another folder and another, and it was all the same. Some women had been mangled or burnt but were still alive when these images were taken. One image had candles and strange symbols I didn't recognize drawn on the wall in the background. This Father Frank was more disturbed than I thought. He was using the cover of the cult that focused on spirituality and twisted it into whatever the fuck this was.

"They have dates and names. I'm surprised someone would do that unless they really didn't think they'd get caught," Roach said, pointing to the long list of folders.

"It's their trophies," Wilder answered. "They probably keep something personal as well, but this will be where he comes to relive the kills. Someplace no one would be watching or catch him jerking off or re-enacting it with others."

"That's fucked up," Roach said.

My pulse began to pound hard as a thought occurred to me. "Is there a folder for Raine Eastman?" Wilder and Roach looked at me, and even though they didn't say it, I knew what they were thinking. "I need to know," I said before they could argue.

The little folders went on and on as he made it down to the Rs, and the little cursor hovered over a file highlighted in blue. My fist clenched on the knife, shaking in my grasp.

"Open it," I growled.

"Buddy, you sure you want to see this?"

My eyes snapped to Roach. "What if this was Lane?"

"I know, but...."

"Open the fucking file or get out of my way and I'll do it," I ordered.

Wilder clicked on the file, and the world narrowed in on the photographs on the screen. There weren't as many as the other files, and the photo quality wasn't as clear, but that didn't matter.

There she was, my precious little Tink at fifteen, tied up and naked just like she said. Roach turned around and crossed his arms over his chest, his face as angry as I felt.

Blood and other bodily fluids coated her body. A dark hood was tied with black tape around her neck, but that didn't stop her eyes from gripping me behind the dark material. I could taste her terror on my tongue and acid in the back of my throat as my body revolted against what I saw.

Wilder clicked through all the photos, most were just of her, but some had Jim and Dave. Frank must have been the one taking the pictures.

A sharp pain pierced my chest like I was being stabbed through the heart. She thought this was me. For eleven long years, she thought I did this to her. Fire and ice sizzled in my veins as rage collided with the realization of the horror she'd felt.

"This is a pattern. It's not random. Some of the others have it too, just in different spots," Wilder said, pointing to the six knife wounds on her naked blood-covered stomach. "If she wasn't his first, she was close to it. That's the only reason she's alive. They're not as clean and precise. The cuts were tentative, and he used a different blade than the others. The wounds are smaller in size, and by some miracle, he missed all her major veins, or she would've bled out in minutes."

My body wouldn't stop shaking, and my heart pounded hard in my chest. I gripped my knees as the room swam and took deep breaths to get myself under control. Roach's hands were on my shoulders, but he didn't say anything.

The fear in Raine's eyes that night, when she found me in her house, came storming to the surface of my mind, and I wanted to throw up. That look on her face would haunt my dreams. She was my it, my all, my everything, and these three had destroyed us both.

"Take the computer. I don't care if he knows it's missing. The families of these people deserve closure." I stood and nodded to Roach that I was okay.

"This guy is fucking dead, and when we find him, he's all mine." Wilder and Roach stayed quiet but locked eyes with me. "Father Frank may have signed a deal with the Devil, but I'm the Reaper, and I intend to fucking collect."

Jace

29

J ace

Kai insisted on coming to the airfield with us. I found him extreme and unpredictable most of the time, but he was downright strange this last week. Kai didn't challenge me or threaten to kill me when I purposely tried to get under his skin. He hardly spoke when we saw him and was more protective and edgy over Raine than I ever wanted to see from an enforcer. I didn't know what was happening, but I would bet money that something set him off.

Raine was splitting her time between us, so we saw Kai every other night, and although he sometimes hung out and ate dinner, it never felt like he was wholly here. He was fine with Raine but would spend most of the time standing at one of the large windows staring outside. I didn't know if this was a residual effect of the night we tag-teamed Raine, but it felt like something else. I hated being in the dark about shit. If he didn't snap out of it by tomorrow night, we were going to have another private conversation.

I glanced out the plane window and watched Raine talk to Kai. He looked panicked, scared she would get on the plane with me and never come back. If he really knew her, he'd know she wouldn't leave unless forced to. She was so much like Avro with her loyalty and undying positivity. Those two were meant to be in each other's orbit, and I was hoping that Raine could get him through his surgery when I couldn't be here.

Kai glanced up at me as they hugged, and our eyes locked. The usual anger brewing in their depths wasn't there. It freaked me out when someone's personality did a one-eighty like this. There was always a reason, and Kai didn't change for sweet, fluffy bunny reasons. He would only have a personality lobotomy if something seriously bad happened.

I looked away first—this was their moment—and answered Allen and the list of questions he was firing at me. They were mixed in with reminders about everything for this evening.

We were supposed to do a concert in Nashville two days ago, but Damon caught the flu and couldn't keep anything down. Not that I wanted Damon to be sick, but I wasn't complaining about the extra time I got. This was the longest stretch I'd been home in years.

"Hey," Raine said, smiling as she walked along the aisle and dropped her carry-on before hanging the garment bag on one of the lockable hooks.

"Hey," I said back. I glanced out the window again, and Kai was still standing in the same spot, staring up at the window. "Did he want to come?" I pointed my thumb out the window. "I mean, he can't come to the awards or anything. But if he's that freaked out about you going to this with me, he can babysit me, I guess."

Raine shook her head before sitting down. "No, I'm not even going to give him that option. He's been...how do I put this?" She bit her lip. "Do you find Kai is acting strange? Like more protective than normal?"

"I have noticed it," I said.

"I wondered if it was because we talked about me moving in with you and Avro, but he said he was fine. In fact, he said it would be safer than living at the old farmhouse so close to the MC property, and he liked that, so I don't know."

She shrugged. "Now that I think about it, they've both been weird. I don't mean they have a thing going on kind of weird," she said quickly, which made me chuckle.

"They've been weird in different ways. I've tried to get them to talk, but neither will say what's bothering them. You're the only one acting normal. You must have some idea what the hell is up. I hate being in the dark." She looked stressed as she stared at me. "I know Avro's knee has been sore. Are we doing too much?"

I sighed and crossed my arms, annoyed that Avro still hadn't talked to Raine, and now I would have to tell her. Probably his damn plan all along.

"If you know anything, please tell me, Jace." She rubbed at her chest. "I'm worried, and it's freaking me out that I'm met with a door slamming in my face the moment I bring it up."

"I know what's going on with Avro, but Kai, I have no clue." I rubbed the back of my neck as I debated whether I should tell her. It should come from Avro, but I wanted Raine to be able to enjoy this experience.

"Avro is acting off. I didn't know if anyone else saw it, so I didn't want to say anything."

The roar of the motorcycle firing up echoed into the plane's cabin, and we watched silently as Kai pulled out into the dark. It was very early, and I wanted to throw my phone as it dinged three more times in a row. Fucking Allen.

"Jace, please tell me about Avro." Raine reached out and placed her hand on my knee.

"I shouldn't. It's not my place to say," I said, and Raine leaned back and crossed her arms over her chest. She was giving me some serious 'fuck you' face, and it was kinda hot. "I'm serious. Avro doesn't like anyone to worry, and I shouldn't say if he hasn't mentioned it yet."

"Jace, are we or are we not all in this together? You made it very clear to me that anything that happened to any of us individually affected us all. I have the right to know."

"Fuck, I hate it when my words are tossed back at me." I leaned my head back against the seat. "Fine, but he may kill me if he finds out I told you."

"I doubt he's going to kill you," she said, shaking her head. "So out with it."

"You know about his knee, right?" Raine nodded. "It started to twinge a few months back, nothing big, just now and then when he'd move too fast the wrong way. He didn't think much of it, just leftover pain from the original surgeries. Then the pain became more frequent. He went to the doctor for testing a couple of weeks back, and he got the call the other night that he needs another surgery. This time they are doing a knee replacement and ACL reconstruction surgery." Raine covered her mouth and swore under her breath.

"What's going on with the knee? Do they know?"

"I don't have technical terms for you, but basically, the bone is breaking apart in the joint." I used my hands to demonstrate Avro's knee and the joint breaking. Raine looked like she was going to cry.

"Oh my god, why is he still dancing at the bar? That has to kill. And why doesn't he want me to know?"

"It's not that he doesn't want you to know. He doesn't want to become someone's problem, and...honestly, I think he's avoiding the topic. The less he talks about it, the less real it becomes."

"So he's opting to stay quiet and pretend he's okay? Jace, come on, that's not healthy," Raine said, and I shrugged.

"I've tried getting him to talk. He's very stubborn when he wants to be. The doc is talking six weeks with zero weight to start and then re-evaluate. That means he is most likely in a wheelchair, then on crutches if all goes well. If it doesn't...I don't know. But stairs will be nearly impossible, so he's been setting up the spare room on the main floor. He definitely won't be able to work behind the bar, and he won't be able to dance. As far as sex goes, I'm guessing that he will be out for a few weeks and can only sit or lay down, so that will bother him too." I ran my thumb across my lip as I pictured the kiss he gave me before I left. I could feel his heart breaking.

I hated that he was going through this for a third time. He didn't like me to know how much pain he was in. When I was home, he'd sneak off to another room. I'd find him silently crying but refusing to take more than one painkiller a day. He was terrified that he'd become addicted. Avro was stronger than he realized, while he always thought he was weak. I didn't get it, but it was another thing he and Raine had in common.

"Anyway, Avro's not taking it very well. That accident was horrible, and his knee was a mess. I was in Germany at the time and didn't get back until two weeks after it happened, but he was...lost, I don't know how better to describe it."

Tears ran steadily down Raine's cheeks as she leaned forward, her hands clasped together. "I feel like such an asshole. How did I not see he was in so much pain? I've been so caught up in my wonderful new bubble with all of you that I just wasn't paying attention." Her eyes snapped up to mine. "Should we even be going on this trip?"

"I have to go, but you can stay if you don't feel like going now. The thing is, Peaches, Avro wouldn't want that. Why do you think he didn't tell you? He doesn't want to be treated differently. It drives him crazy."

Raine slumped back and wiped away the tears. "Is this why he decided not to come?"

"He has an appointment today with the surgeon to go over his surgery plan," I said, and Raine jumped up, her fists clenched tight.

"What? You have to be kidding me? He's going all alone?" I didn't say anything, and she swore and paced the aisle. "I hate this. I have to pretend I don't know when all I want is to be there for him. This is ridiculous. Why are men so stubborn?"

I cocked a brow at her. "Have you ever looked in a mirror?"

"Oh, shut up," she grumbled, making me laugh.

"Look, we are only going for the night. It's why I shortened the trip. We go, do the awards, fly out tomorrow morning, and force him to come clean and accept help. I have to go to this, Peaches. It is an obligation, and I'd prefer to have you with me, but if you want to stay, I won't stop you." I nodded to the Captain and Co-Pilot as they walked in. "But you better hurry and decide. It looks like we're heading out soon."

She nibbled her bottom lip and looked back and forth between the open door and me before sitting down.

"You're right. It's one night, and this way, he won't feel worse that I backed out. Especially since we spent an entire day finding that dress." She looked over at the garment bag. "I thought I was going to kill him. He took me to every store twice."

"I know, you've mentioned it once or twice," I emphasized, and she glared at me.

"You going to turn into asshole Jace again?" She huffed. "I feel like you're a transformer."

"I thought we already settled this. I'm always asshole Jace." Leaning in close to her, I made sure she was wiggling with nervous energy before I spoke again. "And I plan on being very, very much the asshole at the awards. Be prepared to blush for me more than once."

Raine's eyes grew wide, and I heard her swallow. It was so fun to play with her. She'd have the worst-case scenarios running around in her head all flight, and I was sick because I loved it.

"What are you planning?"

The Co-pilot chose that moment to close the door. The lock was loud even over the sound of the engines coming to life. "Too late now. I guess you'll have to wait and see," I said, loving the look of pure horror in her eyes.

This was going to be fun.

Snake

30

Kaivan

My beer bottle tapped on the top of the bar. The clubhouse was extremely noisy with everyone back. I couldn't decide if I enjoyed the background noise that drowned out the voices in my head or preferred when it was quiet and my voices kept me company.

"Hey man, what's going on?" Mannix sat on the stool beside me. I looked at my friend and knew he knew about the cult, the house, and what we'd seen. It was all laid bare in his eyes. Roach—that ass—must have said something, and now Mannix looked worried. The only ones that should be worrying were Dave and Frank or Francois, whatever he was going by. I had plans for them, and the images only got worse with each passing day.

"I'm not going to randomly kill anyone if that's what you're asking," I said, staring at his reflection in the mirror.

"The thought may have crossed my mind. You tend to take your pent-up anger out in interesting ways." Mannix smirked, and the corner of my mouth turned up.

"Lately, I've had another outlet for my frustration," I said, and Mannix clapped a hand on my shoulder.

"I'm happy for you, kid."

"No, don't be callin' me that. I thought I'd finally got you kicked of that habit?" I groaned and then laughed. Strangely, being called by the nickname Mannix gave me in prison felt good. I knew he'd done it to remind me of my place but also that my life wasn't over. The guy was like that, subtle with the things he chose to do, but they always had a purpose.

"I remember the first time you mentioned Raine's name. Even then, with all the anger in you, I saw how much you still loved her. That kind of devotion never dies." I drank the last of my beer and pushed the bottle away.

"Is that so? And how would you know?"

Mannix smiled and chuckled a deep sound that always sounded warm and inviting. "Well, I think that will be a story for another night. As long as you're good, I'm good. We're ride or die, remember that."

"Mannix," I said as he stood. I couldn't look at him as I warred with the emotions swirling in my gut. "I would've been honored to call you dad."

"Asshole," Mannix grumbled, and I watched his reflection as he wiped at his face, which made me smile.

"Hey, Snake! Um…isn't that your old lady on the television?" Kickstand yelled over the noise, and just like that, the room fell silent. "Holy shit! It is. What the hell is she doing on that guy's arm? Isn't he some rockstar or something?"

Oh, this was my worst nightmare. If there was a God, he knew how to fuck with me in all the worst ways. I lifted my head to the massive television that typically showed sports or a car restoration show, but nope, not tonight. Of course, someone had to turn to the awards show, and there they were, Jace and Raine, smiling for cameras.

She looked fucking stunning, and my mouth fell open as I soaked her in. She was wearing a shimmery blue dress the same color as her eyes that sparkled under the lights and clung to every one of her delicious curves. It was cut so low in the front that there was a perfect V that left very little to the imagination. The dress was long with a slit up the side, exposing one leg, and showed off the matching shoes. Her hair was styled in an adorable look that showed off her neck and the jewelry I had no doubt Jace bought for her. My mouth ran dry, the shock of her perfection leaving me speechless.

She looked like a queen and as magical as the nickname I'd given her years ago. My heart beat faster in my chest, my breathing harsh as I tried to draw a deep breath. In the bright lights on Jace Everly's arm, she looked like she'd always belonged. And the fear of not being enough tried to claw its way to the front of my brain.

"Let's kill him!" Kickstand yelled, setting off a chain of hollering.

"Yeah, no one touches one of our old ladies and gets away with it." The crowd of a hundred or more stood in a single motion and headed for the artillery room like a wave coming into shore.

"Shit, shit, shit," I mumbled under my breath and slid off my stool.

"Wait!" There were still a few calls for murder, one unsurprisingly coming from Tanner. "I knew she was going to be there," I said and hoped they would leave it at that. I walked around a few tables and turned to face the room, making sure the exit was right behind me for when this hell was over.

"Does that mean she's no longer your old lady," Tanner asked. "Is she fair game?"

I was going to kill him.

"No," I growled in his direction and slowly turned to glare at the massive group staring at me. This felt very much like my drunken dancing on the bar night...what I could remember of it anyway.

"Raine is still my old lady." The group blinked like they were hooked to the same remote control. Fuck they were going to make me say it.

"Well, don't leave us hanging, Snake. What's going on," Chase asked from where he was sitting playing cards.

This felt worse than everyone staring at me on my first day in prison, and that was saying something. I cleared my throat and rolled out my shoulders. My eyes found Roach and then Mannix.

"I'm in a relationship with Raine and two guys," I said, and no one moved.

Roach's mouth hit the floor, and I felt the heat creeping up my neck. It wasn't that there weren't guys in the clubhouse that liked other guys. It was the fact that this was me. I was a jealous, possessive asshole, and I'd made a very loud statement by fucking Raine in here. It was the kind of statement that said my hands only, and that went for inside the club and out.

"So, you're fucking that hot ass woman and fucking the hot ass rock star," Tanner asked, and I rolled my eyes in his direction. "Holy fuck, you are. You're my mother fucking superhero. I want to be you when I grow up. Damn! Where's my foursome ladies and gents," Tanner yelled, and for the first time, I was happy Tanner was crazier than I was because the tension diffused like a balloon popping.

"To be clear, you're good with this," Chase asked, pointing at the television showing Raine and Jace kissing. I may still murder him when they got back for kissing her like that and putting me through this, but I sighed and nodded.

"Yes, sorta, but...." I paused as my feet vibrated. I looked around the room. "Did you all feel that?" There was a soft rumbling sound, and I turned my head to listen. Was this a gas leak?

"Feel what," Chase asked, standing from the table.

"He looks like his head is going to twist right off his body," Tanner joked.

"Not the time Tanner," Chase said before I could. "What do you feel, Snake?"

"There is an intermittent rumbling and...." The floor vibrated again, but this time so did the walls and dirt sprinkled down from the ceiling. "That."

Pulling my gun, I turned and ran down the stairs, taking them two at a time. The entire room was on the move and following behind me. At the next church meeting, I would bring up how this place was a death trap waiting to happen. We needed a second or even third set of stairs.

The sounds were louder down on the lower level, and it definitely seemed like explosions. I pushed open the metal door just enough to peer out and not get shot if this was an ambush.

"What the fuck is going on out there," Mannix asked at the sound of gunfire.

"I'm not sure. Be ready for anything," I said and darted out the door.

When the door wasn't pelted with a rain of bullets, I turned toward the sounds which were coming from the amusement park. That wasn't normal, but it seemed fitting. With Wilder, anything was possible. I stopped in my tracks as an explosion erupted from under the old Teacups ride and watched a screaming man that seemed to be chased by a flying pink teacup. I cringed as the man and the teacup slammed into an old upright support of a rollercoaster before crashing to the hard concrete below. As if to add insult to injury, the ride groaned and bent in half, the top landing on the already still man, effectively squishing him like a bug.

"Wow, that was...."

"Gnarly as fuck," Tanner said. I couldn't even be bothered looking at him.

"What the fuck is going on," I asked no one as my eyes took in the mass amounts of carnage.

How did Wilder get involved with this blood bath? It looked like an invisible hand was tearing apart bodies and decided to sprinkle them all over the amusement park. I'd seen a lot of shit, but never anything close to this.

The ground was littered with pieces of rides while fires burned in every corner of the large park. There was more gunfire and screaming, but it all seemed contained to that side of the fence.

Just to be safe, I yelled, "Stray bullets are an issue. If you don't have a bulletproof vest on, I'd go in and grab one." Some stayed, but most ran back inside. We'd moved a ton of that downstairs since the last attack, so it didn't take long for everyone to be suited and head back out. Beast walked over and handed vests to Chase, Mannix, and Roach.

"Well, at least I know who you love most," I teased Beast.

"I'm coming back with more. Hang on to yourself," he said, not cracking a smile before wandering off. Beast seemed different since Chase came back. It was almost as if the grief of losing his wife hadn't affected him until he no longer had the club's day-to-day to focus on.

I turned my attention back to the ongoing mayhem. There was so much blood and random flesh decorating the ground and rides left standing that I was reminded of what I'd done at the warehouse to that Weasel guy. But on a much larger scale.

All hell broke loose as a large group of men near the back side of the amusement park came roaring out of nowhere on motorcycles, with even more men screaming and running chaotically in all directions. I had a feeling Wilder let them get that far before raining hell on them. It was like they couldn't decide which way to go.

"If a fucking T-rex appears out of the smoke, you're all on your own," Tanner said. "Because I'm gonna ride that bitch."

I glanced over at him and wondered how we'd collected such a pile of insanity in one location. Wilder next door, Tanner came with Chase, and I couldn't forget Ava at the sorority house. Ava was the strangest of them all. We never knew what she was going to do, when she was going to show up, or who she was going to drag in with her.

"It looks like the Desert Vipers," I said as Chase and Roach, now suited up with their vests, stepped beside me. "Or at least what's left of them."

The ground shook like a miniature earthquake as three more explosions went off, much closer this time. We all turned away and covered our heads as we ran from the debris that included large pieces off of motorcycles.

I pointed to the parking lot. "We need to get the bikes inside," I said to Chase as more debris sailed through the air and crashed down on our side of the fence.

"Beast, get a party organized and move the bikes into the back warehouse," Chase yelled, and Beast jumped into action.

There was a growling noise before men started screaming, and what seemed like tall turrets of steam rose into the air.

"Cover up," I yelled.

It felt like rain hitting us, but I knew that wet feeling was not water.

"Oh shit, that's disgusting," Roach growled as he rubbed red dots off his face and flicked a piece of skin off his leather jacket.

Four men on foot were running for our fence, all screaming as if the devil himself was on their heels. I raised my gun and fired two shots taking out the two guys in the middle.

"Don't shoot," the remaining two yelled. "Please don't shoot." Another dropped dead, but I hadn't taken the shot and looked around, realizing it wasn't any of our guys. I knew who it was, but everyone else was looking for the source of the random bullet. The last guy slipped in some blood and landed hard on the ground. He scrambled to his feet, looking like he'd been dipped in red paint.

"Ohhh look, fireworks!"

I jumped at the sound of Ava's sing-song voice. Where the hell had she come from? It was as if thinking about her had conjured the craziness like she was a demon. I looked down at the small woman who was next-level terrifying. I still had no idea how she survived half the shit she did, and what the hell was she wearing? Today she was in a duck outfit like a mascot at a game who wandered away to end up here. I thought Wilder was random, but Ava took the cake and licked off the icing one finger at a time.

Of course, Tanner was in love with her, but she could never remember his name, which never got old. Anytime Tanner was knocked down a peg from his arrogant horse's back was a day to celebrate.

"It's so pretty," Ava said, her mouth making a little O as another explosion went off, and part of another old ride toppled over with a loud groan and then crashed. All I could think was this would give Wilder more places to hide.

"What the hell else are we supposed to do?" Someone yelled.

"Fucked if I know," Chase mumbled under his breath so only Roach or I could hear before barking orders. "Kill anyone that makes it onto our side of the fence unless they want to join us. They'll need to be willing to take their punishment starting tonight. Spread out and stay back from the property line. I don't know how close those explosions will come in our direction."

People quickly dispersed, just as the last guy running for the fence finally made it after slipping and falling on his ass twice more. He gripped the chain link so hard that his fingers were bright white while his eyes were wide with terror.

"This place…it's alive! Help me, please," he begged.

Chase opened his mouth to answer just as a seemingly ordinary bush came to life and jumped on the man. Even though I knew who it was under the cover of the tree camouflage, I couldn't help feeling creeped out as the screaming man was tackled to the ground and fell silent before the bush ran off into the amusement park. If I had a list of shit in my life that I never thought I'd see, Wilder topped it every single time.

"The bush ate that man," Ava exclaimed. "There are killer bushes." She turned and ran off like that was the craziest thing she'd ever seen. That girl was the walking embodiment of 'what the fuck,' and she was worried about a bush coming to life. Fucking ironic.

"Ava, wait up," Tanner took off hot on her heels, and I shook my head.

"Loyal one you have there, Chase," I said sarcastically. Loving the opportunity to get a dig in at him.

Chase's eyes narrowed. "Don't make me tell you not the time or place," he drawled.

I snorted. "Yes, Daddy," I said, sweet as pie, and smiled at him.

"You had to go there and make it weird," Chase countered. "Prick." It was nice to see him flustered for a change.

"Okay, are we going to ignore the fact that a bush just killed a man? Or did no one else other than me and Ava see that," Roach asked. "Please, dear God, let someone else have seen that."

It wasn't often that I got to mess with Roach, and I was tempted to lean over and ask him what he was talking about, but Mannix ruined my fun.

"Yeah, I saw it," Mannix said, and Roach's shoulders relaxed.

"That's good. I look like shit in white straight jackets."

"When the hell were you ever in a straight jacket," I asked.

"I'm just saying it wouldn't suit me. White is not my color." He shrugged as I continued to stare at him. "Besides, for a moment, I thought I was tripping on drugs I didn't remember taking. That would've led to a few more questions."

I shook my head at him. What the fuck was in the water around this place?

"Sooo, two guys huh?" Chase didn't look at me, but I could feel him wanting to smile and joke about my grand statement, 'No one else will touch Raine.'

I turned and looked at Chase. "You know what...." I rolled out my shoulders as a sense of freedom came over me. "Tonight is a whole lot fucked up, and normally I'd take care of it. Just like I've taken care of it for the last one year, three months, and four weeks, minus a day." Chase looked at me. His brow knitted together. "I'd worry about calling in a favor with the guy I'm blackmailing at the cop shop. I'd kill who I needed to keep this shit quiet and organize a proper cleanup, but since you're back...." I squeezed Chase's shoulder. "Have fun. I'm outta here."

"What?" All three of the guys said at once. I never left when there was club shit to take care of. No matter how angry I'd been, I always put the club first, but tonight, I was getting the hell out of here. I had too much toxic shit doing the backstroke in my brain. The last thing I needed was to handle severed body parts.

"You heard me. I'm gone for the night. I'm sick of cleaning up mass amounts of body parts and stressing over this shit. I need a night off." I looked back at the park. "Besides, I think the Vipers have bigger problems than us," I said as an arm landed on the fence, getting tangled in the barbed wire.

I stared at the swinging body part and smiled, unsure why it was so fucking funny. Revving my bike, I rolled up beside Chase, who still looked shell-shocked at the carnage.

"It's good to have you back, Prez. Call Johnson at the local. He'll sort out the paperwork for a price." I looked back at the mess. "He may need a bonus for this one." Smirking, I rode out the gates to get as far away from whatever the hell that insanity was, only to drive by Ava running down the sidewalk in her duck suit and Tanner jogging right along beside her.

Sometimes I really wondered if it was me that was the common denominator because the craziest shit followed me around like a damn dirt cloud.

Avro

31

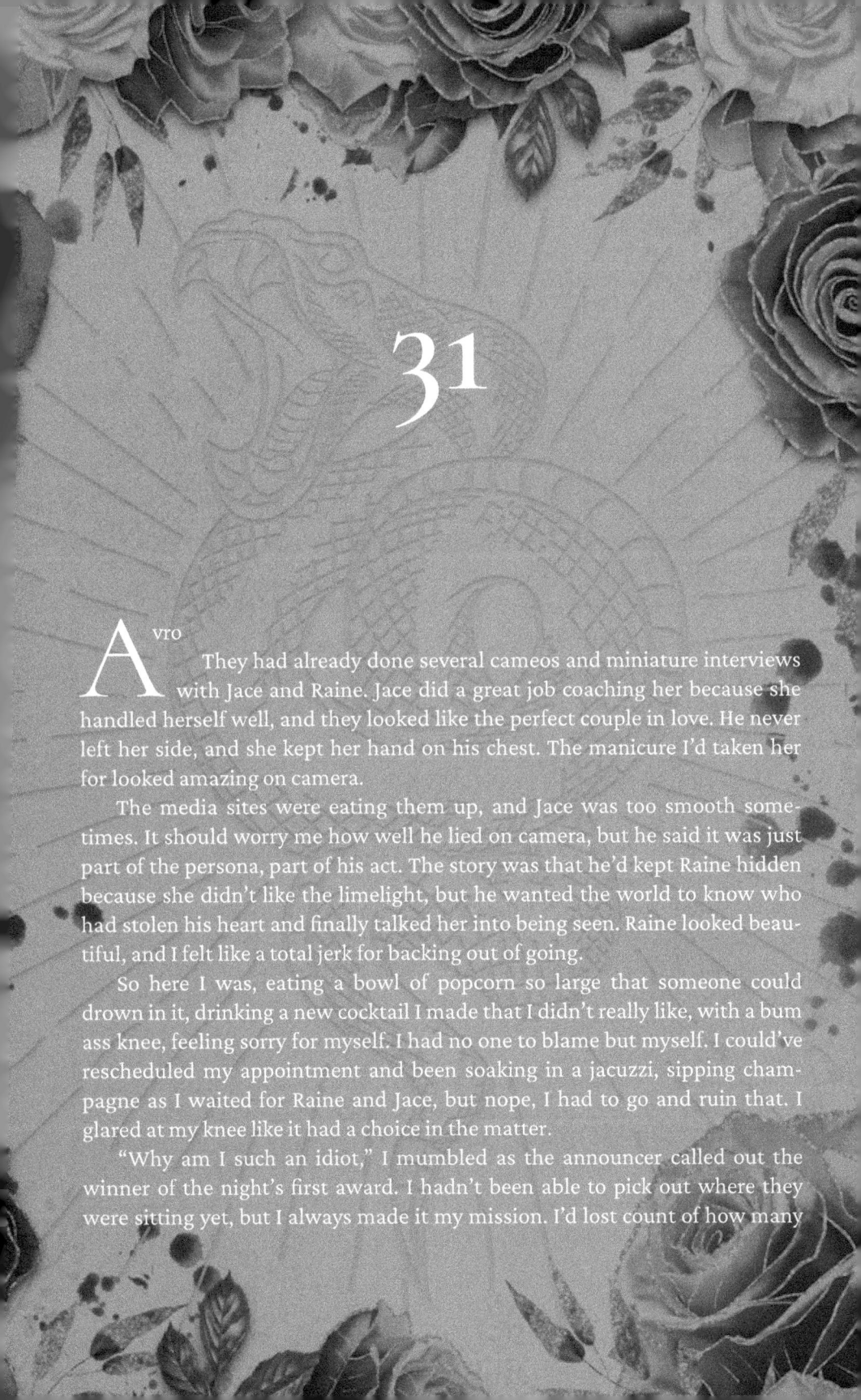

Avro

They had already done several cameos and miniature interviews with Jace and Raine. Jace did a great job coaching her because she handled herself well, and they looked like the perfect couple in love. He never left her side, and she kept her hand on his chest. The manicure I'd taken her for looked amazing on camera.

The media sites were eating them up, and Jace was too smooth sometimes. It should worry me how well he lied on camera, but he said it was just part of the persona, part of his act. The story was that he'd kept Raine hidden because she didn't like the limelight, but he wanted the world to know who had stolen his heart and finally talked her into being seen. Raine looked beautiful, and I felt like a total jerk for backing out of going.

So here I was, eating a bowl of popcorn so large that someone could drown in it, drinking a new cocktail I made that I didn't really like, with a bum ass knee, feeling sorry for myself. I had no one to blame but myself. I could've rescheduled my appointment and been soaking in a jacuzzi, sipping champagne as I waited for Raine and Jace, but nope, I had to go and ruin that. I glared at my knee like it had a choice in the matter.

"Why am I such an idiot," I mumbled as the announcer called out the winner of the night's first award. I hadn't been able to pick out where they were sitting yet, but I always made it my mission. I'd lost count of how many times I watched award shows searching out Jace like a game of *Where's Waldo*. I always hated seeing him standing on the carpet with his arm around someone else, but I didn't feel that with him and Raine tonight.

Jace had a good chance of winning one if not two, awards. It was why Allen was so insistent that Jace be there in person. I took another sip of the drink and gagged, tempted to throw it out and start over. Even my skills at making a new concoction were off tonight.

I stood up to make something else when a knock sounded at the back door, which was strange because very few people used it.

Sitting my popcorn on the table, I limped over. I should not have worked behind the bar last night, but I was the only act right now without Raine. My knee was screaming at me for dancing.

I turned on the outside light and peered out the small window. Kai? Did hell freeze over? When I opened the door, Kai was holding a box of pizza and a six-pack of beer, but it was the blood smattering his face and clothes that had me wondering, *what the fuck*?

"I come with a peace offering. It's only pepperoni cause I didn't know what you liked, but the beer is good and cold," he said, holding up the party-size box like I couldn't see it. Who did he think we were feeding?

"Are more people coming?"

"No, why?"

"No reason. This isn't a 'Hey, come over for a beer, but I'm going to threaten you again, type night,' is it?" I leaned against the door jam, not letting him in.

"No, it is a genuine offer," Kai said, but I was still wary.

"So you have no one else you'd prefer to hang out with? Don't you have an entire motorcycle club of friends?"

Kai sighed. "Okay look, I don't have a television, I didn't want to watch the awards in the clubhouse, and the guys at the club are a little busy at the moment."

"Ah! So I'm the last spot you'd come, but you're desperate. Check. Is whatever the club is busy with the reason you're covered with blood? You know you're covered in blood, right," I asked.

Kai looked down and then shrugged. "I didn't do it." His brow furrowed. "I know you don't believe that, but for once, it's actually true. Probably, why I got the huge discount at the pizza joint, though...huh, oh well."

I stepped out of the way to let him in. "You're not sitting on my brand-new couch like that. Give me the pizza and beer, and you can go shower."

"You're serious?"

"Does this expression look like I'm joking?" I said, sarcasm dripping off every word.

"Wow, when did you become the Jace in the room?"

Sighing, I took the pizza and beer from his hands. "Even the nice guy is allowed to have a bad day. There are flannel pants and T-shirts in the dresser closest to the bathroom. Hunt in the closet for a sweatshirt. I don't really care what you wear," I said, biting my lip and forcing myself to walk normally as I turned around and headed deeper into the kitchen.

"Fine, I'll be back."

"Boots off first. Don't think I didn't notice you stomped up my stairs with your boots the other night—no more of that in my home. I don't care how many nights you stay, but I like my stuff clean, and I refuse to clean up after adults," I said, impressed and shocked that I was being so firm. It was the pain making me ornery.

"Fair," Kai said. I was surprised he wasn't arguing and looked over as he undid his boots. I hit bake on the oven and pulled out a pan to heat the pizza. "I'll be five."

"Kai?"

He stopped just as he walked out into the hall. "Yeah?"

"Thanks for the pizza."

"Who said any of it was for you," he smirked, and I shook my head as Kai disappeared.

Wonders never cease. Kai and I were hanging out and about to eat pizza like civilized adults. The world really has gone mad. I got plates ready and poured the beer into tall steins, then grabbed some other snack food from the cupboard as the pizza was heating. By the time Kai jogged down the stairs wearing my clothes, I had almost everything in the living room. I looked at him in my plaid flannel pants and couldn't figure out where I made the crazy turn in my night, but I felt like taking a picture because Jace and Raine would never believe me.

"Thanks, I feel much better," Kai said, taking the plate I held out and then piling it with six slices of pizza.

"Do I want to know what you did with your dirty clothes?"

"You mean they're not to be washed in the sink and laid out on the bed to dry?"

Kai smirked as I glared at him, but he just chuckled and walked away. It took everything in me not to go check that wasn't exactly what he did. Grumbling, I grabbed my plate.

Taking a deep breath, I walked out to the couch. Kai was staring at me with his brows drawn together in confusion. "Why are you pretending you're not limping?"

I blew the air out of my lungs and groaned. "That noticeable?"

"Is water wet?"

"Whatever. I don't want to talk about it. Besides, you've been fucking odd too." I sat my plate on my lap and turned my head to look at Kai.

"No, I haven't," he argued.

"I mean, broody asshole is your go-to, but nah, I'm not buying it. You're hiding something." Kai didn't bother to answer and stuffed half a slice of pizza in his mouth. "Doesn't look like we have anything to talk about then."

"You think he'll actually win something?" Kai was the first to break the silence.

"As good of a chance of any of them, I guess. His agent is pretty certain that of the three awards the group is nominated for, they will win at least one," I answered. "Aren't we a sad, pathetic pair?"

"Speak for yourself," Kai growled, and I couldn't help but laugh. "What?"

"I gotta tell you that you're far less scary when you're in my flannel pants and Jace's band T-shirt."

Kai looked down at himself. "You have nothing else. Do you even buy other T-shirts that aren't molded to your body? Half of them felt like spandex."

"They're for work. The patrons like to see the goods." I smiled, but sadness was tugging at me. I knew I couldn't dance anymore, at least not until after the surgery, and I was given the all-clear, but it could be months and constant pain.

I took a bite of pizza and pushed the troubling thoughts out of my mind for the night. I smiled and pointed at the television as the camera panned across the first few rows, and I was able to spot Jace and Raine.

"There they are." Raine looked slightly intimidated by all the other celebrities around her, but I could only tell because I knew her so well.

"Okay look, I'll show you mine if you show me yours," I said, and Kai's hand stopped moving halfway to his open mouth. It was annoying me that I didn't know what Kai was hiding. It felt big, and I trusted my gut.

"Um...what are we talking about?"

"Please spare me, we've already seen each other's dicks, and I have no interest in fucking you." I took a big gulp of the beer.

"Why not? I'm totally fuckable," Kai said, and I turned my head to stare at him.

"What the hell is going on with you? Actually, forget it, don't tell me. All I want to know is why you've been so quiet and overprotective this week with Raine, and I will tell you about my knee."

"I'm pretty sure you're getting the better end of this deal. What I have is volatile. Why you're limping doesn't seem to hold any real weight." Kai shifted around to face me and kept eating. It felt like we were playing poker. But who had more chips to push into the center of the table?

"I'm assuming this would be our secret. We are not speaking about this to anyone outside of this room?" Kai continued to devour the food, making me wonder how he ate that much.

"Yes, I'd agree to that," I said.

"Then I need something better than your knee," he said.

I watched the television as they ran through commercials and more awards that I wasn't interested in.

"Okay, how about this? I'll tell you how I hurt my knee," I said.

"I already know how. It was during a training session for a circus performance." Kai smirked and polished off the last of his pizza.

"It wasn't the circus," I said and then waved my hand, dismissing the argument. I knew what people thought, and yes, it was a fancy circus, but it was more than that to me. It was theater. It was living out a dream, on stage, under the lights, and being the star. I felt like I could do anything.

"Never mind that. The point is the accident I have told everyone about is only a half-truth. There is a much larger story that not a soul knows about," I said.

"Not even Jace?"

"Not even Jace," I said and turned my head to look at Kai's profile as he watched the television. He rubbed his chin as he thought.

"Alright, I'll tell you, but if Raine hears about this, all the goodwill we've built between us over the last week will disappear." The crowd clapped and cheered on the television, but my attention remained firmly on Kai.

"She won't hear it from me, and if Jace hears about what I tell you, then the same goes for you," I offered and turned on the couch to face him. "So, what's going on?"

"You first." Kai grabbed the bowl of popcorn I was eating earlier and ate a handful before grabbing the chips and doing the same. Soon he was surrounded by chips, cheeses, pretzels, and popcorn.

"Would you like a bowl you can mix them in?" I offered. I was starting to wonder if he had a tapeworm.

"Can I just put it in with the popcorn?"

"Sure, I was done anyway." I waited until he was settled before I started. "The accident wasn't an accident. My normal partner was off sick, but I think he was threatened or paid off to stay home. The guy in his place let me drop from seventy-five feet in the air."

"What the fuck? Did you piss in his cereal," Kai asked.

"So funny. No, of course not. He wanted my spot and was pissed that I beat him out. I didn't die because we had a hidden emergency net that pulled up if one of us fell. Dying in front of people watching doesn't go over well."

"But you still messed up your knee?" Kai picked up single pieces of each snack and popped them into his mouth. I was morbidly fascinated with his eating. Refocusing, I continued with my story.

"I wouldn't have, but shocker, after my first bounce, the line snapped on one of the corner cords, and I landed on my leg all wrong. It bent one way, and I bent the other." I demonstrated with my hands. "That line is designed to handle more than a dozen of us dropping on it at a time. It never should've snapped. The insurance company ruled it an accident, but I know it was sabotage."

"Did you at least get compensated for it?" Kai seemed very interested in my story, which I appreciated, yet...it was weird. Maybe he was actually trying, but I was skeptical.

"They paid for all my medical and this new surgery I have to have. I didn't want to sue since I knew it wasn't the company, but they offered to pay anything I needed to recover, so I agreed."

"Why did you never tell the cops," Kai asked.

"When I was in the hospital after my first surgery, a delivery guy showed up with a large flower arrangement. When I opened the card, there was a picture of Jace with a red line through his face, and on the back, it said, *One word is all that it will take*." I shrugged. "The fact he knew about Jace at all freaked me out. We are always so careful and back then we rarely saw one another."

"Damn, that's cold," Kai said. "Smart and devious, but definitely cold. I get why you wouldn't say anything. What's this guy's name?"

"I don't know if I should say. After I got out of the hospital, I did some digging, and it turns out his family is part of the mafia," I picked up my beer and gulped the rest. "He ruined my life so he could have fifteen minutes of fame. He did like two shows and quit." I shook my head.

"I hate him. I've had two surgeries, and now I need a third to replace my knee and reconstruct my ACL. They're saying two or three months before I'm okay, and that's only if it takes and I'm diligent with my physio. So much pain, and for what? So this guy could say he got to headline in Vegas and then turned his nose up at it." My hand squeezed the glass hard, and I had to take a deep breath before I broke it. "I try to be a good person, Kai, I really do, but this guy...let's just say I wouldn't mind him going missing."

Turning my head, I looked at Kai. He was quiet, his stare intense. "What's his name?"

I licked my lips. I hadn't said his name since that day. It felt like bringing bad energy around me if I did.

"Julian Fiore."

"Okay."

"What does okay mean?"

"It means okay. Consider it done. Don't ask questions, don't pass go or collect your two hundred dollars. Just let it be, and it will be taken care of," Kai said, his voice calm.

"You mean you'll...you know?"

"I mean, it's best not to ask questions that you really don't want answers to, but I can say he will be taught a lesson, and you can sleep better at night." Kai tossed a piece of popcorn into the air and caught it like he wasn't just talking about killing someone. I stared at him for a long time as my mind took in and chewed on what he said.

"Thanks." Unsure what to say to that right now, I pointed at him. "Okay, your turn."

"I know who attacked Raine." My mouth dropped open. "I also made sure that one of the three would never breathe again. The other two I'm closing in on, and I found pictures of her assault."

He picked up his beer and took a sip before setting all the snacks on the table. It wasn't so much what Kai was doing that freaked me out. It was what he wasn't saying. He would destroy whoever it was until there was nothing left to find.

"Does Raine know who they are?"

Like I hit a light switch, Kai whipped his head in my direction, his lip curled up, and his eyebrows drew tight as the anger radiated off him. "No, and I want it to remain that way. Two of the three men were people she knew and trusted. She already had to live through thinking I hurt her. I don't want to put any more nightmares in her head."

I nibbled on my lower lip. "I'd want to know, Kai. If it were me, I'd want to know," I said softly.

"Well, Raine is not you, and she's been through a lot. I'm not putting this on her as well. I'll find them, and I'll take care of them. When I'm good and ready, and Raine has had more time adjusting to all of this." Kai demonstrated my home with his hands, but I think he meant all the changes in general. Her growth, not just the new walls around her. "Then I will find a way to tell her, but not before." His face grew darker, like he was casting shadows in the room with his glare. "I will deal with them in my way. I owe her that. I owe myself that, and I won't rest until it happens. You wanted us to have a sharing session and a bonding moment, then there it is. You don't say a word to her about this."

We were quiet after that, and one by one, performers walked up to the stage to accept their awards. It seemed like forever before they called the names of those nominated for Best Rock Song. The announcers on stage made a joke, but I just wanted them to hurry up. My heart was pounding faster as I stared at the television.

"And the winner is...Grimhead Crew!"

"Yes!" I yelled and jumped up, pumping my fist into the air, immediately regretting it as pain shot through my knee. "Fuck" I grumbled as I flopped back down and held onto the joint. But even my stupid knee couldn't stop the happiness or the smile from spreading as the camera swung to Jace and Raine.

He gave her a quick kiss and then walked up with the rest of the band. Of course, Marcus didn't bother with the stairs and just jumped onto the stage. That guy was wild.

Jace stepped up to the podium, and my breath caught. He looked so handsome. He raised the award, and the crowd screamed and clapped.

"Wow, this is an honor. Thank you to all the fans that voted for us. This award is for all of us, all of you. I wouldn't be standing here without my band, but they have unwisely elected me to speak."

He smiled at the camera, and my heart flipped. He'd been nominated so many times but never won. I wanted to dance and cry and laugh. The pride I felt for him when I knew how hard he worked not just on his craft but to come back from all that had happened...he amazed me.

"I'd like to thank this group of guys right here. There are no other people I'd rather be with and spend so much time on a bus with." The crowd chuckled. *"In all seriousness, there are just so many people I want to thank, my agent Allen, the many producers, songwriters, those in the industry that have helped get us to this point, and of course the fans, the list is endless."*

He fell silent for a moment as he looked down at the podium. My stomach churned. It wasn't obvious to anyone else, but he was gearing himself up for something.

"*One thing that I learned very early on in my career is that you can't do it alone.*"

You could hear the fan area chanting: *We love Jace, We love Jace.*

A sexy smile pulled at the corner of his mouth. "*I love you too.*"

More screaming but louder now.

"They really do love him, don't they?" Kai said, startling me. I'd forgotten he was sitting on the couch with me.

"Yeah, almost from day one, the fans made it impossible for a label not to notice his talent. He could've done anything. He's always been like that, and it used to make me so fucking mad." I chuckled. "But I've always loved him, no matter what."

Jace signaled for the crowd to quiet down and waited before continuing. "*But I want to come clean on something tonight.*"

Everything stopped, including my breathing, as it became eerily quiet. Jace rubbed his chin, and I slid closer to the front of the couch. What was he up to?

"*You know, my agent is always making sure I'm in the news, with some sort of drama swirling around me. Some of it is true. I'm not always a good guy.*"

He dropped his voice and winked as the fan section went insane. The camera swung in that direction, and I thought for sure someone was going to throw themselves off the second-floor balcony. It sounded like he was at a concert as they drowned out everything else. He waited until the, *We love you, Jace* quieted down again.

"*But sadly, most of the things you've seen have all been staged to sell more songs. I'm not really that exciting. I mean, come on, me with a Princess?*" Jace cocked a brow and smiled before his face grew serious, and my blood pressure spiked.

"What the hell are you doing, Jace? You better not tank your career to stay at home. I will kick your ass," I said to the screen as if he could hear me.

"You do know he can't hear you, right?" Kai held out a new beer for me as he returned from the kitchen. I cracked it and took a swig, not bothering with the glass. I hadn't even seen Kai move from beside me, so engrossed in what Jace was saying.

"Oh, he'll know I'm watching. I always watch. I haven't missed a show he was nominated for."

"You're actually really funny," Kai said, and I looked at him, expecting more from that statement, but he kept his eyes on the television.

"*So here's the thing, I'm tired of the lies and the fake drama. I'm tired of the staged photos and interviews. I want all of you in this room and at home to know right now about something real and very important to me. There are two people in* this world that I love, and they mean more to me than anything. One has been with me for almost seventeen years, has lived with and watched all this unfold, and still stuck with me. The second person is newer to my life but holds my heart in her palm as equally as the other."

My eyes flicked to the band standing right beside Jace. They were smiling and looking like they knew what was coming, so they had to be in on this. I always knew when Marcus or Damon was shocked. They had easy tells. As the camera panned the room, it was easy to see that Raine had no idea what he was up to. She looked like she wanted to bolt from her seat and run out the doors.

"The first of those two couldn't be here with me tonight, although he wanted to be. I'm going to preface this by announcing that I'm bi-sexual and in a menage relationship." He paused and waited for the collective gasp of shock and then wild cheers to stop.

"Holy fuck, I don't think this is what Allen meant when he said he wanted more drama, Jace. What the hell are you doing?" My hand covered my mouth, and I pictured Allen fainting backstage.

Jace held up his hand to quiet the room once more. He had to be over time by now, but the camera didn't cut to commercial.

"He has kept me going through some very, very dark days in my life. Avro Beck, I'm done hiding you in the shadows. I love you, and I wish you could've been here tonight."

My mouth dropped open. "I think I'm going to pass out," I mumbled. My breathing was as fast as my rabbiting heart.

Kai clapped a hand on my shoulder as he laughed at my terrified expression. "Guess you didn't know what he was up to."

"Now for the second person that I love. All of you just learned of Raine and our relationship, and I know this has come as a shock, as I'm sure learning of Avro just now has, but Raine, could you come up here for a minute."

The camera immediately found her in the crowd, her image plastered on the massive screens, and I wasn't the only one who looked like they would pass out. Her blue eyes couldn't have gotten any wider, and all the color was drained from her face.

"What is he doing now," Kai asked.

I looked at Kai. "I didn't know about him outing me to the entire world. You really think I know what he's doing now?"

"Shhh, I want to listen," Kai said, and I thought I might just take my chances and punch him again.

Raine stood and walked along the aisle to loud cheers. Damon met her at the bottom of the stairs and helped her up. When she was by Jace's side, her lips barely moved, but I could tell she was asking him what he was doing. He simply linked their hands together.

"I have one more thing to say, and then I promise to get off this stage so you can all get on with your night. Most of you don't know this, but my entire family was murdered a few years ago." There was once more a collective gasp. "I've managed to keep it quiet until now, but I feel it's important you all know."

So many shocks for one awards show the media had to be salivating with the headlines.

"I'm sure some of you even saw it on the news, but I'm mentioning this because it would've been easy to allow the tragedy of that loss to consume me, drag me down, and make me turn my back on humanity. I was tempted and held a lot of anger for a long time. On top of that, a close personal relationship with depression almost got the best of me, and I never want any of you to feel that way. The band and I will be starting a help group for anyone suffering, and more will be announced in a few days as we launch this endeavor."

"Is what he said true," Kai asked. "I tried looking him up, but nothing other than his music career showed up."

"He pays to keep it off all search engines, but yeah, his mother, sister, and brother were all shot by his stepfather. If we hadn't left to head back to college, we would probably be dead too. Jace lives with that guilt. It's why you bother him so much. It's not your jerk attitude or the time you spent behind bars or even that you want to be in Raine's life. You remind him of what he lost and how easy it can happen again," I answered.

"Fuck," Kai mumbled. "Don't I feel like the asshole now."

I glanced over at Kai. "You said it."

"Jerk."

I smirked even as my hand shook in anticipation. I chugged the beer but kept my eyes on the screen, unable to look away.

"I want to tell everyone to hold those you love tight, never let them go, and fight for what you want." His eyes turned to Raine. "This beautiful woman came into my life, and as reluctant as I was in the beginning, I couldn't stop the warmth of her soul from seeping into my heart. I can breathe for the first time in so long, Raine, with you and Avro in my life. You make everyone around you feel loved and safe with your big heart and kind soul. We should all try to be as gracious and loving as you are. This world would be a far better place."

Jace's hand gripped the little podium, and I could tell he was getting emotional. These weren't just pretty words for the camera. I'd known him long enough to see through the mask and could tell fact from fiction.

"Raine, you make everyone that meets you want to be better without even trying, and I'm blessed that you came into my world. You and Avro are it for me, and I want you to know, in front of all these witnesses, I love you. This world is better for having you in it. I was so lucky to find a diamond like you."

A tear trickled down her cheek, and under the bright lights on stage, diamonds were exactly what the tiny droplets looked like.

"He certainly knows how to captivate everyone," Kai said.

"Yeah, he does."

Jace stepped away from the podium, and it was harder to hear what he said, so I turned the volume on max. He was whispering so low that the mic couldn't pick it up, but I was positive he was warning her that he would kiss her in front of everyone. He was taking a page from my book. I got one hell of an earful for doing that. Jace lowered himself to one knee just as I took a sip of my beer, and it sprayed all over the coffee table.

"What the fuck?" Kai and I said together.

The television suddenly blared at us. "Raine Eastman, you're the light that will always lead me through the darkest of days and keep me warm on the coldest of nights. You have helped the fire inside of me burn brighter and restored my hope. I thought I'd healed from my family being stolen from me, but I realize now that something was still missing, and you are the piece that has completed the puzzle of my heart."

"Holy shit," I mumbled. My mouth hung open as Jace pulled a jewelry box from his pocket. I couldn't believe what I was watching. My entire body shook with the adrenaline racing through my system, and I couldn't decipher if I was happy about this or terrified that I'd just been cut out for good. Had I brought us all together to lose them both?

"Raine Eastman, would you do me the honor of marrying me and becoming my wife?"

The cameras zoomed in on her face, and Raine looked as shocked and confused as I felt. I could feel her brain working from here, which gave me hope that this wasn't a plan of theirs that I was cut out of. It was horrible that I could even think that, but Jace always told me what he was going to do, and this was the biggest of big deals. Why had he felt the need to keep this from me?

Raine licked her lips, her face flashing with anger under the shock, and for the briefest of moments, I thought she would slap him and walk off the stage, but that wasn't Raine. She might kill him after, but to make an even larger spectacle wasn't in her DNA.

"*Yes, of course, I will,*" she said, and the entire place erupted with deafening cheers.

Grabbing the remote, I muted the television as they kissed and sat there staring as they cut to commercial

My head slowly turned to look at Kai as he looked at me.

"I'm going to kill him," Kai and I said together.

Raine

32

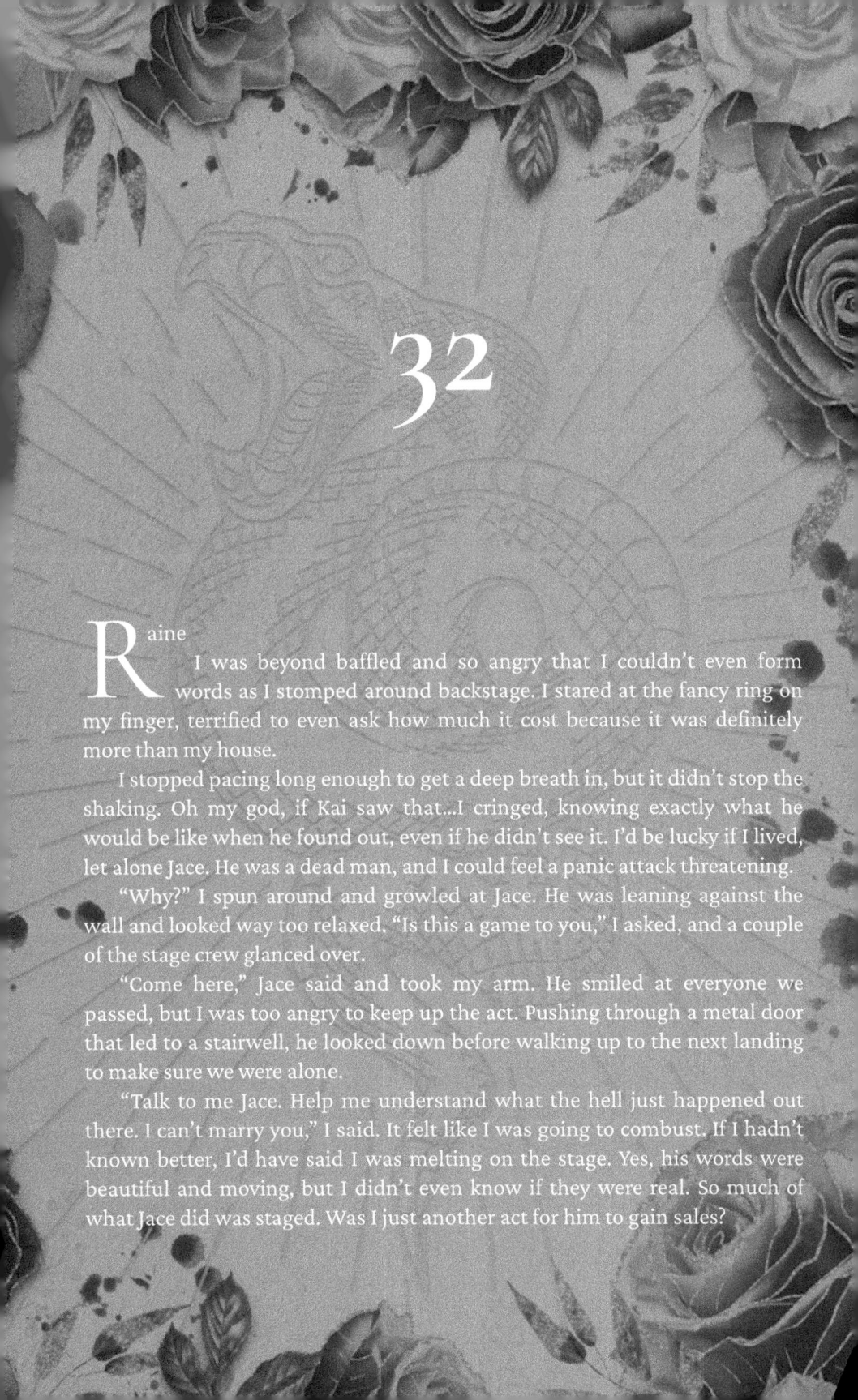

Raine

I was beyond baffled and so angry that I couldn't even form words as I stomped around backstage. I stared at the fancy ring on my finger, terrified to even ask how much it cost because it was definitely more than my house.

I stopped pacing long enough to get a deep breath in, but it didn't stop the shaking. Oh my god, if Kai saw that...I cringed, knowing exactly what he would be like when he found out, even if he didn't see it. I'd be lucky if I lived, let alone Jace. He was a dead man, and I could feel a panic attack threatening.

"Why?" I spun around and growled at Jace. He was leaning against the wall and looked way too relaxed. "Is this a game to you," I asked, and a couple of the stage crew glanced over.

"Come here," Jace said and took my arm. He smiled at everyone we passed, but I was too angry to keep up the act. Pushing through a metal door that led to a stairwell, he looked down before walking up to the next landing to make sure we were alone.

"Talk to me Jace. Help me understand what the hell just happened out there. I can't marry you," I said. It felt like I was going to combust. If I hadn't known better, I'd have said I was melting on the stage. Yes, his words were beautiful and moving, but I didn't even know if they were real. So much of what Jace did was staged. Was I just another act for him to gain sales?

"Why can't you marry me?" Jace crossed his arms, his face the same perfect arrogant mask it always was.

"For starters, we haven't had one discussion about this between us or all of us, and even if I wanted to hop on a plane and fly off into the sunset with you and never see Kai or Avro again, Kai would track us down and kill us both."

"I never thought that. Okay, maybe I did, but we'd bring Avro, but not anymore. I'm not trying to cut them out." Jace crossed his arms over his chest.

"Then what the hell is all this for? Is this just a way to one-up Kai and piss him off? Is that why you decided to bring me? Am I a pawn of drama for you to move around on a board? If it is Jace, so help me, god." I was gearing up for a real rant.

Jace placed his hands on my shoulders and made me look at him. "Stop it, Peaches. Seriously, you look like you're going to pass out."

"Can you blame me? You just proposed to me in front of however many thousands of people out there, and I had no warning at all."

Jace smirked, and it was too sexy for as angry as I was. "First, no one sees a proposal coming. At least if it's done right, they don't. That is kind of the point. Second, it's millions cause everyone watching in their homes just saw too."

My eyes narrowed into a glare, but my stomach flipped at the thought. "Oh god, I think I'm gonna be sick."

Stepping away from Jace, I grabbed the cold railing and closed my eyes. The jittering inside my body wasn't getting better, and it felt like my heart would jump out of my chest. My head swam a little, and I could feel the old panic attack wanting to rear its ugly head. No, I would not pass out. I was stronger than that now. Counting to ten very slowly, I concentrated on my breathing and the seconds between each breath. If Avro were here, he'd help calm me down. Oh no Avro. Wait did he know?

Jace touched my shoulders, but I shrugged him off and stepped away. "Don't touch me Jace." Turning around, I backed away from him until the cool of the concrete stairwell touched my back. "Did Avro know what you were planning?"

"No, no one did because if you want me to be honest, I hadn't planned it myself." My mouth dropped open, and I lifted my trembling hand to look at the ring.

"None of that was real? You made me cry and say yes to a proposal in front of however many people, and none of it was real?" I growled and grabbed the ring to yank it off my finger.

Jace reached out and stopped my hands, cupping them in his. "Stop. I mean it, Peaches. I want to tell you what's going on, but I refuse to talk to this version of you."

"Version of..." My nostrils flared, and I opened my mouth to give him another piece of my mind, but he pushed me up against the wall. The impact shocked me, but not as much as the kiss that followed. I should've been used to the demanding, lightheaded kisses that affected every part of my entire body. My lips moved like he had willed them while my hands gripped his tux jacket.

Every nerve ending was alive and on fire with his touch. I moaned as he deepened the kiss and pressed his body into mine. The air was stolen from my chest as he rubbed his trapped cock against my stomach.

"Fuck I want you right now," Jace growled, his lips still touching mine. "Don't ever take that ring off. I meant every word I said, and it stays on your finger as long as any part of you wanted to say yes. Do you understand?"

I nodded, not sure I could even speak.

"I do love you, Raine. I know it's soon, and I get all the what-ifs and other factors like Avro and, yes, even Kai, but I wouldn't have proposed if I didn't want to marry you."

Pushing himself away from me, he placed a hand on either side of my body, trapping me in place. It reminded me of the first night we met.

I took a shuddering breath and had to look away from his intense stare to think straight. "Then why Jace? Why now? Why like this? Why not tell even Avro? I don't understand."

Jace lowered his voice. "Allen got wind that I've been shopping around to replace him. I didn't like what he was planning and had been arranging for the band lately. Things have been tense. I expected not to see eye-to-eye all the time, but this was different. I wasn't comfortable with the things he wanted me to do." He looked over his shoulder to ensure no one could hear and whispered. "He wanted me to pretend I'd gotten drunk and got this other girl pregnant."

My mouth fell open. "He what? Who?"

"Doesn't matter who, I never let him get that far. I shut him down and told him to forget about it. He'd mapped out how we'd live together for four months, and then she'd pretend to lose the baby, and we'd part ways. It would make a big splash, but this is just too much. A few risqué photos are one thing. This shit he was coming up with was next level." Jace shook his head. "He said as long as it sold records, he didn't care, that everything was repairable, and I could play the part of a broken hearted, wannabe dad." He held out his hands. "I was livid. I mean, that is just...no. Not just for me, it makes a complete mockery of all those who have lost a child. Fuck."

"Shit, I'm sorry. Why didn't you say anything?" I placed my hand on his chest, and his eyes softened.

"I don't lean. I deal. I fix things when they need to be fixed. That's who I am."

There was a whole lot of telling off I wanted to do, but one thing at a time. "So what does that have to do with tonight?"

"After speaking with the guys, we agreed I'd make a few calls and get someone else lined up. I don't know how he found out, but he threatened that if I left him, he'd dig up anything he could on you and release it publicly, making it impossible for us to be together. I know he'd do it too. I could see it in his eyes. I don't know when he turned the corner from having morals to none, but I wasn't following him down that street."

Jace rolled out his shoulder and walked in a circle as he took a few deep breaths. It was easy to see how this was getting to him, and I couldn't blame him. This had to be picking at old memories of his family.

"I decided on the plane, which is why I never spoke to anyone. Besides, even if I had thought of this before leaving, Avro is already dealing with enough. Kai would never have let you get on the plane, and I was unsure what you'd do."

"Son of a bitch. I can't believe Allen did all of this." I groaned, annoyed with myself for not talking to Jace about my gut feeling at the concert. "He was questioning me and promised to find out if I was a gold digger at your concert. Said if I was, he'd ruin me."

Jace glared, and I swallowed hard. "Why didn't you tell me? I asked if he threatened you, and you said no."

I shrugged. "Honestly, I figured you'd blow a gasket. Then he'd have all the ammunition to want me out, make you look bad, or both. I hoped it was better to let the heat die down and have it blow over. Maybe he would end up excited about us. I should've said something, but I thought I was protecting you."

"Guys like Allen don't blow over, not unless you beat them with a big stick first."

"I see that now."

"Anyway, I decided to get ahead of him and his plans. I fired him just before they announced the award winner. Now if he digs up shit, he will look like a petty, bitter ex-employee that just wants to stir up dirt. The millions that were watching will have our back. They will crush him. Having fans has its difficulties, but in a situation like this, there is no one better to have at your back than millions devoted to you."

"But this is a gimmick. Won't your fans just see through what you've done if Allen does do something?"

Jace stood up straight but cupped my chin. "I didn't have time to prep anyone, and yes, this was much faster than I would've done if given the option, but it's not a gimmick. You and what we have are not a joke to me, Raine. I'd be honored if you married me, and I mean that. It's not just placating or pretty words. Avro has always been part of my heart, and now you are as well, and I'm not letting that go. Not for Kai, and definitely not for fucking Allen."

It was not lost on me that he used my name, not Peaches. Butterflies took flight in my stomach, and I tried to picture myself as Mrs. Everly. I smiled and wanted to go all mushy. I mean, who wouldn't? But there were other people in the relationship to consider and there was a gnawing of guilt that was marring the happiness.

"Look, the thing is that no matter what I said out there, we can't get married for any reason without talking to Avro and Kai. We can play it up for the media if you want, but they would be crushed. Not only do I not want to do that to them, but if I'm getting married, I want all of you to be involved," I said.

Jace stepped back and rubbed at his chin. He looked so serious with the furrowed brow and intense stare.

"You're right, I feel the same, but I'm just trying to figure out how to play this."

I grabbed his hands, and they felt so hot compared to mine.

"We don't need to figure it all out now. We can talk about it on the plane and then speak to the guys when we get back. As for right now, we'll go out there and pretend all is normal. What I'm saying is, you don't need to fix it all tonight."

"You're amazing, and I know why Avro fell so hard and why Kai has never stopped. I wasn't certain I wanted anything in my life to change, but you're worth every second of it."

I couldn't stop the blush from spreading. "I can't believe the first time you told me you loved me was on national television." He smirked.

"You always remember your firsts. There is no way you'll ever forget that," he said, tipping my head up and dropping his mouth to nip at my lower lip. "I wish I didn't have one more award to wait for because I've been dying to get you out of this dress all night."

"Now, if it were Kai, he'd have just done it in front of everyone." I teased and loved that, for once, I was getting to poke at him.

Jace's lip curved up. "Don't tempt me 'cause I'm all for it. You must know by now that I love when people watch. Let them drool. Let them hate. I don't fucking care. It all turns me on." Turning my head to the side, he kissed my jumping pulse. "Maybe I should. I'm not sure how I will top that first award speech, and that would definitely do it." He nipped at the sensitive skin, and I shuddered in his hold. "What do you think, Peaches? You want to be my naughty girl and let me fuck you on stage?"

"No amount of begging or pretty words is going to make that happen," I said and then sucked in a sharp breath as his hand easily slipped between the high cut split in the dress, his fingers sliding between my thighs. "Even if you proposed again, I wouldn't do it," I panted as his finger rubbed little circles, teasing me.

"I do love a challenge, Peaches, but you're right. We shouldn't get arrested. At least not tonight. We need to spread out the firsts." Moaning, my hands gripped his shoulders as his finger pushed into me. "Such a good girl not wearing any underwear." Jace sank his finger deeper, and my hands gripped the material of his jacket into my fist. I couldn't even care that it would wrinkle the material.

"We shouldn't be doing this," I said. "What if someone sees us?"

"Then they're going to get a show 'cause I'm not waiting any longer to be inside this sweet pussy of yours. Unzip my cock and pull it out," Jace ordered, his finger never stopping the teasing assault driving me crazy.

"Jace, I don't...."

He stopped any complaint as his lips crashed down on mine, and his finger pressed as deep as it could go. I turned into a panting mess as he added a second finger and swallowed my moans.

"Do it, Peaches, unzip my cock. I know you want it. I will keep you in this fucking stairwell until I get to celebrate with my new fiancé." He smiled. "I'll miss the rest of the awards if I have to, and then I'll tell the media why."

"Are you blackmailing your new fiancé already," I asked, sucking in a ragged breath. He knew exactly what to do to push me toward that sweet bliss and hold off just enough that I couldn't quite get there.

"Call it gentle persuasion."

"This is insane." It might have been, but my hands released the tight hold on the jacket to slide down his body. I already knew he was going commando, it was the deal he talked me into making before we left the hotel, and there was no way he could've walked back out there now. His pants were tented, making it hard to get the zipper down.

I didn't have to reach inside once they were unzipped. That was all the encouragement his cock needed to spring free. I wrapped my hand around that silky, hard length, and Jace groaned.

"Fuck I love it when you touch me, Peaches." My thumb ran over the tip and took the droplets of precum to play with the ring. God, I loved the feel of it. I really wanted all the guys to get one. "Yeah, just like that, fuck, that feels good."

Jace pushed harder into my palm as he pressed me up against the wall. My eyes closed as he slowly fucked my hand until I was begging for more.

"Please Jace."

"Please what, Peaches?" His lips grazed my ear. "You want me to fuck you right here? Spread this tight pussy open and make you cum all over me?" I shivered and moaned. "You're my good girl, aren't you?" I nodded. "Are you going to let me fuck you right now? Say it, Peaches, tell me you want me."

"Yes, I...oh God," I moaned as his fingers picked up the pace.

"What was that, Peaches? I didn't quite catch what you said." I would've told off the arrogant, smirking jerk if I could think straight, but I'd been reduced to nothing more than the feel of his fingers and the need coursing through my body.

"Yes, I want you to fuck me," I blurted out, the words running together. I expected him to make me repeat it, but he pulled his fingers out, and I couldn't stop the excited trembling as he sucked the fingers into his mouth. Everything he did was precise and with intent, and I couldn't look away.

"Gimmie your leg," he said, tapping the one with the slit. I lifted my leg, and his hot hand gripping my thigh made me moan in anticipation. "Move the dress off to the side." Jace's voice dropped, the words coming out like a growl.

My already racing heart tripled in time as I pulled the shimmery material away. I could hear someone talking and getting close to the stairwell door, but if Jace heard, he didn't care. Stepping forward, he teased me for just a second before thrusting in with a groan that vibrated through my body. I buried my face in the crook of his neck and pressed my lips together to keep from yelling out.

As the voice got closer, I realized someone was talking on the phone, and then the door opened. Jace looked over his shoulder, his already dark and intense expression turning into a snarl.

"Get the fuck out, now," he commanded, and I shivered at the tone. I was quickly learning to love this side of him. I couldn't see the person for Jace's body, but the door immediately closed. He turned his heated stare back to me. "Wrap your arms around my neck and hold on, 'cause I'm not holding back." I moaned as I did what he asked. "Fuck I love it when you squeeze my cock like that."

His mouth and the things he said always made me so hot. I was already so close to the edge that it wouldn't take much to push me over. I locked my arms around his neck as he lifted me just enough that my toe was almost not touching the floor. His deep thrusts stole my breath away as I clung tighter to him.

"Fuck, you're always so tight and wet. I can't get enough of you," Jace said. My ass was already pressed into the wall as hard as it could go, and yet Jace was fucking me like he could push me right through the concrete. My body was a quaking disaster of emotions and sensations, quickly pushing me to the peak.

"You gonna cum on me, Peaches? You going to soak my cock and mark me as yours?" I couldn't answer. No words would form, no matter how many times I tried. Jace growled as his hips pounded into me. "Fuck yes, Peaches."

I could only moan as I rode his cock, my body tightening like a spring. I was ready to burst and wanted to scream, but I bit my lip instead.

"I will take my time with you when we get back to the hotel. I want to feast on your sweet pussy until you can't take anymore and then fuck you all over again. You ignite a fire in me, Peaches, and if I don't cum right now, I might burn up and take you with me."

I bit down on his collar and moaned as his pace quickened. His piercing was rubbing me in just the right spot, and with a smothered yell, I came hard. My body arched into his as my arms tightened, and I shuddered with pleasure.

"That's it, Peaches, such a good girl cumming all over my cock. Oh, fuck yes," Jace groaned, his body tensing in my hold, and then I felt him cumming inside me. Something about that sensation always set off smaller climaxes, and the wave I was riding kept going until Jace fell still. He was breathing hard, and I wanted to do it again and not have to head back to our seats.

"I better go get cleaned up," I said as Jace slowly slipped from my body and let my leg drop to the floor.

He smiled wide and stuffed his cock back into his pants. "Oh, no, you're not."

"What? But..."

"I don't care, Peaches. I'm covered in your cum for the rest of the night. So you can sit in mine, besides what you eat right now."

He ran his finger up the inside of my leg and held his finger out to me. His brow cocked, and I opened my mouth, sucking his finger clean. He did it a few more times before the corner of his mouth pulled up in a lopsided grin that showed off the dimple you didn't often see.

"There, that's as clean as you'll get until tonight." He adjusted my dress until it was once more in place.

"You're terrible," I said, shaking my head at him, which only made Jace laugh.

"Maybe, but you love it, and I can't wait to see you out there squirming as everyone stares at you, and you're not sure if it's because you were backstage getting fucked or because you just got engaged."

I glared at him and thought every swear word I could think of, but before I could mouth off, he dropped his lips to mine and kissed me with so much tenderness that it was as breathtaking as when he was demanding.

"I love you, Peaches. I'm proud to have you on my arm tonight." Jace stepped back and held out his arm like a perfect gentleman. There were so many layers to him that my head swam, and my emotions turned inside out.

I put my hand on his arm to see the stunning ring with what looked like a million little diamonds surrounding the large emerald-cut stone. "You're really sure about this? I don't want to be the girl that was proposed to because you were forced to do it."

"I've done many things, Raine, but I wouldn't lie about wanting this. I watched as my mother was beaten down emotionally and physically before her beautiful life was stolen for good. What that taught me, what I want, is a chance at a happy ending, whatever that looks like. You helped complete what was missing in me. Avro knew it from the first moment he met you, and he's been prepping us both for this moment." Taking my hand, he linked our fingers together. "Like keys to my soul, you and Avro hold them all," he softly sang before kissing my hand.

"I love you too, Jace," I said, my body melting at his smile.

Raine

33

Raine

Breathing fast as I held the sheets to my chest, I sat up in bed. It was always the same when the nightmares hit. The attack, running down the alley, the pain and fear mixed with the stench of their bodies and the couch, all in vivid detail.

I closed my eyes and took a deep breath as I forced the old images down. I didn't know why they were still creeping up. It was so long ago, and now that Kai and I were in a different place, I thought they would go away for good.

Jace was sound asleep, his two awards sitting on the nightstand, and I couldn't help but smile. He deserved them, and I was so proud as he walked up on stage to receive the second award of the night. We'd celebrated with the band for a few hours after everything wrapped up before coming back here, where Jace had a very loud conversation with Avro before we did anything else. I'd never heard Avro so angry, but he was livid and didn't let Jace get a word in before he hung up on us. If Avro was that mad, how the heck was Kai going to react?

He said we'd deal with it when we got home and weren't letting it ruin our night. It had taken a while, but once I decided Jace was right and let go, our time together was amazing. I'd made the mistake of thinking that Jace couldn't still be able to go that long, but he kept me panting for him for hours until I couldn't even open my eyes or lift my head. I glanced at the clock and realized I'd only been asleep for a couple of hours.

Swinging my legs out of bed, I pulled on his discarded dress shirt, did up a few buttons, and rolled the sleeves. It smelled like him and immediately calmed the last bit of nerves. I checked my phone to see if there were any answers to the texts I'd sent Kai, but all I saw was my side of the convo staring back at me. He was ignoring me. I tried calling, but he wouldn't pick up. I knew he needed space, but if he just talked to me for five minutes, I could set his mind at ease and explain in detail when we got back. Jace was strict about what was put into texts, so I couldn't just lay it all out there, but I expected an *I don't want to fucking talk to you right now*, at the very least.

I padded into the main part of the suite. I'd never seen anything as extravagant as this before and wasn't sure if I liked the lavishness. The sitting room alone could fit my entire house three times over. It was stunning, and there was no denying that, but I'd never lived like this and didn't see the need for all this unused space.

The kitchen was as large as the sitting room and held fancy appliances I doubted ever got used. Grabbing a glass, I hit the ice button on the fridge, and a few clunks later, I had perfectly round ice balls. Holding up the glass, I stared at the shape. Even the ice cubes couldn't be normal. What the heck? I filled the glass and took a long drink of water that felt good as it hit the back of my throat, reminding me that I'd been screaming half the night.

My stomach flipped with the same butterflies as last night, and my lips curved up as I thought about the jacuzzi and then back in bed afterward.

I sucked in a startled breath as I reached the bedroom door. It took a second to understand what was happening, but someone was dressed in all black with one of Jace's awards in their hands raised to strike Jace.

"Jace, look out!" Without thinking, I threw the glass I was holding. After years of throwing glasses and bottles across the bar to Avro, the glass sailed with accuracy and crashed into the side of the attacker's head.

"Fuck," came the deep growl of a man's voice as the glass hit him, and he slammed into the dresser.

"What the fuck?" Jace yelled, his eyes snapping open. He sat up straight in bed as I ran across the room and slammed my shoulder into the startled attacker like I was playing rugby. Whoever the guy was, he dropped the award as the second one on the nightstand toppled over. He held up his arms as I caught him in the knee with my foot, knocking it to the side at an odd angle.

"Fuck off, you bitch," he growled. He could call me whatever name he wanted. I wasn't letting some robber come in and hurt either of us. Gripping his injured knee, he stumbled to the side and tripped over his feet before smacking into the wall and hitting the ground with a thud.

The same kind of blinding anger was taking over as it had when I saw the girl all over Kai at the bar, and I balled my fists, ready to attack again, but Jace picked me up and turned me away from whoever it was.

I was gearing up to complain when I realized I was in nothing but his dress shirt. Jace had his phone in hand, already glowing with nine-one-one on the screen.

"Who the fuck are you, and what do you want?" Jace growled and held his arm out like he thought I would try something again as I stepped up beside him. The guy on the floor laughed and reached up, pulling down the hood. "Allen? What the hell are you doing?"

My eyes widened, and I stared up at Jace, who looked as shocked as I was. "He was trying to kill you. He had the award ready to smash over your head," I said, and Allen's eyes rolled in my direction.

"I should've done it long ago, you thankless prick," he drawled, his words a little slow like he'd been drinking or was on drugs. "And, wouldn't that be ironic? The girl that put an innocent man in jail ends up in jail for murder, but she is also innocent. Well, you're not innocent, but...you get my drift."

I pressed against Jace's arm. "Why are you doing this? I've never done anything to you."

Allen pointed at Jace. "Bullshit, this is all because of you!" I was shocked by the venom in his voice. "He ruined me because of you and the stupidity of wanting to keep you. I told him you'd bring him down, and you will. The fans will learn about your druggie parents and your lies that sent a man to jail, and they'll turn on you. Or how about your interactions with a known motorcycle club enforcer, the one you happened to put in jail?"

"How the hell...."

Jace grabbed my arm, his look telling me not to confirm or deny. I ground my teeth, livid that he dug into my past and tried to twist all the pain I had suffered into a weapon.

"All my clients have left. Jace wasn't happy just firing me, which was humiliating enough, but he had to ruin my career because of his need to have his playtime with you."

Did he think I was a pet? He acted as if Jace owned me with the way he spoke. It was disturbing, but then again, everything about this was disturbing.

"I didn't have anything to do with that. I have no idea why they left," Jace growled. "But, I'm kinda wishing I'd thought of that now."

"Lies! There is no such thing as coincidences," he yelled and began cursing as he tried to pull himself to his feet. I barely recognized him. He seemed so different from the put-together man I'd met initially. "I've lost everything, and it's all your fault."

Allen reached behind his back, and I sucked in a deep breath, not knowing if he was reaching for a gun or a phone. Jace, obviously thinking the same thing tossed his phone on the bed and jumped on Allen, sending the two men crashing to the floor.

I grabbed Jace's phone and realized an operator was already on the line.

"Hello, is anyone still there?"

"Hi, yes. I think he's going for a weapon. Jace and Allen are fighting."

"Go to the door, the officers are there," the woman on the line said, and I sprinted as fast as I could. Reaching the door, I whipped it open, and four officers walked in.

"This way," I said and ran back to the bedroom with the sound of their heavy boots following me. I went inside and got out of the way as they ran over to where Jace now had Allen pinned face down. A small gun no bigger than my palm was on the floor.

I covered my mouth as I realized this man was willing to kill Jace and me. There was lots of noise and chaos as they got him in cuffs, and all the old memories surfaced one at a time. I saw the officers coming to my house when my parents died and giving my statement over and over about my attack. I didn't notice I was crying until Jace wrapped his arms around me and held me tight.

"Shh, it's going to be okay. He's gone. It's just us. Allen is going to go away for a long time. My lawyers will make sure of it."

"Why does this stuff keep happening? It seems like there is something else every time I turn around. He almost killed you, Jace. If I'd been any longer in the kitchen, he would've. I...oh my god." Wrapping my arms around him, I let out the pent-up emotion, my body trembling as the tears fell harder. Jace held me tight, and for the first time, I really felt the connection between us.

Even last night, with everything that had happened and the wild aftermath of the awards show, it was right now, in this quiet moment, that I felt his kind heart and his love for me.

"I can't answer the why, but maybe it's because we all have crazy shit and terrible pasts that we understand one another so well," Jace said, and as I leaned back to look up at him, he wiped away the tears on my face with his thumbs. "Thank you for saving me," he said, laying his lips against my forehead.

"There was no way I was letting him hit you with that thing." I shuddered at the thought.

"Well, I hope you're prepared to save me again," Jace said, and my eyebrows drew together. "We still have to deal with Kai and Avro."

Laying my head against his chest, I groaned. That was one conversation I was not looking forward to having. No matter how we explained it, he would want to shoot first and ask questions later.

Kaivan

I stomped from one end of Avro and Jace's house to the other so many times that there should've been a groove in the tile floor. I needed to sleep, but hadn't been able too all night. Every time I closed my eyes all I could see was Jace down on one knee and Raine agreeing to marry him. It was my worst nightmare coming true before my eyes. I knew I couldn't trust him and I almost had.

The fact that Avro wasn't bitching about my boots screamed what a foul mood I was in. The moment I stopped moving, all I could think about were the different ways I wanted to kill Jace, and there were many. The current fantasy was me cutting him up and turning him into a human shish kebab that I could lower into the water for the sharks.

"They're here," Avro called down the hall where I'd just turned around, and I marched back, my muscles twitching and hands flexing to wrap around his throat.

I rounded the corner as they stepped through the door, and the first thing my eyes landed on was the rock that looked like an ice cube on Raine's finger. It took every ounce of self-control I had not to leap over Raine and onto the man closing the door behind them.

"I fucking warned you!" I yelled, and Raine stepped back. I stopped moving at the terrified look in her eyes. How times have changed. I wanted that look not so long ago, but now it hurt my heart. I opted to point at Jace instead of getting any closer. "I told you if you tried to take her away, I'd destroy you. I thought we came to an understanding. I never wanted to have to use the information, but I fucking will."

"What is he talking about," Raine asked and looked between us.

"What you think is going on is not what happened, Kai, and I'll explain everything if you give me a minute before you try to kill me." Jace looked down at Raine. "Kai and I agreed not to try and pull you in any one direction.

We each have dirt on the other that we'd prefer not be shared with the world and have been using it as collateral."

"That's just a fancy way of saying you're blackmailing one another," she said and crossed her arms over her chest. "And here I thought you were actually learning to get along."

"So did I, but it looks like I'm going to fucking need that information after all," I growled.

"Slow your fucking roll, Kai, you don't have the slightest clue what happened, and I'm not trying to pull her away from you or Avro. That's the last thing I'm doing."

"You're fucking liar," I growled, marching around Raine. I gripped Jace by the hoodie he was wearing. "It's been what you were pushing for from the first moment I met you."

"I'm pretty fucking sure I'm not the one that stormed into my home and tore it up and waved a gun around threatening to kill you, or have you forgotten that you almost shot us all?" Jace yelled, and I hated the reminder of how close the gun had come to going off and taking Raine forever.

"Now, get your fucking hands off of me," Jace growled but continued to hold his hands up and didn't touch me.

"What's this bullshit? Fight me, you asshole," I said. Jace stood his ground but didn't touch me, and my heart raced faster.

Raine shoved her arms between us, and I snarled at her, my anger shifting and dividing as it rose like an inferno and then tumbled in on itself, only to reform again.

"You agreed to marry him? How could you do that?" My world was narrowing in as I stared down at her. So many years of love and pain were welling up inside of me, and I couldn't think straight looking into her big blue eyes. "After everything we've shared, how could you just decide to say fuck it and turn your back on me? How could you leave and never come back?"

"Whoa! What are you talking about? I'm not turning my back on you. Kai, I'm right here. I came back," Raine said, her eyes searching my face.

"Yeah Kai, we are standing here in front of you on time, exactly when we said we'd be back," Jace said, and the sound of his voice was grating on my nerves.

"Stay out of this. This is all your fault." It was a good thing that Avro said I had to leave all weapons outside because if I had my gun, there was a good chance I would've shot Jace. The image of him bleeding out was so vivid in my mind that my fists tightened until they cracked, and still, he didn't look away or move. "You think you're so fucking smart, don't you?"

"Kai, let Jace go. You don't know what's going on. Let him explain what happened."

"Why, so you can pack a bag and fuck off to wherever you want? So you can have me tossed in prison again. That's what you want, right? You want me out of your life for good. You want to pack a bag and run off to your sister's."

Raine shook her head. "Kai...I don't have a sister. What is happening right now?"

I pushed away from Jace to give Raine my full attention. I pointed my thumb at Jace. "It's pretty obvious who you've decided to choose. I knew this would happen. I knew he'd get to you with his fancy plane and concerts around the world. That you'd be swayed by the five-star restaurants and decide you'd rather not stay at the clubhouse and with me."

"No, of course not. I don't care about money or fancy things. You know that about me. Do you really think I'm that shallow? And what club are we talking about?"

"I knew it, I knew you'd decide to leave me alone for however long without checking on me, and now you come back and expect me to forgive you." I snorted in disgust. "Now you have the cost of everything I own on your finger."

I stomped away from them, needing to put space between us before I did something I'd regret or that landed me in jail. My head was pounding, and a sharp pain was throbbing behind my eye. I couldn't show weakness. You never showed weakness to your enemies. I whipped around to glare at the three sets of eyes trying to stare me down. They were trying to corner me. They'd been waiting for this moment to attack me.

Raine took a step toward me. "Kai...are you okay? I'm not sure what's happening, but you're not making sense," she said. She kept walking in my direction, and I backed away like her hands were poison.

"So, you're saying we're done?"

"What? No. Of course not. What is going on with you? Kai, you're really worrying me right now." Reaching out, Raine laid her hand on my chest, and her brow pulled together. "I love you. I don't want to leave you. Do you hear me?"

"Don't look at me like that." I stepped away from her until her hand fell away. "Your eyes are all full of concern like you fucking care about me. Lies on your tongue that you spill so easily."

"Kai, seriously, what the fuck is going on," Jace asked, his worried voice just as grating as his cocky one. Really him speaking or breathing at all. As I looked at him, my head started to spin.

"I warned you not to divide us. I promised you that I didn't care who crashed and burned. Now she's dead."

"Who's dead? Kai, are you okay," Avro asked and stepped up to my side. "You're really not making much sense. Come sit down. You're all sweaty like you're going to pass out."

"Don't touch me," I jerked away from Avro, my mind for just a moment seeing Red's hand on my bicep. I shook my head to erase the image. What was happening? My head was light, yet my limbs were so heavy it was an effort to point at them.

"Why are all of you looking at me like that? I'm fine. It's all of you that are the problem. I knew this was all a mistake. You can't go into that area without getting hurt, and now the three of us are here together. I had to kill him. It could never work" I stumbled sideways away from them, planning to leave out the back door and never return.

"Kai, stop this." Raine was walking toward me, holding out her hands, but when she touched me, it felt like I'd been burnt, and I jerked away. My mind was clouded with overlapping images, and I ran my hand through my hair, trying to decipher what was real and what wasn't as they merged.

"I said, don't touch me," I grabbed at the door jam to the kitchen, but when I took a step, I tripped on something and landed heavily against the wall. Of course, they took advantage of my weakened position, and all three of them descended on me.

"Don't touch me, no, don't touch me...I'll kill you," I said, or at least I think I said it, but I didn't feel my mouth moving. The pounding in my head worsened as I slid down the cool surface to the floor.

"I said...stop touching me. Stop hurting me, please. No, I don't want to go," I said, and it all went dark.

Raine

34

Raine

I was waiting outside the backdoor for Roach to arrive. Something was going on with Kai, but I didn't know if he could go to a hospital. The worry was eating me alive.

"Hey, are you okay," Avro asked as he stepped outside and wrapped his arm around my shoulders. I leaned into his warm body and shook my head no.

"I'm scared. I expected the anger, but it was like he was talking to someone else part of the time or multiple people...shit Avro, what if something is really wrong with him? I just found him. I can't lose him all over again. I know you two don't like him, but...."

"Shhh, stop. First, you're not going to lose him. Kai is a tough SOB. Second I don't hate him. We actually got along well until the proposal, but that's beside the point." He sighed as he kissed the top of my head. "There is no point stressing or worrying until we know more."

I wished I could be as optimistic as Avro, so many strange and terrible things had happened already. For Kai to come back into my life and, then something might be wrong with him...I couldn't even let myself go there. I wanted to fall to my knees and beg whoever would listen to help him.

"I hope you're right," I said as a black truck pulled into the back lane and parked in the driveway. Two men got out. The driver I recognized, but I didn't know the second man. Roach opened the back door and then walked over.

"Hi, thanks for coming," I said. "I just didn't know who else to call."

"You did the right thing. We have a club doctor who has all the best equipment needed to make sure Snake is okay," the man I didn't know said. He held out his hand, which was as large as my face. "Nice to meet you finally, Raine. My name is Mannix. I have heard a lot about you." I shook his outstretched hand.

"I'm sure not all of it has been nice," I said, and he smirked but didn't confirm or deny it.

"Nice to meet you. I'm Avro." Avro held out his hand for Mannix to shake next.

"So what happened," Roach asked, crossing his arms over his chest. I didn't like the way he was staring at me. It felt like he was blaming me for this happening to Kai. I already held enough blame in my heart. I didn't need this.

"I don't know. One minute he seemed fine but angry. The next, he was arguing, but it felt like he wasn't really talking to us, and then he slowly collapsed to the ground. His pulse was racing, and he was clammy to touch. We got him to the couch and covered him up, then I called you immediately. He's breathing, and his pulse has slowed, but he hasn't woken up."

"Where is he," Mannix asked, and I tore my eyes away from Roach's hard stare.

"He's just inside in the living room," I pulled open the door and led the way to where Kai was lying on the couch, murmuring something while Jace sat in a chair watching him.

"Well shit, you're Jace Everly," Mannix said and smiled. "Nice to meet you." Jace stood, and the pleasantries started all over again.

I stood by the door out of the way, and Roach leaned down and whispered. "You had to know something like this would happen," he said.

I looked up at him. "Excuse me?"

"The very public proposal and you accepting. You had to know that it would send Kai into a tailspin. Why would you do that to him?"

Crossing my arms, I glared at Roach. "You have no right to ask me that. You also have no idea what's going on or why."

"You're right, I don't, but that man is my brother, blood or not, and this shit you have going on, making him play house with you and two other guys, is bullshit."

Roach walked away before I could say anything else, but I was seething mad. Why was it that he thought he got a say in our relationship?

I watched as Mannix and Roach picked Kai up, and my stomach churned to see him like this. Kai was so strong. I expected the anger and to see him fired up, but this was different. Had I pushed him too far? It wasn't like I set out to hurt him. I loved him with every fiber of my being.

"I want to come with you," I said as they approached the living room door.

"Not a chance," Roach said, and I was ready to punch him.

Mannix glared over his shoulder at Roach before turning his eyes on me. Mannix had a calming personality that reminded me a bit of Avro, but where Avro wasn't commanding or liked to be in charge, Mannix's entire aura screamed that he was the man to talk to, and everyone listened.

"Even though Roach has terrible bedside manners, he is right. It's better if we take him to the club doctor alone, but I will personally call you the moment we know anything."

Avro placed his hands on my shoulders as if silently telling me to let it go. I nodded even though I wanted to argue until I was blue in the face. But this wasn't about me. This was about Kai and a doctor seeing him as quickly as possible.

"Thank you," I said, and Roach rolled his eyes.

"Don't do that," I growled at him.

"I said what I said, and I stand by every word. The reason Kai is like this is because of you," Roach said.

"Roach, knock it off," Mannix ordered. "I will call you, but we need to get going." They walked out the back door, and we watched as Kai was loaded into the truck, and they drove away.

Stepping away from Avro, I began to pace, unable to sit still. "So, I take it Jace filled you in?"

"Yes, I'm sorry I blew up and didn't listen last night. I think I'm part of the reason Kai is so agitated." I turned to look at him, and he ran his hand through his hair. "We were both here watching the awards when the proposal happened. We were understandably shocked, hurt, and pissed. We stayed up all night talking and arguing, and then I had the blow-up phone call with Jace, and I think we fed off each other's anxiety. Not a great combo."

"Shit," I moaned. "I should've kept calling until he picked up." I rubbed my face. This whole thinking about so many people at once was harder than it looked. I turned to Jace, who was staring out the window. "You've been awfully quiet. What are you thinking?"

"I don't know. It's been an intense forty-eight hours. I was threatened, I proposed, was almost killed in my sleep, and now this. I'm going to go play and hopefully pump out a new number-one song." He faked a half-hearted smile. Jace was doing that closed-off thing, and I wanted to hit everyone and scream. I might still scream just because it would make me feel better.

Jace stopped walking when he reached me. "I'm sorry about Kai, I may not like him, but I don't want to see him in a bad way either, you know?"

I nodded. "I know, and I know this will blow over when he understands why you did it and that we're not just making plans without him." Jace looked down to the ground and then back up into my eyes. The look gripped my heart and twisted. His face wasn't covered with the arrogant mask, and the sadness laid bare was trying to break the last piece of my heart that was already fracturing.

"Technically, with Allen going to jail, we don't have to get married or pretend to be engaged if you don't want to. If this is going to cause a huge issue with Kai, then we can figure out a way to spin it," he said.

"I wasn't planning on backing out of the agreement we discussed last night. Is that what you want?"

Jace raised one cocky eyebrow. "You already know the answer to that question. I've told you how I feel and what I want. Once you decide, let me know." Jace sauntered away, his hands stuffed in his pockets, and Avro and I were left staring at one another.

"What the fuck?" I resumed my pacing. "Why can't things just be calm? I don't understand why my life is like a hurricane. It goes out to sea, then comes back into shore to destroy everything, then swirls away only to do it all over again."

Avro shrugged. "I don't have any answers to that. I'm sorry, but I have an idea that might help ease the tension and get you out of the house while we wait to hear about Kai."

"What's that," I asked as I walked past where he was leaning against the wall.

"Let's go pack some of your things and bring them over. I know you still had reservations about moving in full-time, but—"

I held up my hand and cut Avro off. "No, let's do it. I need the distraction, or I'm going to go crazy waiting to hear about Kai," I said as the sound of the piano drifted down the stairs. "It seems we all need a distraction."

Avro grabbed his keys, and although the drive to my house was quiet, it felt good to get out, and it felt even better to be around Avro, who'd always been the buoy in stormy waters I clung to.

Pulling up, I stared at my postage stamp house and knew this was the right decision. This place never felt like home. It was a pit-stop, a place to hover while I tried to get my shit together. So much had happened in a very short time, but I'd learned that I was stronger than I gave myself credit for. I was more adventurous than I ever thought, and I had enough love in my heart for three of the best people I'd ever met. I loved them all and would protect them fiercely.

Kai needed to be okay, and I would find a way to make him see that public engagement or not—he was my heart. I loved Avro and Jace, but I wouldn't do anything without Kai involved in the decision. We were two souls destined and fused together long ago.

We walked into the small living room, and I quickly surveyed the furniture purchased at thrift stores or garage sales. None of it was anything I wanted to keep.

Avro's fingers trailed down my arm as he passed, but before he could get far, I pulled on his hand and brought him to a halt. "Why didn't you want to tell me about your surgery?"

Avro's gaze went from shocked to annoyed. "Jace can't keep his mouth shut."

"Don't get angry with him. He told me something you should've." Avro ran his hand through his hair and looked away from my eyes. When he didn't say anything, I knew I would have to poke at him. "Start by telling me how your appointment went yesterday?"

He shrugged and tugged my hand so we could sit down on the couch. "Surgery is set to happen in two weeks. I already took care of the paperwork yesterday to have you come back to Eclipse and explained that your family emergency was a false alarm."

"That's it, business as usual?" I curled up on the couch, leaning my elbow on the back as I stared at the side of his face.

"I just want everything to be ready, and I knew you'd want to head back to work. Look, I didn't say anything because I hate talking about it. I'm going to be useless for months. Just a bum sitting around at home, feeling sorry for myself." Avro rubbed at his eyes. "I know, it's not true, but I won't be able to do even the simplest things easily, things we all take for granted. Like how awkward it is to sit on a toilet and wipe your butt." He smirked, making me smile. "Or doing laundry, making a meal, and taking a shower. Hell, even sex is a problem. I will be useless, and it's a horrible feeling."

Reaching out, I ran my hand through his soft hair. I really did love this raven color. It was so striking with his amber eyes. "Avro, you're never useless. Would you ever think that of anyone else that you saw on crutches, in a wheelchair, or anything else for that matter?"

"No, of course not," he said, his eyes had gone wide with the horrified expression.

"Then why are you placing these unrealistic expectations on yourself and thinking about yourself so negatively?" He pressed his face into my hand.

"I don't know. I'm not a great patient, I guess. I prefer to look after people than be looked after, and with this, I'm going to need help, and I'm so scared to fall back into the dark depression I had before. It's like this monster looming and waiting to strike when I'm at my weakest."

I scooted closer to him, and he turned his head to look at me, so I stole the opportunity to kiss his way too-tempting lips. Avro was so tender and sweet with everything he did, and I knew that if Kai had found me years ago before Avro had helped me trust again, then I wouldn't have been able to handle everything that happened since. Avro pushed me to find my strength and believe in myself. Breaking the kiss, I touched our foreheads together.

"That's not going to happen. Things are different this time. Now that Jace is rid of Allen, he's planning to be around more, and I'm here. You always let us lean on you, so it only seems fair that you lean on us. Besides, I'd look cute in an apron and nothing else."

Avro laughed, his eyes lighting up. "Now, that is definitely worth having a bad knee. I just hate that I've leaned on Jace so much over the years. For so many different things, it feels like it's all I do."

"So what. Do you realize how much Jace and I need and lean on you with things that have nothing to do with your knee or how well you can do doggie style?" Avro chuckled. "I mean think about it. Who is it that Jace calls whenever something is bothering him, when he's excited about news or needs advice? It's you. Who helped me feel safe around men and helped me open up to even having a relationship? That was also you. Who took me shopping for the perfect dress for last night? Who has given me countless pep talks, made me laugh, or anything you do just by being you. So you can't work for a few months, we will be fine. So you can't cook everything you want. It gives you time to look up more recipes you can try. Don't stress. We'll get through this together."

I ran my thumb down his cheek and then over his lips, which should be on a magazine cover.

"I get all that I do, but..." He sighed. "I'm scared and don't even want to say it out loud." He closed his eyes and took a deep breath that shook his whole body. "What if I never dance again?" He opened his eyes, and they were filled with so much worry. "I was lucky I healed as well as I did last time, and my knee is still falling apart. Dancing may seem like nothing to everyone else, but to me...to me, it's the lifeline to my sanity. If that's taken away, what do I have left?"

"I hate to sound like the positivity queen. Especially when I feel anything but and would be just as scared as you are right now if roles were reversed. But... what I do know is that you're Avro, which means that no matter what is thrown at you, you will find a way around it or will figure out a new passion to throw yourself into. I'm not saying it will be easy. I'm just saying you have so many options you can't dream of yet. Dancing may end up reserved for at home, but no matter what, you will be okay. I'm making it my mission."

I smiled and kissed his cheek, then the side of his neck, and his hand snaked around my waist.

"Is that so?"

"Oh, it's very so," I said, slipping my leg over his lap to straddle him. Avro pulled me as close as I could get to his body, the warmth he radiated instantly blanketing me. "But, no more not telling me important things like your knee."

Cupping my face, Avro licked and nipped along my lower lip until I opened for him. Just like the first time he kissed me, the tenderness and emotion behind the kiss wiped everything else away. For a few moments, the world was perfect with candy canes and gumdrops.

"I promise to tell you everything from now on," Avro said, breaking the kiss.

"Do you want to tell me what this dirt is that Kai and Jace have on one another?"

"Nooooo, how about we leave that for another day when we can all talk about it," Avro said, and I could agree with that. It made sense to have them tell me themselves.

"That seems fair enough, but I do want to know." He ran his hands through my hair, and I moaned. He had a magic touch.

"Good, because I suddenly have other things on my mind."

"Is that so? Like what?" I teased and wiggled in his lap. He drew in a sharp breath that ended with a groan.

"Like getting you out of these clothes. Might as well christen the house before you leave it." No one could pull off a sexier and more inviting grin than Avro.

"I think I could be talked into that."

Avro

35

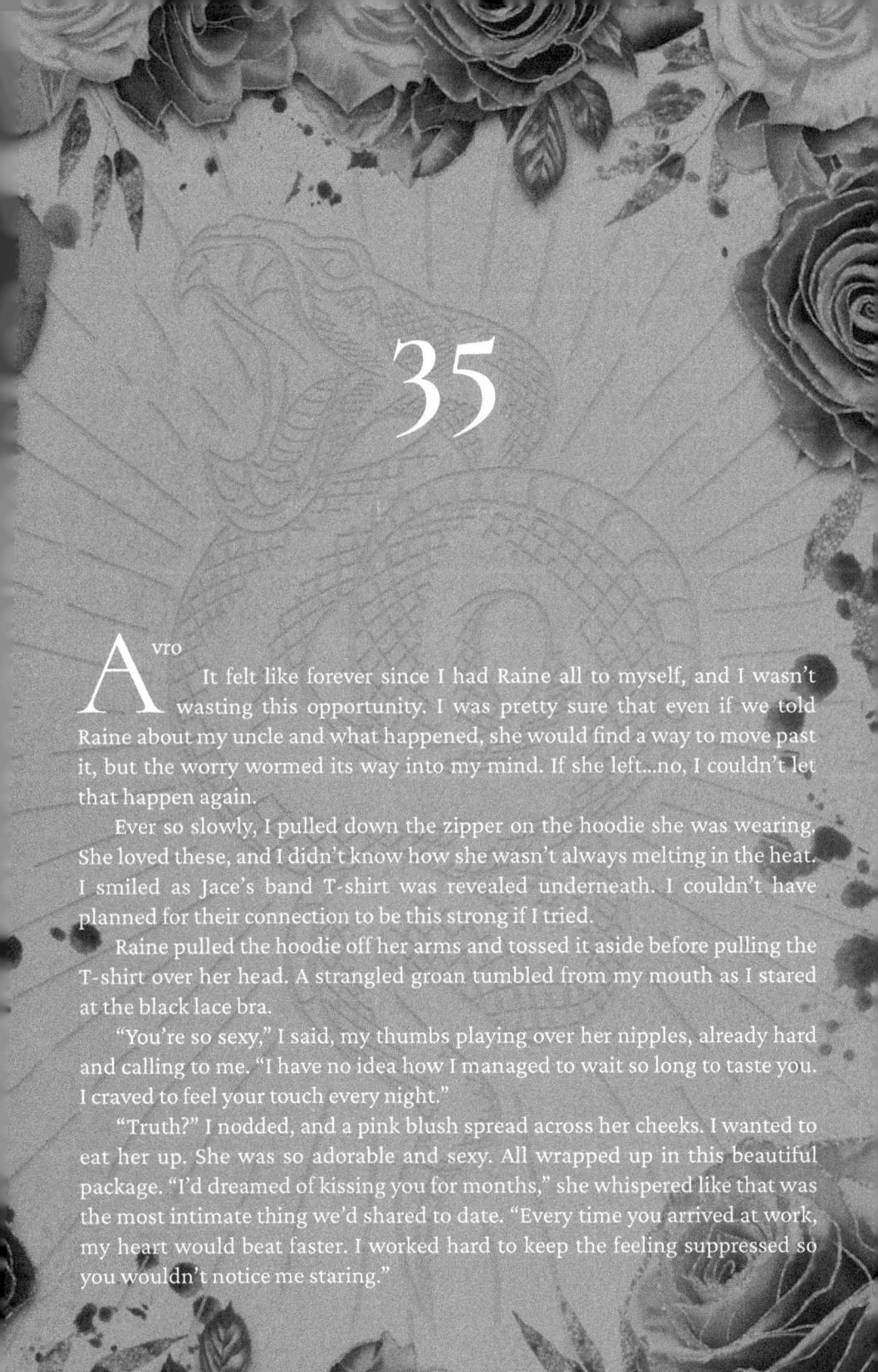

Avro

It felt like forever since I had Raine all to myself, and I wasn't wasting this opportunity. I was pretty sure that even if we told Raine about my uncle and what happened, she would find a way to move past it, but the worry wormed its way into my mind. If she left...no, I couldn't let that happen again.

Ever so slowly, I pulled down the zipper on the hoodie she was wearing. She loved these, and I didn't know how she wasn't always melting in the heat. I smiled as Jace's band T-shirt was revealed underneath. I couldn't have planned for their connection to be this strong if I tried.

Raine pulled the hoodie off her arms and tossed it aside before pulling the T-shirt over her head. A strangled groan tumbled from my mouth as I stared at the black lace bra.

"You're so sexy," I said, my thumbs playing over her nipples, already hard and calling to me. "I have no idea how I managed to wait so long to taste you. I craved to feel your touch every night."

"Truth?" I nodded, and a pink blush spread across her cheeks. I wanted to eat her up. She was so adorable and sexy. All wrapped up in this beautiful package. "I'd dreamed of kissing you for months," she whispered like that was the most intimate thing we'd shared to date. "Every time you arrived at work, my heart would beat faster. I worked hard to keep the feeling suppressed so you wouldn't notice me staring."

Nothing could wipe the smile off my face. "You have no idea how much I love hearing you say that. Not the suppressed part, of course."

"I still can't believe this is real," Raine said and slowly pushed herself to her feet.

"I'd always held out hope this was where we'd end up. I admit I hadn't been prepared for a few of the other surprises along the way," I said and stood, but the pain in my knee flared, and I grimaced.

Raine wrapped her arm around my waist. "You good?"

"Yeah, just moved too fast. I have to keep reminding myself to go slow. I'll be fine." Cupping her face, I smiled, and her eyes filled with mischief.

"I have an idea," Raine tugged at the bottom of my shirt, and I lifted my hands and arms so she could pull it off. "I'm going to take your jeans off, and I want you to lay down on the couch for me." Her smile was wicked and promised a lot more than a hot kiss. I was so ready for all of it.

"I will in a minute. I just want to look at you. You make my heart sing, Raine. I feel so complete having you and Jace. I can't believe I'm going to say this, but I really don't mind Kai either." I looked down at Raine's hands on my arms and let go of her face to look at the ring Jace had given her.

"It's beautiful, isn't it? I mean, it's massive, which scares the crap out of me, but I don't know how he got one so unique so quickly." Raine's eyes told me she'd already made up her mind, even if she hadn't realized it yet.

"So he didn't tell you?"

"Tell me what?"

"This is a family heirloom. He found it in a bank deposit box when his mom was killed. There was a note with it that said it was to go to him, her eldest son if anything ever happened to her. It was his great, great grandmother's ring, and with each generation, something was added." Raine's mouth dropped open as she looked at the ring again. "All true, I swear. When I first saw this ring, it was just the emerald cut center, with two little side diamonds. Now it has the soft blue stones and a new ring of diamonds around it. He had someone put that together for you."

"For me?"

I laughed hard. "You are the one wearing it."

Raine's cheeks flushed a bright red all over again. "I mean, he didn't have it done like this and was just waiting to give it to someone. Not that...that wouldn't be special, but...I'm totally botching this question."

"No, I know for a fact he hadn't changed it before, but how he had it done so quickly...well, that's a Jace question. Knowing Jace, he made friends with a jeweler at some point and called in a favor." I ran my thumb over her fingers.

"I'm happy you said yes, and when Kai finds out, he may not be great with it, but he will understand."

"I'm not so sure about that," she said, her face falling. "You know I'm not marrying Jace unless you're all involved, right? He explained that to you?"

"Yes, and Kai will get it too, even if it takes a hot minute. I just have a feeling about it."

Raine smiled. "See, here you are again, cheering me up. Now for once, do as I tell you to and take your damn clothes off and lay down."

"Yes, ma'am. That is one order I will never decline." I stripped as fast as I could and stroked my cock as I stared at Raine taking her time to get undressed. It was sweet torture to watch her, yet I'd spend all day doing it if given the opportunity. "Fuck girl, I swear you make me so hard. Do you have any idea how many nights I went home and ached as I thought about having you?"

My eyes followed her as she bent over, pushing her sexy little underwear down her legs. "I don't know what I would have done if you broached the topic sooner, but I'm suddenly picturing really hot phone sex." I groaned, my cock throbbing in my hand. "Now lay down, or I'll put my clothes back on."

"Damn, you've been hanging around Jace too much," I teased as I eased myself onto the couch and laid down like she told me to.

"Are you complaining," Raine asked as her bra unclipped and fell to the floor.

"Fuck, no."

I expected her to straddle me, but instead, she turned around, and I groaned as I realized she was getting in position to sixty-nine.

"Oh fuck, yes," I said as her sweet pussy hovered above my mouth. Grabbing her hips, I pulled her down onto my face and loved Raine's immediate moans and whimpers.

"Yes Avro, it feels so good." I held her tighter, burying my tongue as deep as I could. I was addicted to her. My tongue feasted on her while her breathy moans were a feast for my ears.

I growled into her pussy as her hot mouth slid around my cock. The silky feeling of her lips and tongue swirling around my sensitive head made my hips thrust into her mouth to get deeper.

"Fuck Raine," I moaned loudly as she bobbed faster on my aching shaft. She cupped my balls and gently massaged them, driving me wild. I sucked her clit into my mouth like a piece of candy, and Raine's cry of pleasure sent a shiver racing down my spine. Raine moaned and moved back and forth on my mouth as she pressed harder into me.

"God Avro, you're going to make me cum too fast...ah, oh fuck too late, I cumming," she yelled. I swirled my tongue on her clit and sucked harder until she was cumming in my mouth as she screamed my name. I was ravenous for more, and even as her hips bucked with the sensitivity of her orgasm, I held on tight and buried my face deeper.

"Ah! Oh, so not fair, you're too good." Raine said. I was a whore for praise, I could admit it, and I would have her craving my mouth on her pussy. When she laid her head down at night, I wanted my face to be who she pictured between her legs.

"Mmmm," I moaned as she sucked me back into her mouth. Her hand and mouth worked in perfect rhythm as she bobbed her head in time to the stroke of my tongue. We were entirely in sync, and as her body shuddered, I knew she was as close to her second orgasm as I was to cumming. I tried to push the desire down, but I was failing and felt the release pushing past my restraint.

Raine's body quivered as her sucking got faster and more desperate. I growled and bucked my hips up to meet her mouth. She rubbed my balls and then ran her finger along the sensitive skin to my ass. My legs spread further to give her more room, the pleasure of her exploring fingers driving me insane.

"You like that, huh? You want me to do this?" Raine asked and pressed harder on my back door. I groaned loudly as I sucked on her clit hard. "Fuck Avro! You have the best tongue," she said, and my pride swelled along with my cock.

"Cum for me, Raine, cum for me again, and I'll let go." Her hips started to rotate in quick circles. I followed and found the spot she wanted me to lick.

"Yes, oh, yes," the words tumbled from her mouth, even with my cock still in hers. Her body tensed as she sucked hard on my cock, and a wet finger pressed into my ass.

I couldn't hold back and yelled as I came, the first shot so intense it almost hurt, but in the most delicious way possible. With a final flick of my tongue, Raine came as well, and we were left moaning and panting as we drank each other down.

Raine collapsed on my body, her tongue lazily licking at my spent cock.

"Fuck I could eat you all day," I said, and I meant every word. I was tempted to see if I could make her cum a third time, but my knee was starting to throb.

I closed my eyes and gave her the same treatment, making sure every last bit of her release was licked up and earned a few sighs.

"I don't want to get up, but I guess we should get a few things packed," I said, and Raine nodded.

"If I could move."

I laughed as she moaned and slowly stood. She was always stunning, but her entire body was flushed, with her cheeks a bright red, and I loved that I put that look of pure satisfaction on her face. There was nothing more satisfying.

"On the bright side, we can always try another knee-safe position when we're done packing," I said, wanting to throw packing out the window and just fuck the rest of the day away. It seemed like a perfect stress killer.

"I could definitely be talked into that." The corner of Raine's mouth pulled up in a devious grin as she pulled on her underwear. "Shit, I wasn't even thinking. I don't have any boxes."

"That's okay. I'll get some. I know a place not far from here that sells them, and I need to go to the hardware store anyway. The faucets in the lower level bathroom are shot, and I need to get a new set," I said, slipping my T-shirt over my head. "Why don't you start organizing what you want to take and what to throw out?"

"I like that plan. Can you grab me a coffee when you're out?"

"Sure." I finished tying my sneakers and stood. I quickly used the washroom to clean up and then met Raine at her door. "I'll be about forty minutes, I think," I said and gave her a kiss. "I love you."

The smile that always lit up a room beamed up at me. I never wanted to let her go, but it was just the hardware store and coffee. I'd be back soon. Sighing, I kissed her again. "I love you too."

Snake

36

Kaivan

Bang. Bang. Bang.

The beer bottles exploded, and I covered my ears to block the sound, but after being out here for the last one hour and eleven minutes, I couldn't stop my ears from ringing. Father held out his gun to me. "That son, is how you shoot a gun."

"I already told you I don't want to shoot a gun. They kill people," I said, annoyance with this day seeping into my tone. I didn't see his hand coming, but I felt the crack as he smacked me across the face and knocked me to the ground.

"What did I tell you?"

I held my cheek, my eyes stinging, but I refused to cry. My father said that only women and pussies cried, and I wouldn't be either. I glared up at my father. I wanted to ride my bike or surf with my friends, but he told me I needed to learn to be a man instead. What did shooting a gun have to do with being a man?

"Come on, get up. You're still a fucking terrible shot," he said. "Such an embarrassment."

My father's friends from the motorcycle club and their sons laughed as they drank off to the side. They were all older than I was. The youngest of the group was five years, six months, and nine days older than me. None of them wanted me to hang around, and I didn't like them either. They all wanted to be like their dads and be part of the motorcycle club. I had other interests that didn't involve riding around on a Harley and hanging out in a smoky clubhouse.

Mom hated that my father was always gone, and I'd heard them arguing when he was home about sweetbutts. I didn't know what they were until he dragged me to the club to hang out with the other kids for events like Tony's birthday. I quickly learned what they were and what they did when Tony's dad got a sweetbutt to suck his dick for his eighteenth birthday in front of all of us. Of course, my father smiled and said he'd do better for me on my eighteenth. Whatever that was supposed to mean.

I glanced over as they made jokes and laughed. I hated that they always came when my father dragged me out here into the middle of the swamp with the bugs, snakes, and other strange crap. We'd all take turns shooting empty bottles like it was the best thing ever, but I could think of at least ten things I wanted to do instead.

Pushing myself to my feet, I dusted off my hands on my jeans and took the gun that felt heavy compared to my plastic water ones. He pointed his hand toward the target of bottles set up on wooden stumps. For just a moment, I wondered what it would be like to turn the gun on him instead of the bottles. Would he treat me like a man, then?

"Now shoot, and try to hit something this time. The only thing that isn't safe from you is a barn wall," he said, then laughed with multiple voices echoing.

As I raised the gun to shoot the bottles, the stumps and swamp disappeared.

I blinked and stared down at my mom's body lying on the living room floor. I looked at my hand, but the gun was gone, and I dropped to my knees beside her.

The roar of a motorcycle was loud, and I could just make out a man on a bike outside. His laughter was almost as loud as the bike as he rode away into the dark.

"Mom, how can I help?"

"You, you killed me," she said, her voice wet, blood dripping from the corner of her mouth.

"No, no, it wasn't me." I pressed on the wound, but she batted my hands away and started to laugh. "Mom, stop it. I need to stop the bleeding."

"You're a killer, you've always been a killer, and it's what you will always be," she snarled as she pushed my hands away again. "I should've left you with your father years ago. Now look at me. It's all your fault."

Tears streamed from my eyes as I pushed myself away from her body. "It's not true, Mom, it's not true, don't say that," I cried, the tears making it impossible to see.

"You couldn't save yourself, just like you couldn't save Raine." I whipped my head from side to side to see who said that. "Your father was right. You destroy everything you touch."

"Who said that?" I pushed myself to my feet and glanced around the garage filled with boxes. It felt like I was in a crazy game of hide and seek.

"Oh, come now boy, you must recognize my voice. I was part of your life for five years. Five long terrible years where I had to put up with a useless sack of shit like you."

I marched down one long row of boxes and equipment that seemed to go on forever, but when I turned at the end, no one was there.

"Just admit it, Kaivan. Admit that you were never going to be able to save Raine from me that night. You stayed home and let her take your beating for you."

"Shut the fuck up, that's not what happened," I yelled and pushed over some boxes in the direction of the voice. More laughing reached me, and the anger churning in my gut erupted. I slammed my shoulder from side to side and knocked the two stacks down until there were no tall objects to obscure my view.

Dave stood by the garage door without a shirt, zipper down on his dirty jeans, and a knife in hand. "She was always going to be mine that night, Kaivan. You sent her to me, and mmm, was she ever good. That sweet little virgin pussy."

Roaring, I ran at Dave, and he calmly walked inside the house with a smile as he slammed the door. Maniacal laughing was loud in my ears.

"What happened to Raine was all your fault. You have no one to blame but yourself," Dave said through the door as I beat my hands and feet off the metal until my knuckles bled. Breathing hard, I dropped to all fours, my eyes stinging with more tears.

"Don't cry, boy. Cryin' is for pussies," I looked up at the gruff voice and stared into Red's cold glare.

"What the fuck do you want?" I pushed myself to my feet, and he took a step back. "Last I checked, I was off limits to you."

He licked his lips. "Were you, though? Were you ever really off limits?"

"What the fuck are you talking about?" My hands clenched into fists as my gaze flicked to the two men hovering in the doorway.

"I have it under good authority that Mannix lied. You weren't already part of his gang when he came into the bathroom. Technically, he stole from me, not the other way around." Red ran his tongue over his teeth, accentuating the gap where a tooth was missing.

"Is that so? I don't know your source, but they don't know shit. You seem to have a recurring issue with that. Maybe you need a new informant." I would go to my grave telling that lie until it manifested into the truth. There was no fucking way I'd ever let Red know that he had something on Mannix or me.

Red's nostrils flared, his eyes narrowing into slits. "You're full of shit and just as mouthy as the day you arrived. You haven't learned a thing."

"What I've learned is that you're not as big as you like to think you are. You've already lost control of the cigarettes, and I'm working on cell phones next. Soon you'll be nobody. Nothing but the raping piece of shit you are."

Red rubbed at his bottom lip and chuckled low like he was amused, but I knew he was seething inside. Controlling the cigarette import and export was massive. He'd taken a huge hit when I got the guards on my side. That had taken some work, but it was paying off.

"One of these days, you won't be so lucky, and I'll be there waiting," Red said, his eyes promising he wouldn't let this go.

A sharp pain stabbed me behind my eye, and I grabbed at my head. Opening my eyes, I shivered from head to toe as I stared down at Red, a mangled and bloody mess on the floor. My hand was shaking so hard it was hitting the side of my leg.

"Fuck, Kaivan, what the hell did you do? You said you wanted to rough him up a little," Steve, the guard said as he came in and looked down at the bloody corpse. "Give me the weapon, now."

Lifting my hand, I realized I was clenching a shank in my fist, once white, now a bright red. Steve held out his hand, and I dropped the blade into it.

"What the hell happened? I need an answer," he looked over his shoulder at the sound of a door closing and the echo of more guards coming.

"He...he...." I looked up at Steve. "He knocked me out, and when I came to, he was...um...it was self-defense," I managed to say, and Steve shook his head.

"Fuck, go on, get out of here. The cameras to the east wing are off, go shower and leave your clothes in the garbage. I'll get rid of them. But, Snake, after this, we're even."

I glanced down at Red's still face, his pale skin glowing even against the white tile. His head turned in my direction, and I took a startled step back.

"You may have killed me, but you'll never be rid of me. Death sticks to you. I will forever cling to your mind," he said.

"Kai, get the hell out of here," Steve said.

"Did you see that?" I pointed at Red, whose head was perfectly still once more.

"No, they're almost here, go, now," he whispered, his voice harsh.

I took off and ran along the hallway he told me to take and tried to ignore the pain in my body and the humiliation in my soul. Stripping, I stuffed the bloody jumpsuit into the garbage and got in the shower, not caring that the water was ice cold.

With my eyes closed, the icy water pelted me in the face, and I let the tears I'd been holding back fall. Death did cling to me, and no one was safe around me. Everything I touched was corrupted or died. The Devil had marked me at birth to live and breathe, walking among souls already lost. I felt it. I wanted to deny it, to push it away, but eventually, everyone turned on you or died.

"Do it!" My eyes snapped open, and Raine was screaming at me. I stared at the gun in my hand pressed to her chest.

"No."

"Do it," she screamed again as tears streamed down her beautiful face. "I've wasted so much of my life being scared. I can't be that person again. So do it, 'cause I'm done. My heart was ripped from my chest in that warehouse. You might as well destroy my soul too."

I wanted to yell no, that I loved her, that I'd always loved her, but I stood there staring at her saying nothing, my mouth refusing to move. Each tear that slid down her cheek was like a knife to my chest.

"Do it," she whispered.

Bang

Raine stumbled back, her hands going to her chest as blood poured from her and soaked the front of her hoodie. I looked at the gun and then back up to her scared eyes.

"You...." Raine collapsed, and I dropped the gun and grabbed her body before she hit the floor.

"No, no, no. This is not happening. Help her," I yelled at Roach and the two other men in the room. "Why are you just standing there? Help her. Call 911, get me towels, do something." I smoothed back Raine's hair, her hand cool to the touch as I gripped it in mine. "No, Tink, please, it was an accident. I didn't mean to. Please help her," I pleaded again with those standing around, but still, no one moved. They just looked away.

"I love you, Tink. Please stay with me, don't go, don't leave me. Please, I'm sorry." Tears poured down my cheeks, and the pain of her fading eyes ripped out my heart as if she were using her hand.

"I...love...you," she said and then went still.

"No!" I wailed and gripped her lifeless body to my chest, rocking, unable to manage the pain.

"Please."

"What are you crying for, boy?" Red and my father squatted beside me as I held Raine tighter.

"Go away," I yelled at them.

"He still doesn't get it," my father told Red.

"Nope, he definitely doesn't."

"Get what?" Both sets of eyes turned in my direction.

"She was already dead, boy. The moment she met you, the reaper took her soul. Everything you touch is tainted. You're a stain on this earth, and you killed her."

"No, it's not true," I said, but everyone, including my mom, stood around nodding at me.

"Ah!" I screamed and grabbed the gun off the ground. I didn't hesitate as I put the barrel in my mouth.

Bang

My eyes snapped open as I gasped for breath. I didn't know where I was, but I grabbed for Raine, and she wasn't there. There was enough light coming in the window that I recognized my room. I struggled to remember what happened, but all I could see was her fading eyes and the blood all over my hands. What had I done?

I hadn't cried in years, but the tears streamed down my cheeks in relentless lines as I struggled to breathe against the growing pain in my chest. Grabbing the pillow she used when she slept here, I gripped it hard and buried my face in the fabric. I clung to it like I'd clung to her body as the sobs wracked me.

I heard the sound of boots and didn't even care who saw me. My life wasn't worth living if she was dead...if I took her life. I could still taste the metal of my gun in my mouth and would've reached for it if Roach hadn't appeared and gripped my face in his hands.

"Let go..." I pushed at him, but he held me harder. "I killed her. I killed my heart," I said, and he shook his head.

"No, you didn't. Look at me, bro. Raine is okay."

"What?"

"I said, Raine is alright. You didn't hurt her. The doc was here. He said you'll be fine. The stress and lack of sleep brought this on."

"I don't care about me. You promise she's alive?"

"Yes," Roach said, letting go of my face and groaning as his phone rang. He pulled it from his pocket, and I realized it was mine. "This guy never gives up. How do you put up with him?" He hit a button and sat the phone down.

"What? Who?"

"Avro. The guy keeps fucking calling," Roach said.

"Why?" I asked, pushing myself up in bed. Everything ached. Whatever I went through left me feeling like I ran a marathon and then did a round with Mike Tyson.

"I don't know. I didn't answer."

"But Avro never calls me," I said. "Give me my phone."

"The doc said that...."

"I don't fucking care what the doc said. Give me my phone," I growled.

"I don't get it, man. Why are you torturing yourself, allowing them to be in a relationship with you and Raine? I couldn't do it," I looked at the fifty missed calls and then up at Roach.

"I'd do anything for her. That's all there is to it. I'd survive longer without my beating heart than if you took her from me." Roach shook his head like he just couldn't understand. Of course, he couldn't. He'd never loved someone so much they made his blood sing. They became his world.

"Why didn't you answer any of these?"

"I had more important things to worry about, like what the fuck was wrong with you. Besides, Raine was pestering us to let them know how you were before we took you from their house. I may not have bothered to call when Mannix asked me to."

"Why?"

"She hurt you. She fucking deserved it. She can wait a little to find out what's wrong. It won't kill her."

"Fuck man, I swear if something is wrong," I mumbled. I was about to hit the voicemail and listen to the messages when it started to ring again.

"Avro?"

"Kai, thank God. She's gone, she's gone, something happened," he rambled, but I sat up straight and was on the move. Whatever was going on with me could fucking wait.

"Slow down. What do you mean she's gone? Raine took off again, like last time?" I grabbed my leather jacket off the door handle, not slowing my pace. I knew Roach was following, the sound of his boots heavy behind me.

"Fuck Kai. No, not like last time." He sounded like he was hyperventilating. The one thing I'd learned about Avro, he was pretty fucking chill. It was Jace and I that freaked out. To hear the terror in his voice had me gripping the phone tighter.

"Then what happened?"

"After you were taken away, Raine was really upset. I offered to come to her house and pack some of her stuff to keep her mind occupied. I went to get some supplies from the hardware store, and when I got back, she was gone."

"But not like last time?"

"Kai! No!" Avro yelled into the phone. I could hear Jace in the background telling him to take a breath, but his fear spiked my adrenaline, and my heart pounded against my ribs.

"Then how?"

"Give me the phone," Jace said, and there was swearing, but Jace came on the line. "Kai, she's been taken by someone. There were signs of a struggle, and her phone was smashed on the floor. The door was open when Avro got back, but who the fuck would want to take Raine? Is this because of me and the proposal? I just can't see a fan doing this."

I stopped dead as an ice-cold dread snaked down my spine. "No, it's Frank."

Snake

37

8:31PM

Kaivan

Jace stood in the doorway when Roach, Wilder, and I pulled up. His body language seemed calm, but as his silver eyes found mine, I could tell he was on the same edge as me. I turned to Roach as we parked in front of the house, and before I could say a word, Wilder hopped out and jogged up to meet Jace. I'd never admit this out loud, but I felt better having Wilder along. My nerves were shot, and the tremors that started when I learned she was taken had only gotten worse over the last twenty-one minutes.

"Roach, go see if any of the neighbors saw anything," I said. It was probably a long shot. In this neighborhood, people kept their drapes drawn tight and never talked. Not wanting to get involved was a standard MO.

"What am I supposed to say? I'm your friendly neighborhood biker. Just checking in to see if you saw a girl being kidnapped?" I glared at him.

"Just say you're her cousin or something and that you were coming to help her move. I don't care what you say. Just see if they saw anything. If they have a door camera, I'll pay for the footage."

"Fine, whatever," he said, and I grabbed his arm before he could move.

"What the fuck is your problem?" I growled.

"Honestly?" I nodded. "Since the moment you found Raine, it's been nothing but stress and drama. You've been out of your mind, agitated in your skin, anger rolling off you in waves to the point that we're all terrified to go near you. This love or obsession, whatever it is the two of you have with those guys, is toxic as fuck for you. I'm worried you don't see it. I'm worried that without meaning to, Raine will drag you so far down the rabbit hole away from your sanity that there will be no coming back." He turned his eyes away from me and gripped the steering wheel hard.

"I will do whatever you want. I will help however you want 'cause, at the end of the day, you are my ride-or-die. I have some serious reservations that I haven't voiced to be supportive, but the way Mannix and I found you earlier...." Roach turned his head to stare at me again. "It scared the fuck out of me, and you know I don't scare easily."

"Earlier wasn't just Raine. It's been building for a while." I rubbed at the back of my neck. "All the shit, the old memories, the pain that I buried...that crap decided it was coming up faster than projectile vomit. The dream was...fucked. Point is, I get your concern, and coming from you, I respect it, but it's also not your call. So if you want to continue to be my ride-or-die, get the fuck out of the truck and stop wasting time. I love Raine, and if Dave and Frank have her...you saw what they will do to her. You good if that happens?"

"No. No, I'm not. You're right. Let's go," Roach said, hopping out. Getting out of the truck, I jogged toward the front door of Raine's small house.

I got Roach's concern. We'd been looking out for one another since he was arrested and tossed in the same block as the rest of the wild animals. When I saw him and Hollywood, I recognized myself—five years earlier when I was thrown to the wolves—in their terrified expressions. I immediately brought them in before anyone else could, and we'd become kill for one another tight. But he needed to get on board with what I chose to do with my life.

Raine may have laid down what she wanted, but I had the choice to be part of it or leave, and I chose to stay. If I was completely honest with myself, I didn't mind Jace and Avro in her life. They were like those sticky vines that just kept growing on you. The engagement was a crazy shock, and maybe seeing that brought on whatever the fuck that dream shit was, or maybe it had been building for years and would have happened no matter what.

Regardless, I felt clearer, and so much of the anger and jealousy I'd been carrying around like a weighted vest had fallen away. Now it was replaced with a paralyzing fear I was trying really fucking hard to ignore so I didn't lose every last marble left in my head.

I stepped inside the house as Wilder came down from upstairs.

"What can you tell me?"

"They're correct. She was taken. It was quick, so there was more than one person, or they subdued her somehow." Wilder bent over and picked up the smashed phone. "My guess is drugged. The guy left this upstairs on her pillow."

Wilder handed me an instant photo of Raine tied up and laying in the bed of a pickup truck with tape over her mouth and her hands and feet tied together. Anger so volatile burned in my veins. If they touched one hair on her head....

Flipping the picture over, I read the short note:

Payment for taking something important to me, so I'm taking something important to you.
Stop looking, or more people you care about will end up the same way.
JJ

She looked asleep, but I knew better. I handed the picture to Jace, and he growled. I knew exactly how he felt.

"How did you find this? We searched upstairs and didn't see anything," Jace asked, his eyes glued to the picture.

Wilder shrugged. "I looked."

Jace looked up at Wilder, and if I weren't so afraid for Raine, I would've laughed at his confused expression. I now knew what I looked like talking to Wilder.

Roach stepped into the doorway and blocked out the sun. "If someone saw something they aren't saying. Most didn't answer the door." I nodded.

The fear that started when I heard Avro's panicked voice was swirling around in my gut, and I had to push it down and lock it up tight. I could deal with the demons in my head later. For now, they needed to take a back fucking seat.

I glanced at Avro sitting on the couch, his head in his hands as he leaned forward on his knees. His eyes were trained on the floor, and he looked like he was caught between throwing up and having a panic attack.

"Hey, I need you to know before anything else that the proposal wasn't to take her away from you. I can tell you all about the why later, but I needed you to know that, and—"

I held up my hand to stop Jace. "I don't care. None of that is important right now." Jace nodded. "All that matters is getting her back and killing the fuckers that took her."

"Fair enough," Jace said.

"Both of you going to be good with that?"

"Killing them?" Jace asked. He looked at Avro, who lifted his head, and there was a conviction in his eyes that reminded me of the day he came to my house to tell me Raine was gone the first time.

"I don't care what happens to them," Avro said, and we locked stares as we shared an understanding. Whatever happened after we left this house was never to be spoken of to anyone. No cops, no other friends, no drunken nights out and rambling to others because you couldn't deal. It was 'lock it up tight and throw away the key' kind of shit.

I glanced around the small home that seemed extra tiny with the five of us in it and spotted her backpack sitting in the corner.

"Fuck," I growled. "I don't know how to find her."

"We'll track her, but we're going to need a lot more weapons," Wilder said, and I blinked in confusion.

"Her bag is sitting there. How do you propose I track her?" I pointed at the black backpack. "I only had one."

"A tracker? On Raine? Damn man, you're brave. If she found that out...," Jace said, and I glared at him. "What? I didn't say I was going to say anything, just that it's ballsy, but it explains how you found her so quickly."

"We will track her like normal." Wilder tilted his head as he looked at me. "With the other trackers."

"What other trackers?"

"The ones I put on her," he said matter-of-factly, and I wanted to kiss him for doing it and punch him for the same reason.

"You put more trackers on Raine?"

He nodded. "Yes, a bag is okay, but as you can see, it can get left behind. I slipped one into the sole of all her shoes."

Roach whistled. "That's smart. Fucked up, but smart."

"So why do we need more weapons?" I asked, ignoring Roach's shocked appreciation.

Wilder held his phone out to me, and I took it. The screen showed what looked like an overhead view of a really large farm. "What am I looking at?"

"That's where they took her. It's a property about an hour outside the city, but if you zoom in, you'll see the armed men. There is also a security gate with four watch towers. This must be where they take those they decide to keep long term," Wilder said.

"So, who are these guys, and why would they want Raine," Jace asked, and Avro spoke before I could answer.

"They're the fucking guys who attacked her years ago and sent Kai to prison. He's been hunting them down," Avro said. "My guess is you were getting a little too close to finding them, and they've taken her as collateral or punishment."

"Yes, that would be my assumption, as well," Wilder agreed.

"There had to be a camera in the house. We should've sat on it to see when Frank fucking returned." My hand clenched into a fist as I kicked myself.

"Let's go. We need to ride out," I said, and Wilder grabbed my arm and shook his head no. "Don't fucking shake your head at me. I'm going."

"No, you can't, at least not yet. You will be dead before you ever reach the gates. We need a plan and a lot more firepower. I have trusted you with all my questions, but this is my arena. Attacking impenetrable targets and staying alive is what I do best." Wilder let go of my arm. "If you want her alive, and you alive to be with her, then you need to listen to me."

I glanced around the room, and no one else was disagreeing. "Every second Raine's there...they could be doing anything to her," I growled at him, my heart hammering hard.

"True, but if you go alone or with just a few of us and no plan, the chance of success is still zero, but now we are dead and cannot help." His face was void of all emotion, just like it always was, and for once, I wished I could be like him. Not feeling this terror as it tried to choke me out would have been welcome.

"If it makes you feel better, I do not think they will kill her until tomorrow around mid-day."

I swallowed. "Why?"

"All the newer images on the laptop, the lighting is the same. It is as if they wait until the exact same time of day." My left hand shook and I squeezed it into a fist to keep my shit together. There was so many other things they could do to her in that amount of time. "We will get her back alive, is that not what is most important?"

He was right. I slammed the door on my fear so I didn't do something stupid. "Fine. What's the plan?"

LOST SOULS CLUBHOUSE - 2:04 AM

Kaivan

The five of us stood around a large map of the property as Wilder placed pieces from a Risk game on the paper. If the situation were different, I might have laughed at the man moving tiny game pieces around dressed in full camo. His face was painted, and Wilder was strapped with everything from knives to grenades.

I truly thought Avro and Jace would back out, but neither had wavered in their conviction, which earned them points in my 'They're not terrible' book.

Leaning over the table, I focused on my entry point as Wilder reviewed the plan for the last time.

"What the fuck?" Chase's voice echoed as he slammed the door open. Chase, Mannix, Beast, Tanner, and some of the other guys walked into the room and stared at us. "What the fuck are you doing?"

I pushed myself up straight and squared off with my Prez. He wasn't keeping me from going, and I was taking whatever weapons I wanted. I'd earned the right after all the blood, sweat, and hours I'd spent keeping this place safe.

Chase's eyes were narrowed as he glared at me. The muscle in his jaw was twitching as we squared off.

"Answer me, Snake. What the fuck do you think you're doing?" He turned his head to look at Jace and Avro, and even though he knew who they were, he didn't comment.

"I'm going to save Raine. She's been taken, and we're going to get her back. You can't stop me from going, and I'm taking what I need for weapons. If you try to stop me, Chase, you can consider this my official resignation."

Chase shook his head, his brows knitting together. "Why the hell would I try to stop you from going and getting your old lady?"

"The way you came in here, I thought..."

"Well, you thought wrong. I'm fucking pissed off that Roach was the one who texted me what was going on and not you. We're your fucking family. Get that through your head. If your girl is in trouble, we'll all get her back." Chase stepped forward until he could put his hand on my shoulder. "I promised you that I'd prove I was back for good, but more than that, you need to believe that not everything will go to shit. We'll get her back safe. Now, what's the plan?"

I couldn't bring myself to say anything as the room filled with people. Mannix gripped my shoulder on the way past, his eyes locking with mine. He gave me a single nod, and emotion clogged my throat, making it hard to swallow. The world felt like it was painted with blood when it came to my life, but a glimmer of hope sparkled among the gore.

Words that Mannix had said over the years played on a loop in my mind. Even though I'd been part of the MC, it wasn't until now that I felt like I belonged. I turned to see Wilder jump up on the large table and hold up the map as he organized groups to hit the target locations.

"Sorry, but as soon as I saw what we were up against, I texted Chase and told him what was happening. I knew you never would," Roach said.

"Thanks, man."

"We'll get her back," he said before walking away.

I once saw a quote that said love was stronger than revenge, and I spit on the sentiment. I called it a false truth, a fake fact that people liked to say and hide behind when they were too weak to take care of their business.

Tonight, I realized I may have missed the true meaning behind the quote. It wasn't that love was stronger than revenge...love fucking fueled it like gasoline to a naked flame, and I planned on scorching the earth to get back what was mine.

Raine

38

Raine

I shivered, my body cold. The kind of cold that seeped into your bones and made you ache from the inside out. I tried to move or even open my eyes, but my body wouldn't respond. Not my arms, legs, or eyes. My brain raced through the fog as I tried to remember what happened. Was I in an accident? Was I paralyzed?

That didn't make sense because everything hurt. My toes to the top of my head felt like I'd been beaten. The last thing I remembered was going to my house with Avro and kissing him on the couch. We were going to be packing…I think. Pieces of our time and conversation were coming back to me like little images floating by, and I had to grab them, or they would disappear again.

"You got her?"

The remaining fog was instantly wiped away. My heart stopped and then pounded so hard that it felt like it would rip from my chest. I knew that voice. I could never forget that cold and calculating rasp as sharp to my ears as the steel blade he shoved into my stomach. My body trembled, or I thought it did. I still didn't feel like I was moving except for tremors under my skin.

"Yes, but I don't know if anyone saw me. It was a shit time of day to take her, but she was with some guy, and I had to wait for a good moment."

Dave.

It all came rushing back. The doorbell rang, and Dave stood there in tears apologizing for tracking me down, but Irene was in the hospital, and her dying wish was to see me. I didn't want to go without Avro, but when I turned to grab my phone to call him, something sharp stabbed me in the side of the neck, and everything went dark.

"It was worth the risk. You did well, Profit Dave," the man who haunted my dreams said.

How had I ever thought this man was Kai? Hearing his voice again, he sounded so different. There was no comparison, yet for so long my mind had conjured Kai's face and voice every time I thought about the attack.

Did that mean Dave was one of the other men? My stomach flipped and churned with images of him on top of me. I had to push it aside quickly, or I would vomit, and I didn't think I could open my mouth. My pinky twitched, so whatever he'd given me was slowly starting to wear off, but there was no way in hell I was letting them know.

I needed to be smarter than I was at fifteen if there was any chance of getting out of this alive. The two men talked, but none of it was about me, or anything that made sense, and my mind drifted to the men in my life.

If I didn't escape, then what? Would they think I took off again and they just couldn't find me? Or would my body be dropped off somewhere like a discarded bag of garbage, and that's how they would find out?

"When was the last time you re-administered the drugs?"

"Forty minutes ago, just like you asked."

"Excellent. Take her to my wives. They will know what to do. This one needs to be cleansed before the ceremony," the man with the terrifying voice said.

How long had I been here?

"I'll make sure she's ready, Father," Dave said, and if my mouth could move, it would've fallen open. There was no way this other man was his real father, was he supposed to be someone spiritual?

"Good, and be careful the drugs you gave her should be slowly wearing off. We want her able to scream for the ceremony." There was a loud bang, but I remained still even though the adrenaline coursing through my body spiked. "Isn't that right, Raine?"

I tried so hard not to react, but the fear made it nearly impossible. My lungs stopped working for a few seconds, and the man Dave called Father chuckled. I realized then that I was in a cell, and they were both very close. My skin crawled like I was coated in a million insects, even though I was pretty sure there were none.

"She is starting to hear us. Get her prepped quickly. I'm excited to complete the ritual that started so long ago," Father said as he moved away from the cage, his voice getting quieter.

The sound of keys and the scrape of a door reminded me of those old medieval shows and the cells where they kept prisoners. This wasn't much different. I was being held and would be put on display. It might not be a guillotine coming for my head, but that would've been better than whatever these men planned.

I'd already suffered in their clutches once before and barely survived. There was no doubt that if they completed this...ceremony, there would be no coming back.

Rough hands gripped me and picked me up, and as much as I wanted to strike out and make my escape, I couldn't move anything other than my little finger. He stank of sweat and sausage as I was pressed against Dave's meaty body. My stomach rolled again, and to keep from being sick, I counted his steps and tried to follow which direction he went.

"You know, Raine, I was content to let you live your life and never see you again. You were never the intended target that night, but Kai...he needed to be taught a lesson then, and he needs to be stopped now."

They were after Kai that night. What the hell had they planned on doing with him if they got him? I couldn't even fathom the pain they would've caused him, and for the first time, I was happy that they had gotten me instead. Kai would've fought until they killed him.

"But, if I'm honest, I have to admit that I'm excited to finish this and maybe get to fuck you again. You did have a sweet pussy, and it ruined me forever. The only thing that satisfies me now is the taste of a sweet young thing like you were."

Was he really blaming me for him being a sick piece of shit? Oh, hell no. I'd taken on way too much guilt over my life. There was no fucking way that I was allowing him to blame me for his twisted fantasies. He was my foster father, someone that I thought at least cared for me on some level. But it was obvious now he was nothing more than a child molester looking for the right opportunity.

There was a loud knock on what sounded like wood, and I realized we were at a door.

"You want to know something else?" *Did I really have a choice?* "Sometimes when I stroke myself, it's your screams I hear and your pussy, I imagine."

And when I thought about what you did to me, I fantasized about ripping your cock from your body.

The initial terror was still there but slowly shifting into something else.

Something far more lethal, and if I got my hands free, I would make my fantasy come true.

"Come in, Profit Dave, we have the bath prepared," a female voice said. What woman in their right mind would willingly choose to say here? "You can place her in the bath. We will look after her until it's time."

I wanted to scream as Dave sat me down in the water. It was so hot that I was positive it would burn the skin off my body. When he released me, my head lolled to the side, and no matter how hard I tried to lift it, it wouldn't budge. It was like my brain had been disconnected from my body, and none of the controls worked.

"Thank you, Profit Dave. We will summon you when needed." The same female voice said.

"You have been chosen for a very special ceremony. You must feel honored," a new female voice said.

Honored was not how I felt right now. Terrified, creeped out, and angry were all words I would use, but honored was not on my list.

"She is very beautiful. Could we ask to keep her?" A third woman chimed in with a sweeter sing-song voice. What was I a pet? Keep her? The women were more terrifying than Dave or the Father.

"No, we have been given our instructions. We know what we must do. Let's not question the Father's wishes. He does know best," the first woman said.

"Yes, Deist," at least four other voices said in unison. The water around me splashed and moved, and I would've jumped out if I could when multiple hands touched my body. I smelled something flowery and figured it must be soap as the woman directly behind me rubbed the silky lather across my chest and over my breasts. Her fingers softly twisted my nipples between her fingers until they were hard.

"You do have pretty little buds," she said, and squeezed them harder. "To bad we don't have more time." She spent all her time playing with my breasts and would've sworn that she was sucking on them.

Battling back the fear to be able to think straight was almost impossible as time ticked on. They didn't miss a single spot and even held my leg above the water to do my feet. I fought against the drugs and could twitch two fingers now, but it was still not enough. A hand slid between my thighs and rubbed along the sensitive folds of my pussy.

"Check to see if she is satisfactory for the Father," the woman behind me said as she continued rubbing my nipples. I wanted to stand up and yell at them to leave me alone. The finger massaging my pussy slid inside, and once more, I was violated. If I wanted to fuck multiple women, I wanted it to be my choice, not the demand of some lunatic. Instead of feeling dirty or tainted like before, I got angry. No angry wasn't a strong enough word, I wanted them all dead. I didn't care why they were like this, I just wanted them to be wiped from the earth for good.

"If we were allowed, I'd keep you," the one who asked earlier said. She had a distinct voice. "You have a very tight womanhood and I would've enjoyed tasting you. Father will be pleased."

And if I could, I'd cut your tits off. Now get your finger out of me.

I wanted to scream and rage. My foot suddenly flexed, and one eyelid parted slightly. Suddenly I didn't care about the woman and her finger anymore. The only thing that mattered was my body's movements. They were tiny, but the more parts I could move, the greater my chance of getting out of here in one piece.

With my partially opened eye, I glanced at the women leaning over the tub as they touched me with hands, sponges, and coarse scrub brushes. It was hard to focus at first, but one of the women leaned closer, and it was a good thing that I couldn't make a sound. Her neck and the side of her face were carved with patterns and symbols, the scars deep enough to stand out from the rest of her unmarred skin. The closest comparison I could think of was an old Star Trek episode, but those people were supposed to be aliens.

I focused in on the symbol near my eye and it looked like a round circle with a star in the middle and the outline of horns that turned into the letter Y.

Maybe I'd judged them prematurely. Maybe staying here wasn't a choice. Maybe they were victims like me, but the crazy got to them one mutilation at a time.

My body felt raw and sore everywhere by the time they were finished. I thought they would call Dave to get me out of the narrow tub, but instead, they all picked me up at once and laid me out on something hard. I made sure not to try and open my eye any further, but I couldn't help wanting to know that was going on. As if I was a child, they dressed me in a white robe, the material itchy against my sensitive skin.

The first woman, whom the others called Diest, opened the door. "She is prepared for the next stage."

Next stage? How many stages were there? No, this was good. The longer they kept me from going to this Father guy, the better. With each passing second, I felt more of the drug wearing off.

Dave once more picked me up and carried me out, and again I laid like I was dead across his arms. He walked me into another room and put me on a bed where a man in a dark grey outfit chanted and waved smoke over my body that smelt like weed more than anything else. Were they trying to get me high now? I held my breath for as long as possible and only took shallow breaths.

"She is ready to receive the mark," Dave said.

I felt like I was traveling through terrifying magical doors, each one more confusing than the next, but this last stop was where the real panic began to set in. The room was stifling, and as Dave laid me on the uncomfortable table, I noticed the wood-burning stove in the corner. It looked like one you'd see at a hunting cabin on television, but the long black piece of metal the man pulled out was another matter.

Dave pulled up my sleeve as the other man walked toward me with the glowing cattle brand. I recognized the symbol from the side of the girl's face, and it dawned on me they weren't cut. They'd all been branded. I didn't want this, I didn't want any of this, and I tried to command my body to roll off the bed, but other than a few more jerks from my feet, my body didn't respond.

No, no, no

As the man got closer, my legs twitched up to my hips, but it wasn't enough, and a moment later, that bright red poker touched the outside of my shoulder. I screamed, but the sound came out like a weird moan, and the scent of burning flesh tainted the air. Searing pain radiated down my arm, and the room swam.

I braced against the pain, my teeth clenching together.

"You like that, Raine? Feel the evil inside of you leaving your body?" Dave asked. He'd completely lost his mind. There was no other explanation because to believe any of this was a way to cleanse me of evil was ludicrous.

The second man took the brand away, and my head spun more. The pain was immense. I thought I knew what pain was, but I wasn't prepared to have my flesh burned off.

No, you cannot pass out.

Don't pass out.

Dave picked me up again, humming as we walked. His gate had changed from earlier. He walked slowly and deliberately with each exaggerated stride. I flopped around in his outstretched arms and knew I would look asleep or dead to anyone watching, but inside, I was trying hard not to come undone and lose focus on my opportunity.

The humming grew louder as more voices joined in, and a shiver raced down my spine. It was hard to see my surroundings while hanging upside-down, but it was dark with the soft glow of flickering candles and a single sun spot that glowed like a beacon.

There were a lot of people. The humming was so loud that it felt like a thousand voices together as the sound vibrated through my body. I could just make out the bottom edge of what had to be black robes as they swayed against the floor.

This was a cult.

The way Dave and the Father addressed one another, the group of subservient women that Father had called his wives—cleansing, chanting, branding, and now more people in robes.

Dave stopped walking, and my head flopped to the side as he placed me on something cold and hard. My fingers felt like they were touching rock, and the earlier fear I'd managed to control threatened to take over once more. I was in a hysterical fog, trapped inside my body like an animal trapped in a cage, but the cage was my flesh and bones. I didn't need to see to know I'd reached my final destination.

The hum that had turned into a chant reached the end, and the room fell silent. I could feel the tears sliding down my cheek as the weight of my reality settled on my chest. Even if I could get free, this wasn't like the warehouse. There were dozens of voices. I didn't know where I was. I had no weapon, and my body still couldn't respond. With every passing second, more would tingle and twitch, but it wasn't enough to get up and run or fight my way through a crowd of any kind, let alone those hell-bent on making me a sacrifice.

More tears spilled from my eyes and felt cool on my skin as they fell and dried on my cheeks. For eleven years, I'd lived in constant fear of those that had hurt me. Eleven years I blamed the wrong man, and the moment I let myself live and breathe and believe in love and a happily ever after again... they struck. I'd let my guard down and never suspected who the real culprit was. Did Irene know what Dave did? Did she even care? It didn't matter, but so many questions swirled in my head.

It was like they were waiting for the moment I let my walls down to take me and finish what they'd started. The feeling was coming back to my jaw, and my teeth chattered. The longer no one said anything, the more scared I became. I should've been happy that no one touched me, but not knowing where they were and what they were doing was somehow worse.

"Today is a special day," Father said. His loud booming voice pierced my heart with more terror than I ever thought possible, and all I could think about was my guys.

Kai. The first love of my life, the other half of my soul. I could so clearly see our chance to rebuild the future that had been stolen from us. I could feel his hands and how he made me feel protected and safe.

"Today, we will complete a ceremony that was interrupted and left uncompleted. A circle that should have brought us more power from the beginning." He said, and I tried to block him and the crazy out.

Avro. The sweetest man I've ever known. Who was there for me through so many terrible nights and helped me step out of my shell with his unwavering patience.

"By completing this circle, we will feed evil one of its own, and just like a snake eating its tail, its mouth will be too full to bother us and our righteous path that only God can see."

Jace. The way he commanded everything and pushed me hard to step out of the shadows of my fear and become who I wanted to be. Our short time together had shown me there was so much more I wanted to do before it all ended.

This man who claimed to be a Father, a man of God, was no more than a charlatan. The world needed fewer people like this. People who twisted religion into whatever they wanted it to be, whatever served them. They were wolves in sheep's clothing who planned on stealing everything from me—the potential laughs and smiles, the soft touches and stupid arguments over who ate the last cookie. I wanted it all.

My jaw clenched tight, and my shoulders twitched, the muscles firing and coming to life as Father kept talking. Those in the room would call and answer during parts of his ludicrous speech. They had held me down and taken what they wanted, but not this time. I'd fight to my last dying breath.

The room fell silent, and all I could hear was the pounding of my heart and the woosh of air leaving my lungs.

I couldn't stop my whole body from jerking as someone touched my leg. What felt like fingers traveled along my body until a hand gripped my chin.

"And so we meet again, Kitten," Father whispered close to my ear. I no longer wondered what the Devil sounded like. This man had walked straight from hell and into this room.

"Your death was stolen from me once. Your friend Jim couldn't stomach it any longer and called the paramedics. He was weak and undeserving of the robe, but there is no one here to help you today, Kitten," he whispered so only I could hear. "I'm going to enjoy every second of this."

The only Jim I had known was Dave's friend, who was like an uncle to me. My body revolted against the thought that not only Dave but also Jim could do that to me. No other explanation made sense.

He took a deep breath, smelling my skin, and both my legs spasmed and jerked on the table. "Oh yes, you do smell so sweet. We will all fill you with our godly seed to wash away any lingering darkness before your demon body is sacrificed."

"You're..."

"What's that, Kitten? I didn't understand that demon tongue of yours."

My eyes fluttered open, and I stared into the eyes of the man who had worn another's face for too long. His dark eyes felt like they were penetrating my soul and trying to steal it from my body. I hated him. I hated everything he did to me, everything he stood for.

"You're...a...dead...man," I whispered and then swallowed down the dry and smoky taste from the candles in the room.

Father smiled at me, but it was cold and calculating. I could see in his eyes he was envisioning me screaming in pain. There was an edge to his stare that had all my instincts screaming *serial killer* dressed up in religious robes. My hand twitched at my side, and I tested my fingers. They all moved.

"You're still the same, Kitten. I see we didn't break you well enough. Not to worry, we will tonight," he said as he pulled the red hood over his head.

I tried to lift my arm, but it only raised slightly before flopping back to the stone. I was panting hard when he finished lighting the rest of the candles.

"Profit Dave, begin the shackling process."

"Yes, Father," Dave said and stepped up to pull a thick chain and leather cuff from under the table.

"No...don't...touch...me," I growled and coughed. I tried to yank my leg away, but it was heavy and slow. Dave grabbed it easily, holding it in place while he fastened the cuff. I felt an intense combination of panic and rage as Dave gripped my second leg.

The leather was securely in place, and Dave moved toward my arms when we heard a scream that froze everyone. I glanced up at Dave and Father. They looked worried. Or was it just my hopeful imagination?

Like a switch was hit, the sound of gunfire could be heard. The distinct roar of not just one but dozens of motorcycles echoed through the room, and my bottom lip shook.

"Go, all of you, go and fight. This is our home, kill all who try to take it in the name of all that is holy," Father yelled.

As soon as everyone left, Father turned his glare on Dave. "Did you let them follow, you fool?"

He dropped to the floor, and I could just make out the top of his head. "No, Father. I'd never do that. I was careful."

The screams were getting louder along with the gunfire, and an explosion erupted outside. The entire building shook, toppling over a couple of the candles. The shrieks of women reached a new level as they ran into the room where we were and kept going toward the back of the building. Father looked around and then down at Dave.

"Guard her. I'll be right back." Father looked at me, and our eyes locked.

He wasn't coming back.

He was a weak man who hid behind the men and women he manipulated to get what he wanted—the thrill of the kill. I'd gotten away once and could see the emotion in those dark eyes, he was torn, but his self-preservation won out. He sprinted in the direction the women had run.

Dave went to one of the doors and stood to the side, staring out. He didn't consider me a threat, but that was his mistake. I tested my shoulders, lifted my arms, and squeezed my hands to make sure everything worked. I wanted to scream as I forced myself into a sitting position while all my muscles slowly came to life and burned worse than the brand on my arm.

I kept an eye on Dave while my fingers fought with the leather buckle attached to the cuff on my ankle. My fingers were moving but didn't have much strength, and I was sweating by the time I got the first one off. Another explosion shook the building, and a tall candelabra toppled over, hitting the wood paneling along the edge of the room. Within minutes the dry wood caught fire.

My hands shook harder, and I bit my lip to help concentrate on loosening the second cuff. Dave turned and looked over his shoulder in my direction, and there was a brief pause before his brow furrowed.

"What the fuck do you think you're doing?"

A scream rippled up from the depths of my body as I pulled on the strap three times before the buckle gave way. Dave growled as he stomped toward me, and not caring how much pain it caused, I rolled off the other side of the table and landed hard on the floor. I winced with the impact, but something shiny caught my eye. A small table had been set up with various tools for the ceremony, which was really public torture.

Not hesitating, I reached out and gripped the handle of the ceremonial curved knife. The metal felt cool in my palm, and a sense of empowerment washed over me as a hand grabbed my ankle. I screamed and kicked out violently with my heels, catching Dave in the chin with my foot.

"Let go of me!"

My eyes locked on the large hand wrapped around my ankle, the fingers pressing into my skin. Those fingers had gripped me like this once before, but there was no way it would happen again.

11:13 AM

Kaivan

The transport truck pulled up to the meet with something loaded on the back. Wilder jumped out of the driver's seat while Avro got out the passenger side and undid the straps holding the massive canvas covering in place. I stared at the shape.

No...this couldn't be what I thought it was, could it?

"Did they bring a fucking tank?" Roach asked.

Before I could answer, the last strap was freed, and my eyes bugged out at the sight of the massive tan-colored tank.

"I believe they did," I said.

"Wow." I looked at Jace and his surprised expression. "I mean, I knew Avro had family in the army, but I was not expecting this as the favor he asked for," Jace said.

"You and me both."

"Do you think they robbed a museum," Roach asked.

"Anything is fucking possible at this point."

The long line of motorcycles and men waiting for the gates to be opened all stared on as Wilder climbed inside and Avro dropped the ramps down.

Avro walked over, his knee looked like a football with all the supports he had strapped in place, but he wouldn't even consider being left behind.

"Well, that should take their gate down," Avro said as he wiped his hands off.

I didn't give him time to think about it and grabbed him, pulling him into a hug. He held himself perfectly still but then slowly hugged me back. "Thanks, man. I don't know what you had to promise to make this happen, but thank you." Pulling back, I gripped Avro's shoulders.

"Don't look at me like that. I didn't do it for you. I did it for Raine," Avro said. "I'd do anything for her, but...you're welcome too," he tacked onto the end, making me smirk.

Wilder popped out of the top hatch as the tank pulled up beside us.

"Remember, wait for the signal. It will be a big boom. Let's move out," Wilder yelled, and the hatch slammed down. The hair stood on my neck as the powerful machine took the lead the rumble and sound of tracks screaming how lethal it was.

The four of us jumped in Roach's truck and waited for the signal. My nerves had been bad the whole way here. Nothing seemed to be moving fast enough, and the anxiousness made me jumpy and irritable. Now that we were here, a sense of calm had washed over me. The part of me that loved the kill was ready for what was coming, and I wouldn't stop until Dave and Frank were both six feet under.

An explosion went off, the sound of the tank unmistakable, and the truck shook.

"Fuck," I mumbled as smoke rose into the air. That was our cue.

Roach pulled out along with dozens of trucks and an even longer line of motorcycles. All the guys were riding with their guns out, ready for action.

We crested the rise just as the tank smashed into the second watch tower. The people inside tried to hang on as the wooden structure crashed to the ground. The long barrel of the tank's gun swung in the direction of the last tower on the far side of the property, and even though I knew it would be coming, the sound of it going off and the large tower exploding was something I'd never forget.

Roach sped through the gate, clipping a guy running with the front of the truck before speeding across the property to the furthest building on the east side. Cranking the wheel, the ass of the truck slid on the sand before coming to a stop.

"Be careful."

Nodding, I hopped out and ran for the building, looking for a door. One burst open, and two men in black robes ran out. They didn't see me, and I shot them as they ran toward some vehicles parked on this side.

Grabbing the door, I pulled it open and listened, but I couldn't hear anyone coming with the noise out front. Slipping into the dimly lit building, I looked up and down the hallway, not sure which way to go first. I couldn't say why, but I chose the hallway leading to the back of the large steel structure.

I wasn't sure what I expected to find in a cult compound. Maybe a few old farmhouses, a couple of sheds, or a barn, but not something that could double as a jet hanger. Poking my head around the corner, I didn't see anything, but the quiet was eerie.

I paused when I heard a scream, and not just any scream. That was Raine. I knew her voice like it was my own. Not caring how many were in the way or what danger I was running into, I sprinted for the sound as a crippling fear held my heart.

I turned the corner and ran past a few open rooms. A man came running out of one with a fire poker held above his head. I didn't slow or lose my stride as I fired my gun, and he dropped to his knees. I ran around him, not caring if he lived or died. Raine's hysterical screams were all the fuel I needed to put one foot in front of the other.

Bursting through the doors, I ran into a large circular room. The place was on fire at the far end, but it was moving, and it wouldn't take long for the entire building to go up in flames.

My panic reached a new level when Raine's screams echoed in my ears, but I couldn't see her. Running toward the stone slab in the center of the room, I saw something moving and whipped around the end, only to skid to a stop.

Raine was covered in blood, with only her beautiful blue eyes showing through the mask of red. She straddled Dave as the knife she held stabbed into his chest and stomach, even though he was long dead. He wore a black robe like the other men had on, but it was open, exposing his naked body. There was a deep gash across his face showing off the bone. His hands and cock had been severed, and most of his insides were lying around him, but still, Raine screamed as her hand moved in a blur.

Putting my gun away, I inched around so she would see me better and got down into a crouch.

"Raine," I said, but she didn't respond. I knew this level of anger and fear, it made you delusional. She wasn't here in this room. She wasn't anywhere but the room inside her mind playing a movie all its own.

The flicker of flames caught my attention as they licked up the far wall. We needed to get out of here.

"Raine," I tried louder this time, but her wild eyes remained locked on Dave's face. Each plunge of the knife sent blood flying in all directions, his limp body rocking with the harsh blows as she tore him apart.

"Tink!" I yelled, and her hand paused in the air, even though her eyes stayed looking down. She was panting hard, her chest heaving, and her arm shaking violently. "Tink, it's me. Look at me, baby. It's me, Kai. Look up at me."

Her big blue eyes slowly lifted to meet mine, but her hand remained raised above her head. "That's it, keep looking at me." I touched my hand to my chest. "Do you see me? It's Kai," I said, and she blinked a few times. "Tink, we need to go. The building is on fire." I ever so slowly held out my hand so I didn't spook her. Dark smoke drifted in our direction and I coughed as some of it reached my nose. "Give me the knife, Tink."

I coughed a few more times, the taste of smoke itching the back of my throat.

Raine looked down at the man she was straddling and then up at me.

"Kai?"

"Yeah, it's me, Tink. We found you. Jace and Avro are outside. But we need to go."

"He tried to hurt me." She sniffled. "I had to do it. I couldn't let him hurt me again." Her voice hitched, as her bottom lip trembled.

"I know, I'm so fucking happy you did." I kept my hand stretched out and took a deep breath as her arm lowered one inch at a time. "He's dead. I promise you killed him, and he's not coming back, but we need to go." She looked at Dave's face again. "Give me the knife."

Hand trembling, she held out the blade that was dripping red and whimpered as she let go of the handle. I stabbed Dave through the eye up to the decorative hilt. Raine's body slumped, and she looked like she would fall over. Reaching out, I gripped her under the arms like a small child and stood in a single motion.

"Kai," she cried, her arms wrapping around my neck, her body shaking uncontrollably as she clung to me. "You came for me." I hated that even a shadow of doubt existed in her mind.

"Always." I held her tighter. "I'll always come for you." Her crying got louder, but she kept mumbling how much she loved me over and over.

Marching for the door as the fire spread, I kept my eyes open for other threats. I hadn't seen Frank on my way in and hoped that Roach or someone else found him, but I wouldn't be surprised if the coward found a hole to crawl into the moment the fighting started.

The shooting outside had stopped, but I still poked my head out the door to check that all was clear before stepping into the mid-day sun. All those we captured were on their knees with their hands zip-tied behind their back. I didn't know what Chase planned on doing with them, but if it were left up to me, I'd make sure an example was made of them.

"I'm going in, now fucking let go of me," Jace growled as Avro, Roach, and Chase held him back.

"Snake will find her," Roach said, but Jace looked ready to throw down with the three men.

"The fire is getting bigger. What if something happened to them? Let go," Jace roared.

I took a moment to appreciate Jace. He sure didn't act like a celebrity. He was as ornery and ready to fight as any of the guys in the club. I had come to terms and was at peace with them and our relationship. They'd proven their loyalty to Raine, and that was good enough for me. The rest we would figure out.

Before they all ended up in a brawl, I whistled, and they looked over. The relief was evident in their eyes as Avro and Jace ran in my direction. They didn't even wait for me to put her down before we were wrapped up in a hug.

Roach caught my eye, and he shook his head. I knew what that meant. They didn't find Frank.

"I love you guys so much," Raine said.

"We love you too," Avro said. "We were all so scared."

"I didn't think I was ever going to see any of you again," she said, breaking down into sobs that shook her body.

I didn't know what this relationship would look like six months or even a year down the road. What I knew was that all the shit I'd been worrying about didn't matter. All I cared about was Raine. The rest would sort itself out.

The building behind us exploded, and a large pillar of smoke snaked its way up into the sky, blocking out the bright rays of the sun.

In a way, we were back to where it all started, and even though I never wanted Raine to have to defend herself, I hoped it helped her sleep at night, knowing that she'd gotten her revenge. She deserved to see them all burn in hell.

I glanced around at the burning buildings and for trees beyond that. This wasn't over. One day I'd find Frank, and I'd make him pay.

Two down, but still one to go.

Raine

EPILOGUE

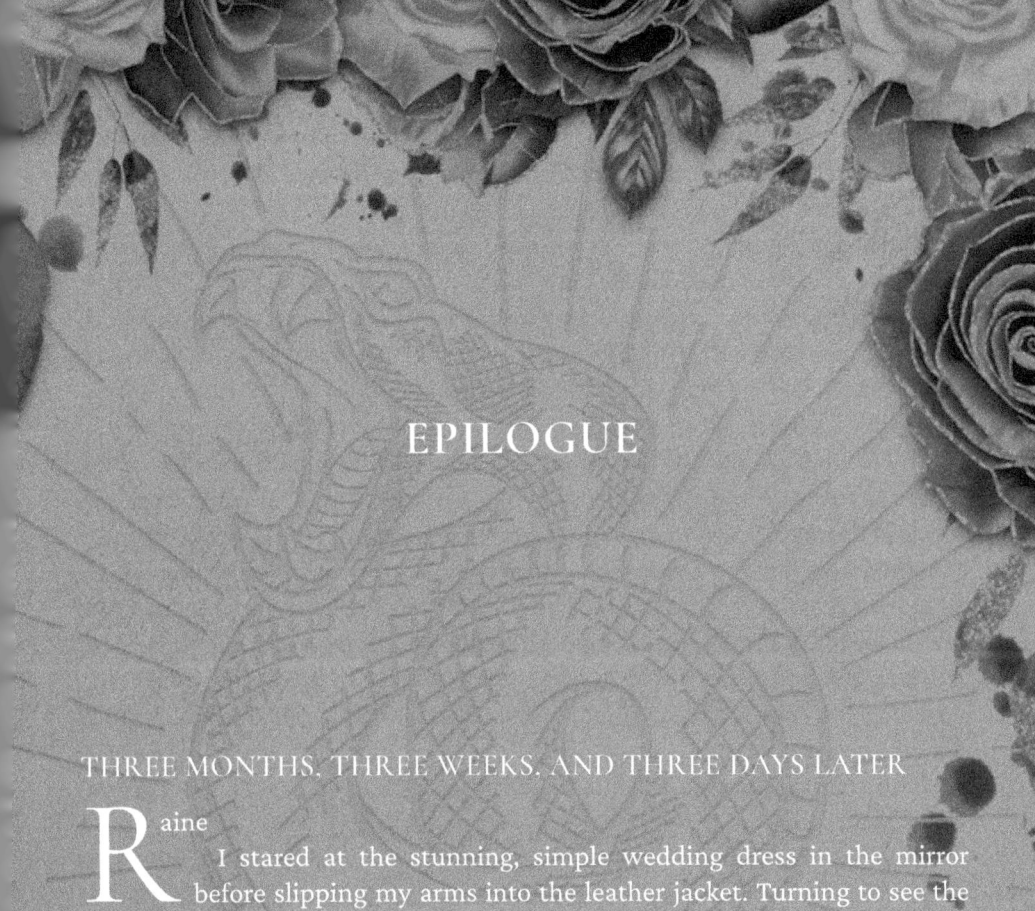

THREE MONTHS, THREE WEEKS, AND THREE DAYS LATER

Raine

I stared at the stunning, simple wedding dress in the mirror before slipping my arms into the leather jacket. Turning to see the back, I smirked at the Lost Souls emblem.

"Are you sure you want to wear a leather jacket for your wedding," Emma, the seamstress, asked.

Smiling, I took it off and turned for her to unzip the dress. "Yeah, I really do. It'll still be ready next week?"

"Yes, all the minor adjustments will be complete." Emma smiled as I walked into the changing room to get dressed. I glanced at the ring Jace had given me and then at the other two rings on the same hand. I looked like I was diamond-obsessed, but fair was fair.

Kai wanted the middle finger for his black diamond arrangement. He said it was a classic fuck you to the social norms.

Avro chose my index finger, and now my hand was worth a fortune and could be used as a weapon.

I kept Jace's on my wedding finger. It had taken the jeweler a while to get the blood off it and put it back together. My overwhelming happiness quickly fell as I pictured it coated in blood. Looking up at the mirror, I couldn't help but turn to stare at the mark on my arm.

I ran my fingers over the area. The brand had been a firm ridge before Jace found a plastic surgeon willing to fix it. Once it was fully healed, I would get a tattoo to finish covering it up.

Dave's face haunted me, but what I'd succumbed to haunted me more. I still remembered everything from the hours I was in Frank and Dave's grasp, and so many times, I woke up in a cold sweat with Dave's mangled body taunting me. I jerked my fingers away from the spot as I felt myself slipping down that hole. I hated to think about that day.

I pulled on my jeans, sneakers, and my Grimhead Crew T-shirt. Shockingly, Jace had added a small reaper to the artwork for Kai. He might be the biggest jerk of the bunch, but he could be a marshmallow that left you breathless and shocked. I turned my mind back to the ceremony next weekend.

We'd decided that I wouldn't officially marry any of them. At least as far as the courts were concerned. But after much arguing, we decided on a fake lavish wedding for the social media sites and a promise ceremony with all three of my guys. The entire motorcycle club was invited, and Chase was handling the service. I'd seen him a few times at the clubhouse and learned almost everyone's name. I was still scratching my head over how Chase ended up with Naomi. She was bit much and we all backed out of the room whenever she arrived.

Roach and I made up. I did end up punching him in the face and told him he would never cut me out again, but he deserved it, and luckily it made Kai laugh. I loved talking to Mannix. He was a wealth of knowledge and wisdom that touched my heart. Kai told me that Mannix helped protect him in prison, and I'd forever be grateful to him for that.

Kai was still just as broody and domineering as he always was, but it had shifted. He was relaxed at home, loved to cuddle, and was letting me in on some of the shit he never shared with me before. He joked around with Avro and seemed to enjoy the constant banter with Jace. I still didn't want to know what he did as an enforcer. It was probably wrong of me to turn the other cheek and ignore it, but so did all the other wives. It was a conscious choice we all needed to make. If I wanted to be with him, I needed to decide what was more important to me, and it always came back to the same answer. I loved Kai more than I cared about my moral compass or my soul after I was dead.

We'd finally gotten Avro to cave and talked into selling his place, and now we were all chipping in to revamp a mansion where all of us could live. It was best to have neutral ground to start fresh and build new memories. I thought it might break his heart since he'd worked so hard to buy it, but since we found the ideal location and he was helping with the remodeling and interior design of the new house, he came around. Of course, we all knew everything was going to be overly labeled.

I'd decided to go back to school rather than work at Eclipse. It was never my dream job. I loved it there because of Avro. He decided he couldn't go back once he got the all-clear, especially with the world knowing he and Jace were involved. Avro shocked me by deciding to be the band's new manager. No one was more suited, with his organization, ability to tell people no—and still sound like it was a maybe—to talk his way into venues for performances, and come up with fun photo-ops and stunts for the band's social media. You've never seen someone more protective, and he kept a tight hold and eye over Jace's finances to make sure no one was taking advantage of him or the band. It was the perfect match, and Jace seemed calmer. His newest songs were all at the top of the charts, and he was home more than ever.

I had to do some serious self-reflection to understand what really made me happy. I wanted to help people, specifically those traumatized or in the system. I had firsthand knowledge of the struggles, and if I could help even one person, that was what I wanted to do. What that job looked like was still undetermined, but it felt right.

Jace and Kai were scaring me. I wasn't sure I liked them getting along. They still sniped at one another and would take every opportunity to piss the other off, but I never felt like it would turn into a fight like it did before. There was an underlying respect now that wasn't there previously.

I grabbed my purse and other bags from the mall and walked out to the front of the store.

"See you next week Emma," I called out.

"See you later, Raine."

I shouldered open the door and did the usual sweep of my surroundings. It always felt like I was still being watched. I was kidnapped twice and almost saw Jace killed, so I found myself looking over my shoulder again, and I hated it. Kai kept telling me it was normal. Avro told me to give myself a break. Jace...well Jace was always pushing me emotionally. But I still had the fear that Frank was hidden around every corner.

Avro was finally walking and working out now. He'd offered to come with me today, but I didn't want him to see the dress and all the other purchases, like their gifts, I'd gotten for the ceremony.

Stuffing all the bags in the trunk, I wandered around the car and hopped into the driver's seat. I couldn't figure out why I'd waited so long to get my driver's license. The feeling of freedom it brought was undeniable. Something thumped as I pulled out of the parking spot, and I jumped. I looked in the back seat, my heart racing, only to find that it was the container of windshield wash I'd picked up earlier and forgot was there.

"Shit, I meant to put you in," I said to the blue liquid as I tried to tame my racing heart. My teeth ground together, the anger seeping in. Whenever I jumped like a scared rabbit, I was angry afterward. Smacking the steering wheel, I finished pulling out and drove to the exit.

"I need to find a way to get over this."

I got over jumping at my shadow once, and I wouldn't let what happened at the ranch hold me back or keep me scared. He didn't get that kind of power.

My cell phone rang, and I hit the answer button, a smile already on my face at the sight of Jace's name.

"Hey there," I answered. "All okay?"

"Define okay," Jace said as something crashed in the background. I could clearly hear Avro and Kai yelling at one another.

"Oh shit. I thought we were past all this. What's wrong?" My heart sank thinking they would be on bad terms for the ceremony.

"Let's just say I'm never agreeing to us doing any of the final renovations again. These two can't make their mind up about anything, and now the brand-new faucets don't work. Avro is blaming Kai 'cause he bought them on clearance, and...anyway. I know it's a lot to ask, but just to keep world war three from breaking out in here, can you please go and pick up a couple of new sets for the bathrooms?"

"I swear to god, Kai, you never listen!" Avro yelled, and I cringed. Avro never yelled, which meant he had to be pretty fired up.

"Yeah, of course, I'll head to the hardware store close to home. I'll get there before they close for the night." I glanced at the time, knowing I'd be cutting it close since they closed at six, and it was already almost five, but I flicked on the turn signal and headed that way.

"Thanks, I'll keep them from killing each other. Fucking children." Jace hung up the phone, and once more, it was like the world had turned upside down. When had Jace become the calm one, and Avro and Kai argued? Men...

"Are you kidding me?" I grumbled when I saw the yellow caution tape blocking off a huge section of the parking lot for repaving. Of course, it was crazy busy, and I found a single parking spot around the corner of the building. "Unbelievable," I said as I pulled into the lone spot at the end.

Sighing, I got out and did my usual sweep for the boogeyman, but there was only the sound of workers, birds, and cars on the road—no sign of any monsters lurking.

It took forever to find and match the right faucets to the images that Jace sent. I swear it was like they were hidden on purpose. Then I ended up stuck in a massive line to check out, and I swear if I got to the front and they said they were now closed, it wouldn't just be Avro going postal.

Bags in hand, I marched for the car. Food was next on my list. The old kitchen was ripped out, and we still had weeks to go before it was functioning again, so I was picking up pizza. I still hadn't found as good of a spot near us as Terry's, but Jace was begging to invest in an expansion. He might get Terry to cave, which was amazing and dangerous. The last thing I needed was a pizza place I could eat at every day within walking distance from the new property.

My phone rang as I got to the trunk of my car, and I stuffed my hand in my pocket. It was like a trap as the rings caught, and I couldn't get my hand back out. The gates to the back of the store opened, and I glanced over my shoulder as a large cube truck left with product.

I didn't hear the other vehicle coming up until the whir and bang of a sliding door opening made me jump. I turned around just as gloved hands grabbed me.

"Ah!" I screamed as I was whipped off my feet. I pulled on my hand but still couldn't get it free, and my other hand was weighed down by the plastic bags around my wrist. "Let go of me," I managed to yell as I was tossed in the back of the van. The door slammed shut, leaving me in complete darkness inside the windowless box.

No, this couldn't be happening again. How fucking unlucky can one person be? I rolled to the end of the van and banged into the back, the faucets banging into me as the van peeled out. The loud squealing of the tires and the rough bump and sharp turn told me we'd just pulled out on the main road.

I'd handcuffed myself.

This was unbelievable.

I was always so careful.

Shaking out my wrist, I got the bags off and then fought with my pocket to free my hand and the cell phone I was after in the first place.

Jumping to my feet, I stumbled from side to side but made my way to the front and banged as hard as I could.

"Frank! Let me out of here," I screamed. Unlocking the phone, I tried Kai first, but it just beeped busy. How the hell was that possible? I tried Jace, and the same thing happened. "Fuck," I mumbled under my breath.

Bang, bang, bang.

"The Lost Souls will hunt you down and kill you! You're a dead man."

Bang, bang, bang.

There was no response other than to turn a corner so fast that I fell to my knees.

"Dammit," I growled with the sudden impact, which was more disorienting than painful. I tried the phone again, including 911, and nothing worked. Could this guy really have a cell jammer? What the fuck? I seriously wanted to know how I managed to piss this guy off so fucking much. He'd tortured me twice now and was aiming for round three.

Standing, I tried hollering again. "Snake will rip your fucking balls off your body while you're still breathing. Let me out of here!"

It was no use. There was zero response, and I was wasting my energy. The vehicle drove on, even when I hit the walls and screamed like a banshee. My throat and fists were sore. The fear that hadn't hit at first with the anger flowing became a crippling terror that wanted me to curl up in a corner and cry.

I tried to figure out where I was taken, but as the ride dragged on, I lost track of the turns and how much time went by. My thumb ran over the rings, and I let myself have a moment to think about Kai, Jace, and Avro. Our worlds were all so different, our traumas significant and fears just as great. Yet we managed to come together and became a unit that worked.

I wiped away the tears running down my cheeks. I wasn't giving up. Frank had taken too much from me, and there was no way that I was letting him take anything else. Even sitting, I braced myself so I didn't fall over as the van turned sharply and began driving over a rough road. We were going slowly now. It felt like an unmaintained service road or a really long driveway.

We had to be getting closer, and my pulse spiked, the blood pumping through my veins as I pictured the fight I would have when those doors opened.

The van made a wide sweeping turn and then started to back up. The sound of the reverse alarm was loud inside the empty cargo area. I got ready to spring the moment the sliding door opened. Thump, thump, thump was all I heard as the van shut off and doors on the other side of the dividing wall opened and closed. I listened hard, trying to track their movements, but I was startled when the back doors suddenly opened.

The setting sunlight poured into the back half of the van, but no one charged in to grab me. I didn't know which was worse. If someone had rushed in, I was prepared to fight, but all the hair stood on the back of my neck, and a cold dread raced down my spine as everything remained quiet.

"Raine Eastman, get out of the van," a loud mechanical voice bellowed. It sounded like he was using a PA system or something. So my hope that they just decided to take me for a joy ride and leave me was definitely not happening. I glanced at my discarded bags of faucets and wondered if I could use one as a weapon, but all those zip ties they used to hold them to the cardboard would be impossible to get off.

"Now, or die sooner," the voice announced.

Swallowing hard, I took a tentative step toward the open doors, and as I got closer, I realized that we were in the middle of nowhere. All I could see were trees and grass. With each step closer, I shook a little more, but still, no one reached in and grabbed me. What the fuck was this guy doing? My brain raced as fast as my heart as I tried to piece this newest torture together.

Poking my head out of the back, I saw no one. It was completely silent aside from the sounds of nature. The main issue was a fence taller than the van, complete with barbed wire running in each direction away from where it was backed up. With a quick look, I could tell that the van just fit, like this entire thing had been designed to screw with someone. As strange of a time as it was to have a movie flashback, all I could picture were the raptors in Jurassic Park being dropped off in their enclosures.

"Get out of the van. This is your last warning," the voice was really loud now, and as I stepped down and looked around, I spotted the speaker on the top of a pole, but still no sign of actual people.

I'd been expecting almost anything, but this...this I wasn't prepared for.

"Now run. If you make it through the forest to the other side, your sins will be forgiven, and you will live. If not...then the demons chasing you will finally catch up."

My eyes swung to the forest. Holy shit. My heart pounded so hard I thought I would pass out.

"You will have a five-minute head start. Three, two, one...go."

I bolted away from the van and glanced back only once, and it only confirmed that there wasn't another option out.

Slow your breathing.

I kept saying to myself as I reached the edge of the tall trees and veered to the path that looked like it was used for biking. Even though it would keep me in sight, I could move faster, and there was less chance I would trip over a vine and fall.

I was plunged into shadows, and the cool evening air made me shiver. The sound of a twig snapping off to my left had my head whipping in that direction. I couldn't see anything, but the trembling in my body told me someone was out there. A yipping sound to my right spiked my heart rate, and when whoever was on my left answered, I knew I was being chased down.

My feet moved faster, and I whipped around a slight bend in the path.

"Get her," the same mechanical voice growled.

"You have nowhere to go," a second voice chimed in.

"I'm going to fuck you so hard," the first one said.

Even though it was getting darker, I could see the gap in the trees. The voice had said if I made it to the other side, I would live—if I could trust that voice. Who knew what Frank really had waiting for me? I glanced around for anything I could use as a weapon, but there were no sticks or branches. I didn't even see any rocks bigger than pebbles you'd skip at the beach.

"Whoop, whoop," the voice to my left said. I looked over and almost screamed as I stared at a black and white devil's face, such a contrast to the surroundings that it practically glowed. The crashing of the person on my right getting closer drew my attention. That person wore the same mask, but this one was black and red.

Fear gripped my throat, making breathing difficult, but I pumped my arms harder for the last few feet to my only hope of freedom. Out of my peripheral vision, I saw the masked men getting closer and knew they were toying with me. Even though I was terrified to run through this gap and find out what was on the other side, it was my only chance.

Holding up my arms to ward off a couple of dangling vines, I burst through the gap into the open grassy area.

"What the?" I gasped as I looked around at the massive backyard and the house I recognized. There was a fancy gazebo with lights hanging all along the edge and off the railings. It was easy to see the man leaning against the entryway with a blue and black mask, no shirt, and jeans.

My pace slowed as my brain tried to understand how I ended up at home. I screamed as arms gripped me around the waist. Instead of tackling me to the ground, the man swung me up into his arms. I reached back, ready to hit him, when all the tattoos on his chest, including my name, caught my eye.

"Kai?"

"Hey, Tink," he said and chuckled.

"Are you kidding me right now?" I looked at the second guy laughing under his mask and knew it was Jace. "I'm going to kill all of you, I swear."

"I did like the part where you wanted me to rip off the guy's balls while he was still breathing," Kai said, and I could feel him smiling at me. "You know me so well."

"You three are unbelievable. I should lock you out of the house."

Kai laughed hard. "You could, but I'd just have to ask Wilder for the key I'm sure he already has made."

The corner of my mouth pulled up. Wilder and his crazy appearances had grown on me. He loved it when I made chocolate chip muffins and would sit and talk for hours, then suddenly disappear as if he'd never been there.

"That is true," I said as we walked up the steps to meet the masked man in blue, who was definitely Avro.

"Okay, then tell me what the hell all this was about?" I held my hand out to the forest as Kai set me on my feet. "I thought I was dead, you bunch of jerks." I was annoyed, but as they closed the screendoor, a different kind of tremor raced down my spine. No one could deny that they looked as sexy as any sinful fantasy. They stood shoulder to shoulder, shirtless with matching black jeans and those masks that promised dark desires.

"You've been having nightmares about being taken again," Avro said.

"And you kept saying you wanted to get over it," Jace said.

Kai stepped forward and wrapped an arm around my waist. "Now, when you think of being kidnapped, the dream will end with the three of us. We are your monsters tonight, ones you'll never get out of your head."

I licked my lips, I wasn't sure this would be in any medical journal anywhere, but I couldn't deny that this was definitely a better outcome to have floating around in my head. I looked over my shoulder to our new home and then around the large gazebo that could easily hold a party. I had no idea when they installed this without me seeing it, but a smile tugged at the corner of my mouth. It screamed Avro with all the lights and a large bed with a million pillows. The pizza I was supposed to get was piled on the table, and there was a built-in brick oven and fridge. This was incredible, a small oasis away from the house.

"You did all this for me?" My eyes went to their jeans. No strip club anywhere could compete with this show.

"Yes. We would do anything to help you, but there are rules tonight," Jace said. I watched as they finished stripping together, and I pulled at the shirt I was wearing, overheating from more than just the run.

"What kind of rules?" I crossed my arms but knew I would play whatever game they had in mind. They were way too tempting, and the surge of fear had left a lasting hangover effect of excitement that made me rub my thighs together.

"Kai is going to be in charge, and the three of us are going to do what he says, no hesitation, no questions asked."

If I hadn't been chased through the woods a few seconds ago, I would've said that those words coming out of Jace's mouth were the most shocking thing to happen. Although Kai and Jace had learned to share me on occasion, this was the one time it felt like anything could happen.

"Don't look so shocked," Kai said. He leaned down and growled into the side of my neck. The strange mask was terrifying, yet as the glacial shivers started, so did the twin inferno that licked up my body from between my thighs. I gripped his shoulders, loving the feel of his muscles flexing under my touch and his hard cock pressing into my stomach.

"Alright, I'll play the game." I bit my lip in anticipation.

"Such a good girl," Kai said, the sound devious from inside the mask.

He grabbed the front of my shirt, and I gasped and moaned as he pulled hard and sent buttons flying in every direction. I felt his eyes on my body even though I couldn't see them, and it was still as intimate as any touch.

"That's much better."

Kai stepped back, and my chest was heaving like I'd gone for another sprint. He casually walked over to a chair off to the side and sat down. I wanted to take a picture of him naked like that, his cock standing up with that mask on. Not even the hottest day could compare to the sight of these three intoxicating men. My heart was full, and my life was nowhere near what I imagined. It had turned out so much better than I thought possible or deserved.

But I was never letting go.

- If you'd like to see the conclusion to the story of Father Frank, then be sure to keep a lookout for the next duet in the series – Hollywood's story - Showbiz and Fealty
- If you'd like to see the conclusion of Happy Harris, the man that murdered Kai's mother, then be sure to keep a look out for – Wilder's duet – Warfare & Dissention by T.L. Hodel
- Would you like to know more about Father Frank, aka Francois Hanson, and his twin brother? – Then make sure to read the Buchan Brother's Duet – Unhinged Cain by Brooklyn Cross and Twisted Abel by T.L. Hodel

THANK YOU

Thank you to all those that decided to pick up this book and read it. It is only with readers continued support that Indie Authors, such as myself, are able to keep writing which is why your reviews mean so much to us. If you enjoyed this book, please consider leaving me a review.

ABOUT THE AUTHOR

Writing is not just a passion for me. It is a lifeline to my sanity.

I have always loved writing but suffer from severe dyslexia and short-term memory retention issues. I struggled in school while I worked every night on re-training my brain.

I was frequently treated like I would never succeed, and I found myself putting my love for writing on a shelf.

Even at the age of six, I found it easier to communicate with animals than people, which was a big reason why I was drawn to dressage horseback riding. I remained focused on my passion for riding until I had to step away from the competition world for personal reasons.

Today, my desire for writing and storytelling has been rekindled. I have published multiple books and will never let anyone or anything hold me back again.
I am a proud romance author who offers my readers morally grey heroes, a ton of spice, epic journeys, and redemption stories.

-Follow Your Dreams-

Brooklyn Cross

Milton Keynes UK
Ingram Content Group UK Ltd.
UKHW040637071124
2653UKWH00025B/204

9 781998 015146